THE FOUNTAINHEAD

THE
FOUNTAINHEAD

By AYN RAND

With Special Introduction by the Author

A Bobbs-Merrill Book
Macmillan Publishing Company
New York

Macmillan Publishing Company
866 Third Avenue, New York, N.Y. 10022
Collier Macmillan Canada, Inc.

Library of Congress Cataloging-in-Publication Data

Rand, Ayn.
The fountainhead.

"A Bobbs-Merrill Book."
I. Title.
PS3535.A547F6   1986   813'.52   86-8760
ISBN 0-02-600910-2 (previously 0-672-50669-6)

First Printing 1943

First Macmillan Printing 1986

10 9 8 7 6 5 4 3 2

Manufactured in the United States of America

I offer my profound gratitude to the great profession of architecture and its heroes who have given us some of the highest expressions of man's genius, yet have remained unknown, undiscovered by the majority of men. And to the architects who gave me their generous assistance in the technical matters of this book.

No person or event in this story is intended as a reference to any real person or event. The titles of the newspaper columns were invented and used by me in the first draft of this novel. They were not taken from and have no reference to any actual newspaper columns or features.

                                        Ayn Rand
March 10, 1943

INTRODUCTION

Many people have asked me how I feel about the fact that *The Fountainhead* has been in print for twenty-five years. I cannot say that I feel anything in particular, except a kind of quiet satisfaction. In this respect, my attitude toward my writing is best expressed by a statement of Victor Hugo: "If a writer wrote merely for his time, I would have to break my pen and throw it away."

Certain writers, of whom I am one, do not live, think or write on the range of the moment. Novels, in the proper sense of the word, are not written to vanish in a month or a year. That most of them do, today, that they are written and published as if they were magazines, to fade as rapidly, is one of the sorriest aspects of today's literature, and one of the clearest indictments of its dominant esthetic philosophy: concrete-bound, journalistic Naturalism which has now reached its dead end in the inarticulate sounds of panic.

Longevity—predominantly, though not exclusively—is the prerogative of a literary school which is virtually non-existent today: Romanticism. This is not the place for a dissertation on the nature of Romantic fiction, so let me state—for the record and for the benefit of those college students who have never been allowed to discover it—only that Romanticism is the *conceptual* school of art. It deals, not with the random trivia of the day, but with the timeless, fundamental, universal problems and *values* of human existence. It does not record or photograph; it creates and projects. It is concerned—in the words of Aristotle—not with things as they are, but with things as they might be and ought to be.

And for the benefit of those who consider relevance to one's own time as of crucial importance, I will add, in regard to our age, that never has there been a time when men have so desperately needed a projection of things as they ought to be.

I do not mean to imply that I knew, when I wrote it, that *The Fountainhead* would remain in print for twenty-five years. I did not think of any specific time period. I knew only that : was a book that *ought to* live. It did.

But that I knew it over twenty-five years ago—that I knew it while *The Fountainhead* was being rejected by twelve publishers, some of whom declared that it was "too intellectual," "too controversial" and would not sell because no audience existed for it—*that* was the difficult part of its history; difficult for me to bear. I mention it here for the sake of any other writer of my kind who might have to face the same battle—as a reminder of the fact that it can be done.

I will not retell here the story of the publication of *The Fountainhead.* But it would be impossible for me to discuss *The Fountainhead* or any part of its history without mentioning the man who made it possible for me to write it: my husband, Frank O'Connor.

In a play I wrote in my early thirties, *Ideal,* the heroine, a screen star, speaks for me when she says: "I want to see, real, living, and in the hours of my own days, that glory I create as an illusion. I want it real. I want to know that there is someone, somewhere, who wants it, too. Or else what is the use of seeing it, and working, and burning oneself for an impossible vision? A spirit, too, needs fuel. It can run dry."

Frank was the fuel. He gave me, in the hours of my own days, the reality of that sense of life which created *The Fountainhead*—and he helped me to maintain it over a long span of years when there was nothing around us but a gray desert of people and events that evoked nothing but contempt and revulsion. The essence of the bond between us is the fact that neither of us has ever wanted or been tempted to settle for anything less than the world presented in *The Fountainhead.* We never will.

If there is in me any touch of the Naturalistic writer who records "real-life" dialogue for use in a novel, it has been exercised only in regard to Frank. For instance, one of the most effective lines in *The Fountainhead* comes at the end of Part II, when, in reply to Toohey's question: "Why don't you tell me what you think of me?" Roark answers: "But I don't think of you." That line was Frank's answer to a different type of person, in a somewhat similar context. "You're casting pearls without getting even a pork chop in return," was said by Frank to me, in regard to my professional position. I gave that line to Dominique at Roark's trial.

I did not feel discouragement very often, and when I did, it did not last longer than overnight. But there was one evening, during the writing of *The Fountainhead,* when I felt so profound an indignation at the state of "things as they are" that it seemed as if I would never regain the energy to move one step farther toward "things as they ought to be." Frank talked to me for hours, that night. He convinced me of why one cannot give up the world to those one despises. By the time he finished, my discouragement was gone; it never came back in so intense a form.

I had been opposed to the practice of dedicating books; I had held that a book is addressed to any reader who proves worthy of it. But, that night, I told Frank that I would dedicate *The Fountainhead* to him because he had saved it. And one of my happiest moments, about two years later, was given to me by the look on his face when he came home, one day, and saw the page-proofs of the book, headed by the page that stated in cold, clear, objective print: *To Frank O'Connor*.

These are some of the reasons why, for me, the most profound *personal* meaning of this new, anniversary edition is the fact that its jacket carries the reproduction of a painting by Frank. It is like the completion, the proper climax of this book's history.

That painting was not done for *The Fountainhead*. It represents Frank's version of a sunrise we had seen once in San Francisco. His title for the painting is *Man Also Rises*.

I have been asked whether I have changed in these past twenty-five years. No, I am the same—only more so. Have my ideas changed? No, my fundamental convictions, my view of life and of man, have never changed, from as far back as I can remember, but my knowledge of their applications has grown, in scope and in precision. What is my present evaluation of *The Fountainhead?* I am as proud of it as I was on the day when I finished writing it.

Was *The Fountainhead* written for the purpose of presenting my philosophy? Here, I shall quote from *The Goal of My Writing*, an address I gave at Lewis and Clark College, on October 1, 1963: "This is the motive and purpose of my writing: *the projection of an ideal man*. The portrayal of a moral ideal, as my ultimate literary goal, as an end in itself—to which any didactic, intellectual or philosophical values contained in a novel are only the means.

"Let me stress this: my purpose is *not* the philosophical enlightenment of my readers . . . My purpose, first cause and prime mover is the portrayal of Howard Roark [or the heroes of *Atlas Shrugged*] *as an end in himself* . . .

"I write—and read—for the sake of the story. . . . My basic test for any story is: 'Would I want to meet these characters and observe these events in real life? Is this story an experience worth living through for its own sake? Is the pleasure of contemplating these characters an end in itself?'

"Since my purpose is the presentation of an ideal man, I had to define and present the conditions which make him possible and which his existence requires. Since man's character is the product of his premises, I had to define and present the kinds of premises and values that create the character of an ideal man and motivate his actions; which means that I had to define and present a rational code of ethics. Since man acts among and deals with other men, I had to present the kind of social system that makes it possible for ideal men to exist and to function—a free, productive, rational system which demands and rewards the best in every man, and which is, obviously, laissez-faire capitalism.

"But neither politics nor ethics nor philosophy is an end in itself, neither in life nor in literature. Only Man is an end in himself."

Are there any substantial changes I would want to make in *The Fountainhead?* No—and, therefore, I have left its text untouched. I want it to stand as it was written. But there is one minor error and one possibly misleading sentence which I should like to clarify, so I shall mention them here.

The error is semantic: the use of the word "egotist" in Roark's courtroom speech, while actually the word should have been "egoist." The error was caused by my reliance on a dictionary which gave such misleading definitions of these two words that "egotist" seemed closer to the meaning I intended (*Webster's Daily Use Dictionary,* 1933). (Modern philosophers, however, are guiltier than lexicographers in regard to these two terms.)

The possibly misleading sentence is in Roark's speech: "From this simplest necessity to the highest religious abstraction, from the wheel to the skyscraper, everything we are and everything we have comes from a single attribute of man—the function of his reasoning mind."

This could be misinterpreted to mean an endorsement of religion or religious ideas. I remember hesitating over that sentence, when I wrote it, and deciding that Roark's and my atheism, as well as the overall spirit of the book, were so clearly established that no one would misunderstand it, particularly since I said that religious abstractions are the product of man's mind, not of supernatural revelation.

But an issue of this sort should not be left to implications. What I was referring to was not religion as such, but a special category of abstractions, the most exalted one, which, for centuries, had been the near-monopoly of religion: *ethics*—not the particular content of religious ethics, but the abstraction "ethics," the realm of values, man's code of good and evil, with the emotional connotations of height, uplift, nobility, reverence, grandeur, which pertain to the realm of man's values, but which religion has arrogated to itself.

The same meaning and considerations were intended and are applicable to another passage of the book, a brief dialogue between Roark and Hopton Stoddard, which may be misunderstood if taken out of context:

" 'You're a profoundly religious man, Mr. Roark—in your own way. I can see that in your buildings.'

" 'That's true,' said Roark."

In the context of that scene, however, the meaning is clear: it is Roark's profound dedication to values, to the highest and best, to the ideal, that Stoddard is referring to (see his explanation of the nature of the proposed temple). The erection of the Stoddard Temple and the subsequent trial state the issue explicitly.

This leads me to a wider issue which is involved in every line of *The Fountainhead* and which has to be understood if one wants to understand the causes of its lasting appeal.

Religion's monopoly in the field of ethics has made it extremely difficult to communicate the emotional meaning and connotations of a rational view of life. Just as religion has pre-empted the field of ethics, turning morality *against* man, so it has usurped the highest moral concepts of our language, placing them outside this earth and beyond man's reach. "Exaltation" is usually taken to mean an emotional state evoked by contemplating the supernatural. "Worship" means the emotional experience of loyalty and dedication to something higher than man. "Reverence" means the emotion of a sacred respect, to be experienced on one's knees. "Sacred" means superior to and not-to-be-touched-by any concerns of man or of this earth. Etc.

But such concepts do name actual emotions, even though no supernatural dimension exists; and these emotions are experienced as uplifting or ennobling, without the self-abasement required by religious definitions. What, then, is their source or referent in reality? It is the entire emotional realm of man's dedication to a moral ideal. Yet apart from the man-degrading aspects introduced by religion, that emotional realm is left unidentified, without concepts, words or recognition.

It is this highest level of man's emotions that has to be redeemed from the murk of mysticism and redirected at its proper object: man.

It is in this sense, with this meaning and intention, that I would identify the sense of life dramatized in *The Fountainhead* as *man-worship*.

It is an emotion that a few—a very few—men experience consistently; some men experience it in rare, single sparks that flash and die without consequences; some do not know what I am talking about; some do and spend their lives as frantically virulent spark-extinguishers.

Do not confuse "man-worship" with the many attempts, not to emancipate morality from religion and bring it into the realm of reason, but to substitute a secular meaning for the worst, the most profoundly irrational elements of religion. For instance, there are all the variants of modern collectivism (communist, fascist, Nazi, etc.), which preserve the religious-altruist ethics in full and merely substitute "society" for

God as the beneficiary of man's self-immolation. There are the various schools of modern philosophy which, rejecting the law of identity, proclaim that reality is an indeterminate flux ruled by miracles and shaped by whims—not God's whims, but man's or "society's." These neo-mystics are not man-worshipers; they are merely the secularizers of as profound a hatred for man as that of their avowedly mystic predecessors.

A cruder variant of the same hatred is represented by those concrete-bound, "statistical" mentalities who—unable to grasp the meaning of man's volition—declare that man cannot be an object of worship, since they have never encountered any specimens of humanity who deserved it.

The man-worshipers, in my sense of the term, are those who see man's highest potential and strive to actualize it. The man-haters are those who regard man as a helpless, depraved, contemptible creature—and struggle never to let him discover otherwise. It is important here to remember that the only direct, introspective knowledge of man anyone possesses is of himself.

More specifically, the essential division between these two camps is: those dedicated to the *exaltation* of man's self-esteem and the *sacredness* of his happiness on earth—and those determined not to allow either to become possible. The majority of mankind spend their lives and psychological energy in the middle, swinging between these two, struggling not to allow the issue to be named. This does not change the nature of the issue.

Perhaps the best way to communicate *The Fountainhead's* sense of life is by means of the quotation which had stood at the head of my manuscript, but which I removed from the final, published book. With this opportunity to explain it, I am glad to bring it back.

I removed it, because of my profound disagreement with the philosophy of its author, Friedrich Nietzsche. Philosophically, Nietzsche is a mystic and an irrationalist. His metaphysics consists of a somewhat "Byronic" and mystically "malevolent" universe; his epistemology subordinates reason to "will," or feeling or instinct or blood or innate virtues of character. But, as a poet, he projects at times (not consistently) a magnificent feeling for man's greatness, expressed in emotional, *not* intellectual, terms.

This is especially true of the quotation I had chosen. I could not endorse its literal meaning: it proclaims an indefensible tenet—psychological determinism. But if one takes it as a poetic projection of an emotional experience (and if, intellectually, one substitutes the concept of an acquired "basic premise" for the concept of an innate "fundamental certainty"), then that quotation communicates the inner state of an exalted self-esteem—and sums up the emotional consequences for which *The Fountainhead* provides the rational, philosophical base:

"It is not the works, but the *belief* which is here decisive and determines the order of rank—to employ once more an old religious formula with a new and deeper meaning,—it is some fundamental certainty which a noble soul has about itself, something which is not to be sought, is not to be found, and perhaps, also, is not to be lost. —*The noble soul has reverence for itself.*—" (Friedrich Nietzsche, *Beyond Good and Evil.)*

This view of man has rarely been expressed in human history. Today, it is virtually non-existent. Yet this is the view with which—in various degrees of longing, wistfulness, passion and agonized confusion —the best of mankind's youth start out in life. It is not even a view, for most of them, but a foggy, groping, undefined sense made of raw pain and incommunicable happiness. It is a sense of enormous expectation, the sense that one's life is important, that great achievements are within one's capacity, and that great things lie ahead.

It is not in the nature of man—nor of any living entity—to start out by giving up, by spitting in one's own face and damning existence; that requires a process of corruption whose rapidity differs from man to man. Some give up at the first touch of pressure; some sell out; some run down by imperceptible degrees and lose their fire, never knowing when or how they lost it. Then all of these vanish in the vast swamp of their elders who tell them persistently that maturity consists of abandoning one's mind; security, of abandoning one's values; practicality, of losing self-esteem. Yet a few hold on and move on, knowing that that fire is not to be betrayed, learning how to give it shape, purpose and reality. But whatever their future, at the dawn of their lives, men seek a noble vision of man's nature and of life's potential.

There are very few guideposts to find. *The Fountainhead* is one of them.

This is one of the cardinal reasons of *The Fountainhead's* lasting appeal: it is a confirmation of the spirit of youth, proclaiming man's glory, showing how much is possible.

It does not matter that only a few in each generation will grasp and achieve the full reality of man's proper stature—and that the rest will betray it. It is those few that move the world and give life its meaning—and it is those few that I have always sought to address. The rest are no concern of mine; it is not me or *The Fountainhead* that they will betray: it is their own souls.

AYN RAND

New York, May 1968

CONTENTS

Part 1

PETER KEATING

I

HOWARD ROARK LAUGHED.

He stood naked at the edge of a cliff. The lake lay far below him. A frozen explosion of granite burst in flight to the sky over motionless water. The water seemed immovable, the stone flowing. The stone had the stillness of one brief moment in battle when thrust meets thrust and the currents are held in a pause more dynamic than motion. The stone glowed, wet with sunrays.

The lake below was only a thin steel ring that cut the rocks in half. The rocks went on into the depth, unchanged. They began and ended in the sky. So that the world seemed suspended in space, an island floating on nothing, anchored to the feet of the man on the cliff.

His body leaned back against the sky. It was a body of long straight lines and angles, each curve broken into planes. He stood, rigid, his hands hanging at his sides, palms out. He felt his shoulder blades drawn tight together, the curve of his neck, and the weight of the blood in his hands. He felt the wind behind him, in the hollow of his spine. The wind waved his hair against the sky. His hair was neither blond nor red, but the exact color of ripe orange rind.

He laughed at the thing which had happened to him that morning and at the things which now lay ahead.

He knew that the days ahead would be difficult. There were questions to be faced and a plan of action to be prepared. He knew that he should think about it. He knew also that he would not think, because everything was clear to him already, because the plan had been set long ago, and because he wanted to laugh.

He tried to consider it. But he forgot. He was looking at the granite.

He did not laugh as his eyes stopped in awareness of the earth around him. His face was like a law of nature—a thing one could not question, alter or implore. It had high cheekbones over gaunt, hollow cheeks; gray eyes, cold and steady; a contemptuous mouth, shut tight, the mouth of an executioner or a saint.

He looked at the granite. To be cut, he thought, and made into walls. He looked at a tree. To be split and made into rafters. He looked at a streak of rust on the stone and thought of iron ore under the ground. To be melted and to emerge as girders against the sky.

These rocks, he thought, are here for me; waiting for the drill, the dynamite and my voice; waiting to be split, ripped, pounded, reborn; waiting for the shape my hands will give them.

Then he shook his head, because he remembered that morning and that there were many things to be done. He stepped to the edge, raised his arms, and dived down into the sky below.

He cut straight across the lake to the shore ahead. He reached the rocks where he had left his clothes. He looked regretfully about him. For three years, ever since he had lived in Stanton, he had come here for his only relaxation, to swim, to rest, to think, to be alone and alive, whenever he could find one hour to spare, which had not been often. In his new freedom the first thing he had wanted to do was to come here, because he knew that he was coming for the last time. That morning he had been expelled from the Architectural School of the Stanton Institute of Technology.

He pulled his clothes on: old denim trousers, sandals, a shirt with short sleeves and most of its buttons missing. He swung down a narrow trail among the boulders, to a path running through a green slope, to the road below.

He walked swiftly, with a loose, lazy expertness of motion. He walked down the long road, in the sun. Far ahead Stanton lay sprawled on the coast of Massachusetts, a little town as a setting for the gem of its existence—the great institute rising on a hill beyond.

The township of Stanton began with a dump. A gray mound of refuse rose in the grass. It smoked faintly. Tin cans glittered in the sun. The road led past the first houses to a church. The church was a Gothic monument of shingles painted pigeon blue. It had stout wooden buttresses supporting nothing. It had stained-glass windows with heavy traceries of imitation stone. It opened the way into long streets edged by tight, exhibitionist lawns. Behind the lawns stood wooden piles tortured out of all shape: twisted into gables, turrets, dormers; bulging with porches; crushed under huge, sloping roofs. White curtains floated at the windows. A garbage can stood at a side door, flowing over. An old Pekinese sat upon a cushion on a door step, its mouth drooling. A line of diapers fluttered in the wind between the columns of a porch.

People turned to look at Howard Roark as he passed. Some remained staring after him with sudden resentment. They could give no reason for it: it was an instinct his presence awakened in most people. Howard Roark saw no one. For him, the streets were empty. He could have walked there naked without concern.

He crossed the heart of Stanton, a broad green edged by shop windows. The windows displayed new placards announcing: WELCOME TO THE CLASS OF '22! GOOD LUCK, CLASS OF '22! The Class of '22 of the Stanton Institute of Technology was holding its commencement exercises that afternoon.

Roark swung into a side street, where at the end of a long row, on a knoll over a green ravine, stood the house of Mrs. Keating. He had boarded at that house for three years.

Mrs. Keating was out on the porch. She was feeding a couple of canaries in a cage suspended over the railing. Her pudgy little hand stopped in mid-air when she saw him. She watched him with curiosity. She tried to pull her mouth into a proper expression of sympathy; she succeeded only in betraying that the process was an effort.

He was crossing the porch without noticing her. She stopped him.

"Mr. Roark!"

"Yes?"

"Mr. Roark, I'm so sorry about—" she hesitated demurely "—about what happened this morning."

"What?" he asked.

"Your being expelled from the Institute. I can't tell you how sorry I am. I only want you to know that I feel for you."

He stood looking at her. She knew that he did not see her. No, she thought, it was not that exactly. He always looked straight at people and his damnable eyes never missed a thing, it was only that he made people feel as if they did not exist. He just stood looking. He would not answer.

"But what I say," she continued, "is that if one suffers in this world, it's on account of error. Of course, you'll have to give up the architect profession now, won't you? But then a young man can always earn a decent living clerking or selling or something."

He turned to go.

"Oh, Mr. Roark!" she called.

"Yes?"

"The Dean phoned for you while you were out."

For once, she expected some emotion from him; and an emotion would be the equivalent of seeing him broken. She did not know what it was about him that had always made her want to see him broken.

"Yes?" he asked.

"The Dean," she repeated uncertainly, trying to recapture her effect. "The Dean himself through his secretary."

"Well?"

"She said to tell you that the Dean wanted to see you immediately the moment you got back."

"Thank you."

"What do you suppose he can want *now?*"

"I don't know."

He had said: "I don't know." She had heard distinctly: "I don't give a damn." She stared at him incredulously.

"By the way," she said, "Petey is graduating today." She said it without apparent relevance.

"Today? Oh, yes."

"It's a great day for me. When I think of how I skimped and slaved to put my boy through school. Not that I'm complaining. I'm not one to complain. Petey's a brilliant boy."

She stood drawn up. Her stout little body was corseted so tightly under the starched folds of her cotton dress that it seemed to squeeze the fat out to her wrists and ankles.

"But of course," she went on rapidly, with the eagerness of her favorite subject, "I'm not one to boast. Some mothers are lucky and others just aren't. We're all in our rightful place. You just watch Petey from now on. I'm not one to want my boy to kill himself with work and I'll thank the Lord for any small success that comes his way. But if that boy isn't the greatest architect of this U.S.A., his mother will want to know the reason why!"

He moved to go.

"But what am I doing, gabbing with you like that!" she said brightly. "You've got to hurry and change and run along. The Dean's waiting for you."

She stood looking after him through the screen door, watching his gaunt figure move across the rigid neatness of her parlor. He always made her uncomfortable in the house, with a vague feeling of apprehension, as if she were waiting to see him swing out suddenly and smash her coffee tables, her Chinese vases, her framed photographs. He had never shown any inclination to do so. She kept expecting it, without knowing why.

Roark went up the stairs to his room. It was a large, bare room, made luminous by the clean glow of whitewash. Mrs. Keating had never had the feeling that Roark really lived there. He had not added a single object to the bare necessities of furniture which she had provided; no pictures, no pennants, no cheering human touch. He had brought nothing to the room but his clothes and his drawings; there were few clothes and too many drawings; they were stacked high in one corner; sometimes she thought that the drawings lived there, not the man.

Roark walked now to these drawings; they were the first things to be packed. He lifted one of them, then the next, then another. He stood looking at the broad sheets.

They were sketches of buildings such as had never stood on the face of the earth. They were as the first houses built by the first man born, who had never heard of others building before him. There was nothing to be said of them, except that each structure was inevitably what it had to be. It was not as if the draftsman had sat over them, pondering laboriously, piecing together doors, windows and columns, as his whim dictated and as the books prescribed. It was as if the buildings had sprung from the earth and from some living force, complete, unalterably right. The hand that had made the sharp pencil lines still had much to learn. But not a line seemed superfluous, not a needed plane was missing. The structures were austere and simple, until one looked at them and realized what work, what complexity of method, what tension of thought had achieved the simplicity. No laws had dictated a single detail. The buildings were not Classical, they were not Gothic, they were not Renaissance. They were only Howard Roark.

He stopped, looking at a sketch. It was one that had never satisfied him. He had designed it as an exercise he had given himself, apart from his schoolwork; he did that often when he found some particular site and stopped before it to think of what building it should bear. He had spent nights staring at this sketch, wondering what he had missed. Glancing at it now, unprepared, he saw the mistake he had made.

He flung the sketch down on the table, he bent over it, he slashed lines straight through his neat drawing. He stopped once in a while and stood looking at it, his finger tips pressed to the paper; as if his hands held the building. His hands had long fingers, hard veins, prominent joints and wristbones.

An hour later he heard a knock at his door.

"Come in!" he snapped, without stopping.

"Mr. Roark!" gasped Mrs. Keating, staring at him from the threshold. "What on earth are you doing?"

He turned and looked at her, trying to remember who she was.

"How about the Dean?" she moaned. "The Dean that's waiting for you?"

"Oh," said Roark. "Oh, yes. I forgot."

"You . . . *forgot?*"

"Yes." There was a note of wonder in his voice, astonished by her astonishment.

"Well, all I can say," she choked, "is that it serves you right! It just serves you right. And with the commencement beginning at four-thirty, how do you expect him to have time to see you?"

"I'll go at once, Mrs. Keating."

It was not her curiosity alone that prompted her to action; it was a secret fear that the sentence of the Board might be revoked. He went to the bathroom at the end of the hall; she watched him washing his hands, throwing his loose, straight hair back into a semblance of order. He came out again, he was on his way to the stairs before she realized that he was leaving.

"Mr. Roark!" she gasped, pointing at his clothes. "You're not going like *this?*"

"Why not?"

"But it's your *Dean!*"

"Not any more, Mrs. Keating."

She thought, aghast, that he said it as if he were actually happy.

The Stanton Institute of Technology stood on a hill, its crenelated walls raised as a crown over the city stretched below. It looked like a medieval fortress, with a Gothic cathedral grafted to its belly. The fortress was eminently suited to its purpose, with stout, brick walls, a few slits wide enough for sentries, ramparts behind which defending archers could hide, and corner turrets from which boiling oil could be poured upon the attacker—should such an emergency arise in an institute of learning. The cathedral rose over it in lace splendor, a fragile defense against two great enemies: light and air.

The Dean's office looked like a chapel, a pool of dreamy twilight fed by one tall window of stained glass. The twilight flowed in through the garments of stiff saints, their arms contorted at the elbows. A red spot of light and a purple one rested respectively upon two genuine gargoyles squatting at the corners of a fireplace that had never been used. A green spot stood in the center of a picture of the Parthenon, suspended over the fireplace.

When Roark entered the office, the outlines of the Dean's figure swam dimly behind his desk, which was carved like a confessional. He was a short, plumpish gentleman whose spreading flesh was held in check by an indomitable dignity.

"Ah, yes, Roark," he smiled. "Do sit down, please."

Roark sat down. The Dean entwined his fingers on his stomach and waited for the plea he expected. No plea came. The Dean cleared his throat.

"It will be unnecessary for me to express my regret at the unfortunate event of this morning," he began, "since I take it for granted that you have always known my sincere interest in your welfare."

"Quite unnecessary," said Roark.

The Dean looked at him dubiously, but continued:

"Needless to say, I did not vote against you. I abstained entirely. But you may be glad to know that you had quite a determined little group of defenders at the meeting. Small, but determined. Your professor of structural engineering acted quite the crusader on your behalf. So did your professor of mathematics. Unfortunately, those who felt it their duty to vote for your expulsion quite outnumbered the others. Professor Peterkin, your critic of design, made an issue of the matter. He went so far as to threaten us with his resignation unless you were expelled. You must realize that you have given Professor Peterkin great provocation."

"I do," said Roark.

"That, you see, was the trouble. I am speaking of your attitude towards the subject of architectural design. You have never given it the attention it deserves. And yet, you have been excellent in all the engineering sciences. Of course, no one denies the importance of structural engineering to a future architect, but why go to extremes? Why neglect what may be termed the artistic and inspirational side of your profession and concentrate on all those dry, technical, mathematical subjects? You intended to become an architect, not a civil engineer."

"Isn't this superfluous?" Roark asked. "It's past. There's no point in discussing my choice of subjects now."

"I am endeavoring to be helpful, Roark. You must be fair about this. You cannot say that you were not given many warnings before this happened."

"I was."

The Dean moved in his chair. Roark made him uncomfortable. Roark's eyes were fixed on him politely. The Dean thought, there's nothing wrong with the way he's looking at me, in fact it's quite correct, most properly attentive; only, it's as if I were not here.

"Every problem you were given," the Dean went on, "every project you had to design—what did you do with it? Every one of them done in that—well, I cannot call it a style—in that incredible manner of yours. It is contrary to every principle we have tried to teach you, contrary to all established precedents and traditions of Art. You may think you are what is called a modernist, but it isn't even that. It is . . . it is sheer insanity, if you don't mind."

"I don't mind."

"When you were given projects that left the choice of style up to you and you turned in one of your wild stunts—well, frankly, your teachers passed you because they did not know what to make of it. *But*, when you were given an exercise in the historical styles, a Tudor chapel or a French opera house to design—and you turned in something that looked like a lot of boxes piled together without rhyme or reason—would you say it was an answer to an assignment or plain insubordination?"

"It was insubordination," said Roark.

"We wanted to give you a chance—in view of your brilliant record in all other subjects. But when you turn in this—" the Dean slammed his fist down on a sheet spread before him—*"this* as a Renaissance villa for your final project of the year—really, my boy, it was too much!"

The sheet bore a drawing—a house of glass and concrete. In the corner there was a sharp, angular signature: Howard Roark.

"How do you expect us to pass you after this?"

"I don't."

"You left us no choice in the matter. Naturally, you would feel bitterness toward us at this moment, but . . ."

"I feel nothing of the kind," said Roark quietly. "I owe you an apology. I don't usually let things happen to me. I made a mistake this time. I shouldn't have waited for you to throw me out. I should have left long ago."

"Now, now, don't get discouraged. This is not the right attitude to take. Particularly in view of what I am going to tell you."

The Dean smiled and leaned forward confidentially, enjoying the overture to a good deed.

"Here is the real purpose of our interview. I was anxious to let you know as soon as possible. I did not wish to leave you disheartened. Oh, I did, personally, take a chance with the President's temper when I mentioned this to him, but . . . Mind you, he did not commit himself, but . . . Here is how things stand: now that you realize how serious it is, if you take a year off, to rest, to think it over—shall we say to grow up?—there might be a chance of our taking you back. Mind you, I cannot promise anything—this is strictly unofficial—it would be most unusual, but in view of the circumstances and of your brilliant record, there might be a very good chance."

Roark smiled. It was not a happy smile, it was not a grateful one. It was a simple, easy smile and it was amused.

"I don't think you understood me," said Roark. "What made you suppose that I want to come back?"

"Eh?"

"I won't be back. I have nothing further to learn here."

"I *don't* understand you," said the Dean stiffly.

"Is there any point in explaining? It's of no interest to you any longer."

"You will kindly explain yourself."

"If you wish. I want to be an architect, not an archeologist. I see no purpose in doing Renaissance villas. Why learn to design them, when I'll never build them?"

"My dear boy, the great style of the Renaissance is far from dead. Houses of that style are being erected every day."

"They are. And they will be. But not by me."

"Come, come, now, this is childish."

"I came here to learn about building. When I was given a project, its only value to me was to learn to solve it as I would solve a real one in the future. I did them the way I'll build them. I've learned all I could learn here—in the structural sciences of which you don't approve. One more year of drawing Italian post cards would give me nothing."

An hour ago the Dean had wished that this interview would proceed as calmly as possible. Now he wished that Roark would display some emotion; it seemed unnatural for him to be so quietly natural in the circumstances.

"Do you mean to tell me that you're thinking seriously of building *that way*, when and *if* you are an architect?"

"Yes."

"My dear fellow, who will let you?"

"That's not the point. The point is, who will stop me?"

"Look here, this is serious. I am sorry that I haven't had a long, earnest talk with you much earlier. . . . I know, I know, I know, don't interrupt me, you've seen a modernistic building or two, and it gave you ideas. But do you realize what a passing fancy that whole so-called modern movement is? You must learn to understand—and it has been proved by all authorities—that everything beautiful in architecture has been done already. There is a treasure mine in every style of the past. We can only choose from the great masters. Who are we to improve upon them? We can only attempt, respectfully, to repeat."

"Why?" asked Howard Roark.

No, thought the Dean, no, he hasn't said anything else; it's a perfectly innocent word; he's not threatening me.

"But it's self-evident!" said the Dean.

"Look," said Roark evenly, and pointed at the window. "Can you see the campus and the town? Do you see how many men are walking and living down there? Well, I don't give a damn what any or all of them think about architecture—or about anything else, for that matter. Why should I consider what their grandfathers thought of it?"

"That is our sacred tradition."

"Why?"

"For heaven's sake, can't you stop being so naïve about it?"

"But I don't understand. Why do you want me to think that *this* is great architecture?" He pointed to the picture of the Parthenon.

"That," said the Dean, "is the Parthenon."

"So it is."

"I haven't the time to waste on silly questions."

"All right, then." Roark got up, he took a long ruler from the desk, he walked to the picture. "Shall I tell you what's rotten about it?"

"It's the *Parthenon!"* said the Dean.

"Yes, God damn it, the Parthenon!"

The ruler struck the glass over the picture.

"Look," said Roark. "The famous flutings on the famous columns— what are they there for? To hide the joints in wood—when columns were made of wood, only these aren't, they're marble. The triglyphs, what are they? *Wood.* Wooden beams, the way they had to be laid when people began to build wooden shacks. Your Greeks took marble and they made copies of their wooden structures out of it, because others had done it that way. Then your masters of the Renaissance came along and made copies in plaster of copies in marble of copies in wood. Now here we are, making copies in steel and concrete of copies in plaster of copies in marble of copies in wood. Why?"

The Dean sat watching him curiously. Something puzzled him, not in the words, but in Roark's manner of saying them.

"Rules?" said Roark. "Here are my rules: what can be done with one substance must never be done with another. No two materials are alike. No two sites on earth are alike. No two buildings have the same purpose. The purpose, the site, the material determine the shape. Nothing can be reasonable or beautiful unless it's made by one central idea, and the idea sets every detail. A building is alive, like a man. Its integrity is to follow its own truth, its one single theme, and to serve its own single purpose. A man doesn't borrow pieces of his body. A building doesn't borrow hunks of its soul. Its maker gives it the soul and every wall, window and stairway to express it."

"But all the proper forms of expression have been discovered long ago."

"Expression—of what? The Parthenon did not serve the same purpose as its wooden ancestor. An airline terminal does not serve the same purpose as the Parthenon. Every form has its own meaning. Every man creates his meaning and form and goal. Why is it so important—what others have done? Why does it become sacred by the mere fact of not being your own? Why is anyone and everyone right—so long as it's not yourself? Why does the number of those others take the place of truth? Why is truth made a mere matter of arithmetic—and only of addition at that? Why is everything twisted out of all sense to fit everything else?

There must be some reason. I don't know. I've never known it. I'd like to understand."

"For heaven's sake," said the Dean. "Sit down. . . . That's better. . . . Would you mind very much putting that ruler down? . . . Thank you. . . . Now listen to me. No one has ever denied the importance of modern technique to an architect. We must learn to adapt the beauty of the past to the needs of the present. The voice of the past is the voice of the people. Nothing has ever been invented by one man in architecture. The proper creative process is a slow, gradual, anonymous, collective one, in which each man collaborates with all the others and subordinates himself to the standards of the majority."

"But you see," said Roark quietly, "I have, let's say, sixty years to live. Most of that time will be spent working. I've chosen the work I want to do. If I find no joy in it, then I'm only condemning myself to sixty years of torture. And I can find the joy only if I do my work in the best way possible to me. But the best is a matter of standards—and I set my own standards. I inherit nothing. I stand at the end of no tradition. I may, perhaps, stand at the beginning of one."

"How old are you?" asked the Dean.

"Twenty-two," said Roark.

"Quite excusable," said the Dean; he seemed relieved. "You'll outgrow all that." He smiled. "The old standards have lived for thousands of years and nobody has been able to improve upon them. What are your modernists? A transient mode, exhibitionists trying to attract attention. Have you observed the course of their careers? Can you name one who has achieved any permanent distinction? Look at Henry Cameron. A great man, a leading architect twenty years ago. What is he today? Lucky if he gets—once a year—a garage to remodel. A bum and a drunkard, who . . ."

"We won't discuss Henry Cameron."

"Oh? Is he a friend of yours?"

"No. But I've seen his buildings."

"And you found them . . ."

"I said we won't discuss Henry Cameron."

"Very well. You must realize that I am allowing you a great deal of . . . shall we say, latitude? I am not accustomed to hold a discussion with a student who behaves in your manner. However, I am anxious to forestall, if possible, what appears to be a tragedy, the spectacle of a young man of your obvious mental gifts setting out deliberately to make a mess of his life."

The Dean wondered why he had promised the professor of mathematics to do all he could for this boy. Merely because the professor had said: "This," and pointed to Roark's project, "is a great man." A great man, thought the Dean, or a criminal. The Dean winced. He did not approve of either.

He thought of what he had heard about Roark's past. Roark's father had been a steel puddler somewhere in Ohio and had died long ago. The boy's entrance papers showed no record of nearest relatives. When asked about it, Roark had said indifferently: "I don't think I have any relatives. I may have. I don't know." He had seemed astonished that he should be expected to have any interest in the matter. He had not made or sought a single friend on the campus. He had refused to join a fraternity. He had worked his way through high school and through the three years here at the Institute. He had worked as a common laborer in the building trades since childhood. He had done plastering, plumbing, steel work, anything he could get, going from one small town to another, working his way east, to the great cities. The Dean had seen him, last summer, on his vacation, catching rivets on a skyscraper in construction in Boston; his long body relaxed under greasy overalls, only his eyes intent, and his right arm swinging forward, once in a while, expertly, without effort, to catch the flying ball of fire at the last moment, when it seemed that the hot rivet would miss the bucket and strike him in the face.

"Look here, Roark," said the Dean gently. "You have worked hard for your education. You had only one year left to go. There is something important to consider, particularly for a boy in your position. There's the *practical* side of an architect's career to think about. An architect is not an end in himself. He is only a small part of a great social whole. *Co-operation* is the key word to our modern world and to the profession of architecture in particular. Have you thought of your potential clients?"

"Yes," said Roark.

"The *Client*," said the Dean. "The Client. Think of that above all. He's the one to live in the house you build. Your only purpose is to serve him. You must aspire to give the proper artistic expression to his wishes. Isn't that all one can say on the subject?"

"Well, I could say that I must aspire to build for my client the most comfortable, the most logical, the most beautiful house that can be built. I could say that I must try to sell him the best I have and also teach him to know the best. I could say it, but I won't. Because I don't intend to build in order to serve or help anyone. I don't intend to build in order to have clients. I intend to have clients in order to build."

"How do you propose to force your ideas on them?"

"I don't propose to force or be forced. Those who want me will come to me."

Then the Dean understood what had puzzled him in Roark's manner.

"You know," he said, "you would sound much more convincing if you spoke as if you cared whether I agreed with you or not."

"That's true," said Roark. "I don't care whether you agree with me or not." He said it so simply that it did not sound offensive, it sounded like the statement of a fact which he noticed, puzzled, for the first time.

"You don't care what others think—which might be understandable. But you don't care even to make them think as you do?"

"No."

"But that's . . . that's monstrous."

"Is it? Probably. I couldn't say."

"I'm glad of this interview," said the Dean, suddenly, too loudly. "It has relieved my conscience. I believe, as others stated at the meeting, that the profession of architecture is not for you. I have tried to help you. Now I agree with the Board. You are a man not to be encouraged. You are dangerous."

"To whom?" asked Roark.

But the Dean rose, indicating that the interview was over.

Roark left the room. He walked slowly through the long halls, down the stairs, out to the lawn below. He had met many men such as the Dean; he had never understood them. He knew only that there was some important difference between his actions and theirs. It had ceased to disturb him long ago. But he always looked for a central theme in buildings and he looked for a central impulse in men. He knew the source of his actions; he could not discover theirs. He did not care. He had never learned the process of thinking about other people. But he wondered, at times, what made them such as they were. He wondered again, thinking of the Dean. There was an important secret involved somewhere in that question, he thought. There was a principle which he must discover.

But he stopped. He saw the sunlight of late afternoon, held still in the moment before it was to fade, on the gray limestone of a stringcourse running along the brick wall of the Institute building. He forgot men, the Dean and the principle behind the Dean, which he wanted to discover. He thought only of how lovely the stone looked in the fragile light and of what he could have done with that stone.

He thought of a broad sheet of paper, and he saw, rising on the paper, bare walls of gray limestone with long bands of glass, admitting the glow of the sky into the classrooms. In the corner of the sheet stood a sharp, angular signature—HOWARD ROARK.

II

" . . . Architecture, my friends, is a great art based on two cosmic principles: Beauty and Utility. In a broader sense, these are but part of the three eternal entities: Truth, Love and Beauty. Truth—to the traditions of our Art, Love—for our fellow men whom we are to serve, Beauty—ah, Beauty is a compelling goddess to all artists, be it in the shape of a lovely woman or a building. . . . Hm. . . . Yes. . . . In conclusion, I should like to say to you, who are about to embark upon your careers in architecture, that you are now the custodians of a sacred heritage. . . . Hm. . . . Yes. . . . So, go forth into the world, armed with the three eternal enti—armed with courage and vision, loyal to the standards this great school has represented for many years. May you all serve faithfully, neither as slaves to the past nor as those parvenus who preach originality for its own sake, which attitude is only ignorant vanity. May you all have many rich, active years before you and leave, as you depart from this world, your mark on the sands of time!"

Guy Francon ended with a flourish, raising his right arm in a sweeping salute; informal, but with an air, that gay, swaggering air which Guy Francon could always permit himself. The huge hall before him came to life in applause and approval.

A sea of faces, young, perspiring and eager, had been raised solemnly —for forty-five minutes—to the platform where Guy Francon had held forth as the speaker at the commencement exercises of the Stanton Institute of Technology, Guy Francon who had brought his own person from New York for the occasion; Guy Francon, of the illustrious firm of Francon & Heyer, vice-president of the Architects' Guild of America, member of the American Academy of Arts and Letters, member of the National Fine Arts Commission, Secretary of the Arts and Crafts League of New York, chairman of the Society for Architectural Enlightenment of the U.S.A.; Guy Francon, knight of the Legion of Honor of France, decorated by the governments of Great Britain, Belgium, Monaco and Siam; Guy Francon, Stanton's greatest alumnus, who had designed the famous Frink National Bank Building of New York City, on the top of which, twenty-five floors above the pavements, there burned in a miniature replica of the Hadrian Mausoleum a wind-blown torch made of glass and the best General Electric bulbs.

Guy Francon descended from the platform, fully conscious of his timing and movements. He was of medium height and not too heavy, with just an unfortunate tendency to stoutness. Nobody, he knew, would

16

give him his real age, which was fifty-one. His face bore not a wrinkle nor a single straight line; it was an artful composition in globes, circles, arcs and ellipses, with bright little eyes twinkling wittily. His clothes displayed an artist's infinite attention to details. He wished, as he descended the steps, that this were a co-educational school.

The hall before him, he thought, was a splendid specimen of architecture, made a bit stuffy today by the crowd and by the neglected problem of ventilation. But it boasted green marble dados, Corinthian columns of cast iron painted gold, and garlands of gilded fruit on the walls; the pineapples particularly, thought Guy Francon, had stood the test of years very well. It is, thought Guy Francon, touching; it was I who built this annex and this very hall, twenty years ago; and here I am.

The hall was packed with bodies and faces, so tightly that one could not distinguish at a glance which faces belonged to which bodies. It was like a soft, shivering aspic made of mixed arms, shoulders, chests and stomachs. One of the heads, pale, dark haired and beautiful, belonged to Peter Keating.

He sat, well in front, trying to keep his eyes on the platform, because he knew that many people were looking at him and would look at him later. He did not glance back, but the consciousness of those centered glances never left him. His eyes were dark, alert, intelligent. His mouth, a small upturned crescent faultlessly traced, was gentle and generous, and warm with the faint promise of a smile. His head had a certain classical perfection in the shape of the skull, in the natural wave of black ringlets about finely hollowed temples. He held his head in the manner of one who takes his beauty for granted, but knows that others do not. He was Peter Keating, star student of Stanton, president of the student body, captain of the track team, member of the most important fraternity, voted the most popular man on the campus.

The crowd was there, thought Peter Keating, to see him graduate, and he tried to estimate the capacity of the hall. They knew of his scholastic record and no one would beat his record today. Oh, well, there was Shlinker. Shlinker had given him stiff competition, but he had beaten Shlinker this last year. He had worked like a dog, because he had wanted to beat Shlinker. He had no rivals today. . . . Then he felt suddenly as if something had fallen down, inside his throat, to his stomach, something cold and empty, a blank hole rolling down and leaving that feeling on its way: not a thought, just the hint of a question asking him whether he was really as great as this day would proclaim him to be. He looked for Shlinker in the crowd; he saw his yellow face and gold-rimmed glasses. He stared at Shlinker warmly, in relief, in reassurance, in gratitude. It was obvious that Shlinker could never hope to equal his own appearance or ability; he had nothing to doubt; he would always beat Shlinker and all the Shlinkers of the world; he would let no one achieve what he could not achieve. Let them all watch him. He would give them good reason to stare. He felt the hot breaths about him and the expectation, like a tonic. It was wonderful, thought Peter Keating, to be alive.

His head was beginning to reel a little. It was a pleasant feeling. The feeling carried him, unresisting and unremembering, to the platform in front of all those faces. He stood—slender, trim, athletic—and let the deluge break upon his head. He gathered from its roar that he had graduated with honors, that the Architects' Guild of America had presented him with a gold medal and that he had been awarded the Prix de Paris by the Society for Architectural Enlightenment of the U.S.A.—a four-year scholarship at the Ecole des Beaux Arts in Paris.

Then he was shaking hands, scratching the perspiration off his face with the end of a rolled parchment, nodding, smiling, suffocating in his black gown and hoping that people would not notice his mother sobbing with her arms about him. The President of the Institute shook his hand, booming: "Stanton will be proud of you, my boy." The Dean shook his hand, repeating: ". . . a glorious future . . . a glorious future . . . a glorious future . . ." Professor Peterkin shook his hand, and patted his shoulder, saying: ". . . and you'll find it absolutely essential; for example, I had the experience when I built the Peabody Post Office . . ." Keating did not listen to the rest, because he had heard the story of the Peabody Post Office many times. It was the only structure anyone had ever known Professor Peterkin to have erected, before he sacrificed his practice to the responsibilities of teaching. A great deal was said about Keating's final project—a Palace of Fine Arts. For the life of him, Keating could not remember at the moment what that project was.

Through all this, his eyes held the vision of Guy Francon shaking his hand, and his ears held the sounds of Francon's mellow voice: ". . . as I have told you, it is still open, my boy. Of course, now that you have this scholarship . . . you will have to decide . . . a Beaux-Arts diploma is very important to a young man . . . but I should be delighted to have you in our office. . . ."

The banquet of the class of '22 was long and solemn. Keating listened to the speeches with interest; when he heard the endless sentences about "young men as the hope of American Architecture" and "the future opening its golden gates," he knew that he was the hope and his was the future, and it was pleasant to hear this confirmation from so many eminent lips. He looked at the gray-haired orators and thought of how much younger he would be when he reached their positions, theirs and beyond them.

Then he thought suddenly of Howard Roark. He was surprised to find that the flash of that name in his memory gave him a sharp little twinge of pleasure, before he could know why. Then he remembered: Howard Roark had been expelled this morning. He reproached himself silently; he made a determined effort to feel sorry. But the secret glow came back, whenever he thought of that expulsion. The event proved conclusively that he had been a fool to imagine Roark a dangerous rival; at one time, he had worried about Roark more than about Shlinker, even though Roark was two years younger and one class below him. If he had ever entertained any doubts on their respective gifts, hadn't this day settled it all? And, he remembered, Roark had been very nice to him, helping him whenever he was stuck on a problem . . . not stuck, really, just did not have the time to think it out, a plan or something. Christ! how Roark could untangle a plan, like pulling a string and it was open . . . well, what if he could? What did it get him? He was done for now. And knowing this, Peter Keating experienced at last a satisfying pang of sympathy for Howard Roark.

When Keating was called upon to speak, he rose confidently. He could not show that he was terrified. He had nothing to say about architecture. But he spoke, his head high, as an equal among equals, just subtly diffident, so that no great name present could take offense. He remembered saying: "Architecture is a great art . . . with our eyes to the future and the reverence of the past in our hearts . . . of all the crafts, the most important one sociologically . . . and, as the man who is an inspiration to us all has said today, the three eternal entities are: Truth, Love and Beauty. . . ."

Then, in the corridors outside, in the noisy confusion of leave-taking, a boy had thrown an arm about Keating's shoulders and whispered: "Run on home and get out of the soup-and-fish, Pete, and it's Boston for us tonight, just our own gang; I'll pick you up in an hour." Ted Shlinker had urged: "Of course you're coming, Pete. No fun without you. And, by the way, congratulations and all that sort of thing. No hard feelings. May the best man win." Keating had thrown his arm about Shlinker's shoulders; Keating's eyes had glowed with an insistent kind of warmth, as if Shlinker were his most precious friend; Keating's eyes glowed like that on everybody. He had said: "Thanks, Ted, old man. I really do feel awful about that A.G.A. medal—I think you were the one for it, but you never can tell what possesses those old fogies." And now Keating was on his way home through the soft darkness, wondering how to get away from his mother for the night.

His mother, he thought, had done a great deal for him. As she pointed out frequently, she was a lady and had graduated from high school; yet she had worked hard, had taken boarders into their home, a concession unprecedented in her family.

His father had owned a stationery store in Stanton. Changing times had ended the business and a hernia had ended Peter Keating, Sr., twelve years ago. Louisa Keating had been left with the home that stood at the end of a respectable street, an annuity from an insurance kept up accurately—she had seen to that—and her son. The annuity was a modest one, but with the help of the boarders and of a tenacious purpose Mrs. Keating had managed. In the summers her son helped, clerking in hotels or posing for hat advertisements. Her son, Mrs. Keating had decided, would assume his rightful place in the world, and she had clung to this as softly, as inexorably as a leech. . . . It's funny, Keating remembered, at one time he had wanted to be an artist. It was his mother who had chosen a better field in which to exercise his talent for drawing. "Architecture," she had said, "is such a respectable profession. Besides, you meet the best people in it." She had pushed him into his career, he had never known when or how. It's funny, thought Keating, he had not remembered that youthful ambition of his for years. It's funny that it should hurt him now—to remember. Well, this was the night to remember it—and to forget it forever.

Architects, he thought, always made brilliant careers. And once on top, did they ever fail? Suddenly, he recalled Henry Cameron; builder of skyscrapers twenty years ago; old drunkard with offices on some waterfront today. Keating shuddered and walked faster.

He wondered, as he walked, whether people were looking at him. He watched the rectangles of lighted windows; when a curtain fluttered and a head leaned out, he tried to guess whether it had leaned to watch his passing; if it hadn't, some day it would; some day, they all would.

Howard Roark was sitting on the porch steps when Keating approached the house. He was leaning back against the steps, propped up on his elbows, his long legs stretched out. A morning-glory climbed over the porch pillars, as a curtain between the house and the light of a lamppost on the corner.

It was strange to see an electric globe in the air of a spring night. It made the street darker and softer; it hung alone, like a gap, and left nothing to be seen but a few branches heavy with leaves, standing still at the gap's edges. The small hint became immense, as if the darkness held nothing but a flood of leaves. The mechanical ball of glass made the leaves seem more living; it took away their color and gave the promise that in daylight they would be a brighter green than had ever existed; it took away one's sight and left a new sense instead, neither smell nor touch, yet both, a sense of spring and space.

Keating stopped when he recognized the preposterous orange hair in the darkness of the porch. It was the one person whom he had wanted to see tonight. He was glad to find Roark alone, and a little afraid of it.

"Congratulations, Peter," said Roark.

"Oh . . . Oh, thanks. . . ." Keating was surprised to find that he felt more pleasure than from any other compliment he had received today. He was timidly glad that Roark approved, and he called himself inwardly a fool for it. ". . . I mean . . . do you know or . . ." He added sharply: "Has mother been telling you?"

"She has."

"She shouldn't have!"

"Why not?"

"Look, Howard, you know that I'm terribly sorry about your being . . ."

Roark threw his head back and looked up at him.

"Forget it," said Roark.

"I . . . there's something I want to speak to you about, Howard, to ask your advice. Mind if I sit down?"

"What is it?"

Keating sat down on the steps beside him. There was no part that he could ever play in Roark's presence. Besides, he did not feel like playing a part now. He heard a leaf rustling in its fall to the earth; it was a thin, glassy, spring sound.

He knew, for the moment, that he felt affection for Roark; an affection that held pain, astonishment and helplessness.

"You won't think," said Keating gently, in complete sincerity, "that it's awful of me to be asking about my business, when you've just been . . . ?"

"I said forget about that. What is it?"

"You know," said Keating honestly and unexpectedly even to himself, "I've often thought that you're crazy. But I know that you know many things about it—architecture, I mean—which those fools never knew. And I know that you love it as they never will."

"Well?"

"Well, I don't know why I should come to you, but—Howard, I've never said it before, but you see, I'd rather have your opinion on things than the Dean's—I'd probably follow the Dean's, but it's just that yours means more to me myself, I don't know why. I don't know why I'm saying this, either."

Roark turned over on his side, looked at him, and laughed. It was a young, kind, friendly laughter, a thing so rare to hear from Roark that Keating felt as if someone had taken his hand in reassurance; and he forgot that he had a party in Boston waiting for him.

"Come on," said Roark, "you're not being afraid of me, are you? What do you want to ask about?"

"It's about my scholarship. The Paris prize I got."

"Yes?"

"It's for four years. But, on the other hand, Guy Francon offered me a job with him some time ago. Today he said it's still open. And I don't know which to take."

Roark looked at him; Roark's fingers moved in slow rotation, beating against the steps.

"If you want my advice, Peter," he said at last, "you've made a mistake already. By asking me. By asking anyone. Never ask people. Not about your work. Don't you know what you want? How can you stand it, not to know?"

"You see, that's what I admire about you, Howard. You always know."

"Drop the compliments."

"But I mean it. How do you always manage to decide?"

"How can you let others decide for you?"

"But you see, I'm not sure, Howard. I'm never sure of myself. I don't know whether I'm as good as they all tell me I am. I wouldn't admit that to anyone but you. I think it's because you're always so sure that I . . ."

"Petey!" Mrs. Keating's voice exploded behind them. "Petey, sweetheart! What *are* you doing there?"

She stood in the doorway, in her best dress of burgundy taffeta, happy and angry.

"And here I've been sitting all alone, waiting for you! What on earth are you doing on those filthy steps in your dress suit? Get up this minute! Come on in the house, boys. I've got hot chocolate and cookies ready for you."

"But, Mother, I wanted to speak to Howard about something important," said Keating. But he rose to his feet.

She seemed not to have heard. She walked into the house. Keating followed.

Roark looked after them, shrugged, rose and went in also.

Mrs. Keating settled down in an armchair, her stiff skirt crackling.

"Well?" she asked. "What were you two discussing out there?"

Keating fingered an ash tray, picked up a matchbox and dropped it, then, ignoring her, turned to Roark.

"Look, Howard, drop the pose," he said, his voice high. "Shall I junk the scholarship and go to work, or let Francon wait and grab the Beaux-Arts to impress the yokels? What do you think?"

Something was gone. The one moment was lost.

"Now, Petey, let me get this straight . . ." began Mrs. Keating.

"Oh, wait a minute, Mother! . . . Howard, I've got to weigh it carefully. It isn't everyone who can get a scholarship like that. You're pretty good when you rate that. A course at the Beaux Arts—you know how important that is."

"I don't," said Roark.

"Oh, hell, I know your crazy ideas, but I'm speaking practically, for a man in *my* position. Ideals aside for a moment, it certainly is . . ."

"You don't want my advice," said Roark.

"Of course I do! I'm asking you!"

But Keating could never be the same when he had an audience, any audience. Something was gone. He did not know it, but he felt that Roark knew; Roark's eyes made him uncomfortable and that made him angry.

"I want to *practice* architecture," snapped Keating, "not talk about it! Gives you a great prestige—the old Ecole. Puts you above the rank and file of the ex-plumbers who think they can build. On the other hand, an opening with Francon—Guy Francon himself offering it!"

Roark turned away.

"How many boys will match that?" Keating went on blindly. "A year from now they'll be boasting they're working for Smith or Jones if they find work at all. While I'll be with *Francon & Heyer!*"

"You're quite right, Peter," said Mrs. Keating, rising. "On a question like that you don't want to consult your mother. It's too important. I'll leave you to settle it with Mr. Roark."

He looked at his mother. He did not want to hear what she thought of this; he knew that his only chance to decide was to make the decision before he heard her; she had stopped, looking at him, ready to turn and leave the room; he knew it was not a pose—she would leave if he wished it; he wanted her to go; he wanted it desperately. He said:

"Why, Mother, how can you say that? Of course I want your opinion. What . . . what do you think?"

She ignored the raw irritation in his voice. She smiled.

"Petey, I never think anything. It's up to you. It's always been up to you."

"Well . . ." he began hesitantly, watching her, "if I go to the Beaux-Arts . . ."

"Fine," said Mrs. Keating, "go to the Beaux-Arts. It's a grand place. A whole ocean away from your home. Of course, if you go, Mr. Francon will take somebody else. People will talk about that. Everybody knows that Mr. Francon picks out the best boy from Stanton every year for his office. I wonder how it'll look if some other boy gets the job? But I guess that doesn't matter."

"What . . . what will people say?"

"Nothing much, I guess. Only that the other boy was the best man of his class. I guess he'll take Shlinker."

"No!" he gulped furiously. "Not Shlinker!"

"Yes," she said sweetly. "Shlinker."

"But . . ."

"But why should you care what people will say? All you have to do is please yourself."

"And you think that Francon . . ."

"Why should I think of Mr. Francon? It's nothing to me."

"Mother, you want me to take the job with Francon?"

"I don't want anything, Petey. You're the boss."

He wondered whether he really liked his mother. But she was his mother and this fact was recognized by everybody as meaning automatically that he loved her, and so he took for granted that whatever he felt for her was love. He did not know whether there was any reason why he should respect her judgment. She was his mother; this was supposed to take the place of reasons.

"Yes, of course, Mother. . . . But . . . Yes, I know, but . . . Howard?"

It was a plea for help. Roark was there, on a davenport in the corner, half lying, sprawled limply like a kitten. It had often astonished Keating; he had seen Roark moving with the soundless tension, the control, the precision of a cat; he had seen him relaxed, like a cat, in shapeless ease, as if his body held no single solid bone. Roark glanced up at him. He said:

"Peter, you know how I feel about either one of your opportunities. Take your choice of the lesser evil. What will you learn at the Beaux-Arts? Only more Renaissance palaces and operetta settings. They'll kill everything you might have in you. You do good work, once in a while, when somebody lets you. If you really want to learn, go to work. Francon is a bastard and a fool, but you will be building. It will prepare you for going on your own that much sooner."

"Even Mr. Roark can talk sense sometimes," said Mrs. Keating, "even if he does talk like a truck driver."

"Do you really think that I do good work?" Keating looked at him, as if his eyes still held the reflection of that one sentence—and nothing else mattered.

"Occasionally," said Roark. "Not often."

"Now that it's all settled . . ." began Mrs. Keating.

"I . . . I'll have to think it over, Mother."

"Now that it's all settled, how about the hot chocolate? I'll have it out to you in a jiffy!"

She smiled at her son, an innocent smile that declared her obedience and gratitude, and she rustled out of the room.

Keating paced nervously, stopped, lighted a cigarette, stood spitting the smoke out in short jerks, then looked at Roark.

"What are you going to do now, Howard?"

"I?"

"Very thoughtless of me, I know, going on like that about myself. Mother means well, but she drives me crazy. . . . Well, to hell with that. What are you going to do?"

"I'm going to New York."

"Oh, swell. To get a job?"

"To get a job."

"In . . . in architecture?"

"In architecture, Peter."

"That's grand. I'm glad. Got any definite prospects?"

"I'm going to work for Henry Cameron."

"Oh, no, Howard!"

Roark smiled slowly, the corners of his mouth sharp, and said nothing.

"Oh, no, Howard!"

"Yes."

"But he's nothing, nobody any more! Oh, I know he has a name, but he's done for! He never gets any important buildings, hasn't had any for years! They say he's got a dump for an office. What kind of future will you get out of him? What will you learn?"

"Not much. Only how to build."

"For God's sake, you can't go on like that, deliberately ruining yourself! I thought . . . well, yes, I thought you'd learned something today!"

"I have."

"Look, Howard, if it's because you think that no one else will have you now, no one better, why, I'll help you. I'll work old Francon and I'll get connections and . . ."

"Thank you, Peter. But it won't be necessary. It's settled."

"What did he say?"

"Who?"

"Cameron."

"I've never met him."

Then a horn screamed outside. Keating remembered, started off to change his clothes, collided with his mother at the door and knocked a cup off her loaded tray.

"Petey!"

"Never mind, Mother!" He seized her elbows. "I'm in a hurry, sweetheart. A little party with the boys—now, now, don't say anything—I won't be late and—look! We'll celebrate my going with Francon & Heyer!"

He kissed her impulsively, with the gay exuberance that made him irresistible at times, and flew out of the room, up the stairs. Mrs. Keating shook her head, flustered, reproving and happy.

In his room, while flinging his clothes in all directions, Keating thought suddenly of a wire he would send to New York. That particular subject had not been in his mind all day, but it came to him with a sense of desperate urgency; he wanted to send that wire now, at once. He scribbled it down on a piece of paper:

"Katie dearest coming New York job Francon love ever
"Peter"

That night Keating raced toward Boston, wedged in between two boys, the wind and the road whistling past him. And he thought that the world was opening to him now, like the darkness fleeing before the bobbing headlights. He was free. He was ready. In a few years—so very soon, for time did not exist in the speed of that car—his name would ring like a horn, ripping people out of sleep. He was ready to do great things, magnificent things, things unsurpassed in . . . in . . . oh, hell . . . in architecture.

III

Peter Keating looked at the streets of New York. The people, he observed, were extremely well dressed.

He had stopped for a moment before the building on Fifth Avenue, where the office of Francon & Heyer and his first day of work awaited him. He looked at the men who hurried past. Smart, he thought, smart as hell. He glanced regretfully at his own clothes. He had a great deal to learn in New York.

When he could delay it no longer, he turned to the door. It was a miniature Doric portico, every inch of it scaled down to the exact proportions decreed by the artists who had worn flowing Grecian tunics; between the marble perfection of the columns a revolving door sparkled with nickel-plate, reflecting the streaks of automobiles flying past. Keating walked through the revolving door, through the lustrous marble lobby, to an elevator of gilt and red lacquer that brought him, thirty floors later, to a mahogany door. He saw a slender brass plate with delicate letters:

FRANCON & HEYER, ARCHITECTS.

The reception room of the office of Francon & Heyer, Architects, looked like a cool, intimate ballroom in a Colonial mansion. The silver white walls were paneled with flat pilasters; the pilasters were fluted and curved into Ionic snails; they supported little pediments broken in the middle to make room for half a Grecian urn plastered against the wall. Etchings of Greek temples adorned the panels, too small to be distinguished, but presenting the unmistakable columns, pediments and crumbling stone.

Quite incongruously, Keating felt as if a conveyer belt was under his feet, from the moment he crossed the threshold. It carried him to the reception clerk who sat at a telephone switchboard behind the white balustrade of a Florentine balcony. It transferred him to the threshold of a huge drafting room. He saw long, flat tables, a forest of twisted rods descending from the ceiling to end in green-shaded lamps, enormous blueprint files, towers of yellow drawers, papers, tin boxes, sample bricks, pots of glue and calendars from construction companies, most of them bearing pictures of naked women. The chief draftsman snapped at Keating, without quite seeing him. He was bored and crackling with purpose simultaneously. He jerked his thumb in the direction of a locker room, thrust his chin out toward the door of a locker, and stood, rocking from heels to toes, while Keating pulled a pearl-gray smock over his stiff, uncertain body. Francon had insisted on that smock. The conveyor belt stopped at a table in a corner of the drafting room, where Keating found himself with a set of plans to expand, the scraggy back of the chief draftsman retreating from him in the unmistakable manner of having forgotten his existence.

Keating bent over his task at once, his eyes fixed, his throat rigid. He saw nothing but the pearly shimmer of the paper before him. The steady lines he drew surprised him, for he felt certain that his hand was jerking an inch back and forth across the sheet. He followed the lines, not knowing where they led or why. He knew only that the plan was some-one's tremendous achievement which he could neither question nor equal. He wondered why he had ever thought of himself as a potential architect.

Much later, he noticed the wrinkles of a gray smock sticking to a pair of shoulder blades over the next table. He glanced about him, cautiously at first, then with curiosity, then with pleasure, then with contempt. When he reached this last, Peter Keating became himself again and felt love for mankind. He noticed sallow cheeks, a funny nose, a wart on a receding chin, a stomach squashed against the edge of a table. He loved these sights. What these could do, he could do better. He smiled. Peter Keating needed his fellow men.

When he glanced at his plans again, he noticed the flaws glaring at him from the masterpiece. It was the floor of a private residence, and he noted the twisted hallways that sliced great hunks of space for no appar-ent reason, the long, rectangular sausages of rooms doomed to darkness. Jesus, he thought, they'd have flunked me for this in the first term. After which, he proceeded with his work swiftly, easily, expertly—and hap-pily.

Before lunchtime, Keating had made friends in the room, not any definite friends, but a vague soil spread and ready from which friend-ships would spring. He had smiled at his neighbors and winked in under-standing over nothing at all. He had used each trip to the water cooler to caress those he passed with the soft, cheering glow of his eyes, the brilliant eyes that seemed to pick each man in turn out of the room, out of the universe, as the most important specimen of humanity and as Keating's dearest friend. There goes—there seemed to be left in his wake—a smart boy and a hell of a good fellow.

Keating noticed that a tall blond youth at the next table was doing the elevation of an office building. Keating leaned with chummy respect against the boy's shoulder and looked at the laurel garlands entwined about fluted columns three floors high.

"Pretty good for the old man," said Keating with admiration.

"Who?" asked the boy.

"Why, Francon," said Keating.

"Francon hell," said the boy placidly. "He hasn't designed a dog-house in eight years." He jerked his thumb over his shoulder, at a glass door behind them. "Him."

"What?" asked Keating, turning.

"Him," said the boy. "Stengel. He does all these things."

Behind the glass door Keating saw a pair of bony shoulders above the edge of a desk, a small, triangular head bent intently, and two blank pools of light in the round frames of glasses.

It was late in the afternoon when a presence seemed to have passed beyond the closed door, and Keating learned from the rustle of whispers around him that Guy Francon had arrived and had risen to his office on the floor above. Half an hour later the glass door opened and Stengel came out, a huge piece of cardboard dangling between his fingers.

"Hey, you," he said, his glasses stoppping on Keating's face. "You doing the plans for this?" He swung the cardboard forward. "Take this up to the boss for the okay. Try to listen to what he'll say and try to look intelligent. Neither of which matters anyway."

He was short and his arms seemed to hang down to his ankles; arms swinging like ropes in the long sleeves, with big, efficient hands. Keating's eyes froze, darkening, for one-tenth of a second, gathered in a tight stare at the blank lenses. Then Keating smiled and said pleasantly:

"Yes, sir."

He carried the cardboard on the tips of his ten fingers, up the crimson-plushed stairway to Guy Francon's office. The cardboard displayed a water-color perspective of a gray granite mansion with three tiers of dormers, five balconies, four bays, twelve columns, one flagpole and two lions at the entrance. In the corner, neatly printed by hand, stood: "Residence of Mr. and Mrs. James S. Whattles. Francon & Heyer, Architects." Keating whistled softly: James S. Whattles was the multimillionaire manufacturer of shaving lotions.

Guy Francon's office was polished. No, thought Keating, not polished, but shellacked; no, not shellacked, but liquid with mirrors melted and poured over every object. He saw splinters of his own reflection let loose like a swarm of butterflies, following him across the room, on the Chippendale cabinets, on the Jacobean chairs, on the Louis XV mantelpiece. He had time to note a genuine Roman statue in a corner, sepia photographs of the Parthenon, of Rheims Cathedral, of Versailles and of the Frink National Bank Building with the eternal torch.

He saw his own legs approaching him in the side of the massive mahogany desk. Guy Francon sat behind the desk. Guy Francon's face was yellow and his cheeks sagged. He looked at Keating for an instant as if he had never seen him before, then remembered and smiled expansively.

"Well, well, well, Kittredge, my boy, here we are, all set and at home! So glad to see you. Sit down, boy, sit down, what have you got there? Well, there's no hurry, no hurry at all. Sit down. How do you like it here?"

"I'm afraid, sir, that I'm a little too happy," said Keating, with an expression of frank, boyish helplessness. "I thought I could be business-like on my first job, but starting in a place like this . . . I guess it knocked me out a little. . . . I'll get over it, sir," he promised.

"Of course," said Guy Francon. "It might be a bit overwhelming for a boy, just a bit. But don't you worry. I'm sure you'll make good."

"I'll do my best, sir."

"Of course you will. What's this they sent me?" Francon extended his hand to the drawing, but his fingers came to rest limply on his forehead instead. "It's so annoying, this headache. . . . No, no, nothing serious—" he smiled at Keating's prompt concern—"just a little *mal de tête*. One works so hard."

"Is there anything I can get for you, sir?"

"No, no, thank you. It's not anything you can get for me, it's if only you could take something away from me." He winked. "The champagne. *Entre nous*, that champagne of theirs wasn't worth a damn last night. I've never cared for champagne anyway. Let me tell you, Kittredge, it's very important to know about wines, for instance when you'll take a client out to dinner and will want to be sure of the proper thing to order. Now I'll tell you a professional secret. Take quail, for instance. Now most people would order Burgundy with it. What do you do? You call for Clos Vougeot 1904. See? Adds that certain touch. Correct, but original. One must always be original. . . . Who sent you up, by the way?"

"Mr. Stengel, sir."

"Oh, Stengel." The tone in which he pronounced the name clicked like a shutter in Keating's mind: it was a permission to be stored away for future use. "Too grand to bring his own stuff up, eh? Mind you, he's a great designer, the best designer in New York City, but he's just getting to be a bit too grand lately. He thinks he's the only one doing any work around here, just because I give him ideas and let him work them out for me. Just because he smudges at a board all day long. You'll learn, my boy, when you've been in the business longer, that the real work of an office is done beyond its walls. Take last night, for instance. Banquet of the Clarion Real Estate Association. Two hundred guests—dinner and champagne—oh, yes, champagne!" He wrinkled his nose fastidiously, in self-mockery. "A few words to say informally in a little after-dinner speech—you know, nothing blatant, no vulgar sales talk—only a few well-chosen thoughts on the responsibility of realtors to society, on the importance of selecting architects who are competent, respected and well established. You know, a few bright little slogans that will stick in the mind."

"Yes, sir, like 'Choose the builder of your home as carefully as you choose the bride to inhabit it.' "

"Not bad. Not bad at all, Kittredge. Mind if I jot it down?"

"My name is Keating, sir," said Keating firmly. "You are very welcome to the idea. I'm very happy if it appeals to you."

"Keating, of course! Why, of course, Keating," said Francon with a disarming smile. "Dear me, one meets so many people. How did you say it? Choose the builder . . . It was very well put."

He made Keating repeat it and wrote it down on a pad, picking a pencil from an array before him, new, many-colored pencils, sharpened to a professional needle point, ready, unused.

Then he pushed the pad aside, sighed, patted the smooth waves of his hair and said wearily:

"Well, all right, I suppose I'll have to look at the thing."

Keating extended the drawing respectfully. Francon leaned back, held the cardboard out at arm's length and looked at it. He closed his left eye, then his right eye, then moved the cardboard an inch farther. Keating expected wildly to see him turn the drawing upside down. But Francon just held it and Keating knew suddenly that he had long since stopped seeing it. Francon was studying it for his, Keating's benefit; and then Keating felt light, light as air, and he saw the road to his future, clear and open.

"Hm . . . yes," Francon was saying, rubbing his chin with the tips of two soft fingers. "Hm . . . yes . . ."

He turned to Keating.

"Not bad," said Francon. "Not bad at all. . . . Well . . . perhaps . . . it could have been more distinguished, you know, but . . . well, the drawing is done so neatly. . . . What do you think, Keating?"

Keating thought that four of the windows faced four mammoth granite columns. But he looked at Francon's fingers playing with a petunia-mauve necktie, and decided not to mention it. He said instead:

"If I may make a suggestion, sir, it seems to me that the cartouches between the fourth and fifth floors are somewhat too modest for so imposing a building. It would appear that an ornamented stringcourse would be so much more appropriate."

"That's it. I was just going to say it. An ornamented stringcourse. . . . But . . . but look, it would mean diminishing the fenestration, wouldn't it?"

"Yes," said Keating, a faint coating of diffidence over the tone he had used in discussions with his classmates, "but windows are less important than the dignity of a building's façade."

"That's right. Dignity. We must give our clients dignity above all.

Yes, definitely, an ornamented stringcourse. . . . Only . . . look, I've approved the preliminary drawings, and Stengel has had this done up so neatly."

"Mr. Stengel will be delighted to change it if you advise him to."

Francon's eyes held Keating's for a moment. Then Francon's lashes dropped and he picked a piece of lint off his sleeve.

"Of course, of course . . ." he said vaguely. "But . . . do you think the stringcourse is really important?"

"I think," said Keating slowly, "it is more important to make changes you find necessary than to okay every drawing just as Mr. Stengel designed it."

Because Francon said nothing, but only looked straight at him, because Francon's eyes were focused and his hands limp, Keating knew that he had taken a terrible chance and won; he became frightened by the chance after he knew he had won.

They looked silently across the desk, and both saw that they were two men who could understand each other.

"We'll have an ornamented stringcourse," said Francon with calm, genuine authority. "Leave this here. Tell Stengel that I want to see him."

He had turned to go. Francon stopped him. Francon's voice was gay and warm:

"Oh, Keating, by the way, may I make a suggestion? Just between us, no offense intended, but a burgundy necktie would be so much better than blue with your gray smock, don't you think so?"

"Yes, sir," said Keating easily. "Thank you. You'll see it tomorrow."

He walked out and closed the door softly.

On his way back through the reception room, Keating saw a distinguished, gray-haired gentleman escorting a lady to the door. The gentleman wore no hat and obviously belonged to the office; the lady wore a mink cape, and was obviously a client.

The gentleman was not bowing to the ground, he was not unrolling a carpet, he was not waving a fan over her head; he was only holding the door for her. It merely seemed to Keating that the gentleman was doing all of that.

The Frink National Bank Building rose over Lower Manhattan, and its long shadow moved, as the sun traveled over the sky, like a huge clock hand across grimy tenements, from the Aquarium to Manhattan Bridge. When the sun was gone, the torch of Hadrian's Mausoleum flared up in its stead, and made glowing red smears on the glass of windows for miles around, on the top stories of buildings high enough to reflect it. The Frink National Bank Building displayed the entire history of Roman art in well-chosen specimens; for a long time it had been considered the best building of the city, because no other structure could boast a single Classical item which it did not possess. It offered so many columns, pediments, friezes, tripods, gladiators, urns and volutes that it looked as if it had not been built of white marble, but squeezed out of a pastry tube. It was, however, built of white marble. No one knew that but the owners who had paid for it. It was now of a streaked, blotched, leprous color, neither brown nor green but the worst tones of both, the color of slow rot, the color of smoke, gas fumes and acids eating into a delicate stone intended for clean air and open country. The Frink National Bank Building, however, was a great success. It had been so great a success that it was the last structure Guy Francon ever designed; its prestige spared him the bother from then on.

Three blocks east of the Frink National Bank stood the Dana Building. It was some stories lower and without any prestige whatever. Its lines were hard and simple, revealing, emphasizing the harmony of the steel skeleton within, as a body reveals the perfection of its bones. It had no other ornament to offer. It displayed nothing but the precision of its sharp angles, the modeling of its planes, the long streaks of its windows like streams of ice running down from the roof to the pavements. New Yorkers seldom looked at the Dana Building. Sometimes, a rare country visitor would come upon it unexpectedly in the moonlight and stop and wonder from what dream that vision had come. But such visitors were rare. The tenants of the Dana Building said that they would not exchange it for any structure on earth; they appreciated the light, the air, the beautiful logic of the plan in their halls and offices. But the tenants of the Dana Building were not numerous; no prominent man wished his business to be located in a building that looked "like a warehouse."

The Dana Building had been designed by Henry Cameron.

In the eighteen-eighties, the architects of New York fought one another for second place in their profession. No one aspired to the first. The first was held by Henry Cameron. Henry Cameron was hard to get in those days. He had a waiting list two years in advance; he designed personally every structure that left his office. He chose what he wished to build. When he built, a client kept his mouth shut. He demanded of all people the one thing he had never granted anybody: obedience. He went through the years of his fame like a projectile flying to a goal no one could guess. People called him crazy. But they took what he gave them, whether they understood it or not, because it was a building "by Henry Cameron."

At first, his buildings were merely a little different, not enough to frighten anyone. He made startling experiments, once in a while, but people expected it and one did not argue with Henry Cameron. Something was growing in him with each new building, struggling, taking shape, rising dangerously to an explosion. The explosion came with the birth of the skyscraper. When structures began to rise not in tier on ponderous tier of masonry, but as arrows of steel shooting upward without weight or limit, Henry Cameron was among the first to understand this new miracle and to give it form. He was among the first and the few who accepted the truth that a tall building must look tall. While architects cursed, wondering how to make a twenty-story building look like an old brick mansion, while they used every horizontal device available in order to cheat it of its height, shrink it down to tradition, hide the shame of its steel, make it small, safe and ancient—Henry Cameron designed skyscrapers in straight, vertical lines, flaunting their steel and height. While architects drew friezes and pediments, Henry Cameron decided that the skyscraper must not copy the Greeks. Henry Cameron decided that no building must copy any other.

He was thirty-nine years old then, short, stocky, unkempt; he worked like a dog, missed his sleep and meals, drank seldom but then brutally, called his clients unprintable names, laughed at hatred and fanned it deliberately, behaved like a feudal lord and a longshoreman, and lived in a passionate tension that stung men in any room he entered, a fire neither they nor he could endure much longer. It was the year 1892.

The Columbian Exposition of Chicago opened in the year 1893.

The Rome of two thousand years ago rose on the shores of Lake Michigan, a Rome improved by pieces of France, Spain, Athens and every style that followed it. It was a "Dream City" of columns, triumphal arches, blue lagoons, crystal fountains and popcorn. Its architects competed on who could steal best, from the oldest source and from the most sources at once. It spread before the eyes of a new country every structural crime ever committed in all the old ones. It was white as a plague, and it spread as such.

People came, looked, were astounded, and carried away with them, to the cities of America, the seeds of what they had seen. The seeds sprouted into weeds; into shingled post offices with Doric porticos, brick mansions with iron pediments, lofts made of twelve Parthenons piled on top of one another. The weeds grew and choked everything else.

Henry Cameron had refused to work for the Columbian Exposition, and had called it names that were unprintable, but repeatable, though not in mixed company. They were repeated. It was repeated also that he had thrown an inkstand at the face of a distinguished banker who had asked him to design a railroad station in the shape of the temple of Diana at Ephesus. The banker never came back. There were others who never came back.

Just as he reached the goal of long, struggling years, just as he gave shape to the truth he had sought—the last barrier fell closed before him. A young country had watched him on his way, had wondered, had begun to accept the new grandeur of his work. A country flung two thousand years back in an orgy of Classicism could find no place for him and no use.

It was not necessary to design buildings any longer, only to photograph them; the architect with the best library was the best architect. Imitators copied imitations. To sanction it there was Culture; there were twenty centuries unrolling in moldering ruins; there was the great Exposition; there was every European post card in every family album.

Henry Cameron had nothing to offer against this; nothing but a faith he held merely because it was his own. He had nobody to quote and nothing of importance to say. He said only that the form of a building must follow its function; that the structure of a building is the key to its beauty; that new methods of construction demand new forms; that he wished to build as he wished and for that reason only. But people could not listen to him when they were discussing Vitruvius, Michelangelo and Sir Christopher Wren.

Men hate passion, any great passion. Henry Cameron made a mistake: he loved his work. That was why he fought. That was why he lost.

People said he never knew that he had lost. If he did, he never let them see it. As his clients became rarer, his manner to them grew more overbearing. The less the prestige of his name, the more arrogant the sound of his voice pronouncing it. He had had an astute business manager, a mild, self-effacing little man of iron who, in the days of his glory, faced quietly the storms of Cameron's temper and brought him clients; Cameron insulted the clients, but the little man made them accept it and come back. The little man died.

Cameron had never known how to face people. They did not matter to him, as his own life did not matter, as nothing mattered but buildings. He had never learned to give explanations, only orders. He had never been liked. He had been feared. No one feared him any longer.

He was allowed to live. He lived to loathe the streets of the city he had dreamed of rebuilding. He lived to sit at the desk in his empty office, motionless, idle, waiting. He lived to read in a well-meaning newspaper account a reference to "the late Henry Cameron." He lived to begin drinking, quietly, steadily, terribly, for days and nights at a time; and to hear those who had driven him to it say, when his name was mentioned for a commission: "Cameron? I should say not. He drinks like a fish. That's why he never gets any work." He lived to move from the offices that occupied three floors of a famous building to one floor on a less expensive street, then to a suite farther downtown, then to three rooms facing an air shaft, near the Battery. He chose these rooms because, by pressing his face to the window of his office, he could see, over a brick wall, the top of the Dana Building.

Howard Roark looked at the Dana Building beyond the windows, stopping at each landing, as he mounted the six flights of stairs to Henry Cameron's office; the elevator was out of order. The stairs had been painted a dirty file-green a long time ago; a little of the paint remained to grate under shoe soles in crumbling patches. Roark went up swiftly, as if he had an appointment, a folder of his drawings under his arm, his eyes on the Dana Building. He collided once with a man descending the stairs; this had happened to him often in the last two days; he had walked through the streets of the city, his head thrown back, noticing nothing but the buildings of New York.

In the dark cubbyhole of Cameron's anteroom stood a desk with a telephone and a typewriter. A gray-haired skeleton of a man sat at the desk, in his shirt sleeves, with a pair of limp suspenders over his shoulders. He was typing specifications intently, with two fingers and incredible speed. The light from a feeble bulb made a pool of yellow on his back, where the damp shirt stuck to his shoulder blades.

The man raised his head slowly, when Roark entered. He looked at Roark, said nothing and waited, his old eyes weary, unquestioning, incurious.

"I should like to see Mr. Cameron," said Roark.

"Yeah?" said the man, without challenge, offense or meaning. "About what?"

"About a job."

"What job?"

"Drafting."

The man sat looking at him blankly. It was a request that had not confronted him for a long time. He rose at last, without a word, shuffled to a door behind him and went in.

He left the door half open. Roark heard him drawling:

"Mr. Cameron, there's a fellow outside says he's looking for a job here."

Then a voice answered, a strong, clear voice that held no tones of age:

"Why, the damn fool! Throw him out . . . Wait! Send him in!"

The old man returned, held the door open and jerked his head at it silently. Roark went in. The door closed behind him.

Henry Cameron sat at his desk at the end of a long, bare room. He sat bent forward, his forearms on the desk, his two hands closed before him. His hair and his beard were coal black, with coarse threads of white. The muscles of his short, thick neck bulged like ropes. He wore a white shirt with the sleeves rolled above the elbows; the bare arms were hard, heavy and brown. The flesh of his broad face was rigid, as if it had aged by compression. The eyes were dark, young, living.

Roark stood on the threshold and they looked at each other across the long room.

The light from the air shaft was gray, and the dust on the drafting table, on the few green files, looked like fuzzy crystals deposited by the light. But on the wall, between the windows, Roark saw a picture. It was the only picture in the room. It was the drawing of a skyscraper that had never been erected.

Roark's eyes moved first and they moved to the drawing. He walked across the office, stopped before it and stood looking at it. Cameron's eyes followed him, a heavy glance, like a long, thin needle held fast at one end, describing a slow circle, its point piercing Roark's body, keeping it pinned firmly. Cameron looked at the orange hair, at the hand hanging by his side, its palm to the drawing, the fingers bent slightly, forgotten not in a gesture but in the overture to a gesture of asking or seizing something.

"Well?" said Cameron at last. "Did you come to see me or did you come to look at pictures?"

Roark turned to him.

"Both," said Roark.

He walked to the desk. People had always lost their sense of existence in Roark's presence; but Cameron felt suddenly that he had never been as real as in the awareness of the eyes now looking at him.

"What do you want?" snapped Cameron.

"I should like to work for you," said Roark quietly. The voice said: "I should like to work for you." The tone of the voice said: "I'm going to work for you."

"Are you?" said Cameron, not realizing that he answered the unpronounced sentence. "What's the matter? None of the bigger and better fellows will have you?"

"I have not applied to anyone else."

"Why not? Do you think this is the easiest place to begin? Think anybody can walk in here without trouble? Do you know who I am?"

"Yes. That's why I'm here."

"Who sent you?"

"No one."

"Why the hell should you pick me?"

"I think you know that."

"What infernal impudence made you presume that I'd want you? Have you decided that I'm so hard up that I'd throw the gates open for any punk who'd do me the honor? 'Old Cameron,' you've said to yourself, 'is a has-been, a drunken . . .' Come on, you've said it! . . . 'a drunken failure who can't be particular!' Is that it? . . . Come on, answer me! Answer me, damn you! What are you staring at? Is that it? Go on! Deny it!"

"It's not necessary."

"Where have you worked before?"

"I'm just beginning."

"What have you done?"

"I've had three years at Stanton."

"Oh? The gentleman was too lazy to finish?"

"I have been expelled."

"Great!" Cameron slapped the desk with his fist and laughed. "Splendid! You're not good enough for the lice nest at Stanton, but you'll work for Henry Cameron! You've decided this is the place for refuse! What did they kick you out for? Drink? Women? What?"

"These," said Roark, and extended his drawings.

Cameron looked at the first one, then at the next, then at every one of them to the bottom. Roark heard the paper rustling as Cameron slipped one sheet behind another. Then Cameron raised his head.

"Sit down."

Roark obeyed. Cameron stared at him, his thick fingers drumming against the pile of drawings.

"So you think they're good?" said Cameron. "Well, they're awful. It's unspeakable. It's a crime. Look," he shoved a drawing at Roark's face, "look at that. What in Christ's name was your idea? What possessed you to indent that plan here? Did you just want to make it pretty, because you had to patch something together? Who do you think you are? Guy Francon, God help you? . . . Look at this building, you fool! You get an idea like this and you don't know what to do with it! You stumble on a magnificent thing and you have to ruin it! Do you know how much you've got to learn?"

"Yes. That's why I'm here."

"And look at that one! I wish I'd done that at your age! But why did you have to botch it? Do you know what I'd do with that? Look, to hell with your stairways and to hell with your furnace room! When you lay the foundations . . ."

He spoke furiously for a long time. He cursed. He did not find one sketch to satisfy him. But Roark noticed that he spoke as of buildings that were in construction.

He broke off abruptly, pushed the drawings aside, and put his fist over them. He asked:

"When did you decide to become an architect?"

"When I was ten years old."

"Men don't know what they want so early in life, if ever. You're lying."

"Am I?"

"Don't stare at me like that! Can't you look at something else? Why did you decide to be an architect?"

"I didn't know it then. But it's because I've never believed in God."

"Come on, talk sense."

"Because I love this earth. That's all I love. I don't like the shape of things on this earth. I want to change them."

"For whom?"

"For myself."

"How old are you?"

"Twenty-two."

"Where did you hear all that?"

"I didn't."

"Men don't talk like that at twenty-two. You're abnormal."

"Probably."

"I didn't mean it as a compliment."

"I didn't either."

"Got any family?"

"No."

"Worked through school?"

"Yes."

"At what?"

"In the building trades."

"How much money have you got left?"

"Seventeen dollars and thirty cents."

"When did you come to New York?"

"Yesterday."

Cameron looked at the white pile under his fist.

"God damn you," said Cameron softly.

"God damn you!" roared Cameron suddenly, leaning forward. "I didn't ask you to come here! I don't need any draftsmen! There's nothing here to draft! I don't have enough work to keep myself and my men out of the Bowery Mission! I don't want any fool visionaries starving around here! I don't want the responsibility. I didn't ask for it. I never thought I'd see it again. I'm through with it. I was through with that many years ago. I'm perfectly happy with the drooling dolts I've got here, who never had anything and never will have and it makes no difference what becomes of them. That's all I want. Why did you have to come here? You're setting out to ruin yourself, you know that, don't you? And I'll help you to do it. I don't want to see you. I don't like you. I don't like your face. You look like an insufferable egotist. You're impertinent. You're too sure of yourself. Twenty years ago I'd have punched your face with the greatest of pleasure. You're coming to work here tomorrow at nine o'clock sharp."

"Yes," said Roark, rising.

"Fifteen dollars a week. That's all I can pay you."

"Yes."

"You're a damn fool. You should have gone to someone else. I'll kill you if you go to anyone else. What's your name?"

"Howard Roark."

"If you're late, I'll fire you."

"Yes."

Roark extended his hand for the drawings.

"Leave these here!" bellowed Cameron. "Now get out!"

IV

"TOOHEY," SAID GUY FRANCON, "ELLSWORTH TOOHEY. PRETTY decent of him, don't you think? Read it, Peter."

Francon leaned jovially across his desk and handed to Keating the August issue of *New Frontiers*. *New Frontiers* had a white cover with a black emblem that combined a palette, a lyre, a hammer, a screw driver and a rising sun; it had a circulation of thirty thousand and a following that described itself as the intellectual vanguard of the country; no one had ever risen to challenge the description. Keating read from an article entitled "Marble and Mortar," by Ellsworth M. Toohey:

". . . And now we come to another notable achievement of the metropolitan skyline. We call the attention of the discriminating to the new Melton Building by Francon & Heyer. It stands in white serenity as an eloquent witness to the triumph of Classical purity and common sense. The discipline of an immortal tradition has served here as a cohesive factor in evolving a structure whose beauty can reach, simply and lucidly, the heart of every man in the street. There is no freak exhibitionism here, no perverted striving for novelty, no orgy of unbridled egotism. Guy Francon, its designer, has known how to subordinate himself to the mandatory canons which generations of craftsmen behind him have proved inviolate, and at the same time how to display his own creative originality, not in spite of, but precisely *because of* the classical dogma he has accepted with the humility of a true artist. It may be worth mentioning, in passing, that dogmatic discipline is the only thing which makes true originality possible. . . .

"More important, however, is the symbolic significance of a building such as this rising in our imperial city. As one stands before its southern façade, one is stricken with the realization that the stringcourses, repeated with deliberate and gracious monotony from the third to the eighteenth story, these long, straight, horizontal lines are the moderating, leveling principle, the lines of equality. They seem to bring the towering structure down to the humble level of the observer. They are the lines of the earth, of the people, of the great masses. They seem to tell us that none may rise too high above the restraint of the common human level, that all is held and shall be checked, even as this proud edifice, by the stringcourses of men's brotherhood. . . ."

There was more. Keating read it all, then raised his head. "Gee!" he said, awed.

Francon smiled happily.

41

"Pretty good, eh? And from *Toohey,* no less. Not many people might have heard the name, but they will, mark my word, they will. I know the signs. . . . So he doesn't think I'm so bad? And he's got a tongue like an icepick, when he feels like using it. You should see what he says about others, more often than not. You know Durkin's latest mousetrap? Well, I was at a party where Toohey said—" Francon chuckled—"he said: 'If Mr. Durkin suffers under the delusion that he is an architect, someone should mention to him the broad opportunities offered by the shortage of skilled plumbers.' That's what he said, imagine, in public!"

"I wonder," said Keating wistfully, "what he'll say about *me,* when the time comes."

"What on earth does he mean by that symbolic significance stuff and the stringcourses of men's brotherhood? . . . Oh, well, if that's what he praises us for, we should worry!"

"It's the critic's job to interpret the artist, Mr. Francon, even to the artist himself. Mr. Toohey has merely stated the hidden significance that was subconsciously in your own mind."

"Oh," said Francon vaguely. "Oh, do you think so?" he added brightly. "Quite possible. . . . Yes, quite possible. . . . You're a smart boy, Peter."

"Thank you, Mr. Francon." Keating made a movement to rise.

"Wait. Don't go. One more cigarette and then we'll both return to the drudgery."

Francon was smiling over the article, reading it again. Keating had never seen him so pleased; no drawing in the office, no work accomplished had ever made him as happy as these words from another man on a printed page to be read by other eyes.

Keating sat easily in a comfortable chair. His month with the firm had been well spent. He had said nothing and done nothing, but the impression had spread through the office that Guy Francon liked to see this particular boy sent to him whenever anyone had to be sent. Hardly a day passed without the pleasant interlude of sitting across the desk from Guy Francon, in a respectful, growing intimacy, listening to Francon's sighs about the necessity of being surrounded by men who understood him.

Keating had learned all he could learn about Guy Francon, from his fellow draftsmen. He had learned that Guy Francon ate moderately and exquisitely, and prided himself on the title of gourmet; that he had graduated with distinction from the Ecole des Beaux Arts; that he had married a great deal of money and that the marriage had not been a happy one; that he matched meticulously his socks with his handkerchiefs, but never with his neckties; that he had a great preference for designing buildings of gray granite; that he owned a quarry of gray granite in Connecticut, which did a thriving business; that he maintained a magnificent bachelor apartment done in plum-colored Louis XV; that his wife, of a distinguished old name, had died, leaving her fortune to their only daughter; that the daughter, now nineteen, was away at college.

These last facts interested Keating a great deal. He mentioned to Francon, tentatively, in passing, the subject of his daughter. "Oh, yes . . ." Francon said thinly. "Yes, indeed . . ." Keating abandoned all further research into the matter, for the time being; Francon's face had declared that the thought of his daughter was painfully annoying to him, for some reason which Keating could not discover.

Keating had met Lucius N. Heyer, Francon's partner, and had seen him come to the office twice in three weeks, but had been unable to learn what service Heyer rendered to the firm. Heyer did not have haemophilia, but looked as though he should have it. He was a withered aristocrat, with a long, thin neck, pale, bulging eyes and a manner of frightened sweetness toward everyone. He was the relic of an ancient family, and it was suspected that Francon had taken him into partnership for the sake of his social connections. People felt sorry for poor dear Lucius, admired him for the effort of undertaking a professional career, and thought it would be nice to let him build their homes. Francon built them and required no further service from Lucius. This satisfied everybody.

The men in the drafting rooms loved Peter Keating. He made them feel as if he had been there for a long time; he had always known how to become part of any place he entered; he came soft and bright as a sponge to be filled, unresisting, with the air and the mood of the place. His warm smile, his gay voice, the easy shrug of his shoulders seemed to say that nothing weighed too much within his soul and so he was not one to blame, to demand, to accuse anything.

As he sat now, watching Francon read the article, Francon raised his head to glance at him. Francon saw two eyes looking at him with immense approval—and two bright little points of contempt in the corners of Keating's mouth, like two musical notes of laughter visible the second before they were to be heard. Francon felt a great wave of comfort. The comfort came from the contempt. The approval, together with that wise half-smile, granted him a grandeur he did not have to earn; a blind admiration would have been precarious; a deserved admiration would have been a responsibility; an undeserved admiration was precious.

"When you go, Peter, give this to Miss Jeffers to put in my scrapbook."

On his way down the stairs, Keating flung the magazine high in the air and caught it smartly, his lips pursed to whistle without sound.

In the drafting room he found Tim Davis, his best friend, slouched despondently over a drawing. Tim Davis was the tall, blond boy at the next table, whom Keating had noticed long ago, because he had known, with no tangible evidence, but with certainty, as Keating always knew such things, that this was the favored draftsman of the office. Keating managed to be assigned, as frequently as possible, to do parts of the projects on which Davis worked. Soon they were going out to lunch together, and to a quiet little speak-easy after the day's work, and Keating was listening with breathless attention to Davis' talk about his love for one Elaine Duffy, not a word of which Keating ever remembered afterward.

He found Davis now in black gloom, his mouth chewing furiously a cigarette and a pencil at once. Keating did not have to question him. He merely bent his friendly face over Davis' shoulder. Davis spit out the cigarette and exploded. He had just been told that he would have to work overtime tonight, for the third time this week.

"Got to stay late, God knows how late! Gotta finish this damn tripe tonight!" He slammed the sheets spread before him. "Look at it! Hours and hours and hours to finish it! What am I going to do?"

"Well, it's because you're the best man here, Tim, and they need you."

"To hell with that! I've got a date with Elaine tonight! How'm I going to break it? Third time! She won't believe me! She told me so last time! That's the end! I'm going up to Guy the Mighty and tell him where he can put his plans and his job! I'm through!"

"Wait," said Keating, and leaned closer to him. "Wait! There's another way. I'll finish them for you."

"Huh?"

"I'll stay. I'll do them. Don't be afraid. No one'll tell the difference."

"Pete! Would you?"

"Sure. I've nothing to do tonight. You just stay till they all go home, then skip."

"Oh, gee, Pete!" Davis sighed, tempted. "But look, if they find out, they'll can me. You're too new for this kind of job."

"They won't find out."

"I can't lose my job, Pete. You know I can't. Elaine and I are going to be married soon. If anything happens . . ."

"Nothing will happen."

Shortly after six, Davis departed furtively from the empty drafting room, leaving Keating at his table.

Bending under a solitary green lamp, Keating glanced at the desolate expanse of three long rooms, oddly silent after the day's rush, and he felt that he owned them, that he would own them, as surely as the pencil moved in his hand.

It was half past nine when he finished the plans, stacked them neatly on Davis' table, and left the office. He walked down the street, glowing with a comfortable, undignified feeling, as though after a good meal. Then the realization of his loneliness struck him suddenly. He had to share this with someone tonight. He had no one. For the first time he wished his mother were in New York. But she had remained in Stanton, awaiting the day when he would be able to send for her. He had nowhere to go tonight, save to the respectable little boarding house on West Twenty-Eighth Street, where he could climb three flights of stairs to his clean, airless little room. He had met people in New York, many people, many girls, with one of whom he remembered spending a pleasant night, though he could not remember her last name; but he wished to see none of them. And then he thought of Catherine Halsey.

He had sent her a wire on the night of his graduation and forgotten her ever since. Now he wanted to see her; the desire was intense and immediate with the first sound of her name in his memory. He leaped into a bus for the long ride to Greenwich Village, climbed to the deserted top and, sitting alone on the front bench, cursed the traffic lights whenever they turned to red. It had always been like this where Catherine was concerned; and he wondered dimly what was the matter with him.

He had met her a year ago in Boston, where she had lived with her widowed mother. He had found Catherine homely and dull, on that first meeting, with nothing to her credit but her lovely smile, not a sufficient reason ever to see her again. He had telephoned her the next evening. Of the countless girls he had known in his student years she was the only one with whom he had never progressed beyond a few kisses. He could have any girl he met and he knew it; he knew that he could have Catherine; he wanted her; she loved him and had admitted it simply, openly, without fear or shyness, asking nothing of him, expecting nothing; somehow, he had never taken advantage of it. He had felt proud of the girls whom he escorted in those days, the most beautiful girls, the most popular, the best dressed, and he had delighted in the envy of his schoolmates. He had been ashamed of Catherine's thoughtless sloppiness and of the fact that no other boy would look at her twice. But he had never been as happy as when he took her to fraternity dances. He had had many violent loves, when he swore he could not live without this girl or that; he forgot Catherine for weeks at a time and she never reminded him. He had always come back to her, suddenly, inexplicably, as he did tonight.

Her mother, a gentle little schoolteacher, had died last winter. Catherine had gone to live with an uncle in New York. Keating had answered some of her letters immediately, others—months later. She had always replied at once, and never written during his long silences, waiting patiently. He had felt, when he thought of her, that nothing would ever replace her. Then, in New York, within reach of a bus or a telephone, he had forgotten her again for a month.

He never thought, as he hurried to her now, that he should have announced his visit. He never wondered whether he would find her at home. He had always come back like this and she had always been there. She was there again tonight.

She opened the door for him, on the top floor of a shabby, pretentious brownstone house. "Hello, Peter," she said, as if she had seen him yesterday.

She stood before him, too small, too thin for her clothes. The short black skirt flared out from the slim band of her waist; the boyish shirt collar hung loosely, pulled to one side, revealing the knob of a thin collarbone; the sleeves were too long over the fragile hands. She looked at him, her head bent to one side; her chestnut hair was gathered carelessly at the back of her neck, but it looked as though it were bobbed, standing, light and fuzzy, as a shapeless halo about her face. Her eyes were gray, wide and nearsighted; her mouth smiled slowly, delicately, enchantingly, her lips glistening.

"Hello, Katie," he said.

He felt at peace. He felt he had nothing to fear, in this house or anywhere outside. He had prepared himself to explain how busy he'd been in New York; but explanations seemed irrelevant now.

"Give me your hat," she said, "be careful of that chair, it's not very steady, we have better ones in the living room, come in."

The living room, he noticed, was modest but somehow distinguished, and in surprisingly good taste. He noticed the books; cheap shelves rising to the ceiling, loaded with precious volumes; the volumes stacked carelessly, actually being used. He noticed, over a neat, shabby desk, a Rembrandt etching, stained and yellow, found, perhaps, in some junk shop by the eyes of a connoisseur who had never parted with it, though its price would have obviously been of help to him. He wondered what business her uncle could be in; he had never asked.

He stood looking vaguely at the room, feeling her presence behind him, enjoying that sense of certainty which he found so rarely. Then he turned and took her in his arms and kissed her; her lips met his softly, eagerly; but she was neither frightened nor excited, too happy to accept this in any way save by taking it for granted.

"God, I've missed you!" he said, and knew that he had, every day since he'd seen her last and most of all, perhaps, on the days when he had not thought of her.

"You haven't changed much," she said. "You look a little thinner. It's becoming. You'll be very attractive when you're fifty, Peter."

"That's not very complimentary—by implication."

"Why? Oh, you mean I think you're not attractive now? Oh, but you are."

"You shouldn't say that right out to me like that."

"Why not? You know you are. But I've been thinking of what you'll look like at fifty. You'll have gray temples and you'll wear a gray suit—I saw one in a window last week and I thought that would be the one—and you'll be a very great architect."

"You really think so?"

"Why, yes." She was not flattering him. She did not seem to realize that it could be flattery. She was merely stating a fact, too certain to need emphasis.

He waited for the inevitable questions. But instead, they were talking suddenly of their old Stanton days together, and he was laughing, holding her across his knees, her thin shoulders leaning against the circle of his arm, her eyes soft, contented. He was speaking of their old bathing suits, of the runs in her stockings, of their favorite ice-cream parlor in Stanton, where they had spent so many summer evenings together—and he was thinking dimly that it made no sense at all; he had more pertinent things to tell and to ask her; people did not talk like that when they hadn't seen each other for months. But it seemed quite normal to her; she did not appear to know that they had been parted.

He was first to ask finally:

"Did you get my wire?"

"Oh, yes. Thanks."

"Don't you want to know how I'm getting along in the city?"

"Sure. How are you getting along in the city?"

"Look here, you're not terribly interested."

"Oh, but I am! I want to know everything about you."

"Why don't you ask?"

"You'll tell me when you want to."

"It doesn't matter much to you, does it?"

"What?"

"What I've been doing."

"Oh . . . Yes, it does, Peter. No, not too much."

"That's sweet of you!"

"But, you see, it's not what you do that matters really. It's only you."

"Me what?"

"Just you here. Or you in the city. Or you somewhere in the world. I don't know. Just that."

"You know, you're a fool, Katie. Your technique is something awful."

"My what?"

"Your technique. You can't tell a man so shamelessly, like that, that you're practically crazy about him."

"But I am."

"But you can't say so. Men won't care for you."

"But I don't want men to care for me."

"You want me to, don't you?"

"But you do, don't you?"

"I do," he said, his arms tightening about her. "Damnably. I'm a bigger fool than you are."

"Well, then it's perfectly all right," she said, her fingers in his hair, "isn't it?"

"It's always been perfectly all right, that's the strangest part about it. . . . But look, I want to tell you about what's happened to me, because it's important."

"I'm really very interested, Peter."

"Well, you know I'm working for Francon & Heyer and . . . Oh, hell, you don't even know what that means!"

"Yes, I do. I've looked them up in *Who's Who in Architecture*. It said some very nice things about them. And I asked Uncle. He said they were tops in the business."

"You bet they are. Francon—he's the greatest designer in New York, in the whole country, in the world maybe. He's put up seventeen skyscrapers, eight cathedrals, six railroad terminals and God knows what else. . . . Of course, you know, he's an old fool and a pompous fraud who oils his way into everything and . . ."

He stopped, his mouth open, staring at her. He had not intended to say that. He had never allowed himself to think that before.

She was looking at him serenely.

"Yes?" she asked. "And . . . ?"

"Well . . . and . . ." he stammered, and he knew that he could not speak differently, not to her, "and that's what I really think of him. And I have no respect for him at all. And I'm delighted to be working for him. See?"

"Sure," she said quietly. "You're ambitious, Peter."

"Don't you despise me for it?"

"No. That's what you wanted."

"Sure, that's what I wanted. Well, actually, it's not as bad as that. It's a tremendous firm, the best in the city. I'm really doing work, and Francon is very pleased with me. I'm getting ahead. I think I can have any job I want in the place eventually. . . . Why, only tonight I took over a man's work and he doesn't know that he'll be useless soon, because . . . Katie! What am I saying?"

"It's all right, dear. I understand."

"If you did, you'd call me the names I deserve and make me stop it."

"No, Peter. I don't want to change you. I love you, Peter."

"God help you!"

"I know that."

"You know *that?* And you say it *like this?* Like you'd say, 'Hello, it's a beautiful evening'?"

"Well, why not? Why worry about it? I love you."

"No, don't worry about it! Don't ever worry about it! . . . Katie. . . . I'll never love anyone else. . . ."

"I know that too."

He held her close, anxiously, afraid that her weightless little body would vanish. He did not know why her presence made him confess things unconfessed in his own mind. He did not know why the victory he came here to share had faded. But it did not matter. He had a peculiar sense of freedom—her presence always lifted from him a pressure he could not define—he was alone—he was himself. All that mattered to him now was the feeling of her coarse cotton blouse against his wrist.

Then he was asking her about her own life in New York and she was speaking happily about her uncle.

"He's wonderful, Peter. He's really wonderful. He's quite poor, but he took me in and he was so gracious about it, he gave up his study to make a room for me and now he has to work here, in the living room. You must meet him, Peter. He's away now, on a lecture tour, but you must meet him when he comes back."

"Sure, I'd love to."

"You know, I wanted to go to work and be on my own, but he wouldn't let me. 'My dear child,' he said, 'not at seventeen. You don't want me to be ashamed of myself, do you? I don't believe in child labor.' That was kind of a funny idea, don't you think? He has so many funny ideas—I don't understand them all, but they say he's a brilliant man. So he made it look as if I were doing him a favor by letting him keep me, and I think that was really very decent of him."

"What do you do with yourself all day long?"

"Nothing much of anything now. I read books. On architecture. Uncle has tons of books on architecture. But when he's here I type his lectures for him. I really don't think he likes me to do it, he prefers the typist he had, but I love it and he lets me. And he pays me her salary. I didn't want to take it, but he made me."

"What does he do for a living?"

"Oh, so many things, I don't know, I can't keep track of them. He teaches art history, for one thing, he's a kind of professor."

"And when are you going to college, by the way?"

"Oh . . . Well . . . well, you see, I don't think Uncle approves of the idea. I told him how I'd always planned to go and that I'd work my own way through, but he seems to think it's not for me. He doesn't say much, only: 'God made the elephant for toil and the mosquito for flitting about, and it's not advisable, as a rule, to experiment with the laws of nature, however, if you want to try it, my dear child . . .' But he's not objecting really, it's up to me, only . . ."

"Well, don't let him stop you."

"Oh, he wouldn't want to stop me. Only, I was thinking, I was never any great shakes in high school, and, darling, I'm really quite utterly lousy at mathematics, and so I wonder . . . But then, there's no hurry, I've got plenty of time to decide."

"Listen, Katie, I don't like that. You've always planned on college. If that uncle of yours . . ."

"You shouldn't say it like this. You don't know him. He's the most amazing man. I've never met anyone quite like him. He's so kind, so understanding. And he's such fun, always joking, he's so clever at it, nothing that you thought was serious ever seems to be when he's around, and yet he's a very serious man. You know, he spends hours talking to me, he's never too tired and he's not bored with my stupidity, he tells me all about strikes, and conditions in the slums, and the poor people in sweatshops, always about others, never about himself. A friend of his told me that Uncle could be a very rich man if he tried, he's so clever, but he won't, he just isn't interested in money."

"That's not human."

"Wait till you see him. Oh, he wants to meet you, too. I've told him about you. He calls you 'the T-square Romeo.' "

"Oh, he does, does he?"

"But you don't understand. He means it kindly. It's the way he says things. You'll have a lot in common. Maybe he could help you. He knows something about architecture, too. You'll love Uncle Ellsworth."

"*Who?*" said Keating.

"My uncle."

"Say," Keating asked, his voice a little husky, "what's your uncle's name?"

"Ellsworth Toohey. Why?"

His hands fell limply. He sat staring at her.

"What's the matter, Peter?"

He swallowed. She saw the jerking motion of his throat. Then he said, his voice hard:

"Listen, Katie, I don't want to meet your uncle."

"But why?"

"I don't want to meet him. Not through you. . . . You see, Katie, you don't know me. I'm the kind that uses people. I don't want to use you. Ever. Don't let me. Not you."

"Use me how? What's the matter? Why?"

"It's just this: I'd give my eyeteeth to meet Ellsworth Toohey, that's all." He laughed harshly. "So he knows something about architecture, does he? You little fool! He's the most important man in architecture. Not yet, maybe, but that's what he'll be in a couple of years—ask Francon, that old weasel knows. He's on his way to becoming the Napoleon of all architectural critics, your Uncle Ellsworth is, just watch him. In the first place, there aren't many to bother writing about our profession, so he's the smart boy who's going to corner the market. You should see the big shots in our office lapping up every comma he puts out in print! So you think maybe he could help me? Well, he could make me, and he will, and I'm going to meet him some day, when I'm ready for him, as I met Francon, but not here, not through you. Understand? Not from you!"

"But, Peter, why not?"

"Because I don't want it that way! Because it's filthy and I hate it, all of it, my work and my profession, and what I'm doing and what I'm going to do! It's something I want to keep you out of. You're all I really have. Just keep out of it, Katie!"

"Out of what?"

"I don't know!"

She rose and stood in the circle of his arms, his face hidden against her hip; she stroked his hair, looking down at him.

"All right, Peter. I think I know. You don't have to meet him until you want to. Just tell me when you want it. You can use me, if you have to. It's all right. It won't change anything."

When he raised his head, she was laughing softly.

"You've worked too hard, Peter. You're a little unstrung. Suppose I make you some tea?"

"Oh, I'd forgotten all about it, but I've had no dinner today. Had no time."

"Well, of all things! Well, how perfectly disgusting! Come on to the kitchen, this minute, I'll see what I can fix up for you!"

He left her two hours later, and he walked away feeling light, clean, happy, his fears forgotten, Toohey and Francon forgotten. He thought only that he had promised to come again tomorrow and that it was an unbearably long time to wait. She stood at the door, after he had gone, her hand on the knob he had touched, and she thought that he might come tomorrow—or three months later.

"When you finish tonight," said Henry Cameron, "I want to see you in my office."

"Yes," said Roark.

Cameron veered sharply on his heels and walked out of the drafting room. It had been the longest sentence he had addressed to Roark in a month.

Roark had come to this room every morning, had done his task, and had heard no word of comment. Cameron would enter the drafting room and stand behind Roark for a long time, looking over his shoulder. It was as if his eyes concentrated deliberately on trying to throw the steady hand off its course on the paper. The two other draftsmen botched their work from the mere thought of such an apparition standing behind them. Roark did not seem to notice it. He went on, his hand unhurried, he took his time about discarding a blunted pencil and picking out another. "Uh-huh," Cameron would grunt suddenly. Roark would turn his head then, politely attentive. "What is it?" he would ask. Cameron would turn away without a word, his narrowed eyes underscoring contemptuously the fact that he considered an answer unnecessary, and would leave the drafting room. Roark would go on with his drawing.

"Looks bad," Loomis, the young draftsman, confided to Simpson, his ancient colleague. "The old man doesn't like this guy. Can't say that I blame him, either. Here's one that won't last long."

Simpson was old and helpless; he had survived from Cameron's three-floor office, had stuck and had never understood it. Loomis was young, with the face of a drugstore-corner lout; he was here because he had been fired from too many other places.

Both men disliked Roark. He was usually disliked, from the first sight of his face, anywhere he went. His face was closed like the door of a safety vault; things locked in safety vaults are valuable; men did not care to feel that. He was a cold, disquieting presence in the room; his presence had a strange quality: it made itself felt and yet it made them feel that he was not there; or perhaps that he was and they weren't.

After work he walked the long distance to his home, a tenement near the East River. He had chosen that tenement because he had been able to get, for two-fifty a week, its entire top floor, a huge room that had been used for storage: it had no ceiling and the roof leaked between its naked beams. But it had a long row of windows, along two of its walls, some panes filled with glass, others with cardboard, and the windows opened high over the river on one side and the city on the other.

A week ago Cameron had come into the drafting room and had thrown down on Roark's table a violent sketch of a country residence. "See if you can make a house out of this!" he had snapped and gone without further explanation. He had not approached Roark's table during the days that followed. Roark had finished the drawings last night and left them on Cameron's desk. This morning, Cameron had come in, thrown some sketches of steel joints to Roark, ordered him to appear in his office later and had not entered the drafting room again for the rest of the day.

The others were gone. Roark pulled an old piece of oil cloth over his table and went to Cameron's office. His drawings of the country house were spread on the desk. The light of the lamp fell on Cameron's cheek, on his beard, the white threads glistening, on his fist, on a corner of the drawing, its black lines bright and hard as if embossed on the paper.

"You're fired," said Cameron.

Roark stood, halfway across the long room, his weight on one leg, his arms hanging by his sides, one shoulder raised.

"Am I?" he asked quietly, without moving.

"Come here," said Cameron. "Sit down."

Roark obeyed.

"You're too good," said Cameron. "You're too good for what you want to do with yourself. It's no use, Roark. Better now than later."

"What do you mean?"

"It's no use wasting what you've got on an ideal that you'll never reach, that they'll never let you reach. It's no use, taking that marvelous thing you have and making a torture rack for yourself out of it. Sell it, Roark. Sell it now. It won't be the same, but you've got enough in you. You've got what they'll pay you for, and pay plenty, if you use it their way. Accept them, Roark. Compromise. Compromise now, because you'll have to later, anyway, only then you'll have gone through things you'll wish you hadn't. You don't know. I do. Save yourself from that. Leave me. Go to someone else."

"Did you do that?"

"You presumptuous bastard! How good do you think I said you were? Did I tell you to compare yourself to . . ." He stopped because he saw that Roark was smiling.

He looked at Roark, and suddenly smiled in answer, and it was the most painful thing that Roark had ever seen.

"No," said Cameron softly, "that won't work, huh? No, it won't . . . Well, you're right. You're as good as you think you are. But I want to speak to you. I don't know exactly how to go about it. I've lost the habit of speaking to men like you. Lost it? Maybe I've never had it. Maybe that's what frightens me now. Will you try to understand?"

"I understand. I think you're wasting your time."

"Don't be rude. Because I can't be rude to you now. I want you to listen. Will you listen and not answer me?"

"Yes. I'm sorry. I didn't intend it as rudeness."

"You see, of all men, I'm the last one to whom you should have come. I'll be committing a crime if I keep you here. Somebody should have warned you against me. I won't help you at all. I won't discourage you. I won't teach you any common sense. Instead, I'll push you on. I'll drive you the way you're going now. I'll beat you into remaining what you are, and I'll make you worse. . . . Don't you see? In another month I won't be able to let you go. I'm not sure I can now. So don't argue with me and go. Get out while you can."

"But can I? Don't you think it's too late for both of us? It was too late for me twelve years ago."

"Try it, Roark. Try to be reasonable for once. There's plenty of big fellows who'll take you, expulsion or no expulsion, if I say so. They may laugh at me in their luncheon speeches, but they steal from me when it suits them, and they know that I know a good draftsman when I see one. I'll give you a letter to Guy Francon. He worked for me once, long ago. I think I fired him, but that wouldn't matter. Go to him. You won't like it at first, but you'll get used to it. And you'll thank me for it many years from now."

"Why are you saying all this to me? That's not what you want to say. That's not what you did."

"That's why I'm saying it! Because that's not what I did! . . . Look, Roark, there's one thing about you, the thing I'm afraid of. It's not just the kind of work you do; I wouldn't care, if you were an exhibitionist who's being different as a stunt, as a lark, just to attract attention to himself. It's a smart racket, to oppose the crowd and amuse it and collect admission to the side show. If you did that, I wouldn't worry. But it's not that. You love your work. God help you, you love it! And that's the curse. That's the brand on your forehead for all of them to see. You love it, and they know it, and they know they have you. Do you ever look at the people in the street? Aren't you afraid of them? I am. They move past you and they wear hats and they carry bundles. But that's not the substance of them. The substance of them is hatred for any man who loves his work. That's the only kind they fear. I don't know why. You're opening yourself up, Roark, for each and every one of them."

"But I never notice the people in the streets."

"Do you notice what they've done to me?"

"I notice only that you weren't afraid of them. Why do you ask me to be?"

"That's just why I'm asking it!" He leaned forward, his fists closing on the desk before him. "Roark, do you want me to say it? You're cruel, aren't you? All right, I'll say it: do you want to end up like this? Do you want to be what I am?"

Roark got up and stood against the edge of light on the desk.

"If," said Roark, "at the end of my life, I'll be what you are today, here, in this office, I shall consider it an honor that I could not have deserved."

"Sit down!" roared Cameron. "I don't like demonstrations!"

Roark looked down at himself, at the desk, astonished to find himself standing. He said: "I'm sorry. I didn't know I got up."

"Well, sit down. Listen. I understand. And it's very nice of you. But you don't know. I thought a few days here would be enough to take the hero worship out of you. I see it wasn't. Here you are, saying to yourself how grand old Cameron is, a noble fighter, a martyr to a lost cause, and you'd just love to die on the barricades with me and to eat in dime lunchwagons with me for the rest of your life. I know, it looks pure and beautiful to you now, at your great old age of twenty-two. But do you know what it means? Thirty years of a lost cause, that sounds beautiful, doesn't it? But do you know how many days there are in thirty years? Do you know what happens in those days? Roark! Do you know what happens?"

"You don't want to speak of that."

"No! I don't want to speak of that! But I'm going to. I want you to hear. I want you to know what's in store for you. There will be days when you'll look at your hands and you'll want to take something and smash every bone in them, because they'll be taunting you with what they could do, if you found a chance for them to do it, and you can't find that chance, and you can't bear your living body because it has failed those hands somewhere. There will be days when a bus driver will snap at you as you enter a bus, and he'll be only asking for a dime, but that won't be what you'll hear; you'll hear that you're nothing, that he's laughing at you, that it's written on your forehead, that thing they hate you for. There will be days when you'll stand in the corner of a hall and listen to a creature on a platform talking about buildings, about that work which you love, and the things he'll say will make you wait for somebody to rise and crack him open between two thumbnails; and then you'll hear the people applauding him, and you'll want to scream, because you won't know whether they're real or you are, whether you're in a room full of gored skulls, or whether someone has just emptied your own head, and you'll say nothing, because the sounds you could make—they're not a language in that room any longer; but if you'd want to speak, you won't anyway, because you'll be brushed aside, you who have nothing to tell them about buildings! Is that what you want?"

Roark sat still, the shadows sharp on his face, a black wedge on a sunken cheek, a long triangle of black cutting across his chin, his eyes on Cameron.

"Not enough?" asked Cameron. "All right. Then, one day, you'll see on a piece of paper before you a building that will make you want to kneel; you won't believe that you've done it, but you will have done it; then you'll think that the earth is beautiful and the air smells of spring and you love your fellow men, because there is no evil in the world. And you'll set out from your house with this drawing, to have it erected, because you won't have any doubt that it will be erected by the first man to see it. But you won't get very far from your house. Because you'll be stopped at the door by the man who's come to turn off the gas. You hadn't had much food, because you saved money to finish your drawing, but still you had to cook something and you hadn't paid for it. . . . All right, that's nothing, you can laugh at that. But finally you'll get into a man's office with your drawing, and you'll curse yourself for taking so much space of his air with your body, and you'll try to squeeze yourself out of his sight, so that he won't see you, but only hear your voice begging him, pleading, your voice licking his knees; you'll loathe yourself for it, but you won't care, if only he'd let you put up that building, you won't care, you'll want to rip your insides open to show him, because if he saw what's there he'd have to let you put it up. But he'll say that he's very sorry, only the commission has just been given to Guy Francon. And you'll go home, and do you know what you'll do there? You'll cry. You'll cry like a woman, like a drunkard, like an animal. That's your future, Howard Roark. Now, do you want it?"

"Yes," said Roark.

Cameron's eyes dropped; then his head moved down a little, then a little farther; his head went on dropping slowly, in long, single jerks, then stopped; he sat still, his shoulders hunched, his arms huddled together in his lap.

"Howard," whispered Cameron, "I've never told it to anyone. . . ."

"Thank you. . . ." said Roark.

After a long time, Cameron raised his head.

"Go home now," said Cameron, his voice flat. "You've worked too much lately. And you have a hard day ahead." He pointed to the drawings of the country house. "This is all very well, and I wanted to see what you'd do, but it's not good enough to build. You'll have to do it over. I'll show you what I want tomorrow."

V

A YEAR WITH THE FIRM OF FRANCON & HEYER HAD GIVEN KEATING the whispered title of crown prince without portfolio. Still only a draftsman, he was Francon's reigning favorite. Francon took him out to lunch—an unprecedented honor for an employee. Francon called him to be present at interviews with clients. The clients seemed to like seeing so decorative a young man in an architect's office.

Lucius N. Heyer had the annoying habit of asking Francon suddenly: "When did you get the new man?" and pointing to an employee who had been there for three years. But Heyer surprised everybody by remembering Keating's name and by greeting him, whenever they met, with a smile of positive recognition. Keating had had a long conversation with him, one dreary November afternoon, on the subject of old porcelain. It was Heyer's hobby; he owned a famous collection, passionately gathered. Keating displayed an earnest knowledge of the subject, though he had never heard of old porcelain till the night before, which he had spent at the public library. Heyer was delighted; nobody in the office cared about his hobby, few ever noticed his presence. Heyer remarked to his partner: "You're certainly good at picking your men, Guy. There's one boy I wish we wouldn't lose, what's his name?—Keating." "Yes, indeed," Francon answered, smiling, "yes, indeed."

In the drafting room, Keating concentrated on Tim Davis. Work and drawings were only unavoidable details on the surface of his days; Tim Davis was the substance and the shape of the first step in his career.

Davis let him do most of his own work; only night work, at first, then parts of his daily assignments as well; secretly, at first, then openly. Davis had not wanted it to be known. Keating made it known, with an air of naïve confidence which implied that he was only a tool, no more than Tim's pencil or T-square, that his help enhanced Tim's importance rather than diminished it and, therefore, he did not wish to conceal it.

At first, Davis relayed instructions to Keating; then the chief draftsman took the arrangement for granted and began coming to Keating with orders intended for Davis. Keating was always there, smiling, saying: "I'll do it, don't bother Tim with those little things, I'll take care of it." Davis relaxed and let himself be carried along; he smoked a great deal, he lolled about, his legs twisted loosely over the rungs of a stool, his eyes closed, dreaming of Elaine; he uttered once in a while: "Is the stuff ready, Pete?"

Davis had married Elaine that spring. He was frequently late for work. He had whispered to Keating: "You're in with the old man, Pete, slip a good word for me, once in a while, will you?—so they'll overlook a few things. God, do I hate to have to be working right now!" Keating would say to Francon: "I'm sorry, Mr. Francon, that the Murray job subbasement plans were so late, but Tim Davis had a quarrel with his wife last night, and you know how newlyweds are, you don't want to be too hard on them," or: "It's Tim Davis again, Mr. Francon, do forgive him, he can't help it, he hasn't got his mind on his work at all!"

When Francon glanced at the list of his employees' salaries, he noticed that his most expensive draftsman was the man least needed in the office.

When Tim Davis lost his job, no one in the drafting room was surprised but Tim Davis. He could not understand it. He set his lips defiantly in bitterness against a world he would hate forever. He felt he had no friend on earth save Peter Keating.

Keating consoled him, cursed Francon, cursed the injustice of humanity, spent six dollars in a speak-easy, entertaining the secretary of an obscure architect of his acquaintance and arranged a new job for Tim Davis.

Whenever he thought of Davis afterward, Keating felt a warm pleasure; he had influenced the course of a human being, had thrown him off one path and pushed him into another; a human being—it was not Tim Davis to him any longer, it was a living frame and a mind, a conscious mind—why had he always feared that mysterious entity of consciousness within others?—and he had twisted that frame and that mind to his own will. By a unanimous decision of Francon, Heyer and the chief draftsman, Tim's table, position and salary were given to Peter Keating. But this was only part of his satisfaction; there was another sense of it, warmer and less real—and more dangerous. He said brightly and often: "Tim Davis? Oh yes, *I* got him his present job."

He wrote to his mother about it. She said to her friends: "Petey is such an unselfish boy."

He wrote to her dutifully, each week; his letters were short and respectful; hers, long, detailed and full of advice which he seldom finished reading.

He saw Catherine Halsey occasionally. He had not gone to her on that following evening, as he had promised. He had awakened in the morning and remembered the things he had said to her, and hated her for his having said them. But he had gone to her again, a week later; she had not reproached him and they had not mentioned her uncle. He saw her after that every month or two; he was happy when he saw her, but he never spoke to her of his career.

He tried to speak of it to Howard Roark; the attempt failed. He called on Roark twice; he climbed, indignantly, the five flights of stairs to Roark's room. He greeted Roark eagerly; he waited for reassurance, not knowing what sort of reassurance he needed nor why it could come only from Roark. He spoke of his job and he questioned Roark, with sincere concern, about Cameron's office. Roark listened to him, answered all his questions willingly, but Keating felt that he was knocking against a sheet of iron in Roark's unmoving eyes, and that they were not speaking about the same things at all. Before the visit was over, Keating was taking notice of Roark's frayed cuffs, of his shoes, of the patch on the knee of his trousers, and he felt satisfied. He went away chuckling, but he went away miserably uneasy, and wondered why, and swore never to see Roark again, and wondered why he knew that he would have to see him.

"Well," said Keating, "I couldn't quite work it to ask her to lunch, but she's coming to Mawson's exhibition with me day after tomorrow. Now what?"

He sat on the floor, his head resting against the edge of a couch, his bare feet stretched out, a pair of Guy Francon's chartreuse pyjamas floating loosely about his limbs.

Through the open door of the bathroom he saw Francon standing at the washstand, his stomach pressed to its shining edge, brushing his teeth.

"That's splendid," said Francon, munching through a thick foam of toothpaste. "That'll do just as well. Don't you see?"

"No."

"Lord, Pete, I explained it to you yesterday before we started. Mrs. Dunlop's husband's planning to build a home for her."

"Oh, yeah," said Keating weakly, brushing the matted black curls off his face. "Oh, yeah . . . I remember now . . . Jesus, Guy, I got a head on me! . . ."

He remembered vaguely the party to which Francon had taken him the night before, he remembered the caviar in a hollow iceberg, the black net evening gown and the pretty face of Mrs. Dunlop, but he could not remember how he had come to end up in Francon's apartment. He shrugged; he had attended many parties with Francon in the past year and had often been brought here like this.

"It's not a very large house," Francon was saying, holding the toothbrush in his mouth; it made a lump on his cheek and its green handle stuck out. "Fifty thousand or so, I understand. They're small fry anyway. But Mrs. Dunlop's brother-in-law is Quimby—you know, the big real estate fellow. Won't hurt to get a little wedge into that family, won't hurt at all. You're to see where that commission ends up, Pete. Can I count on you, Pete?"

"Sure," said Keating, his head drooping. "You can always count on me, Guy. . . ."

He sat still, watching his bare toes and thinking of Stengel, Francon's designer. He did not want to think, but his mind leaped to Stengel automatically, as it always did, because Stengel represented his next step.

Stengel was impregnable to friendship. For two years, Keating's attempts had broken against the ice of Stengel's glasses. What Stengel thought of him was whispered in the drafting rooms, but few dared to repeat it save in quotes; Stengel said it aloud, even though he knew that the corrections his sketches bore, when they returned to him from Francon's office, were made by Keating's hand. But Stengel had a vulnerable point: he had been planning for some time to leave Francon and open an office of his own. He had selected a partner, a young architect of no talent but of great inherited wealth. Stengel was waiting only for a chance. Keating had thought about this a great deal. He could think of nothing else. He thought of it again, sitting there on the floor of Francon's bedroom.

Two days later, when he escorted Mrs. Dunlop through the gallery exhibiting the paintings of one Frederic Mawson, his course of action was set. He piloted her through the sparse crowd, his fingers closing over her elbow once in a while, letting her catch his eyes directed at her young face more often than at the paintings.

"Yes," he said as she stared obediently at a landscape featuring an auto dump and tried to compose her face into the look of admiration expected of her, "magnificent work. Note the colors, Mrs. Dunlop. . . . They say this fellow Mawson had a terribly hard time. It's an old story—trying to get recognition. Old and heartbreaking. It's the same in all the arts. My own profession included."

"Oh, indeed?" said Mrs. Dunlop, who quite seemed to prefer architecture at the moment.

"Now this," said Keating, stopping before the depiction of an old hag picking at her bare toes on a street curb, "this is art as a social document. It takes a person of courage to appreciate this."

"It's simply wonderful," said Mrs. Dunlop.

"Ah, yes, courage. It's a rare quality. . . . They say Mawson was starving in a garret when Mrs. Stuyvesant discovered him. It's glorious to be able to help young talent on its way."

"It must be wonderful," agreed Mrs. Dunlop.

"If I were rich," said Keating wistfully, "I'd make it my hobby: to arrange an exhibition for a new artist, to finance the concert of a new pianist, to have a house built by a new architect. . . ."

"Do you know, Mr. Keating?—my husband and I are planning to build a little home on Long Island."

"Oh, are you? How very charming of you, Mrs. Dunlop, to confess such a thing to me. You're so young, if you'll forgive my saying this. Don't you know that you run the danger of my becoming a nuisance and trying to interest you in my firm? Or are you safe and have chosen an architect already?"

"No, I'm not safe at all," said Mrs. Dunlop prettily, "and I wouldn't mind the danger really. I've thought a great deal about the firm of Francon & Heyer in these last few days. And I've heard they are so terribly good."

"Why, thank you, Mrs. Dunlop."

"Mr. Francon is a great architect."

"Oh, yes."

"What's the matter?"

"Nothing. Nothing really."

"No, what's the matter?"

"Do you really want me to tell you?"

"Why, certainly."

"Well, you see, Guy Francon—it's only a name. He would have nothing to do with your house. It's one of those professional secrets that I shouldn't divulge, but I don't know what it is about you that makes me want to be honest. All the best buildings in our office are designed by Mr. Stengel."

"Who?"

"Claude Stengel. You've never heard the name, but you will, when someone has the courage to discover him. You see, he does all the work, he's the real genius behind the scenes, but Francon puts his signature on it and gets all the credit. That's the way it's done everywhere."

"But why does Mr. Stengel stand for it?"

"What can he do? No one will give him a start. You know how most people are, they stick to the beaten path, they pay three times the price for the same thing, just to have the trademark. Courage, Mrs. Dunlop, they lack courage. Stengel is a great artist, but there are so few discerning people to see it. He's ready to go on his own, if only he could find some outstanding person like Mrs. Stuyvesant to give him a chance."

"Really?" said Mrs. Dunlop. "How very interesting! Tell me more about it."

He told her a great deal more about it. By the time they had finished the inspection of the works of Frederic Mawson, Mrs. Dunlop was shaking Keating's hand and saying:

"It's so kind, so very unusually kind of you. Are you sure that it won't embarrass you with your office if you arrange for me to meet Mr. Stengel? I didn't quite dare to suggest it and it was so kind of you not to be angry at me. It's so unselfish of you and more than anyone else would have done in your position."

When Keating approached Stengel with the suggestion of a proposed luncheon, the man listened to him without a word. Then he jerked his head and snapped:

"What's in it for you?"

Before Keating could answer, Stengel threw his head back suddenly.

"Oh," said Stengel. "Oh, I see."

Then he leaned forward, his mouth drawn thin in contempt:

"Okay. I'll go to that lunch."

When Stengel left the firm of Francon & Heyer to open his own office and proceed with the construction of the Dunlop house, his first commission, Guy Francon smashed a ruler against the edge of his desk and roared to Keating:

"The bastard! The abysmal bastard! After all I've done for him."

"What did you expect?" said Keating, sprawled in a low armchair before him. "Such is life."

"But what beats me is how did that little skunk ever hear of it? To snatch it right from under our nose!"

"Well, I've never trusted him anyway." Keating shrugged. "Human nature . . ."

The bitterness in his voice was sincere. He had received no gratitude from Stengel. Stengel's parting remark to him had been only: "You're a worse bastard than I thought you were. Good luck. You'll be a great architect some day."

Thus Keating achieved the position of chief designer for Francon & Heyer.

Francon celebrated the occasion with a modest little orgy at one of the quieter and costlier restaurants. "In a coupla years," he kept repeating, "in a coupla years you'll see things happenin', Pete. . . . You're a good boy and I like you and I'll do things for you. . . . Haven't I done things for you? . . . You're going places, Pete . . . in a coupla years. . . ."

"Your tie's crooked, Guy," said Keating dryly, "and you're spilling brandy all over your vest. . . ."

Facing his first task of designing, Keating thought of Tim Davis, of Stengel, of many others who had wanted it, had struggled for it, had tried, had been beaten—by him. It was a triumphant feeling. It was a tangible affirmation of his greatness. Then he found himself suddenly in his glass-enclosed office, looking down at a blank sheet of paper—alone. Something rolled in his throat down to his stomach, cold and empty, his old feeling of the dropping hole. He leaned against the table, closing his eyes. It had never been quite real to him before that this was the thing actually expected of him—to fill a sheet of paper, to create something on a sheet of paper.

It was only a small residence. But instead of seeing it rise before him, he saw it sinking; he saw its shape as a pit in the ground; and as a pit within him; as emptiness, with only Davis and Stengel rattling uselessly within it. Francon had said to him about the building: "It must have dignity, you know, dignity . . . nothing freaky . . . a structure of elegance . . . and stay within the budget," which was Francon's conception of giving his designer ideas and letting him work them out. Through a cold stupor, Keating thought of the clients laughing in his face; he heard the thin, omnipotent voice of Ellsworth Toohey calling his attention to the opportunities open to him in the field of plumbing. He hated every piece of stone on the face of the earth. He hated himself for having chosen to be an architect.

When he began to draw, he tried not to think of the job he was doing; he thought only that Francon had done it, and Stengel, even Heyer, and all the others, and that he could do it, if they could.

He spent many days on his preliminary sketches. He spent long hours in the library of Francon & Heyer, selecting from Classic photographs the appearance of his house. He felt the tension melting in his mind. It was right and it was good, that house growing under his hand, because men were still worshiping the masters who had done it before him. He did not have to wonder, to fear or to take chances; it had been done for him.

When the drawings were ready, he stood looking at them uncertainly. Were he to be told that this was the best or the ugliest house in the world, he would agree with either. He was not sure. He had to be sure. He thought of Stanton and of what he had relied upon when working on his assignments there. He telephoned Cameron's office and asked for Howard Roark.

He came to Roark's room, that night, and spread before him the plans, the elevations, the perspective of his first building. Roark stood over it, his arms spread wide, his hands holding the edge of the table, and he said nothing for a long time.

Keating waited anxiously; he felt anger growing with his anxiety— because he could see no reason for being so anxious. When he couldn't stand it, he spoke:

"You know, Howard, everybody says Stengel's the best designer in town, and I don't think he was really ready to quit, but I made him and I took his place. I had to do some pretty fine thinking to work that, I . . ."

He stopped. It did not sound bright and proud, as it would have sounded anywhere else. It sounded like begging.

Roark turned and looked at him. Roark's eyes were not contemptuous; only a little wider than usual, attentive and puzzled. He said nothing and turned back to the drawings.

Keating felt naked. Davis, Stengel, Francon meant nothing here. People were his protection against people. Roark had no sense of people. Others gave Keating a feeling of his own value. Roark gave him nothing. He thought that he should seize his drawings and run. The danger was not Roark. The danger was that he, Keating, remained.

Roark turned to him.

"Do you enjoy doing this sort of thing, Peter?" he asked.

"Oh, I know," said Keating, his voice shrill, "I know you don't approve of it, but this is business, I just want to know what you think of this *practically,* not philosophically, not . . ."

"No, I'm not going to preach to you. I was only wondering."

"If you could help me, Howard, if you could just help me with it a little. It's my first house, and it means so much to me at the office, and I'm not sure. What do you think? Will you help me, Howard?"

"All right."

Roark threw aside the sketch of the graceful façade with the fluted pilasters, the broken pediments, the Roman fasces over the windows and the two eagles of Empire by the entrance. He picked up the plans. He took a sheet of tracing paper, threw it over the plan and began to draw. Keating stood watching the pencil in Roark's hand. He saw his imposing entrance foyer disappearing, his twisted corridors, his lightless corners; he saw an immense living room growing in the space he had thought too limited; a wall of giant windows facing the garden, a spacious kitchen. He watched for a long time.

"And the façade?" he asked, when Roark threw the pencil down.

"I can't help you with that. If you must have it Classic, have it good Classic at least. You don't need three pilasters where one will do. And take those ducks off the door, it's too much."

Keating smiled at him gratefully, when he was leaving, his drawings under his arm; he descended the stairs, hurt and angry; he worked for three days making new plans from Roark's sketches, and a new, simpler elevation; and he presented his house to Francon with a proud gesture that looked like a flourish.

"Well," said Francon, studying it, "well, I declare! . . . What an imagination you have, Peter . . . I wonder . . . It's a bit daring, but I wonder . . ." He coughed and added: "It's just what I had in mind."

"Of course," said Keating. "I studied your buildings, and I tried to think of what you'd do, and if it's good, it's because I think I know how to catch your ideas."

Francon smiled. And Keating thought suddenly that Francon did not really believe it and knew that Keating did not believe it, and yet they were both contented, bound tighter together by a common method and a common guilt.

The letter on Cameron's desk informed him regretfully that after earnest consideration, the board of directors of the Security Trust Company had not been able to accept his plans for the building to house the new Astoria branch of the Company and that the commission had been awarded to the firm of Gould & Pettingill. A check was attached to the letter, in payment for his preliminary drawings, as agreed; the amount was not enough to cover the expense of making those drawings.

The letter lay spread out on the desk. Cameron sat before it, drawn back, not touching the desk, his hands gathered in his lap, the back of one in the palm of the other, the fingers tight. It was only a small piece of paper, but he sat huddled and still, because it seemed to be a supernatural thing, like radium, sending forth rays that would hurt him if he moved and exposed his skin to them.

For three months, he had awaited the commission of the Security Trust Company. One after another, the chances that had loomed before him at rare intervals, in the last two years, had vanished, looming in vague promises, vanishing in firm refusals. One of his draftsmen had had to be discharged long ago. The landlord had asked questions, politely at first, then dryly, then rudely and openly. But no one in the office had minded that nor the usual arrears in salaries: there had been the commission of the Security Trust Company. The vice-president, who had asked Cameron to submit drawings, had said: "I know, some of the directors won't see it as I do. But go ahead, Mr. Cameron. Take the chance with me and I'll fight for you."

Cameron had taken the chance. He and Roark had worked savagely —to have the plans ready on time, before time, before Gould & Pettingill could submit theirs. Pettingill was a cousin of the Bank president's wife and a famous authority on the ruins of Pompeii; the Bank president was an ardent admirer of Julius Caesar and had once, while in Rome, spent an hour and a quarter in reverent inspection of the Colosseum.

Cameron and Roark and a pot of black coffee had lived in the office from dawn till frozen dawn for many days, and Cameron had thought involuntarily of the electric bill, but made himself forget it. The lights still burned in the drafting room in the early hours when he sent Roark out for sandwiches, and Roark found gray morning in the streets while it was still night in the office, in the windows facing a high brick wall. On the last day, it was Roark who had ordered Cameron home after midnight, because Cameron's hands were jerking and his knees kept seeking the tall drafting stool for support, leaning against it with a slow, cautious, sickening precision. Roark had taken him down to a taxi and in the light of a street lamp Cameron had seen Roark's face, drawn, the eyes kept wide artificially, the lips dry. The next morning Cameron had entered the drafting room, and found the coffee pot on the floor, on its side over a black puddle, and Roark's hand in the puddle, palm up, fingers half closed, Roark's body stretched out on the floor, his head thrown back, fast asleep. On the table, Cameron had found the plans, finished. . . .

He sat looking at the letter on his desk. The degradation was that he could not think of those nights behind him, he could not think of the building that should have risen in Astoria and of the building that would now take its place; it was that he thought only of the bill unpaid to the electric company. . . .

In these last two years Cameron had disappeared from his office for weeks at a time, and Roark had not found him at home, and had known what was happening, but could only wait, hoping for Cameron's safe return. Then, Cameron had lost even the shame of his agony, and had come to his office reeling, recognizing no one, openly drunk and flaunting it before the walls of the only place on earth he had respected.

Roark learned to face his own landlord with the quiet statement that he could not pay him for another week; the landlord was afraid of him and did not insist. Peter Keating heard of it somehow, as he always heard everything he wanted to know. He came to Roark's unheated room, one evening, and sat down, keeping his overcoat on. He produced a wallet, pulled out five ten-dollar bills, and handed them to Roark. "You need it, Howard. I know you need it. Don't start protesting now. You can pay me back any time." Roark looked at him, astonished, took the money, saying: "Yes, I need it. Thank you, Peter." Then Keating said: "What in hell are you doing, wasting yourself on old Cameron? What do you want to live like this for? Chuck it, Howard, and come with us. All I have to do is say so. Francon'll be delighted. We'll start you at sixty a week." Roark took the money out of his pocket and handed it back to him. "Oh, for God's sake, Howard! I . . . I didn't mean to offend you." "I didn't either." "But please, Howard, keep it anyway." "Good night, Peter."

Roark was thinking of that when Cameron entered the drafting room, the letter from the Security Trust Company in his hand. He gave the letter to Roark, said nothing, turned and walked back to his office. Roark read the letter and followed him. Whenever they lost another commission Roark knew that Cameron wanted to see him in the office, but not to speak of it; just to see him there, to talk of other things, to lean upon the reassurance of his presence.

On Cameron's desk Roark saw a copy of the New York *Banner*.

It was the leading newspaper of the great Wynand chain. It was a paper he would have expected to find in a kitchen, in a barbershop, in a third-rate drawing room, in the subway; anywhere but in Cameron's office. Cameron saw him looking at it and grinned.

"Picked it up this morning, on my way here. Funny, isn't it? I didn't know we'd . . . get that letter today. And yet it seems appropriate together—this paper and that letter. Don't know what made me buy it. A sense of symbolism, I suppose. Look at it, Howard. It's interesting."

Roark glanced through the paper. The front page carried the picture of an unwed mother with thick glistening lips, who had shot her lover; the picture headed the first installment of her autobiography and a detailed account of her trial. The other pages ran a crusade against utility companies; a daily horoscope; extracts from church sermons; recipes for young brides; pictures of girls with beautiful legs; advice on how to hold a husband; a baby contest; a poem proclaiming that to wash dishes was nobler than to write a symphony; an article proving that a woman who had borne a child was automatically a saint.

"That's our answer, Howard. That's the answer given to you and to me. This paper. That it exists and that it's liked. Can you fight that? Have you any words to be heard and understood by that? They shouldn't have sent us the letter. They should have sent a copy of Wynand's *Banner*. It would be simpler and clearer. Do you know that in a few years that incredible bastard, Gail Wynand, will rule the world? It will be a beautiful world. And perhaps he's right."

Cameron held the paper outstretched, weighing it on the palm of his hand.

"To give them what they want, Howard, and to let them worship you for it, for licking their feet—or . . . or what? What's the use? . . . Only it doesn't matter, nothing matters, not even that it doesn't matter to me any more. . . ."

Then he looked at Roark. He added:

"If only I could hold on until I've started you on your own, Howard. . . ."

"Don't speak of that."

"I want to speak of that. . . . It's funny, Howard, next spring it will be three years that you've been here. Seems so much longer, doesn't it? Well, have I taught you anything? I'll tell you: I've taught you a great deal and nothing. No one can teach you anything, not at the core, at the source of it. What you're doing—it's yours, not mine, I can only teach you to do it better. I can give you the means, but the aim—the aim's your own. You won't be a little disciple putting up anemic little things in early Jacobean or late Cameron. What you'll be . . . if only I could live to see it!"

"You'll live to see it. And you know it now."

Cameron stood looking at the bare walls of his office, at the white piles of bills on his desk, at the sooty rain trickling slowly down the windowpanes.

"I have no answer to give them, Howard. I'm leaving you to face them. You'll answer them. All of them, the Wynand papers and what makes the Wynand papers possible and what lies behind that. It's a strange mission to give you. I don't know what our answer is to be. I know only that there is an answer and that you're holding it, that you're the answer, Howard, and some day you'll find the words for it."

VI

SERMONS IN STONE BY ELLSWORTH M. TOOHEY WAS PUBLISHED IN January of the year 1925.

It had a fastidious jacket of midnight blue with plain silver letters and a silver pyramid in one corner. It was subtitled "Architecture for Everybody" and its success was sensational. It presented the entire history of architecture, from mud hut to skyscraper, in the terms of the man in the street, but it made these terms appear scientific. Its author stated in his preface that it was an attempt "to bring architecture where it belongs—to the people." He stated further that he wished to see the average man "think and speak of architecture as he speaks of baseball." He did not bore his readers with the technicalities of the Five Orders, the post and lintel, the flying buttress or reinforced concrete. He filled his pages with homey accounts of the daily life of the Egyptian housekeeper, the Roman shoe-cobbler, the mistress of Louis XIV, what they ate, how they washed, where they shopped and what effect their buildings had upon their existence. But he gave his readers the impression that they were learning all they had to know about the Five Orders and the reinforced concrete. He gave his readers the impression that there were no problems, no achievements, no reaches of thought beyond the common daily routine of people nameless in the past as they were in the present; that science had no goal and no expression beyond its influence on this routine; that merely by living through their own obscure days his readers were representing and achieving all the highest objectives of any civilization. His scientific precision was impeccable and his erudition astounding; no one could refute him on the cooking utensils of Babylon or the doormats of Byzantium. He wrote with the flash and the color of a first-hand observer. He did not plod laboriously through the centuries; he danced, said the critics, down the road of the ages, as a jester, a friend and a prophet.

He said that architecture was truly the greatest of the arts, because it was anonymous, as all greatness. He said that the world had many famous buildings, but few renowned builders, which was as it should be, since no one man had ever created anything of importance in architecture, or elsewhere, for that matter. The few whose names had lived were really impostors, expropriating the glory of the people as others expropriated its wealth. "When we gaze at the magnificence of an ancient monument and ascribe its achievement to one man, we are guilty of spiritual embezzlement. We forget the army of craftsmen, unknown and

69

unsung, who preceded him in the darkness of the ages, who toiled humbly—all heroism is humble—each contributing his small share to the common treasure of his time. A great building is not the private invention of some genius or other. It is merely a condensation of the spirit of a people."

He explained that the decadence of architecture had come when private property replaced the communal spirit of the Middle Ages, and that the selfishness of individual owners—who built for no purpose save to satisfy their own bad taste, "all claim to an individual taste is bad taste"—had ruined the planned effect of cities. He demonstrated that there was no such thing as free will, since men's creative impulses were determined, as all else, by the economic structure of the epoch in which they lived. He expressed admiration for all the great historical styles, but admonished against their wanton mixture. He dismissed modern architecture, stating that: "So far, it has represented nothing but the whim of isolated individuals, has borne no relation to any great, spontaneous mass movement, and as such is of no consequence." He predicted a better world to come, where all men would be brothers and their buildings would become harmonious and all alike, in the great tradition of Greece, "the Mother of Democracy." When he wrote this, he managed to convey—with no tangible break in the detached calm of his style—that the words now seen in ordered print had been blurred in manuscript by a hand unsteady with emotion. He called upon architects to abandon their selfish quest for individual glory and dedicate themselves to the embodiment of the mood of their people. "Architects are servants, not leaders. They are not to assert their little egos, but to express the soul of their country and the rhythm of their time. They are not to follow the delusions of their personal fancy, but to seek the common denominator, which will bring their work close to the heart of the masses. Architects—ah, my friends, theirs is not to reason why. Theirs is not to command, but to be commanded."

The advertisements for *Sermons in Stone* carried quotations from critics: "Magnificent!" "A stupendous achievement!" "Unequaled in all art history!" "Your chance to get acquainted with a charming man and a profound thinker." "Mandatory reading for anyone aspiring to the title of intellectual."

There seemed to be a great many aspiring to that title. Readers acquired erudition without study, authority without cost, judgment without effort. It was pleasant to look at buildings and criticize them with a professional manner and with the memory of page 439; to hold artistic discussions and exchange the same sentences from the same paragraphs. In distinguished drawing rooms one could soon hear it said: "Architecture? Oh, yes, Ellsworth Toohey."

According to his principles, Ellsworth M. Toohey listed no architect by name in the text of his book—"the myth-building, hero-worshiping method of historical research has always been obnoxious to me." The names appeared only in footnotes. Several of these referred to Guy Francon, "who has a tendency to the overornate, but must be commended for his loyalty to the strict tradition of Classicism." One note referred to Henry Cameron, "prominent once as one of the fathers of the so-called modern school of architecture and relegated since to a well-deserved oblivion. *Vox populi vox dei.*"

In February of 1925 Henry Cameron retired from practice.

For a year, he had known that the day would come. He had not spoken of it to Roark, but they both knew and went on, expecting nothing save to go on as long as it was still possible. A few commissions had dribbled into their office in the past year, country cottages, garages, remodeling of old buildings. They took anything. But the drops stopped. The pipes were dry. The water had been turned off by a society to whom Cameron had never paid his bill.

Simpson and the old man in the reception room had been dismissed long ago. Only Roark remained, to sit still through the winter evenings and look at Cameron's body slumped over his desk, arms flung out, head on arms, a bottle glistening under the lamp.

Then, one day in February, when Cameron had touched no alcohol for weeks, he reached for a book on a shelf and collapsed at Roark's feet, suddenly, simply, finally. Roark took him home and the doctor stated that an attempt to leave his bed would be all the death sentence Cameron needed. Cameron knew it. He lay still on his pillow, his hands dropped obediently one at each side of his body, his eyes unblinking and empty. Then he said:

"You'll close the office for me, Howard, will you?"

"Yes," said Roark.

Cameron closed his eyes, and would say nothing else, and Roark sat all night by his bed, not knowing whether the old man slept or not.

A sister of Cameron's appeared from somewhere in New Jersey. She was a meek little old lady with white hair, trembling hands and a face one could never remember, quiet, resigned and gently hopeless. She had a meager little income and she assumed the responsibility of taking her brother to her home in New Jersey; she had never married and had no one else in the world; she was neither glad nor sorry of the burden; she had lost all capacity for emotion many years ago.

On the day of his departure Cameron handed to Roark a letter he had written in the night, written painfully, an old drawing board on his knees, a pillow propping his back. The letter was addressed to a prominent architect; it was Roark's introduction to a job. Roark read it and,

THE FOUNTAINHEAD · 72

looking at Cameron, not at his own hands, tore the letter across, folded the pieces and tore it again.

"No," said Roark. "You're not going to ask them for anything. Don't worry about me."

Cameron nodded and kept silent for a long time.

Then he said:

"You'll close up the office, Howard. You'll let them keep the furniture for their rent. But you'll take the drawing that's on the wall in my room there and you'll ship it to me. Only that. You'll burn everything else. All the papers, the files, the drawings, the contracts, everything."

"Yes," said Roark.

Miss Cameron came with the orderlies and the stretcher, and they rode in an ambulance to the ferry. At the entrance to the ferry, Cameron said to Roark:

"You're going back now." He added: "You'll come to see me, Howard. . . . Not too often . . ."

Roark turned and walked away, while they were carrying Cameron to the pier. It was a gray morning and there was the cold, rotting smell of the sea in the air. A gull dipped low over the street, gray like a floating piece of newspaper, against a corner of damp, streaked stone.

That evening, Roark went to Cameron's closed office. He did not turn on the lights. He made a fire in the Franklin heater in Cameron's room, and emptied drawer after drawer into the fire, not looking down at them. The papers rustled dryly in the silence, a thin odor of mold rose through the dark room, and the fire hissed, crackling, leaping in bright streaks. At times a white flake with charred edges would flutter out of the flames. He pushed it back with the end of a steel ruler.

There were drawings of Cameron's famous buildings and of buildings unbuilt; there were blueprints with the thin white lines that were girders still standing somewhere; there were contracts with famous signatures; and at times, from out of the red glow, there flashed a sum of seven figures written on yellowed paper, flashed and went down, in a thin burst of sparks.

From among the letters in an old folder, a newspaper clipping fluttered to the floor. Roark picked it up. It was dry, brittle and yellow, and it broke at the folds, in his fingers. It was an interview given by Henry Cameron, dated May 7, 1892. It said: "Architecture is not a business, not a career, but a crusade and a consecration to a joy that justifies the existence of the earth." He dropped the clipping into the fire and reached for another folder.

He gathered every stub of pencil from Cameron's desk and threw them in also.

He stood over the heater. He did not move, he did not look down; he felt the movement of the glow, a faint shudder at the edge of his vision. He looked at the drawing of the skyscraper that had never been built, hanging on the wall before him.

It was Peter Keating's third year with the firm of Francon & Heyer. He carried his head high, his body erect with studied uprightness; he looked like the picture of a successful young man in advertisements for high-priced razors or medium-priced cars.

He dressed well and watched people noticing it. He had an apartment off Park Avenue, modest but fashionable, and he bought three valuable etchings as well as a first edition of a classic he had never read nor opened since. Occasionally, he escorted clients to the Metropolitan Opera. He appeared, once, at a fancy-dress Arts Ball and created a sensation by his costume of a medieval stonecutter, scarlet velvet and tights; he was mentioned in a society-page account of the event—the first mention of his name in print—and he saved the clipping.

He had forgotten his first building, and the fear and doubt of its birth. He had learned that it was so simple. His clients would accept anything, so long as he gave them an imposing façade, a majestic entrance and a regal drawing room, with which to astound their guests. It worked out to everyone's satisfaction: Keating did not care so long as his clients were impressed, the clients did not care so long as their guests were impressed, and the guests did not care anyway.

Mrs. Keating rented her house in Stanton and came to live with him in New York. He did not want her; he could not refuse—because she was his mother and he was not expected to refuse. He met her with some eagerness; he could at least impress her by his rise in the world. She was not impressed; she inspected his rooms, his clothes, his bank books and said only: "It'll do, Petey—for the time being."

She made one visit to his office and departed within a half-hour. That evening he had to sit still, squeezing and cracking his knuckles, for an hour and a half, while she gave him advice. "That fellow Whithers had a much more expensive suit than yours, Petey. That won't do. You've got to watch your prestige before those boys. The little one who brought in those blueprints—I didn't like the way he spoke to you. . . . Oh, nothing, nothing, only I'd keep my eye on him. . . . The one with the long nose is no friend of yours. . . . Never mind, I just know. . . . Watch out for the one they called Bennett. I'd get rid of him if I were you. He's ambitious. I know the signs. . . ."

Then she asked:

"Guy Francon . . . has he any children?"

"One daughter."

"Oh . . ." said Mrs. Keating. "What is she like?"

"I've never met her."

"Really, Peter," she said, "it's downright rude to Mr. Francon if you've made no effort to meet his family."

"She's been away at college, Mother. I'll meet her some day. It's getting late, Mother, and I've got a lot of work to do tomorrow. . . ."

But he thought of it that night and the following day. He had thought of it before and often. He knew that Francon's daugher had graduated from college long ago and was now working on the *Banner*, where she wrote a small column on home decoration. He had been able to learn nothing else about her. No one in the office seemed to know her. Francon never spoke of her.

On that following day, at luncheon, Keating decided to face the subject.

"I hear such nice things about your daughter," he said to Francon.

"Where did you hear nice things about her?" Francon asked ominously.

"Oh, well, you know how it is, one hears things. And she writes brilliantly."

"Yes, she writes brilliantly." Francon's mouth snapped shut.

"Really, Guy, I'd love to meet her."

Francon looked at him and sighed wearily.

"You know she's not living with me," said Francon. "She has an apartment of her own—I'm not sure that I even remember the address. . . . Oh, I suppose you'll meet her some day. You won't like her, Peter."

"Now, why do you say that?"

"It's one of those things, Peter. As a father I'm afraid I'm a total failure. . . . Say, Peter, what did Mrs. Mannering say about that new stairway arrangement?"

Keating felt angry, disappointed—and relieved. He looked at Francon's squat figure and wondered what appearance his daughter must have inherited to earn her father's so obvious disfavor. Rich and ugly as sin—like most of them, he decided. He thought that this need not stop him—some day. He was glad only that the day was postponed. He thought, with new eagerness, that he would go to see Catherine tonight.

Mrs. Keating had met Catherine in Stanton. She had hoped that Peter would forget. Now she knew that he had not forgotten, even though he seldom spoke of Catherine and never brought her to his home. Mrs. Keating did not mention Catherine by name. But she chatted about penniless girls who hooked brilliant young men, about promising boys whose careers had been wrecked by marriage to the wrong woman; and she read to him every newspaper account of a celebrity divorcing his plebeian wife who could not live up to his eminent position.

Keating thought, as he walked toward Catherine's house that night, of the few times he had seen her; they had been such unimportant occasions, but they were the only days he remembered of his whole life in New York.

He found, in the middle of her uncle's living room, when she let him in, a mess of letters spread all over the carpet, a portable typewriter, newspapers, scissors, boxes and a pot of glue.

"Oh dear!" said Catherine, flopping limply down on her knees in the midst of the litter. "Oh dear!"

She looked up at him, smiling disarmingly, her hands raised and spread over the crinkling white piles. She was almost twenty now and looked no older than she had looked at seventeen.

"Sit down, Peter. I thought I'd be through before you came, but I guess I'm not. It's Uncle's fan mail and his press clippings. I've got to sort it out, and answer it and file it and write notes of thanks and . . . Oh, you should see some of the things people write to him! It's wonderful. Don't stand there. Sit down, will you? I'll be through in a minute."

"You're through right now," he said, picking her up in his arms, carrying her to a chair.

He held her and kissed her and she laughed happily, her head buried on his shoulder. He said:

"Katie, you're an impossible little fool and your hair smells so nice!"

She said: "Don't move, Peter. I'm comfortable."

"Katie, I want to tell you, I had a wonderful time today. They opened the Bordman Building officially this afternoon. You know, down on Broadway, twenty-two floors and a Gothic spire. Francon had indigestion, so I went there as his representative. I designed that building anyway and . . . Oh, well, you know nothing about it."

"But I do, Peter. I've seen all your buildings. I have pictures of them. I cut them out of the papers. And I'm making a scrapbook, just like Uncle's. Oh, Peter, it's so wonderful!"

"What?"

"Uncle's scrapbooks, and his letters . . . all this . . ." She stretched her hands out over the papers on the floor, as if she wanted to embrace them. "Think of it, all these letters coming from all over the country, perfect strangers and yet he means so much to them. And here I am, helping him, me, just nobody, and look what a responsibility I have! It's so touching and so big, what do they matter—all the little things that can happen to us?—when this concerns a whole nation!"

"Yeah? Did he tell you that?"

"He told me nothing at all. But you can't live with him for years without getting some of that . . . that wonderful selflessness of his."

He wanted to be angry, but he saw her twinkling smile, her new kind of fire, and he had to smile in answer.

"I'll say this, Katie: it's becoming to you, becoming as hell. You know, you could look stunning if you learned something about clothes. One of these days, I'll take you bodily and drag you down to a good dressmaker. I want you to meet Guy Francon some day. You'll like him."

"Oh? I thought you said once that I wouldn't."

"Did I say that? Well, I didn't really know him. He's a grand fellow. I want you meet them all. You'd be . . . hey, where are you going?" She had noticed the watch on his wrist and was edging away from him.

"I . . . It's almost nine o'clock, Peter, and I've got to have this finished before Uncle Ellsworth gets home. He'll be back by eleven, he's making a speech at a labor meeting tonight. I can work while we're talking, do you mind?"

"I certainly do! To hell with your dear uncle's fans! Let him untangle it all himself. You stay just where you are."

She sighed, but put her head on his shoulder obediently. "You mustn't talk like that about Uncle Ellsworth. You don't understand him at all. Have you read his book?"

"Yes! I've read his book and it's grand, it's stupendous, but I've heard nothing but talk of his damn book everywhere I go, so do you mind if we change the subject?"

"You still don't want to meet Uncle Ellsworth?"

"Why? What makes you say that? I'd love to meet him."

"Oh . . ."

"What's the matter?"

"You said once that you didn't want to meet him through me."

"Did I? How do you always remember all the nonsense I happen to say?"

"Peter, I don't want you to meet Uncle Ellsworth."

"Why not?"

"I don't know. It's kind of silly of me. But now I just don't want you to. I don't know why."

"Well, forget it then. I'll meet him when the time comes. Katie, listen, yesterday I was standing at the window in my room, and I thought of you, and I wanted so much to have you with me, I almost called you, only it was too late. I get so terribly lonely for you like that, I . . ."

She listened, her arms about his neck. And then he saw her looking suddenly past him, her mouth opened in consternation; she jumped up, dashed across the room, and crawled on her hands and knees to reach a lavender envelope lying under a desk.

"Now what on earth?" he demanded angrily.

"It's a very important letter," she said, still kneeling, the envelope held tightly in her little fist, "it's a very important letter and there it was, practically in the wastebasket, I might have swept it out without noticing. It's from a poor widow who has five children and her eldest son wants to be an architect and Uncle Ellsworth is going to arrange a scholarship for him."

"Well," said Keating, rising, "I've had just about enough of this. Let's get out of here, Katie. Let's go for a walk. It's beautiful out tonight. You don't seem to belong to yourself in here."

"Oh, fine! Let's go for a walk."

Outside, there was a mist of snow, a dry, fine, weightless snow that hung still in the air, filling the narrow tanks of streets. They walked together, Catherine's arm pressed to his, their feet leaving long brown smears on the white sidewalks.

They sat down on a bench in Washington Square. The snow enclosed the Square, cutting them off from the houses, from the city beyond. Through the shadow of the arch, little dots of light rolled past them, steel-white, green and smeared red.

She sat huddled close to him. He looked at the city. He had always been afraid of it and he was afraid of it now; but he had two fragile protections: the snow and the girl beside him.

"Katie," he whispered, "Katie . . ."

"I love you, Peter. . . ."

"Katie," he said, without hesitation, without emphasis, because the certainty of his words allowed no excitement, "we're engaged, aren't we?"

He saw her chin move faintly as it dropped and rose to form one word.

"Yes," she said calmly, so solemnly that the word sounded indifferent.

She had never allowed herself to question the future, for a question would have been an admission of doubt. But she knew, when she pronounced the "yes," that she had waited for this and that she would shatter it if she were too happy.

"In a year or two," he said holding her hand tightly, "we'll be married. Just as soon as I'm on my feet and set with the firm for good. I have mother to take care of, but in another year it will be all right." He tried to speak as coldly, as practically as he could, not to spoil the wonder of what he felt.

"I'll wait, Peter," she whispered. "We don't have to hurry."

"We won't tell anyone, Katie. . . . It's our secret, just ours until . . ." And suddenly a thought came to him, and he realized, aghast, that he could not prove it had never occurred to him before; yet he knew, in complete honesty, even though it did astonish him, that he had never thought of this before. He pushed her aside. He said angrily: "Katie! You won't think that it's because of that great, damnable uncle of yours?"

She laughed; the sound was light and unconcerned, and he knew that he was vindicated.

"Lord, no, Peter! He won't like it, of course, but what do we care?"

"He won't like it? Why?"

"Oh, I don't think he approves of marriage. Not that he preaches anything immoral, but he's always told me marriage is old-fashioned, an economic device to perpetuate the institution of private property, or something like that or anyway that he doesn't like it."

"Well, that's wonderful! We'll show him."

In all sincerity, he was glad of it. It removed, not from his mind which he knew to be innocent, but from all other minds where it could occur, the suspicion that there had been in his feeling for her any hint of such considerations as applied to . . . to Francon's daughter, for instance. He thought it was strange that this should seem so important; that he should wish so desperately to keep his feeling for her free from ties to all other people.

He let his head fall back, he felt the bite of snowflakes on his lips. Then he turned and kissed her. The touch of her mouth was soft and cold with the snow.

Her hat had slipped to one side, her lips were half open, her eyes round, helpless, her lashes glistening. He held her hand, palm up, and looked at it: she wore a black woolen glove and her fingers were spread out clumsily like a child's; he saw beads of melted snow in the fuzz of the glove; they sparkled radiantly once in the light of a car flashing past.

VII

THE BULLETIN OF THE ARCHITECTS' GUILD OF AMERICA CARRIED, IN its Miscellaneous Department, a short item announcing Henry Cameron's retirement. Six lines summarized his achievements in architecture and misspelled the names of his two best buildings.

Peter Keating walked into Francon's office and interrupted Francon's well-bred bargaining with an antique dealer over a snuffbox that had belonged to Madame Pompadour. Francon was precipitated into paying nine dollars and twenty-five cents more than he had intended to pay. He turned to Keating testily, after the dealer had left, and asked:

"Well, what is it, Peter, what is it?"

Keating threw the bulletin down on Francon's desk, his thumbnail underscoring the paragraph about Cameron.

"I've got to have that man," said Keating.

"What man?"

"Howard Roark."

"Who the hell," asked Francon, "is Howard Roark?"

"I've told you about him. Cameron's designer."

"Oh . . . oh, yes, I believe you did. Well, go and get him."

"Do you give me a free hand on how I hire him?"

"What the hell? What is there about hiring another draftsman? Incidentally, did you have to interrupt me for *that?*"

"He might be difficult. And I want to get him before he decides on anyone else."

"Really? He's going to be difficult about it, is he? Do you intend to beg him to come *here* after Cameron's? Which is not great recommendation for a young man anyway."

"Come on, Guy. Isn't it?"

"Oh well . . . well, speaking structurally, not esthetically, Cameron does give them a thorough grounding and . . . Of course, Cameron was pretty important in his day. As a matter of fact, I was one of his best draftsmen myself once, long ago. There's something to be said for old Cameron when you need that sort of thing. Go ahead. Get your Roark if you think you need him."

"It's not that I really need him. But he's an old friend of mine, and out of a job, and I thought it would be a nice thing to do for him."

"Well, do anything you wish. Only don't bother me about it. . . . Say, Peter, don't you think this is as lovely a snuffbox as you've ever seen?"

That evening, Keating climbed, unannounced, to Roark's room and knocked, nervously, and entered cheerfully. He found Roark sitting on the window sill, smoking.

"Just passing by," said Keating, "with an evening to kill and happened to think that that's where you live, Howard, and thought I'd drop in to say hello, haven't seen you for such a long time."

"I know what you want," said Roark. "All right. How much?"

"What do you mean, Howard?"

"You know what I mean."

"Sixty-five a week," Keating blurted out. This was not the elaborate approach he had prepared, but he had not expected to find that no approach would be necessary. "Sixty-five to start with. If you think it's not enough, I could maybe . . ."

"Sixty-five will do."

"You . . . you'll come with us, Howard?"

"When do you want me to start?"

"Why . . . as soon as you can! Monday?"

"All right."

"Thanks, Howard!"

"On one condition," said Roark. "I'm not going to do any designing. Not any. No details. No Louis XV skyscrapers. Just keep me off esthetics if you want to keep me at all. Put me in the engineering department. Send me on inspections, out in the field. Now, do you still want me?"

"Certainly. Anything you say. You'll like the place, just wait and see. You'll like Francon. He's one of Cameron's men himself."

"He shouldn't boast about it."

"Well . . ."

"No. Don't worry. I won't say it to his face. I won't say anything to anyone. Is that what you wanted to know?"

"Why, no, I wasn't worried, I wasn't even thinking of that."

"Then it's settled. Good night. See you Monday."

"Well, yes . . . but I'm in no special hurry, really I came to see you and . . ."

"What's the matter, Peter? Something bothering you?"

"No . . . I . . ."

"You want to know why I'm doing it?" Roark smiled, without resentment or interest. "Is that it? I'll tell you, if you want to know. I don't give a damn where I work next. There's no architect in town that I'd want to work for. But I have to work somewhere, so it might as well be your Francon—if I can get what I want from you. I'm selling myself, and I'll play the game that way—for the time being."

"Really, Howard, you don't have to look at it like that. There's no limit to how far you can go with us, once you get used to it. You'll see, for a change, what a real office looks like. After Cameron's dump . . ."

"We'll shut up about that, Peter, and we'll do it damn fast."

"I didn't mean to criticize or . . . I didn't mean anything." He did not know what to say nor what he should feel. It was a victory, but it seemed hollow. Still, it was a victory and he felt that he wanted to feel affection for Roark.

"Howard, let's go out and have a drink, just sort of to celebrate the occasion."

"Sorry, Peter. That's not part of the job."

Keating had come here prepared to exercise caution and tact to the limit of his ability; he had achieved a purpose he had not expected to achieve; he knew he should take no chances, say nothing else and leave. But something inexplicable, beyond all practical considerations, was pushing him on. He said unheedingly:

"Can't you be human for once in your life?"

"What?"

"Human! Simple. Natural."

"But I am."

"Can't you ever relax?"

Roark smiled, because he was sitting on the window sill, leaning sloppily against the wall, his long legs hanging loosely, the cigarette held without pressure between limp fingers.

"That's not what I mean!" said Keating. "Why can't you go out for a drink with me?"

"What for?"

"Do you always have to have a purpose? Do you always have to be so damn serious? Can't you ever do things without reason, just like every-body else? You're so serious, so old. Everything's important with you, everything's great, significant in some way, every minute, even when you keep still. Can't you ever be comfortable—and unimportant?"

"No."

"Don't you get tired of the heroic?"

"What's heroic about me?"

"Nothing. Everything. I don't know. It's not what you do. It's what you make people feel around you."

"What?"

"The un-normal. The strain. When I'm with you—it's always like a choice. Between you—and the rest of the world. I don't want that kind of a choice. I don't want to be an outsider. I want to belong. There's so much in the world that's simple and pleasant. It's not all fighting and renunciation. It is—with you."

"What have I ever renounced?"

"Oh, you'll never renounce anything! You'd walk over corpses for what you want. But it's what you've renounced by never wanting it."

"That's because you can't want both."

"Both what?"

"Look, Peter. I've never told you any of those things about me. What makes you see them? I've never asked you to make a choice between me and anything else. What makes you feel that there is a choice involved? What makes you uncomfortable when you feel that—since you're so sure I'm wrong?"

"I . . . I don't know." He added: "I don't know what you're talking about." And then he asked suddenly:

"Howard, why do you hate me?"

"I don't hate you."

"Well, that's it! Why don't you hate me at least?"

"Why should I?"

"Just to give me something. I know you can't like me. You can't like anybody. So it would be kinder to acknowledge people's existence by hating them."

"I'm not kind, Peter."

And as Keating found nothing to say, Roark added:

"Go home, Peter. You got what you wanted. Let it go at that. See you Monday."

Roark stood at a table in the drafting room of Francon & Heyer, a pencil in his hand, a strand of orange hair hanging down over his face, the prescribed pearl-gray smock like a prison uniform on his body.

He had learned to accept his new job. The lines he drew were to be the clean lines of steel beams, and he tried not to think of what these beams would carry. It was difficult, at times. Between him and the plan of the building on which he was working stood the plan of that building as it should have been. He saw what he could make of it, how to change the lines he drew, where to lead them in order to achieve a thing of splendor. He had to choke the knowledge. He had to kill the vision. He had to obey and draw the lines as instructed. It hurt him so much that he shrugged at himself in cold anger. He thought: difficult?— well, learn it.

But the pain remained—and a helpless wonder. The thing he saw was so much more real than the reality of paper, office and commission. He could not understand what made others blind to it, and what made their indifference possible. He looked at the paper before him. He wondered why ineptitude should exist and have its say. He had never known that.

And the reality which permitted it could never become quite real to him.

But he knew that this would not last—he had to wait—it was his only assignment, to wait—what he felt didn't matter—it had to be done—he had to wait.

"Mr. Roark, are you ready with the steel cage for the Gothic lantern for the American Radio Corporation Building?"

He had no friends in the drafting room. He was there like a piece of furniture, as useful, as impersonal and as silent. Only the chief of the engineering department, to which Roark was assigned, had said to Keating after the first two weeks: "You've got more sense than I gave you credit for, Keating. Thanks." "For what?" asked Keating. "For nothing that was intentional, I'm sure," said the chief.

Once in a while, Keating stopped by Roark's table to say softly: "Will you drop in at my office when you're through tonight, Howard? Nothing important."

When Roark came, Keating began by saying: "Well, how do you like it here, Howard? If there's anything you want, just say so and I'll . . ." Roark interrupted to ask: "Where is it, this time?" Keating produced sketches from a drawer and said: "I know it's perfectly right, just as it is, but what do you think of it, generally speaking?" Roark looked at the sketches, and even though he wanted to throw them at Keating's face and resign, one thought stopped him: the thought that it was a building and that he had to save it, as others could not pass a drowning man without leaping in to the rescue.

Then he worked for hours, sometimes all night, while Keating sat and watched. He forgot Keating's presence. He saw only a building and his chance to shape it. He knew that the shape would be changed, torn, distorted. Still, some order and reason would remain in its plan. It would be a better building than it would have been if he refused.

Sometimes, looking at the sketch of a structure simpler, cleaner, more honest than the others, Roark would say: "That's not so bad, Peter. You're improving." And Keating would feel an odd little jolt inside, something quiet, private and precious, such as he never felt from the compliments of Guy Francon, of his clients, of all others. Then he would forget it and feel much more substantially pleased when a wealthy lady murmured over a teacup: "You're the coming architect of America, Mr. Keating," though she had never seen his buildings.

He found compensations for his submission to Roark. He would enter the drafting room in the morning, throw a tracing boy's assignment down on Roark's table and say: "Howard, do this up for me, will you?—and make it fast." In the middle of the day, he would send a boy to Roark's table to say loudly: "Mr. Keating wishes to see you in his office at once." He would come out of the office and walk in Roark's direction and say to the room at large: "Where the hell are those Twelfth Street plumbing specifications? Oh, Howard, will you look through the files and dig them up for me?"

At first, he was afraid of Roark's reaction. When he saw no reaction, only a silent obedience, he could restrain himself no longer. He felt a sensual pleasure in giving orders to Roark; and he felt also a fury of resentment at Roark's passive compliance. He continued, knowing that he could continue only so long as Roark exhibited no anger, yet wishing desperately to break him down to an explosion. No explosion came.

Roark liked the days when he was sent out to inspect buildings in construction. He walked through the steel hulks of buildings more naturally than on pavements. The workers observed with curiosity that he walked on narrow planks, on naked beams hanging over empty space, as easily as the best of them.

It was a day in March, and the sky was a faint green with the first hint of spring. In Central Park, five hundred feet below, the earth caught the tone of the sky in a shade of brown that promised to become green, and the lakes lay like splinters of glass under the cobwebs of bare branches. Roark walked through the shell of what was to be a gigantic apartment hotel, and stopped before an electrician at work.

The man was toiling assiduously, bending conduits around a beam. It was a task for hours of strain and patience, in a space overfilled against all calculations. Roark stood, his hands in his pockets, watching the man's slow, painful progress.

The man raised his head and turned to him abruptly. He had a big head and a face so ugly that it became fascinating; it was neither old nor flabby, but it was creased in deep gashes and the powerful jowls drooped like a bulldog's; the eyes were startling—wide, round and china-blue.

"Well?" the man asked angrily, "What's the matter, Bricktop?"

"You're wasting your time," said Roark.

"Yeah?"

"Yeah."

"You don't say!"

"It will take you hours to get your pipes around that beam."

"Know a better way to do it?"

"Sure."

"Run along, punk. We don't like college smarties around here."

"Cut a hole in that beam and put your pipes through."

"*What?*"

"Cut a hole through the beam."

"The hell I will!"

"The hell you won't."

"It ain't done that way."

"I've done it."

"*You?*"

"It's done everywhere."

"It ain't gonna be done here. Not by me."

"Then I'll do it for you."

The man roared. "That's rich! When did office boys learn to do a man's work?"

"Give me your torch."

"Look out, boy! It'll burn your pretty pink toes!"

Roark took the man's gloves and goggles, took the acetylene torch, knelt, and sent a thin jet of blue fire at the center of the beam. The man stood watching him. Roark's arm was steady, holding the tense, hissing streak of flame in leash, shuddering faintly with its violence, but holding it aimed straight. There was no strain, no effort in the easy posture of his body, only in his arm. And it seemed as if the blue tension eating slowly through metal came not from the flame but from the hand holding it.

He finished, put the torch down, and rose.

"Jesus!" said the electrician. "Do you know how to handle a torch!"

"Looks like it, doesn't it?" He removed the gloves, the goggles, and handed them back. "Do it that way from now on. Tell the foreman I said so."

The electrician was staring reverently at the neat hole cut through the beam. He muttered: "Where did you learn to handle it like that, Red?"

Roark's slow, amused smile acknowledged this concession of victory. "Oh, I've been an electrician, and a plumber, and a rivet catcher, and many other things."

"And went to school besides?"

"Well, in a way."

"Gonna be an architect?"

"Yes."

"Well, you'll be the first one that knows something besides pretty pictures and tea parties. You should see the teacher's pets they send us down from the office."

"If you're apologizing, don't. I don't like them either. Go back to the pipes. So long."

"So long, Red."

The next time Roark appeared on that job, the blue-eyed electrician waved to him from afar, and called him over, and asked advice about his work which he did not need; he stated that his name was Mike and that he had missed Roark for several days. On the next visit the day shift was leaving, and Mike waited outside for Roark to finish the inspection. "How about a glass of beer, Red?" he invited, when Roark came out. "Sure," said Roark, "thanks."

They sat together at a table in the corner of a basement speak-easy, and they drank beer, and Mike related his favorite tale of how he had fallen five stories when a scaffolding gave way under him, how he had broken three ribs but lived to tell it, and Roark spoke of his days in the building trades. Mike did have a real name, which was Sean Xavier Donnigan, but everyone had forgotten it long ago; he owned a set of tools and an ancient Ford, and existed for the sole purpose of traveling around the country from one big construction job to another. People meant very little to Mike, but their performance a great deal. He worshiped expertness of any kind. He loved his work passionately and had no tolerance for anything save for other single-track devotions. He was a master in his own field and he felt no sympathy except for mastery. His view of the world was simple: there were the able and there were the incompetent; he was not concerned with the latter. He loved buildings. He despised, however, all architects.

"There was one, Red," he said earnestly, over his fifth beer, "one only and you'd be too young to know about him, but that was the only man that knew building. I worked for him when I was your age."

"Who was that?"

"Henry Cameron was his name. He's dead, I guess, these many years."

Roark looked at him for a long time, then said: "He's not dead, Mike," and added: "I've worked for him."

"*You did?*"

"For almost three years."

They looked at each other silently, and that was the final seal on their friendship.

Weeks later, Mike stopped Roark, one day, at the building, his ugly face puzzled, and asked:

"Say, Red, I heard the super tell a guy from the contractor's that you're stuck-up and stubborn and the lousiest bastard he's ever been up against. What did you do to him?"

"Nothing."

"What the hell did he mean?"

"I don't know," said Roark. "Do you?"

Mike looked at him, shrugged and grinned.

"No," said Mike.

VIII

EARLY IN MAY, PETER KEATING DEPARTED FOR WASHINGTON, TO supervise the construction of a museum donated to the city by a great philanthropist easing his conscience. The museum building, Keating pointed out proudly, was to be decidedly different: it was not a reproduction of the Parthenon, but of the Maison Carrée at Nîmes.

Keating had been away for some time when an office boy approached Roark's table and informed him that Mr. Francon wished to see him in his office. When Roark entered the sanctuary, Francon smiled from behind the desk and said cheerfully: "Sit down, my friend. Sit down . . ." but something in Roark's eyes, which he had never seen at close range before, made Francon's voice shrink and stop, and he added dryly: "Sit down."

Roark obeyed. Francon studied him for a second, but could reach no conclusion beyond deciding that the man had a most unpleasant face, yet looked quite correctly attentive.

"You're the one who's worked for Cameron, aren't you?" Francon asked.

"Yes," said Roark.

"Mr. Keating has been telling me very nice things about you," Francon tried pleasantly and stopped. It was wasted courtesy; Roark just sat looking at him, waiting.

"Listen . . . what's your name?"

"Roark."

"Listen, Roark. We have a client who is a little . . . odd, but he's an important man, a *very* important man, and we have to satisfy him. He's given us a commission for an eight-million-dollar office building, but the trouble is that he has very definite ideas on what he wants it to look like. He wants it—" Francon shrugged apologetically, disclaiming all blame for the preposterous suggestion—"he wants it to look like *this*." He handed Roark a photograph. It was a photograph of the Dana Building.

Roark sat quite still, the photograph hanging between his fingers.

"Do you know that building?" asked Francon.

"Yes."

"Well, that's what he wants. And Mr. Keating's away. I've had Bennett and Cooper and Williams make sketches, but he's turned them down. So I thought I'd give you a chance."

Francon looked at him, impressed by the magnanimity of his own offer. There was no reaction. There was only a man who still looked as if he'd been struck on the head.

"Of course," said Francon, "it's quite a jump for you, quite an assignment, but I thought I'd let you try. Don't be afraid. Mr. Keating and I will go over it afterward. Just draw up the plans and a good sketch of it. You must have an idea of what the man wants. You know Cameron's tricks. But of course, we can't let a crude thing like this come out of our office. We must please him, but we must also preserve our reputation and not frighten all our other clients away. The point is to make it simple and in the general mood of this, but also artistic. You know, the more severe kind of Greek. You don't have to use the Ionic order, use the Doric. Plain pediments and simple moldings, or something like that. Get the idea? Now take this along and show me what you can do. Bennett will give you all the particulars and . . . What's the mat——"

Francon's voice cut itself off.

"Mr. Francon, please let me design it the way the Dana Bulding was designed."

"Huh?"

"Let me do it. Not copy the Dana Building, but design it as Henry Cameron would have wanted it done, as I will."

"You mean modernistic?"

"I . . . well, call it that."

"Are you crazy?"

"Mr. Francon, please listen to me." Roark's words were like the steps of a man walking a tightwire, slow, strained, groping for the only right spot, quivering over an abyss, but precise. "I don't blame you for the things you're doing. I'm working for you, I'm taking your money, I have no right to express objections. But this time . . . this time the client is asking for it. You're risking nothing. He wants it. Think of it, there's a man, one man who sees and understands and wants it and has the power to build it. Are you going to fight a client for the first time in your life—and fight for what? To cheat him and to give him the same old trash, when you have so many others asking for it, and one, only one, who comes with a request like this?"

"Aren't you forgetting yourself?" asked Francon, coldly.

"What difference would it make to you? Just let me do it my way and show it to him. Only show it to him. He's already turned down three sketches, what if he turns down a fourth? But if he doesn't . . . if he doesn't . . ."

Roark had never known how to entreat and he was not doing it well; his voice was hard, toneless, revealing the effort, so that the plea became an insult to the man who was making him plead. Keating would have given a great deal to see Roark in that moment. But Francon could not appreciate the triumph he was the first ever to achieve; he recognized only the insult.

"Am I correct in gathering," Francon asked, "that you are criticizing me and teaching me something about architecture?"

"I'm begging you," said Roark, closing his eyes.

"If you weren't a protégé of Mr. Keating's, I wouldn't bother to discuss the matter with you any further. But since you are quite obviously naïve and inexperienced, I shall point out to you that I am not in the habit of asking for the esthetic opinions of my draftsmen. You will kindly take this photograph—and I do not wish any building as Cameron *might have* designed it, I wish the scheme of *this* adapted to our site—and you will follow my instructions as to the Classic treatment of the façade."

"I can't do it," said Roark, very quietly.

"What? Are you speaking to me? Are you actually saying: 'Sorry, I can't do it'?"

"I haven't said 'sorry,' Mr. Francon."

"What did you say?"

"That I can't do it."

"Why?"

"You don't want to know why. Don't ask me to do any designing. I'll do any other kind of job you wish. But not that. And not to Cameron's work."

"What do you mean, no designing? You expect to be an architect some day—or do you?"

"Not like this."

"Oh . . . I see . . . So you can't do it? You mean you won't?"

"If you prefer."

"Listen, you impertinent fool, this is incredible!"

Roark got up.

"May I go, Mr. Francon?"

"In all my life," roared Francon, "in all my experience, I've never seen anything like it! Are you here to tell me what you'll do and what you won't do? Are you here to give me lessons and criticize my taste and pass judgment?"

"I'm not criticizing anything," said Roark quietly. "I'm not passing judgment. There are some things that I can't do. Let it go at that. May I leave now?"

"You may leave this room and this firm now and from now on! You may go straight to the devil! Go and find yourself another employer! Try and find him! Go get your check and get out!"

"Yes, Mr. Francon."

That evening Roark walked to the basement speak-easy where he could always find Mike after the day's work. Mike was now employed on the construction of a factory by the same contractor who was awarded most of Francon's biggest jobs. Mike had expected to see Roark on an inspection visit to the factory that afternoon, and greeted him angrily:

"What's the matter, Red? Lying down on the job?"

When he heard the news, Mike sat still and looked like a bulldog baring its teeth. Then he swore savagely.

"The bastards," he gulped between stronger names, "the bastards . . ."

"Keep still, Mike."

"Well . . . what now, Red?"

"Someone else of the same kind, until the same thing happens again."

When Keating returned from Washington he went straight up to Francon's office. He had not stopped in the drafting room and had heard no news. Francon greeted him expansively:

"Boy, it's great to see you back! What'll you have? A whisky-and-soda or a little brandy?"

"No, thanks. Just give me a cigarette."

"Here. . . . Boy, you look fine! Better than ever. How do you do it, you lucky bastard? I have so many things to tell you! How did it go down in Washington? Everything all right?" And before Keating could answer, Francon rushed on: "Something dreadful's happened to me. Most disappointing. Do you remember Lili Landau? I thought I was all set with her, but last time I saw her, did I get the cold shoulder! Do you know who's got her? You'll be surprised. Gail Wynand, no less! The girl's flying high. You should see her pictures and her legs all over his newspapers. Will it help her show or won't it! What can I offer against that? And do you know what he's done? Remember how she always said that nobody could give her what she wanted most—her childhood home, the dear little Austrian village where she was born? Well, Wynand bought it, long ago, the whole damn village, and had it shipped here—every bit of it!—and had it assembled again down on the Hudson, and there it stands now, cobbles, church, apple trees, pigsties and all! Then he springs it on Lili, two weeks ago. Wouldn't you just know it? If the King of Babylon could get hanging gardens for his homesick lady, why not Gail Wynand? Lili's all smiles and gratitude—but the poor girl was really miserable. She'd have much preferred a mink coat. She never wanted the damn village. And Wynand knew it, too. But there it stands, on the Hudson. Last week, he gave a party for her, right there, in that village—a costume party, with Mr. Wynand dressed as Cesare Borgia—wouldn't he, though?—and what a party!—if you can believe what you hear, but you know how it is, you can never prove anything on Wynand. Then what does he do the next day but pose up there himself with little schoolchildren who'd never seen an Austrian village—the philanthropist!—and plasters the photos all over his papers with plenty of sob stuff about educational values, and gets mush notes from women's clubs! I'd like to know what he'll do with the village when he gets rid of Lili! He will, you know, they never last long with him. Do you think I'll have a chance with her then?"

"Sure," said Keating. "Sure, you will. How's everything here in the office?"

"Oh, fine. Same as usual. Lucius had a cold and drank up all of my best Bas Armagnac. It's bad for his heart, and a hundred dollars a case! . . . Besides, Lucius got himself caught in a nasty little mess. It's that phobia of his, his damn porcelain. Seems he went and bought a teapot from a fence. He knew it was stolen goods, too. Took me quite a bit of bother to save us from a scandal. . . . Oh, by the way, I fired that friend of yours, what's his name?—Roark."

"Oh," said Keating, and let a moment pass, then asked: "Why?"

"The insolent bastard! Where did you ever pick him up?"

"What happened?"

"I thought I'd be nice to him, give him a real break. I asked him to make a sketch for the Farrell Building—you know, the one Brent finally managed to design and we got Farrell to accept, you know, the simplified Doric—and your friend just up and refused to do it. It seems he has ideals or something. So I showed him the gate. . . . What's the matter? What are you smiling at?"

"Nothing. I can just see it."

"Now don't you ask me to take him back!"

"No, of course not."

For several days, Keating thought that he should call on Roark. He did not know what he would say, but felt dimly that he should say something. He kept postponing it. He was gaining assurance in his work. He felt that he did not need Roark, after all. The days went by, and he did not call on Roark, and he felt relief in being free to forget him.

Beyond the windows of his room Roark saw the roofs, the water tanks, the chimneys, the cars speeding far below. There was a threat in the silence of his room, in the empty days, in his hands hanging idly by his sides. And he felt another threat rising from the city below, as if each window, each strip of pavement, had set itself closed grimly, in wordless resistance. It did not disturb him. He had known and accepted it long ago.

He made a list of the architects whose work he resented least, in the order of their lesser evil, and he set out upon the search for a job, coldly, systematically, without anger or hope. He never knew whether these days hurt him; he knew only that it was a thing which had to be done.

The architects he saw differed from one another. Some looked at him across the desk, kindly and vaguely, and their manner seemed to say that it was touching, his ambition to be an architect, touching and laudable and strange and attractively sad as all the delusions of youth. Some smiled at him with thin, drawn lips and seemed to enjoy his presence in the room, because it made them conscious of their own accomplishment. Some spoke coldly, as if his ambition were a personal insult. Some were brusque, and the sharpness of their voices seemed to say that they needed good draftsmen, they always needed good draftsmen, but this qualification could not possibly apply to him, and would he please refrain from being rude enough to force them to express it more plainly.

It was not malice. It was not a judgment passed upon his merit. They did not think he was worthless. They simply did not care to find out whether he was good. Sometimes, he was asked to show his sketches; he extended them across a desk, feeling a contraction of shame in the muscles of his hand; it was like having the clothes torn off his body, and the shame was not that his body was exposed, but that it was exposed to indifferent eyes.

Once in a while he made a trip to New Jersey, to see Cameron. They sat together on the porch of a house on a hill, Cameron in a wheel chair, his hands on an old blanket spread over his knees. "How is it, Howard? Pretty hard?" "No." "Want me to give you a letter to one of the bastards?" "No."

Then Cameron would not speak of it any more, he did not want to speak of it, he did not want the thought of Roark rejected by their city to become real. When Roark came to him, Cameron spoke of architecture with the simple confidence of a private possession. They sat together, looking at the city in the distance, on the edge of the sky, beyond the river. The sky was growing dark and luminous as blue-green glass; the buildings looked like clouds condensed on the glass, gray-blue clouds frozen for an instant in straight angles and vertical shafts, with the sunset caught in the spires. . . .

As the summer months passed, as his list was exhausted and he returned again to the places that had refused him once, Roark found that a few things were known about him and he heard the same words— spoken bluntly or timidly or angrily or apologetically—"You were kicked out of Stanton. You were kicked out of Francon's office." All the different voices saying it had one note in common: a note of relief in the certainty that the decision had been made for them.

He sat on the window sill, in the evening, smoking, his hand spread on the pane, the city under his fingers, the glass cold against his skin.

In September, he read an article entitled "Make Way For Tomorrow" by Gordon L. Prescott, A.G.A., in the *Architectural Tribune*. The article stated that the tragedy of the profession was the hardships placed in the way of its talented beginners; that great gifts had been lost in the struggle, unnoticed; that architecture was perishing from a lack of new blood and new thought, a lack of originality, vision and courage; that the author of the article made it his aim to search for promising beginners, to encourage them, develop them and give them the chance they deserved. Roark had never heard of Gordon L. Prescott, but there was a tone of honest conviction in the article. He allowed himself to start for Prescott's office with the first hint of hope.

The reception room of Gordon L. Prescott's office was done in gray, black and scarlet; it was correct, restrained and daring all at once. A young and very pretty secretary informed Roark that one could not see Mr. Prescott without an appointment, but that she would be very glad to make an appointment for next Wednesday at two-fifteen. On Wednesday at two-fifteen, the secretary smiled at Roark and asked him please to be seated for just a moment. At four forty-five he was admitted into Gordon L. Prescott's office.

Gordon L. Prescott wore a brown checkered tweed jacket and a white turtle-neck sweater of angora wool. He was tall, athletic and thirty-five, but his face combined a crisp air of sophisticated wisdom with the soft skin, the button nose, the small, puffed mouth of a college hero. His face was sun-scorched, his blond hair clipped short, in a military Prussian haircut. He was frankly masculine, frankly unconcerned about elegance and frankly conscious of the effect.

He listened to Roark silently, and his eyes were like a stop watch registering each separate second consumed by each separate word of Roark's. He let the first sentence go by; on the second he interrupted to say curtly: "Let me see your drawings," as if to make it clear that anything Roark might say was quite well known to him already.

He held the drawings in his bronzed hands. Before he looked down at them, he said: "Ah, yes, so many young men come to me for advice, so many." He glanced at the first sketch, but raised his head before he had seen it. "Of course, it's the combination of the practical and the transcendental that is so hard for beginners to grasp." He slipped the sketch to the bottom of the pile. "Architecture is primarily a utilitarian conception, and the problem is to elevate the principle of pragmatism into the realm of esthetic abstraction. All else is nonsense." He glanced at two sketches and slipped them to the bottom. "I have no patience with visionaries who see a holy crusade in architecture for architecture's sake. The great dynamic principle is the common principle of the human equation." He glanced at a sketch and slipped it under. "The public taste and the public heart are the final criteria of the artist. The genius is the one who knows how to express the general. The exception is to tap the unexceptional." He weighed the pile of sketches in his hand, noted that he had gone through half of them and dropped them down on the desk.

"Ah, yes," he said, "your work. Very interesting. But not practical. Not mature. Unfocused and undisciplined. Adolescent. Originality for originality's sake. Not at all in the spirit of the present day. If you want an idea of the sort of thing for which there is a crying need—here—let me show you." He took a sketch out of a drawer of the desk. "Here's a young man who came to me totally unrecommended, a beginner who had never worked before. When you can produce stuff like this, you won't find it necessary to look for a job. I saw this one sketch of his and I took him on at once, started him at twenty-five a week, too. There's no question but that he is a potential genius." He extended the sketch to Roark. The sketch represented a house in the shape of a grain silo incredibly merged with the simplified, emaciated shadow of the Parthenon.

"That," said Gordon L. Prescott, "is originality, the new in the eternal. Try toward something like this. I can't really say that I predict a great deal for your future. We must be frank, I wouldn't want to give you illusions based on my authority. You have a great deal to learn. I couldn't venture a guess on what talent you might possess or develop later. But with hard work, perhaps . . . Architecture is a difficult profession, however, and the competition is stiff, you know, very stiff . . . And now, if you'll excuse me, my secretary has an appointment waiting for me. . . ."

Roark walked home late on an evening in October. It had been another of the many days that stretched into months behind him, and he could not tell what had taken place in the hours of that day, whom he had seen, what form the words of refusal had taken. He concentrated fiercely on the few minutes at hand, when he was in an office, forgetting everything else; he forgot these minutes when he left the office; it had to be done, it had been done, it concerned him no longer. He was free once more on his way home.

A long street stretched before him, its high banks coming close together ahead, so narrow that he felt as if he could spread his arms, seize the spires and push them apart. He walked swiftly, the pavements as a springboard throwing his steps forward.

He saw a lighted triangle of concrete suspended somewhere hundreds of feet above the ground. He could not see what stood below, supporting it; he was free to think of what he'd want to see there, what he would have made to be seen. Then he thought suddenly that now, in this moment, according to the city, according to everyone save that hard certainty within him, he would never build again, never—before he had begun. He shrugged. Those things happening to him, in those offices of strangers, were only a kind of sub-reality, unsubstantial incidents in the path of a substance they could not reach or touch.

He turned into side streets leading to the East River. A lonely traffic light hung far ahead, a spot of red in a bleak darkness. The old houses crouched low to the ground, hunched under the weight of the sky. The street was empty and hollow, echoing to his footsteps. He went on, his collar raised, his hands in his pockets. His shadow rose from under his heels, when he passed a light, and brushed a wall in a long black arc, like the sweep of a windshield wiper.

IX

JOHN ERIK SNYTE LOOKED THROUGH ROARK'S SKETCHES, FLIPPED
three of them aside, gathered the rest into an even pile, glanced
again at the three, tossed them down one after another on top of the
pile, with three sharp thuds, and said:

"Remarkable. Radical, but remarkable. What are you doing tonight?"

"Why?" asked Roark, stupefied.

"Are you free? Mind starting in at once? Take your coat off, go to the
drafting room, borrow tools from somebody and do me up a sketch for a
department store we're remodeling. Just a quick sketch, just a general
idea, but I must have it tomorrow. Mind staying late tonight? The heat's
on and I'll have Joe send you up some dinner. Want black coffee or
Scotch or what? Just tell Joe. Can you stay?"

"Yes," said Roark, incredulously. "I can work all night."

"Fine! Splendid! That's just what I've always needed—a Cameron
man. I've got every other kind. Oh, yes, what did they pay you at
Francon's?"

"Sixty-five."

"Well, I can't splurge like Guy the Epicure. Fifty's tops. Okay? Fine.
Go right in. I'll have Billings explain about the store to you. I want
something modern. Understand? Modern, violent, crazy, to knock their
eye out. Don't restrain yourself. Go the limit. Pull any stunt you can
think of, the goofier the better. Come on!"

John Erik Snyte shot to his feet, flung a door open into a huge drafting
room, flew in, skidded against a table, stopped, and said to a stout man
with a grim moon-face: "Billings—Roark. He's our modernist. Give
him the Benton store. Get him some instruments. Leave him your keys
and show him what to lock up tonight. Start him as of this morning.
Fifty. What time was my appointment with Dolson Brothers? I'm late
already. So long, I won't be back tonight."

He skidded out, slamming the door. Billings evinced no surprise. He
looked at Roark as if Roark had always been there. He spoke impas-
sively, in a weary drawl. Within twenty minutes, he left Roark at a
drafting table with paper, pencils, instruments, a set of plans and photographs of the department store, a set of charts and a long list of instructions.

Roark looked at the clean white sheet before him, his fist closed
tightly about the thin stem of a pencil. He put the pencil down, and
picked it up again, his thumb running softly up and down the smooth

96

shaft; he saw that the pencil was trembling. He put it down quickly, and he felt anger at himself for the weakness of allowing this job to mean so much to him, for the sudden knowledge of what the months of idleness behind him had really meant. His finger tips were pressed to the paper, as if the paper held them, as a surface charged with electricity will hold the flesh of a man who has brushed against it, hold and hurt. He tore his fingers off the paper. Then he went to work. . . .

John Erik Snyte was fifty years old; he wore an expression of quizzical amusement, shrewd and unwholesome, as if he shared with each man he contemplated a lewd secret which he would not mention because it was so obvious to them both. He was a prominent architect; his expression did not change when he spoke of this fact. He considered Guy Francon an impractical idealist; he was not restrained by any Classic dogma; he was much more skillful and liberal; he built anything. He had no distaste for modern architecture and built cheerfully, when a rare client asked for it, bare boxes with flat roofs, which he called progressive; he built Roman mansions which he called fastidious; he built Gothic churches which he called spiritual. He saw no difference among any of them. He never became angry, except when somebody called him eclectic.

He had a system of his own. He employed five designers of various types and he staged a contest among them on each commission he received. He chose the winning design and improved it with bits of the four others. "Six minds," he said, "are better than one."

When Roark saw the final drawing of the Benton Department Store, he understood why Snyte had not been afraid to hire him. He recognized his own planes of space, his windows, his system of circulation; he saw, added to it, Corinthian capitals, Gothic vaulting, Colonial chandeliers and incredible moldings, vaguely Moorish. The drawing was done in water color, with miraculous delicacy, mounted on cardboard, covered with a veil of tissue paper. The men in the drafting room were not allowed to look at it, except from a safe distance; all hands had to be washed, all cigarettes discarded. John Erik Snyte attached a great importance to the proper appearance of a drawing for submission to clients, and kept a young Chinese student of architecture employed solely upon the execution of these masterpieces.

Roark knew what to expect of his job. He would never see his work erected, only pieces of it, which he preferred not to see; but he would be free to design as he wished and he would have the experience of solving actual problems. It was less than he wanted and more than he could expect. He accepted it at that. He met his fellow designers, the four other contestants, and learned that they were unofficially nicknamed in the drafting room as "Classic," "Gothic," "Renaissance" and "Miscellaneous." He winced a little when he was addressed as "Hey, Modernistic."

The strike of the building-trades unions infuriated Guy Francon. The strike had started against the contractors who were erecting the Noyes-Belmont Hotel, and had spread to all the new structures of the city. It had been mentioned in the press that the architects of the Noyes-Belmont were the firm of Francon & Heyer.

Most of the press helped the fight along, urging the contractors not to surrender. The loudest attacks against the strikers came from the powerful papers of the great Wynand chain.

"We have always stood," said the Wynand editorials, "for the rights of the common man against the yellow sharks of privilege, but we cannot give our support to the destruction of law and order." It had never been discovered whether the Wynand papers led the public or the public led the Wynand papers; it was known only that the two kept remarkably in step. It was not known to anyone, however, save to Guy Francon and a very few others, that Gail Wynand owned the corporation which owned the corporation which owned the Noyes-Belmont Hotel.

This added greatly to Francon's discomfort. Gail Wynand's real-estate operations were rumored to be vaster than his journalistic empire. It was the first chance Francon had ever had at a Wynand commission and he grasped it avidly, thinking of the possibilities which it could open. He and Keating had put their best efforts into designing the most ornate of all Rococo palaces for future patrons who could pay twenty-five dollars per day per room and who were fond of plaster flowers, marble cupids and open elevator cages of bronze lace. The strike had shattered the future possibilities; Francon could not be blamed for it, but one could never tell whom Gail Wynand would blame and for what reason. The unpredictable, unaccountable shifts of Wynand's favor were famous, and it was well known that few architects he employed once were ever employed by him again.

Francon's sullen mood led him to the unprecedented breach of snapping over nothing in particular at the one person who had always been immune from it—Peter Keating. Keating shrugged, and turned his back to him in silent insolence. Then Keating wandered aimlessly through the halls, snarling at young draftsmen without provocation. He bumped into Lucius N. Heyer in a doorway and snapped: "Look where you're going!" Heyer stared after him, bewildered, blinking.

There was little to do in the office, nothing to say and everyone to avoid. Keating left early and walked home through a cold December twilight.

At home, he cursed aloud the thick smell of paint from the overheated radiators. He cursed the chill, when his mother opened a window. He could find no reason for his restlessness, unless it was the sudden inactivity that left him alone. He could not bear to be left alone.

He snatched up the telephone receiver and called Catherine Halsey. The sound of her clear voice was like a hand pressed soothingly against his hot forehead. He said: "Oh, nothing important, dear, I just wondered if you'd be home tonight. I thought I'd drop in after dinner." "Of course, Peter. I'll be home." "Swell. About eight-thirty?" "Yes . . . Oh, Peter, have you heard about Uncle Ellsworth?" "Yes, God damn it, I've heard about your Uncle Ellsworth! . . . I'm sorry, Katie . . . Forgive me, darling, I didn't mean to be rude, but I've been hearing about your uncle all day long. I know, it's wonderful and all that, only look, we're not going to talk about him again tonight!" "No, of course not. I'm sorry. I understand. I'll be waiting for you." "So long, Katie."

He had heard the latest story about Ellsworth Toohey, but he did not want to think of it because it brought him back to the annoying subject of the strike. Six months ago, on the wave of his success with *Sermons in Stone,* Ellsworth Toohey had been signed to write "One Small Voice," a daily syndicated column for the Wynand papers. It appeared in the *Banner* and had started as a department of art criticism, but grown into an informal tribune from which Ellsworth M. Toohey pronounced verdicts on art, literature, New York restaurants, international crises and sociology—mainly sociology. It had been a great success. But the building strike had placed Ellsworth M. Toohey in a difficult position. He made no secret of his sympathy with the strikers, but he had said nothing in his column, for no one could say what he pleased on the papers owned by Gail Wynand save Gail Wynand. However, a mass meeting of strike sympathizers had been called for this evening. Many famous men were to speak, Ellsworth Toohey among them. At least, Toohey's name had been announced.

The event caused a great deal of curious speculation and bets were made on whether Toohey would dare to appear. "He will," Keating had heard a draftsman insist vehemently, "he'll sacrifice himself. He's that kind. He's the only honest man in print." "He won't," another had said. "Do you realize what it means to pull a stunt like that on Wynand? Once Wynand gets it in for a man, he'll break the guy sure as hell's fire. Nobody knows when he'll do it or how he'll do it, but he'll do it, and nobody'll prove a thing on him, and you're done for once you get Wynand after you." Keating did not care about the issue one way or another, and the whole matter annoyed him.

He ate his dinner, that evening, in grim silence and when Mrs. Keating began, with an "Oh, by the way . . ." to lead the conversation in a direction he recognized, he snapped: "You're not going to talk about Catherine. Keep still." Mrs. Keating said nothing further and concentrated on forcing more food on his plate.

He took a taxi to Greenwich Village. He hurried up the stairs. He jerked at the bell. He waited. There was no answer. He stood, leaning against the wall, ringing, for a long time. Catherine wouldn't be out when she knew he was coming; she couldn't be. He walked incredulously down the stairs, out to the street, and looked up at the windows of her apartment. The windows were dark.

He stood, looking up at the windows as at a tremendous betrayal. Then came a sick feeling of loneliness, as if he were homeless in a great city; for the moment, he forgot his own address or its existence. Then he thought of the meeting, the great mass meeting where her uncle was publicly to make a martyr of himself tonight. That's where she went, he thought, the damn little fool! He said aloud: "To hell with her!". . . And he was walking rapidly in the direction of the meeting hall.

There was one naked bulb of light over the square frame of the hall's entrance, a small, blue-white lump glowing ominously, too cold and too bright. It leaped out of the dark street, lighting one thin trickle of rain from some ledge above, a glistening needle of glass, so thin and smooth that Keating thought crazily of stories where men had been killed by being pierced with an icicle. A few curious loafers stood indifferently in the rain around the entrance, and a few policemen. The door was open. The dim lobby was crowded with people who could not get into the packed hall; they were listening to a loud-speaker installed there for the occasion. At the door three vague shadows were handing out pamphlets to passers-by. One of the shadows was a consumptive, unshaved young man with a long, bare neck; the other was a trim youth with a fur collar on an expensive coat; the third was Catherine Halsey.

She stood in the rain, slumped, her stomach jutting forward in weariness, her nose shiny, her eyes bright with excitement. Keating stopped, staring at her.

Her hand shot toward him mechanically with a pamphlet, then she raised her eyes and saw him. She smiled without astonishment, and said happily:

"Why, Peter! How sweet of you to come here!"

"Katie . . ." he choked a little. "Katie, what the hell . . ."

"But I had to, Peter." Her voice had no trace of apology. "You don't understand, but I . . ."

"Get out of the rain. Get inside."

"But I can't! I have to . . ."

"Get out of the rain at least, you fool!" He pushed her roughly through the door, into a corner of the lobby.

"Peter darling, you're not angry, are you? You see, it was like this: I didn't think Uncle would let me come here tonight, but at the last minute he said I could if I wanted to, and that I could help with the pamphlets. I knew you'd understand, and I left you a note on the living room table, explaining, and . . ."

"You left me a note? *Inside?*"

"Yes . . . Oh . . . Oh, dear me, I never thought of that, you couldn't get in of course, how silly of me, but I was in such a rush! No, you're not going to be angry, you can't! Don't you see what this means to him? Don't you know what he's sacrificing by coming here? And I knew he would. I told them so, those people who said not a chance, it'll be the end of him—and it might be, but he doesn't care. That's what he's like. I'm frightened and I'm terribly happy, because what he's done—it makes me believe in all human beings. But I'm frightened, because you see, Wynand will . . ."

"Keep still! I know it all. I'm sick of it. I don't want to hear about your uncle or Wynand or the damn strike. Let's get out of here."

"Oh, no, Peter! We can't! I want to hear him and . . ."

"Shut up over there!" someone hissed at them from the crowd.

"We're missing it all," she whispered. "That's Austen Heller speaking. Don't you want to hear Austen Heller?"

Keating looked up at the loud-speaker with a certain respect, which he felt for all famous names. He had not read much of Austen Heller, but he knew that Heller was the star columnist of the *Chronicle*, a brilliant, independent newspaper, arch-enemy of the Wynand publications; that Heller came from an old, distinguished family and had graduated from Oxford; that he had started as a literary critic and ended by becoming a quiet fiend devoted to the destruction of all forms of compulsion, private or public, in heaven or on earth; that he had been cursed by preachers, bankers, clubwomen and labor organizers; that he had better manners than the social elite whom he usually mocked, and a tougher constitution than the laborers whom he usually defended; that he could discuss the latest play on Broadway, medieval poetry or international finance; that he never donated to charity, but spent more of his own money than he could afford, on defending political prisoners anywhere.

The voice coming from the loud-speaker was dry, precise, with the faint trace of a British accent.

". . . and we must consider," Austen Heller was saying unemotionally, "that since—unfortunately—we are forced to live together, the most important thing for us to remember is that the only way in which we can have any law at all is to have as little of it as possible. I see no ethical standard by which to measure the whole unethical conception of a State, except in the amount of time, of thought, of money, of effort and of obedience, which a society extorts from its every member. Its value and its civilization are in inverse ratio to that extortion. There is no conceivable law by which a man can be forced to work on any terms except those he chooses to set. There is no conceivable law to prevent him from setting them—just as there is none to force his employer to accept them. The freedom to agree or disagree is the foundation of our kind of society—and the freedom to strike is a part of it. I am mentioning this as a reminder to a certain Petronius from Hell's Kitchen, an exquisite bastard who has been rather noisy lately about telling us that this strike represents a destruction of law and order."

The loud-speaker coughed out a high, shrill sound of approval and a clatter of applause. There were gasps among the people in the lobby. Catherine grasped Keating's arm. "Oh, Peter!" she whispered. "He means Wynand! Wynand was born in Hell's Kitchen. He can afford to say that, but Wynand will take it out on Uncle Ellsworth!"

Keating could not listen to the rest of Heller's speech, because his head was swimming in so violent an ache that the sound hurt his eyes and he had to keep his eyelids shut tightly. He leaned against the wall.

He opened his eyes with a jerk, when he became aware of the peculiar silence around him. He had not noticed the end of Heller's speech. He saw the people in the lobby standing in tense, solemn expectation, and the blank rasping of the loud-speaker pulled every glance into its dark funnel. Then a voice came through the silence, loudly and slowly:

"Ladies and gentlemen, I have the great honor of presenting to you now Mr. Ellsworth Monkton Toohey!"

Well, thought Keating, Bennett's won his six bits down at the office. There were a few seconds of silence. Then the thing which happened hit Keating on the back of the head; it was not a sound nor a blow, it was something that ripped time apart, that cut the moment from the normal one preceding it. He knew only the shock, at first; a distinct, conscious second was gone before he realized what it was and that it was applause. It was such a crash of applause that he waited for the loud-speaker to explode; it went on and on and on, pressing against the walls of the lobby, and he thought he could feel the walls buckling out to the street. The people around him were cheering. Catherine stood, her lips parted, and he felt certain that she was not breathing at all.

It was a long time before silence came suddenly, as abrupt and shocking as the roar; the loud-speaker died, choking on a high note. Those in the lobby stood still. Then came the voice.

"My friends," it said, simply and solemnly. "My brothers," it added softly, involuntarily, both full of emotion and smiling apologetically at the emotion. "I am more touched by this reception than I should allow myself to be. I hope I shall be forgiven for a trace of the vain child which is in all of us. But I realize—and in that spirit I accept it—that this tribute was paid not to my person, but to a principle which chance has granted me to represent in all humility tonight."

It was not a voice, it was a miracle. It unrolled as a velvet banner. It spoke English words, but the resonant clarity of each syllable made it sound like a new language spoken for the first time. It was the voice of a giant.

Keating stood, his mouth open. He did not hear what the voice was saying. He heard the beauty of the sounds without meaning. He felt no need to know the meaning; he could accept anything, he would be led blindly anywhere.

". . . and so, my friends," the voice was saying, "the lesson to be learned from our tragic struggle is the lesson of unity. We shall unite or we shall be defeated. Our will—the will of the disinherited, the forgotten, the oppressed—shall weld us into a solid bulwark, with a common faith and a common goal. This is the time for every man to renounce the thoughts of his petty little problems, of gain, of comfort, of self-gratification. This is the time to merge his self in a great current, in the rising tide which is approaching to sweep us all, willing or unwilling, into the future. History, my friends, does not ask questions or acquiescence. It is irrevocable, as the voice of the masses that determine it. Let us listen to the call. Let us organize, my brothers. Let us organize. Let us organize. Let us organize."

Keating looked at Catherine. There was no Catherine; there was only a white face dissolving in the sounds of the loud-speaker. It was not that she heard her uncle; Keating could feel no jealousy of him; he wished he could. It was not affection. It was something cold and impersonal that left her empty, her will surrendered and no human will holding hers, but a nameless thing in which she was being swallowed.

"Let's get out of here," he whispered. His voice was savage. He was afraid.

She turned to him, as if she were emerging from unconsciousness. He knew that she was trying to recognize him and everything he implied. She whispered:

"Yes. Let's get out."

They walked through the streets, through the rain, without direction. It was cold, but they went on, to move, to feel the movement, to know the sensation of their own muscles moving.

"We're getting drenched," Keating said at last, as bluntly and naturally as he could; their silence frightened him; it proved that they both knew the same thing and that the thing had been real. "Let's find some place where we can have a drink."

"Yes," said Catherine, "let's. It's so cold. . . . Isn't it stupid of me? Now I've missed Uncle's speech and I wanted so much to hear it." It was all right. She had mentioned it. She had mentioned it quite naturally, with a healthy amount of proper regret. The thing was gone. "But I wanted to be with you, Peter . . . I want to be with you always." The thing gave a last jerk, not in the meaning of what she said, but in the reason that had prompted her to say it. Then it was gone, and Keating smiled; his fingers sought her bare wrist between her sleeve and glove, and her skin was warm against his. . . .

Many days later Keating heard the story that was being told all over town. It was said that on the day after the mass meeting Gail Wynand had given Ellsworth Toohey a raise in salary. Toohey had been furious and had tried to refuse it. "You cannot bribe me, Mr. Wynand," he had said. "I'm not bribing you," Wynand had answered; "don't flatter yourself."

When the strike was settled, interrupted construction went forward with a spurt throughout the city, and Keating found himself spending days and nights at work, with new commissions pouring into the office. Francon smiled happily at everybody and gave a small party for his staff, to erase the memory of anything he might have said. The palatial residence of Mr. and Mrs. Dale Ainsworth on Riverside Drive, a pet project of Keating's, done in Late Renaissance and gray granite, was completed at last. Mr. and Mrs. Dale Ainsworth gave a formal reception as a housewarming, to which Guy Francon and Peter Keating were invited, but Lucius N. Heyer was ignored, quite accidentally, as always happened to him of late. Francon enjoyed the reception, because every square foot of granite in the house reminded him of the stupendous payment received by a certain granite quarry in Connecticut. Keating enjoyed the reception, because the stately Mrs. Ainsworth said to him with a disarming smile: "But I was *certain* that you were Mr. Francon's partner! It's Francon and Heyer, of course! How perfectly careless of me! All I can offer by way of excuse is that if you aren't his partner, one would certainly say you were *entitled* to be!" Life in the office rolled on smoothly, in one of those periods when everything seemed to go well.

Keating was astonished, therefore, one morning shortly after the Ainsworth reception, to see Francon arrive at the office with a countenance of nervous irritation. "Oh, nothing," he waved his hand at Keating impatiently, "nothing at all." In the drafting room Keating noticed three draftsmen, their heads close together, bent over a section of the New York *Banner*, reading with a guilty kind of avid interest; he heard an unpleasant chuckle from one of them. When they saw him the paper disappeared, too quickly. He had no time to inquire into this; a contractor's job runner was waiting for him in his office, also a stack of mail and drawings to be approved.

He had forgotten the incident three hours later in a rush of appointments. He felt light, clear-headed, exhilarated by his own energy. When he had to consult his library on a new drawing which he wished to compare with its best prototypes, he walked out of his office, whistling, swinging the drawing gaily.

His motion had propelled him halfway across the reception room, when he stopped short; the drawing swung forward and flapped back against his knees. He forgot that it was quite improper for him to pause there like that in the circumstances.

A young woman stood before the railing, speaking to the reception clerk. Her slender body seemed out of all scale in relation to a normal human body; its lines were so long, so fragile, so exaggerated that she looked like a stylized drawing of a woman and made the correct proportions of a normal being appear heavy and awkward beside her. She wore a plain gray suit; the contrast between its tailored severity and her appearance was deliberately exorbitant—and strangely elegant. She let the finger tips of one hand rest on the railing, a narrow hand ending the straight imperious line of her arm. She had gray eyes that were not ovals, but two long, rectangular cuts edged by parallel lines of lashes; she had an air of cold serenity and an exquisitely vicious mouth. Her face, her pale gold hair, her suit seemed to have no color, but only a hint, just on the verge of the reality of color, making the full reality seem vulgar. Keating stood still, because he understood for the first time what it was that artists spoke about when they spoke of beauty.

"I'll see him now, if I see him at all," she was saying to the reception clerk. "He asked me to come and this is the only time I have." It was not a command; she spoke as if it were not necessary for her voice to assume the tones of commanding.

"Yes, but . . ." A light buzzed on the clerk's switchboard; she plugged the connection through, hastily. "Yes, Mr. Francon . . ." She listened and nodded with relief. "Yes, Mr. Francon." She turned to the visitor: "Will you go right in, please?"

The young woman turned and looked at Keating as she passed him on her way to the stairs. Her eyes went past him without stopping. Something ebbed from his stunned admiration. He had had time to see her eyes; they seemed weary and a little contemptuous, but they left him with a sense of cold cruelty.

He heard her walking up the stairs, and the feeling vanished, but the admiration remained. He approached the reception clerk eagerly.

"Who was that?" he asked.

The clerk shrugged:

"That's the boss's little girl."

"Why, the lucky stiff!" said Keating. "He's been holding out on me."

"You misunderstood me," the clerk said coldly. "It's his daughter. It's Dominique Francon."

"Oh," said Keating. "Oh, Lord!"

"Yeah?" the girl looked at him sarcastically. "Have you read this morning's *Banner?*"

"No. Why?"

"Read it."

Her switchboard buzzed and she turned away from him.

He sent a boy for a copy of the *Banner* and turned anxiously to the column, "Your House," by Dominique Francon. He had heard that she'd been quite successful lately with descriptions of the homes of prominent New Yorkers. Her field was confined to home decoration, but she ventured occasionally into architectural criticism. Today her subject was the new residence of Mr. and Mrs. Dale Ainsworth on Riverside Drive. He read, among many other things, the following:

"You enter a magnificent lobby of golden marble and you think that this is the City Hall or the Main Post Office, but it isn't. It has, however, everything: the mezzanine with the colonnade and the stairway with a goitre and the cartouches in the form of looped leather belts. Only it's not leather, it's marble. The dining room has a splendid bronze gate, placed by mistake on the ceiling, in the shape of a trellis entwined with fresh bronze grapes. There are dead ducks and rabbits hanging on the wall panels, in bouquets of carrots, petunias and string beans. I do not think these would have been very attractive if real, but since they are bad plaster imitations, it is all right. . . . The bedroom windows face a brick wall, not a very neat wall, but nobody needs to see the bedrooms. . . . The front windows are large enough and admit plenty of light, as well as the feet of the marble cupids that roost on the outside. The cupids are well fed and present a pretty picture to the street, against the severe granite of the façade; they are quite commendable, unless you just can't stand to look at dimpled soles every time you glance out to see whether it's raining. If you get tired of it, you can always look out of the central windows of the third floor, and into the cast-iron rump of Mercury who sits on top of the pediment over the entrance. It's a very beautiful entrance. Tomorrow, we shall visit the home of Mr. and Mrs. Smythe-Pickering."

Keating had designed the house. But he could not help chuckling through his fury when he thought of what Francon must have felt reading this, and of how Francon was going to face Mrs. Dale Ainsworth. Then he forgot the house and the article. He remembered only the girl who had written it.

He picked three sketches at random from his table and started for Francon's office to ask his approval of the sketches, which he did not need.

On the stair landing outside Francon's closed door he stopped. He heard Francon's voice behind the door, loud, angry and helpless, the voice he always heard when Francon was beaten.

". . . to expect such an outrage! From my own daughter! I'm used to anything from you, but this beats it all. What am I going to do? How am I going to explain? Do you have any kind of a vague idea of my position?"

Then Keating heard her laughing; it was a sound so gay and so cold that he knew it was best not to go in. He knew he did not want to go in, because he was afraid again, as he had been when he'd seen her eyes.

He turned and descended the stairs. When he had reached the floor below, he was thinking that he would meet her, that he would meet her soon and that Francon would not be able to prevent it now. He thought of it eagerly, laughing in relief at the picture of Francon's daughter as he had imagined her for years, revising his vision of his future; even though he felt dimly that it would be better if he never met her again.

X

RALSTON HOLCOMBE HAD NO VISIBLE NECK, BUT HIS CHIN TOOK care of that. His chin and jaws formed an unbroken arc, resting on his chest. His cheeks were pink, soft to the touch, with the irresilient softness of age, like the skin of a peach that has been scalded. His rich white hair rose over his forehead and fell to his shoulders in the sweep of a medieval mane. It left dandruff on the back of his collar.

He walked through the streets of New York, wearing a broad-brimmed hat, a dark business suit, a pale green satin shirt, a vest of white brocade, a huge black bow emerging from under his chin, and he carried a staff, not a cane, but a tall ebony staff surmounted by a bulb of solid gold. It was as if his huge body were resigned to the conventions of a prosaic civilization and to its drab garments, but the oval of his chest and stomach sallied forth, flying the colors of his inner soul.

These things were permitted to him, because he was a genius. He was also president of the Architects' Guild of America.

Ralston Holcombe did not subscribe to the views of his colleagues in the organization. He was not a grubbing builder nor a businessman. He was, he stated firmly, a man of ideals.

He denounced the deplorable state of American architecture and the unprincipled eclecticism of its practitioners. In any period of history, he declared, architects built in the spirit of their own time, and did not pick designs from the past; we could be true to history only in heeding her law, which demanded that we plant the roots of our art firmly in the reality of our own life. He decried the stupidity of erecting buildings that were Greek, Gothic or Romanesque; let us, he begged, be modern and build in the style that belongs to our days. He had found that style. It was Renaissance.

He stated his reasons clearly. Inasmuch, he pointed out, as nothing of great historical importance had happened in the world since the Renaissance, we should consider ourselves still living in that period; and all the outward forms of our existence should remain faithful to the examples of the great masters of the sixteenth century.

He had no patience with the few who spoke of a modern architecture in terms quite different from his own; he ignored them; he stated only that men who wanted to break with *all* of the past were lazy ignoramuses, and that one could not put originality above Beauty. His voice trembled reverently on that last word.

He accepted nothing but stupendous commissions. He specialized in the eternal and the monumental. He built a great many memorials and capitols. He designed for International Expositions.

He built like a composer improvising under the spur of a mystic guidance. He had sudden inspirations. He would add an enormous dome to the flat roof of a finished structure, or encrust a long vault with gold-leaf mosaic, or rip off a façade of limestone to replace it with marble. His clients turned pale, stuttered—and paid. His imperial personality carried him to victory in any encounter with a client's thrift; behind him stood the stern, unspoken, overwhelming assertion that he was an *Artist*. His prestige was enormous.

He came from a family listed in the *Social Register*. In his middle years he had married a young lady whose family had not made the *Social Register*, but made piles of money instead, in a chewing-gum empire left to an only daughter.

Ralston Holcombe was now sixty-five, to which he added a few years, for the sake of his friends' compliments on his wonderful physique; Mrs. Ralston Holcombe was forty-two, from which she deducted considerably.

Mrs. Ralston Holcombe maintained a salon that met informally every Sunday afternoon. "Everybody who is anybody in architecture drops in on us," she told her friends. "They'd better," she added.

On a Sunday afternoon in March, Keating drove to the Holcombe mansion—a reproduction of a Florentine *palazzo*—dutifully, but a little reluctantly. He had been a frequent guest at these celebrated gatherings and he was beginning to be bored, for he knew everybody he could expect to find there. He felt, however, that he had to attend this time, because the occasion was to be in honor of the completion of one more capitol by Ralston Holcombe in some state or another.

A substantial crowd was lost in the marble ballroom of the Holcombes, scattered in forlorn islets through an expanse intended for court receptions. The guests stood about, self-consciously informal, working at being brilliant. Steps rang against the marble with the echoing sound of a crypt. The flames of tall candles clashed desolately with the gray of the light from the street; the light made the candles seem dimmer, the candles gave to the day outside a premonitory tinge of dusk. A scale model of the new state capitol stood displayed on a pedestal in the middle of the room, ablaze with tiny electric bulbs.

Mrs. Ralston Holcombe presided over the tea table. Each guest accepted a fragile cup of transparent porcelain, took two delicate sips and vanished in the direction of the bar. Two stately butlers went about collecting the abandoned cups.

Mrs. Ralston Holcombe, as an enthusiastic girl friend had described her, was "petite, but intellectual." Her diminutive stature was her secret sorrow, but she had learned to find compensations. She could talk, and did, of wearing dresses size ten and of shopping in the junior departments. She wore high-school garments and short socks in summer, displaying spindly legs with hard blue veins. She adored celebrities. That was her mission in life. She hunted them grimly; she faced them with wide-eyed admiration and spoke of her own insignificance, of her humility before achievement; she shrugged, tight-lipped and rancorous, whenever one of them did not seem to take sufficient account of her own views on life after death, the theory of relativity, Aztec architecture, birth control and the movies. She had a great many poor friends and advertised the fact. If a friend happened to improve his financial position, she dropped him, feeling that he had committed an act of treason. She hated the wealthy in all sincerity: they shared her only badge of distinction. She considered architecture her private domain. She had been christened "Constance" and found it awfully clever to be known as "Kiki," a nickname she had forced on her friends when she was well past thirty.

Keating had never felt comfortable in Mrs. Holcombe's presence, because she smiled at him too insistently and commented on his remarks by winking and saying: "Why, Peter, how naughty of you!" when no such intention had been in his mind at all. He bowed over her hand, however, this afternoon as usual, and she smiled from behind the silver teapot. She wore a regal gown of emerald velvet, and a magenta ribbon in her bobbed hair with a cute little bow in front. Her skin was tanned and dry, with enlarged pores showing on her nostrils. She handed a cup to Keating, a square-cut emerald glittering on her finger in the candlelight.

Keating expressed his admiration for the capitol and escaped to examine the model. He stood before it for a correct number of minutes, scalding his lips with the hot liquid that smelled of cloves. Holcombe, who never looked in the direction of the model and never missed a guest stopping before it, slapped Keating's shoulder and said something appropriate about young fellows learning the beauty of the style of the Renaissance. Then Keating wandered off, shook a few hands without enthusiasm, and glanced at his wrist watch, calculating the time when it would be permissible to leave. Then he stopped.

Beyond a broad arch, in a small library, with three young men beside her, he saw Dominique Francon.

She stood leaning against a column, a cocktail glass in her hand. She wore a suit of black velvet; the heavy cloth, which transmitted no light rays, held her anchored to reality by stopping the light that flowed too freely through the flesh of her hands, her neck, her face. A white spark of fire flashed like a cold metallic cross in the glass she held, as if it were a lens gathering the diffused radiance of her skin.

Keating tore forward and found Francon in the crowd.

"Well, Peter!" said Francon brightly. "Want me to get you a drink? Not so hot," he added, lowering his voice, "but the Manhattans aren't too bad."

"No," said Keating, "thanks."

"*Entre nous*," said Francon, winking at the model of the capital, "it's a holy mess, isn't it?"

"Yes," said Keating. "Miserable proportions. . . . That dome looks like Holcombe's face imitating a sunrise on the roof. . . ." They had stopped in full view of the library and Keating's eyes were fixed on the girl in black, inviting Francon to notice it; he enjoyed having Francon in a trap.

"And the plan! The plan! Do you see that on the second floor . . . oh," said Francon, noticing.

He looked at Keating, then at the library, then at Keating again.

"Well," said Francon at last, "don't blame me afterward. You've asked for it. Come on."

They entered the library together. Keating stopped, correctly, but allowing his eyes an improper intensity, while Francon beamed with unconvincing cheeriness:

"Dominique, my dear! May I present?—this is Peter Keating, my own right hand. Peter—my daughter."

"How do you do," said Keating, his voice soft.

Dominique bowed gravely.

"I have waited to meet you for such a long time, Miss Francon."

"This will be interesting," said Dominique. "You will want to be nice to me, of course, and yet that won't be diplomatic."

"What do you mean, Miss Francon?"

"Father would prefer you to be horrible with me. Father and I don't get along at all."

"Why, Miss Francon, I . . ."

"I think it's only fair to tell you this at the beginning. You may want to redraw some conclusions." He was looking for Francon, but Francon had vanished. "No," she said softly, "Father doesn't do these things well at all. He's too obvious. You asked him for the introduction, but he shouldn't have let me notice that. However, it's quite all right, since we both admit it. Sit down."

She slipped into a chair and he sat down obediently beside her. The young men whom he did not know stood about for a few minutes, trying to be included in the conversation by smiling blankly, then wandered off.

Keating thought with relief that there was nothing frightening about her; there was only a disquieting contrast between her words and the candid innocence of the manner she used to utter them; he did not know which to trust.

"I admit I asked for the introduction," he said. "That's obvious anyway, isn't it? Who wouldn't ask for it? But don't you think that the conclusions I'll draw may have nothing to do with your father?"

"Don't say that I'm beautiful and exquisite and like no one you've ever met before and that you're very much afraid that you're going to fall in love with me. You'll say it eventually, but let's postpone it. Apart from that, I think we'll get along very nicely."

"But you're trying to make it very difficult for me, aren't you?"

"Yes. Father should have warned you."

"He did."

"You should have listened. Be very considerate of Father. I've met so many of his own right hands that I was beginning to be skeptical. But you're the first one who's lasted. And who looks like he's going to last. I've heard a great deal about you. My congratulations."

"I've been looking forward to meeting you for years. And I've been reading your column with so much . . ." He stopped. He knew he shouldn't have mentioned that; and, above all, he shouldn't have stopped.

"So much . . . ?" she asked gently.

". . . so much pleasure," he finished, hoping that she would let it go at that.

"Oh, yes," she said. "The Ainsworth house. You designed it. I'm sorry. You just happened to be the victim of one of my rare attacks of honesty. I don't have them often. As you know, if you've read my stuff yesterday."

"I've read it. And—well, I'll follow your example and I'll be perfectly frank. Don't take it as a complaint—one must never complain against one's critics. But really that capitol of Holcombe's is much worse in all those very things that you blasted us for. Why did you give him such a glowing tribute yesterday? Or did you have to?"

"Don't flatter me. Of course I didn't have to. Do you think anyone on the paper pays enough attention to a column on home decoration to care what I say in it? Besides, I'm not even supposed to write about capitols. Only I'm getting tired of home decorations."

"Then why did you praise Holcombe?"

"Because that capitol of his is so awful that to pan it would have been an anticlimax. So I thought it would be amusing to praise it to the sky. It was."

"Is that the way you go about it?"

"That's the way I go about it. But no one reads my column, except housewives who can never afford to decorate their homes, so it doesn't matter at all."

"But what do you really like in architecture?"

"I don't like anything in architecture."

"Well, you know of course that I won't believe that. Why do you write if you have nothing you want to say?"

"To have something to do. Something more disgusting than many other things I could do. And more amusing."

"Come on, that's not a good reason."

"I never have any good reasons."

"But you must be enjoying your work."

"I am. Don't you see that I am?"

"You know, I've actually envied you. Working for a magnificent enterprise like the Wynand papers. The largest organization in the country, commanding the best writing talent and . . ."

"Look," she said, leaning toward him confidentially, "let me help you. If you had just met Father, and he were working for the Wynand papers, that would be exactly the right thing to say. But not with me. That's what I'd expect you to say and I don't like to hear what I expect. It would be much more interesting if you said that the Wynand papers are a contemptible dump heap of yellow journalism and all their writers put together aren't worth two bits."

"Is that what you really think of them?"

"Not at all. But I don't like people who try to say only what they think I think."

"Thanks. I'll need your help. I've never met anyone . . . oh, no, of course, that's what you didn't want me to say. But I really meant it about your papers. I've always admired Gail Wynand. I've always wished I could meet him. What is he like?"

"Just what Austen Heller called him—an exquisite bastard."

He winced. He remembered where he had heard Austen Heller say that. The memory of Catherine seemed heavy and vulgar in the presence of the thin white hand he saw hanging over the arm of the chair before him.

"But, I mean," he asked, "what's he like in person?"

"I don't know. I've never met him."

"You *haven't?*"

"No."

"Oh, I've heard he's so interesting!"

"Undoubtedly. When I'm in a mood for something decadent I'll probably meet him."

"Do you know Toohey?"

"Oh," she said. He saw what he had seen in her eyes before, and he did not like the sweet gaiety of her voice. "Oh, Ellsworth Toohey. Of course I know him. He's wonderful. He's a man I always enjoy talking to. He's such a perfect blackguard."

"Why, Miss Francon! You're the first person who's ever . . ."

"I'm not trying to shock you. I meant all of it. I admire him. He's so complete. You don't meet perfection often in this world one way or the other, do you? And he's just that. Sheer perfection in his own way. Everyone else is so unfinished, broken up into so many different pieces that don't fit together. But not Toohey. He's a monolith. Sometimes, when I feel bitter against the world, I find consolation in thinking that it's all right, that I'll be avenged, that the world will get what's coming to it—because there's Ellsworth Toohey."

"What do you want to be avenged for?"

She looked at him, her eyelids lifted for a moment, so that her eyes did not seem rectangular, but soft and clear.

"That was very clever of you," she said. "That was the first clever thing you've said."

"Why?"

"Because you knew what to pick out of all the rubbish I uttered. So I'll have to answer you. I'd like to be avenged for the fact that I have nothing to be avenged for. Now let's go on about Ellsworth Toohey."

"Well, I've always heard, from everybody, that he's a sort of saint, the one pure idealist, utterly incorruptible and . . ."

"That's quite true. A plain grafter would be much safer. But Toohey is like a testing stone for people. You can learn about them by the way they take him."

"Why? What do you actually mean?"

She leaned back in her chair, and stretched her arms down to her knees, twisting her wrists, palms out, the fingers of her two hands entwined. She laughed easily.

"Nothing that one should make a subject of discussion at a tea party. Kiki's right. She hates the sight of me, but she's got to invite me once in a while. And I can't resist coming, because she's so obvious about not wanting me. You know, I told Ralston tonight what I really thought of his capitol, but he wouldn't believe me. He only beamed and said that I was a very nice little girl."

"Well, aren't you?"

"What?"

"A very nice little girl."

"No. Not today. I've made you thoroughly uncomfortable. So I'll make up for it. I'll tell you what I think of you, because you'll be worrying about that. I think you're smart and safe and obvious and quite ambitious and you'll get away with it. And I like you. I'll tell Father that I approve of his right hand very much, so you see you have nothing to fear from the boss's daughter. Though it would be better if I didn't say anything to Father, because my recommendation would work the other way with him."

"May I tell you only one thing that I think about you?"

"Certainly. Any number of them."

"I think it would have been better if you hadn't told me that you liked me. Then I would have had a better chance of its being true."

She laughed.

"If you understand that," she said, "then we'll get along beautifully. Then it might even be true."

Gordon L. Prescott appeared in the arch of the ballroom, glass in hand. He wore a gray suit and a turtle-neck sweater of silver wool. His boyish face looked freshly scrubbed, and he had his usual air of soap, tooth paste and the outdoors.

"Dominique, darling!" he cried, waving his glass. "Hello, Keating," he added curtly. "Dominique, where have you been hiding yourself? I heard you were here and I've had a hell of a time looking for you!"

"Hello, Gordon," she said. She said it quite correctly; there was nothing offensive in the quiet politeness of her voice; but following his high note of enthusiasm, her voice struck a tone that seemed flat and deadly in its indifference—as if the two sounds mingled into an audible counterpoint around the melodic thread of her contempt.

Prescott had not heard. "Darling," he said, "you look lovelier every time I see you. One wouldn't think it were possible."

"Seventh time," said Dominique.

"What?"

"Seventh time that you've said it when meeting me, Gordon. I'm counting them."

"You simply won't be serious, Dominique. You'll never be serious."

"Oh, yes, Gordon. I was just having a very serious conversation here with my friend Peter Keating."

A lady waved to Prescott and he accepted the opportunity, escaping, looking very foolish. And Keating delighted in the thought that she had dismissed another man for a conversation she wished to continue with her friend Peter Keating.

But when he turned to her, she asked sweetly: "What was it we were talking about, Mr. Keating?" And then she was staring with too great an interest across the room, at the wizened figure of a little man coughing over a whisky glass.

"Why," said Keating, "we were . . ."

"Oh, there's Eugene Pettingill. My great favorite. I must say hello to Eugene."

And she was up, moving across the room, her body leaning back as she walked, moving toward the most unattractive septuagenarian present.

Keating did not know whether he had been made to join the brotherhood of Gordon L. Prescott, or whether it had been only an accident.

He returned to the ballroom reluctantly. He forced himself to join groups of guests and to talk. He watched Dominique Francon as she moved through the crowd, as she stopped in conversation with others. She never glanced at him again. He could not decide whether he had succeeded with her or failed miserably.

He managed to be at the door when she was leaving.

She stopped and smiled at him enchantingly.

"No," she said, before he could utter a word, "you can't take me home. I have a car waiting. Thank you just the same."

She was gone and he stood at the door, helpless and thinking furiously that he believed he was blushing.

He felt a soft hand on his shoulder and turned to find Francon beside him.

"Going home, Peter? Let me give you a lift."

"But I thought you had to be at the club by seven."

"Oh, that's all right, I'll be a little late, doesn't matter, I'll drive you home, no trouble at all." There was a peculiar expression of purpose on Francon's face, quite unusual for him and unbecoming.

Keating followed him silently, amused, and said nothing when they were alone in the comfortable twilight of Francon's car.

"Well?" Francon asked ominously.

Keating smiled. "You're a pig, Guy. You don't know how to appreciate what you've got. Why didn't you tell me? She's the most beautiful woman I've ever seen."

"Oh, yes," said Francon darkly. "Maybe that's the trouble."

"What trouble? Where do you see any trouble?"

"What do you really think of her, Peter? Forget the looks. You'll see how quickly you'll forget that. What do you think?"

"Well, I think she has a great deal of character."

"Thanks for the understatement."

Francon was gloomily silent, and then he said with an awkward little note of something like hope in his voice:

"You know, Peter, I was surprised. I watched you, and you had quite a long chat with her. That's amazing. I fully expected her to chase you away with one nice, poisonous crack. Maybe you could get along with her, after all. I've concluded that you just can't tell anything about her. Maybe . . . You know, Peter, what I wanted to tell you is this: Don't pay any attention to what she said about my wanting you to be horrible with her."

The heavy earnestness of that sentence was such a hint that Keating's lips moved to shape a soft whistle, but he caught himself in time. Francon added heavily: "I don't want you to be horrible with her at all."

"You know, Guy," said Keating, in a tone of patronizing reproach, "you shouldn't have run away like that."

"I never know how to speak to her." He sighed. "I've never learned to. I can't understand what in blazes is the matter with her, but something is. She just won't behave like a human being. You know, she's been expelled from two finishing schools. How she ever got through college I can't imagine, but I can tell you that I dreaded to open my mail for four solid years, waiting for word of the inevitable. Then I thought, well, once she's on her own I'm through and I don't have to worry about it, but she's worse than ever."

"What do you find to worry about?"

"I don't. I try not to. I'm glad when I don't have to think of her at all. I can't help it, I just wasn't cut out for a father. But sometimes I get to feel that it's my responsibility after all, though God knows I don't want it, but still there it is, I should do something about it, there's no one else to assume it."

"You've let her frighten you, Guy, and really there's nothing to be afraid of."

"You don't think so?"

"No."

"Maybe you're the man to handle her. I don't regret your meeting her now, and you know that I didn't want you to. Yes, I think you're the one man who could handle her. You . . . you're quite determined—aren't you, Peter?—when you're after something?"

"Well," said Keating, throwing one hand up in a careless gesture, "I'm not afraid very often."

Then he leaned back against the cushions, as if he were tired, as if he had heard nothing of importance, and he kept silent for the rest of the drive. Francon kept silent also.

"Boys," said John Erik Snyte, "don't spare yourselves on this. It's the most important thing we've had this year. Not much money, you understand, but the prestige, the connections! If we do land it, won't some of those great architects turn green! You see, Austen Heller has told me frankly that we're the third firm he's approached. He would have none of what those big fellows tried to sell him. So it's up to us, boys. You know, something different, unusual, but in good taste, and you know, *different*. Now do your best."

His five designers sat in a semicircle before him. "Gothic" looked bored and "Miscellaneous" looked discouraged in advance; "Renaissance" was following the course of a fly on the ceiling. Roark asked:

"What did he actually say, Mr. Snyte?"

Snyte shrugged and looked at Roark with amusement, as if he and Roark shared a shameful secret about the new client, not worth mentioning.

"Nothing that makes great sense—quite between us, boys," said Snyte. "He was somewhat inarticulate, considering his great command of the English language in print. He admitted he knew nothing about architecture. He didn't say whether he wanted it modernistic or period or what. He said something to the effect that he wanted a house of his own, but he's hesitated for a long time about building one because all houses look alike to him and they all look like hell and he doesn't see how anyone can become enthusiastic about any house, and yet he has the idea that he wants a building he could love. 'A building that would mean something' is what he said, though he added that he 'didn't know what or how.' There. That's about all he said. Not much to go on, and I wouldn't have undertaken to submit sketches if it weren't Austen Heller. But I grant you that it doesn't make sense. . . . What's the matter, Roark?"

"Nothing," said Roark.

This ended the first conference on the subject of a residence for Austen Heller.

Later that day Snyte crowded his five designers into a train, and they went to Connecticut to see the site Heller had chosen. They stood on a lonely, rocky stretch of shore, three miles beyond an unfashionable little town; they munched sandwiches and peanuts, and they looked at a cliff rising in broken ledges from the ground to end in a straight, brutal, naked drop over the sea, a vertical shaft of rock forming a cross with the long, pale horizontal of the sea.

"There," said Snyte. "That's it." He twirled a pencil in his hand. "Damnable, eh?" He sighed. "I tried to suggest a more respectable location, but he didn't take it so well so I had to shut up." He twirled the pencil. "That's where he wants the house, right on the top of that rock." He scratched the tip of his nose with the point of the pencil. "I tried to suggest setting it farther back from the shore and keeping the damn rock for a view, but that didn't go so well either." He bit the eraser between the tips of his teeth. "Just think of the blasting, the leveling one's got to do on that top." He cleaned his fingernail with the lead, leaving a black mark. "Well, that's that. . . . Observe the grade, and the quality of the stone. The approach will be difficult. . . . I have all the surveys and the photographs in the office. . . . Well . . . Who's got a cigarette? . . . Well, I think that's about all. . . . I'll help you with suggestions anytime. . . . Well . . . What time is that damn train back?"

Thus the five designers were started on their task. Four of them proceeded immediately at their drawing boards. Roark returned alone to the site, many times.

Roark's five months with Snyte stretched behind him like a blank. Had he wished to ask himself what he had felt, he would have found no answer, save in the fact that he remembered nothing of these months. He could remember each sketch he had made. He could, if he tried, remember what had happened to those sketches; he did not try.

But he had not loved any of them as he loved the house of Austen Heller. He stayed in the drafting room through evening after evening, alone with a sheet of paper and the thought of a cliff over the sea. No one saw his sketches until they were finished.

When they were finished, late one night, he sat at his table, with the sheets spread before him, sat for many hours, one hand propping his forehead, the other hanging by his side, blood gathering in the fingers, numbing them, while the street beyond the window became deep blue, then pale gray. He did not look at the sketches. He felt empty and very tired.

The house on the sketches had been designed not by Roark, but by the cliff on which it stood. It was as if the cliff had grown and completed itself and proclaimed the purpose for which it had been waiting. The house was broken into many levels, following the ledges of the rock, rising as it rose, in gradual masses, in planes flowing together up into one consummate harmony. The walls, of the same granite as the rock, continued its vertical lines upward; the wide, projecting terraces of concrete, silver as the sea, followed the line of the waves, of the straight horizon.

Roark was still sitting at his table when the men returned to begin their day in the drafting room. Then the sketches were sent to Snyte's office.

Two days later, the final version of the house to be submitted to Austen Heller, the version chosen and edited by John Erik Snyte, executed by the Chinese artist, lay swathed in tissue paper on a table. It was Roark's house. His competitors had been eliminated. It was Roark's house, but its walls were now of red brick, its windows were cut to conventional size and equipped with green shutters, two of its projecting wings were omitted, the great cantilevered terrace over the sea was replaced by a little wrought-iron balcony, and the house was provided with an entrance of Ionic columns supporting a broken pediment, and with a little spire supporting a weather vane.

John Erik Snyte stood by the table, his two hands spread in the air over the sketch, without touching the virgin purity of its delicate colors. "That is what Mr. Heller had in mind, I'm sure," he said. "Pretty good... Yes, pretty good . . . Roark, how many times do I have to ask you not to smoke around a final sketch? Stand away. You'll get ashes on it."

Austen Heller was expected at twelve o'clock. But at half past eleven Mrs. Symington arrived unannounced and demanded to see Mr. Snyte immediately. Mrs. Symington was an imposing dowager who had just moved into her new residence, designed by Mr. Snyte; besides, Snyte expected a commission for an apartment house from her brother. He could not refuse to see her and he bowed her into his office, where she proceeded to state without reticence of expression that the ceiling of her library had cracked and the bay windows of her drawing room were hidden under a perpetual veil of moisture which she could not combat. Snyte summoned his chief engineer and they launched together into detailed explanations, apologies and damnations of contractors. Mrs. Symington showed no sign of relenting when a signal buzzed on Snyte's desk and the reception clerk's voice announced Austin Heller.

It would have been impossible to ask Mrs. Symington to leave or Austin Heller to wait. Snyte solved the problem by abandoning her to the soothing speech of his engineer and excusing himself for a moment. Then he emerged into the reception room, shook Heller's hand and suggested: "Would you mind stepping into the drafting room, Mr. Heller? Better light in there, you know, and the sketch is all ready for you, and I didn't want to take the chance of moving it."

Heller did not seem to mind. He followed Snyte obediently into the drafting room, a tall, broad-shouldered figure in English tweeds, with sandy hair and a square face drawn in countless creases around the ironical calm of the eyes.

The sketch lay on the Chinese artist's table, and the artist stepped aside diffidently, in silence. The next table was Roark's. He stood with his back to Heller; he went on with his drawing, and did not turn. The employees had been trained not to intrude on the occasions when Snyte brought a client into the drafting room.

Snyte's finger tips lifted the tissue paper, as if raising the veil of a bride. Then he stepped back and watched Heller's face. Heller bent down and stood hunched, drawn, intent, saying nothing for a long time.

"Listen, Mr. Snyte," he began at last. "Listen, I think . . ." and stopped.

Snyte waited patiently, pleased, sensing the approach of something he didn't want to disturb.

"This," said Heller suddenly, loudly, slamming his fist down on the drawing, and Snyte winced, "this is the nearest anyone's ever come to it!"

"I knew you'd like it, Mr. Heller," said Snyte.

"I don't," said Heller.

Snyte blinked and waited.

"It's so near somehow," said Heller regretfully, "but it's not right. I don't know where, but it's not. Do forgive me, if this sounds vague, but I like things at once or I don't. I know that I wouldn't be comfortable, for instance, with that entrance. It's a lovely entrance, but you won't even notice it because you've seen it so often."

"Ah, but allow me to point out a few considerations, Mr. Heller. One wants to be modern, of course, but one wants to preserve the appearance of a home. A combination of stateliness and coziness, you understand, a very austere house like this must have a few softening touches. It is strictly correct architecturally."

"No doubt," said Heller. "I wouldn't know about that. I've never been strictly correct in my life."

"Just let me explain this scheme and you'll see that it's . . ."

"I know," said Heller wearily. "I know. I'm sure you're right. Only . . ." His voice had a sound of the eagerness he wished he could feel. "Only, if it had some unity, some . . . some central idea . . . which is there and isn't . . . if it seemed to live . . . which it doesn't . . . It lacks something and it has too much. . . . If it were cleaner, more clear-cut . . . what's the word I've heard used?—if it were integrated. . . ."

Roark turned. He was at the other side of the table. He seized the sketch, his hand flashed forward and a pencil ripped across the drawing, slashing raw black lines over the untouchable water-color. The lines blasted off the Ionic columns, the pediment, the entrance, the spire, the blinds, the bricks; they flung up two wings of stone; they rent the windows wide; they splintered the balcony and hurled a terrace over the sea.

It was being done before the others had grasped the moment when it began. Then Snyte jumped forward, but Heller seized his wrist and stopped him. Roark's hand went on razing walls, splitting, rebuilding in furious strokes.

Roark threw his head up once, for a flash of a second, to look at Heller across the table. It was all the introduction they needed; it was like a handshake. Roark went on, and when he threw the pencil down, the house—as he had designed it—stood completed in an ordered pattern of black streaks. The performance had not lasted five minutes.

Snyte made an attempt at a sound. As Heller said nothing, Snyte felt free to whirl on Roark and scream: "You're fired, God damn you! Get out of here! You're fired!"

"We're both fired," said Austen Heller, winking to Roark. "Come on. Have you had any lunch? Let's go some place. I want to talk to you."

Roark went to his locker to get his hat and coat. The drafting room witnessed a stupefying act and all work stopped to watch it: Austen Heller picked up the sketch, folded it over four times, cracking the sacred cardboard, and slipped it into his pocket.

"But, Mr. Heller . . ." Snyte stammered, "let me explain . . . It's perfectly all right if that's what you want, we'll do the sketch over . . . let me explain . . ."

"Not now," said Heller. "Not now." He added at the door: "I'll send you a check."

Then Heller was gone, and Roark with him; and the door, as Heller swung it shut behind them, sounded like the closing paragraph in one of Heller's articles.

Roark had not said a word.

In the softly lighted booth of the most expensive restaurant that Roark had ever entered, across the crystal and silver glittering between them, Heller was saying:

". . . because that's the house I want, because that's the house I've always wanted. Can you build it for me, draw up the plans and supervise the construction?"

"Yes," said Roark.

"How long will it take if we start at once?"

"About eight months."

"I'll have the house by late fall?"

"Yes."

"Just like that sketch?"

"Just like that."

"Look, I have no idea what kind of a contract one makes with an architect and you must know, so draw up one and let my lawyer okay it this afternoon, will you?"

"Yes."

Heller studied the man who sat facing him. He saw the hand lying on the table before him. Heller's awareness became focused on that hand. He saw the long fingers, the sharp joints, the prominent veins. He had the feeling that he was not hiring this man, but surrendering himself into his employment.

"How old are you," asked Heller, "whoever you are?"

"Twenty-six. Do you want any references?"

"Hell, no. I have them, here in my pocket. What's your name?"

"Howard Roark."

Heller produced a checkbook, spread it open on the table and reached for his fountain pen.

"Look," he said, writing, "I'll give you five hundred dollars on account. Get yourself an office or whatever you have to get, and go ahead."

He tore off the check and handed it to Roark, between the tips of two straight fingers, leaning forward on his elbow, swinging his wrist in a sweeping curve. His eyes were narrowed, amused, watching Roark quizzically. But the gesture had the air of a salute.

The check was made out to "Howard Roark, Architect."

XI

HOWARD ROARK OPENED HIS OWN OFFICE.
It was one large room on the top of an old building, with a broad window high over the roofs. He could see the distant band of the Hudson at his window sill, with the small streaks of ships moving under his finger tips when he pressed them to the glass. He had a desk, two chairs, and a huge drafting table. The glass entrance door bore the words: "Howard Roark, Architect." He stood in the hall for a long time, looking at the words. Then he went in, and slammed his door; he picked up a T-square from the table and flung it down again, as if throwing an anchor.

John Erik Snyte had objected. When Roark came to the office for his drawing instruments Snyte emerged into the reception room, shook his hand warmly and said: "Well, Roark! Well, how are you? Come in, come right in, I want to speak to you!"

And with Roark seated before his desk Snyte proceeded loudly:

"Look, fellow, I hope you've got sense enough not to hold it against me, anything that I might've said yesterday. You know how it is, I lost my head a little, and it wasn't what you did, but that you had to go and do it on that sketch, *that sketch* . . . well, never mind. No hard feelings?"

"No," said Roark. "None at all."

"Of course, you're not fired. You didn't take me seriously, did you? You can go right back to work here this very minute."

"What for, Mr. Snyte?"

"What do you mean, what for? Oh, you're thinking of the Heller house? But you're not taking Heller seriously, are you? You saw how he is, that madman can change his mind sixty times a minute. He won't really give you that commission, you know, it isn't as simple as that, it isn't being done that way."

"We've signed the contract yesterday."

"Oh, you have? Well, that's splendid! Well, look, Roark, I'll tell you what we'll do: you bring the commission back to us and I'll let you put your name on it with mine—'John Erik Snyte & Howard Roark.' And we'll split the fee. That's in addition to your salary—and you're getting a raise, incidentally. Then we'll have the same arrangement on any other commission you bring in. And . . . Lord, man, what are you laughing at?"

"Excuse me, Mr. Snyte. I'm sorry."

"I don't believe you understand," said Snyte, bewildered. "Don't you see? It's your insurance. You don't want to break loose just yet. Commissions won't fall into your lap like this. Then what will you do? This way, you'll have a steady job and you'll be building toward independent practice, if that's what you're after. In four or five years, you'll be ready to take the leap. That's the way everybody does it. You see?"

"Yes."

"Then you agree?"

"No."

"But, good Lord, man, you've lost your mind! To set up alone *now?* Without experience, without connections, without . . . well, without anything at all! I never heard of such a thing. Ask anybody in the profession. See what they'll tell you. It's preposterous!"

"Probably."

"Listen, Roark, won't you please listen?"

"I'll listen if you want me to, Mr. Snyte. But I think I should tell you now that nothing you can say will make any difference. If you don't mind that, I don't mind listening."

Snyte went on speaking for a long time and Roark listened, without objecting, explaining or answering.

"Well, if that's how you are, don't expect me to take you back when you find yourself on the pavement."

"I don't expect it, Mr. Snyte."

"Don't expect anyone else in the profession to take you in, after they hear what you've done to me."

"I don't expect that either."

For a few days Snyte thought of suing Roark and Heller. But he decided against it, because there was no precedent to follow under the circumstances; because Heller had paid him for his efforts, and the house had been actually designed by Roark; and because no one ever sued Austen Heller.

The first visitor to Roark's office was Peter Keating.

He walked in, without warning, one noon, walked straight across the room and sat down on Roark's desk, smiling gaily, spreading his arms wide in a sweeping gesture:

"Well, Howard!" he said. "Well, fancy that!"

He had not seen Roark for a year.

"Hello, Peter," said Roark.

"You're own office, your own name and everything! Already! Just imagine!"

"Who told you, Peter?"

"Oh, one hears things. You wouldn't expect me not to keep track of your career, now would you? You know what I've always thought of you. And I don't have to tell you that I congratulate you and wish you the very best."

"No, you don't have to."

"Nice place you got here. Light and roomy. Not quite as imposing as it should be, perhaps, but what can one expect at the beginning? And then, the prospects are uncertain, aren't they, Howard?"

"Quite."

"It's an awful chance you've taken."

"Probably."

"Are you really going to go through with it? I mean, on your own?"

"Looks that way, doesn't it?"

"Well, it's not too late, you know. I thought, when I heard the story, that you'd surely turn it over to Snyte and make a smart deal with him."

"I didn't."

"Aren't you really going to?"

"No."

Keating wondered why he should experience that sickening feeling of resentment; why he had come here hoping to find the story untrue, hoping to find Roark uncertain and willing to surrender. That feeling had haunted him ever since he'd heard the news about Roark; the sensation of something unpleasant that remained after he'd forgotten the cause. The feeling would come back to him, without reason, a blank wave of anger, and he would ask himself: now what the hell?—what was it I heard today? Then he would remember: Oh, yes, Roark— Roark's opened his own office. He would ask himself impatiently: So what?—and know at the same time that the words were painful to face, and humiliating like an insult.

"You know, Howard, I admire your courage. Really, you know, I've had much more experience and I've got more of a standing in the profession, don't mind saying it—I'm only speaking objectively—but I wouldn't dare take such a step."

"No, you wouldn't."

"So you've made the jump first. Well, well. Who would have thought it? . . . I wish you all the luck in the world."

"Thank you, Peter."

"I know you'll succeed. I'm sure of it."

"Are you?"

"Of course! Of course, I am. Aren't you?"

"I haven't thought of it."

"You haven't thought of it?"

"Not much."

"Then you're not sure, Howard? You aren't?"

"Why do you ask that so eagerly?"

"What? Why . . . no, not eagerly, but of course, I'm concerned. Howard, it's bad psychology not to be certain now, in your position. So you have doubts?"

"None at all."

"But you said . . ."

"I'm quite sure of things, Peter."

"Have you thought about getting your registration?"

"I've applied for it."

"You've got no college degree, you know. They'll make it difficult for you at the examination."

"Probably."

"What are you going to do if you don't get the license?"

"I'll get it."

"Well, I guess I'll be seeing you now at the A.G.A., if you don't go high hat on me, because you'll be a full-fledged member and I'm only a junior."

"I'm not joining the A.G.A."

"What do you mean, you're not joining? You're eligible now."

"Possibly."

"You'll be invited to join."

"Tell them not to bother."

"What!"

"You know, Peter, we had a conversation just like this seven years ago, when you tried to talk me into joining your fraternity at Stanton. Don't start it again."

"You won't join the A.G.A. when you have a chance to?"

"I won't join anything, Peter, at any time."

"But don't you realize how it helps?"

"In what?"

"In being an architect."

"I don't like to be helped in being an architect."

"You're just making things harder for yourself."

"I am."

"And it will be plenty hard, you know."

"I know."

"You'll make enemies of them if you refuse such an invitation."

"I'll make enemies of them anyway."

The first person to whom Roark had told the news was Henry Cameron. Roark went to New Jersey the day after he signed the contract with Heller. It had rained and he found Cameron in the garden, shuffling slowly down the damp paths, leaning heavily on a cane. In the past winter, Cameron had improved enough to walk a few hours each day. He walked with effort, his body bent. He looked at the first shoots of green on the earth under his feet. He lifted his cane, once in a while, bracing his legs to stand firm for a moment; with the tip of the cane, he touched a folded green cup and watched it spill a glistening drop in the twilight. He saw Roark coming up the hill, and frowned. He had seen Roark only a week ago, and because these visits meant too much to both of them, neither wished the occasions to be too frequent.

"Well?" Cameron asked gruffly. "What do you want here again?"

"I have something to tell you."

"It can wait."

"I don't think so."

"Well?"

"I'm opening my own office. I've just signed for my first building."

Cameron rotated his cane, the tip pressed into the earth, the shaft describing a wide circle, his two hands bearing down on the handle, the palm of one on the back of the other. His head nodded slowly, in rhythm with the motion, for a long time, his eyes closed. Then he looked at Roark and said:

"Well, don't brag about it."

He added: "Help me to sit down." It was the first time Cameron had ever pronounced this sentence; his sister and Roark had long since learned that the one outrage forbidden in his presence was any intention of helping him to move.

Roark took his elbow and led him to a bench. Cameron asked harshly, staring ahead at the sunset:

"What? For whom? How much?"

He listened silently to Roark's story. He looked for a long time at the sketch on cracked cardboard with the pencil lines over the water color. Then he asked many questions about the stone, the steel, the roads, the contractors, the costs. He offered no congratulations. He made no comment.

Only when Roark was leaving, Cameron said suddenly:

"Howard, when you open your office, take snapshots of it—and show them to me."

Then he shook his head, looked away guiltily, and swore.

"I'm being senile. Forget it."

Roark said nothing.

Three days later he came back. "You're getting to be a nuisance," said Cameron. Roark handed him an envelope, without a word. Cameron looked at the snapshots, at the one of the broad, bare office, of the wide window, of the entrance door. He dropped the others, and held the one of the entrance door for a long time.

"Well," he said at last, "I did live to see it."

He dropped the snapshot.

"Not quite exactly," he added. "Not in the way I had wanted to, but I did. It's like the shadows some say we'll see of the earth in that other world. Maybe that's how I'll see the rest of it. I'm learning."

He picked up the snapshot.

"Howard," he said. "Look at it."

He held it between them.

"It doesn't say much. Only 'Howard Roark, Architect.' But it's like those mottoes men carved over the entrance of a castle and died for. It's a challenge in the face of something so vast and so dark, that all the pain on earth—and do you know how much suffering there is on earth?—all the pain comes from that thing you are going to face. I don't know what it is, I don't know why it should be unleashed against you. I know only that it will be. And I know that if you carry these words through to the end, it will be a victory, Howard, not just for you, but for something that should win, that moves the world—and never wins acknowledgment. It will vindicate so many who have fallen before you, who have suffered as you will suffer. May God bless you—or whoever it is that is alone to see the best, the highest possible to human hearts. You're on your way into hell, Howard."

Roark walked up the path to the top of the cliff where the steel hulk of the Heller house rose into a blue sky. The skeleton was up and the concrete was being poured; the great mats of the terraces hung over the silver sheet of water quivering far below; plumbers and electricians had started laying their conduits.

He looked at the squares of sky delimited by the slender lines of girders and columns, the empty cubes of space he had torn out of the sky. His hands moved involuntarily, filling in the planes of walls to come, enfolding the future rooms. A stone clattered from under his feet and went bouncing down the hill, resonant drops of sound rolling in the sunny clarity of the summer air.

He stood on the summit, his legs planted wide apart, leaning back against space. He looked at the materials before him, the knobs of rivets in steel, the sparks in blocks of stone, the weaving spirals in fresh, yellow planks.

Then he saw a husky figure enmeshed in electric wires, a bulldog face spreading into a huge grin and china-blue eyes gloating in a kind of unholy triumph.

"Mike!" he said incredulously.

THE FOUNTAINHEAD • 130

Mike had left for a big job in Philadelphia months ago, long before the appearance of Heller in Snyte's office, and Mike had never heard the news—or so he supposed.

"Hello, Red," said Mike, much too casually, and added: "Hello, boss."

"Mike, how did you . . . ?"

"You're a hell of an architect. Neglecting the job like that. It's my third day here, waiting for you to show up."

"Mike, how did you get here? Why such a come-down?" He had never known Mike to bother with small private residences.

"Don't play the sap. You know how I got here. You didn't think I'd miss it, your first house, did you? And you think it's a come-down? Well, maybe it is. And maybe it's the other way around."

Roark extended his hand and Mike's grimy fingers closed about it ferociously, as if the smudges he left implanted in Roark's skin said everything he wanted to say. And because he was afraid that he might say it, Mike growled:

"Run along, boss, run along. Don't clog up the works like that."

Roark walked through the house. There were moments when he could be precise, impersonal, and stop to give instructions as if this were not his house but only a mathematical problem; when he felt the existence of pipes and rivets, while his own person vanished.

There were moments when something rose within him, not a thought nor a feeling, but a wave of some physical violence, and then he wanted to stop, to lean back, to feel the reality of his person heightened by the frame of steel that rose dimly about the bright, outstanding existence of his body as its center. He did not stop. He went on calmly. But his hands betrayed what he wanted to hide. His hands reached out, ran slowly down the beams and joints. The workers in the house had noticed it. They said: "That guy's in love with the thing. He can't keep his hands off."

The workers liked him. The contractor's superintendents did not. He had had trouble in finding a contractor to erect the house. Several of the better firms had refused the commission. "We don't do that kinda stuff." "Nah, we won't bother. Too complicated for a small job like that." "Who the hell wants that kind of a house? Most likely we'll never collect from the crank afterwards. To hell with it." "Never did anything like it. Wouldn't know how to go about it. I'll stick to construction that is construction." One contractor had looked at the plans briefly and thrown them aside, declaring with finality: "It won't stand." "It will," said Roark. The contractor drawled indifferently. "Yeah? And who are you to tell me, Mister?"

He had found a small firm that needed the work and undertook it, charging more than the job warranted—on the ground of the chance they were taking with a queer experiment. The construction went on, and the foremen obeyed sullenly, in disapproving silence, as if they were waiting for their predictions to come true and would be glad when the house collapsed about their heads.

Roark had bought an old Ford and drove down to the job more often than was necessary. It was difficult to sit at a desk in his office, to stand at a table, forcing himself to stay away from the construction site. At the site there were moments when he wished to forget his office and his drawing board, to seize the men's tools and go to work on the actual erection of the house, as he had worked in his childhood, to build that house with his own hands.

He walked through the structure, stepping lightly over piles of planks and coils of wire, he made notes, he gave brief orders in a harsh voice. He avoided looking in Mike's direction. But Mike was watching him, following his progress through the house. Mike winked at him in understanding, whenever he passed by. Mike said once:

"Control yourself, Red. You're open like a book. God, it's indecent to be so happy!"

Roark stood on the cliff, by the structure, and looked at the countryside, at the long, gray ribbon of the road twisting past along the shore. An open car drove by, fleeing into the country. The car was overfilled with people bound for a picnic. There was a jumble of bright sweaters, and scarfs fluttering in the wind; a jumble of voices shrieking without purpose over the roar of the motor, and overstressed hiccoughs of laughter; a girl sat sidewise, her legs flung over the side of the car; she wore a man's straw hat slipping down to her nose and she yanked savagely at the strings of a ukelele, ejecting raucous sounds, yelling "Hey!" These people were enjoying a day of their existence; they were shrieking to the sky their release from the work and the burdens of the days behind them; they had worked and carried the burdens in order to reach a goal—and this was the goal.

He looked at the car as it streaked past. He thought that there was a difference, some important difference, between the consciousness of this day in him and in them. He thought that he should try to grasp it. But he forgot. He was looking at a truck panting up the hill, loaded with a glittering mound of cut granite.

Austen Heller came to look at the house frequently, and watched it grow, curious, still a little astonished. He studied Roark and the house with the same meticulous scrutiny; he felt as if he could not quite tell them apart.

Heller, the fighter against compulsion, was baffled by Roark, a man so impervious to compulsion that he became a kind of compulsion himself, an ultimatum against things Heller could not define. Within a week, Heller knew that he had found the best friend he would ever have; and he knew that the friendship came from Roark's fundamental indifference. In the deeper reality of Roark's existence there was no consciousness of Heller, no need for Heller, no appeal, no demand. Heller felt a line drawn, which he could not touch; beyond that line, Roark asked nothing of him and granted him nothing. But when Roark looked at him with approval, when Roark smiled, when Roark praised one of his articles, Heller felt the strangely clean joy of a sanction that was neither a bribe nor alms.

In the summer evenings they sat together on a ledge halfway up the hill, and talked while darkness mounted slowly up the beams of the house above them, the last sunrays retreating to the tips of the steel uprights.

"What is it that I like so much about the house you're building for me, Howard?"

"A house can have integrity, just like a person," said Roark, "and just as seldom."

"In what way?"

"Well, look at it. Every piece of it is there because the house needs it—and for no other reason. You see it from here as it is inside. The rooms in which you'll live made the shape. The relation of masses was determined by the distribution of space within. The ornament was determined by the method of construction, an emphasis of the principle that makes it stand. You can see each stress, each support that meets it. Your own eyes go through a structural process when you look at the house, you can follow each step, you see it rise, you know what made it and why it stands. But you've seen buildings with columns that support nothing, with purposeless cornices, with pilasters, mouldings, false arches, false windows. You've seen buildings that look as if they contained a single large hall, they have solid columns and single, solid windows six floors high. But you enter and find six stories inside. Or buildings that contain a single hall, but with a façade cut up into floor lines, band courses, tiers of windows. Do you understand the difference? Your house is made by its own needs. Those others are made by the need to impress. The determining motive of your house is in the house. The determining motive of the other is in the audience."

"Do you know that that's what I've felt in a way? I've felt that when I move into this house, I'll have a new sort of existence, and even my simple daily routine will have a kind of honesty or dignity that I can't quite define. Don't be astonished if I tell you that I feel as if I'll have to live up to that house."

"I intended that," said Roark.

"And, incidentally, thank you for all the thought you seem to have taken about my comfort. There are so many things I notice that had never occurred to me before, but you've planned them as if you knew all my needs. For instance, my study is the room I'll need most and you've given it the dominant spot—and, incidentally, I see where you've made it the dominant mass from the outside, too. And then the way it connects with the library, and the living room well out of my way, and the guest rooms where I won't hear too much of them—and all that. You were very considerate of me."

"You know," said Roark, "I haven't thought of you at all. I thought of the house." He added: "Perhaps that's why I knew how to be considerate of you."

The Heller house was completed in November of 1926.

In January of 1927 the *Architectural Tribune* published a survey of the best American homes erected during the past year. It devoted twelve large, glossy pages to photographs of the twenty-four houses its editors had selected as the worthiest architectural achievements. The Heller house was not mentioned.

The real-estate sections of the New York papers presented, each Sunday, brief accounts of the notable new residences in the vicinity. There was no account of the Heller house.

The year book of the Architects' Guild of America, which presented magnificent reproductions of what it chose as the best buildings of the country, under the title "Looking Forward," gave no reference to the Heller house.

There were many occasions when lecturers rose to platforms and addressed trim audiences on the subject of the progress of American architecture. No one spoke of the Heller house.

In the club rooms of the A.G.A. some opinions were expressed.

"It's a disgrace to the country," said Ralston Holcombe, "that a thing like that Heller house is allowed to be erected. It's a blot on the profession. There ought to be a law."

"That's what drives clients away," said John Erik Snyte. "They see a house like that and they think all architects are crazy."

"I see no cause for indignation," said Gordon L. Prescott. "I think it's screamingly funny. It looks like a cross between a filling station and a comic-strip idea of a rocket ship to the moon."

"You watch it in a couple of years," said Eugene Pettingill, "and see what happens. The thing'll collapse like a house of cards."

"Why speak in terms of years?" said Guy Francon. "Those modernistic stunts never last more than a season. The owner will get good and sick of it and he'll come running home to a good old early Colonial."

The Heller house acquired fame throughout the countryside surrounding it. People drove out of their way to park on the road before it, to stare, point and giggle. Gas-station attendants snickered when Heller's car drove past. Heller's cook had to endure the derisive glances of shopkeepers when she went on her errands. The Heller house was known in the neighborhood as "The Booby Hatch."

Peter Keating told his friends in the profession, with an indulgent smile: "Now, now, you shouldn't say that about him. I've known Howard Roark for a long time, and he's got quite a talent, quite. He's even worked for me once. He's just gone haywire on that house. He'll learn. He has a future. . . . Oh, you don't think he has? You really don't think he has?"

Ellsworth M. Toohey, who let no stone spring from the ground of America without his comment, did not know that the Heller house had been erected, as far as his column was concerned. He did not consider it necessary to inform his readers about it, if only to damn it. He said nothing.

XII

A COLUMN ENTITLED "OBSERVATIONS AND MEDITATIONS" BY ALVAH
Scarret appeared daily on the front page of the New York
Banner. It was a trusted guide, a source of inspiration and a molder of
public philosophy in small towns throughout the country. In this column
there had appeared, years ago, the famous statement: "We'd all be a
heap sight better off if we'd forget the highfalutin notions of our fancy
civilization and mind more what the savages knew long before us: to
honor our mother." Alvah Scarret was a bachelor, had made two million
dollars, played golf expertly and was editor-in-chief of the Wynand
papers.

It was Alvah Scarret who conceived the idea of the campaign against
living conditions in the slums and "Landlord Sharks," which ran in the
Banner for three weeks. This was material such as Alvah Scarret rel-
ished. It had human appeal and social implications. It lent itself to
Sunday-supplement illustrations of girls leaping into rivers, their skirts
flaring well above their knees. It boosted circulation. It embarrassed the
sharks who owned a stretch of blocks by the East River, selected as the
dire example of the campaign. The sharks had refused to sell these
blocks to an obscure real-estate company; at the end of the campaign
they surrendered and sold. No one could prove that the real-estate company was owned by a company owned by Gail Wynand.

The Wynand papers could not be left without a campaign for long.
They had just concluded one on the subject of modern aviation. They
had run scientific accounts of the history of aviation in the Sunday
Family Magazine supplement, with pictures ranging from Leonardo da
Vinci's drawings of flying machines to the latest bomber; with the added
attraction of Icarus writhing in scarlet flames, his nude body blue-green,
his wax wings yellow and the smoke purple; also of a leprous hag with
flaming eyes and a crystal ball, who had predicted in the XIth century
that man would fly; also of bats, vampires and werewolves.

They had run a model plane construction contest; it was open to all
boys under the age of ten who wished to send in three new subscriptions
to the *Banner*. Gail Wynand, who was a licensed pilot, had made a solo
flight from Los Angeles to New York, establishing a transcontinental
speed record, in a small, specially built craft costing one hundred thousand dollars. He had made a slight miscalculation on reaching New
York and had been forced to land in a rocky pasture; it had been a hair-
raising landing, faultlessly executed; it had just so happened that a

135

battery of photographers from the *Banner* were present in the neighborhood. Gail Wynand had stepped out of the plane. An ace pilot would have been shaken by the experience. Gail Wynand had stood before the cameras, an immaculate gardenia in the lapel of his flying jacket, his hand raised with a cigarette held between two fingers that did not tremble. When questioned about his first wish on returning to earth, he had expressed the desire to kiss the most attractive woman present, had chosen the dowdiest old hag from the crowd and bent to kiss her gravely on the forehead, explaining that she reminded him of his mother.

Later, at the start of the slum campaign, Gail Wynand had said to Alvah Scarret: "Go ahead. Squeeze all you can out of the thing," and had departed on his yacht for a world cruise, accompanied by an enchanting aviatrix of twenty-four to whom he had made a present of his transcontinental plane.

Alvah Scarret went ahead. Among many other steps of his campaign he assigned Dominique Francon to investigate the condition of homes in the slums and to gather human material. Dominique Francon had just returned from a summer in Biarritz; she always took a whole summer's vacation and Alvah Scarret granted it, because she was one of his favorite employees, because he was baffled by her and because he knew that she could quit her job whenever she pleased.

Dominique Francon went to live for two weeks in the hall bedroom of an East-Side tenement. The room had a skylight, but no windows; there were five flights of stairs to climb and no running water. She cooked her own meals in the kitchen of a numerous family on the floor below; she visited neighbors, she sat on the landings of fire escapes in the evenings and went to dime movies with the girls of the neighborhood.

She wore frayed skirts and blouses. The abnormal fragility of her normal appearance made her look exhausted with privation in these surroundings; the neighbors felt certain that she had T.B. But she moved as she had moved in the drawing room of Kiki Holcombe—with the same cold poise and confidence. She scrubbed the floor of her room, she peeled potatoes, she bathed in a tin pan of cold water. She had never done these things before; she did them expertly. She had a capacity for action, a competence that clashed incongruously with her appearance. She did not mind this new background; she was indifferent to the slums as she had been indifferent to the drawing rooms.

At the end of two weeks she returned to her penthouse apartment on the roof of a hotel over Central Park, and her articles on life in the slums appeared in the *Banner*. They were a merciless, brilliant account.

She heard baffled questions at a dinner party. "My dear, you didn't actually write those things?" "Dominique, you didn't really live in that place?" "Oh, yes," she answered. "The house you own on East Twelfth Street, Mrs. Palmer," she said, her hand circling lazily from under the cuff of an emerald bracelet too broad and heavy for her thin wrist, "has a sewer that gets clogged every other day and runs over, all through the courtyard. It looks blue and purple in the sun, like a rainbow." "The block you control for the Claridge estate, Mr. Brooks, has the most attractive stalactites growing on all the ceilings," she said, her golden head leaning to her corsage of white gardenias with drops of water sparkling on the lusterless petals.

She was asked to speak at a meeting of social workers. It was an important meeting, with a militant, radical mood, led by some of the most prominent women in the field. Alvah Scarret was pleased and gave her his blessing. "Go to it, kid," he said, "lay it on thick. We want the social workers." She stood in the speaker's pulpit of an unaired hall and looked at a flat sheet of faces, faces lecherously eager with the sense of their own virtue. She spoke evenly, without inflection. She said, among many other things: "The family on the first floor rear do not bother to pay their rent, and the children cannot go to school for lack of clothes. The father has a charge account at a corner speak-easy. He is in good health and has a good job. . . . The couple on the second floor have just purchased a radio for sixty-nine dollars and ninety-five cents cash. In the fourth-floor front, the father of the family has not done a whole day's work in his life, and does not intend to. There are nine children, supported by the local parish. There is a tenth one on its way. . . ." When she finished there were a few claps of angry applause. She raised her hand and said: "You don't have to applaud. I don't expect it." She asked politely: "Are there any questions?" There were no questions.

When she returned home she found Alvah Scarret waiting for her. He looked incongruous in the drawing room of her penthouse, his huge bulk perched on the edge of a delicate chair, a hunched gargoyle against the glowing spread of the city beyond a solid wall of glass. The city was like a mural designed to illuminate and complete the room: the fragile lines of spires on a black sky continued the fragile lines of the furniture; the lights glittering in distant windows threw reflections on the bare, lustrous floor; the cold precision of the angular structures outside answered the cold, inflexible grace of every object within. Alvah Scarret broke the harmony. He looked like a kindly country doctor and like a cardsharp. His heavy face bore the benevolent, paternal smile that had always been his passkey and his trademark. He had the knack of making the kindliness of his smile add to, not detract from his solemn appearance of dignity; his long, thin, hooked nose did detract from the kindliness, but it added to the dignity; his stomach, cantilevered over his legs, did detract from the dignity, but it added to the kindliness.

He rose, beamed and held Dominique's hand.

"Thought I'd drop in on my way home," he said. "I've got something to tell you. How did it go, kid?"

"As I expected it."

She tore her hat off and threw it down on the first chair in sight. Her hair slanted in a flat curve across her forehead and fell in a straight line to her shoulders; it looked smooth and tight, like a bathing cap of pale, polished metal. She walked to the window and stood looking out over the city. She asked without turning: "What did you want to tell me?"

Alvah Scarret watched her pleasurably. He had long since given up any attempts beyond holding her hand when not necessary or patting her shoulder; he had stopped thinking of the subject, but he had a dim, half-conscious feeling which he summed up to himself in the words: You never can tell.

"I've got good news for you, child," he said. "I've been working out a little scheme, just a bit of reorganization, and I've figured where I'll consolidate a few things together into a Women's Welfare Department. You know, the schools, the home economics, the care of babies, the juvenile delinquents and all the rest of it—all to be under one head. And I see no better woman for the job than my little girl."

"Do you mean me?" she asked, without turning.

"No one else but. Just as soon as Gail comes back, I'll get his okay."

She turned and looked at him, her arms crossed, her hands holding her elbows. She said:

"Thank you, Alvah. But I don't want it."

"What do you mean, you don't want it?"

"I mean that I don't want it."

"For heaven's sake, do you realize what an advance that would be?"

"Toward what?"

"Your career."

"I never said I was planning a career."

"But you don't want to be running a dinky back-page column forever!"

"Not forever. Until I get bored with it."

"But think of what you could do in the real game! Think of what Gail could do for you once you come to his attention!"

"I have no desire to come to his attention."

"But, Dominique, we need you. The women will be for you solid after tonight."

"I don't think so."

"Why, I've ordered two columns held for a yarn on the meeting and your speech."

She reached for the telephone and handed the receiver to him. She said:

"You'd better tell them to kill it."

"Why?"

She searched through a litter of papers on a desk, found some type-written sheets and handed them to him. "Here's the speech I made tonight," she said.

He glanced through it. He said nothing, but clasped his forehead once. Then he seized the telephone and gave orders to run as brief an account of the meeting as possible, and not to mention the speaker by name.

"All right," said Dominique, when he dropped the receiver. "Am I fired?"

He shook his head dolefully. "Do you want to be?"

"Not necessarily."

"I'll squash the business," he muttered. "I'll keep it from Gail."

"If you wish. I really don't care one way or the other."

"Listen, Dominque—oh I know, I'm not to ask any questions—only why on earth are you always doing things like that?"

"For no reason on earth."

"Look, you know, I've heard about that swank dinner where you made certain remarks on this same subject. And then you go and say things like these at a radical meeting."

"They're true, though, both sides of it, aren't they?"

"Oh, sure, but couldn't you have reversed the occasions when you chose to express them?"

"There wouldn't have been any point in that."

"Was there any in what you've done?"

"No. None at all. But it amused me."

"I can't figure you out, Dominique. You've done it before. You go along so beautifully, you do brilliant work and just when you're about to make a real step forward—you spoil it by pulling something like this. Why?"

"Perhaps that is precisely why."

"Will you tell me—as a friend, because I like you and I'm interested in you—what are you really after?"

"I should think that's obvious. I'm after nothing at all."

He spread his hands open, shrugging helplessly.

She smiled gaily.

"What is there to look so mournful about? I like you, too, Alvah, and I'm interested in you. I even like to talk to you, which is better. Now sit still and relax and I'll get you a drink. You need a drink, Alvah."

She brought him a frosted glass with ice cubes ringing in the silence. "You're just a nice child, Dominique," he said.

"Of course. That's what I am."

She sat down on the edge of a table, her hands flat behind her, leaning back on two straight arms, swinging her legs slowly. She said:

"You know, Alvah, it would be terrible if I had a job I really wanted."

"Well, of all things! Well, of all fool things to say! What do you mean?"

"Just that. That it would be terrible to have a job I enjoyed and did not want to lose."

"Why?"

"Because I would have to depend on you—you're a wonderful person, Alvah, but not exactly inspiring and I don't think it would be beautiful to cringe before a whip in your hand—oh, don't protest, it would be such a polite little whip, and that's what would make it uglier. I would have to depend on our boss Gail—he's a great man, I'm sure, only I'd just as soon never set eyes on him."

"Whatever gives you such a crazy attitude? When you know that Gail and I would do anything for you, and I personally . . ."

"It's not only that, Alvah. It's not you alone. If I found a job, a project, an idea or a person I wanted—I'd have to depend on the whole world. Everything has strings leading to everything else. We're all so tied together. We're all in a net, the net is waiting, and we're pushed into it by one single desire. You want a thing and it's precious to you. Do you know who is standing ready to tear it out of your hands? You can't know, it may be so involved and so far away, but someone is ready, and you're afraid of them all. And you cringe and you crawl and you beg and you accept them—just so they'll let you keep it. And look at whom you come to accept."

"If I'm correct in gathering that you're criticizing mankind in general . . ."

"You know, it's such a peculiar thing—our idea of mankind in general. We all have a sort of vague, glowing picture when we say that, something solemn, big and important. But actually all we know of it is the people we meet in our lifetime. Look at them. Do you know any you'd feel big and solemn about? There's nothing but housewives haggling at pushcarts, drooling brats who write dirty words on the sidewalks, and drunken debutantes. Or their spiritual equivalents. As a matter of fact, one can feel some respect for people when they suffer. They have a certain dignity. But have you ever looked at them when they're enjoying themselves? That's when you see the truth. Look at those who spend the money they've slaved for—at amusement parks and side shows.

Look at those who're rich and have the whole world open to them. Observe what they pick out for enjoyment. Watch them in the smarter speak-easies. That's your mankind in general. I don't want to touch it."

"But hell! That's not the way to look at it. That's not the whole picture. There's some good in the worst of us. There's always a redeeming feature."

"So much the worse. Is it an inspiring sight to see a man commit a heroic gesture, and then learn that he goes to vaudeville shows for relaxation? Or see a man who's painted a magnificent canvas—and learn that he spends his time sleeping with every slut he meets?"

"What do you want? Perfection?"

"—or nothing. So, you see, I take the nothing."

"That doesn't make sense."

"I take the only desire one can really permit oneself. Freedom, Alvah, freedom."

"You call that freedom?"

"To ask nothing. To expect nothing. To depend on nothing."

"What if you found something you wanted?"

"I won't find it. I won't choose to see it. It would be part of that lovely world of yours. I'd have to share it with all the rest of you—and I wouldn't. You know, I never open again any great book I've read and loved. It hurts me to think of the other eyes that have read it and of what they were. Things like that can't be shared. Not with people like that."

"Dominique, it's abnormal to feel so strongly about anything."

"That's the only way I can feel. Or not at all."

"Dominique, my dear," he said, with earnest, sincere concern, "I wish I'd been your father. What kind of a tragedy did you have in your childhood?"

"Why, none at all. I had a wonderful childhood. Free and peaceful and not bothered too much by anybody. Well, yes, I did feel bored very often. But I'm used to that."

"I suppose you're just an unfortunate product of our times. That's what I've always said. We're too cynical, too decadent. If we went back in all humility to the simple virtues . . ."

"Alvah, how can you start on that stuff? That's only for your editorials and . . ." She stopped, seeing his eyes; they looked puzzled and a little hurt. Then she laughed. "I'm wrong. You really do believe all that. If it's actually believing, or whatever it is you do that takes its place. Oh, Alvah! That's why I love you. That's why I'm doing again right now what I did tonight at the meeting."

"What?" he asked, bewildered.

"Talking as I am talking—to you as you are. It's nice, talking to you about such things. Do you know, Alvah, that primitive people made statues of their gods in man's likeness? Just think of what a statue of you would look like—of you nude, your stomach and all."

"Now what's that in relation to?"

"To nothing at all, darling. Forgive me." She added: "You know, I love statues of naked men. Don't look so silly. I said statues. I had one in particular. It was supposed to be Helios. I got it out of a museum in Europe. I had a terrible time getting it—it wasn't for sale, of course. I think I was in love with it, Alvah. I brought it home with me."

"Where is it? I'd like to see something you like, for a change."

"It's broken."

"Broken? A museum piece? How did that happen?"

"I broke it."

"How?"

"I threw it down the air shaft. There's a concrete floor below."

"Are you totally crazy? Why?"

"So that no one else would ever see it."

"Dominique!"

She jerked her head, as if to shake off the subject; the straight mass of her hair stirred in a heavy ripple, like a wave through a half-liquid pool of mercury. She said:

"I'm sorry, darling. I didn't want to shock you. I thought I could speak to you because you're the one person who's impervious to any sort of shock. I shouldn't have. It's no use, I guess."

She jumped lightly off the table.

"Run on home, Alvah," she said. "It's getting late. I'm tired. See you tomorrow."

Guy Francon read his daughter's articles; he heard of the remarks she had made at the reception and at the meeting of social workers. He understood nothing of it, but he understood that it had been precisely the sequence of events to expect from his daughter. It preyed on his mind, with the bewildered feeling of apprehension which the thought of her always brought him. He asked himself whether he actually hated his daughter.

But one picture came back to his mind, irrelevantly, whenever he asked himself that question. It was a picture of her childhood, of a day from some forgotten summer on his country estate in Connecticut long ago. He had forgotten the rest of that day and what had led to the one moment he remembered. But he remembered how he stood on the terrace and saw her leaping over a high green hedge at the end of the lawn. The hedge seemed too high for her little body; he had time to think that she could not make it, in the very moment when he saw her flying triumphantly over the green barrier. He could not remember the beginning nor the end of that leap; but he still saw, clearly and sharply, as on a square of movie film cut out and held motionless forever, the one instant when her body hung in space, her long legs flung wide, her thin arms thrown up, hands braced against the air, her white dress and blond hair spread in two broad, flat mats on the wind, a single moment, the flash of a small body in the greatest burst of ecstatic freedom he had ever witnessed in his life.

He did not know why that moment remained with him, what significance, unheeded at the time, had preserved it for him when so much else of greater import had been lost. He did not know why he had to see that moment again whenever he felt bitterness for his daughter, nor why, seeing it, he felt that unbearable twinge of tenderness. He told himself merely that his paternal affection was asserting itself quite against his will. But in an awkward, unthinking way he wanted to help her, not knowing, not wanting to know what she had to be helped against.

So he began to look more frequently at Peter Keating. He began to accept the solution which he never quite admitted to himself. He found comfort in the person of Peter Keating, and he felt that Keating's simple, stable wholesomeness was just the support needed by the unhealthy inconstancy of his daughter.

Keating would not admit that he had tried to see Dominique again, persistently and without results. He had obtained her telephone number from Francon long ago, and he had called her often. She had answered, and laughed gaily, and told him that of course she'd see him, she knew she wouldn't be able to escape it, but she was so busy for weeks to come and would he give her a ring by the first of next month?

Francon guessed it. He told Keating he would ask Dominique to lunch and bring them together again. "That is," he added, "I'll try to ask her. She'll refuse, of course." Dominique surprised him again: she accepted, promptly and cheerfully.

She met them at a restaurant, and she smiled as if this were a reunion she welcomed. She talked gaily, and Keating felt enchanted, at ease, wondering why he had ever feared her. At the end of a half hour she looked at Francon and said:

"It was wonderful of you to take time off to see me, Father. Particularly when you're so busy and have so many appointments."

Francon's face assumed a look of consternation.

"My God, Dominique, that reminds me!"

"You have an appointment you forgot?" she asked gently.

"Confound it, yes! It slipped my mind entirely. Old Andrew Colson phoned this morning and I forgot to make a note of it and he insisted on seeing me at two o'clock, you know how it is, I just simply can't refuse to see Andrew Colson, confound it!—today of all . . ." He added, suspiciously: "How did you know it?"

"Why, I didn't know it at all. It's perfectly all right, Father. Mr. Keating and I will excuse you, and we'll have a lovely luncheon together, and I have no appointments at all for the day, so you don't have to be afraid that I'll escape from him."

Francon wondered whether she knew that that had been the excuse he'd prepared in advance in order to leave her alone with Keating. He could not be sure. She was looking straight at him; her eyes seemed just a bit too candid. He was glad to escape.

Dominique turned to Keating with a glance so gentle that it could mean nothing but contempt.

"Now let's relax," she said. "We both know what Father is after, so it's perfectly all right. Don't let it embarrass you. It doesn't embarrass me. It's nice that you've got Father on a leash. But I know it's not helpful to you to have him pulling ahead of the leash. So let's forget it and eat our lunch."

He wanted to rise and walk out; and knew, in furious helplessness, that he wouldn't. She said:

"Don't frown, Peter. You might as well call me Dominique, because we'll come to that anyway, sooner or later. I'll probably see a great deal of you, I see so many people, and if it will please Father to have you as one of them—why not?"

For the rest of the luncheon she spoke to him as to an old friend, gaily and openly; with a disquieting candor which seemed to show that there was nothing to conceal, but showed that it was best to attempt no probe. The exquisite kindliness of her manner suggested that their relationship was of no possible consequence, that she could not pay him the tribute of hostility. He knew that he disliked her violently. But he watched the shape of her mouth, the movements of her lips framing words; he watched the way she crossed her legs, a gesture smooth and exact, like an expensive instrument being folded; and he could not escape the feeling of incredulous admiration he had experienced when he had seen her for the first time.

When they were leaving, she said:

"Will you take me to the theater tonight, Peter? I don't care what play, any one of them. Call for me after dinner. Tell Father about it. It will please him."

"Though, of course, he should know better than to be pleased," said Keating, "and so should I, but I'll be delighted just the same, Dominique."

"Why should you know better?"

"Because you have no desire to go to a theater or to see me tonight."

"None whatever. I'm beginning to like you, Peter. Call for me at half past eight."

When Keating returned to the office, Francon called him upstairs at once.

"Well?" Francon asked anxiously.

"What's the matter, Guy?" said Keating, his voice innocent. "Why are you so concerned?"

"Well, I . . . I'm just . . . frankly, I'm interested to see whether you two could get together at all. I think you'd be a good influence for her. What happened?"

"Nothing at all. We had a lovely time. You know your restaurants—the food was wonderful . . . Oh, yes, I'm taking your daughter to a show tonight."

"No!"

"Why, yes."

"How did you ever manage that?"

Keating shrugged. "I told you one mustn't be afraid of Dominique."

"I'm not afraid, but . . . Oh, is it 'Dominique' already? My congratulations, Peter. . . . I'm not afraid, it's only that I can't figure her out. No one can approach her. She's never had a single girl friend, not even in kindergarten. There's always a mob around her, but never a friend. I don't know what to think. There she is now, living all alone, always with a crowd of men around and . . ."

"Now, Guy, you mustn't think anything dishonorable about your own daughter."

"I don't! That's just the trouble—that I don't. I wish I could. But she's twenty-four, Peter, and she's a virgin—I know, I'm sure of it. Can't you tell just by looking at a woman? I'm no moralist, Peter, and I think that's abnormal. It's unnatural at her age, with her looks, with the kind of utterly unrestricted existence that she leads. I wish to God she'd get married. I honestly do. . . . Well, now, don't repeat that, of course, and don't misinterpret it, I didn't mean it as an invitation."

"Of course not."

"By the way, Peter, the hospital called while you were out. They said poor Lucius is much better. They think he'll pull through." Lucius N. Heyer had had a stroke, and Keating had exhibited a great deal of concern for his progress, but had not gone to visit him at the hospital.

"I'm so glad," said Keating.

"But I don't think he'll ever be able to come back to work. He's getting old, Peter. . . . Yes, he's getting old. . . . One reaches an age when one can't be burdened with business any longer." He let a paper knife hang between two fingers and tapped it pensively against the edge of a desk calendar. "It happens to all of us, Peter, sooner or later. . . . One must look ahead. . . ."

Keating sat on the floor by the imitation logs in the fireplace of his living room, his hands clasped about his knees, and listened to his mother's questions on what did Dominique look like, what did she wear, what had she said to him and how much money did he suppose her mother had actually left her.

He was meeting Dominique frequently now. He had just returned from an evening spent with her on a round of night clubs. She always accepted his invitations. He wondered whether her attitude was deliberate proof that she could ignore him more completely by seeing him often than by refusing to see him. But each time he met her, he planned eagerly for the next meeting. He had not seen Catherine for a month. She was busy with research work which her uncle had entrusted to her, in preparation for a series of his lectures.

Mrs. Keating sat under a lamp, mending a slight tear in the lining of Peter's dinner jacket, reproaching him, between questions, for sitting on the floor in his dress trousers and best formal shirt. He paid no attention to the reproaches or the questions. But under his bored annoyance he felt an odd sense of relief; as if the stubborn stream of her words were pushing him on and justifying him. He answered once in a while: "Yes. . . . No. . . . I don't know. . . . Oh, yes, she's lovely. She's very lovely. . . . It's awfully late, Mother. I'm tired. I think I'll go to bed. . . ."

The doorbell rang.

"Well," said Mrs. Keating. "What can that be, at this hour?"

Keating rose, shrugging, and ambled to the door.

It was Catherine. She stood, her two hands clasped on a large, old, shapeless pocketbook. She looked determined and hesitant at once. She drew back a little. She said: "Good evening, Peter. Can I come in? I've got to speak to you."

"Katie! Of course! How nice of you! Come right in. Mother, it's Katie."

Mrs. Keating looked at the girl's feet which stepped as if moving on the rolling deck of a ship; she looked at her son, and she knew that something had happened, to be handled with great caution.

"Good evening, Catherine," she said softly.

Keating was conscious of nothing save the sudden stab of joy he had felt on seeing her; the joy told him that nothing had changed, that he was safe in certainty, that her presence resolved all doubts. He forgot to wonder about the lateness of the hour, about her first, uninvited appearance in his apartment.

"Good evening, Mrs. Keating," she said, her voice bright and hollow. "I hope I'm not disturbing you, it's late probably, is it?"

"Why, not at all, child," said Mrs. Keating.

Catherine hurried to speak, senselessly, hanging on to the sound of words:

"I'll just take my hat off. . . . Where can I put it, Mrs. Keating? Here on the table? Would that be all right? . . . No, maybe I'd better put it on this bureau, though it's a little damp from the street, the hat is, it might hurt the varnish, it's a nice bureau, I hope it doesn't hurt the varnish. . . ."

"What's the matter, Katie?" Keating asked, noticing at last.

She looked at him and he saw that her eyes were terrified. Her lips parted; she was trying to smile.

"Katie!" he gasped.

She said nothing.

"Take your coat off. Come here, get yourself warm by the fire."

He pushed a low bench to the fireplace, he made her sit down. She was wearing a black sweater and an old black skirt, schoolgirlish house garments which she had not changed for her visit. She sat hunched, her knees drawn tight together. She said, her voice lower and more natural, with the first released sound of pain in it:

"You have such a nice place. . . . So warm and roomy. . . . Can you open the windows any time you want to?"

"Katie darling," he said gently, "what happened?"

"Nothing. It's not that anything really happened. Only I had to speak to you. Now. Tonight."

He looked at Mrs. Keating. "If you'd rather . . ."

"No. It's perfectly all right. Mrs. Keating can hear it. Maybe it's better if she hears it." She turned to his mother and said very simply: "You see, Mrs. Keating, Peter and I are engaged." She turned to him and added, her voice breaking: "Peter, I want to be married now, tomorrow, as soon as possible."

Mrs. Keating's hand descended slowly to her lap. She looked at Catherine, her eyes expressionless. She said quietly, with a dignity Keating had never expected of her:

"I didn't know it. I am very happy, my dear."

"You don't mind? You really don't mind at all?" Catherine asked desperately.

"Why, child, such things are to be decided only by you and my son."

"Katie!" he gasped, regaining his voice. "What happened? Why as soon as possible?"

"Oh! oh, it did sound as if . . . as if I were in the kind of trouble girls are supposed to . . ." She blushed furiously. "Oh, my God! No! It's not that! You know it couldn't be! Oh, you couldn't think, Peter, that I . . . that . . ."

"No, of course not," he laughed, sitting down on the floor by her side, slipping an arm around her. "But pull yourself together. What is it? You know I'd marry you tonight if you wanted me to. Only what happened?"

"Nothing. I'm all right now. I'll tell you. You'll think I'm crazy. I just suddenly had the feeling that I'd never marry you, that something dreadful was happening to me and I had to escape from it."

"What was happening to you?"

"I don't know. Not a thing. I was working on my research notes all day, and nothing had happened at all. No calls or visitors. And then suddenly tonight, I had that feeling, it was like a nightmare, you know, the kind of horror that you can't describe, that's not like anything normal at all. Just the feeling that I was in mortal danger, that something was closing in on me, that I'd never escape it, because it wouldn't let me and it was too late."

"That you'd never escape what?"

"I don't know exactly. Everything. My whole life. You know, like quicksand. Smooth and natural. With not a thing that you can notice about it or suspect. And you walk on it easily. When you've noticed, it's too late. . . . And I felt that it would get me, that I'd never marry you, that I had to run, now, now or never. Haven't you ever had a feeling like that, just fear that you couldn't explain?"

"Yes," he whispered.

"You don't think I'm crazy?"

"No, Katie. Only what was it exactly that started it? Anything in particular?"

"Well . . . it seems so silly now." She giggled apologetically. "It was like this: I was sitting in my room and it was a little chilly, so I didn't open the window. I had so many papers and books on the table, I hardly had room to write and every time I made a note my elbow'd push something off. There were piles of things on the floor all around me, all paper, and it rustled a little, because I had the door to the living room half open and there was a little draft, I guess. Uncle was working too, in the living room. I was getting along fine, I'd been at it for hours, didn't even know what time it was. And then suddenly it got me. I don't know why. Maybe the room was stuffy, or maybe it was the silence. I couldn't hear a thing, not a sound in the living room, and there was that paper rustling, so softly, like somebody being choked to death. And then I looked around and . . . and I couldn't see Uncle in the living room, but I saw his shadow on the wall, a huge shadow, all hunched, and it didn't move, only it was so huge!"

She shuddered. The thing did not seem silly to her any longer. She whispered:

"That's when it got me. It wouldn't move, that shadow, but I thought all that paper was moving, I thought it was rising very slowly off the floor, and it was going to come to my throat and I was going to drown. That's when I screamed. And, Peter, he didn't hear. He didn't hear it! Because the shadow didn't move. Then I seized my hat and coat and I ran. When I was running through the living room, I think he said: 'Why, Catherine, what time is it?—Where are you going?' Something like that, I'm not sure. But I didn't look back and I didn't answer—I couldn't. I was afraid of him. Afraid of Uncle Ellsworth who's never said a harsh word to me in his life! . . . That was all, Peter. I can't understand it, but I'm afraid. Not so much any more, not here with you, but I'm afraid. . . ."

Mrs. Keating spoke, her voice dry and crisp:

"Why, it's plain what happened to you, my dear. You worked too hard and overdid it, and you just got a mite hysterical."

"Yes . . . probably . . ."

"No," said Keating dully, "no, it wasn't that. . . ." He was thinking of the loud-speaker in the lobby of the strike meeting. Then he added quickly: "Yes, Mother's right. You're killing yourself with work, Katie. That uncle of yours—I'll wring his neck one of these days."

"Oh, but it's not his fault! He doesn't want me to work. He often takes the books away from me and tells me to go to the movies. He's said that himself, that I work too hard. But I like it. I think that every note I make, every little bit of information—it's going to be taught to hundreds of young students, all over the country, and I think it's me who's helping to educate people, just my own little bit in such a big cause—and I feel proud and I don't want to stop. You see? I've really got nothing to complain about. And then . . . then, like tonight . . . I don't know what's the matter with me."

"Look, Katie, we'll get the license tomorrow morning and then we'll be married at once, anywhere you wish."

"Let's, Peter," she whispered. "You really don't mind? I have no real reasons, but I want it. I want it so much. Then I'll know that everything's all right. We'll manage. I can get a job if you . . . if you're not quite ready or . . ."

"Oh, nonsense. Don't talk about that. We'll manage. It doesn't matter. Only let's get married and everything else will take care of itself."

"Darling, you understand? You do understand?"

"Yes, Katie."

"Now that it's all settled," said Mrs. Keating, "I'll fix you a cup of hot tea, Catherine. You'll need it before you go home."

She prepared the tea, and Catherine drank it gratefully and said, smiling:

"I . . . I've often been afraid that you wouldn't approve, Mrs. Keating."

"Whatever gave you that idea," Mrs. Keating drawled, her voice not in the tone of a question. "Now you run on home like a good girl and get a good night's sleep."

"Mother, couldn't Katie stay here tonight? She could sleep with you."

"Well, now, Peter, don't get hysterical. What would her uncle think?"

"Oh, no, of course not. I'll be perfectly all right, Peter. I'll go home."

"Not if you . . ."

"I'm not afraid. Not now. I'm fine. You don't think that I'm really scared of Uncle Ellsworth?"

"Well, all right. But don't go yet."

"Now, Peter," said Mrs. Keating, "you don't want her to be running around the streets later than she has to."

"I'll take her home."

"No," said Catherine. "I don't want to be sillier than I am. No, I won't let you."

He kissed her at the door and he said: "I'll come for you at ten o'clock tomorrow morning and we'll go for the license." "Yes, Peter," she whispered.

He closed the door after her and he stood for a moment, not noticing that he was clenching his fists. Then he walked defiantly back to the living room, and he stopped, his hands in his pockets, facing his mother. He looked at her, his glance a silent demand. Mrs. Keating sat looking at him quietly, without pretending to ignore the glance and without answering it.

Then she asked:

"Do you want to go to bed, Peter?"

He had expected anything but that. He felt a violent impulse to seize the chance, to turn, leave the room and escape. But he had to learn what she thought; he had to justify himself.

"Now, Mother, I'm not going to listen to any objections."

"I've made no objections," said Mrs. Keating.

"Mother, I want you to understand that I love Katie, that nothing can stop me now, and that's that."

"Very well, Peter."

"I don't see what it is that you dislike about her."

"What I like or dislike is of no importance to you any more."

"Oh yes, Mother, of course it is! You know it is. How can you say that?"

"Peter, I have no likes or dislikes as far as I'm concerned. I have no thought for myself at all, because nothing in the world matters to me, except you. It might be old-fashioned, but that's the way I am. I know I shouldn't be, because children don't appreciate it nowadays, but I can't help it."

"Oh, Mother, you know that I appreciate it! You know that I wouldn't want to hurt you."

"You can't hurt me, Peter, except by hurting yourself. And that . . . that's hard to bear."

"How am I hurting myself?"

"Well, if you won't refuse to listen to me . . ."

"I've never refused to listen to you!"

"If you do want to hear my opinion, I'll say that this is the funeral of twenty-nine years of my life, of all the hopes I've had for you."

"But why? Why?"

"It's not that I dislike Catherine, Peter. I like her very much. She's a nice girl—if she doesn't let herself go to pieces often and pick things out of thin air like that. But she's a respectable girl and I'd say she'd make a good wife for anybody. For any nice, plodding, respectable boy. But to think of it for you, Peter! For you!"

"But . . ."

"You're modest, Peter. You're too modest. That's always been your trouble. You don't appreciate yourself. You think you're just like anybody else."

"I certainly don't! And I won't have anyone think that!"

"Then use your head! Don't you know what's ahead of you? Don't you see how far you've come already and how far you're going? You have a chance to become—well, not the very best, but pretty near the top in the architectural profession, and . . ."

"Pretty near the top? Is that what you think? If I can't be the very best, if I can't be the one architect of this country in my day—I don't want any damn part of it!"

"Ah, but one doesn't get to that, Peter, by falling down on the job. One doesn't get to be first in anything without the strength to make some sacrifices."

"But . . ."

"Your life doesn't belong to you, Peter, if you're really aiming high. You can't allow yourself to indulge every whim, as ordinary people can, because with them it doesn't matter anyway. It's not you or me or what we feel, Peter. It's your career. It takes strength to deny yourself in order to win other people's respect."

"You just dislike Katie and you let your own prejudice . . ."

"Whatever would I dislike about her? Well, of course, I can't say that I approve of a girl who has so little consideration for her man that she'll run to him and upset him over nothing at all, and ask him to chuck his future out the window just because she gets some crazy notion. That shows what help you can expect from a wife like that. But as far as I'm concerned, if you think that I'm worried about myself—well, you're just blind, Peter. Don't you see that for me personally it would be a perfect match? Because I'd have no trouble with Catherine, I could get along with her beautifully, she'd be respectful and obedient to her mother-in-law. While, on the other hand, Miss Francon . . ."

He winced. He had known that this would come. It was the one subject he had been afraid to hear mentioned.

"Oh yes, Peter," said Mrs. Keating quietly, firmly, "we've got to speak of that. Now, I'm sure I could never manage Miss Francon, and an elegant society girl like that wouldn't even stand for a dowdy, uneducated mother like me. She'd probably edge me out of the house. Oh, yes, Peter. But you see, it's not me that I'm thinking of."

"Mother," he said harshly, "that part of it is pure drivel—about my having a chance with Dominique. That hell-cat—I'm not sure she'd ever look at me."

"You're slipping, Peter. There was a time when you wouldn't have admitted that there was anything you couldn't get."

"But I don't want her, Mother."

"Oh, you don't, don't you? Well, there you are. Isn't that what I've been saying? Look at yourself! There you've got Francon, the best architect in town, just where you want him! He's practically begging you to take a partnership—at your age, over how many other, older men's heads? He's not permitting, he's *asking* you to marry his daughter! And you'll walk in tomorrow and you'll present to him the little nobody you've gone and married! Just stop thinking of yourself for a moment and think of others a bit! How do you suppose he'll like that? How will he like it when you show him the little guttersnipe that you've preferred to his daughter?"

"He won't like it," Keating whispered.

"You bet your life he won't! You bet your life he'll kick you right out on the street! He'll find plenty who'll jump at the chance to take your place. How about that Bennett fellow?"

"Oh, no!" Keating gasped so furiously that she knew she had struck right. "Not Bennett!"

"Yes," she said triumphantly. "Bennett! That's what it'll be—Francon & Bennett, while you'll be pounding the pavements looking for a job! But you'll have a wife! Oh, yes, you'll have a wife!"

"Mother, please . . ." he whispered, so desperately that she could allow herself to go on without restraint.

"This is the kind of wife you'll have. A clumsy little girl who won't know where to put her hands or feet. A sheepish little thing who'll run and hide from any important person that you'll want to bring to the house. So you think you're so good? Don't kid yourself, Peter Keating! No great man ever got there alone. Don't you shrug it off, how much the right woman's helped the best of them. Your Francon didn't marry a chambermaid, you bet your life he didn't! Just try to see things through other people's eyes for a bit. What will they think of your wife? What will they think of you? You don't make your living building chicken coops for soda jerkers, don't you forget that! You've got to play the game as the big men of this world see it. You've got to live up to them. What will they think of a man who's married to a common little piece of baggage like that? Will they admire you? Will they trust you? Will they respect you?"

"Shut up!" he cried.

But she went on. She spoke for a long time, while he sat, cracking his knuckles savagely, moaning once in a while: "But I love her. . . . I can't, Mother! I can't. . . . I love her. . . ."

She released him when the streets outside were gray with the light of morning. She let him stumble off to his room, to the accompaniment of the last, gentle, weary sounds of her voice:

"At least, Peter, you can do that much. Just a few months. Ask her to wait just a few months. Heyer might die any moment and then, once you're a partner, you can marry her and you might get away with it. She won't mind waiting just that little bit longer, if she loves you. . . . Think it over, Peter. . . . And while you're thinking it over, think just a bit that if you do this now, you'll be breaking your mother's heart. It's not important, but take just a tiny notice of that. Think of yourself for an hour, but give one minute to the thought of others. . . ."

He did not try to sleep. He did not undress, but sat on his bed for hours, and the thing clearest in his mind was the wish to find himself transported a year ahead when everything would have been settled, he did not care how.

He had decided nothing when he rang the door bell of Catherine's apartment at ten o'clock. He felt dimly that she would take his hand, that she would lead him, that she would insist—and thus the decision would be made.

Catherine opened the door and smiled, happily and confidently, as if nothing had happened. She led him to her room, where broad shafts of sunlight flooded the columns of books and papers stacked neatly on her desk. The room was clean, orderly, the pile of the rug still striped in bands left by a carpet sweeper. Catherine wore a crisp organdy blouse, with sleeves standing stiffly, cheerfully about her shoulders; little fluffy needles glittered through her hair in the sunlight. He felt a brief wrench of disappointment that no menace met him in her house; a wrench of relief also, and of disappointment.

"I'm ready, Peter," she said. "Get me my coat."

"Did you tell your uncle?" he asked.

"Oh, yes. I told him last night. He was still working when I got back."

"What did he say?"

"Nothing. He just laughed and asked me what I wanted for a wedding present. But he laughed so much!"

"Where is he? Didn't he want to meet me at least?"

"He had to go to his newspaper office. He said he'd have plenty of time to see more than enough of you. But he said it so nicely!"

"Listen, Katie, I . . . there's one thing I wanted to tell you." He hesitated, not looking at her. His voice was flat. "You see, it's like this: Lucius Heyer, Francon's partner, is very ill and they don't expect him to live. Francon's been hinting quite openly that I'm to take Heyer's place. But Francon has the crazy idea that he wants me to marry his daughter. Now don't misunderstand me, you know there's not a chance, but I can't tell him so. And I thought . . . I thought that if we waited . . . for just a few weeks . . . I'd be set with the firm and then Francon could do nothing to me when I come and tell him that I'm married. . . . But, of course it's up to you." He looked at her and his voice was eager. "If you want to do it now, we'll go at once."

"But, Peter," she said calmly, serene and astonished. "But of course. We'll wait."

He smiled in approval and relief. But he closed his eyes.

"Of course, we'll wait," she said firmly. "I didn't know this and it's very important. There's really no reason to hurry at all."

"You're not afraid that Francon's daughter might get me?"

She laughed. "Oh, Peter! I know you too well."

"But if you'd rather . . ."

"No, it's much better. You see, to tell you the truth, I thought this morning that it would be better if we waited, but I didn't want to say anything if you had made up your mind. Since you'd rather wait, I'd much rather too, because, you see, we got word this morning that Uncle's invited to repeat this same course of lectures at a terribly important university on the West Coast this summer. I felt horrible about leaving him flat, with the work unfinished. And then I thought also that perhaps we were being foolish, we're both so young. And Uncle Ellsworth laughed so much. You see, it's really wiser to wait a little."

"Yes. Well, that's fine. But, Katie, if you feel as you did last night . . ."

"But I don't! I'm so ashamed of myself. I can't imagine what ever happened to me last night. I try to remember it and I can't understand. You know how it is, you feel so silly afterward. Everything's so clear and simple the next day. Did I say a lot of awful nonsense last night?"

"Well, forget it. You're a sensible little girl. We're both sensible. And we'll wait just a while, it won't be long."

"Yes, Peter."

He said suddenly, fiercely:

"*Insist* on it now, Katie."

And then he laughed stupidly, as if he had not been quite serious.

She smiled gaily in answer. "You see?" she said, spreading her hands out.

"Well . . ." he muttered. "Well, all right, Katie. We'll wait. It's better, of course. I . . . I'll run along then. I'll be late at the office." He felt he had to escape her room for the moment, for that day. "I'll give you a ring. Let's have dinner together tomorrow."

"Yes, Peter. That will be nice."

He went away, relieved and desolate, cursing himself for the dull, persistent feeling that told him he had missed a chance which would never return; that something was closing in on them both and they had surrendered. He cursed, because he could not say what it was that they should have fought. He hurried on to his office where he was being late for an appointment with Mrs. Moorehead.

Catherine stood in the middle of the room, after he had left, and wondered why she suddenly felt empty and cold; why she hadn't known until this moment that she had hoped he would force her to follow him. Then she shrugged, and smiled reproachfully at herself, and went back to the work on her desk.

XIII

O N A DAY IN OCTOBER, WHEN THE HELLER HOUSE WAS NEARING
completion, a lanky young man in overalls stepped out of a
small group that stood watching the house from the road and approached
Roark.

"You the fellow who built the Booby Hatch?" he asked, quite diffidently.

"If you mean this house, yes," Roark answered.

"Oh, I beg your pardon, sir. It's only that that's what they call the
place around here. It's not what I'd call it. You see, I've got a building
job . . . well, not exactly, but I'm going to build a filling station of my
own about ten miles from here, down on the Post Road. I'd like to talk to
you."

Later, on a bench in front of the garage where he worked, Jimmy
Gowan explained in detail. He added: "And how I happened to think of
you, Mr. Roark, is that I like it, that funny house of yours. Can't say
why, but I like it. It makes sense to me. And then again I figured
everybody's gaping at it and talking about it, well, that's no use to a
house, but that'd be plenty smart for a business, let them giggle, but let
them talk about it. So I thought I'd get you to build it, and then they'll
all say I'm crazy, but do you care? I don't."

Jimmy Gowan had worked like a mule for fifteen years, saving money
for a business of his own. People voiced indignant objections to his choice
of architect; Jimmy uttered no word of explanation or self-defense; he
said politely: "Maybe so, folks, maybe so," and proceeded to have
Roark build his station.

The station opened on a day in late December. It stood on the edge of
the Boston Post Road, two small structures of glass and concrete forming a semicircle among the trees: the cylinder of the office and the long,
low oval of the diner, with the gasoline pumps as the colonnade of a
forecourt between them. It was a study in circles; there were no angles
and no straight lines; it looked like shapes caught in a flow, held still at
the moment of being poured, at the precise moment when they formed a
harmony that seemed too perfect to be intentional. It looked like a
cluster of bubbles hanging low over the ground, not quite touching it, to
be swept aside in an instant on a wind of speed; it looked gay, with
the hard, bracing gaity of efficiency, like a powerful airplane engine.

Roark stayed at the station on the day of its opening. He drank coffee
in a clean, white mug, at the counter of the diner, and he watched the

156

cars stopping at the door. He left late at night. He looked back once, driving down the long, empty road. The lights of the station winked, flowing away from him. There it stood, at the crossing of two roads, and cars would be streaming past it day and night, cars coming from cities in which there was no room for buildings such as this, going to cities in which there would be no buildings such as this. He turned his face to the road before him, and he kept his eyes off the mirror which still held, glittering softly, dots of light that moved away far behind him. . . .

He drove back to months of idleness. He sat in his office each morning, because he knew that he had to sit there, looking at a door that never opened, his fingers forgotten on a telephone that never rang. The ash trays he emptied each day, before leaving, contained nothing but the stubs of his own cigarettes.

"What are you doing about it, Howard?" Austen Heller asked him at dinner one evening.

"Nothing."

"But you must."

"There's nothing I can do."

"You must learn how to handle people."

"I can't."

"Why?"

"I don't know how. I was born without some one particular sense."

"It's something one acquires."

"I have no organ to acquire it with. I don't know whether it's something I lack, or something extra I have that stops me. Besides, I don't like people who have to be handled."

"But you can't sit still and do nothing now. You've got to go after commissions."

"What can I tell people in order to get commissions? I can only show my work. If they don't hear that, they won't hear anything I say. I'm nothing to them, but my work—my work is all we have in common. And I have no desire to tell them anything else."

"Then what are you going to do? You're not worried?"

"No. I expected it. I'm waiting."

"For what?"

"My kind of people."

"What kind is that?"

"I don't know. Yes, I do know, but I can't explain it. I've often wished I could. There must be some one principle to cover it, but I don't know what it is."

"Honesty?"

"Yes . . . no, only partly. Guy Francon is an honest man, but it isn't that. Courage? Ralston Holcombe has courage, in his own manner. . . . I don't know. I'm not that vague on other things. But I can tell my kind of people by their faces. By something in their faces. There will be thousands passing by your house and by the gas station. If out of those thousands, one stops and sees it—that's all I need."

"Then you do need other people, after all, don't you, Howard?"

"Of course. What are you laughing at?"

"I've always thought that you were the most anti-social animal I've ever had the pleasure of meeting."

"I need people to give me work. I'm not building mausoleums. Do you suppose I should need them in some other way? In a closer, more personal way?"

"You don't need anyone in a very personal way."

"No."

"You're not even boasting about it."

"Should I?"

"You can't. You're too arrogant to boast."

"Is that what I am?"

"Don't you know what you are?"

"No. Not as far as you're seeing me, or anyone else."

Heller sat silently, his wrist describing circles with a cigarette. Then Heller laughed, and said:

"That was typical."

"What?"

"That you didn't ask me to tell you what you are as I see you. Anybody else would have."

"I'm sorry. It wasn't indifference. You're one of the few friends I want to keep. I just didn't think of asking."

"I know you didn't. That's the point. You're a self-centered monster, Howard. The more monstrous because you're utterly innocent about it."

"That's true."

"You should show a little concern when you admit that."

"Why?"

"You know, there's a thing that stumps me. You're the coldest man I know. And I can't understand why—knowing that you're actually a fiend in your quiet sort of way—why I always feel, when I see you, that you're the most life-giving person I've ever met."

"What do you mean?"

"I don't know. Just that."

The weeks went by, and Roark walked to his office each day, sat at his desk for eight hours, and read a great deal. At five o'clock, he walked home. He had moved to a better room, near the office; he spent little; he had enough money for a long time to come.

On a morning in February the telephone rang in his office. A brisk, emphatic feminine voice asked for an appointment with Mr. Roark, the architect. That afternoon, a brisk, small, dark-skinned woman entered the office; she wore a mink coat and exotic earrings that tinkled when she moved her head. She moved her head a great deal, in sharp little birdlike jerks. She was Mrs. Wayne Wilmot of Long Island and she wished to build a country house. She had selected Mr. Roark to build it, she explained, because he had designed the home of Austen Heller. She adored Austen Heller; he was, she stated, an oracle to all those pretending just the tiniest bit to the title of progressive intellectual, she thought—"don't you?"—and she followed Heller like a zealot, "yes, literally, like a zealot." Mr. Roark was very young, wasn't he?—but she didn't mind that, she was very liberal and glad to help youth. She wanted a large house, she had two children, she believed in expressing their individuality—"don't you?"—and each had to have a separate nursery, she had to have a library—"I read to distraction"—a music room, a conservatory—"we grow lilies-of-the-valley, my friends tell me it's my flower"—a den for her husband, who trusted her implicitly and let her plan the house—"because I'm so good at it, if I weren't a woman I'm sure I'd be an architect"—servants' rooms and all that, and a three-car garage. After an hour and a half of details and explanations, she said:

"And of course, as to the style of the house, it will be English Tudor. I adore English Tudor."

He looked at her. He asked slowly:

"Have you seen Austen Heller's house?"

"No, though I did want to see it, but how could I?—I've never met Mr. Heller, I'm only his fan, just that, a plain, ordinary fan, what is he like in person?—you must tell me, I'm dying to hear it—no, I haven't seen his house, it's somewhere up in Maine, isn't it?"

Roark took photographs out of the desk drawer and handed them to her.

"This," he said, "is the Heller house."

She looked at the photographs, her glance like water skimming off their glossy surfaces, and threw them down on the desk.

"Very interesting," she said. "Most unusual. Quite stunning. But, of course, that's not what I want. That kind of a house wouldn't express my personality. My friends tell me I have the Elizabethan personality."

Quietly, patiently, he tried to explain to her why she should not build a Tudor house. She interrupted him in the middle of a sentence.

"Look here, Mr. Roark, you're not trying to teach me something, are you? I'm quite sure that I have good taste, and I know a great deal about architecture, I've taken a special course at the club. My friends tell me that I know more than many architects. I've quite made up my mind that I shall have an English Tudor house. I do not care to argue about it."

"You'll have to go to some other architect, Mrs. Wilmot."

She stared at him incredulously.

"You mean, you're refusing the commission?"

"Yes."

"You don't want *my* commission?"

"No."

"But why?"

"I don't do this sort of thing."

"But I thought architects . . ."

"Yes. Architects will build you anything you ask for. Any other architect in town will."

"But I gave you first chance."

"Will you do me a favor, Mrs. Wilmot? Will you tell me why you came to me if all you wanted was a Tudor house?"

"Well, I certainly thought you'd appreciate the opportunity. And then, I thought I could tell my friends that I had Austen Heller's architect."

He tried to explain and to convince. He knew, while he spoke, that it was useless, because his words sounded as if they were hitting a vacuum. There was no such person as Mrs. Wayne Wilmot; there was only a shell containing the opinions of her friends, the picture postcards she had seen, the novels of country squires she had read; it was this that he had to address, this immateriality which could not hear him or answer, deaf and impersonal like a wad of cotton.

"I'm sorry," said Mrs. Wayne Wilmot, "but I'm not accustomed to dealing with a person utterly incapable of reason. I'm quite sure I shall find plenty of bigger men who'll be glad to work for me. My husband was opposed to my idea of having you, in the first place, and I'm sorry to see that he was right. Good day, Mr. Roark."

She walked out with dignity, but she slammed the door. He slipped the photographs back into the drawer of his desk.

Mr. Robert L. Mundy, who came to Roark's office in March, had been sent by Austen Heller. Mr. Mundy's voice and hair were gray as steel, but his eyes were blue, gentle and wistful. He wanted to build a house in Connecticut, and he spoke of it tremulously, like a young bridegroom and like a man groping for his last, secret goal.

"It's not just a house, Mr. Roark," he said with timid diffidence, as if he were speaking to a man older and more prominent than himself, "it's like . . . like a symbol to me. It's what I've been waiting and working for all these years. It's so many years now. . . . I must tell you this, so you'll understand. I have a great deal of money now, more than I care to think about. I didn't always have it. Maybe it came too late. I don't know. Young people think that you forget what happens on the way when you get there. But you don't. Something stays. I'll always remember how I was a boy—in a little place down in Georgia, that was—and how I ran errands for the harness maker, and the kids laughed when carriages drove by and splashed mud all over my pants. That's how long ago I decided that some day I'd have a house of my own, the kind of a house that carriages stop before. After that, no matter how hard it got to be at times, I'd always think of that house, and it helped. Afterward, there were years when I was afraid of it—I could have built it, but I was afraid. Well, now the time has come. Do you understand, Mr. Roark? Austen said you'd be just the man who'd understand."

"Yes," said Roark eagerly, "I do."

"There was a place," said Mr. Mundy, "down there, near my home town. The mansion of the whole county. The Randolph place. An old plantation house, as they don't build them any more. I used to deliver things there sometimes, at the back door. That's the house I want, Mr. Roark. Just like it. But not back there in Georgia. I don't want to go back. Right here, near the city. I've bought the land. You must help me to have it landscaped just like the Randolph place. We'll plant trees and shrubs, the kind they have in Georgia, the flowers and everything. We'll find a way to make them grow. I don't care how much it costs. Of course, we'll have electric lights and garages now, not carriages. But I want the electric lights made like candles and I want the garages to look like the stables. Everything, just as it was. I have photographs of the Randolph place. And I've bought some of their old furniture."

When Roark began to speak Mr. Mundy listened, in polite astonishment. He did not seem to resent the words. They did not penetrate.

"Don't you see?" Roark was saying. "It's a monument you want to build, but not to yourself. Not to your life or your own achievement. To other people. To their supremacy over you. You're not challenging that supremacy. You're immortalizing it. You haven't thrown it off—you're putting it up forever. Will you be happy if you seal yourself for the rest of your life in that borrowed shape? Or if you strike free, for once, and build a new house, your own? You don't want the Randolph place. You want what it stood for. But what it stood for is what you've fought all your life."

Mr. Mundy listened blankly. And Roark felt again a bewildered helplessness before unreality: there was no such person as Mr. Mundy;

there were only the remnants, long dead, of the people who had inhabited the Randolph place; one could not plead with remnants or convince them.

"No," said Mr. Mundy, at last. "No. You may be right, but that's not what I want at all. I don't say you haven't got your reasons, and they sound like good reasons, but I like the Randolph place."

"Why?"

"Just because I like it. Just because that's what I like."

When Roark told him that he would have to select another architect, Mr. Mundy said unexpectedly:

"But I like you. Why can't you build it for me? What difference would it make to you?"

Roark did not explain.

Later, Austen Heller said to him: "I expected it. I was afraid you'd turn him down. I'm not blaming you, Howard. Only he's so rich. It could have helped you so much. And, after all, you've got to live."

"Not that way," said Roark.

In April Mr. Nathaniel Janss, of the Janss-Stuart Real Estate Company, called Roark to his office. Mr. Janss was frank and blunt. He stated that his company was planning the erection of a small office building—thirty stories—on lower Broadway, and that he was not sold on Roark as the architect, in fact he was more or less opposed to him, but his friend Austen Heller had insisted that he should meet Roark and talk to him about it; Mr. Janss did not think very much of Roark's stuff, but Heller had simply bullied him and he would listen to Roark before deciding on anyone, and what did Roark have to say on the subject?

Roark had a great deal to say. He said it calmly, and this was difficult, at first, because he wanted that building, because what he felt was the desire to wrench that building out of Mr. Janss at the point of a gun, if he'd had one. But after a few minutes, it became simple and easy, the thought of the gun vanished, and even his desire for the building; it was not a commission to get and he was not there to get it; he was only speaking of buildings.

"Mr. Janss, when you buy an automobile, you don't want it to have rose garlands about the windows, a lion on each fender and an angel sitting on the roof. Why don't you?"

"That would be silly," stated Mr. Janss.

"Why would it be silly? Now I think it would be beautiful. Besides, Louis the Fourteenth had a carriage like that and what was good enough for Louis is good enough for us. We shouldn't go in for rash innovations and we shouldn't break with tradition."

"Now you know damn well you don't believe anything of the sort!"

"I know I don't. But that's what you believe, isn't it? Now take a human body. Why wouldn't you like to see a human body with a curling tail with a crest of ostrich feathers at the end? And with ears shaped like acanthus leaves? It would be ornamental, you know, instead of the stark, bare ugliness we have now. Well, why don't you like the idea? Because it would be useless and pointless. Because the beauty of the human body is that it hasn't a single muscle which doesn't serve its purpose; that there's not a line wasted; that every detail of it fits one idea, the idea of a man and the life of a man. Will you tell me why, when it comes to a building, you don't want it to look as if it had any sense or purpose, you want to choke it with trimmings, you want to sacrifice its purpose to its envelope—not knowing even why you want that kind of an envelope? You want it to look like a hybrid beast produced by crossing the bastards of ten different species until you get a creature without guts, without heart or brain, a creature all pelt, tail, claws and feathers? Why? You must tell me, because I've never been able to understand it."

"Well," said Mr. Janss, "I've never thought of it that way." He added, without great conviction: "But we want our building to have dignity, you know, and beauty, what they call real beauty."

"What who calls what beauty?"

"Well-l-l . . ."

"Tell me, Mr. Janss, do you really think that Greek columns and fruit baskets are beautiful on a modern, steel office building?"

"I don't know that I've ever thought anything about why a building was beautiful, one way or another," Mr. Janss confessed, "but I guess that's what the public wants."

"Why do you suppose they want it?"

"I don't know."

"Then why should you care what they want?"

"You've got to consider the public."

"Don't you know that most people take most things because that's what's given them, and they have no opinion whatever? Do you wish to be guided by what they expect you to think they think or by your own judgment?"

"You can't force it down their throats."

"You don't have to. You must only be patient. Because on your side you have reason—oh, I know, it's something no one really wants to have on his side—and against you, you have just a vague, fat, blind inertia."

"Why do you think that I don't want reason on my side?"

"It's not you, Mr. Janss. It's the way most people feel. They have to take a chance, everything they do is taking a chance, but they feel so much safer when they take it on something they know to be ugly, vain and stupid."

"That's true, you know," said Mr. Janss.

At the conclusion of the interview, Mr. Janss said thoughtfully:

"I can't say that it doesn't make sense, Mr. Roark. Let me think it over. You'll hear from me shortly."

Mr. Janss called him a week later. "It's the Board of Directors that will have to decide. Are you willing to try, Roark? Draw up the plans and some preliminary sketches. I'll submit them to the Board. I can't promise anything. But I'm for you and I'll fight them on it."

Roark worked on the plans for two weeks of days and nights. The plans were submitted. Then he was called before the board of directors of the Janss-Stuart Real Estate Company. He stood at the side of a long table and he spoke, his eyes moving slowly from face to face. He tried not to look down at the table, but on the lower rim of his vision there remained the white spot of his drawings spread before the twelve men. He was asked a great many questions. Mr. Janss jumped up at times to answer instead, to pound the table with his fist, to snarl: "Don't you see? Isn't it clear? . . . What of it, Mr. Grant? What if no one has ever built anything like it? . . . Gothic, Mr. Hubbard? Why *must* we have Gothic? . . . I've a jolly good mind to resign if you turn this down!"

Roark spoke quietly. He was the only man in the room who felt certain of his own words. He felt also that he had no hope. The twelve faces before him had a variety of countenances, but there was something, neither color nor feature, upon all of them, as a common denominator, something that dissolved their expressions, so that they were not faces any longer but only empty ovals of flesh. He was addressing everyone. He was addressing no one. He felt no answer, not even the echo of his own words striking against the membrane of an eardrum. His words were falling down a well, hitting stone salients on their way, and each salient refused to stop them, threw them farther, tossed them from one another, sent them to seek a bottom that did not exist.

He was told that he would be informed of the Board's decision. He knew that decision in advance. When he received the letter, he read it without feeling. The letter was from Mr. Janss and it began: "Dear Mr. Roark, I am sorry to inform you that our Board of Directors find themselves unable to grant you the commission for . . ." There was a plea in the letter's brutal, offensive formality: the plea of a man who could not face him.

John Fargo had started in life as a pushcart peddler. At fifty he owned a modest fortune and a prosperous department store on lower Sixth Avenue. For years he had fought successfully against a larger store across the street, one of many inherited by a numerous family. In the fall of last year the family had moved that particular branch to new quarters, farther uptown. They were convinced that the center of the city's retail business was shifting north and they had decided to hasten the downfall of their former neighborhood by leaving their old store vacant, a grim reminder and embarrassment to their competitor across the street. John Fargo had answered by announcing that he would build a new store of his own, on the very same spot, next door to his old one; a store newer and smarter than any the city had seen; he would, he declared, keep the prestige of his old neighborhood.

When he called Roark to his office he did not say that he would have to decide later or think things over. He said: "You're the architect." He sat, his feet on his desk, smoking a pipe, snapping out words and puffs of smoke together. "I'll tell you what space I need and how much I want to spend. If you need more—say so. The rest is up to you. I don't know much about buildings. But I know a man who knows when I see him. Go ahead."

Fargo had chosen Roark because Fargo had driven, one day, past Gowan's Service Station, and stopped, and gone in, and asked a few questions. After that, he bribed Heller's cook to show him through the house in Heller's absence. Fargo needed no further argument.

Late in May, when the drafting table in Roark's office was buried deep in sketches for the Fargo store, he received another commission.

Mr. Whitford Sanborn, the client, owned an office building that had been built for him many years ago by Henry Cameron. When Mr. Sanborn decided that he needed a new country residence he rejected his wife's suggestions of other architects; he wrote to Henry Cameron. Cameron wrote a ten-page letter in answer; the first three lines of the letter stated that he had retired from practice; the rest of it was about Howard Roark. Roark never learned what had been said in that letter; Sanborn would not show it to him and Cameron would not tell him. But Sanborn signed him to build the country residence, in spite of Mrs. Sanborn's violent objections.

Mrs. Sanborn was the president of many charity organizations and this had given her an addiction to autocracy such as no other avocation could develop. Mrs. Sanborn wished a French chateau built upon their new estate on the Hudson. She wished it to look stately and ancient, as if it had always belonged to the family; of course, she admitted, people would know that it hadn't, but it would *appear* as if it had.

Mr. Sanborn signed the contract after Roark had explained to him in detail the kind of a house he was to expect; Mr. Sanborn had agreed to it readily, had not wished even to wait for sketches. "But of course,

Fanny," Mr. Sanborn said wearily, "I want a modern house. I told you that long ago. That's what Cameron would have designed." "What in heaven's name does Cameron mean now?" she asked. "I don't know, Fanny. I know only that there's no building in New York like the one he did for me."

The arguments continued for many long evenings in the dark, cluttered, polished mahogany splendor of the Sanborns' Victorian drawing room. Mr. Sanborn wavered. Roark asked, his arm sweeping out at the room around them: "Is *this* what you want?" "Well, if you're going to be impertinent . . ." Mrs. Sanborn began, but Mr. Sanborn exploded: "Christ, Fanny! He's right! That's just what I *don't* want! That's just what I'm sick of!"

Roark saw no one until his sketches were ready. The house—of plain field stone, with great windows and many terraces—stood in the gardens over the river, as spacious as the spread of water, as open as the gardens, and one had to follow its lines attentively to find the exact steps by which it was tied to the sweep of the gardens, so gradual was the rise of the terraces, the approach to and the full reality of the walls; it seemed only that the trees flowed into the house and through it; it seemed that the house was not a barrier against sunlight, but a bowl to gather it, to concentrate it into brighter radiance than that of the air outside.

Mr. Sanborn was first to see the sketches. He studied them, and then he said: "I . . . I don't know quite how to say it, Mr. Roark. It's great. Cameron was right about you."

After others had seen the sketches Mr. Sanborn was not certain of this any longer. Mrs. Sanborn said that the house was awful. And the long evening arguments were resumed. "Now why, *why* can't we add turrets there, on the corners?" Mrs. Sanborn asked. "There's plenty of room on those flat roofs." When she had been talked out of the turrets, she inquired: "Why can't we have mullioned windows? What difference would that make? God knows, the windows are large enough—though why they have to be so large I fail to see, it gives one no privacy at all—but I'm willing to accept your windows, Mr. Roark, if you're so stubborn about it, but why can't you put mullions on the panes? It will soften things, and it gives a regal air, you know, a feudal sort of mood."

The friends and relatives to whom Mrs. Sanborn hurried with the sketches did not like the house at all. Mrs. Walling called it preposterous, and Mrs. Hooper—crude. Mr. Melander said he wouldn't have it as a present. Mrs. Applebee stated that it looked like a shoe factory. Miss Davitt glanced at the sketches and said with approval: "Oh, how very artistic, my dear! Who designed it? . . . Roark? . . . Roark? . . . Never heard of him. . . . Well, frankly, Fanny, it looks like something phony."

The two children of the family were divided on the question. June Sanborn, aged nineteen, had always thought that all architects were romantic, and she had been delighted to learn that they would have a very young architect; but she did not like Roark's appearance and his indifference to her hints, so she declared that the house was hideous and she, for one, would refuse to live in it. Richard Sanborn, aged twenty-four, who had been a brilliant student in college and was now slowly drinking himself to death, startled his family by emerging from his usual lethargy and declaring that the house was magnificent. No one could tell whether it was esthetic appreciation or hatred of his mother or both.

Whitford Sanborn swayed with every new current. He would mutter: "Well, now, not mullions, of course, that's utter rubbish, but couldn't you give her a cornice, Mr. Roark, to keep peace in the family? Just a kind of a crenelated cornice, it wouldn't spoil anything. Or would it?"

The arguments ended when Roark declared that he would not build the house unless Mr. Sanborn approved the sketches just as they were and signed his approval on every sheet of the drawings. Mr. Sanborn signed.

Mrs. Sanborn was pleased to learn, shortly afterward, that no reputable contractor would undertake the erection of the house. "You see?" she started triumphantly. Mr. Sanborn refused to see. He found an obscure firm that accepted the commission grudgingly and as a special favor to him. Mrs. Sanborn learned that she had an ally in the contractor, and she broke social precedent to the extent of inviting him for tea. She had long since lost all coherent ideas about the house; she merely hated Roark. Her contractor hated all architects on principle.

The construction of the Sanborn house proceeded through the months of summer and fall, each day bringing new battles. "But, of course, Mr. Roark, I told you I wanted three closets in my bedroom, I remember distinctly, it was on a Friday and we were sitting in the drawing room and Mr. Sanborn was sitting in the big chair by the window and I was . . . What about the plans? What plans? How do you expect me to understand plans?" "Aunt Rosalie says she can't possibly climb a circular stairway, Mr. Roark. What are we going to do? Select our guests to fit your house?" "Mr. Hulburt says that kind of a ceiling won't hold. . . . Oh, yes, Mr. Hulburt knows a lot about architecture. He's spent two summers in Venice." "June, poor darling, says her room will be dark as a cellar. . . . Well, that's the way she feels, Mr. Roark. Even if it isn't dark, but if it makes her *feel* dark, it's the same thing." Roark stayed up nights, redrafting the plans for the alterations which he could not avoid. It meant days of tearing down floors, stairways, partitions already erected; it meant extras piling up on the contractor's budget. The contractor shrugged and said: "I told you so. That's what always happens when you get one of those fancy architects. You wait and see what this thing will cost you before he gets through."

Then, as the house took shape, it was Roark who found that he wanted to make a change. The eastern wing had never quite satisfied him. Watching it rise, he saw the mistake he had made and the way to correct it; he knew it would bring the house into a more logical whole. He was making his first steps in building and they were his first experiments. He could admit it openly. But Mr. Sanborn refused to allow the change; it was his turn. Roark pleaded with him; once the picture of that new wing had become clear in Roark's mind he could not bear to look at the house as it stood. "It's not that I disagree with you," Mr. Sanborn said coldly, "in fact, I do think you're right. But we cannot afford it. Sorry." "It will cost you less than the senseless changes Mrs. Sanborn has forced me to make." "Don't bring that up again." "Mr. Sanborn," Roark asked slowly, "will you sign a paper that you authorize this change provided it costs you nothing?" "Certainly. If you can conjure up a miracle to work that."

He signed. The eastern wing was rebuilt. Roark paid for it himself. It cost him more than the fee he received. Mr. Sanborn hesitated: he wanted to repay it. Mrs. Sanborn stopped him. "It's just a low trick," she said, "just a form of high-pressure. He's blackmailing you on your better feelings. He expects you to pay. Wait and see. He'll ask for it. Don't let him get away with that." Roark did not ask for it. Mr. Sanborn never paid him.

When the house was completed, Mrs. Sanborn refused to live in it. Mr. Sanborn looked at it wistfully, too tired to admit that he loved it, that he had always wanted a home just like it. He surrendered. The house was not furnished. Mrs. Sanborn took herself, her husband and her daughter off to Florida for the winter, "where," she said, "we have a house that's a decent Spanish, thank God!—because we bought it ready-made. This is what happens when you venture to build for yourself, with some half-baked idiot of an architect!" Her son, to everybody's amazement, exhibited a sudden burst of savage will power: he refused to go to Florida; he liked the new house, he would live nowhere else. So three of the rooms were furnished for him. The family left and he moved alone into the house on the Hudson. At night, one could see from the river a single rectangle of yellow, small and lost, among the windows of the huge, dead house.

The bulletin of the Architects' Guild of America carried a small item:

"A curious incident, which would be amusing if it were not deplorable, is reported to us about a home recently built by Mr. Whitford Sanborn, noted industrialist. Designed by one Howard Roark and erected at a cost of well over $100,000, this house was found by the family to be uninhabitable. It stands now, abandoned, as an eloquent witness to professional incompetence."

XIV

LUCIUS N. HEYER STUBBORNLY REFUSED TO DIE. HE HAD RECOVERED
from the stroke and returned to his office, ignoring the objections
of his doctor and the solicitous protests of Guy Francon. Francon offered to buy him out. Heyer refused, his pale, watering eyes staring
obstinately at nothing at all. He came to his office every two or three
days; he read the copies of correspondence left in his letter basket
according to custom; he sat at his desk and drew flowers on a clean pad;
then he went home. He walked, dragging his feet slowly; he held his
elbows pressed to his sides and his forearms thrust forward, with the
fingers half closed, like claws; the fingers shook; he could not use his
left hand at all. He would not retire. He liked to see his name on
the firm's stationery.

He wondered dimly why he was no longer introduced to prominent
clients, why he never saw the sketches of their new buildings, until they
were half erected. If he mentioned this, Francon protested: "But Lucius,
I couldn't think of bothering you in your condition. Any other man
would have retired, long ago."

Francon puzzled him mildly. Peter Keating baffled him. Keating
barely bothered to greet him when they met, and then as an after-
thought; Keating walked off in the middle of a sentence addressed to
him; when Heyer issued some minor order to one of the draftsmen, it
was not carried out and the draftsman informed him that the order had
been countermanded by Mr. Keating. Heyer could not understand it; he
always remembered Keating as the diffident boy who had talked to him
so nicely about old porcelain. He excused Keating at first; then he tried
to mollify him, humbly and clumsily; then he conceived an unreasoning
fear of Keating. He complained to Francon. He said, petulantly, assum-
ing the tone of an authority he could never have exercised: "That boy of
yours, Guy, that Keating fellow, he's getting to be impossible. He's rude
to me. You ought to get rid of him." "Now you see, Lucius," Francon
answered dryly, "why I say that you should retire. You're overstraining
your nerves and you're beginning to imagine things."

Then came the competition for the Cosmo-Slotnick Building.

Cosmo-Slotnick Pictures of Hollywood, California, had decided to
erect a stupendous home office in New York, a skyscraper to house a
motion-picture theater and forty floors of offices. A world-wide competition for the selection of the architect had been announced a year in
advance. It was stated that Cosmo-Slotnick were not merely the leaders

169

in the art of the motion picture, but embraced all the arts, since all contributed to the creation of the films; and architecture being a lofty, though neglected, branch of esthetics, Cosmo-Slotnick were ready to put it on the map.

With the latest news of the casting of *I'll Take a Sailor* and the shooting of *Wives for Sale,* came stories about the Parthenon and the Pantheon. Miss Sally O'Dawn was photographed on the steps of the Rheims Cathedral—in a bathing suit, and Mr. Pratt ("Pardner") Purcell gave an interview, stating that he had always dreamed of being a master builder, if he hadn't been a movie actor. Ralston Holcombe, Guy Francon and Gordon L. Prescott were quoted on the future of American architecture—in an article written by Miss Dimples Williams, and an imaginary interview quoted what Sir Christopher Wren would have said about the motion picture. In the Sunday supplements there were photographs of Cosmo-Slotnick starlets in shorts and sweaters, holding T-squares and slide-rules, standing before drawing boards that bore the legend: "Cosmo-Slotnick Building" over a huge question mark.

The competition was open to all architects of all countries; the building was to rise on Broadway and to cost ten million dollars; it was to symbolize the genius of modern technology and the spirit of the American people; it was announced in advance as "the most beautiful building in the world." The jury of award consisted of Mr. Shupe, representing Cosmo, Mr. Slotnick, representing Slotnick, Professor Peterkin of the Stanton Institute of Technology, the Mayor of the City of New York, Ralston Holcombe, president of the A.G.A., and Ellsworth M. Toohey.

"Go to it, Peter!" Francon told Keating enthusiastically. "Do your best. Give me all you've got. This is your great chance. You'll be known the world over if you win. And here's what we'll do: we'll put your name on our entry, along with the firm's. If we win, you'll get one fifth of the prize. The grand prize is sixty thousand dollars, you know."

"Heyer will object," said Keating cautiously.

"Let him object. That's why I'm doing it. He might get it through his head what's the decent thing for him to do. And I . . . well, you know how I feel, Peter. I think of you as my partner already. I owe it to you. You've earned it. This might be your key to it."

Keating redrew his project five times. He hated it. He hated every girder of that building before it was born. He worked, his hand trembling. He did not think of the drawing under his hand. He thought of all the other contestants, of the man who might win and be proclaimed publicly as his superior. He wondered what that other one would do, how the other would solve the problem and surpass him. He had to beat that man; nothing else mattered; there was no Peter Keating, there was only a suction chamber, like the kind of tropical plant he'd heard about, a plant that drew an insect into its vacuum and sucked it dry and thus acquired its own substance.

He felt nothing but immense uncertainty when his sketches were ready and the delicate perspective of a white marble edifice lay, neatly finished, before him. It looked like a Renaissance palace made of rubber and stretched to the height of forty stories. He had chosen the style of the Renaissance because he knew the unwritten law that all architectural juries liked columns, and because he remembered Ralston Holcombe on the jury. He had borrowed from all of Holcombe's favorite Italian palaces. It looked good . . . it might be good . . . he was not sure. He had no one to ask.

He heard these words in his own mind and he felt a wave of blind fury. He felt it before he knew the reason, but he knew the reason almost in the same instant: there was someone whom he could ask. He did not want to think of that name; he would not go to him; the anger rose to his face and he felt the hot, tight patches under his eyes. He knew that he would go.

He pushed the thought out of his mind. He was not going anywhere. When the time came, he slipped his drawings into a folder and went to Roark's office.

He found Roark alone, sitting at the desk in the large room that bore no signs of activity.

"Hello, Howard!" he said brightly. "How are you? I'm not interrupting anything, am I?"

"Hello, Peter," said Roark. "You aren't."

"Not awfully busy, are you?"

"No."

"Mind if I sit down for a few minutes?"

"Sit down."

"Well, Howard, you've been doing great work. I've seen the Fargo Store. It's splendid. My congratulations."

"Thank you."

"You've been forging straight ahead, haven't you? Had three commissions already?"

"Four."

"Oh, yes, of course, four. Pretty good. I hear you've been having a little trouble with the Sanborns."

"I have."

"Well, it's not all smooth sailing, not all of it, you know. . . . No new commissions since? Nothing?"

"No. Nothing."

"Well, it will come. I've always said that architects don't have to cut one another's throat, there's plenty of work for all of us, we must develop a spirit of professional unity and co-operation. For instance, take that competition—have you sent your entry in already?"

"What competition?"

"Why, *the* competition. The Cosmo-Slotnick competition."

"I'm not sending any entry."

"You're . . . not? Not at all?"

"No."

"Why?"

"I don't enter competitions."

"Why, for heaven's sake?"

"Come on, Peter. You didn't come here to discuss that."

"As a matter of fact I did think I'd show you my own entry, you understand I'm not asking you to help me, I just want your reaction, just a general opinion."

He hastened to open the folder.

Roark studied the sketches. Keating snapped: "Well? Is it all right?"

"No. It's rotten. And you know it."

Then, for hours, while Keating watched and the sky darkened and lights flared up in the windows of the city, Roark talked, explained, slashed lines through the plans, untangled the labyrinth of the theater's exits, cut windows, unraveled halls, smashed useless arches, straightened stairways. Keating stammered once: "Jesus, Howard! Why don't you enter the competition, if you can do it like this?" Roark answered: "Because I can't. I couldn't if I tried. I dry up. I go blank. I can't give them what they want. But I can straighten someone else's damn mess when I see it."

It was morning when he pushed the plans aside. Keating whispered: "And the elevation?"

"Oh, to hell with your elevation! I don't want to look at your damn Renaissance elevations!" But he looked. He could not prevent his hand from cutting lines across the perspective. "All right, damn you, give them good Renaissance if you must and if there is such a thing! Only I can't do that for you. Figure it out yourself. Something like this. Simpler, Peter, simpler, more direct, as honest as you can make of a dishonest thing. Now go home and try to work out something on this order."

Keating went home. He copied Roark's plans. He worked out Roark's hasty sketch of the elevation into a neat, finished perspective. Then the drawings were mailed, properly addressed, to:

"The Most Beautiful Building in the World" Competition
Cosmo-Slotnick Pictures, Inc.
New York City.

The envelope, accompanying the entry, contained the names: "Francon & Heyer, architects, Peter Keating, associated designer."

Through the months of that winter Roark found no other chances, no offers, no prospects of commissions. He sat at his desk and forgot, at times, to turn on the lights in the early dusk. It was as if the heavy immobility of all the hours that had flowed through the office, of its door, of its air, were beginning to seep into his muscles. He would rise and fling a book at the wall, to feel his arm move, to hear the burst of sound. He smiled, amused, picked up the book, and laid it neatly back on the desk. He turned on the desk lamp. Then he stopped, before he had withdrawn his hands from the cone of light under the lamp, and he looked at his hands; he spread his fingers out slowly. Then he remembered what Cameron had said to him long ago. He jerked his hands away. He reached for his coat, turned the lights off, locked the door and went home.

As spring approached he knew that his money would not last much longer. He paid the rent on his office promptly on the first of each month. He wanted the feeling of thirty days ahead, during which he would still own the office. He entered it calmly each morning. He found only that he did not want to look at the calendar when it began to grow dark and he knew that another day of the thirty had gone. When he noticed this, he made himself look at the calendar. It was a race he was running now, a race between his rent money and . . . he did not know the name of the other contestant. Perhaps it was every man whom he passed on the street.

When he went up to his office, the elevator operators looked at him in a queer, lazy, curious sort of way; when he spoke, they answered, not insolently, but in an indifferent drawl that seemed to say it would become insolent in a moment. They did not know what he was doing or why; they knew only that he was a man to whom no clients ever came. He attended, because Austen Heller asked him to attend, the few parties Heller gave occasionally; he was asked by guests: "Oh, you're an architect? You'll forgive me, I haven't kept up with architecture—what have you built?" When he answered, he heard them say: "Oh, yes, indeed," and he saw the conscious politeness of their manner tell him that he was an architect by presumption. They had never seen his buildings; they did not know whether his buildings were good or worthless; they knew only that they had never heard of these buildings.

It was a war in which he was invited to fight nothing, yet he was pushed forward to fight, he had to fight, he had no choice—and no adversary.

He passed by buildings under construction. He stopped to look at the steel cages. He felt at times as if the beams and girders were shaping themselves not into a house, but into a barricade to stop him; and the few steps on the sidewalk that separated him from the wooden fence enclosing the construction were the steps he would never be able to take. It was pain, but it was a blunted, unpenetrating pain. It's true, he would tell himself; it's not, his body would answer, the strange, untouchable healthiness of his body.

The Fargo Store had opened. But one building could not save a neighborhood; Fargo's competitors had been right, the tide had turned, was flowing uptown, his customers were deserting him. Remarks were made openly on the decline of John Fargo, who had topped his poor business judgment by an investment in a preposterous kind of a building; which proved, it was stated, that the public would not accept these architectural innovations. It was not stated that the store was the cleanest and brightest in the city; that the skill of its plan made its operation easier than had ever been possible; that the neighborhood had been doomed before its erection. The building took the blame.

Athelstan Beasely, the wit of the architectural profession, the court jester of the A.G.A., who never seemed to be building anything, but organized all the charity balls, wrote in his column entitled "Quips and Quirks" in the *A.G.A. Bulletin:*

"Well, lads and lassies, here's a fairy tale with a moral: seems there was, once upon a time, a little boy with hair the color of a Hallowe'en pumpkin, who thought that he was better than all you common boys and girls. So to prove it, he up and built a house, which is a very nice house, except that nobody can live in it, and a store, which is a very lovely store, except that it's going bankrupt. He also erected a very eminent structure, to wit: a dogcart on a mud road. This last is reported to be doing very well indeed, which, perhaps, is the right field of endeavor for that little boy."

At the end of March Roark read in the papers about Roger Enright. Roger Enright possessed millions, an oil concern and no sense of restraint. This made his name appear in the papers frequently. He aroused a half-admiring, half-derisive awe by the incoherent variety of his sudden ventures. The latest was a project for a new type of residential development—an apartment building, with each unit complete and isolated like an expensive private home. It was to be known as the Enright House. Enright had declared that he did not want it to look like anything anywhere else. He had approached and rejected several of the best architests in town.

Roark felt as if this newspaper item were a personal invitation; the kind of chance created expressly for him. For the first time he attempted to go after a commission. He requested an interview with Roger Enright.

He got an interview with a secretary. The secretary, a young man who looked bored, asked him several questions about his experience; he asked them slowly, as if it required an effort to decide just what it would be appropriate to ask under the circumstances, since the answers would make no difference whatever; he glanced at some photographs of Roark's buildings, and declared that Mr. Enright would not be interested.

In the first week of April, when Roark had paid his last rental for one more month at the office, he was asked to submit drawings for the new building of the Manhattan Bank Company. He was asked by Mr. Weidler, a member of the board of directors, who was a friend of young Richard Sanborn. Weidler told him: "I've had a stiff fight, Mr. Roark, but I think I've won. I've taken them personally through the Sanborn house, and Dick and I explained a few things. However, the board must see the drawings before they make a decision. So it's not quite certain as yet, I must tell you frankly, but it's almost certain. They've turned down two other architects. They're very much interested in you. Go ahead. Good luck!"

Henry Cameron had had a relapse and the doctor warned his sister that no recovery could be expected. She did not believe it. She felt a new hope, because she saw that Cameron, lying still in bed, looked serene and—almost happy, a word she had never found it possible to associate with her brother.

But she was frightened, one evening, when he said suddenly: "Call Howard. Ask him to come here." In the three years since his retirement he had never called for Roark, he had merely waited for Roark's visits.

Roark arrived within an hour. He sat by the side of Cameron's bed, and Cameron talked to him as usual. He did not mention the special invitation and did not explain. The night was warm and the window of Cameron's bedroom stood open to the dark garden. When he noticed, in a pause between sentences, the silence of the trees outside, the unmoving silence of late hours, Cameron called his sister and said: "Fix the couch in the living room for Howard. He's staying here." Roark looked at him and understood. Roark inclined his head in agreement; he could acknowledge what Cameron had just declared to him only by a quiet glance as solemn as Cameron's.

Roark remained at the house for three days. No reference was made to his staying there—nor to how long he would have to stay. His presence was accepted as a natural fact requiring no comment. Miss Cameron understood—and knew that she must say nothing. She moved about silently, with the meek courage of resignation.

Cameron did not want Roark's continuous presence in his room. He would say: "Go out, take a walk through the garden, Howard. It's beautiful, the grass is coming up." He would lie in bed and watch, with contentment, through the open window, Roark's figure moving among the bare trees that stood against a pale blue sky.

He asked only that Roark eat his meals with him. Miss Cameron would put a tray on Cameron's knees, and serve Roark's meal on a small table by the bed. Cameron seemed to take pleasure in what he had never had nor sought: a sense of warmth in performing a daily routine, the sense of family.

On the evening of the third day Cameron lay back on his pillow, talking as usual, but the words came slowly and he did not move his head. Roark listened and concentrated on not showing that he knew what went on in the terrible pauses between Cameron's words. The words sounded natural, and the strain they cost was to remain Cameron's last secret, as he wished.

Cameron spoke about the future of building materials. "Watch the light metals industry, Howard. . . . In a few . . . years . . . you'll see them do some astounding things. . . . Watch the plastics, there's a whole new era . . . coming from that. . . . You'll find new tools, new means, new forms. . . . You'll have to show . . . the damn fools . . . what wealth the human brain has made for them . . . what possibilities. . . . Last week I read about a new kind of composition tile . . . and I've thought of a way to use it where nothing . . . else would do . . . take, for instance, a small house . . . about five thousand dollars . . . ."

After a while he stopped and remained silent, his eyes closed. Then Roark heard him whisper suddenly:

"Gail Wynand . . ."

Roark leaned closer to him, bewildered.

"I don't . . . hate anybody any more . . . only Gail Wynand . . . No, I've never laid eyes on him. . . . But he represents . . . everything that's wrong with the world . . . the triumph . . . of overbearing vulgarity. . . . It's Gail Wynand that you'll have to fight, Howard. . . ."

Then he did not speak for a long time. When he opened his eyes again, he smiled. He said:

"I know . . . what you're going through at your office just now. . . ." Roark had never spoken to him of that. "No . . . don't deny and . . . don't say anything. . . . I know. . . . But . . . it's all right. . . . Don't be afraid. . . . Do you remember the day when I tried to fire you? . . . Forget what I said to you then. . . . It was not the whole story. . . . This is . . . Don't be afraid. . . . It was worth it. . . ."

His voice failed and he could not use it any longer. But the faculty of sight remained untouched and he could lie silently and look at Roark without effort. He died half an hour later.

Keating saw Catherine often. He had not announced their engagement, but his mother knew, and it was not a precious secret of his own any longer. Catherine thought, at times, that he had dropped the sense of significance in their meetings. She was spared the loneliness of waiting for him; but she had lost the reassurance of his inevitable returns.

Keating had told her: "Let's wait for the results of that movie competition, Katie. It won't be long, they'll announce the decision in May. If I win—I'll be set for life. Then we'll be married. And that's when I'll meet your uncle—and he'll want to meet me. And I've got to win."

"I know you'll win."

"Besides, old Heyer won't last another month. The doctor told us that we can expect a second stroke at any time and that will be that. If it doesn't get him to the graveyard, it'll certainly get him out of the office."

"Oh, Peter, I don't like to hear you talk like that. You mustn't be so . . . so terribly selfish."

"I'm sorry, dear. Well . . . yes, I guess I'm selfish. Everybody is."

He spent more time with Dominique. Dominique watched him complacently, as if he presented no further problem to her. She seemed to find him suitable as an inconsequential companion for an occasional, inconsequential evening. He thought that she liked him. He knew that this was not an encouraging sign.

He forgot at times that she was Francon's daughter; he forgot all the reasons that prompted him to want her. He felt no need to be prompted. He wanted her. He needed no reasons now but the excitement of her presence.

Yet he felt helpless before her. He refused to accept the thought that a woman could remain indifferent to him. But he was not certain even of her indifference. He waited and tried to guess her moods, to respond as he supposed she wished him to respond. He received no answer.

On a spring night they attended a ball together. They danced, and he drew her close, he stressed the touch of his fingers on her body. He knew that she noticed and understood. She did not withdraw; she looked at him with an unmoving glance that was almost expectation. When they were leaving, he held her wrap and let his fingers rest on her shoulders; she did not move or draw the wrap closed; she waited; she let him lift his hands. Then they walked together down to the cab.

She sat silently in a corner of the cab; she had never before considered his presence important enough to require silence. She sat, her legs crossed, her wrap gathered tightly, her finger tips beating in slow rotation against her knee. He closed his hand softly about her forearm. She did not resist; she did not answer; only her fingers stopped beating. His lips touched her hair; it was not a kiss, he merely let his lips rest against her hair for a long time.

When the cab stopped, he whispered: "Dominique . . . let me come up . . . for just a moment . . ."

"Yes," she answered. The word was flat, impersonal, with no sound of invitation. But she had never allowed it before. He followed her, his heart pounding.

There was one fragment of a second, as she entered her apartment, when she stopped, waiting. He stared at her helplessly, bewildered, too happy. He noticed the pause only when she was moving again, walking away from him, into the drawing room. She sat down, and her hands fell limply one at each side, her arms away from her body, leaving her unprotected. Her eyes were half closed, rectangular, empty.

"Dominique . . ." he whispered, "Dominique . . . how lovely you are! . . ."

Then he was beside her, whispering incoherently:

"Dominique . . . Dominique, I love you . . . Don't laugh at me, please don't laugh! . . . My whole life . . . anything you wish . . . Don't you know how beautiful you are? . . . Dominique . . . I love you . . ."

He stopped, with his arms around her and his face over hers, to catch some hint of response or resistance; he saw nothing. He jerked her violently against him and kissed her lips.

His arms fell open. He let her body fall back against the seat, and he stared at her, aghast. It had not been a kiss; he had not held a woman in his arms; what he had held and kissed had not been alive. Her lips had not moved in answer against his; her arms had not moved to embrace him; it was not revulsion—he could have understood revulsion. It was as if he could hold her forever or drop her, kiss her again or go further to satisfy his desire—and her body would not know it, would not notice it. She was looking at him, past him. She saw a cigarette stub that had fallen off a tray on a table beside her, she moved her hand and slipped the cigarette back into the tray.

"Dominique," he whispered stupidly, "didn't you want me to kiss you?"

"Yes." She was not laughing at him; she was answering simply and helplessly.

"Haven't you ever been kissed before?"

"Yes. Many times."

"Do you always act like that?"

"Always. Just like that."

"Why did you want me to kiss you?"

"I wanted to try it."

"You're not human, Dominique."

She lifted her head, she got up and the sharp precision of the movement was her own again. He knew he would hear no simple, confessing helplessness in her voice; he knew the intimacy was ended, even though her words, when she spoke, were more intimate and revealing than anything she had said; but she spoke as if she did not care what she revealed or to whom:

"I suppose I'm one of those freaks you hear about, an utterly frigid woman. I'm sorry, Peter. You see? You have no rivals, but that includes you also. A disappointment, darling?"

"You . . . you'll outgrow it . . . some day . . ."

"I'm really not so young, Peter. Twenty-five. It must be an interesting experience to sleep with a man. I've wanted to want it. I should think it would be exciting to become a dissolute woman. I am, you know, in everything but in fact. . . . Peter, you look as if you were going to blush in a moment, and that's very amusing."

"Dominique! Haven't you ever been in love at all? Not even a little?"

"I haven't. I really wanted to fall in love with you. I thought it would be convenient. I'd have no trouble with you at all. But you see? I can't feel anything. I can't feel any difference, whether it's you or Alvah Scarret or Lucius Heyer."

He got up. He did not want to look at her. He walked to a window and stood, staring out, his hands clasped behind his back. He had forgotten his desire and her beauty, but he remembered now that she was Francon's daughter.

"Dominique, will you marry me?"

He knew he had to say it now; if he let himself think of her, he would never say it; what he felt for her did not matter any longer; he could not let it stand between him and his future; and what he felt for her was growing into hatred.

"You're not serious?" she asked.

He turned to her. He spoke rapidly, easily; he was lying now, and so he was sure of himself and it was not difficult:

"I love you, Dominique. I'm crazy about you. Give me a chance. If there's no one else, why not? You'll learn to love me—because I understand you. I'll be patient. I'll make you happy."

She shuddered suddenly, and then she laughed. She laughed simply, completely; he saw the pale foam of her dress trembling; she stood straight, her head thrown back, like a string shaking with the vibrations of a blinding insult to him; an insult, because her laughter was not bitter or mocking, but quite simply gay.

Then it stopped. She stood looking at him. She said earnestly:

"Peter, if I ever want to punish myself for something terrible, if I ever want to punish myself disgustingly—I'll marry you." She added: "Consider it a promise."

"I'll wait—no matter what reason you choose for it."

Then she smiled gaily, the cold, gay smile he dreaded.

"Really, Peter, you don't have to do it, you know. You'll get that partnership anyway. And we'll always be good friends. Now it's time for you to go home. Don't forget, you're taking me to the horse show Wednesday. Oh, yes, we're going to the horse show Wednesday. I adore horse shows. Good night, Peter."

He left and walked home through the warm spring night. He walked savagely. If, at that moment, someone had offered him sole ownership of the firm of Francon & Heyer at the price of marrying Dominique, he would have refused it. He knew also, hating himself, that he would not refuse, if it were offered to him on the following morning.

XV

THIS WAS FEAR. THIS WAS WHAT ONE FEELS IN NIGHTMARES, THOUGHT
Peter Keating, only then one awakens when it becomes unbearable, but he could neither awaken nor bear it any longer. It had been growing, for days, for weeks, and now it had caught him: this lewd, unspeakable dread of defeat. He would lose the competition, he was certain that he would lose it, and the certainty grew as each day of waiting passed. He could not work; he jerked when people spoke to him; he had not slept for nights.

He walked toward the house of Lucius Heyer. He tried not to notice the faces of the people he passed, but he had to notice; he had always looked at people; and people looked at him, as they always did. He wanted to shout at them and tell them to turn away, to leave him alone. They were staring at him, he thought, because he was to fail and they knew it.

He was going to Heyer's house to save himself from the coming disaster in the only way he saw left to him. If he failed in that competition—and he knew he was to fail—Francon would be shocked and disillusioned; then if Heyer died, as he could die at any moment, Francon would hesitate—in the bitter aftermath of a public humiliation—to accept Keating as his partner; if Francon hesitated, the game was lost. There were others waiting for the opportunity: Bennett, whom he had been unable to get out of the office; Claude Stengel, who had been doing very well on his own, and had approached Francon with an offer to buy Heyer's place. Keating had nothing to count on, except Francon's uncertain faith in him. Once another partner replaced Heyer, it would be the end of Keating's future. He had come too close and had missed. That was never forgiven.

Through the sleepless nights the decision had become clear and hard in his mind: he had to close the issue at once; he had to take advantage of Francon's deluded hopes before the winner of the competition was announced; he had to force Heyer out and take his place; he had only a few days left.

He remembered Francon's gossip about Heyer's character. He looked through the files in Heyer's office and found what he had hoped to find. It was a letter from a contractor, written fifteen years ago; it stated merely that the contractor was enclosing a check for twenty thousand dollars due Mr. Heyer. Keating looked up the records for that particular building; it did seem that the structure had cost more than it should have

181

cost. That was the year when Heyer had started his collection of porcelain.

He found Heyer alone in his study. It was a small, dim room and the air in it seemed heavy, as if it had not been disturbed for years. The dark mahogany paneling, the tapestries, the priceless pieces of old furniture were kept faultlessly clean, but the room smelt, somehow, of indigence and of decay. There was a single lamp burning on a small table in a corner, and five delicate, precious cups of ancient porcelain on the table. Heyer sat hunched, examining the cups in the dim light, with a vague, pointless enjoyment. He shuddered a little when his old valet admitted Keating, and he blinked in vapid bewilderment, but he asked Keating to sit down.

When he heard the first sounds of his own voice, Keating knew he had lost the fear that had followed him on his way through the streets; his voice was cold and steady. Tim Davis, he thought, Claude Stengel, and now just one more man to be removed.

He explained what he wanted, spreading upon the still air of the room one short, concise, complete paragraph of thought, perfect as a gem with clean edges.

"And so, unless you inform Francon of your retirement tomorrow morning," he concluded, holding the letter by a corner between two fingers, "*this* goes to the A.G.A."

He waited. Heyer sat still, with his pale, bulging eyes blank and his mouth open in a perfect circle. Keating shuddered and wondered whether he was speaking to an idiot.

Then Heyer's mouth moved and his pale pink tongue showed, flickering against his lower teeth.

"But I don't want to retire." He said it simply, guilelessly, in a little petulant whine.

"You will have to retire."

"I don't want to. I'm not going to. I'm a famous architect. I've always been a famous architect. I wish people would stop bothering me. They all want me to retire. I'll tell you a secret." He leaned forward; he whispered slyly: "You may not know it, but I know, he can't deceive me: Guy wants me to retire. He thinks he's outwitting me, but I can see through him. That's a good one on Guy." He giggled softly.

"I don't think you understood me. Do you understand this?" Keating pushed the letter into Heyer's half-closed fingers.

He watched the thin sheet trembling as Heyer held it. Then it dropped to the table and Heyer's left hand with the paralyzed fingers jabbed at it blindly, purposelessly, like a hook. He said, gulping:

"You can't send this to the A.G.A. They'll have my license taken away."

"Certainly," said Keating, "they will."

"And it will be in the papers."

"In all of them."

"You can't do that."

"I'm going to—unless you retire."

Heyer's shoulders drew down to the edge of the table. His head remained above the edge, timidly, as if he were ready to draw it also out of sight.

"You won't do that please you won't," Heyer mumbled in one long whine without pauses. "You're a nice boy you're a very nice boy you won't do it will you?"

The yellow square of paper lay on the table. Heyer's useless left hand reached for it, crawling slowly over the edge. Keating leaned forward and snatched the letter from under his hand.

Heyer looked at him, his head bent to one side, his mouth open. He looked as if he expected Keating to strike him; with a sickening, pleading glance that said he would allow Keating to strike him.

"Please," whispered Heyer, "you won't do that, will you? I don't feel very well. I've never hurt you. I seem to remember, I did something very nice for you once."

"What?" snapped Keating. "What did you do for me?"

"Your name's Peter Keating . . . Peter Keating . . . remember . . . I did something nice for you. . . . You're the boy Guy has so much faith in. Don't trust Guy. I don't trust him. But I like you. We'll make you a designer one of these days." His mouth remained hanging open on the word. A thin strand of saliva trickled down from the corner of his mouth. "Please . . . don't . . ."

Keating's eyes were bright with disgust; aversion goaded him on; he had to make it worse because he couldn't stand it.

"You'll be exposed publicly," said Keating, the sounds of his voice glittering. "You'll be denounced as a grafter. People will point at you. They'll print your picture in the papers. The owners of that building will sue you. They'll throw you in jail."

Heyer said nothing. He did not move. Keating heard the cups on the table tinkling suddenly. He could not see the shaking of Heyer's body. He heard a thin, glassy ringing in the silence of the room, as if the cups were trembling of themselves.

"Get out!" said Keating, raising his voice, not to hear that sound. "Get out of the firm! What do you want to stay for? You're no good. You've never been any good."

The yellow face at the edge of the table opened its mouth and made a wet, gurgling sound like a moan.

Keating sat easily, leaning forward, his knees spread apart, one elbow resting on his knee, the hand hanging down, swinging the letter.

"I . . ." Heyer choked. "I . . ."

"Shut up! You've got nothing to say, except yes or no. Think fast now. I'm not here to argue with you."

Heyer stopped trembling. A shadow cut diagonally across his face. Keating saw one eye that did not blink, and half a mouth, open, the darkness flowing in through the hole, into the face, as if it were drowning.

"Answer me!" Keating screamed, frightened suddenly. "Why don't you answer me?"

The half-face swayed and he saw the head lurch forward; it fell down on the table, and went on, and rolled to the floor, as if cut off; two of the cups fell after it, cracking softly to pieces on the carpet. The first thing Keating felt was relief to see that the body had followed the head and lay crumpled in a heap on the floor, intact. There had been no sound; only the muffled, musical bursting of porcelain.

He'll be furious, thought Keating, looking down at the cups. He had jumped to his feet, he was kneeling, gathering the pieces pointlessly; he saw that they were broken beyond repair. He knew he was thinking also, at the same time, that it had come, that second stroke they had been expecting, and that he would have to do something about it in a moment, but that it was all right, because Heyer would have to retire now.

Then he moved on his knees closer to Heyer's body. He wondered why he did not want to touch it. "Mr. Heyer," he called. His voice was soft, almost respectful. He lifted Heyer's head, cautiously. He let it drop. He heard no sound of its falling. He heard the hiccough in his own throat. Heyer was dead.

He sat beside the body, his buttocks against his heels, his hands spread on his knees. He looked straight ahead; his glance stopped on the folds of the hangings by the door; he wondered whether the gray sheen was dust or the nap of velvet and was it velvet and how old-fashioned it was to have hangings by a door. Then he felt himself shaking. He wanted to vomit. He rose, walked across the room and threw the door open, because he remembered that there was the rest of the apartment somewhere and a valet in it, and he called, trying to scream for help.

Keating came to the office as usual. He answered questions, he explained that Heyer had asked him, that day, to come to his house after dinner; Heyer had wanted to discuss the matter of his retirement. No one doubted the story and Keating knew that no one ever would. Heyer's end had come as everybody had expected it to come. Francon felt nothing but relief. "We knew he would, sooner or later," said Francon. "Why regret that he spared himself and all of us a prolonged agony?"

Keating's manner was calmer than it had been for weeks. It was the calm of blank stupor. The thought followed him, gentle, unstressed, monotonous, at his work, at home, at night: he was a murderer . . . no, but almost a murderer . . . almost a murderer . . . He knew that it had not been an accident; he knew he had counted on the shock and the terror; he had counted on that second stroke which would send Heyer to the hospital for the rest of his days. But was that all he had expected? Hadn't he known what else a second stroke could mean? Had he counted on that? He tried to remember. He tried, wringing his mind dry. He felt nothing. He expected to feel nothing, one way or another. Only he wanted to know. He did not notice what went on in the office around him. He forgot that he had but a short time left to close the deal with Francon about the partnership.

A few days after Heyer's death Francon called him to his office.

"Sit down, Peter," he said with a brighter smile than usual. "Well, I have some good news for you, kid. They read Lucius' will this morning. He had no relatives left, you know. Well, I was surprised, I didn't give him enough credit, I guess, but it seems he could make a nice gesture on occasion. He's left everything to you. . . . Pretty grand, isn't it? Now you won't have to worry about investment when we make arrangements for . . . What's the matter, Peter? . . . Peter, my boy, are you sick?"

Keating's face fell upon his arm on the corner of the desk. He could not let Francon see his face. He was going to be sick; sick, because through the horror, he had caught himself wondering how much Heyer had actually left. . . .

The will had been made out five years ago; perhaps in a senseless spurt of affection for the only person who had shown Heyer consideration in the office; perhaps as a gesture against his partner; it had been made and forgotten. The estate amounted to two hundred thousand dollars, plus Heyer's interest in the firm and his porcelain collection.

Keating left the office early, that day, not hearing the congratulations. He went home, told the news to his mother, left her gasping in the middle of the living room, and locked himself in his bedroom. He went out, saying nothing, before dinner. He had no dinner that night, but he drank himself into a ferocious lucidity, at his favorite speak-easy. And in that heightened state of luminous vision, his head nodding over a glass but his mind steady, he told himself that he had nothing to regret; he had done what anyone would have done; Catherine had said it, he was selfish; everybody was selfish; it was not a pretty thing, to be selfish, but he was not alone in it; he had merely been luckier than most; he had been, because he was better than most; he felt fine; he hoped the useless questions would never come back to him again; every man for himself, he muttered, falling asleep on the table.

The useless questions never came back to him again. He had no time for them in the days that followed. He had won the Cosmo-Slotnick competition.

Peter Keating had known it would be a triumph, but he had not expected the thing that happened. He had dreamed of a sound of trumpets; he had not foreseen a symphonic explosion.

It began with the thin ringing of a telephone, announcing the names of the winners. Then every phone in the office joined in, screaming, bursting from under the fingers of the operator who could barely control the switchboard; calls from every paper in town, from famous architects, questions, demands for interviews, congratulations. Then the flood rushed out of the elevators, poured through the office doors, the messages, the telegrams, the people Keating knew, the people he had never seen before, the reception clerk losing all sense, not knowing whom to admit or refuse, and Keating shaking hands, an endless stream of hands like a wheel with soft moist cogs flapping against his fingers. He did not know what he said at that first interview, with Francon's office full of people and cameras; Francon had thrown the doors of his liquor cabinet wide-open. Francon gulped to all these people that the Cosmo-Slotnick building had been created by Peter Keating alone; Francon did not care; he was magnanimous in a spurt of enthusiasm; besides, it made a good story.

It made a better story than Francon had expected. From the pages of newspapers the face of Peter Keating looked upon the country, the handsome, wholesome, smiling face with the brilliant eyes and the dark curls; it headed columns of print about poverty, struggle, aspiration and unremitting toil that had won their reward; about the faith of a mother who had sacrificed everything to her boy's success; about the "Cinderella of Architecture."

Cosmo-Slotnick were pleased; they had not thought that prize-winning architects could also be young, handsome and poor—well, so recently poor. They had discovered a boy genius; Cosmo-Slotnick adored boy geniuses; Mr. Slotnick was one himself, being only forty-three.

Keating's drawings of the "most beautiful skyscraper on earth" were reproduced in the papers, with the words of the award underneath: ". . . for the brilliant skill and simplicity of its plan . . . for its clean, ruthless efficiency . . . for its ingenious economy of space . . . for the masterful blending of the modern with the traditional in Art . . . to Francon & Heyer and Peter Keating . . ."

Keating appeared in newsreels, shaking hands with Mr. Shupe and Mr. Slotnick, and the subtitle announced what these two gentlemen thought of his building. Keating appeared in newsreels, shaking hands with Miss Dimples Williams, and the subtitle announced what he thought of her current picture. He appeared at architectural banquets and at film banquets, in the place of honor, and he had to make speeches, forgetting whether he was to speak of buildings or of movies. He appeared at architectural clubs and at fan clubs. Cosmo-Slotnick put out a composite picture of Keating and of his building, which could be had for a self-addressed, stamped envelope, and two bits. He made a personal appearance each evening, for a week, on the stage of the Cosmo Theater, with the first run of the latest Cosmo-Slotnick special; he bowed over the footlights, slim and graceful in a black tuxedo, and he spoke for two minutes on the significance of architecture. He presided as judge at a beauty contest in Atlantic City, the winner to be awarded a screen test by Cosmo-Slotnick. He was photographed with a famous prizefighter, under the caption: "Champions." A scale model of his building was made and sent on tour, together with the photographs of the best among the other entries, to be exhibited in the foyers of Cosmo-Slotnick theaters throughout the country.

Mrs. Keating had sobbed at first, clasped Peter in her arms and gulped that she could not believe it. She had stammered, answering questions about Petey and she had posed for pictures, embarrassed, eager to please. Then she became used to it. She told Peter, shrugging, that of course he had won, it was nothing to gape at, no one else could have won. She acquired a brisk little tone of condescension for the reporters. She was distinctly annoyed when she was not included in the photographs taken of Petey. She acquired a mink coat.

Keating let himself be carried by the torrent. He needed the people and the clamor around him. There were no questions and no doubts when he stood on a platform over a sea of faces; the air was heavy, compact, saturated with a single solvent—admiration; there was no room for anything else. He was great; great as the number of people who told him so. He was right; right as the number of people who believed it. He looked at the faces, at the eyes; he saw himself born in them, he saw himself being granted the gift of life. That was Peter Keating, that, the reflection in those staring pupils, and his body was only its reflection.

He found time to spend two hours with Catherine, one evening. He held her in his arms and she whispered radiant plans for their future; he glanced at her with contentment; he did not hear her words; he was thinking of how it would look if they were photographed like this together and in how many papers it would be syndicated.

He saw Dominque once. She was leaving the city for the summer. Dominque was disappointing. She congratulated him, quite correctly; but she looked at him as she had always looked, as if nothing had happened. Of all architectural publications, her column had been the only one that had never mentioned the Cosmo-Slotnick competition or its winner.

"I'm going to Connecticut," she told him. "I'm taking over Father's place down there for the summer. He's letting me have it all to myself. No, Peter, you can't come to visit me. Not even once. I'm going there so I won't have to see anybody." He was disappointed, but it did not spoil the triumph of his days. He was not afraid of Dominique any longer. He felt confident that he could bring her to change her attitude, that he would see the change when she came back in the fall.

But there was one thing which did spoil his triumph; not often and not too loudly. He never tired of hearing what was said about him; but he did not like to hear too much about his building. And when he had to hear it, he did not mind the comments on "the masterful blending of the modern with the traditional" in its façade; but when they spoke of the plan—and they spoke so much of the plan—when he heard about "the brilliant skill and simplicity . . . the clean, ruthless efficiency . . . the ingenious economy of space . . ." when he heard it and thought of . . . He did not think it. There were no words in his brain. He would not allow them. There was only a heavy, dark feeling—and a name.

For two weeks after the award he pushed this thing out of his mind, as a thing unworthy of his concern, to be buried as his doubting, humble past was buried. All winter long he had kept his own sketches of the building with the pencil lines cut across them by another's hand; on the evening of the award he had burned them; it was the first thing he had done.

But the thing would not leave him. Then he grasped suddenly that it was not a vague threat, but a practical danger; and he lost all fear of it. He could deal with a practical danger, he could dispose of it quite simply. He chuckled with relief, he telephoned Roark's office, and made an appointment to see him.

He went to that appointment confidently. For the first time in his life he felt free of the strange uneasiness which he had never been able to explain or escape in Roark's presence. He felt safe now. He was through with Howard Roark.

Roark sat at the desk in his office, waiting. The telephone had rung once, that morning, but it had been only Peter Keating asking for an appointment. He had forgotten now that Keating was coming. He was waiting for the telephone. He had become dependent on that telephone in the last few weeks. He was to hear at any moment about his drawings for the Manhattan Bank Company.

His rent on the office was long since overdue. So was the rent on the room where he lived. He did not care about the room; he could tell the landlord to wait; the landlord waited; it would not have mattered greatly if he had stopped waiting. But it mattered at the office. He told the rental agent that he would have to wait; he did not ask for the delay; he only said flatly, quietly, that there would be a delay, which was all he knew how to do. But his knowledge that he needed this alms from the rental agent, that too much depended on it, had made it sound like begging in his own mind. That was torture. All right, he thought, it's torture. What of it?

The telephone bill was overdue for two months. He had received the final warning. The telephone was to be disconnected in a few days. He had to wait. So much could happen in a few days.

The answer of the bank board, which Weidler had promised him long ago, had been postponed from week to week. The board could reach no decision; there had been objectors and there had been violent supporters; there had been conferences; Weidler told him eloquently little, but he could guess much; there had been days of silence, of silence in the office, of silence in the whole city, of silence within him. He waited.

He sat, slumped across the desk, his face on his arm, his fingers on the stand of the telephone. He thought dimly that he should not sit like that; but he felt very tired today. He thought that he should take his hand off that phone; but he did not move it. Well, yes, he depended on that phone; he could smash it, but he would still depend on it; he and every breath in him and every bit of him. His fingers rested on the stand without moving. It was this and the mail; he had lied to himself also about the mail; he had lied when he had forced himself not to leap, as a rare letter fell through the slot in the door, not to run forward, but to wait, to stand looking at the white envelope on the floor, then to walk to it slowly and pick it up. The slot in the door and the telephone—there was nothing else left to him of the world.

He raised his head, as he thought of it, to look down at the door, at the foot of the door. There was nothing. It was late in the afternoon, probably past the time of the last delivery. He raised his wrist to glance at his watch; he saw his bare wrist; the watch had been pawned. He turned to the window; there was a clock he could distinguish on a distant tower; it was half past four; there would be no other delivery today.

He saw that his hand was lifting the telephone receiver. His fingers were dialing the number.

"No, not yet," Weidler's voice told him over the wire. "We had that meeting scheduled for yesterday, but it had to be called off. . . . I'm keeping after them like a bulldog. . . . I can promise you that we'll have a definite answer tomorrow. I can *almost* promise you. If not tomorrow, then it will have to wait over the week end, but by Monday I promise it for certain. . . . You've been wonderfully patient with us, Mr. Roark. We appreciate it." Roark dropped the receiver. He closed his eyes. He thought he would allow himself to rest, just to rest blankly like this for a few minutes, before he would begin to think of what the date on the telephone notice had been and in what way he could manage to last until Monday.

"Hello, Howard," said Peter Keating.

He opened his eyes. Keating had entered and stood before him, smiling. He wore a light tan spring coat, thrown open, the loops of its belt like handles at his sides, a blue cornflower in his button hole. He stood, his legs apart, his fists on his hips, his hat on the back of his head, his black curls so bright and crisp over his pale forehead that one expected to see drops of spring dew glistening on them as on the cornflower.

"Hello, Peter," said Roark.

Keating sat down comfortably, took his hat off, dropped it in the middle of the desk, and clasped one hand over each knee with a brisk little slap.

"Well, Howard, things are happening, aren't they?"

"Congratulations."

"Thanks. What's the matter, Howard? You look like hell. Surely, you're not overworking yourself, from what I hear?"

This was not the manner he had intended to assume. He had planned the interview to be smooth and friendly. Well, he decided, he'd switch back to that later. But first he had to show that he was not afraid of Roark, that he'd never be afraid again.

"No, I'm not overworking."

"Look, Howard, why don't you drop it?"

That was something he had not intended saying at all. His mouth remained open a little, in atonishment.

"Drop what?"

"The pose. Oh, the ideals, if you prefer. Why don't you come down to earth? Why don't you start working like everybody else? Why don't you stop being a damn fool?" He felt himself rolling down a hill, without brakes. He could not stop.

"What's the matter, Peter?"

"How do you expect to get along in the world? You have to live with people, you know. There are only two ways. You can join them or you can fight them. But you don't seem to be doing either."

"No. Not either."

"And people don't want you. They *don't want you!* Aren't you afraid?"

"No."

"You haven't worked for a year. And you won't. Who'll ever give you work? You might have a few hundreds left—and then it's the end."

"That's wrong, Peter. I have fourteen dollars left, and fifty-seven cents."

"Well? And look at me! I don't care if it's crude to say that myself. That's not the point. I'm not boasting. It doesn't matter who says it. But look at me! Remember how we started? Then look at us now. And then think that it's up to you. Just drop that fool delusion that you're better than everybody else—and go to work. In a year, you'll have an office that'll make you blush to think of this dump. You'll have people running after you, you'll have clients, you'll have friends, you'll have an army of draftsmen to order around! . . . Hell, Howard, it's nothing to me—what can it mean to me?—but this time I'm not fishing for anything for myself, in fact I know that you'd make a dangerous competitor, but I've got to say this to you. Just think, Howard, think of it! you'll be rich, you'll be famous, you'll be respected, you'll be praised, you'll be admired —you'll be one of us! . . . Well? . . . Say something! Why don't you say something?"

He saw that Roark's eyes were not empty and scornful, but attentive and wondering. It was close to some sort of surrender for Roark, because he had not dropped the iron sheet in his eyes, because he allowed his eyes to be puzzled and curious—and almost helpless.

"Look, Peter. I believe you. I know that you have nothing to gain by saying this. I know more than that. I know that you don't want me to succeed—it's all right, I'm not reproaching you, I've always known it—you don't want me ever to reach these things you're offering me. And yet you're pushing me on to reach them, quite sincerely. And you know that if I take your advice, I'll reach them. And it's not love for me, because that wouldn't make you so angry—and so frightened. . . . Peter, what is it that disturbs you about me as I am?"

"I don't know . . ." whispered Keating.

He understood that it was a confession, that answer of his, and a terrifying one. He did not know the nature of what he had confessed and he felt certain that Roark did not know it either. But the thing had been bared; they could not grasp it, but they felt its shape. And it made them sit silently, facing each other, in astonishment, in resignation.

"Pull yourself together, Peter," said Roark gently, as to a comrade. "We'll never speak of that again."

Then Keating said suddenly, his voice clinging in relief to the bright vulgarity of its new tone:

"Aw hell, Howard, I was only talking good plain horse sense. Now if you wanted to work like a normal person——"

"Shut up!" snapped Roark.

Keating leaned back, exhausted. He had nothing else to say. He had forgotten what he had come here to discuss.

"Now," said Roark, "what did you want to tell me about the competition?"

Keating jerked forward. He wondered what had made Roark guess that. And then it became easier, because he forgot the rest in a sweeping surge of resentment.

"Oh, yes!" said Keating crisply, a bright edge of irritation in the sound of his voice. "Yes, I did want to speak to you about that. Thanks for reminding me. Of course, you'd guess it, because you know that I'm not an ungrateful swine. I really came here to thank you, Howard. I haven't forgotten that you had a share in that building, you did give me some advice on it. I'd be the first one to give you part of the credit."

"That's not necessary."

"Oh, it's not that I'd mind, but I'm sure you wouldn't want me to say anything about it. And I'm sure you don't want to say anything your-self, because you know how it is, people are so funny, they misin-terpret everything in such a stupid way. . . . But since I'm getting part of the award money, I thought it's only fair to let you have some of it. I'm glad that it comes at a time when you need it so badly."

He produced his billfold, pulled from it a check he had made out in advance and put it down on the desk. It read: "Pay to the order of Howard Roark—the sum of five hundred dollars."

"Thank you, Peter," said Roark, taking the check.

Then he turned it over, took his fountain pen, wrote on the back: "Pay to the order of Peter Keating," signed and handed the check to Keating.

"And here's my bribe to you, Peter," he said. "For the same purpose. To keep your mouth shut."

Keating stared at him blankly.

"That's all I can offer you now," said Roark. "You can't extort anything from me at present, but later, when I'll have money, I'd like to ask you please not to blackmail me. I'm telling you frankly that you could. Because I don't want anyone to know that I had anything to do with that building."

He laughed at the slow look of comprehension on Keating's face.

"No?" said Roark. "You don't want to blackmail me on that? . . . Go home, Peter. You're perfectly safe. I'll never say a word about it. It's yours, the building and every girder of it and every foot of plumbing and every picture of your face in the papers."

Then Keating jumped to his feet. He was shaking.

"God damn you!" he screamed. "God damn you! Who do you think you are? Who told you that you could do this to people? So you're too good for that building? You want to make me ashamed of it? You rotten, lousy, conceited bastard! Who are you? You don't even have the wits to know that you're a flop, an incompetent, a beggar, a failure, a failure, a failure! And you stand there pronouncing judgment! You, against the whole country! You against everybody! Why should I listen to you? You can't frighten me. You can't touch me. I have the whole world with me! . . . Don't stare at me like that! I've always hated you! You didn't know that, did you? I've always hated you! I always will! I'll break you some day, I swear I will, if it's the last thing I do!"

"Peter," said Roark, "why betray so much?"

Keating's breath failed on a choked moan. He slumped down on a chair, he sat still, his hands clasping the sides of the seat under him.

After a while he raised his head. He asked woodenly:

"Oh God, Howard, what have I been saying?"

"Are you all right now? Can you go?"

"Howard, I'm sorry. I apologize, if you want me to." His voice was raw and dull, without conviction. "I lost my head. Guess I'm just unstrung. I didn't mean any of it. I don't know why I said it. Honestly, I don't."

"Fix your collar. It's unfastened."

"I guess I was angry about what you did with that check. But I suppose you were insulted, too. I'm sorry. I'm stupid like that sometimes. I didn't mean to offend you. We'll just destroy the damn thing."

He picked up the check, struck a match, cautiously watched the paper burn till he had to drop the last scrap.

"Howard, we'll forget it?"

"Don't you think you'd better go now?"

Keating rose heavily, his hands poked about in a few useless gestures, and he mumbled:

"Well . . . well, goodnight, Howard. I . . . I'll see you soon. . . . It's because so much's happened to me lately. . . . Guess I need a rest. . . . So long, Howard. . . ."

When he stepped out into the hall and closed the door behind him, Keating felt an icy sense of relief. He felt heavy and very tired, but drearily sure of himself. He had acquired the knowledge of one thing: he hated Roark. It was not necessary to doubt and wonder and squirm in uneasiness any longer. It was simple. He hated Roark. The reasons? It was not necessary to wonder about the reasons. It was necessary only to hate, to hate blindly, to hate patiently, to hate without anger; only to hate, and let nothing intervene, and not let oneself forget, ever.

The telephone rang late on Monday afternoon.

"Mr. Roark?" said Weidler. "Can you come right over? I don't want to say anything over the phone, but get here at once." The voice sounded clear, gay, radiantly premonitory.

Roark looked at the window, at the clock on the distant tower. He sat laughing at that clock, as at a friendly old enemy; he would not need it any longer, he would have a watch of his own again. He threw his head back in defiance to that pale, gray dial hanging high over the city.

He rose and reached for his coat. He threw his shoulders back, slipping the coat on; he felt pleasure in the jolt of his muscles.

In the street outside, he took a taxi which he could not afford.

The chairman of the board was waiting for him in his office, with Weidler and with the vice-president of the Manhattan Bank Company. There was a long conference table in the room, and Roark's drawings were spread upon it. Weidler rose when he entered and walked to meet him, his hand outstretched. It was in the air of the room, like an overture to the words Weidler uttered, and Roark was not certain of the moment when he heard them, because he thought he had heard them the instant he entered.

"Well, Mr. Roark, the commission's yours," said Weidler.

Roark bowed. It was best not to trust his voice for a few minutes.

The chairman smiled amiably, inviting him to sit down. Roark sat down by the side of the table that supported his drawings. His hand rested on the table. The polished mahogany felt warm and living under his fingers; it was almost as if he were pressing his hand against the foundations of his building; his greatest building, fifty stories to rise in the center of Manhattan.

"I must tell you," the chairman was saying, "that we've had a hell of a fight over that building of yours. Thank God it's over. Some of our members just couldn't swallow your radical innovations. You know how stupidly conservative some people are. But we've found a way to please them, and we got their consent. Mr. Weidler here was really magnificently convincing on your behalf."

A great deal more was said by the three men. Roark barely heard it. He was thinking of the first bite of machine into earth that begins an excavation. Then he heard the chairman saying: ". . . and so it's yours, on one minor condition." He heard that and looked at the chairman.

"It's a small compromise, and when you agree to it we can sign the contract. It's only an inconsequential matter of the building's appearance. I understand that you modernists attach no great importance to a mere façade, it's the plan that counts with you, quite rightly, and we wouldn't think of altering your plan in any way, it's the logic of the plan that sold us on the building. So I'm sure you won't mind."

"What do you want?"

"It's only a matter of a slight alteration in the façade. I'll show you. Our Mr. Parker's son is studying architecture and we had him draw us up a sketch, just a rough sketch to illustrate what we had in mind and to show the members of the board, because they couldn't have visualized the compromise we offered. Here it is."

He pulled a sketch from under the drawings on the table and handed it to Roark.

It was Roark's building on the sketch, very neatly drawn. It was his building, but it had a simplified Doric portico in front, a cornice on top, and his ornament was replaced by a stylized Greek ornament.

Roark got up. He had to stand. He concentrated on the effort of standing. It made the rest easier. He leaned on one straight arm, his hand closed over the edge of the table, the tendons showing under the skin of his wrist.

"You see the point?" said the chairman soothingly. "Our conservatives simply refused to accept a queer stark building like yours. And they claim that the public won't accept it either. So we hit upon a middle course. In this way, though it's not traditional architecture of course, it will give the public the *impression* of what they're accustomed to. It adds a certain air of sound, stable dignity—and that's what we want in a bank, isn't it? It does seem to be an unwritten law that a bank must have a Classic portico—and a bank is not exactly the right institution to parade law-breaking and rebellion. Undermines that intangible feeling of confidence, you know. People don't trust novelty. But this is the scheme that pleased everybody. Personally, I wouldn't insist on it, but I really don't see that it spoils anything. And that's what the board has decided. Of course, we don't mean that we want you to follow this sketch. But it gives you our general idea and you'll work it out yourself, make your own adaptation of the Classic motive to the façade."

Then Roark answered. The men could not classify the tone of his voice; they could not decide whether it was too great a calm or too great an emotion. They concluded that it was calm, because the voice moved forward evenly, without stress, without color, each syllable spaced as by a machine; only the air in the room was not the air that vibrates to a calm voice.

They concluded that there was nothing abnormal in the manner of the man who was speaking, except the fact that his right hand would not leave the edge of the table, and when he had to move the drawings, he did it with his left hand, like a man with one arm paralyzed.

He spoke for a long time. He explained why this structure could not have a Classic motive on its façade. He explained why an honest building, like an honest man, had to be of one piece and one faith; what constituted the life source, the idea in any existing thing or creature, and why—if one smallest part committed treason to that idea—the thing or the creature was dead; and why the good, the high and the noble on earth was only that which kept its integrity.

The chairman interrupted him:

"Mr. Roark, I agree with you. There's no answer to what you're saying. But unfortunately, in practical life, one can't always be so flaw-lessly consistent. There's always the incalculable human element of emo-tion. We can't fight that with cold logic. This discussion is actually superfluous. I can agree with you, but I can't help you. The matter is closed. It was the board's final decision—after more than usually pro-longed consideration, as you know."

"Will you let me appear before the board and speak to them?"

"I'm sorry, Mr. Roark, but the board will not re-open the question for further debate. It was final. I can only ask you to state whether you agree to accept the commission on our terms or not. I must admit that the board has considered the possibility of your refusal. In which case, the name of another architect, one Gordon L. Prescott, has been men-tioned most favorably as an alternative. But I told the board that I felt certain you would accept."

He waited. Roark said nothing.

"You understand the situation, Mr. Roark?"

"Yes," said Roark. His eyes were lowered. He was looking down at the drawings.

"Well?"

Roark did not answer.

"Yes or no, Mr. Roark?"

Roark's head leaned back. He closed his eyes.

"No," said Roark.

After a while the chairman asked:

"Do you realize what you're doing?"

"Quite," said Roark.

"Good God!" Weidler cried suddenly. "Don't you know how big a commission this is? You're a young man, you won't get another chance like this. And . . . all right, damn it all, I'll say it! You need this! I know how badly you need it!"

Roark gathered the drawings from the table, rolled them together and put them under his arm.

"It's sheer insanity!" Weidler moaned. "I want you. We want your building. You need the commission. Do you have to be quite so fanati-cal and selfless about it?"

"What?" Roark asked incredulously.

"Fanatical and selfless."

Roark smiled. He looked down at his drawings. His elbow moved a little, pressing them to his body. He said:

"That was the most selfish thing you've ever seen a man do."

He walked back to his office. He gathered his drawing instruments and the few things he had there. It made one package and he carried it under his arm. He locked the door and gave the key to the rental agent.

He told the agent that he was closing his office. He walked home and left the package there. Then he went to Mike Donnigan's house.

"No?" Mike asked, after one look at him.

"No," said Roark.

"What happened?"

"I'll tell you some other time."

"The bastards!"

"Never mind that, Mike."

"How about the office now?"

"I've closed the office."

"For good?"

"For the time being."

"God damn them all, Red! God damn them!"

"Shut up. I need a job, Mike. Can you help me?"

"Me?"

"I don't know anyone in those trades here. Not anyone that would want me. You know them all."

"In what trades? What are you talking about?"

"In the building trades. Structural work. As I've done before."

"You mean—a plain workman's job?"

"I mean a plain workman's job."

"You're crazy, you God-damn fool!"

"Cut it, Mike. Will you get me a job?"

"But why in hell? You can get a decent job in an architect's office. You know you can."

"I won't, Mike. Not ever again."

"Why?"

"I don't want to touch it. I don't want to see it. I don't want to help them do what they're doing."

"You can get a nice clean job in some other line."

"I would have to think on a nice clean job. I don't want to think. Not their way. It will have to be their way, no matter where I go. I want a job where I won't have to think."

"Architects don't take workmen's jobs."

"That's all this architect can do."

"You can learn something in no time."

"I don't want to learn anything."

"You mean you want me to get you into a construction gang, here, in town?"

"That's what I mean."

"No, God damn you! I can't! I won't! I won't do it!"

"Why?"

"Red, to be putting yourself up like a show for all the bastards in this town to see? For all the sons of bitches to know they brought you down like that? For all of them to gloat?"

Roark laughed.

"I don't give a damn about that, Mike. Why should you?"

"Well, I'm not letting you. I'm not giving the sons of bitches that kinda treat."

"Mike," Roark said softly, "there's nothing else for me to do."

"Hell, yes, there is. I told you before. You'll be listening to reason now. I got all the dough you need until . . ."

"I'll tell you what I've told Austen Heller: If you ever offer me money again, that'll be the end between us."

"But why?"

"Don't argue, Mike."

"But . . ."

"I'm asking you to do me a bigger favor. I want that job. You don't have to feel sorry for me. I don't."

"But . . . but what'll happen to you, Red?"

"Where?"

"I mean . . . your future?"

"I'll save enough money and I'll come back. Or maybe someone will send for me before then."

Mike looked at him. He saw something in Roark's eyes which he knew Roark did not want to be there.

"Okay, Red," said Mike softly.

He thought it over for a long time. He said:

"Listen, Red, I won't get you a job in town. I just can't. It turns my stomach to think of it. But I'll get you something in the same line."

"All right. Anything. It doesn't make any difference to me."

"I've worked for all of that bastard Francon's pet contractors for so long I know everybody ever worked for him. He's got a granite quarry down in Connecticut. One of the foremen's a great pal of mine. He's in town right now. Ever worked in a quarry before?"

"Once. Long ago."

"Think you'll like that?"

"Sure."

"I'll go see him. We won't be telling him who you are, just a friend of mine, that's all."

"Thanks, Mike."

Mike reached for his coat, and then his hands fell back, and he looked at the floor.

"Red . . ."

"It will be all right, Mike."

Roark walked home. It was dark and the street was deserted. There was a strong wind. He could feel the cold, whistling pressure strike his cheeks. It was the only evidence of the flow ripping the air. Nothing moved in the stone corridor about him. There was not a tree to stir, no curtains, no awnings; only naked masses of stone, glass, asphalt and sharp corners. It was strange to feel that fierce movement against his face. But in a trash basket on a corner a crumpled sheet of newspaper was rustling, beating convulsively against the wire mesh. It made the wind real.

In the evening, two days later, Roark left for Connecticut.

From the train, he looked back once at the skyline of the city as it flashed into sight and was held for some moments beyond the windows. The twilight had washed off the details of the buildings. They rose in thin shafts of a soft, porcelain blue, a color not of real things, but of evening and distance. They rose in bare outlines, like empty molds waiting to be filled. The distance had flattened the city. The single shafts stood immeasurably tall, out of scale to the rest of the earth. They were of their own world, and they held up to the sky the statement of what man had conceived and made possible. They were empty molds. But man had come so far; he could go farther. The city on the edge of the sky held a question—and a promise.

Little pinheads of light flared up about the peak of one famous tower, in the windows of the Star Roof Restaurant. Then the train swerved around a bend and the city vanished.

That evening, in the banquet hall of the Star Roof Restaurant, a dinner was held to celebrate the admittance of Peter Keating to partnership in the firm to be known henceforward as Francon & Keating.

At the long table that seemed covered, not with a tablecloth, but with a sheet of light, sat Guy Francon. Somehow, tonight, he did not mind the streaks of silver that appeared on his temples; they sparkled crisply against the black of his hair and they gave him an air of cleanliness and elegance, like the rigid white of his shirt against his black evening clothes. In the place of honor sat Peter Keating. He leaned back, his shoulders straight, his hand closed about the stem of a glass. His black curls glistened against his white forehead. In that one moment of silence, the guests felt no envy, no resentment, no malice. There was a grave feeling of brotherhood in the room, in the presence of the pale, handsome boy who looked solemn as at his first communion. Ralston Holcombe had risen to speak. He stood, his glass in hand. He had prepared his speech, but he was astonished to hear himself saying something quite different, in a voice of complete sincerity. He said:

"We are the guardians of a great human function. Perhaps of the greatest function among the endeavors of man. We have achieved much and we have erred often. But we are willing in all humility to make way for our heirs. We are only men and we are only seekers. But we seek for truth with the best there is in our hearts. We seek with what there is of the sublime granted to the race of men. It is a great quest. To the future of American Architecture!"

Part 2

ELLSWORTH M. TOOHEY

I

To HOLD HIS FISTS CLOSED TIGHT, AS IF THE SKIN OF HIS PALMS had grown fast to the steel he clasped—to keep his feet steady, pressed down hard, the flat rock an upward thrust against his soles—not to feel the existence of his body, but only a few clots of tension: his knees, his wrists, his shoulders and the drill he held—to feel the drill trembling in a long convulsive shudder—to feel his stomach trembling, his lungs trembling, the straight lines of the stone ledges before him dissolving into jagged streaks of trembling—to feel the drill and his body gathered into the single will of pressure, that a shaft of steel might sink slowly into granite—this was all of life for Howard Roark, as it had been in the days of the two months behind him.

He stood on the hot stone in the sun. His face was scorched to bronze. His shirt stuck in long, damp patches to his back. The quarry rose about him in flat shelves breaking against one another. It was a world without curves, grass or soil, a simplified world of stone planes, sharp edges and angles. The stone had not been made by patient centuries welding the sediment of winds and tides; it had come from a molten mass cooling slowly at unknown depth; it had been flung, forced out of the earth, and it still held the shape of violence against the violence of the men on its ledges.

The straight planes stood witness to the force of each cut; the drive of each blow had run in an unswerving line; the stone had cracked open in unbending resistance. Drills bored forward with a low, continuous drone, the tension of the sound cutting through nerves, through skulls, as if the quivering tools were shattering slowly both the stone and the men who held them.

He liked the work. He felt at times as if it were a match of wrestling between his muscles and the granite. He was very tired at night. He liked the emptiness of his body's exhaustion.

Each evening he walked the two miles from the quarry to the little town where the workers lived. The earth of the woods he crossed was soft and warm under his feet; it was strange, after a day spent on the granite ridges; he smiled as at a new pleasure, each evening, and looked down to watch his feet crushing a surface that responded, gave way and conceded faint prints to be left behind.

There was a bathroom in the garret of the house where he roomed; the paint had peeled off the floor long ago and the naked boards were gray-white. He lay in the tub for a long time and let the cool water soak the stone dust out of his skin. He let his head hang back, on the edge of the tub, his eyes closed. The greatness of the weariness was its own relief: it allowed no sensation but the slow pleasure of the tension leaving his muscles.

He ate his dinner in a kitchen, with other quarry workers. He sat alone at a table in a corner; the fumes of the grease, crackling eternally on the vast gas range, hid the rest of the room in a sticky haze. He ate little. He drank a great deal of water; the cold, glittering liquid in a clean glass was intoxicating.

He slept in a small wooden cube under the roof. The boards of the ceiling slanted down over his bed. When it rained, he could hear the burst of each drop against the roof, and it took an effort to realize why he did not feel the rain beating against his body.

Sometimes, after dinner, he would walk into the woods that began behind the house. He would stretch down on the ground, on his stomach, his elbows planted before him, his hands propping his chin, and he would watch the patterns of veins on the green blades of grass under his face; he would blow at them and watch the blades tremble then stop again. He would roll over on his back and lie still, feeling the warmth of the earth under him. Far above, the leaves were still green, but it was a thick, compressed green, as if the color were condensed in one last effort before the dusk coming to dissolve it. The leaves hung without motion against a sky of polished lemon yellow; its luminous pallor emphasized that its light was failing. He pressed his hips, his back into the earth under him; the earth resisted, but it gave way; it was a silent victory; he felt a dim, sensuous pleasure in the muscles of his legs.

Sometimes, not often, he sat up and did not move for a long time; then he smiled, the slow smile of an executioner watching a victim. He thought of his days going by, of the buildings he could have been doing, should have been doing and, perhaps, never would be doing again. He watched the pain's unsummoned appearance with a cold, detached curiosity; he said to himself: Well, here it is again. He waited to see how long it would last. It gave him a strange, hard pleasure to watch his fight against it, and he could forget that it was his own suffering; he could smile in contempt, not realizing that he smiled at his own agony. Such moments were rare. But when they came, he felt as he did in the quarry: that he had to drill through granite, that he had to drive a wedge and blast the thing within him which persisted in calling to his pity.

Dominique Francon lived alone, that summer, in the great Colonial mansion of her father's estate, three miles beyond the quarry town. She received no visitors. An old caretaker and his wife were the only human beings she saw, not too often and merely of necessity; they lived some distance from the mansion, near the stables; the caretaker attended to the grounds and the horses; his wife attended to the house and cooked Dominique's meals.

The meals were served with the gracious severity the old woman had learned in the days when Dominique's mother lived and presided over the guests in that great dining room. At night Dominique found her solitary place at the table laid out as for a formal banquet, the candles lighted, the tongues of yellow flame standing motionless like the shining metal spears of a guard of honor. The darkness stretched the room into a hall, the big windows rose like a flat colonnade of sentinels. A shallow crystal bowl stood in a pool of light in the center of the long table, with a single water lily spreading white petals about a heart yellow like a drop of candle fire.

The old woman served the meal in unobtrusive silence, and disappeared from the house as soon as she could afterward. When Dominique walked up the stairs to her bedroom, she found the fragile lace folds of her nightgown laid out on the bed. In the morning she entered her bathroom and found water in the sunken bathtub, the hyacinth odor of her bath salts, the aquamarine tiles polished, shining under her feet, the huge towels spread out like snowdrifts to swallow her body—yet she heard no steps and felt no living presence in the house. The old woman's treatment of Dominique had the same reverent caution with which she handled the pieces of Venetian glass in the drawing-room cabinets.

Dominique had spent so many summers and winters, surrounding herself with people in order to feel alone, that the experiment of actual solitude was an enchantment to her and a betrayal into a weakness she had never allowed herself: the weakness of enjoying it. She stretched her arms and let them drop lazily, feeling a sweet, drowsy heaviness above her elbows, as after a first drink. She was conscious of her summer dresses, she felt her knees, her thighs encountering the faint resistance of cloth when she moved, and it made her conscious not of the cloth, but of her knees and thighs.

The house stood alone amidst vast grounds, and the woods stretched beyond; there were no neighbors for miles. She rode on horseback down long, deserted roads, down hidden paths leading nowhere. Leaves glittered in the sun and twigs snapped in the wind of her flying passage. She caught her breath at times from the sudden feeling that something magnificent and deadly would meet her beyond the next turn of the road; she could give no identity to what she expected, she could not say whether it was a sight, a person or an event; she knew only its quality—the sensation of a defiling pleasure.

Sometimes she started on foot from the house and walked for miles, setting herself no goal and no hour of return. Cars passed her on the road; the people of the quarry town knew her and bowed to her; she was considered the chatelaine of the countryside, as her mother had been long ago. She turned off the road into the woods and walked on, her arms swinging loosely, her head thrown back, watching the tree tops. She saw clouds swimming behind the leaves; it looked as if a giant tree before her were moving, slanting, ready to fall and crush her; she stopped, she waited, her head thrown back, her throat pulled tight; she felt as if she wanted to be crushed. Then she shrugged and went on. She flung thick branches impatiently out of her way and let them scratch her bare arms. She walked on long after she was exhausted, she drove herself forward against the weariness of her muscles. Then she fell down on her back and lay still, her arms and legs flung out like a cross on the ground, breathing in release, feeling empty and flattened, feeling the weight of the air like a pressure against her breasts.

Some mornings, when she awakened in her bedroom, she heard the explosions of blasting at the granite quarry. She stretched, her arms flung back above her head on the white silk pillow, and she listened. It was the sound of destruction and she liked it.

Because the sun was too hot, that morning, and she knew it would be hotter at the granite quarry, because she wanted to see no one and knew she would face a gang of workers, Dominique walked to the quarry. The thought of seeing it on that blazing day was revolting; she enjoyed the prospect.

When she came out of the woods to the edge of the great stone bowl, she felt as if she were thrust into an execution chamber filled with scalding steam. The heat did not come from the sun, but from that broken cut in the earth, from the reflectors of flat ridges. Her shoulders, her head, her back, exposed to the sky, seemed cool while she felt the hot breath of the stone rising up her legs, to her chin, to her nostrils. The air shimmered below, sparks of fire shot through the granite; she thought the stone was stirring, melting, running in white trickles of lava. Drills and hammers cracked the still weight of the air. It was obscene to see men on the shelves of the furnace. They did not look like workers, they looked like a chain gang serving an unspeakable penance for some unspeakable crime. She could not turn away.

She stood, as an insult to the place below. Her dress—the color of water, a pale green-blue, too simple and expensive, its pleats exact like edges of glass—her thin heels planted wide apart on the boulders, the smooth helmet of her hair, the exaggerated fragility of her body against the sky—flaunted the fastidious coolness of the gardens and drawing rooms from which she came.

She looked down. Her eyes stopped on the orange hair of a man who raised his head and looked at her.

She stood very still, because her first perception was not of sight, but of touch: the consciousness, not of a visual presence, but of a slap in the face. She held one hand awkwardly away from her body, the fingers spread wide on the air, as against a wall. She knew that she could not move until he permitted her to.

She saw his mouth and the silent contempt in the shape of his mouth; the planes of his gaunt, hollow cheeks; the cold, pure brilliance of the eyes that had no trace of pity. She knew it was the most beautiful face she would ever see, because it was the abstraction of strength made visible. She felt a convulsion of anger, of protest, of resistance—and of pleasure. He stood looking up at her; it was not a glance, but an act of ownership. She thought she must let her face give him the answer he deserved. But she was looking, instead, at the stone dust on his burned arms, the wet shirt clinging to his ribs, the lines of his long legs. She was thinking of those statues of men she had always sought; she was wondering what he would look like naked. She saw him looking at her as if he knew that. She thought she had found an aim in life—a sudden, sweeping hatred for that man.

She was first to move. She turned and walked away from him. She saw the superintendent of the quarry on the path ahead, and she waved.

The superintendent rushed forward to meet her. "Why, Miss Francon!" he cried. "Why, how do you do, Miss Francon!"

She hoped the words were heard by the man below. For the first time in her life, she was glad of being Miss Francon, glad of her father's position and possessions, which she had always despised. She thought suddenly that the man below was only a common worker, owned by the owner of this place, and she was almost the owner of this place.

The superintendent stood before her respectfully. She smiled and said:

"I suppose I'll inherit the quarry some day, so I thought I should show some interest in it once in a while."

The superintendent preceded her down the path, displayed his domain to her, explained the work. She followed him far to the other side of the quarry; she descended to the dusty green dell of the work sheds; she inspected the bewildering machinery. She allowed a convincingly sufficient time to elapse. Then she walked back, alone, down the edge of the granite bowl.

She saw him from a distance as she approached. He was working. She saw one strand of red hair that fell over his face and swayed with the trembling of the drill. She thought—hopefully—that the vibrations of the drill hurt him, hurt his body, everything inside his body.

When she was on the rocks above him, he raised his head and looked at her; she had not caught him noticing her approach; he looked up as if he expected her to be there, as if he knew she would be back. She saw the hint of a smile, more insulting than words. He sustained the insolence of looking straight at her, he would not move, he would not grant the concession of turning away—of acknowledging that he had no right to look at her in such manner. He had not merely taken that right, he was saying silently that she had given it to him.

She turned sharply and walked on, down the rocky slope, away from the quarry.

It was not his eyes, not his mouth that she remembered, but his hands. The meaning of that day seemed held in a single picture she had noted: the simple instant of his one hand resting against granite. She saw it again: his finger tips pressed to the stone, his long fingers continuing the straight lines of the tendons that spread in a fan from his wrist to his knuckles. She thought of him, but the vision present through all her thoughts was the picture of that hand on the granite. It frightened her; she could not understand it.

He's only a common worker, she thought, a hired man doing a convict's labor. She thought of that, sitting before the glass shelf of her dressing table. She looked at the crystal objects spread before her; they were like sculptures in ice—they proclaimed her own cold, luxurious fragility; and she thought of his strained body, of his clothes drenched in dust and sweat, of his hands. She stressed the contrast, because it degraded her. She leaned back, closing her eyes. She thought of the many distinguished men whom she had refused. She thought of the quarry worker. She thought of being broken—not by a man she admired, but by a man she loathed. She let her head fall down on her arm; the thought left her weak with pleasure.

For two days she made herself believe that she would escape from this place; she found old travel folders in her trunk, studied them, chose the resort, the hotel and the particular room in that hotel, selected the train she would take, the boat and the number of the stateroom. She found a vicious amusement in doing that, because she knew she would not take this trip she wanted; she would go back to the quarry.

She went back to the quarry three days later. She stopped over the ledge where he worked and she stood watching him openly. When he raised his head, she did not turn away. Her glance told him that she knew the meaning of her action, but did not respect him enough to conceal it. His glance told her only that he had expected her to come. He bent over his drill and went on with his work. She waited. She wanted him to look up. She knew that he knew it. He would not look again.

She stood, watching his hands, waiting for the moments when he touched stone. She forgot the drill and the dynamite. She liked to think of the granite being broken by his hands.

She heard the superintendent calling her name, hurrying to her up the path. She turned to him when he approached.

"I like to watch the men working," she explained.

"Yes, quite a picture, isn't it?" the superintendent agreed. "There's the train starting over there with another load."

She was not watching the train. She saw the man below looking at her, she saw the insolent hint of amusement tell her that he knew she did not want him to look at her now. She turned her head away. The superintendent's eyes traveled over the pit and stopped on the man below them.

"Hey, you down there!" he shouted. "Are you paid to work or to gape?"

The man bent silently over his drill. Dominique laughed aloud.

The superintendent said: "It's a tough crew we got down here, Miss Francon. . . . Some of 'em even with jail records."

"Has that man a jail record?" she asked, pointing down.

"Well, I couldn't say. Wouldn't know them all by sight."

She hoped he had. She wondered whether they whipped convicts nowadays. She hoped they did. At the thought of it, she felt a sinking gasp such as she had felt in childhood, in dreams of falling down a long stairway; but she felt the sinking in her stomach.

She turned brusquely and left the quarry.

She came back many days later. She saw him, unexpectedly, on a flat stretch of stone before her, by the side of the path. She stopped short. She did not want to come too close. It was strange to see him before her, without the defense and excuse of distance.

He stood looking straight at her. Their understanding was too offensively intimate, because they had never said a word to each other. She destroyed it by speaking to him.

"Why do you always stare at me?" she asked sharply.

She thought with relief that words were the best means of estrangement. She had denied everything they both knew by naming it. For a moment, he stood silently, looking at her. She felt terror at the thought that he would not answer, that he would let his silence tell her too clearly why no answer was necessary. But he answered. He said:

"For the same reason you've been staring at me."

"I don't know what you're talking about."

"If you didn't, you'd be much more astonished and much less angry, Miss Francon."

"So you know my name?"

"You've been advertising it loudly enough."

"You'd better not be insolent. I can have you fired at a moment's notice, you know."

He turned his head, looking for someone among the men below. He asked: "Shall I call the superintendent?"

She smiled contemptuously.

"No, of course not. It would be too simple. But since you know who I am, it would be better if you stopped looking at me when I come here. It might be misunderstood."

"I don't think so."

She turned away. She had to control her voice. She looked over the stone ledges. She asked: "Do you find it very hard to work here?"

"Yes. Terribly."

"Do you get tired?"

"Inhumanly."

"How does that feel?"

"I can hardly walk when the day's ended. I can't move my arms at night. When I lie in bed, I can count every muscle in my body by the number of separate, different pains."

She knew suddenly that he was not telling her about himself; he was speaking of her, he was saying the things she wanted to hear and telling her that he knew why she wanted to hear these particular sentences.

She felt anger, a satisfying anger because it was cold and certain. She felt also a desire to let her skin touch his; to let the length of her bare arm press against the length of his; just that; the desire went no further.

She was asking calmly:

"You don't belong here, do you? You don't talk like a worker. What were you before?"

"An electrician. A plumber. A plasterer. Many things."

"Why are you working here?"

"For the money you're paying me, Miss Francon."

She shrugged. She turned and walked away from him up the path. She knew that he was looking after her. She did not glance back. She continued on her way through the quarry, and she left it as soon as she could, but she did not go back down the path where she would have to see him again.

II

DOMINIQUE AWAKENED EACH MORNING TO THE PROSPECT OF A DAY made significant by the existence of a goal to be reached: the goal of making it a day on which she would not go to the quarry.

She had lost the freedom she loved. She knew that a continuous struggle against the compulsion of a single desire was compulsion also, but it was the form she preferred to accept. It was the only manner in which she could let him motivate her life. She found a dark satisfaction in pain—because that pain came from him.

She went to call on her distant neighbors, a wealthy, gracious family who had bored her in New York; she had visited no one all summer. They were astonished and delighted to see her. She sat among a group of distinguished people at the edge of a swimming pool. She watched the air of fastidious elegance around her. She watched the deference of these people's manner when they spoke to her. She glanced at her own reflection in the pool: she looked more delicately austere than any among them.

And she thought, with a vicious thrill, of what these people would do if they read her mind in this moment; if they knew that she was thinking of a man in a quarry, thinking of his body with a sharp intimacy as one does not think of another's body but only of one's own. She smiled; the cold purity of her face prevented them from seeing the nature of that smile. She came back again to visit these people—for the sake of such thoughts in the presence of their respect for her.

One evening, a guest offered to drive her back to her house. He was an eminent young poet. He was pale and slender; he had a soft, sensitive mouth, and eyes hurt by the whole universe. She had not noticed the wistful attention with which he had watched her for a long time. As they drove through the twilight she saw him leaning hesitantly closer to her. She heard his voice whispering the pleading, incoherent things she had heard from many men. He stopped the car. She felt his lips pressed to her shoulder.

She jerked away from him. She sat still for an instant, because she would have to brush against him if she moved and she could not bear to touch him. Then she flung the door open, she leaped out, she slammed the door behind her as if the crash of sound could wipe him out of existence, and she ran blindly. She stopped running after a while, and she walked on, shivering, walked down the dark road until she saw the roof line of her own house.

She stopped, looking about her with her first coherent thought of astonishment. Such incidents had happened to her often in the past; only then she had been amused; she had felt no revulsion; she had felt nothing.

She walked slowly across the lawn, to the house. On the stairs to her room she stopped. She thought of the man in the quarry. She thought, in clear, formed words, that the man in the quarry wanted her. She had known it before; she had known it with his first glance at her. But she had never stated the knowledge to herself.

She laughed. She looked about her, at the silent splendor of her house. The house made the words preposterous. She knew what would never happen to her. And she knew the kind of suffering she could impose on him.

For days she walked with satisfaction through the rooms of her house. It was her defense. She heard the explosions of blasting from the quarry and smiled.

But she felt too certain and the house was too safe. She felt a desire to underscore the safety by challenging it.

She chose the marble slab in front of the fireplace in her bedroom. She wanted it broken. She knelt, hammer in hand, and tried to smash the marble. She pounded it, her thin arm sweeping high over her head, crashing down with ferocious helplessness. She felt the pain in the bones of her arms, in her shoulder sockets. She succeeded in making a long scratch across the marble.

She went to the quarry. She saw him from a distance and walked straight to him.

"Hello," she said casually.

He stopped the drill. He leaned against a stone shelf. He answered:

"Hello."

"I have been thinking of you," she said softly, and stopped, then added, her voice flowing on in the same tone of compelling invitation, "because there's a bit of a dirty job to be done at my house. Would you like to make some extra money?"

"Certainly, Miss Francon."

"Will you come to my house tonight? The way to the servants' entrance is off Ridgewood Road. There's a marble piece at a fireplace that's broken and has to be replaced. I want you to take it out and order a new one made for me."

She expected anger and refusal. He asked:

"What time shall I come?"

"At seven o'clock. What are you paid here?"

"Sixty-two cents an hour."

"I'm sure you're worth that. I'm quite willing to pay you at the same rate. Do you know how to find my house?"

"No, Miss Francon."

"Just ask anyone in the village to direct you."

"Yes, Miss Francon."

She walked away, disappointed. She felt that their secret understanding was lost; he had spoken as if it were a simple job which she could have offered to any other workman. Then she felt the sinking gasp inside, that feeling of shame and pleasure which he always gave her: she realized that their understanding had been more intimate and flagrant than ever—in his natural acceptance of an unnatural offer; he had shown her how much he knew—by his lack of astonishment.

She asked her old caretaker and his wife to remain in the house that evening. Their diffident presence completed the picture of a feudal mansion. She heard the bell of the servants' entrance at seven o'clock. The old woman escorted him to the great front hall where Dominique stood on the landing of a broad stairway.

She watched him approaching, looking up at her. She held the pose long enough to let him suspect that it was a deliberate pose deliberately planned; she broke it at the exact moment before he could become certain of it. She said: "Good evening." Her voice was austerely quiet.

He did not answer, but inclined his head and walked on up the stairs toward her. He wore his work clothes and he carried a bag of tools. His movements had a swift, relaxed kind of energy that did not belong here, in her house, on the polished steps, between the delicate, rigid banisters. She had expected him to seem incongruous in her house; but it was the house that seemed incongruous around him.

She moved one hand, indicating the door of her bedroom. He followed obediently. He did not seem to notice the room when he entered. He entered it as if it were a workshop. He walked straight to the fireplace.

"There it is," she said, one finger pointing to the marble slab.

He said nothing. He knelt, took a thin metal wedge from his bag, held its point against the scratch on the slab, took a hammer and struck one blow. The marble split in a long, deep cut.

He glanced up at her. It was the look she dreaded, a look of laughter that could not be answered, because the laughter could not be seen, only felt. He said:

"Now it's broken and has to be replaced."

She asked calmly:

"Would you know what kind of marble this is and where to order another piece like it?"

"Yes, Miss Francon."

"Go ahead, then. Take it out."

"Yes, Miss Francon."

She stood watching him. It was strange to feel a senseless necessity to watch the mechanical process of the work as if her eyes were helping it. Then she knew that she was afraid to look at the room around them. She made herself raise her head.

She saw the shelf of her dressing table, its glass edge like a narrow green satin ribbon in the semidarkness, and the crystal containers; she saw a pair of white bedroom slippers, a pale blue towel on the floor by a mirror, a pair of stockings thrown over the arm of a chair; she saw the white satin cover of her bed. His shirt had damp stains and gray patches of stone dust; the dust made streaks on the skin of his arms. She felt as if each object in the room had been touched by him, as if the air were a heavy pool of water into which they had been plunged together, and the water that touched him carried the touch to her, to every object in the room. She wanted him to look up. He worked, without raising his head.

She approached him and stood silently over him. She had never stood so close to him before. She looked down at the smooth skin on the back of his neck; she could distinguish single threads of his hair. She glanced down at the tip of her sandal. It was there, on the floor, an inch away from his body; she needed but one movement, a very slight movement of her foot, to touch him. She made a step back.

He moved his head, but not to look up, only to pick another tool from the bag, and bent over his work again.

She laughed aloud. He stopped and glanced at her.

"Yes?" he asked.

Her face was grave, her voice gentle when she answered:

"Oh, I'm sorry. You might have thought that I was laughing at you. But I wasn't, of course."

She added:

"I didn't want to disturb you. I'm sure you're anxious to finish and get out of here. I mean, of course, because you must be tired. But then, on the other hand, I'm paying you by the hour, so it's quite all right if you stretch your time a little, if you want to make more out of it. There must be things you'd like to talk about."

"Oh, yes, Miss Francon."

"Well?"

"I think this is an atrocious fireplace."

"Really? This house was designed by my father."

"Yes, of course, Miss Francon."

"There's no point in your discussing the work of an architect."

"None at all."

"Surely we could choose some other subject."

"Yes, Miss Francon."

She moved away from him. She sat down on the bed, leaning back on straight arms, her legs crossed and pressed close together in a long, straight line. Her body, sagging limply from her shoulders, contradicted the inflexible precision of the legs; the cold austerity of her face contradicted the pose of her body.

He glanced at her occasionally, as he worked. He was speaking obediently. He was saying:

"I shall make certain to get a piece of marble of precisely the same quality, Miss Francon. It is very important to distinguish between the various kinds of marble. Generally speaking, there are three kinds. The white marbles, which are derived from the recrystallization of limestone, the onyx marbles which are chemical deposits of calcium carbonate, and the green marbles which consist mainly of hydrous magnesium silicate or serpentine. This last must not be considered as true marble. True marble is a metamorphic form of limestone, produced by heat and pressure. Pressure is a powerful factor. It leads to consequences which, once started, cannot be controlled."

"What consequences?" she asked, leaning forward.

"The recrystallization of the particles of limestone and the infiltration of foreign elements from the surrounding soil. These constitute the colored streaks which are to be found in most marbles. Pink marble is caused by the presence of manganese oxides, gray marble is due to carbonaceous matter, yellow marble is attributed to a hydrous oxide of iron. This piece here is, of course, white marble. There are a great many varieties of white marble. You should be very careful, Miss Francon . . ."

She sat leaning forward, gathered into a dim black huddle; the lamp light fell on one hand she had dropped limply on her knees, palm up, the fingers half-closed, a thin edge of fire outlining each finger, the dark cloth of her dress making the hand too naked and brilliant.

". . . to make certain that I order a new piece of precisely the same quality. It would not be advisable, for instance, to substitute a piece of white Georgia marble which is not as fine-grained as the white marble of Vermont, which is not as fine-grained as the white marble of Alabama. This is Alabama marble. Very high grade. Very expensive."

He saw her hand close and drop down, out of the light. He continued his work in silence.

When he had finished, he rose, asking:

"Where shall I put the stone?"

"Leave it there. I'll have it removed."

"I'll order a new piece cut to measure and delivered to you C.O.D. Do you wish me to set it?"

"Yes, certainly. I'll let you know when it comes. How much do I owe you?" She glanced at a clock on her bedside table. "Let me see, you've been here three quarters of an hour. That's forty-eight cents." She reached for her bag, she took out a dollar bill, she handed it to him. "Keep the change," she said.

She hoped he would throw it back in her face. He slipped the bill into his pocket. He said:

"Thank you, Miss Francon."

He saw the edge of her long black sleeve trembling over her closed fingers.

"Good night," she said, her voice hollow in anger.

He bowed: "Good night, Miss Francon."

He turned and walked down the stairs, out of the house.

She stopped thinking of him. She thought of the piece of marble he had ordered. She waited for it to come, with the feverish intensity of a sudden mania; she counted the days; she watched the rare trucks on the road beyond the lawn.

She told herself fiercely that she merely wanted the marble to come; just that; nothing else; no hidden reasons; no reasons at all. It was a last, hysterical aftermath; she was free of everything else. The stone would come and that would be the end.

When the stone came, she barely glanced at it. The delivery truck had not left the grounds, when she was at her desk, writing a note on a piece of exquisite stationery. She wrote:

"The marble is here. I want it set tonight."

She sent her caretaker with the note to the quarry. She ordered it delivered to: "I don't know his name. The redheaded workman who was here."

The caretaker came back and brought her a scrap torn from a brown paper bag, bearing in pencil:

"You'll have it set tonight."

She waited, in the suffocating emptiness of impatience, at the window of her bedroom. The servants' entrance bell rang at seven o'clock. There was a knock at her door. "Come in," she snapped—to hide the strange sound of her own voice. The door opened and the caretaker's wife entered, motioning for someone to follow. The person who followed was a short, squat, middle-aged Italian with bow legs, a gold hoop in one ear and a frayed hat held respectfully in both hands.

"The man sent from the quarry, Miss Francon," said the caretaker's wife.

Dominique asked, her voice not a scream and not a question:

"Who are you?"

"Pasquale Orsini," the man answered obediently, bewildered.

"What do you want?"

"Well, I . . . Well, Red down at the quarry said fireplace gotta be fix, he said you wanta I fix her."

"Yes. Yes, of course," she said, rising. "I forgot. Go ahead."

She had to get out of the room. She had to run, not to be seen by anyone, not to be seen by herself if she could escape it.

She stopped somewhere in the garden and stood trembling, pressing her fists against her eyes. It was anger. It was a pure, single emotion that swept everything clean; everything but the terror under the anger; terror, because she knew that she could not go near the quarry now and that she would go.

It was early evening, many days later, when she went to the quarry. She returned on horseback from a long ride through the country, and she saw the shadows lengthening on the lawn; she knew that she could not live through another night. She had to get there before the workers left. She wheeled about. She rode to the quarry, flying, the wind cutting her cheeks.

He was not there when she reached the quarry. She knew at once that he was not there, even though the workers were just leaving and a great many of them were filing down the paths from the stone bowl. She stood, her lips tight, and she looked for him. But she knew that he had left.

She rode into the woods. She flew at random between walls of leaves that melted ahead in the gathering twilight. She stopped, broke a long, thin branch off a tree, tore the leaves off, and went on, using the flexible stick as a whip, lashing her horse to fly faster. She felt as if the speed would hasten the evening on, force the hours ahead to pass more quickly, let her leap across time to catch the coming morning before it came. And then she saw him walking alone on the path before her.

She tore ahead. She caught up with him and stopped sharply, the jolt throwing her forward then back like the release of a spring. He stopped.

They said nothing. They looked at each other. She thought that every silent instant passing was a betrayal; this wordless encounter was too eloquent, this recognition that no greeting was necessary.

She asked, her voice flat:

"Why didn't you come to set the marble?"

"I didn't think it would make any difference to you who came. Or did it, Miss Francon?"

She felt the words not as sounds, but as a blow flat against her mouth. The branch she held went up and slashed across his face. She started off in the sweep of the same motion.

* * * * *

Dominique sat at the dressing table in her bedroom. It was very late. There was no sound in the vast, empty house around her. The French windows of the bedroom were open on a terrace and there was no sound of leaves in the dark garden beyond.

The blankets on her bed were turned down, waiting for her, the pillow white against the tall, black windows. She thought she would try to sleep. She had not seen him for three days. She ran her hands over her head, the curves of her palms pressing against the smooth planes of hair. She pressed her finger tips, wet with perfume, to the hollows of her temples, and held them there for a moment; she felt relief in the cold, contracting bite of the liquid on her skin. A spilled drop of perfume remained on the glass of the dressing table, a drop sparkling like a gem and as expensive.

She did not hear the sound of steps in the garden. She heard them only when they rose up the stairs to the terrace. She sat up, frowning. She looked at the French windows.

He came in. He wore his work clothes, the dirty shirt with rolled sleeves, the trousers smeared with stone dust. He stood looking at her. There was no laughing understanding in his face. His face was drawn, austere in cruelty, ascetic in passion, the cheeks sunken, the lips pulled down, set tight. She jumped to her feet, she stood, her arms thrown back, her fingers spread apart. He didn't move. She saw a vein of his neck rise, beating, and fall down again.

Then he walked to her. He held her as if his flesh had cut through hers and she felt the bones of his arms on the bones of her ribs, her legs jerked tight against his, his mouth on hers.

She did not know whether the jolt of terror shook her first and she thrust her elbows at his throat, twisting her body to escape, or whether she lay still in his arms, in the first instant, in the shock of feeling his skin against hers, the thing she had thought about, had expected, had never known to be like this, could not have known, because this was not part of living, but a thing one could not bear longer than a second.

She tried to tear herself away from him. The effort broke against his arms that had not felt it. Her fists beat against his shoulders, against his face. He moved one hand, took her two wrists, pinned them behind her, under his arm, wrenching her shoulder blades. She twisted her head back. She felt his lips on her breast. She tore herself free.

She fell back against the dressing table, she stood crouching, her hands clasping the edge behind her, her eyes wide, colorless, shapeless in terror. He was laughing. There was the movement of laughter on his face, but no sound. Perhaps he had released her intentionally. He stood, his legs apart, his arms hanging at his sides, letting her be more sharply aware of his body across the space between them than she had been in his arms. She looked at the door behind him, he saw the first hint of movement, no more than a thought of leaping toward that door. He extended his arm, not touching her, and she fell back. Her shoulders moved faintly, rising. He took a step forward and her shoulders fell. She huddled lower, closer to the table. He let her wait. Then he approached. He lifted her without effort. She let her teeth sink into his hand and felt blood on the tip of her tongue. He pulled her head back and he forced her mouth open against his.

She fought like an animal. But she made no sound. She did not call for help. She heard the echoes of her blows in a gasp of his breath, and she knew that it was a gasp of pleasure. She reached for the lamp on the dressing table. He knocked the lamp out of her hand. The crystal burst to pieces in the darkness.

He had thrown her down on the bed and she felt the blood beating in her throat, in her eyes, the hatred, the helpless terror in her blood. She felt the hatred and his hands; his hands moving over her body, the hands that broke granite. She fought in a last convulsion. Then the sudden pain shot up, through her body, to her throat, and she screamed. Then she lay still.

It was an act that could be performed in tenderness, as a seal of love, or in contempt, as a symbol of humiliation and conquest. It could be the act of a lover or the act of a soldier violating an enemy woman. He did it as an act of scorn. Not as love, but as defilement. And this made her lie still and submit. One gesture of tenderness from him—and she would have remained cold, untouched by the thing done to her body. But the act of a master taking shameful, contemptuous possession of her was the kind of rapture she had wanted. Then she felt him shaking with the agony of a pleasure unbearable even to him, she knew that she had given that to him, that it came from her, from her body, and she bit his lips and she knew what he had wanted her to know.

He lay still across the bed, away from her, his head hanging back over the edge. She heard the slow, ending gasps of his breath. She lay on her back, as he had left her, not moving, her mouth open. She felt empty, light and flat.

She saw him get up. She saw his silhouette against the window. He went out, without a word or a glance at her. She noticed that, but it did not matter. She listened blankly to the sound of his steps moving away in the garden.

She lay still for a long time. Then she moved her tongue in her open mouth. She heard a sound that came from somewhere within her, and it was the dry, short, sickening sound of a sob, but she was not crying, her eyes were held paralyzed, dry and open. The sound became motion, a jolt running down her throat to her stomach. It flung her up, she stood awkwardly, bent over, her forearms pressed to her stomach. She heard the small table by the bed rattling in the darkness, and she looked at it, in empty astonishment that a table should move without reason. Then she understood that she was shaking. She was not frightened; it seemed foolish to shake like that, in short, separate jerks, like soundless hiccoughs. She thought she must take a bath. The need was unbearable, as if she had felt it for a long time. Nothing mattered, if only she would take a bath. She dragged her feet slowly to the door of her bathroom.

She turned the light on in the bathroom. She saw herself in a tall mirror. She saw the purple bruises left on her body by his mouth. She heard a moan muffled in her throat, not very loud. It was not the sight, but the sudden flash of knowledge. She knew that she would not take a bath. She knew that she wanted to keep the feeling of his body, the traces of his body on hers, knowing also what such a desire implied. She fell on her knees, clasping the edge of the bathtub. She could not make herself crawl over that edge. Her hands slipped, she lay still on the floor. The tiles were hard and cold under her body. She lay there till morning.

Roark awakened in the morning and thought that last night had been like a point reached, like a stop in the movement of his life. He was moving forward for the sake of such stops; like the moments when he had walked through the half-finished Heller house; like last night. In some unstated way, last night had been what building was to him; in some quality of reaction within him, in what it gave to his consciousness of existence.

They had been united in an understanding beyond the violence, beyond the deliberate obscenity of his action; had she meant less to him, he would not have taken her as he did; had he meant less to her, she would not have fought so desperately. The unrepeatable exaltation was in knowing that they both understood this.

He went to the quarry and he worked that day as usual. She did not come to the quarry and he did not expect her to come. But the thought of her remained. He watched it with curiosity. It was strange to be conscious of another person's existence, to feel it as a close, urgent necessity; a necessity without qualifications, neither pleasant nor painful, merely final like an ultimatum. It was important to know that she existed in the world; it was important to think of her, of how she had awakened this morning, of how she moved, with her body still his, now his forever, of what she thought.

That evening, at dinner in the sooted kitchen, he opened a newspaper and saw the name of Roger Enright in the lines of a gossip column. He read the short paragraph:

"It looks like another grand project on its way to the wastebasket.

Roger Enright, the oil king, seems to be stumped this time. He'll have to call a halt to his latest pipe dream of an Enright House. Architect trouble, we are told. Seems as if half a dozen of the big building boys have been shown the gate by the unsatisfiable Mr. Enright. Top-notchers, all of them."

Roark felt the wrench he had tried so often to fight, not to let it hurt him too much: the wrench of helplessness before the vision of what he could do, what should have been possible and was closed to him. Then, without reason, he thought of Dominique Francon. She had no relation to the things in his mind; he was shocked only to know that she could remain present even among these things.

A week passed. Then, one evening, he found a letter waiting for him at home. It had been forwarded from his former office to his last New York address, from there to Mike, from Mike to Connecticut. The engraved address of an oil company on the envelope meant nothing to him. He opened the letter. He read:

"Dear Mr. Roark,

"I have been endeavoring for some time to get in touch with you, but have been unable to locate you. Please communicate with me at your earliest convenience. I should like to discuss with you my proposed Enright House, if you are the man who built the Fargo Store.

"Sincerely yours,

"Roger Enright."

Half an hour later Roark was on a train. When the train started moving, he remembered Dominique and that he was leaving her behind. The thought seemed distant and unimportant. He was astonished only to know that he still thought of her, even now.

She could accept, thought Dominique, and come to forget in time everything that had happened to her, save one memory: that she had found pleasure in the thing which had happened, that he had known it, and more: that he had known it before he came to her and that he would not have come but for that knowledge. She had not given him the one answer that would have saved her: an answer of simple revulsion—she had found joy in her revulsion, in her terror and in his strength. That was the degradation she had wanted and she hated him for it.

She found a letter one morning, waiting for her on the breakfast table. It was from Alvah Scarret. ". . . When are you coming back, Dominique? I can't tell you how much we miss you here. You're not a comfortable person to have around, I'm actually scared of you, but I might as well inflate your inflated ego some more, at a distance, and confess that we're all waiting for you impatiently. It will be like the homecoming of an Empress."

She read it and smiled. She thought, if they knew . . . those people . . . that old life and that awed reverence before her person . . . I've been raped. . . . I've been raped by some redheaded hoodlum from a stone quarry. . . . I, Dominique Francon. . . . Through the fierce sense of humiliation, the words gave her the same kind of pleasure she had felt in his arms.

She thought of it when she walked through the countryside, when she passed people on the road and the people bowed to her, the chatelaine of the town. She wanted to scream it to the hearing of all.

She was not conscious of the days that passed. She felt content in a strange detachment, alone with the words she kept repeating to herself. Then, one morning, standing on the lawn in her garden, she understood that a week had passed and that she had not seen him for a week. She turned and walked rapidly across the lawn to the road. She was going to the quarry.

She walked the miles to the quarry, down the road, bareheaded in the sun. She did not hurry. It was not necessary to hurry. It was inevitable. To see him again. . . . She had no purpose. The need was too great to name a purpose. . . . Afterward . . . There were other things, hideous, important things behind her and rising vaguely in her mind, but first, above all, just one thing: to see him again . . .

She came to the quarry and she looked slowly, carefully, stupidly about her, stupidly because the enormity of what she saw would not penetrate her brain: she saw at once that he was not there. The work was in full swing, the sun was high over the busiest hour of the day, there was not an idle man in sight, but he was not among the men. She stood, waiting numbly, for a long time.

Then she saw the foreman and she motioned for him to approach.

"Good afternoon, Miss Francon. . . . Lovely day, Miss Francon, isn't it? Just like the middle of summer again and yet fall's not far away, yes, fall's coming, look at the leaves, Miss Francon."

She asked:

"There was a man you had here . . . a man with very bright orange hair . . . where is he?"

"Oh yes. That one. He's gone."

"Gone?"

"Quit. Left for New York, I think. Very suddenly too."

"When? A week ago?"

"Why, no. Just yesterday."

"Who was . . ."

Then she stopped. She was going to ask: "Who was he?" She asked instead:

"Who was working here so late last night? I heard blasting."

"That was for a special order for Mr. Francon's building. The Cosmo-Slotnick Building, you know. A rush job."

"Yes . . . I see. . . ."

"Sorry it disturbed you, Miss Francon."

"Oh, not at all. . . ."

She walked away. She would not ask for his name. It was her last chance of freedom.

She walked swiftly, easily, in sudden relief. She wondered why she had never noticed that she did not know his name and why she had never asked him. Perhaps because she had known everything she had to know about him from that first glance. She thought, one could not find some nameless worker in the city of New York. She was safe. If she knew his name, she would be on her way to New York now.

The future was simple. She had nothing to do except never to ask for his name. She had a reprieve. She had a chance to fight. She would break it—or it would break her. If it did, she would ask for his name.

III

WHEN PETER KEATING ENTERED THE OFFICE, THE OPENING OF the door sounded like a single high blast on a trumpet. The door flew forward as if it had opened of itself to the approach of a man before whom all doors were to open in such manner.

His day in the office began with the newspapers. There was a neat pile of them waiting, stacked on his desk by his secretary. He liked to see what new mentions appeared in print about the progress of the Cosmo-Slotnick Building or the firm of Francon & Keating.

There were no mentions in the papers this morning, and Keating frowned. He saw, however, a story about Ellsworth M. Toohey. It was a startling story. Thomas L. Foster, noted philanthropist, had died and had left, among larger bequests, the modest sum of one hundred thousand dollars to Ellsworth M. Toohey, "my friend and spiritual guide—in appreciation of his noble mind and true devotion to humanity." Ellsworth M. Toohey had accepted the legacy and had turned it over, intact, to the "Workshop of Social Study," a progressive institute of learning where he held the post of lecturer on "Art as a Social Symptom." He had given the simple explanation that he "did not believe in the institution of private inheritance." He had refused all further comment. "No, my friends," he had said, "not about this." And had added, with his charming knack for destroying the earnestness of his own moment: "I like to indulge in the luxury of commenting solely upon interesting subjects. I do not consider myself one of these."

Peter Keating read the story. And because he knew that it was an action which he would never have committed, he admired it tremendously.

Then he thought, with a familiar twinge of annoyance, that he had not been able to meet Ellsworth Toohey. Toohey had left on a lecture tour shortly after the award in the Cosmo-Slotnick competition, and the brilliant gatherings Keating had attended ever since were made empty by the absence of the one man he'd been most eager to meet. No mention of Keating's name had appeared in Toohey's column. Keating turned hopefully, as he did each morning, to "One Small Voice" in the *Banner*. But "One Small Voice" was subtitled "Songs and Things" today, and was devoted to proving the superiority of folk songs over any other form of musical art, and of choral singing over any other manner of musical rendition.

Keating dropped the *Banner*. He got up and paced viciously across

225

the office, because he had to turn now to a disturbing problem. He had been postponing it for several mornings. It was the matter of choosing a sculptor for the Cosmo-Slotnick Building. Months ago the commission for the giant statue of "Industry" to stand in the main lobby of the building had been awarded—tentatively—to Steven Mallory. The award had puzzled Keating, but it had been made by Mr. Slotnick, so Keating had approved of it. He had interviewed Mallory and said: ". . . in recognition of your unusual ability . . . of course you have no name, but you will have, after a commission like this . . . they don't come every day like this building of mine."

He had not liked Mallory. Mallory's eyes were like black holes left after a fire not quite put out, and Mallory had not smiled once. He was twenty-four years old, had had one show of his work, but not many commissions. His work was strange and too violent. Keating remembered that Ellsworth Toohey had said once, long ago, in "One Small Voice": "Mr. Mallory's human figures would have been very fine were it not for the hypothesis that God created the world and the human form. Had Mr. Mallory been entrusted with the job, he might, perhaps, have done better than the Almighty, if we are to judge by what he passes as human bodies in stone. Or would he?"

Keating had been baffled by Mr. Slotnick's choice, until he heard that Dimples Williams had once lived in the same Greenwich Village tenement with Steven Mallory, and Mr. Slotnick could refuse nothing to Dimples Williams at the moment. Mallory had been hired, had worked and had submitted a model of his statue of "Industry." When he saw it, Keating knew that the statue would look like a raw gash, like a smear of fire in the neat elegance of his lobby. It was the slender naked body of a man who looked as if he coud break through the steel plate of a battleship and through any barrier whatever. It stood like a challenge. It left a strange stamp on one's eyes. It made the people around it seem smaller and sadder than usual. For the first time in his life, looking at that statue, Keating thought he understood what was meant by the word "heroic."

He said nothing. But the model was sent on to Mr. Slotnick and many people said, with indignation, what Keating had felt. Mr. Slotnick asked him to select another sculptor and left the choice in his hands.

Keating flopped down in an armchair, leaned back and clicked his tongue against his palate. He wondered whether he should give the commission to Bronson, the sculptor who was a friend of Mrs. Shupe, wife of the president of Cosmo; or to Palmer, who had been recommended by Mr. Huseby who was planning the erection of a new five-million dollar cosmetic factory. Keating discovered that he liked this process of hesitation; he held the fate of two men and of many potential others; their fate, their work, their hope, perhaps even the amount of food in their stomachs. He could choose as he pleased, for any reason, without reasons; he could flip a coin, he could count them off on the buttons of his vest. He was a great man—by the grace of those who depended on him.

Then he noticed the envelope.

It lay on top of a pile of letters on his desk. It was a plain, thin, narrow envelope, but it bore the small masthead of the *Banner* in one corner. He reached for it hastily. It contained no letter; only a strip of proofs for tomorrow's *Banner*. He saw the familiar *"One Small Voice" by Ellsworth M. Toohey*, and under it a single word as subtitle, in large, spaced letters, a single word, blatant in its singleness, a salute by dint of omission:

" K E A T I N G "

He dropped the paper strip and seized it again and read, choking upon great unchewed hunks of sentences, the paper trembling in his hand, the skin on his forehead drawing into tight pink spots. Toohey had written:

"Greatness is an exaggeration, and like all exaggerations of dimension it connotes at once the necessary corollary of emptiness. One thinks of an inflated toy balloon, does one not? There are, however, occasions when we are forced to acknowledge the promise of an approach—brilliantly close—to what we designate loosely by the term of greatness. Such a promise is looming on our architectural horizon in the person of a mere boy named Peter Keating.

"We have heard a great deal—and with justice—about the superb Cosmo-Slotnick Building which he has designed. Let us glance, for once, beyond the building, at the man whose personality is stamped upon it.

"There is no personality stamped upon that building—and in this, my friends, lies the greatness of the personality. It is the greatness of a selfless young spirit that assimilates all things and returns them to the world from which they came, enriched by the gentle brilliance of its own talent. Thus a single man comes to represent, not a lone freak, but the multitude of all men together, to embody the reach of all aspirations in his own. . . .

". . . Those gifted with discrimination will be able to hear the message which Peter Keating addresses to us in the shape of the Cosmo-Slotnick Building, to see that the three simple, massive ground floors are the solid bulk of our working classes which support all of society; that the rows of identical windows offering their panes to the sun are the souls of the common people, of the countless anonymous ones alike in the uniformity of brotherhood, reaching for the light; that the graceful pilasters rising from their firm base in the ground floors and bursting into the gay effervescence of their Corinthian capitals, are the flowers of Culture which blossom only when rooted in the rich soil of the broad masses. . . .

". . . In answer to those who consider all critics as fiends devoted solely to the destruction of sensitive talent, this column wishes to thank Peter Keating for affording us the rare—oh, so rare!—opportunity to prove our delight in our true mission, which is to discover young talent —*when* it is there to be discovered. And if Peter Keating should chance to read these lines, we expect no gratitude from him. The gratitude is ours."

It was when Keating began to read the article for the third time that he noticed a few lines written in red pencil across the space by its title:

"Dear Peter Keating,
"Drop in to see me at my office one of these days. Would love to discover what you look like.

"E.M.T."

He let the clipping flutter down to his desk, and he stood over it, running a strand of hair between his fingers, in a kind of happy stupor. Then he whirled around to his drawing of the Cosmo-Slotnick Building, that hung on the wall between a huge photograph of the Parthenon and one of the Louvre. He looked at the pilasters of his building. He had never thought of them as Culture flowering from out of the broad masses, but he decided that one could very well think that and all the rest of the beautiful stuff.

Then he seized the telephone, he spoke to a high, flat voice which belonged to Ellsworth Toohey's secretary, and he made an appointment to see Toohey at four-thirty of the next afternoon.

In the hours that followed, his daily work assumed a new relish. It was as if his usual activity had been only a bright, flat mural and had now become a noble bas-relief, pushed forward, given a three-dimensional reality by the words of Ellsworth Toohey.

Guy Francon descended from his office once in a while, for no ascertainable purpose. The subtler shades of his shirts and socks matched the gray of his temples. He stood smiling benevolently in silence. Keating flashed past him in the drafting room and acknowledged his presence, not stopping, but slowing his steps long enough to plant a crackling bit of newspaper into the folds of the mauve handkerchief in Francon's breast-pocket, with "Read that when you have time, Guy." He added, his steps half-way across the next room: "Want to have lunch with me today, Guy? Wait for me at the Plaza."

When he came back from lunch, Keating was stopped by a young draftsman who asked, his voice high with excitement:

"Say, Mr. Keating, who's it took a shot at Ellsworth Toohey?"

Keating managed to gasp out:

"Who is it did *what?*"

"Shot Mr. Toohey."

"Who?"

"That's what I want to know, who."

"Shot . . . *Ellsworth Toohey?*"

"That's what I saw in the paper in the restaurant a guy had. Didn't have time to get one."

"He's . . . *killed?*"

"That's what I don't know. Saw only it said about a shot."

"If he's dead, does that mean they won't publish his column tomorrow?"

"Dunno. Why, Mr. Keating?"

"Go get me a paper."

"But I've got to . . ."

"Get me that paper, you damned idiot!"

The story was there, in the afternoon papers. A shot had been fired at Ellsworth Toohey that morning, as he stepped out of his car in front of a radio station where he was to deliver an address on "The Voiceless and the Undefended." The shot had missed him. Ellsworth Toohey had remained calm and sane throughout. His behavior had been theatrical only in too complete an absence of anything theatrical. He had said: "We cannot keep a radio audience waiting," and had hurried on upstairs to the microphone where, never mentioning the incident, he delivered a half-hour's speech from memory, as he always did. The assailant had said nothing when arrested.

Keating stared—his throat dry—at the name of the assailant. It was Steven Mallory.

Only the inexplicable frightened Keating, particularly when the inexplicable lay, not in tangible facts, but in that causeless feeling of dread within him. There was nothing to concern him directly in what had happened, except his wish that it had been someone else, anyone but Steven Mallory; and that he didn't know why he should wish this.

Steven Mallory had remained silent. He had given no explanation of his act. At first, it was supposed that he might have been prompted by despair at the loss of his commission for the Cosmo-Slotnick Building, since it was learned that he lived in revolting poverty. But it was learned, beyond any doubt, that Ellsworth Toohey had had no connection whatever with his loss. Toohey had never spoken to Mr. Slotnick about Steven Mallory. Toohey had not seen the statue of "Industry." On this point Mallory had broken his silence to admit that he had never met Toohey nor seen him in person before, nor known any of Toohey's friends. "Do you think that Mr. Toohey was in some way responsible for your losing that commission?" he was asked. Mallory had answered: "No." "Then why?" Mallory said nothing.

Toohey had not recognized his assailant when he saw him seized by policemen on the sidewalk outside the radio station. He did not learn his name until after the broadcast. Then, stepping out of the studio into an anteroom full of waiting newsmen, Toohey said: "No, of course I won't press any charges. I wish they'd let him go. Who is he, by the way?" When he heard the name, Toohey's glance remained fixed somewhere between the shoulder of one man and the hat brim of another. Then Toohey—who had stood calmly while a bullet struck an inch from his face against the glass of the entrance door below—uttered one word and the word seemed to fall at his feet, heavy with fear: *"Why?"*

No one could answer. Presently, Toohey shrugged, smiled, and said: "If it was an attempt at free publicity—well, what atrocious taste!" But nobody believed this explanation, because all felt that Toohey did not believe it either. Through the interviews that followed, Toohey answered questions gaily. He said: "I had never thought myself important enough to warrant assassination. It would be the greatest tribute one could possibly expect—if it weren't so much in the style of an operetta." He managed to convey the charming impression that nothing of importance had happened because nothing of importance ever happened on earth.

Mallory was sent to jail to await trial. All efforts to question him failed.

The thought that kept Keating uneasily awake for many hours, that night, was the groundless certainty that Toohey felt exactly as he did. He knows, thought Keating, and I know, that there is—in Steven Mallory's motive—a greater danger than in his murderous attempt. But we shall never know his motive. Or shall we? . . . And then he touched the core of fear: it was the sudden wish that he might be guarded, through the years to come, to the end of his life, from ever learning that motive.

Ellsworth Toohey's secretary rose in a leisurely manner, when Keating entered, and opened for him the door into Ellsworth Toohey's office.

Keating had grown past the stage of experiencing anxiety at the prospect of meeting a famous man, but he experienced it in the moment when he saw the door opening under her hand. He wondered what

Toohey really looked like. He remembered the magnificent voice he had heard in the lobby of the strike meeting, and he imagined a giant of a man, with a rich mane of hair, perhaps, just turning gray, with bold, broad features of an ineffable benevolence, something vaguely like the countenance of God the Father.

"Mr. Peter Keating—Mr. Toohey," said the secretary and closed the door behind him.

At a first glance upon Ellsworth Monkton Toohey one wished to offer him a heavy, well-padded overcoat—so frail and unprotected did his thin little body appear, like that of a chicken just emerging from the egg, in all the sorry fragility of unhardened bones. At a second glance one wished to be sure that the overcoat should be an exceedingly good one—so exquisite were the garments covering that body. The lines of the dark suit followed frankly the shape within it, apologizing for nothing: they sank with the concavity of the narrow chest, they slid down from the long, thin neck with the sharp slope of the shoulders. A great forehead dominated the body. The wedge-shaped face descended from the broad temples to a small, pointed chin. The hair was black, lacquered, divided into equal halves by a thin white line. This made the skull look tight and trim, but left too much emphasis to the ears that flared out in solitary nakedness, like the handles of a bouillon cup. The nose was long and thin, prolonged by the small dab of a black mustache. The eyes were dark and startling. They held such a wealth of intellect and of twinkling gaiety that his glasses seemed to be worn not to protect his eyes but to protect other men from their excessive brilliance.

"Hello, Peter Keating," said Ellsworth Monkton Toohey in his compelling, magical voice. "What do you think of the temple of Nike Apteros?"

"How . . . do you do, Mr. Toohey," said Keating, stopped, stupefied. "What do I think . . . of what?"

"Sit down, my friend. Of the temple of Nike Apteros."

"Well . . . Well . . . I . . ."

"I feel certain that you couldn't have overlooked that little gem. The Parthenon has usurped the recognition which—and isn't that usually the case? the bigger and stronger appropriating all the glory, while the beauty of the unprepossessing goes unsung—which should have been awarded to that magnificent little creation of the great free spirit of Greece. You've noted, I'm sure, the fine balance of its mass, the supreme perfection of its modest proportions—ah, yes, you know, the supreme in the modest—the delicate craftsmanship of detail?"

"Yes, of course," muttered Keating, "that's always been my favorite —the temple of Nike Apteros."

"Really?" said Ellsworth Toohey, with a smile which Keating could not quite classify. "I was certain of it. I was certain you'd say it. You have a very handsome face, Peter Keating, when you don't stare like this—which is really quite unnecessary."

And Toohey was laughing suddenly, laughing quite obviously, quite insultingly, at Keating and at himself; it was as if he were underscoring the falseness of the whole procedure. Keating sat aghast for an instant; and then he found himself laughing easily in answer, as if at home with a very old friend.

"That's better," said Toohey. "Don't you find it advisable not to talk too seriously in an important moment? And this might be a very important moment—who knows?—for both of us. And, of course, I knew you'd be a little afraid of me and—oh, I admit—I was quite a bit afraid of you, so isn't this much better?"

"Oh, yes, Mr. Toohey," said Keating happily. His normal assurance in meeting people had vanished; but he felt at ease, as if all responsibility were taken away from him and he did not have to worry about saying the right things, because he was being led gently into saying them without any effort on his part. "I've always known it would be an important moment when I met you, Mr. Toohey. Always. For years."

"Really?" said Ellsworth Toohey, the eyes behind the glasses attentive. "Why?"

"Because I'd always hoped that I would please you, that you'd approve to me . . . of my work . . . when the time came . . . why, I even . . ."

"Yes?"

". . . I even thought, so often, when drawing, is this the kind of a building that Ellsworth Toohey would say is good? I tried to see it like that, through your eyes . . . I . . . I've . . ." Toohey listened watchfully. "I've always wanted to meet you because you're such a profound thinker and a man of such cultural distinc——"

"Now," said Toohey, his voice kindly but a little impatient; his interest had dropped on that last sentence. "None of that. I don't mean to be ungracious, but we'll dispense with that sort of thing, shall we? Unnatural as this may sound, I really don't like to hear personal praise."

It was Toohey's eyes, thought Keating, that put him at ease. There was such a vast understanding in Toohey's eyes and such an unfastidious kindness—no, what a word to think of—such an unlimited kindness. It was as if one could hide nothing from him, but it was not necessary to hide it, because he would forgive anything. They were the most unaccusing eyes that Keating had ever seen.

"But, Mr. Toohey," he muttered, "I did want to . . ."

"You wanted to thank me for my article," said Toohey and made a little grimace of gay despair. "And here I've been trying so hard to prevent you from doing it. Do let me get away with it, won't you?

There's no reason why you should thank me. If you happened to deserve the things I said—well, the credit belongs to you, not to me. Doesn't it?"

"But I was so happy that you thought I'm . . ."

". . . a great architect? But surely, my boy, you knew that. Or weren't you quite sure? Never quite sure of it?"

"Well, I . . ."

It was only a second's pause. And it seemed to Keating that this pause was all Toohey had wanted to hear from him; Toohey did not wait for the rest, but spoke as if he had received a full answer, and an answer that pleased him.

"And as for the Cosmo-Slotnick Building, who can deny that it's an extraordinary achievement? You know, I was greatly intrigued by its plan. It's a most ingenious plan. A brilliant plan. Very unusual. Quite different from what I have observed in your previous work. Isn't it?"

"Naturally," said Keating, his voice clear and hard for the first time, "the problem was different from anything I'd done before, so I worked out that plan to fit the particular requirements of the problem."

"Of course," said Toohey gently. "A beautiful piece of work. You should be proud of it."

Keating noticed that Toohey's eyes stood centered in the middle of the lenses and the lenses stood focused straight on his pupils, and Keating knew suddenly that Toohey knew he had not designed the plan of the Cosmo-Slotnick Building. This did not frighten him. What frightened him was that he saw approval in Toohey's eyes.

"If you must feel—no, not gratitude, gratitude is such an embarrassing word—but, shall we say, appreciation?" Toohey continued, and his voice had grown softer, as if Keating were a fellow conspirator who would know that the words used were to be, from now on, a code for a private meaning, "you might thank me for understanding the symbolic implications of your building and for stating them in words as you stated them in marble. Since, of course, you are not just a common mason, but a thinker in stone."

"Yes," said Keating, "that was my abstract theme, when I designed the building—the great masses and the flowers of culture. I've always believed that true culture springs from the common man. But I had no hope that anyone would ever understand me."

Toohey smiled. His thin lips slid open, his teeth showed. He was not looking at Keating. He was looking down at his own hand, the long slender, sensitive hand of a concert pianist, moving a sheet of paper on the desk. Then he said: "Perhaps we're brothers of the spirit, Keating. The human spirit. That is all that matters in life"—not looking at Keating, but past him, the lenses raised flagrantly to a line over Keating's face.

And Keating knew that Toohey knew he had never thought of any abstract theme until he'd read that article, and more: that Toohey approved again. When the lenses moved slowly to Keating's face, the eyes were sweet with affection, an affection very cold and very real. Then Keating felt as if the walls of the room were moving gently in upon him, pushing him into a terrible intimacy, not with Toohey, but with some unknown guilt. He wanted to leap to his feet and run. He sat still, his mouth half open.

And without knowing what prompted him, Keating heard his own voice in the silence:

"And I did want to say how glad I was that you escaped that maniac's bullet yesterday, Mr. Toohey."

"Oh? . . . Oh, thanks. That? Well! Don't let it upset you. Just one of the minor penalties one pays for prominence in public life."

"I've never liked Mallory. A strange sort of person. Too tense. I don't like people who're tense. I've never liked his work either."

"Just an exhibitionist. Won't amount to much."

"It wasn't my idea, of course, to give him a try. It was Mr. Slotnick's. Pull, you know. But Mr. Slotnick knew better in the end."

"Did Mallory ever mention my name to you?"

"No. Never."

"I haven't even met him, you know. Never saw him before. Why did he do it?"

And then it was Toohey who sat still, before what he saw on Keating's face; Toohey, alert and insecure for the first time. This was it, thought Keating, this was the bond between them, and the bond was fear, and more, much more than that, but fear was the only recognizable name to give it. And he knew, with unreasoning finality, that he liked Toohey better than any man he had ever met.

"Well, you know how it is," said Keating brightly, hoping that the commonplace he was about to utter would close the subject. "Mallory is an incompetent and knows it and he decided to take it out on you as on a symbol of the great and the able."

But instead of a smile, Keating saw the shot of Toohey's sudden glance at him; it was not a glance, it was a fluoroscope, he thought he could feel it crawling searchingly inside his bones. Then Toohey's face seemed to harden, drawing together again in composure, and Keating knew that Toohey had found relief somewhere, in his bones or in his gaping, bewildered face, that some hidden immensity of ignorance within him had given Toohey reassurance. Then Toohey said slowly, strangely, derisively:

"You and I, we're going to be great friends, Peter."

Keating let a moment pass before he caught himself to answer hastily:

"Oh, I hope so, Mr. Toohey!"

"Really, Peter! I'm not as old as all that, am I? 'Ellsworth' is the monument to my parents' peculiar taste in nomenclature."

"Yes . . . Ellsworth."

"That's better. I really don't mind the name, when compared to some of the things I've been called privately—and publicly—these many years. Oh, well. Flattering. When one makes enemies one knows that one's dangerous where it's necessary to be dangerous. There are things that must be destroyed—or they'll destroy us. We'll see a great deal of each other, Peter." The voice was smooth and sure now, with the finality of a decision tested and reached, with the certainty that never again would anything in Keating be a question mark to him. "For instance, I've been thinking for some time of getting together a few young architects—I know so many of them—just an informal little organization, to exchange ideas, you know, to develop a spirit of co-operation, to follow a common line of action for the common good of the profession if necessity arises. Nothing as stuffy as the A.G.A. Just a youth group. Think you'd be interested?"

"Why, of course! And you'd be the chairman?"

"Oh dear, no. I'm never chairman of anything, Peter. I dislike titles. No, I rather thought you'd make the right chairman for us, can't think of anyone better."

"Me?"

"You, Peter. Oh, well, it's only a project—nothing definite—just an idea I've been toying with in odd moments. We'll talk about it some other time. There's something I'd like you to do—and that's really one of the reasons why I wanted to meet you."

"Oh, sure, Mr. Too—sure, Ellsworth. Anything I can do for you . . ."

"It's not for me. Do you know Lois Cook?"

"Lois . . . who?"

"Cook. You don't. But you will. That young woman is the greatest literary genius since Goethe. You must read her, Peter. I don't suggest that as a rule except to the discriminating. She's so much above the heads of the middle-class who love the obvious. She's planning to build a house. A little private residence on the Bowery. Yes, on the Bowery. Just like Lois. She's asked me to recommend an architect. I'm certain that it will take a person like you to understand a person like Lois. I'm going to give her your name—if you're interested in what is to be a small, though quite costly, residence."

"But of course! That's . . . very kind of you, Ellsworth! You know, I thought when you said . . . and when I read your note, that you wanted —well, some favor from me, you know, a good turn for a good turn, and here you're . . ."

"My dear Peter, how naïve you are!"

"Oh, I suppose I shouldn't have said that! I'm sorry. I didn't mean to offend you, I . . ."

"I don't mind. You must learn to know me better. Strange as it may sound, a totally selfless interest in one's fellow men *is* possible in this world, Peter."

Then they talked about Lois Cook and her three published works— "Novels? No, Peter, not exactly novels. . . . No, not collections of stories either . . . that's just it, just Lois Cook—a new form of literature entirely . . ."—about the fortune she had inherited from a long line of successful tradesmen, and about the house she planned to build.

It was only when Toohey had risen to escort Keating to the door— and Keating noted how precariously erect he stood on his very small feet—that Toohey paused suddenly to say:

"Incidentally, it seems to me as if I should remember some personal connection between us, though for the life of me I can't quite place . . . oh, yes, of course. My niece. Little Catherine."

Keating felt his face tighten, and knew he must not allow this to be discussed, but smiled awkwardly instead of protesting.

"I understand you're engaged to her?"

"Yes."

"Charming," said Toohey. "Very charming. Should enjoy being your uncle. You love her very much?"

"Yes," said Keating. "Very much."

The absence of stress in his voice made the answer solemn. It was, laid before Toohey, the first bit of sincerity and of importance within Keating's being.

"How pretty," said Toohey. "Young love. Spring and dawn and heaven and drugstore chocolates at a dollar and a quarter a box. The prerogative of the gods and of the movies. . . . Oh, I do approve, Peter. I think it's lovely. You couldn't have made a better choice than Catherine. She's just the kind for whom the world is well lost—the world with all its problems and all its opportunities for greatness—oh, yes, well lost because she's innocent and sweet and pretty and anemic."

"If you're going to . . ." Keating began, but Toohey smiled with a luminous sort of kindliness.

"Oh, Peter, of course I understand. And I approve. I'm a realist. Man has always insisted on making an ass of himself. Oh, come now, we must never lose our sense of humor. Nothing's really sacred but a sense of humor. Still, I've always loved the tale of Tristan and Isolde. It's the most beautiful story ever told—next to that of Mickey and Minnie Mouse."

IV

"... TOOTHBRUSH IN THE JAW TOOTHBRUSH BRUSH BRUSH tooth jaw foam dome in the foam Roman dome come home home in the jaw Rome dome tooth toothbrush toothpick pickpocket socket rocket . . ."

Peter Keating squinted his eyes, his glance unfocused as for a great distance, but put the book down. The book was thin and black, with scarlet letters forming: *Clouds and Shrouds by Lois Cook*. The jacket said that it was a record of Miss Cook's travels around the world.

Keating leaned back with a sense of warmth and well-being. He liked this book. It had made the routine of his Sunday morning breakfast a profound spiritual experience; he was certain that it was profound, because he didn't understand it.

Peter Keating had never felt the need to formulate abstract convictions. But he had a working substitute. "A thing is not high if one can reach it; it is not great if one can reason about it; it is not deep if one can see its bottom"—this had always been his credo, unstated and unquestioned. This spared him any attempt to reach, reason or see; and it cast a nice reflection of scorn on those who made the attempt. So he was able to enjoy the work of Lois Cook. He felt uplifted by the knowledge of his own capacity to respond to the abstract, the profound, the ideal. Toohey had said: "That's just it, sound as sound, the poetry of words as words, style as a revolt against style. But only the finest spirit can appreciate it, Peter." Keating thought he could talk of this book to his friends, and if they did not understand he would know that he was superior to them. He would not need to explain that superiority—that's just it, "superiority as superiority"—automatically denied to those who asked for explanations. He loved the book.

He reached for another piece of toast. He saw, at the end of the table, left there for him by his mother, the heavy pile of the Sunday paper. He picked it up, feeling strong enough, in this moment, in the confidence of his secret spiritual grandeur, to face the whole world contained in that pile. He pulled out the rotogravure section. He stopped. He saw the reproduction of a drawing: the Enright House by Howard Roark.

He did not need to see the caption or the brusque signature in the corner of the sketch; he knew that no one else had conceived that house and he knew the manner of drawing, serene and violent at once, the pencil lines like high-tension wires on the paper, slender and innocent to see, but not to be touched. It was a structure on a broad space by the East River. He did not grasp it as a building, at first glance, but as a

237

rising mass of rock crystal. There was the same severe, mathematical order holding together a free, fantastic growth; straight lines and clean angles, space slashed with a knife, yet in a harmony of formation as delicate as the work of a jeweler; an incredible variety of shapes, each separate unit unrepeated, but leading inevitably to the next one and to the whole; so that the future inhabitants were to have, not a square cage out of a square pile of cages, but each a single house held to the other houses like a single crystal to the side of a rock.

Keating looked at the sketch. He had known for a long time that Howard Roark had been chosen to build the Enright House. He had seen a few mentions of Roark's name in the papers; not much, all of it to be summed up only as "some young architect chosen by Mr. Enright for some reason, probably an interesting young architect." The caption under the drawing announced that the construction of the project was to begin at once. Well, thought Keating, and dropped the paper, so what? The paper fell beside the black and scarlet book. He looked at both. He felt dimly as if Lois Cook were his defense against Howard Roark.

"What's that, Petey?" his mother's voice asked behind him.

He handed the paper to her over his shoulder. The paper fell past him back to the table in a second.

"Oh," shrugged Mrs. Keating. "Huh . . ."

She stood beside him. Her trim silk dress was fitted too tightly, revealing the solid rigidity of her corset; a small pin glittered at her throat, small enough to display ostentatiously that it was made of real diamonds. She was like the new apartment into which they had moved: conspicuously expensive. The apartment's decoration had been Keating's first professional job for himself. It had been furnished in fresh, new mid-Victorian. It was conservative and stately. Over the fireplace in the drawing room hung a large old painting of what was not but looked like an illustrious ancestor.

"Petey sweetheart, I do hate to rush you on a Sunday morning, but isn't it time to dress up? I've got to run now and I'd hate you to forget the time and be late, it's so nice of Mr. Toohey asking you to his house!"

"Yes, Mother."

"Any famous guests coming too?"

"No. No guests. But there will be one other person there. Not famous." She looked at him expectantly. He added: "Katie will be there."

The name seemed to have no effect on her whatever. A strange assurance had coated her lately, like a layer of fat through which that particular question could penetrate no longer.

"Just a family tea," he emphasized. "That's what he said."

"Very nice of him. I'm sure Mr. Toohey is a very intelligent man."

"Yes, Mother."
He rose impatiently and went to his room.

It was Keating's first visit to the distinguished residential hotel where Catherine and her uncle had moved recently. He did not notice much about the apartment, beyond remembering that it was simple, very clean and smartly modest, that it contained a great number of books and very few pictures, but these authentic and precious. One never remembered the apartment of Ellsworth Toohey, only its host. The host, on this Sunday afternoon, wore a dark gray suit, correct as a uniform, and bedroom slippers of black patent leather trimmed with red; the slippers mocked the severe elegance of the suit, yet completed the elegance as an audacious anti-climax. He sat in a broad, low chair and his face wore an expression of cautious gentleness, so cautious that Keating and Catherine felt, at times, as if they were insignificant soap bubbles.

Keating did not like the way Catherine sat on the edge of a chair, hunched, her legs drawn awkwardly together. He wished she would not wear the same suit for the third season, but she did. She kept her eyes on one point somewhere in the middle of the carpet. She seldom looked at Keating. She never looked at her uncle. Keating found no trace of that joyous admiration with which she had always spoken of Toohey, which he had expected to see her display in his presence. There was something heavy and colorless about Catherine, and very tired.

Toohey's valet brought in the tea tray.

"You will pour, won't you please, my dear?" said Toohey to Catherine. "Ah, there's nothing like tea in the afternoon. When the British Empire collapses, historians will find that it had made but two invaluable contributions to civilization—this tea ritual and the detective novel. Catherine, my dear, do you have to grasp that pot handle as if it were a meat axe? But never mind, it's charming, it's really what we love you for, Peter and I, we wouldn't love you if you were graceful as a duchess —who wants a duchess nowadays?"

Catherine poured the tea and spilled it on the glass table top, which she had never done before.

"I did want to see you two together for once," said Toohey, holding a delicate cup balanced nonchalantly. "Perfectly silly of me, isn't it? There's really nothing to make an occasion of, but then I'm silly and sentimental at times, like all of us. My compliments on your choice, Catherine. I owe you an apology, I never suspected you of such good taste. You and Peter make a wonderful couple. You'll do a great deal for him. You'll cook his Cream of Wheat, launder his handkerchiefs and bear his children, though of course the children will all have measles at one time or another, which is a nuisance."

"But, after all, you . . . you do approve of it?" Keating asked anxiously.

"Approve of it? Of what, Peter?"

"Of our marriage . . . eventually."

"What a superfluous question, Peter! Of course, I approve of it. But how young you are! That's the way of young people—they make an issue where none exists. You asked that as if the whole thing were important enough to disapprove of."

"Katie and I met seven years ago," said Keating defensively.

"And it was love at first sight of course!"

"Yes," said Keating and felt himself being ridiculous.

"It must have been spring," said Toohey. "It usually is. There's always a dark movie theater, and two people lost to the world, their hands clasped together—but hands do perspire when held too long, don't they? Still, it's beautiful to be in love. The sweetest story ever told—and the tritest. Don't turn away like that, Catherine. We must never allow ourselves to lose our sense of humor."

He smiled. The kindliness of his smile embraced them both. The kindliness was so great that it made their love seem small and mean, because only something contemptible could evoke such immensity of compassion. He asked:

"Incidentally, Peter, when do you intend to get married?"

"Oh, well . . . we've never really set a definite date, you know how it's been, all the things happening to me and now Katie has this work of hers and . . . And, by the way," he added sharply, because that matter of Katie's work irritated him without reason, "when we're married, Katie will have to give that up. I don't approve of it."

"But of course," said Toohey, "I don't approve of it either, if Catherine doesn't like it."

Catherine was working as day nursery attendant at the Clifford Settlement House. It had been her own idea. She had visited the settlement often with her uncle, who conducted classes in economics there, and she had become interested in the work.

"But I do like it!" she said with sudden excitement. "I don't see why you resent it, Peter!" There was a harsh little note in her voice, defiant and unpleasant. "I've never enjoyed anything so much in my life. Helping people who're helpless and unhappy. I went there this morning—I didn't *have* to, but I *wanted* to—and then I rushed so on my way home, I didn't have time to change my clothes, but that doesn't matter, who cares what I look like? And"—the harsh note was gone, she was speaking eagerly and very fast—"Uncle Ellsworth, imagine! little Billy Hansen had a sore throat—you remember Billy? And the nurse wasn't there, and I had to swab his throat with Argyrol, the poor thing! He had the most awful white mucous patches down in his throat!"

Her voice seemed to shine, as if she were speaking of great beauty. She looked at her uncle. For the first time Keating saw the affection he had expected. She went on speaking about her work, the children, the settlement. Toohey listened gravely. He said nothing. But the earnest attention in his eyes changed him, his mocking gaiety vanished and he forgot his own advice, he was being serious, very serious indeed. When he noticed that Catherine's plate was empty, he offered her the sandwich tray with a simple gesture and made it, somehow, a gracious gesture of respect.

Keating waited impatiently till she paused for an instant. He wanted to change the subject. He glanced about the room and saw the Sunday papers. This was a question he had wanted to ask for a long time. He asked cautiously:

"Ellsworth . . . what do you think of Roark?"

"Roark? Roark?" asked Toohey. "Who is Roark?"

The too innocent, too trifling manner in which he repeated the name, with the faint, contemptuous question mark quite audible at the end, made Keating certain that Toohey knew the name well. One did not stress total ignorance of a subject if one were in total ignorance of it. Keating said:

"Howard Roark. You know, the architect. The one who's doing the Enright House."

"Oh? Oh, yes, someone's doing that Enright House at last, isn't he?"

"There's a picture of it in the *Chronicle* today."

"Is there? I did glance through the *Chronicle*."

"And . . . what do you think of that building?"

"If it were important, I should have remembered it."

"Of course!" Keating's syllables danced, as if his breath caught at each one in passing: "It's an awful, crazy thing! Like nothing you ever saw or want to see!"

He felt a sense of deliverance. It was as if he had spent his life believing that he carried a congenital disease, and suddenly the words of the greatest specialist on earth had pronounced him healthy. He wanted to laugh, freely, stupidly, without dignity. He wanted to talk.

"Howard's a friend of mine," he said happily.

"A friend of yours? You know him?"

"Do I know him! Why we went to school together—Stanton, you know—why, he lived at our house for three years, I can tell you the color of his underwear and how he takes a shower—I've seen him!"

"He lived at your house in Stanton?" Toohey repeated. Toohey spoke with a kind of cautious precision. The sounds of his voice were small and dry and final, like the cracks of matches being broken.

It was very peculiar, thought Keating. Toohey was asking him a great many questions about Howard Roark. But the questions did not make sense. They were not about buildings, they were not about architecture at all. They were pointless personal questions—strange to ask about a man of whom he had never heard before.

"Does he laugh often?"

"Very rarely."

"Does he seem unhappy?"

"Never."

"Did he have many friends at Stanton?"

"He's never had any friends anywhere."

"The boys didn't like him?"

"Nobody can like him."

"Why?"

"He makes you feel it would be an impertinence to like him."

"Did he go out, drink, have a good time?"

"Never."

"Does he like money?"

"No."

"Does he like to be admired?"

"No."

"Does he believe in God?"

"No."

"Does he talk much?"

"Very little."

"Does he listen if others discuss any . . . idea with him?"

"He listens. It would be better if he didn't."

"Why?"

"It would be less insulting—if you know what I mean, when a man listens like that and you know it hasn't made the slightest bit of difference to him."

"Did he always want to be an architect?"

"He . . ."

"What's the matter, Peter?"

"Nothing. It just occurred to me how strange it is that I've never asked myself that about him before. Here's what's strange: you can't ask that about him. He's a maniac on the subject of architecture. It seems to mean so damn much to him that he's lost all human perspective. He just has no sense of humor about himself at all—now there's a man without a sense of humor, Ellsworth. You don't ask what he'd do if he didn't want to be an architect."

"No," said Toohey. "You ask what he'd do if he couldn't be an architect."

"He'd walk over corpses. Any and all of them. All of us. But he'd be an architect."

Toohey folded his napkin, a crisp little square of cloth on his knee; he folded it accurately, once across each way, and he ran his fingernail along the edges to make a sharp crease.

"Do you remember our little youth group of architects, Peter?" he asked. "I'm making arrangements for a first meeting soon. I've spoken to many of our future members and you'd be flattered by what they said about you as our prospective chairman."

They talked pleasantly for another half hour. When Keating rose to go, Toohey declared:

"Oh, yes. I did speak to Lois Cook about you. You'll hear from her shortly."

"Thank you so much, Ellsworth. By the way, I'm reading *Clouds and Shrouds.*"

"And?"

"Oh, it's tremendous. You know, Ellsworth, it . . . it makes you think so differently about everything you've thought before."

"Yes," said Toohey, "doesn't it?"

He stood at the window, looking out at the last sunshine of a cold, bright afternoon. Then he turned and said:

"It's a lovely day. Probably one of the last this year. Why don't you take Catherine out for a little walk, Peter?"

"Oh, I'd love to!" said Catherine eagerly.

"Well, go ahead." Toohey smiled gaily. "What's the matter, Catherine? Do you have to wait for my permission?"

When they walked out together, when they were alone in the cold brilliance of streets flooded with late sunlight, Keating felt himself recapturing everything Catherine had always meant to him, the strange emotion that he could not keep in the presence of others. He closed his hand over hers. She withdrew her hand, took off her glove and slipped her fingers into his. And then he thought suddenly that hands did perspire when held too long, and he walked faster in irritation. He thought that they were walking there like Mickey and Minnie Mouse and that they probably appeared ridiculous to the passers-by. To shake himself free of these thoughts he glanced down at her face. She was looking straight ahead at the gold light, he saw her delicate profile and the faint crease of a smile in the corner of her mouth, a smile of quiet happiness. But he noticed that the edge of her eyelid was pale and he began to wonder whether she was anemic.

Lois Cook sat on the floor in the middle of her living room, her legs crossed Turkish fashion, showing large bare knees, gray stockings rolled over tight garters, and a piece of faded pink drawers. Peter Keating sat on the edge of a violet satin chaise longue. Never before had he felt uncomfortable at a first interview with a client.

Lois Cook was thirty-seven. She had stated insistently, in her publicity and in private conversation, that she was sixty-four. It was repeated as a whimsical joke and it created about her name a vague impression of eternal youth. She was tall, dry, narrow-shouldered and broad-hipped. She had a long, sallow face, and eyes set close together. Her hair hung about her ears in greasy strands. Her fingernails were broken. She looked offensively unkempt, with studied slovenliness as careful as grooming—and for the same purpose.

She talked incessantly, rocking back and forth on her haunches:

". . . yes, on the Bowery. A private residence. The shrine on the Bowery. I have the site, I wanted it and I bought it, as simple as that, or my fool lawyer bought it for me, you must meet my lawyer, he has halitosis. I don't know what you'll cost me, but it's unessential, money is commonplace. Cabbage is commonplace too. It must have three stories and a living room with a tile floor."

"Miss Cook, I've read *Clouds and Shrouds* and it was a spiritual revelation to me. Allow me to include myself among the few who understand the courage and significance of what you're achieving single-handed while . . ."

"Oh, can the crap," said Lois Cook and winked at him.

"But I mean it!" he snapped angrily. "I loved your book. I . . ."

She looked bored.

"It is so commonplace," she drawled, "to be understood by everybody."

"But Mr. Toohey said . . ."

"Ah, yes. Mr. Toohey." Her eyes were alert now, insolently guilty, like the eyes of a child who has just perpetrated some nasty little joke. "Mr. Toohey. I'm chairman of a little youth group of writers in which Mr. Toohey is very interested."

"You are?" he said happily. It seemed to be the first direct communication between them. "Isn't that interesting! Mr. Toohey is getting together a little youth group of architects, too, and he's kind enough to have me in mind for chairman."

"Oh," she said and winked. "One of us?"

"Of whom?"

He did not know what he had done, but he knew that he had disappointed her in some way. She began to laugh. She sat there, looking up at him, laughing deliberately in his face, laughing ungraciously and not gaily.

"What the . . . !" He controlled himself. "What's the matter, Miss Cook?"

"Oh my!" she said. "You're such a sweet, sweet boy and so pretty!"

"Mr. Toohey is a great man," he said angrily. "He's the most . . . the noblest personality I've ever . . ."

"Oh, yes. Mr. Toohey is a wonderful man." Her voice was strange by omission, it was flagrantly devoid of respect. "My best friend. The most wonderful man on earth. There's the earth and there's Mr. Toohey—a law of nature. Besides, think how nicely you can rhyme it: Toohey—gooey—phooey—hooey. Nevertheless, he's a saint. That's very rare. As rare as genius. I'm a genius. I want a living room without windows. No windows at all, remember that when you draw up the plans. No windows, a tile floor and a black ceiling. And no electricity. I want no electricity in my house, just kerosene lamps. Kerosene lamps with chimneys, and candles. To hell with Thomas Edison! Who was he anyway?"

Her words did not disturb him as much as her smile. It was not a smile, it was a permanent smirk raising the corners of her long mouth, making her look like a sly, vicious imp.

"And, Keating, I want the house to be *ugly*. Magnificently ugly. I want it to be the ugliest house in New York."

"The . . . *ugliest,* Miss Cook?"

"Sweetheart, the beautiful is so commonplace!"

"Yes, but . . . but I . . . well, I don't see how I could permit myself to . . ."

"Keating, where's your courage? Aren't you capable of a sublime gesture on occasion? They all work so hard and struggle and suffer, trying to achieve beauty, trying to surpass one another in beauty. Let's surpass them all! Let's throw their sweat in their face. Let's destroy them at one stroke. Let's be gods. Let's be ugly."

He accepted the commission. After a few weeks he stopped feeling uneasy about it. Wherever he mentioned this new job, he met a respectful curiosity. It was an amused curiosity, but it was respectful. The name of Lois Cook was well known in the best drawing rooms he visited. The titles of her books were flashed in conversation like the diamonds in the speaker's intellectual crown. There was always a note of challenge in the voices pronouncing them. It sounded as if the speaker were being very brave. It was a satisfying bravery; it never aroused antagonism. For an author who did not sell, her name seemed strangely famous and honored. She was the standard-bearer of a vanguard of intellect and revolt. Only it was not quite clear to him just exactly what the revolt was against. Somehow, he preferred not to know.

He designed the house as she wished it. It was a three-floor edifice, part marble, part stucco, adorned with gargoyles and carriage lanterns. It looked like a structure from an amusement park.

His sketch of it was reproduced in more publications than any other drawing he had ever made, with the exception of the Cosmo-Slotnick Building. One commentator expressed the opinion that "Peter Keating is showing a promise of being more than just a bright young man with a knack for pleasing stuffy moguls of big business. He is venturing into the field of intellectual experimentation with a client such as Lois Cook." Toohey referred to the house as "a cosmic joke."

But a peculiar sensation remained in Keating's mind: the feeling of an aftertaste. He would experience a dim flash of it while working on some important structure he liked; he would experience it in the moments when he felt proud of his work. He could not identify the quality of the feeling; but he knew that part of it was a sense of shame.

Once, he confessed it to Ellsworth Toohey. Toohey laughed. "That's good for you, Peter. One must never allow oneself to acquire an exaggerated sense of one's own importance. There's no necessity to burden oneself with absolutes."

V

DOMINIQUE HAD RETURNED TO NEW YORK. SHE RETURNED WITH-out purpose, merely because she could not stay in her country house longer than three days after her last visit to the quarry. She had to be in the city; it was a sudden necessity, irresistible and sense-less. She expected nothing of the city. But she wanted the feeling of the streets and the buildings holding her there. In the morning, when she awakened and heard the muffled roar of traffic far below, the sound was a humiliation, a reminder of where she was and why. She stood at the window, her arms spread wide, holding on to each side of the frame; it was as if she held a piece of the city, all the streets and rooftops outlined on the glass between her two hands.

She went out alone for long walks. She walked fast, her hands in the pockets of an old coat, its collar raised. She had told herself that she was not hoping to meet him. She was not looking for him. But she had to be out in the streets, blank, purposeless, for hours at a time.

She had always hated the streets of a city. She saw the faces streaming past her, the faces made alike by fear—fear as a common denominator, fear of themselves, fear of all and of one another, fear making them ready to pounce upon whatever was held sacred by any single one they met. She could not define the nature or the reason of that fear. But she had always felt its presence. She had kept herself clean and free in a single passion—to touch nothing. She had liked facing them in the streets, she had liked the impotence of their hatred, because she offered them nothing to be hurt.

She was not free any longer. Each step through the streets hurt her now. She was tied to him—and he was tied to every part of the city. He was a nameless worker doing some nameless job, lost in these crowds, dependent on them, to be hurt by any one of them, to be shared by her with the whole city. She hated the thought of him on the sidewalks people had used. She hated the thought of a clerk handing to him a package of cigarettes across a counter. She hated the elbows touching his elbows in a subway train. She came home, after these walks, shaking with fever. She went out again the next day.

When the term of her vacation expired, she went to the office of the *Banner* in order to resign. Her work and her column did not seem amusing to her any longer. She stopped Alvah Scarret's effusive greet-ings. She said: "I just came back to tell you that I'm quitting, Alvah." He looked at her stupidly. He uttered only: "Why?"

247

It was the first sound from the outside world to reach her in a long time. She had always acted on the impulse of the moment, proud of the freedom to need no reasons for her actions. Now she had to face a "why?" that carried an answer she could not escape. She thought: Because of him, because she was letting him change the course of her life. It would be another violation; she could see him smiling as he had smiled on the path in the woods. She had no choice. Either course taken would be taken under compulsion: she could leave her work, because he had made her want to leave it, or she could remain, hating it, in order to keep her life unchanged, in defiance of him. The last was harder.

She raised her head. She said: "Just a joke, Alvah. Just wanted to see what you'd say. I'm not quitting."

She had been back at work for a few days when Ellsworth Toohey walked into her office.

"Hello, Dominique," he said. "Just heard you're back."

"Hello, Ellsworth."

"I'm glad. You know, I've always had the feeling that you'll walk out on us some morning without any reason."

"The feeling, Ellsworth? Or the hope?"

He was looking at her, his eyes as kindly, his smile as charming as ever; but there was a tinge of self-mockery in the charm, as if he knew that she did not approve of it, and a tinge of assurance, as if he were showing that he would look kindly and charming just the same.

"You know, you're wrong there," he said, smiling peacefully. "You've always been wrong about that."

"No. I don't fit, Ellsworth. Do I?"

"I could, of course, ask: Into what? But supposing I don't ask it. Supposing I just say that people who don't fit have their uses also, as well as those who do? Would you like that better? Of course, the simplest thing to say is that I've always been a great admirer of yours and always will be."

"That's not a compliment."

"Somehow, I don't think we'll ever be enemies, Dominique, if that's what you'd like."

"No, I don't think we'll ever be enemies, Ellsworth. You're the most comforting person I know."

"Of course."

"In the sense I mean?"

"In any sense you wish."

On the desk before her lay the rotogravure section of the Sunday Chronicle. It was folded on the page that bore the drawing of the Enright House. She picked it up and held it out to him, her eyes narrowed in a silent question. He looked at the drawing, then his glance moved to her face and returned to the drawing. He let the paper drop back on the desk.

"As independent as an insult, isn't it?" he said.

"You know, Ellsworth, I think the man who designed this should have committed suicide. A man who can conceive a thing as beautiful as this should never allow it to be erected. He should not want it to exist. But he will let it be built, so that women will hang diapers on his terraces, so that men will spit on his stairways and draw dirty pictures on his walls. He's given it to them and he's made it part of them, part of everything. He shouldn't have offered it for men like you to look at. For men like you to talk about. He's defiled his own work by the first word you'll utter about it. He's made himself worse than you are. You'll be committing only a mean little indecency, but he's committed a sacrilege. A man who knows what he must have known to produce this should not have been able to remain alive."

"Going to write a piece about this?" he asked.

"No. That would be repeating his crime."

"And talking to me about it?"

She looked at him. He was smiling pleasantly.

"Yes of course," she said, "that's part of the same crime also."

"Let's have dinner together one of these days, Dominique," he said. "You really don't let me see enough of you."

"All right," she said. "Any time you wish."

At his trial for the assault on Ellsworth Toohey, Steven Mallory refused to disclose his motive. He made no statement. He seemed indifferent to any possible sentence. But Ellsworth Toohey created a minor sensation when he appeared, unsolicited, in Mallory's defense. He pleaded with the judge for leniency; he explained that he had no desire to see Mallory's future and career destroyed. Everybody in the courtroom was touched—except Steven Mallory. Steven Mallory listened and looked as if he were enduring some special process of cruelty. The judge gave him two years and suspended the sentence.

There was a great deal of comment on Toohey's extraordinary generosity. Toohey dismissed all praise, gaily and modestly. "My friends," was his remark—the one to appear in all the papers—"I refuse to be an accomplice in the manufacturing of martyrs."

At the first meeting of the proposed organization of young architects Keating concluded that Toohey had a wonderful ability for choosing people who fitted well together. There was an air about the eighteen persons present which he could not define, but which gave him a sense of comfort, a security he had not experienced in solitude or in any other gathering; and part of the comfort was the knowledge that all the others felt the same way for the same unaccountable reason. It was a feeling of brotherhood, but somehow not of a sainted or noble brotherhood; yet this precisely was the comfort—that one felt, among them, no necessity for being sainted or noble.

Were it not for this kinship, Keating would have been disappointed in the gathering. Of the eighteen seated about Toohey's living room, none was an architect of distinction, except himself and Gordon L. Prescott, who wore a beige turtle-neck sweater and looked faintly patronizing, but eager. Keating had never heard the names of the others. Most of them were beginners, young, poorly dressed and belligerent. Some were only draftsmen. There was one woman architect who had built a few small private homes, mainly for wealthy widows; she had an aggressive manner, a tight mouth and a fresh petunia in her hair. There was a boy with pure, innocent eyes. There was an obscure contractor with a fat, expressionless face. There was a tall, dry woman who was an interior decorator, and another woman of no definite occupation at all.

Keating could not understand what exactly was to be the purpose of the group, though there was a great deal of talk. None of the talk was too coherent, but all of it seemed to have the same undercurrent. He felt that the undercurrent was the one thing clear among all the vague generalities, even though nobody would mention it. It held him there, as it held the others, and he had no desire to define it.

The young men talked a great deal about injustice, unfairness, the cruelty of society toward youth, and suggested that everyone should have his future commissions guaranteed when he left college. The woman architect shrieked briefly something about the iniquity of the rich. The contractor barked that it was a hard world and that "fellows gotta help one another." The boy with the innocent eyes pleaded that "we could do so much good . . ." His voice had a note of desperate sincerity which seemed embarrassing and out of place. Gordon L. Prescott declared that the A.G.A. was a bunch of old fogies with no conception of social responsibility and not a drop of virile blood in the lot of them, and that it was time to kick them in the pants anyway. The woman of indefinite occupation spoke about ideals and causes, though nobody could gather just what these were.

Peter Keating was elected chairman, unanimously. Gordon L. Prescott was elected vice-chairman and treasurer. Toohey declined all nominations. He declared that he would act only as an unofficial advisor. It was decided that the organization would be named the "Council of American Builders." It was decided that membership would not be restricted to architects, but would be open to "allied crafts" and to "all those holding the interests of the great profession of building at heart."

Then Toohey spoke. He spoke at some length, standing up, leaning on the knuckles of one hand against a table. His great voice was soft and persuasive. It filled the room, but it made his listeners realize that it could have filled a Roman amphitheater; there was something subtly flattering in this realization, in the sound of the powerful voice being held in check for their benefit.

". . . and thus, my friends, what the architectural profession lacks is an understanding of its own social importance. This lack is due to a double cause: to the anti-social nature of our entire society and to your own inherent modesty. You have been conditioned to think of yourselves merely as breadwinners with no higher purpose than to earn your fees and the means of your own existence. Isn't it time, my friends, to pause and to redefine your position in society? Of all the crafts, yours is the most important. Important, not in the amount of money you might make, not in the degree of artistic skill you might exhibit, but in the service you render to your fellow men. You are those who provide mankind's shelter. Remember this and then look at our cities, at our slums, to realize the gigantic task awaiting you. But to meet this challenge you must be armed with a broader vision of yourselves and of your work. You are not hired lackeys of the rich. You are crusaders in the cause of the underprivileged and the unsheltered. Not by what we are shall we be judged, but by those we serve. Let us stand united in this spirit. Let us—in all matters—be faithful to this new, broader, higher perspective. Let us organize—well, my friends, shall I say—a nobler dream?"

Keating listened avidly. He had always thought of himself as a breadwinner bent upon earning his fees, in a profession he had chosen because his mother had wanted him to choose it. It was gratifying to discover that he was much more than this; that his daily activity carried a nobler significance. It was pleasant and it was drugging. He knew that all the others in the room felt it also.

". . . and when our system of society collapses, the craft of builders will not be swept under, it will be swept up to greater prominence and greater recognition . . ."

The doorbell rang. Then Toohey's valet appeared for an instant, holding the door of the living room open to admit Dominique Francon.

By the manner in which Toohey stopped, on a half-uttered word, Keating knew that Dominique had not been invited or expected. She smiled at Toohey, shook her head and moved one hand in a gesture telling him to continue. He managed a faint bow in her direction, barely more than a movement of his eyebrows, and went on with his speech. It was a pleasant greeting and its informality included the guest in the intimate brotherhood of the occasion, but it seemed to Keating that it had come just one beat too late. He had never before seen Toohey miss the right moment.

Dominique sat down in a corner, behind the others. Keating forgot to listen for a while, trying to attract her attention. He had to wait until her eyes had traveled thoughtfully about the room, from face to face, and stopped on his. He bowed and nodded vigorously, with the smile of greeting a private possession. She inclined her head, he saw her lashes touching her cheeks for an instant as her eyes closed, and then she looked at him again. She sat looking at him for a long moment, without smiling, as if she were rediscovering something in his face. He had not seen her since spring. He thought that she looked a little tired and lovelier than his memory of her.

Then he turned to Ellsworth Toohey once more and he listened. The words he heard were as stirring as ever, but his pleasure in them had an edge of uneasiness. He looked at Dominique. She did not belong in this room, at this meeting. He could not say why, but the certainty of it was enormous and oppressive. It was not her beauty, it was not her insolent elegance. But something made her an outsider. It was as if they had all been comfortably naked, and a person had entered fully clothed, suddenly making them self-conscious and indecent. Yet she did nothing. She sat listening attentively. Once, she leaned back, crossing her legs, and lighted a cigarette. She shook the flame off the match with a brusque little jerk of her wrist and she dropped the match into an ash tray on a table beside her. He saw her drop the match into the ash tray; he felt as if that movement of her wrist had tossed the match into all their faces. He thought that he was being preposterous. But he noticed that Ellsworth Toohey never looked at her as he spoke.

When the meeting ended, Toohey rushed over to her.

"Dominique, my dear!" he said brightly. "Shall I consider myself flattered?"

"If you wish."

"Had I known that you were interested, I would have sent you a very special invitation."

"But you didn't think I'd be interested?"

"No, frankly, I . . ."

"That was a mistake, Ellsworth. You discounted my newspaper-woman's instinct. Never miss a scoop. It's not often that one has the chance to witness the birth of a felony."

"Just exactly what do you mean, Dominique?" asked Keating, his voice sharp.

She turned to him. "Hello, Peter."

"You know Peter Keating of course?" Toohey smiled at her.

"Oh, yes. Peter was in love with me once."

"You're using the wrong tense, Dominique," said Keating.

"You must never take seriously anything Dominique chooses to say, Peter. She does not intend us to take it seriously. Would you like to join our little group, Dominique? Your professional qualifications make you eminently eligible."

"No, Ellsworth. I wouldn't like to join your little group. I really don't hate you enough to do that."

"Just why do you disapprove of it?" snapped Keating.

"Why, Peter!" she drawled. "Whatever gave you that idea? I don't disapprove of it at all. Do I, Ellsworth? I think it's a proper undertaking in answer to an obvious necessity. It's just what we all need—and deserve."

"Can we count on your presence at our next meeting?" Toohey asked. "It is pleasant to have so understanding a listener who will not be in the way at all—at our next meeting, I mean."

"No, Ellsworth. Thank you. It was merely curiosity. Though you do have an interesting group of people here. Young builders. By the way, why didn't you invite that man who designed the Enright House—what's his name?—Howard Roark?"

Keating felt his jaw snap tight. But she looked at them innocently, she had said it lightly, in the tone of a casual remark—surely, he thought, she did not mean . . . what? he asked himself and added: she did not mean whatever it was he'd thought for a moment she meant, whatever had terrified him in that moment.

"I have never had the pleasure of meeting Mr. Roark," Toohey answered gravely.

"Do you know him?" Keating asked her.

"No," she answered. "I've merely seen a sketch of the Enright House."

"And?" Keating insisted. "What do you think of it?"

"I don't think of it," she answered.

When she turned to leave, Keating accompanied her. He looked at her in the elevator, on their way down. He saw her hand, in a tight black glove, holding the flat corner of a pocketbook. The limp carelessness of her fingers was insolent and inviting at once. He felt himself surrendering to her again.

"Dominique, why did you actually come here today?"

"Oh, I haven't been anywhere for a long time and I decided to start in with that. You know, when I go swimming I don't like to torture myself getting into cold water by degrees. I dive right in and it's a nasty shock, but after that the rest is not so hard to take."

"What do you mean? What do you really see that's so wrong with that meeting? After all, we're not planning to do anything definite. We don't have any actual program. I don't even know what we were there for."

"That's it, Peter. You don't even know what you were there for."

"It's only a group for fellows to get together. Mostly to talk. What harm is there in that?"

"Peter, I'm tired."

"Well, did your appearance tonight mean at least that you're coming out of your seclusion?"

"Yes. Just that . . . My seclusion?"

"I've tried and tried to get in touch with you, you know."

"Have you?"

"Shall I begin to tell you how happy I am to see you again?"

"No. Let's consider that you've told me."

"You know, you've changed, Dominique. I don't know exactly in what way, but you've changed."

"Have I?"

"Let's consider that I've told you how lovely you are, because I can't find words to say it."

The streets were dark. He called a cab. Sitting close to her, he turned and looked at her directly, his glance compelling like an open hint, hoping to make the silence significant between them. She did not turn away. She sat studying his face. She seemed to be wondering, attentive to some thought of her own which he could not guess. He reached over slowly and took her hand. He felt an effort in her hand, he could feel through her rigid fingers the effort of her whole arm, not an effort to withdraw her hand, but to let him hold it. He raised the hand, turned it over and pressed his lips to her wrist.

Then he looked at her face. He dropped her hand and it remained suspended in the air for an instant, the fingers stiff, half closed. This was not the indifference he remembered. This was revulsion, so great that it became impersonal, it could not offend him, it seemed to include more than his person. He was suddenly aware of her body; not in desire or resentment, but just aware of its presence close to him, under her dress. He whispered involuntarily:

"Dominique, who was he?"

She whirled to face him. Then he saw her eyes narrowing. He saw her lips relaxing, growing fuller, softer, her mouth lengthening slowly into a faint smile, without opening. She answered, looking straight at him:

"A workman in the granite quarry."

She succeeded; he laughed aloud.

"Serves me right, Dominique. I shouldn't suspect the impossible."

"Peter, isn't it strange? It was you that I thought I could make myself want, at one time."

"Why is that strange?"

"Only in thinking how little we know about ourselves. Some day you'll know the truth about yourself too, Peter, and it will be worse for you than for most of us. But you don't have to think about it. It won't come for a long time."

"You did want me, Dominique?"

"I thought I could never want anything and you suited that so well."

"I don't know what you mean. I don't know what you ever think you're saying. I know that I'll always love you. And I won't let you disappear again. Now that you're back . . ."

"Now that I'm back, Peter, I don't want to see you again. Oh, I'll have to see you when we run into each other, as we will, but don't call on me. Don't come to see me. I'm not trying to offend you, Peter. It's not that. You've done nothing to make me angry. It's something in myself that I don't want to face again. I'm sorry to choose you as the example. But you suit so well. You—Peter, you're everything I despise in the world and I don't want to remember how much I despise it. If I let myself remember—I'll return to it. This is not an insult to you, Peter. Try to understand that. You're not the worst of the world. You're its best. That's what's frightening. If I ever come back to you—don't let me come. I'm saying this now because I can, but if I come back to you, you won't be able to stop me, and now is the only time when I can warn you."

"I don't know," he said in cold fury, his lips stiff, "what you're talking about."

"Don't try to know. It doesn't matter. Let's just stay away from each other. Shall we?"

"I'll never give you up."

She shrugged. "All right, Peter. This is the only time I've ever been kind to you. Or to anyone."

VI

ROGER ENRIGHT HAD STARTED LIFE AS A COAL MINER IN PENNSYL-
vania. On his way to the millions he now owned, no one had
ever helped him. "That," he explained, "is why no one has ever stood
in my way." A great many things and people had stood in his way,
however; but he had never noticed them. Many incidents of his long
career were not admired; none was whispered about. His career had
been glaring and public like a billboard. He made a poor subject for
blackmailers or debunking biographers. Among the wealthy he was
disliked for having become wealthy so crudely.

He hated bankers, labor unions, women, evangelists and the stock
exchange. He had never bought a share of stock nor sold a share in any
of his enterprises, and he owned his fortune singlehanded, as simply as if
he carried all his cash in his pocket. Beside his oil business he owned a
publishing house, a restaurant, a radio shop, a garage, a plant manufacturing electric refrigerators. Before each new venture he studied the field
for a long time, then proceeded to act as if he had never heard of it,
upsetting all precedent. Some of his ventures were successful, others
failed. He continued running them all with ferocious energy. He worked
twelve hours a day.

When he decided to erect a building, he spent six months looking for
an architect. Then he hired Roark at the end of their first interview,
which lasted half an hour. Later, when the drawings were made, he gave
orders to proceed with construction at once. When Roark began to
speak about the drawings, Enright interrupted him: "Don't explain. It's
no use explaining abstract ideals to me. I've never had any ideals. People say I'm completely immoral. I go only by what I like. But I do know
what I like."

Roark never mentioned the attempt he had made to reach Enright,
nor his interview with the bored secretary. Enright learned of it somehow. Within five minutes the secretary was discharged, and within ten
minutes he was walking out of the office, as ordered, in the middle of a
busy day, a letter left half typed in his machine.

Roark reopened his office, the same big room on the top of an old
building. He enlarged it by the addition of an adjoining room—for the
draftsmen he hired in order to keep up with the planned lightning schedule of construction. The draftsmen were young and without much
experience. He had never heard of them before and he did not ask for
letters of recommendation. He chose them from among many appli-
cants, merely by glancing at their drawings for a few minutes.

In the crowded tension of the days that followed he never spoke to them, except of their work. They felt, entering the office in the morning, that they had no private lives, no significance and no reality save the overwhelming reality of the broad sheets of paper on their tables. The place seemed cold and soulless like a factory, until they looked at him; then they thought that it was not a factory, but a furnace fed on their bodies, his own first.

There were times when he remained in the office all night. They found him still working when they returned in the morning. He did not seem tired. Once he stayed there for two days and two nights in succession. On the afternoon of the third day he fell asleep, half lying across his table. He awakened in a few hours, made no comment and walked from one table to another, to see what had been done. He made corrections, his words sounding as if nothing had interrupted a thought begun some hours ago.

"You're unbearable when you're working, Howard," Austen Heller told him one evening, even though he had not spoken of his work at all.

"Why?" he asked astonished.

"It's uncomfortable to be in the same room with you. Tension is contagious, you know."

"What tension? I feel completely natural only when I'm working."

"That's it. You're completely natural only when you're one inch from bursting into pieces. What in hell are you really made of, Howard? After all, it's only a building. It's not the combination of holy sacrament, Indian torture and sexual ecstasy that you seem to make of it."

"Isn't it?"

He did not think of Dominique often, but when he did, the thought was not a sudden recollection, it was the acknowledgment of a continuous presence that needed no acknowledgment. He wanted her. He knew where to find her. He waited. It amused him to wait, because he knew that the waiting was unbearable to her. He knew that his absence bound her to him in a manner more complete and humiliating than his presence could enforce. He was giving her time to attempt an escape, in order to let her know her own helplessness when he chose to see her again. She would know that the attempt itself had been of his choice, that it had been only another form of mastery. Then she would be ready either to kill him or to come to him of her own will. The two acts would be equal in her mind. He wanted her brought to this. He waited.

The construction of the Enright House was about to begin, when Roark was summoned to the office of Joel Sutton. Joel Sutton, a successful businessman, was planning the erection of a huge office building.

Joel Sutton had based his success on the faculty of understanding nothing about people. He loved everybody. His love admitted no distinctions. It was a great leveler; it could hold no peaks and no hollows, as the surface of a bowl of molasses could not hold them.

Joel Sutton met Roark at a dinner given by Enright. Joel Sutton liked Roark. He admired Roark. He saw no difference between Roark and anyone else. When Roark came to his office, Joel Sutton declared:

"Now I'm not sure, I'm not sure, I'm not sure at all, but I thought that I might consider you for that little building I have in mind. Your Enright House is sort of . . . peculiar, but it's attractive, all buildings are attractive, love buildings, don't you?—and Rog Enright is a very smart man, an exceedingly smart man, he coins money where nobody else'd think it grew. I'll take a tip from Rog Enright any time, what's good enough for Rog Enright is good enough for me."

Roark waited for weeks after that first interview. Joel Sutton never made up his mind in a hurry.

On an evening in December Austen Heller called on Roark without warning and declared that he must accompany him next Friday to a formal party given by Mrs. Ralston Holcombe.

"Hell, no, Austen," said Roark.

"Listen, Howard, just exactly why not? Oh, I know, you hate that sort of thing, but that's not a good reason. On the other hand, I can give you many excellent ones for going. The place is a kind of house of assignation for architects and, of course, you'd sell anything there is to you for a building—oh, I know, for *your* kind of a building, but still you'd sell the soul you haven't got, so can't you stand a few hours of boredom for the sake of future possibilities?"

"Certainly. Only I don't believe that this sort of thing ever leads to any possibilities."

"Will you go this time?"

"Why particularly this time?"

"Well, in the first place, that infernal pest Kiki Holcombe demands it. She spent two hours yesterday demanding it and made me miss a luncheon date. It spoils her reputation to have a building like the Enright House going up in town and not be able to display its architect in her salon. It's a hobby. She collects architects. She insisted that I must bring you and I promised I would."

"What for?"

"Specifically, she's going to have Joel Sutton there next Friday. Try, if it kills you, to be nice to him. He's practically decided to give you that building, from what I hear. A little personal contact might be all that's needed to set it. He's got a lot of others after him. They'll all be there. I want you there. I want you to get that building. I don't want to hear anything about granite quarries for the next ten years. I don't like granite quarries."

Roark sat on a table, his hands clasping the table's edge to keep himself still. He was exhausted after fourteen hours spent in his office, he thought he should be exhausted, but he could not feel it. He made his shoulders sag in an effort to achieve a relaxation that would not come; his arms were tense, drawn, and one elbow shuddered in a thin, continuous quiver. His long legs were spread apart, one bent and still, with the knee resting on the table, the other hanging down straight from the hip over the table's edge, swinging impatiently. It was so difficult these days to force himself to rest.

His new home was one large room in a small, modern apartment house on a quiet street. He had chosen the house because it had no cornices over the windows and no paneling on the walls inside. His room contained a few pieces of simple furniture; it looked clean, vast and empty; one expected to hear echoes from its corners.

"Why not go, just once?" said Heller. "It won't be too awful. It might even amuse you. You'll see a lot of your old friends there. John Erik Snyte, Peter Keating, Guy Francon and his daughter—you should meet his daughter. Have you ever read her stuff?"

"I'll go," said Roark abruptly.

"You're unpredictable enough even to be sensible at times. I'll call for you at eight-thirty Friday. Black tie. Do you own a tux, by the way?"

"Enright made me get one."

"Enright is a very sensible man."

When Heller left, Roark remained sitting on the table for a long time. He had decided to go to the party, because he knew that it would be the last of all places where Dominique could wish to meet him again.

"There is nothing as useless, my dear Kiki," said Ellsworth Toohey, "as a rich woman who makes herself a profession of entertaining. But then, all useless things have charm. Like aristocracy, for instance, the most useless conception of all."

Kiki Holcombe wrinkled her nose in a cute little pout of reproach, but she liked the comparison to aristocracy. Three crystal chandeliers blazed over her Florentine ballroom, and when she looked up at Toohey the lights stood reflected in her eyes, making them a moist collection of sparks between heavy, beaded lashes.

"You say disgusting things, Ellsworth. I don't know why I keep on inviting you."

"That is precisely why, my dear. I think I shall be invited here as often as I wish."

"What can a mere woman do against that?"

"Never start an argument with Mr. Toohey," said Mrs. Gillespie, a tall woman wearing a necklace of large diamonds, the size of the teeth she bared when she smiled. "It's no use. We're beaten in advance."

"Argument, Mrs. Gillespie," he said, "is one of the things that has neither use nor charm. Leave it to the men of brains. Brains, of course, are a dangerous confession of weakness. It had been said that men develop brains when they have failed in everything else."

"Now you don't mean that at all," said Mrs. Gillespie, while her smile accepted it as a pleasant truth. She took possession of him triumphantly and led him away as a prize stolen from Mrs. Holcombe who had turned aside for a moment to greet new guests. "But you men of intellect are such children. You're so sensitive. One must pamper you."

"I wouldn't do that, Mrs. Gillespie. We'll take advantage of it. And to display one's brains is so vulgar. It's even more vulgar than to display one's wealth."

"Oh dear, you would get that in, wouldn't you? Now of course I've heard that you're some sort of a radical, but I won't take it seriously. Not one bit. How do you like that?"

"I like it very much," said Toohey.

"You can't kid me. You can't make me think that you're one of the dangerous kind. The dangerous kind are all dirty and use bad grammar. And you have such a beautiful voice!"

"Whatever made you think that I aspired to be dangerous, Mrs. Gillespie? I'm merely—well, shall we say? that mildest of all things, a conscience. Your own conscience, conveniently personified in the body of another person and attending to your concern for the less fortunate of this world, thus leaving you free not to attend to it."

"Well, what a quaint idea! I don't know whether it's horrible or very wise indeed."

"Both, Mrs. Gillespie. As all wisdom."

Kiki Holcombe surveyed her ballroom with satisfaction. She looked up at the twilight of the ceiling, left untouched above the chandeliers, and she noted how far it was above the guests, how dominant and undisturbed. The huge crowd of guests did not dwarf her hall; it stood over them like a square box of space, grotesquely out of scale; and it was this wasted expanse of air imprisoned above them that gave the occasion an aspect of regal luxury; it was like the lid of a jewel case, unnecessarily large over a flat bottom holding a single small gem.

The guests moved in two broad, changing currents that drew them all, sooner or later, toward two whirlpools; at the center of one stood Ellsworth Toohey, of the other—Peter Keating. Evening clothes were not becoming to Ellsworth Toohey; the rectangle of white shirt front prolonged his face, stretching him out into two dimensions; the wings of his tie made his thin neck look like that of a plucked chicken, pale, bluish and ready to be twisted by a single movement of some strong fist. But he wore his clothes better than any man present. He wore them with the careless impertinence of utter ease in the unbecoming, and the very grotesqueness of his appearance became a declaration of his superiority, superiority great enough to warrant disregard of so much ungainliness.

He was saying to a somber young female who wore glasses and a lowcut evening gown: "My dear, you will never be more than a dilettante of the intellect, unless you submerge yourself in some cause greater than yourself."

He was saying to an obese gentleman with a face turning purple in the heat of an argument: "But, my friend, I might not like it either. I merely said that such happens to be the inevitable course of history. And who are you or I to oppose the course of history?"

He was saying to an unhappy young architect: "No, my boy, what I have against you is not the bad building you designed, but the bad taste you exhibited in whining about my criticism of it. You should be careful. Someone might say that you can neither dish it out nor take it."

He was saying to a millionaire's widow: "Yes, I do think it would be a good idea if you made a contribution to the Workshop of Social Study. It would be a way of taking part in the great human stream of cultural achievement, without upsetting your routine or your digestion."

Those around him were saying: "Isn't he witty? And such courage!"

Peter Keating smiled radiantly. He felt the attention and admiration flowing toward him from every part of the ballroom. He looked at the people, all these trim, perfumed, silk-rustling people lacquered with light, dripping with light, as they had all been dripping with shower water a few hours ago, getting ready to come here and stand in homage before a man named Peter Keating. There were moments when he forgot that he was Peter Keating and he glanced at a mirror, at his own figure, he wanted to join in the general admiration for it.

Once the current left him face to face with Ellsworth Toohey. Keating smiled like a boy emerging from a stream on a summer day, glowing, invigorated, restless with energy. Toohey stood looking at him; Toohey's hands had slipped negligently into his trouser pockets, making his jacket flare out over his thin hips; he seemed to teeter faintly on his small feet; his eyes were attentive in enigmatic appraisal.

"Now this, Ellsworth . . . this . . . isn't it a wonderful evening?" said Keating, like a child to a mother who would understand, and a little like a drunk.

"Being happy, Peter? You're quite the sensation tonight. Little Peter seems to have crossed the line into a big celebrity. It happens like this, one can never tell exactly when or why . . . There's someone here, though, who seems to be ignoring you quite flagrantly, doesn't she?"

Keating winced. He wondered when and how Toohey had had the time to notice that.

"Oh, well," said Toohey, "the exception proves the rule. Regrettable, however. I've always had the absurd idea that it would take a most unusual man to attract Dominique Francon. So of course I thought of you. Just an idle thought. Still, you know, the man who'll get her will have something you won't be able to match. He'll beat you there."

"No one's got her," snapped Keating.

"No, undoubtedly not. Not yet. That's rather astonishing. Oh, I suppose it will take an extraordinary kind of man."

"Look here, what in hell are you doing? You don't like Dominique Francon. Do you?"

"I never said I did."

A little later Keating heard Toohey saying solemnly in the midst of some earnest discussion: "Happiness? But that is so middle-class. What is happiness? There are so many things in life so much more important than happiness."

Keating made his way slowly toward Dominique. She stood leaning back, as if the air were a support solid enough for her thin, naked shoulder blades. Her evening gown was the color of glass. He had the feeling that he should be able to see the wall behind her, through her body. She seemed too fragile to exist; and that very fragility spoke of some frightening strength which held her anchored to existence with a body insufficient for reality.

When he approached, she made no effort to ignore him; she turned to him, she answered; but the monotonous precision of her answers stopped him, made him helpless, made him leave her in a few moments.

When Roark and Heller entered, Kiki Holcombe met them at the door. Heller presented Roark to her, and she spoke as she always did, her voice like a shrill rocket sweeping all opposition aside by sheer speed.

"Oh, Mr. Roark, I've been so eager to meet you! We've all heard so much about you! Now I must warn you that my husband doesn't approve of you—oh, purely on artistic grounds, you understand—but don't let that worry you, you have an ally in this household, an enthusiastic ally!"

"It's very kind, Mrs. Holcombe," said Roark. "And perhaps unnecessary."

"Oh, I *adore* your Enright House! of course, I can't say that it represents my own esthetic convictions, but people of culture must keep their minds open to anything, I mean, to include any viewpoint in creative art, we must be broad-minded above all, don't you think so?"

"I don't know," said Roark. "I've never been broad-minded."

She was certain that he intended no insolence; it was not in his voice nor his manner; but insolence had been her first impression of him. He wore evening clothes and they looked well on his tall, thin figure, but somehow it seemed that he did not belong in them; the orange hair looked preposterous with formal dress; besides, she did not like his face; that face suited a work gang or an army, it had no place in her drawing room. She said:

"We've all been so interested in your work. Your first building?"

"My fifth."

"Oh, indeed? Of course. How interesting."

She clasped her hands, and turned to greet a new arrival. Heller said:

"Whom do you want to meet first? . . . There's Dominique Francon looking at us. Come on."

Roark turned; he saw Dominique standing alone across the room. There was no expression on her face, not even an effort to avoid expression; it was strange to see a human face presenting a bone structure and an arrangement of muscles, but no meaning, a face as a simple anatomical feature, like a shoulder or an arm, not a mirror of sensate perception any longer. She looked at them as they approached. Her feet stood posed oddly, two small triangles pointed straight and parallel, as if there were no floor around her but the few square inches under her soles and she were safe so long as she did not move or look down. He felt a violent pleasure, because she seemed too fragile to stand the brutality of what he was doing; and because she stood it so well.

"Miss Francon, may I present Howard Roark?" said Heller.

He had not raised his voice to pronounce the name; he wondered why it had sounded so stressed; then he thought that the silence had caught the name and held it still; but there had been no silence: Roark's face was politely blank and Dominique was saying correctly:

"How do you do, Mr. Roark."

Roark bowed: "How do you do, Miss Francon."

She said: "The Enright House . . ."

She said it as if she had not wanted to pronounce these three words; and as if they named, not a house, but many things beyond it.

Roark said: "Yes, Miss Francon."

Then she smiled, the correct, perfunctory smile with which one greets an introduction. She said:

"I know Roger Enright. He is almost a friend of the family."

"I haven't had the pleasure of meeting many friends of Mr. Enright."

"I remember once Father invited him to dinner. It was a miserable dinner. Father is called a brilliant conversationalist, but he couldn't bring a sound out of Mr. Enright. Roger just sat there. One must know Father to realize what a defeat it was for him."

"I have worked for your father"—her hand had been moving and it stopped in mid-air—"a few years ago, as a draftsman."

Her hand dropped. "Then you can see that Father couldn't possibly get along with Roger Enright."

"No. He couldn't."

"I think Roger almost liked me, though, but he's never forgiven me for working on a Wynand paper."

Standing between them, Heller thought that he had been mistaken; there was nothing strange in this meeting; in fact, there simply was nothing. He felt annoyed that Dominique did not speak of architecture, as one would have expected her to do; he concluded regretfully that she disliked this man, as she disliked most people she met.

Then Mrs. Gillespie caught hold of Heller and led him away. Roark and Dominique were left alone. Roark said:

"Mr. Enright reads every paper in town. They are all brought to his office—with the editorial pages cut out."

"He's always done that. Roger missed his real vocation. He should have been a scientist. He has such a love for facts and such contempt for commentaries."

"On the other hand, do you know Mr. Fleming?" he asked.

"No."

"He's a friend of Heller's. Mr. Fleming never reads anything but editorial pages. People like to hear him talk."

She watched him. He was looking straight at her, very politely, as any man would have looked, meeting her for the first time. She wished she could find some hint in his face, if only a hint of his old derisive smile; even mockery would be an acknowledgment and a tie; she found nothing. He spoke as a stranger. He allowed no reality but that of a man introduced to her in a drawing room, flawlessly obedient to every convention of deference. She faced this respectful formality, thinking that her dress had nothing to hide from him, that he had used her for a need more intimate than the use of the food he ate—while he stood now at a distance of a few feet from her, like a man who could not possibly permit himself to come closer. She thought that this was his form of mockery, after what he had not forgotten and would not acknowledge. She thought that he wanted her to be first to name it, he would bring her to the humiliation of accepting the past—by being first to utter the word recalling it to reality; because he knew that she could not leave it unrecalled.

"And what does Mr. Fleming do for a living?" she asked.

"He's a manufacturer of pencil sharpeners."

"Really? A friend of Austen's?"

"Austen knows many people. He says that's his business."

"Is he successful?"

"Who, Miss Francon? I'm not sure about Austen, but Mr. Fleming is very successful. He has branch factories in New Jersey, Connecticut and Rhode Island."

"You're wrong about Austen, Mr. Roark. He's very successful. In his profession and mine you're successful if it leaves you untouched."

"How does one achieve that?"

"In one of two ways: by not looking at people at all or by looking at everything about them."

"Which is preferable, Miss Francon?"

"Whichever is hardest."

"But a desire to choose the hardest might be a confession of weakness in itself."

"Of course, Mr. Roark. But it's the least offensive form of confession."

"If the weakness is there to be confessed at all."

Then someone came flying through the crowd, and an arm fell about Roark's shoulders. It was John Erik Snyte.

"Roark, well of all people to see here!" he cried. "So glad, so glad! Ages, hasn't it been? Listen, I want to talk to you! Let me have him for a moment, Dominique."

Roark bowed to her, his arms at his sides, a strand of hair falling forward, so that she did not see his face, but only the orange head bowed courteously for a moment, and he followed Snyte into the crowd.

Snyte was saying: "God, how you've come up these last few years! Listen, do you know whether Enright's planning to go into real estate in a big way, I mean, any other buildings up his sleeve?"

It was Heller who forced Snyte away and brought Roark to Joel Sutton. Joel Sutton was delighted. He felt that Roark's presence here removed the last of his doubts; it was a stamp of safety on Roark's person. Joel Sutton's hand closed about Roark's elbow, five pink, stubby fingers on the black sleeve. Joel Sutton gulped confidentially:

"Listen, kid, it's all settled. You're it. Now don't squeeze the last pennies out of me, all you architects are cutthroats and highway robbers, but I'll take a chance on you, you're a smart boy, snared old Rog, didn't you? So here you've got me swindled too, just about almost, that is, I'll give you a ring in a few days and we'll have a dogfight over the contract!"

Heller looked at them and thought that it was almost indecent to see them together: Roark's tall, ascetic figure, with that proud cleanliness peculiar to long-lined bodies, and beside him the smiling ball of meat whose decision could mean so much.

Then Roark began to speak about the future building, but Joel Sutton looked up at him, astonished and hurt. Joel Sutton had not come here to talk about buildings; parties were given for the purpose of enjoying oneself, and what greater joy could there be but to forget the important things of one's life? So Joel Sutton talked about badminton; that was his hobby; it was a patrician hobby, he explained, he was not being common like other men who wasted time on golf. Roark listened politely. He had nothing to say.

"You do play badminton, don't you?" Joel Sutton asked suddenly.

"No," said Roark.

"You don't?" gulped Joel Sutton. "You don't? Well, what a pity, oh what a rotten pity! I thought sure you did, with that lanky frame of yours you'd be good, you'd be a wow, I thought sure we'd beat the pants off of old Tompkins anytime while that building's being put up."

"While that building's being put up, Mr. Sutton, I wouldn't have the time to play anyway."

"What d'you mean, wouldn't have the time? What've you got draftsmen for? Hire a couple extra, let them worry, I'll be paying you enough, won't I? But then, you don't play, what a rotten shame, I thought sure . . . The architect who did my building down on Canal Street was a whiz at badminton, but he died last year, got himself cracked up in an auto accident, damn him, was a fine architect, too. And here you don't play."

"Mr. Sutton, you're not really upset about it, are you?"

"I'm very seriously disappointed, my boy."

"But what are you actually hiring me for?"

"What am I what?"

"Hiring me for?"

"Why, to do a building of course."

"Do you really think it would be a better building if I played badminton?"

"Well, there's business and there's fun, there's the practical and there's the human end of it, oh, I don't mind, still I thought with a skinny frame like yours you'd surely . . . but all right, all right, we can't have everything. . . ."

When Joel Sutton left him, Roark heard a bright voice saying: "Congratulations, Howard," and turned to find Peter Keating smiling at him radiantly and derisively.

"Hello, Peter. What did you say?"

"I said, congratulations on landing Joel Sutton. Only, you know, you didn't handle that very well."

"What?"

"Old Joel. Oh, of course, I heard most of it—why shouldn't I?—it was very entertaining. That's no way to go about it, Howard. You know what I would have done? I'd have sworn I'd played badminton since I was two years old and how it's the game of kings and earls and it takes a soul of rare distinction to appreciate it and by the time he'd put me to the test I'd have made it my business to play like an earl, too. What would it cost you?"

"I didn't think of it."

"It's a secret, Howard. A rare one. I'll give it to you free of charge with my compliments: always be what people want you to be. Then you've got them where you want them. I'm giving it free because you'll never make use of it. You'll never know how. You're brilliant in some respects, Howard, I've always said that—and terribly stupid in others."

"Possibly."

"You ought to try and learn a few things, if you're going in for playing the game through the Kiki Holcombe salon. Are you? Growing up, Howard? Though it did give me a shock to see you here of all places. Oh, and yes, congratulations on the Enright job, beautiful job as usual —where have you been all summer?—remind me to give you a lesson on how to wear a tux, God, but it looks silly on you! That's what I like, I like to see you looking silly, we're old friends, aren't we, Howard?"

"You're drunk, Peter."

"Of course I am. But I haven't touched a drop tonight, not a drop. What I'm drunk on—you'll never learn, never, it's not for you, and that's also part of what I'm drunk on, that it's not for you. You know, Howard, I love you. I really do. I do—tonight."

"Yes, Peter. You always will, you know."

Roark was introduced to many people and many people spoke to him. They smiled and seemed sincere in their efforts to approach him as a friend, to express appreciation, to display good will and cordial interest. But what he heard was: "The Enright House is magnificent. It's almost as good as the Cosmo-Slotnick Building." "I'm sure you have a great future, Mr. Roark, believe me, I know the signs, you'll be another Ralston Holcombe." He was accustomed to hostility; this kind of benevolence was more offensive than hostility. He shrugged; he thought that he would be out of here soon and back in the simple, clean reality of his own office.

He did not look at Dominique again for the rest of the evening. She watched him in the crowd. She watched those who stopped him and spoke to him. She watched his shoulders stooped courteously as he listened. She thought that this, too, was his manner of laughing at her; he let her see him being delivered to the crowd before her eyes, being surrendered to any person who wished to own him for a few moments. He knew that this was harder for her to watch than the sun and the drill in the quarry. She stood obediently, watching. She did not expect him to notice her again; she had to remain there as long as he was in this room.

There was another person, that night, abnormally aware of Roark's presence, aware from the moment Roark had entered the room. Ellsworth Toohey had seen him enter. Toohey had never set eyes on him before and did not know him. But Toohey stood looking at him for a long time.

Then Toohey moved through the crowd, and smiled at his friends. But between smiles and sentences, his eyes went back to the man with the orange hair. He looked at the man as he looked occasionally at the pavement from a window on the thirtieth floor, wondering about his own body were it to be hurled down and what would happen when it struck against that pavement. He did not know the man's name, his profession or his past; he had no need to know; it was not a man to him, but only a force; Toohey never saw men. Perhaps it was the fascination of seeing that particular force so explicitly personified in a human body.

After a while he asked John Erik Snyte, pointing:

"Who is that man?"

"That?" said Snyte. "Howard Roark. You know, the Enright House."

"Oh," said Toohey.

"What?"

"Of course. It would be."

"Want to meet him?"

"No," said Toohey. "No, I don't want to meet him."

For the rest of the evening, whenever some figure obstructed Toohey's view of the hall, his head would jerk impatiently to find Roark again. He did not want to look at Roark; he had to look; just as he always had to look down at that distant pavement, dreading the sight.

That evening, Ellsworth Toohey was conscious of no one but Roark. Roark did not know that Toohey existed in the room.

When Roark left, Dominique stood counting the minutes, to be certain that he would be lost to sight in the streets before she could trust herself to go out. Then she moved to leave.

Kiki Holcombe's thin, moist fingers clasped her hand in parting, clasped it vaguely and slipped up to hold her wrist for a moment.

"And, my dear," asked Kiki Holcombe, "what did you think of that new one, you know, I saw you talking to him, that Howard Roark?"

"I think," said Dominique firmly, "that he is the most revolting person I've ever met."

"Oh, now, really?"

"Do you care for that sort of unbridled arrogance? I don't know what one could say for him, unless it's that he's terribly good-looking, if that matters."

"*Good-looking?* Are you being funny, Dominique?"

Kiki Holcombe saw Dominique being stupidly puzzled for once. And Dominique realized that what she saw in his face, what made it the face of a god to her, was not seen by others; that it could leave them indifferent; that what she had thought to be the most obvious, inconsequential remark was, instead, a confession of something within her, some quality not shared by others.

"Why, my dear," said Kiki, "he's not good-looking at all, but extremely masculine."

"Don't let it astonish you, Dominique," said a voice behind her. "Kiki's esthetic judgment is not yours—nor mine."

Dominique turned. Ellsworth Toohey stood there, smiling, watching her face attentively.

"You . . ." she began and stopped.

"Of course," said Toohey, bowing faintly in understanding affirmative of what she had not said. "Do give me credit for discernment, Dominique, somewhat equal to yours. Though not for esthetic enjoyment. I'll leave that part of it to you. But we do see things, at times, which are not obvious, don't we—you and I?"

"What things?"

"My dear, what a long philosophical discussion that would take, and how involved, and how—unnecessary. I've always told you that we should be good friends. We have so much in common intellectually. We start from opposite poles, but that makes no difference, because you see, we meet in the same point. It was a very interesting evening, Dominique."

"What are you driving at?"

"For instance, it was interesting to discover what sort of thing appears good-looking to you. It's nice to have you classified firmly, concretely. Without words—just with the aid of a certain face."

"If . . . if you can see what you're talking about, you can't be what you are."

"No, my dear. I *must* be what I am, precisely because of what I see."

"You know, Ellsworth, I think you're much worse than I thought you were."

"And perhaps much worse than you're thinking now. But useful. We're all useful to one another. As you will be to me. As, I think, you will want to be."

"What are you talking about?"

"That's bad, Dominique. Very bad. So pointless. If you don't know what I'm talking about, I couldn't possibly explain it. If you do—I have you, already, without saying anything further."

"What kind of a conversation is this?" asked Kiki, bewildered.

"Just our way of kidding each other," said Toohey brightly. "Don't let it bother you, Kiki. Dominique and I are always kidding each other. Not very well, though, because you see—we can't."

"Some day, Ellsworth," said Dominique, "you'll make a mistake."

"Quite possible. And you, my dear, have made yours already."

"Good night, Ellsworth."

"Good night, Dominique."

Kiki turned to him when Dominique had gone.

"What's the matter with both of you, Ellsworth? Why such talk—over nothing at all? People's faces and first impressions don't mean a thing."

"That, my dear Kiki," he answered, his voice soft and distant, as if he were giving an answer, not to her, but to a thought of his own, "is one of our greatest common fallacies. There's nothing as significant as a human face. Nor as eloquent. We can never really know another person, except by our first glance at him. Because, in that glance, we know everything. Even though we're not always wise enough to unravel the knowledge. Have you ever thought about the style of a soul, Kiki?"

"The . . . what?"

"The style of a soul. Do you remember the famous philosopher who spoke of the style of a civilization? He called it 'style.' He said it was the nearest word he could find for it. He said that every civilization has its one basic principle, one single, supreme, determining conception, and every endeavor of men within that civilization is true, unconsciously and irrevocably, to that one principle. . . . I think, Kiki, that every human soul has a style of its own, also. Its one basic theme. You'll see it reflected in every thought, every act, every wish of that person. The one absolute, the one imperative in that living creature. Years of studying a man won't show it to you. His face will. You'd have to write volumes to describe a person. Think of his face. You need nothing else."

"That sounds fantastic, Ellsworth. And unfair, if true. It would leave people naked before you."

"It's worse than that. It also leaves you naked before them. You betray yourself by the manner in which you react to a certain face. To a certain kind of face. . . . The style of your soul . . . There's nothing important on earth, except human beings. There's nothing as important about human beings as their relations to one another. . . ."

"Well, what do you see in my face?"

He looked at her, as if he had just noticed her presence.

"What did you say?"

"I said, what do you see in my face?"

"Oh . . . yes . . . well, tell me the movie stars you like and I'll tell you what you are."

"You know, I just love to be analyzed. Now let's see. My greatest favorite has always been . . ."

But he was not listening. He had turned his back on her, he was walking away without apology. He looked tired. She had never seen him being rude before—except by intention.

A little later, from among a group of friends, she heard his rich, vibrant voice saying:

". . . and, therefore, the noblest conception on earth is that of men's absolute equality."

VII

"**. . .**" $\mathbf{A}$ND THERE IT WILL STAND, AS A MONUMENT TO nothing but the egotism of Mr. Enright and of Mr. Roark. It will stand between a row of brownstone tenements on one side and the tanks of a gashouse on the other. This, perhaps, is not an accident, but a testimonial to fate's sense of fitness. No other setting could bring out so eloquently the essential insolence of this building. It will rise as a mockery to all the structures of the city and to the men who built them. Our structures are meaningless and false; this building will make them more so. But the contrast will not be to its advantage. By creating the contrast it will have made itself a part of the great ineptitude, its most ludicrous part. If a ray of light falls into a pigsty, it is the ray that shows us the muck and it is the ray that is offensive. Our structures have the great advantage of obscurity and timidity. Besides, they suit us. The Enright House is bright and bold. So is a feather-boa. It *will* attract attention—but only to the immense audacity of Mr. Roark's conceit. When this building is erected, it will be a wound on the face of our city. A wound, too, is colorful."

This appeared in the column "Your House" by Dominique Francon, a week after the party at the home of Kiki Holcombe.

On the morning of its appearance Ellsworth Toohey walked into Dominique's office. He held a copy of the *Banner,* with the page bearing her column turned toward her. He stood silently, rocking a little on his small feet. It seemed as if the expression of his eyes had to be heard, not seen: it was a visual roar of laughter. His lips were folded primly, innocently.

"Well?" she asked.

"Where did you meet Roark before that party?"

She sat looking at him, one arm flung over the back of her chair, a pencil dangling precariously between the tips of her fingers. She seemed to be smiling. She said:

"I had never met Roark before that party."

"My mistake. I was just wondering about . . ." he made the paper rustle, ". . . the change of sentiment."

"Oh, that? Well, I didn't like him when I met him—at the party."

"So I noticed."

"Sit down, Ellsworth. You don't look your best standing up."

"Do you mind? Not busy?"

272

"Not particularly."

He sat down on the corner of her desk. He sat, thoughtfully tapping his knee with the folded paper.

"You know, Dominique," he said, "it's not well done. Not well at all."

"Why?"

"Don't you see what can be read between the lines? Of course, not many will notice that. He will. I do."

"It's not written for him or for you."

"But for the others?"

"For the others."

"Then it's a rotten trick on him and me."

"You see? I thought it was well done."

"Well, everyone to his own methods."

"What are you going to write about it?"

"About what?"

"About the Enright House."

"Nothing."

"Nothing?"

"Nothing."

He threw the paper down on the desk, without moving, just flicking his wrist forward. He said:

"Speaking of architecture, Dominique, why haven't you ever written anything about the Cosmo-Slotnick Building?"

"Is it worth writing about?"

"Oh, decidedly. There are people whom it would annoy very much."

"And are those people worth annoying?"

"So it seems."

"What people?"

"Oh, I don't know. How can we know who reads our stuff? That's what makes it so interesting. All those strangers we've never seen before, have never spoken to, or *can't* speak to—and here's this paper where they can read our answer, if we want to give an answer. I really think you should dash off a few nice things about the Cosmo-Slotnick Building."

"You do seem to like Peter Keating very much."

"I? I'm awfully fond of Peter. You will be, too—eventually, when you know him better. Peter is a useful person to know. Why don't you take time, one of these days, to get him to tell you the story of his life. You'll learn many interesting things."

"For instance?"

"For instance, that he went to Stanton."

"I know that."

"You don't think it's interesting? I do. Wonderful place, Stanton. Remarkable example of Gothic architecture. The stained-glass window in the Chapel is really one of the finest in this country. And then, think, so many young students. All so different. Some graduating with high honors. Others being expelled."

"Well?"

"Did you know that Peter Keating is an old friend of Howard Roark?"

"No. Is he?"

"He is."

"Peter Keating is an old friend of everybody."

"Quite true. A remarkable boy. But this is different. You didn't know that Roark went to Stanton?"

"No."

"You don't seem to know very much about Mr. Roark."

"I don't know anything about Mr. Roark. We weren't discussing Mr. Roark."

"Weren't we? No, of course, we were discussing Peter Keating. Well, you see, one can make one's point best by contrast, by comparison. As you did in your pretty little article today. To appreciate Peter as he should be appreciated, let's follow up a comparison. Let's take two parallel lines. I'm inclined to agree with Euclid, I don't think these two parallels will ever meet. Well, they both went to Stanton. Peter's mother ran a sort of boardinghouse and Roark lived with them for three years. This doesn't really matter, except that it makes the contrast more eloquent and—well—more personal, later on. Peter graduated with high honors, the highest of his class. Roark was expelled. Don't look like that. I don't have to explain why he was expelled, we understand, you and I. Peter went to work for your father and he's a partner now. Roark worked for your father and got kicked out. Yes, he did. Isn't that funny, by the way?—he did, without any help from you at all—that time. Peter has the Cosmo-Slotnick Building to his credit—and Roark has a hot-dog stand in Connecticut. Peter signs autographs—and Roark is not known even to all the bathroom fixtures manufacturers. Now Roark's got an apartment house to do and it's precious to him like an only son—while Peter wouldn't even have noticed it had he got the Enright House, he gets them every day. Now, I don't think that Roark thinks very much of Peter's work. He never has and he never will, no matter what happens. Follow this a step further. No man likes to be beaten. But to be beaten by the man who has always stood as the particular example of mediocrity in his eyes, to start by the side of this mediocrity and to watch it shoot up, while he struggles and gets nothing but a boot in his face, to see the mediocrity snatch from him, one after another, the chances he'd give his life for, to see the mediocrity worshiped, to miss the place he wants and to see the mediocrity enshrined upon it, to lose, to be sacrificed, to be ignored, to be beaten, beaten, beaten—not by a greater genius, not by a god, but by a Peter Keating—well, my little amateur, do you think the Spanish Inquisition ever thought of a torture to equal this?"

"Ellsworth!" she screamed. "Get out of here!"

She had shot to her feet. She stood straight for a moment, then she slumped forward, her two palms flat on the desk, and she stood, bent over; he saw her smooth mass of hair swinging heavily, then hanging still, hiding her face.

"But, Dominique," he said pleasantly, "I was only telling you why Peter Keating is such an interesting person."

Her hair flew back like a mop, and her face followed, she dropped down on her chair, looking at him, her mouth loose and very ugly.

"Dominique," he said softly, "you're obvious. Much too obvious."

"Get out of here."

"Well, I've always said that you underestimated me. Call on me next time you need some help."

At the door, he turned to add:

"Of course, personally, I think Peter Keating is the greatest architect we've got."

That evening, when she came home, the telephone rang.

"Dominique, my dear," a voice gulped anxiously over the wire, "did you really mean all that?"

"Who is this?"

"Joel Sutton. I . . ."

"Hello, Joel. Did I mean what?"

"Hello, dear, how are you? How is your charming father? I mean, did you mean all that about the Enright House and that fellow Roark? I mean, what you said in your column today. I'm quite a bit upset, quite a bit. You know about my building? Well, we're all ready to go ahead and it's such a bit of money, I thought I was very careful about deciding, but I trust you of all people, I've always trusted you, you're a smart kid, plenty smart, if you work for a fellow like Wynand I guess you know your stuff. Wynand knows buildings, why, that man's made more in real estate than on all his papers, you bet he did, it's not supposed to be known, but I know it. And you working for him, and now I don't know what to think. Because, you see, I had decided, yes, I had absolutely and definitely decided—almost—to have this fellow Roark, in fact I told him so, in fact he's coming over tomorrow afternoon to sign the contract, and now . . . Do you really think it will look like a feather-boa?"

"Listen, Joel," she said, her teeth set tight together, "can you have lunch with me tomorrow?"

She met Joel Sutton in the vast, deserted dining room of a distinguished hotel. There were few, solitary guests among the white tables, so that each stood out, the empty tables serving as an elegant setting that proclaimed the guest's exclusiveness. Joel Sutton smiled broadly. He had never escorted a woman as decorative as Dominique.

"You know, Joel," she said, facing him across a table, her voice quiet, set, unsmiling, "it was a brilliant idea, your choosing Roark."

"Oh, do you think so?"

"I think so. You'll have a building that will be beautiful, like an anthem. A building that will take your breath away—also your tenants. A hundred years from now they will write about you in history—and search for your grave in Potter's Field."

"Good heavens, Dominique, what are you talking about?"

"About your building. About the kind of building that Roark will design for you. It will be a great building, Joel."

"You mean, good?"

"I don't mean good. I mean great."

"It's not the same thing."

"No, Joel, no, it's not the same thing."

"I don't like this 'great' stuff."

"No. You don't. I didn't think you would. Then what do you want with Roark? You want a building that won't shock anybody. A building that will be folksy and comfortable and safe, like the old parlor back home that smells of clam chowder. A building that everybody will like, everybody and anybody. It's very uncomfortable to be a hero, Joel, and you don't have the figure for it."

"Well, of course I want a building that people will like. What do you think I'm putting it up for, for my health?"

"No, Joel. Nor for your soul."

"You mean, Roark's no good?"

She sat straight and stiff, as if all her muscles were drawn tight against pain. But her eyes were heavy, half closed, as if a hand were caressing her body. She said:

"Do you see many buildings that he's done? Do you see many people hiring him? There are six million people in the city of New York. Six million people can't be wrong. Can they?"

"Of course not."

"Of course."

"But I thought Enright . . ."

"You're not Enright, Joel. For one thing, he doesn't smile so much. Then, you see, Enright wouldn't have asked my opinion. You did. That's what I like you for."

"Do you really like me, Dominique?"

"Didn't you know that you've always been one of my great favorites?"

"I . . . I've always trusted you. I'll take your word anytime. What do you really think I should do?"

"It's simple. You want the best that money can buy—of what money can buy. You want a building that will be—what it deserves to be. You want an architect whom other people have employed, so that you can show them that you're just as good as they are."

"That's right. That's exactly right. . . . Look, Dominique, you've hardly touched your food."

"I'm not hungry."

"Well, what architect would you recommend?"

"Think, Joel. Who is there, at the moment, that everybody's talking about? Who gets the pick of all commissions? Who makes the most money for himself and his clients? Who's young and famous and safe and popular?"

"Why, I guess . . . I guess Peter Keating."

"Yes, Joel. Peter Keating."

"I'm so sorry, Mr. Roark, so terribly sorry, believe me, but after all, I'm not in business for my health . . . not for my health nor for my soul . . . that is, I mean, well, I'm sure you can understand my position. And it's not that I have anything against you, quite the contrary, I think you're a great architect. You see that's just the trouble, greatness is fine but it's not practical. That's the trouble, Mr. Roark, not practical, and after all you must admit that Mr. Keating has much the better name and he's got that . . . that popular touch which you haven't been able to achieve."

It disturbed Mr. Sutton that Roark did not protest. He wished Roark would try to argue; then he could bring forth the unanswerable justifications which Dominique had taught him a few hours ago. But Roark said nothing; he had merely inclined his head when he heard the decision. Mr. Sutton wanted desperately to utter the justifications, but it seemed pointless to try to convince a man who seemed convinced. Still, Mr. Sutton loved people and did not want to hurt anyone.

"As a matter of fact, Mr. Roark, I'm not alone in this decision. As a matter of fact, I did want you, I had decided on you, honestly I had, but it was Miss Dominique Francon, whose judgment I value most highly, who convinced me that you were not the right choice for this commission—and she was fair enough to allow me to tell you that she did."

He saw Roark looking at him suddenly. Then he saw the hollows of Roark's cheeks twisted, as if drawn in deeper and his mouth open: he was laughing, without sound but for one sharp intake of breath.

"What on earth are you laughing at, Mr. Roark?"

"So Miss Francon wanted you to tell me this?"

"She didn't *want* me to, why should she?—she merely said that I could tell you if I wished."

"Yes, of course."

"Which only shows her honesty and that she has good reasons for her convictions and will stand by them openly."

"Yes."

"Well, what's the matter?"

"Nothing, Mr. Sutton."

"Look, it's not decent to laugh like that."

"No."

His room was half dark around him. A sketch of the Heller house was tacked, unframed, on a long, blank wall; it made the room seem emptier and the wall longer. He did not feel the minutes passing, but he felt time as a solid thing enclosed and kept apart within the room; time clear of all meaning save the unmoving reality of his body.

When he heard the knock at the door, he said: "Come in," without rising.

Dominique came in. She entered as if she had entered this room before. She wore a black suit of heavy cloth, simple like a child's garment, worn as mere protection, not as ornament; she had a high masculine collar raised to her cheeks, and a hat cutting half her face out of sight. He sat looking at her. She waited to see the derisive smile, but it did not come. The smile seemed implicit in the room itself, in her standing there, halfway across that room. She took her hat off, like a man entering a house, she pulled it off by the brim with the tips of stiff fingers and held it hanging down at the end of her arm. She waited, her face stern and cold; but her smooth pale hair looked defenseless and humble. She said:

"You are not surprised to see me."

"I expected you tonight."

She raised her hand, bending her elbow with a tight economy of motion, the bare minimum needed, and flung her hat across to a table. The hat's long flight showed the violence in that controlled jerk of her wrist.

He asked: "What do you want?"

She answered: "You know what I want," her voice heavy and flat.

"Yes. But I want to hear you say it. All of it."

"If you wish." Her voice had the sound of efficiency, obeying an order with metallic precision. "I want to sleep with you. Now, tonight, and at any time you may care to call me. I want your naked body, your skin, your mouth, your hands. I want you—like this—not hysterical with desire—but coldly and consciously—without dignity and without regrets —I want you—I have no self-respect to bargain with me and divide me—I want you—I want you like an animal, or a cat on a fence, or a whore."

She spoke on a single, level tone, as if she were reciting an austere catechism of faith. She stood without moving, her feet in flat shoes planted apart, her shoulders thrown back, her arms hanging straight at her sides. She looked impersonal, untouched by the words she pronounced, chaste like a young boy.

"You know that I hate you, Roark. I hate you for what you are, for wanting you, for having to want you. I'm going to fight you—and I'm going to destroy you—and I tell you this as calmly as I told you that I'm a begging animal. I'm going to pray that you can't be destroyed—I tell you this, too—even though I believe in nothing and have nothing to pray to. But I will fight to block every step you take. I will fight to tear every chance you want away from you. I will hurt you through the only thing that can hurt you—through your work. I will fight to starve you, to strangle you on the things you won't be able to reach. I have done it to you today—and that is why I shall sleep with you tonight."

He sat deep in his chair, stretched out, his body relaxed, and taut in relaxation, a stillness being filled slowly with the violence of future motion.

"I have hurt you today. I'll do it again. I'll come to you whenever I have beaten you—whenever I know that I have hurt you—and I'll let you own me. I want to be owned, not by a lover, but an an adversary who will destroy my victory over him, not with honorable blows, but with the touch of his body on mine. That is what I want of you, Roark. That is what I am. You wanted to hear it all. You've heard it. What do you wish to say now?"

"Take your clothes off."

She stood still for a moment; two hard spots swelled and grew white under the corners of her mouth. Then she saw a movement in the cloth of his shirt, one jolt of controlled breath—and she smiled in her turn, derisively, as he had always smiled at her.

She lifted her two hands to her collar and unfastened the buttons of her jacket, simply, precisely, one after another. She threw the jacket down on the floor, she took off a thin white blouse, and she noticed the tight black gloves on the wrists of her naked arms. She took the gloves off, pulling at each finger in turn. She undressed indifferently, as if she were alone in her own bedroom.

Then she looked at him. She stood naked, waiting, feeling the space between them like a pressure against her stomach, knowing that it was torture for him also and that it was as they both wanted it. Then he got up, he walked to her, and when he held her, her arms rose willingly and she felt the shape of his body imprinted into the skin on the inside of her arm as it encircled him, his ribs, his armpit, his back, his shoulder blade under her fingers, her mouth on his, in a surrender more violent than her struggle had been.

Afterward, she lay in bed by his side, under his blanket, looking at his room, and she asked:

"Roark, why were you working in that quarry?"

"You know it."

"Yes. Anyone else would have taken a job in an architect's office."

"And then you'd have no desire at all to destroy me."

"You understand that?"

"Yes. Keep still. It doesn't matter now."

"Do you know that the Enright House is the most beautiful building in New York?"

"I know that you know it."

"Roark, you worked in that quarry when you had the Enright House in you, and many other Enright Houses, and you were drilling granite like a . . ."

"You're going to weaken in a moment, Dominique, and then you'll regret it tomorrow."

"Yes."

"You're very lovely, Dominique."

"Don't."

"You're lovely."

"Roark, I . . . I'll still want to destroy you."

"Do you think I would want you if you didn't?"

"Roark . . ."

"You want to hear that again? Part of it? I want you, Dominique. I want you. I want you."

"I . . ." She stopped, the word on which she stopped almost audible in her breath.

"No," he said. "Not yet. You won't say that yet. Go to sleep."

"Here? With you?"

"Here. With me. I'll fix breakfast for you in the morning. Did you know that I fix my own breakfast? You'll like seeing that. Like the work in the quarry. Then you'll go home and think about destroying me. Good night, Dominique."

VIII

THE BLINDS RAISED OVER THE WINDOWS OF HER LIVING ROOM, THE lights of the city rising to a black horizon halfway up the glass panes, Dominique sat at her desk, correcting the last sheets of an article, when she heard the doorbell. Guests did not disturb her without warning —and she looked up, the pencil held in mid-air, angry and curious. She heard the steps of the maid in the hall, then the maid came in, saying: "A gentleman to see you, madam," a faint hostility in her voice explaining that the gentleman had refused to give his name.

A man with orange hair?—Dominique wanted to ask, but didn't; the pencil jerked stiffly and she said: "Have him come in."

Then the door opened; against the light of the hall she saw a long neck and sloping shoulders, like the silhouette of a bottle; a rich, creamy voice said, "Good evening, Dominique," and she recognized Ellsworth Toohey whom she had never asked to her house.

She smiled. She said: "Good evening, Ellsworth. I haven't seen you for such a long time."

"You should have expected me now, don't you think so?" He turned to the maid: "Cointreau, please, if you have it, and I'm sure you do."

The maid glanced at Dominique, wide-eyed; Dominique nodded silently, and the maid went out, closing the door.

"Busy, of course?" said Toohey, glancing at the littered desk. "Very becoming, Dominique. Gets results, too. You've been writing much better lately."

She let the pencil fall, and threw an arm over the back of her chair, half turning to him, watching him placidly. "What do you want, Ellsworth?"

He did not sit down, but stood examining the place with the unhurried curiosity of an expert.

"Not bad, Dominique. Just about as I'd expect you to have it. A little cold. You know, I wouldn't have that ice-blue chair over there. Too obvious. Fits in too well. Just what people would expect in just that spot. I'd have it carrot red. An ugly, glaring, outrageous red. Like Mr. Howard Roark's hair. That's quite *en passant*—merely a convenient figure of speech—nothing personal at all. Just one touch of the wrong color would make the whole room. The sort of thing that gives a place elegance. Your flower arrangements are nice. The pictures, too—not bad."

"All right, Ellsworth, all right, what is it?"

"But don't you know that I've never been here before? Somehow,

281

you've never asked me. I don't know why." He sat down comfortably, resting an ankle on a knee, one thin leg stretched horizontally across the other, the full length of a tight, gun-metal sock exposed under the trouser cuff, and a patch of skin showing above the sock, bluish-white with a few black hairs. "But then, you've been so unsociable. The past tense, my dear, the past tense. Did you say that we haven't seen each other for a long time? That's true. You've been so busy—in such an unusual way. Visits, dinners, speak-easies and giving tea parties. Haven't you?"

"I have."

"Tea parties—I though that was tops. This is a good room for parties —large—plenty of space to stuff people into—particularly if you're not particular whom you stuff it with—and you're not. Not now. What do you serve them? Anchovy paste and minced egg cut out like hearts?"

"Caviar and minced onion cut out like stars."

"What about the old ladies?"

"Cream cheese and chopped walnuts—in spirals."

"I'd like to have seen you taking care of things like that. It's wonderful how thoughtful you've become of old ladies. Particularly the filthy rich—with sons-in-law in real estate. Though I don't think that's as bad as going to see *Knock Me Flat* with Commodore Higbee who has false teeth and a nice vacant lot on the corner of Broadway and Chambers."

The maid came in with the tray. Toohey took a glass and held it delicately, inhaling, while the maid went out.

"Will you tell me why the secret service department—I won't ask who—and why the detailed reports on my activities?" Dominique said indifferently.

"You can ask who. Anyone and everyone. Don't you suppose people are talking about Miss Dominique Francon in the role of famous hostess —so suddenly? Miss Dominique Francon as a sort of second Kiki Holcombe, but much better—oh much!—much subtler, much abler, and then, just think, how much more beautiful. It's about time you made some use of that superlative appearance of yours that any woman would cut your throat for. It's still being wasted, of course, if one thinks of form in relation to its proper function, but at least some people are getting some good out of it. Your father, for instance. I'm sure he's delighted with this new life of yours. Little Dominique being friendly to people. Little Dominique who's become normal at last. He's wrong, of course, but it's nice to make him happy. A few others, too. Me, for instance. Though you'd never do anything just to make me happy, but then, you see, that's my lucky faculty—to extract joy from what was not intended for me at all, in a purely selfless way."

"You're not answering my question."

"But I am. You asked why the interest in your activities—and I answer: because they make me happy. Besides, look, one could be astonished—though shortsightedly—if I were gathering information on the activities of my enemies. But not to be informed about the actions of my own side—really, you know, you didn't think I'd be so unskilled a general, and whatever else you might think of me, you've never thought me unskilled."

"*Your side,* Ellsworth?"

"Look, Dominique, that's the trouble with your written—and spoken —style: you use too many question marks. Bad, in any case. Particularly bad when unnecessary. Let's drop the quiz technique—and just talk. Since we both understand and there aren't any questions to be asked between us. If there were—you'd have thrown me out. Instead, you gave me a very expensive liqueur."

He held the rim of the glass under his nose and inhaled with a loose kind of sensual relish, which, at a dinner table, would have been equivalent to a loud lip-smacking, vulgar there, superlatively elegant here, over a cut-crystal edge pressed to a neat little mustache.

"All right," she said. "Talk."

"That's what I've been doing. Which is considerate of me—since you're not ready to talk. Not yet, for a while. Well, let's talk—in a purely contemplative manner—about how interesting it is to see people welcoming you into their midst so eagerly, accepting you, flocking to you. Why is it, do you suppose? They do plenty of snubbing on their own, but just let someone who's snubbed them all her life suddenly break down and turn gregarious—and they all come rolling on their backs with their paws folded, for you to rub their bellies. Why? There could be two explanations, I think. The nice one would be that they are generous and wish to honor you with their friendship. Only the nice explanations are never the true ones. The other one is that they know you're degrading yourself by needing them, you're coming down off a pinnacle—every loneliness is a pinnacle—and they're delighted to drag you down through their friendship. Though, of course, none of them knows it consciously, except yourself. That's why you go through agonies, doing it, and you'd never do it for a noble cause, you'd never do it except for the end you've chosen, an end viler than the means and making the means endurable."

"You know, Ellsworth, you've said a sentence there you'd never use in your column."

"Did I? Undoubtedly. I can say a great many things to you that I'd never use in my column. Which one?"

"Every loneliness is a pinnacle."

"That? Yes, quite right. I wouldn't. You're welcome to it—though it's not too good. Fairly crude. I'll give you better ones some day, if you wish. Sorry, however, that that's all you picked out of my little speech."

"What did you want me to pick?"

"Well, my two explanations, for instance. There's an interesting question there. What is kinder—to believe the best of people and burden them with a nobility beyond their endurance—or to see them as they are, and accept it because it makes them comfortable? Kindness being more important than justice, of course."

"I don't give a damn, Ellsworth."

"Not in a mood for abstract speculation? Interested only in concrete results? All right. How many commissions have you landed for Peter Keating in the last three months?"

She rose, walked to the tray which the maid had left, poured herself a drink, and said: "Four," raising the glass to her mouth. Then she turned to look at him, standing, glass in hand, and added: "And that was the famous Toohey technique. Never place your punch at the beginning of a column nor at the end. Sneak it in where it's least expected. Fill a whole column with drivel, just to get in that one important line."

He bowed courteously. "Quite. That's why I like to talk to you. It's such a waste to be subtle and vicious with people who don't even know that you're being subtle and vicious. But the drivel is never accidental, Dominique. Also, I didn't know that the technique of my column was becoming obvious. I will have to think of a new one."

"Don't bother. They love it."

"Of course. They'll love anything I write. So it's four? I missed one. I counted three."

"I can't understand why you had to come here if that's all you wanted to know. You're so fond of Peter Keating, and I'm helping him along beautifully, better than you could, so if you wanted to give me a pep talk about Petey—it wasn't necessary, was it?"

"You're wrong there twice in one sentence, Dominique. One honest error and one lie. The honest error is the assumption that I wish to help Petey Keating—and, incidentally, I can help him much better than you can, and I have and will, but that's long-range contemplation. The lie is that I came here to talk about Peter Keating—you knew what I came here to talk about when you saw me enter. And—oh my!—you'd allow someone more obnoxious than myself to barge in on you, just to talk about that subject. Though I don't know who could be more obnoxious to you than myself, at the moment."

"Peter Keating," she said.

He made a grimace, wrinkling his nose: "Oh, no. He's not big enough for that. But let's talk about Peter Keating. It's such a convenient coincidence that he happens to be your father's partner. You're merely working your head off to procure commissions for your father, like a dutiful daughter, nothing more natural. You've done wonders for the firm of Francon & Keating in these last three months. Just by smiling at a few dowagers and wearing stunning models at some of our better gatherings. Wonder what you'd accomplish if you decided to go all the way and sell your matchless body for purposes other than esthetic contemplation—in exchange for commissions for Peter Keating." He paused, she said nothing, and he added: "My compliments, Dominique, you've lived up to my best opinion of you—by not being shocked at this."

"What was that intended for, Ellsworth? Shock value or hint value?"

"Oh, it could have been a number of things—a preliminary feeler, for instance. But, as a matter of fact, it was nothing at all. Just a touch of vulgarity. Also the Toohey technique—you know, I always advise the wrong touch at the right time. I am—essentially—such an earnest, single-toned Puritan that I must allow myself another color occasionally—to relieve the monotony."

"Are you, Ellsworth? I wonder what you are—essentially. I don't know."

"I dare say nobody does," he said pleasantly. "Although really, there's no mystery about it at all. It's very simple. All things are simple when you reduce them to fundamentals. You'd be surprised if you knew how few fundamentals there are. Only two, perhaps. To explain all of us. It's the untangling, the reducing that's difficult—that's why people don't like to bother. I don't think they'd like the results, either."

"I don't mind. I know what I am. Go ahead and say it. I'm just a bitch."

"Don't fool yourself, my dear. You're much worse than a bitch. You're a saint. Which shows why saints are dangerous and undesirable."

"And you?"

"As a matter of fact, I know exactly what I am. That alone can explain a great deal about me. I'm giving you a helpful hint—if you care to use it. You don't, of course. You might, though—in the future."

"Why should I?"

"You need me, Dominique. You might as well understand me a little. You see, I'm not afraid of being understood. Not by you."

"I need you?"

"Oh, come on, show a little courage, too."

She sat up and waited coldly, silently. He smiled, obviously with pleasure, making no effort to hide the pleasure.

"Let's see," he said, studying the ceiling with casual attention, "those commissions you got for Peter Keating. The Cryson office building was mere nuisance value—Howard Roark never had a chance at that. The Lindsay home was better—Roark was definitely considered, I think he would have got it but for you. The Stonebrook Clubhouse also—he had a chance at that, which you ruined." He looked at her and chuckled softly. "No comments on techniques and punches, Dominique?" The smile was like cold grease floating over the fluid sounds of his voice. "You slipped up on the Norris country house—he got that last week, you know. Well, you can't be a hundred per cent successful. After all, the Enright House is a big job; it's creating a lot of talk, and quite a few people are beginning to show interest in Mr. Howard Roark. But you've done remarkably well. My congratulations. Now don't you think I'm being nice to you? Every artist needs appreciation—and there's nobody to compliment you, since nobody knows what you're doing, but Roark and me, and he won't thank you. On second thought, I don't think Roark knows what you're doing, and that spoils the fun, doesn't it?"

She asked: "How do you know what I'm doing?"—her voice tired.

"My dear, surely you haven't forgotten that it was I who gave you the idea in the first place?"

"Oh, yes," she said absently. "Yes."

"And now you know why I came here. Now you know what I meant when I spoke about my side."

"Yes," she said. "Of course."

"This is a pact, my dear. An alliance. Allies never trust each other, but that doesn't spoil their effectiveness. Our motives might be quite opposite. In fact, they are. But it doesn't matter. The result will be the same. It is not necessary to have a noble aim in common. It is necessary only to have a common enemy. We have."

"Yes."

"That's why you need me. I've been helpful once."

"Yes."

"I can hurt your Mr. Roark much better than any tea party you'll ever give."

"What for?"

"Omit the what-fors, I don't inquire into yours."

"All right."

"Then it's to be understood between us? We're allies in this?"

She looked at him, she slouched forward, attentive, her face empty. Then she said: "We're allies."

"Fine, my dear. Now listen. Stop mentioning him in your column every other day or so. I know, you take vicious cracks at him each time, but it's too much. You're keeping his name in print, and you don't want to do that. Further: you'd better invite me to those parties of yours. There are things I can do which you can't. Another tip: Mr. Gilbert Colton—you know, the California pottery Coltons—is planning a branch factory in the east. He's thinking of a good modernist. In fact, he's thinking of Mr. Roark. Don't let Roark get it. It's a huge job—with lots of publicity. Go and invent a new tea sandwich for Mrs. Colton. Do anything you wish. But don't let Roark get it."

She got up, dragged her feet to a table, her arms swinging loosely, and took a cigarette. She lighted it, turned to him, and said indifferently: "You can talk very briefly and to the point—when you want to."

"When I find it necessary."

She stood at the window, looking out over the city. She said: "You've never actually done anything against Roark. I didn't know you cared quite so much."

"Oh, my dear. Haven't I?"

"You've never mentioned him in print."

"That, my dear, is what I've done against Mr. Roark. So far."

"When did you first hear of him?"

"When I saw drawings of the Heller house. You didn't think I'd miss that, did you? And you?"

"When I saw drawings of the Enright House."

"Not before?"

"Not before."

She smoked in silence; then she said, without turning to him:

"Ellsworth, if one of us tried to repeat what we said here tonight, the other would deny it and it could never be proved. So it doesn't matter if we're sincere with each other, does it? It's quite safe. Why do you hate him?"

"I never said I hated him."

She shrugged.

"As for the rest," he added, "I think you can answer that yourself."

She nodded slowly to the bright little point of her cigarette's reflection on the glass pane.

He got up, walked over to her, and stood looking at the lights of the city below them, at the angular shapes of buildings, at the dark walls made translucent by the glow of the windows, as if the walls were only a checkered veil of thin black gauze over a solid mass of radiance. And Ellsworth Toohey said softly:

"Look at it. A sublime achievement, isn't it? A heroic achievement. Think of the thousands who worked to create this and of the millions who profit by it. And it is said that but for the spirit of a dozen men, here and there down the ages, but for a dozen men—less, perhaps—none of this would have been possible. And that might be true. If so, there are—again—two possible attitudes to take. We can say that these twelve were great benefactors, that we are all fed by the overflow of the magnificent wealth of their spirit, and that we are glad to accept it in gratitude and brotherhood. Or, we can say that by the splendor of their achievement which we can neither equal nor keep, these twelve have shown us what we are, that we do not want the free gifts of their grandeur, that a cave by an oozing swamp and a fire of sticks rubbed together are preferable to skyscrapers and neon lights—if the cave and the sticks are the limit of our own creative capacities. Of the two attitudes, Dominique, which would you call the truly humanitarian one? Because, you see, I'm a humanitarian."

After a while Dominique found it easier to associate with people. She learned to accept self-torture as an endurance test, urged on by the curiosity to discover how much she could endure. She moved through formal receptions, theater parties, dinners, dances—gracious and smiling, a smile that made her face brighter and colder, like the sun on a winter day. She listened emptily to empty words uttered as if the speaker would be insulted by any sign of enthusiastic interest from his listener, as if oily boredom were the only bond possible between people, the only preservative of their precarious dignity. She nodded to everything and accepted everything.

"Yes, Mr. Holt, I think Peter Keating is the man of the century—our century."

"No, Mr. Inskip, not Howard Roark, you don't want Howard Roark. . . . A phony? Of course, he's a phony—it takes your sensitive honesty to evaluate the integrity of a man. . . . Nothing much? No, Mr. Inskip, of course, Howard Roark is nothing much. It's all a matter of size and distance—and distance. . . . No, I don't drink very much, Mr. Inskip—I'm glad you like my eyes—yes, they always look like that when I'm enjoying myself—and it made me so happy to hear you say that Howard Roark is nothing much."

"You've met Mr. Roark, Mrs. Jones? And you didn't like him? . . . Oh, he's the type of man for whom one can feel no compassion? How true. Compassion is a wonderful thing. It's what one feels when one looks at a squashed caterpillar. An elevating experience. One can let oneself go and spread—you know, like taking a girdle off. You don't have to hold your stomach, your heart or your spirit up—when you feel compassion. All you have to do is look down. It's much easier. When you look up, you get a pain in the neck. Compassion is the greatest virtue. It justifies suffering. There's got to be suffering in the world, else how would we be virtuous and feel compassion? . . . Oh, it has an antithesis—but such a hard, demanding one. . . . Admiration, Mrs. Jones, admiration. But that takes more than a girdle. . . . So I say that anyone for whom we can't feel sorry is a vicious person. Like Howard Roark."

Late at night, often, she came to Roark's room. She came unannounced, certain of finding him there and alone. In his room, there was no necessity to spare, lie, agree and erase herself out of being. Here she was free to resist, to see her resistance welcomed by an adversary too strong to fear a contest, strong enough to need it; she found a will granting her the recognition of her own entity, untouched and not to be touched except in clean battle, to win or to be defeated, but to be preserved in victory or defeat, not ground into the meaningless pulp of the impersonal.

When they lay in bed together it was—as it had to be, as the nature of the act demanded—an act of violence. It was surrender, made the more complete by the force of their resistance. It was an act of tension, as the great things on earth are things of tension. It was tense as electricity, the force fed on resistance, rushing through wires of metal stretched tight; it was tense as water made into power by the restraining violence of a dam. The touch of his skin against hers was not a caress, but a wave of pain, it became pain by being wanted too much, by releasing in fulfill-ment all the past hours of desire and denial. It was an act of clenched teeth and hatred, it was the unendurable, the agony, an act of passion— the word born to mean suffering—it was the moment made of hatred, tension, pain—the moment that broke its own elements, inverted them, triumphed, swept into a denial of all suffering, into its antithesis, into ecstasy.

She came to his room from a party, wearing an evening gown expen-sive and fragile like a coating of ice over her body—and she leaned against the wall, feeling the rough plaster under her skin, glancing slowly at every object around her, at the crude kitchen table loaded with sheets of paper, at the steel rulers, at the towels smudged by the black prints of five fingers, at the bare boards of the floor—and she let her glance slide down the length of her shining satin, down to the small triangle of a silver sandal, thinking of how she would be undressed here. She liked to wander about the room, to throw her gloves down among a litter of pencils, rubber erasers and rags, to put her small silver bag on a stained, discarded shirt, to snap open the catch of a diamond bracelet and drop it on a plate with the remnant of a sandwich, by an unfinished drawing.

"Roark," she said, standing behind his chair, her arms over his shoul-ders, her hand under his shirt, fingers spread and pressed flat against his chest, "I made Mr. Symons promise his job to Peter Keating today. Thirty-five floors, and anything he'll wish to make it cost, money no object, just art, free art." She heard the sound of his soft chuckle, but he did not turn to look at her, only his fingers closed over her wrist and he pushed her hand farther down under his shirt, pressing it hard against his skin. Then she pulled his head back, and she bent down to cover his mouth with hers.

She came in and found a copy of the *Banner* spread out on his table, open at the page bearing "Your House" by Dominique Francon. Her column contained the line: "Howard Roark is the Marquis de Sade of architecture. He's in love with his buildings—and look at them." She knew that he disliked the *Banner,* that he put it there only for her sake, that he watched her noticing it, with the half-smile she dreaded on his face. She was angry; she wanted him to read everything she wrote, yet she would have preferred to think that it hurt him enough to make him avoid it. Later, lying across the bed, with his mouth on her breast, she looked past the orange tangle of his head, at that sheet of newspaper on the table, and he felt her trembling with pleasure.

She sat on the floor, at his feet, her head pressed to his knees, holding his hand, closing her fist in turn over each of his fingers, closing it tight and letting it slide slowly down the length of his finger, feeling the hard, small stops at the joints, and she asked softly: "Roark, you wanted to get the Colton Factory? You wanted it very badly?" "Yes, very badly," he answered, without smiling and without pain. Then she raised his hand to her lips and held it there for a long time.

She got out of bed in the darkness, and walked naked across his room to take a cigarette from the table. She bent to the light of a match, her flat stomach rounded faintly in the movement. He said: "Light one for me," and she put a cigarette between his lips; then she wandered through the dark room, smoking, while he lay in bed, propped up on his elbow, watching her.

Once she came in and found him working at his table. He said: "I've got to finish this. Sit down. Wait." He did not look at her again. She waited silently, huddled in a chair at the farthest end of the room. She watched the straight lines of his eyebrows drawn in concentration, the set of his mouth, the vein beating under the tight skin of his neck, the sharp, surgical assurance of his hand. He did not look like an artist, he looked like the quarry worker, like a wrecker demolishing walls, and like a monk. Then she did not want him to stop or glance at her, because she wanted to watch the ascetic purity of his person, the absence of all sensuality; to watch that—and to think of what she remembered.

There were nights when he came to her apartment, as she came to his, without warning. If she had guests, he said: "Get rid of them," and walked into the bedroom while she obeyed. They had a silent agreement, understood without mention, never to be seen together. Her bedroom was an exquisite place of glass and pale ice-green. He liked to come in wearing clothes stained by a day spent on the construction site. He liked to throw back the covers of her bed, then to sit talking quietly for an hour or two, not looking at the bed, not mentioning her writing or buildings or the latest commission she had obtained for Peter Keating, the simplicity of being at ease, here, like this, making the hours more sensual than the moments they delayed.

There were evenings when they sat together in her living room, at the huge window high over the city. She liked to see him at that window. He would stand, half turned to her, smoking, looking at the city below. She would move away from him and sit down on the floor in the middle of the room and watch him.

Once, when he got out of bed, she switched the light on and saw him standing there, naked; she looked at him, then she said, her voice quiet and desperate with the simple despair of complete sincerity: "Roark, everything I've done all my life is because it's the kind of a world that made you work in a quarry last summer."

"I know that."

He sat down at the foot of the bed. She moved over, she pressed her face against his thigh, curled up, her feet on the pillow, her arm hanging down, letting her palm move slowly up the length of his leg, from the ankle to the knee and back again. She said: "But, of course, if it had been up to me, last spring, when you were broke and jobless, I would have sent you precisely to that kind of a job in that particular quarry."

"I know that too. But maybe you wouldn't have. Maybe you'd have had me as washroom attendant in the clubhouse of the A.G.A."

"Yes. Possibly. Put your hand on my back, Roark. Just hold it there. Like that." She lay still, her face buried against his knees, her arm hanging down over the side of the bed, not moving, as if nothing in her were alive but the skin between her shoulder blades under his hand.

In the drawing rooms she visited, in the restaurants, in the offices of the A.G.A. people talked about the dislike of Miss Dominique Francon of the *Banner* for Howard Roark, that architectural freak of Roger Enright's. It gave him a sort of scandalous fame. It was said: "Roark? You know, the guy Dominique Francon can't stand the guts of." "The Francon girl knows her architecture all right, and if she says he's no good, he must be worse than I thought he was." "God, but these two must hate each other! Though I understand they haven't even met." She liked to hear these things. It pleased her when Athelstan Beasely wrote in his column in the *A.G.A. Bulletin,* discussing the architecture of medieval castles: "To understand the grim ferocity of these structures, we must remember that the wars between feudal lords were a savage business—something like the feud between Miss Dominique Francon and Mr. Howard Roark."

Austen Heller, who had been her friend, spoke to her about it. He was angrier than she had ever seen him; his face lost all the charm of his usual sarcastic poise.

"What in hell do you think you're doing, Dominique?" he snapped. "This is the greatest exhibition of journalistic hooliganism I've ever seen swilled out in public print. Why don't you leave that sort of thing to Ellsworth Toohey?"

"Ellsworth is good, isn't he?" she said.

"At least, he's had the decency to keep his unsanitary trap shut about Roark—though, of course, that too is an indecency. But what's happened to you? Do you realize who and what you're talking about? It was all right when you amused yourself by praising some horrible abortion of Grandpaw Holcombe's or panning the pants off your own father and that pretty butcher's-calendar boy that he's got himself for a partner. It didn't matter one way or another. But to bring that same intellectual manner to the appraisal of someone like Roark. . . . You know, I really thought you had integrity and judgment—if ever given a chance to exercise them. In fact, I thought you were behaving like a tramp only to emphasize the mediocrity of the saps whose works you had to write about. I didn't think that you were just an irresponsible bitch."

"You were wrong," she said.

Roger Enright entered her office, one morning, and said, without greeting: "Get your hat. You're coming to see it with me."

"Good morning, Roger," she said. "To see what?"

"The Enright House. As much of it as we've got put up."

"Why, certainly, Roger," she smiled, rising, "I'd love to see the Enright House."

On their way, she asked: "What's the matter, Roger? Trying to bribe me?"

He sat stiffly on the vast, gray cushions of his limousine, not looking at her. He answered: "I can understand stupid malice. I can understand ignorant malice. I can't understand deliberate rottenness. You are free, of course, to write anything you wish—afterward. But it won't be stupidity and it won't be ignorance."

"You overestimate me, Roger," she shrugged, and said nothing else for the rest of the ride.

They walked together past the wooden fence, into the jungle of naked steel and planks that was to be the Enright House. Her high heels stepped lightly over lime-spattered boards and she walked, leaning back, in careless, insolent elegance. She stopped and looked at the sky held in a frame of steel, the sky that seemed more distant than usual, thrust back by the sweeping length of beams. She looked at the steel cages of future projections, at the insolent angles, at the incredible complexity of this shape coming to life as a simple, logical whole, a naked skeleton with planes of air to form the walls, a naked skeleton on a cold winter

day, with a sense of birth and promise, like a bare tree with a first touch
of green.

"Oh, Roger!"

He looked at her and saw the kind of face one should expect to see in
church at Easter.

"I didn't underestimate either one," he said dryly. "Neither you nor
the building."

"Good morning," said a low, hard voice beside them.

She was not shocked to see Roark. She had not heard him approaching, but it would have been unnatural to think of this building without
him. She felt that he simply was there, that he had been there from the
moment she crossed the outside fence, that this structure was he, in a
manner more personal than his body. He stood before them, his hands
thrust into the pockets of a loose coat, his hair hatless in the cold.

"Miss Francon—Mr. Roark," said Enright.

"We have met once," she said, "at the Holcombes. If Mr. Roark
remembers."

"Of course, Miss Francon," said Roark.

"I wanted Miss Francon to see it," said Enright.

"Shall I show you around?" Roark asked him.

"Yes, do, please," she answered first.

The three of them walked together through the structure, and the
workers stared curiously at Dominique. Roark explained the layout of
future rooms, the system of elevators, the heating plant, the arrangement
of windows—as he would have explained it to a contractor's assistant.
She asked questions and he answered. "How many cubic feet of space,
Mr. Roark?" "How many tons of steel?" "Be careful of these pipes,
Miss Francon. Step this way." Enright walked along, his eyes on the
ground, looking at nothing. But then he asked: "How's it going, Howard?" and Roark smiled, answering: "Two days ahead of schedule," and
they stood talking about the job, like brothers, forgetting her for a
moment, the clanging roar of machines around them drowning out their
words.

She thought, standing there in the heart of the building, that if she had
nothing of him, nothing but his body, here it was, offered to her, the rest
of him, to be seen and touched, open to all; the girders and the conduits
and the sweeping reaches of space were his and could not have been
anyone else's in the world; his, as his face, as his soul; here was the
shape he had made and the thing within him which had caused him to
make it, the end and the cause together, the motive power eloquent in
every line of steel, a man's self, hers for this moment, hers by grace of
her seeing it and understanding.

"Are you tired, Miss Francon?" asked Roark, looking at her face.

"No," she said, "no, not at all. I have been thinking—what kind of plumbing fixtures are you going to use here, Mr. Roark?"

A few days later, in his room, sitting on the edge of his drafting table, she looked at a newspaper, at her column and the lines: "I have visited the Enright construction site. I wish that in some future air raid a bomb would blast this house out of existence. It would be a worthy ending. So much better than to see it growing old and soot-stained, degraded by the family photographs, the dirty socks, the cocktail shakers and the grapefruit rinds of its inhabitants. There is not a person in New York City who should be allowed to live in this building."

Roark came to stand beside her, close to her, his legs pressed to her knees, and he looked down at the paper, smiling.

"You have Roger completely bewildered by this," he said.

"Has he read it?"

"I was in his office this morning when he read it. At first, he called you some names I'd never heard before. Then he said, Wait a moment, and he read it again, he looked up, very puzzled, but not angry at all, and he said, if you read it one way . . . but on the other hand . . ."

"What did you say?"

"Nothing. You know, Dominique, I'm very grateful, but when are you going to stop handing me all that extravagant praise? Someone else might see it. And you won't like that."

"Someone else?"

"You knew that I got it, from that first article of yours about the Enright House. You wanted me to get it. But don't you think someone else might understand your way of doing things?"

"Oh yes. But the effect—for you—will be worse than if they didn't. They'll like you the less for it. However, I don't know who'll even bother to understand. Unless it's . . . Roark, what do you think of Ellsworth Toohey?"

"Good God, why should anyone think of Ellsworth Toohey?"

She liked the rare occasions when she met Roark at some gathering where Heller or Enright had brought him. She liked the polite, impersonal "Miss Francon" pronounced by his voice. She enjoyed the nervous concern of the hostess and her efforts not to let them come together. She knew that the people around them expected some explosion, some shocking sign of hostility which never came. She did not seek Roark out and she did not avoid him. They spoke to each other if they happened to be included in the same group, as they would have spoken to anyone else. It required no effort; it was real and right; it made everything right, even this gathering. She found a deep sense of fitness in the fact that here, among people, they should be strangers; strangers and enemies.

She thought, these people can think of many things he and I are to each other—except what we are. It made the moments she remembered greater, the moments not touched by the sight of others, by the words of others, not even by their knowledge. She thought, it has no existence here, except in me and in him. She felt a sense of possession, such as she could feel nowhere else. She could never own him as she owned him in a room among strangers when she seldom looked in his direction.

If she glanced at him across the room and saw him in conversation with blank, indifferent faces, she turned away, unconcerned; if the faces were hostile, she watched for a second, pleased; she was angry when she saw a smile, a sign of warmth or approval on a face turned to him. It was not jealousy; she did not care whether the face was a man's or a woman's; she resented the approval as an impertinence.

She was tortured by peculiar things: by the street where he lived, by the doorstep of his house, by the cars that turned the corner of his block. She resented the cars in particular; she wished she could make them drive on to the next street. She looked at the garbage pail by the stoop next door, and she wondered whether it had stood there when he passed by, on his way to his office this morning, whether he had looked at that crumpled cigarette package on top. Once, in the lobby of his house, she saw a man stepping out of the elevator; she was shocked for a second; she had always felt as if he were the only inhabitant of that house. When she rode up in the small, self-operating elevator, she stood leaning against the wall, her arms crossed over her breast, her hands hugging her shoulders, feeling huddled and intimate, as in a stall under a warm shower.

She thought of that, while some gentleman was telling her about the latest show on Broadway, while Roark was sipping a cocktail at the other end of the room, while she heard the hostess whispering to somebody: "My Lord, I didn't think Gordon would bring Dominique—I know Austen will be furious at me, because of his friend Roark being here, you know."

Later, lying across his bed, her eyes closed, her cheeks flushed, her lips wet, losing the sense of the rules she herself had imposed, losing the sense of her words, she whispered: "Roark, there was a man talking to you out there today, and he was smiling at you, the fool, the terrible fool, last week he was looking at a pair of movie comedians and loving them, I wanted to tell that man: don't look at him, you'll have no right to want to look at anything else, don't like him, you'll have to hate the rest of the world, it's like that, you damn fool, one or the other, not together, not with the same eyes, don't look at him, don't like him, don't approve, that's what I wanted to tell him, not you and the rest of it, I can't bear to see that, I can't stand it, anything to take you away from it, from their world, from all of them, anything, Roark . . ." She did not hear herself saying it, she did not see him smiling, she did not recognize the full understanding in his face, she saw only his face close over hers, and she had nothing to hide from him, nothing to keep unstated, everything was granted, answered, found.

Peter Keating was bewildered. Dominique's sudden devotion to his career seemed dazzling, flattering, enormously profitable; everybody told him so; but there were moments when he did not feel dazzled or flattered; he felt uneasy.

He tried to avoid Guy Francon. "How did you do it, Peter? How did you do it?" Francon would ask. "She must be crazy about you! Who'd ever think that Dominique of all people would . . .? And who'd think she could? She'd have made me a millionaire if she'd done her stuff five years ago. But then, of course, a father is not the same inspiration as a . . ." He caught an ominous look on Keating's face and changed the end of his sentence to: "as her man, shall we say?"

"Listen, Guy," Keating began, and stopped, sighing, and muttered: "Please, Guy, we mustn't . . ."

"I know, I know, I know. We mustn't be premature. But hell, Peter, *entre nous*, isn't it all as public as an engagement? More so. And louder." Then the smile vanished, and Francon's face looked earnest, peaceful, frankly aged, in one of his rare flashes of genuine dignity. "And I'm glad, Peter," he said simply. "That's what I wanted to happen. I guess I always did love Dominique, after all. It makes me happy. I know I'll be leaving her in good hands. Her and everything else eventually . . ."

"Look, old man, will you forgive me? I'm so terribly rushed—had two hours sleep last night, the Colton factory, you know, Jesus, what a job!—thanks to Dominique—it's a killer, but wait till you see it! Wait till you see the check, too!"

"Isn't she wonderful? Will you tell me, *why* is she doing it? I've asked her and I can't make head or tail of what she says, she gives me the craziest gibberish, you know how she talks."

"Oh well, we should worry, so long as she's doing it!"

He could not tell Francon that he had no answer; he couldn't admit that he had not seen Dominique alone for months; that she refused to see him.

He remembered his last private conversation with her—in the cab on their way from Toohey's meeting. He remembered the indifferent calm of her insults to him—the utter contempt of insults delivered without anger. He could have expected anything after that—except to see her turn into his champion, his press agent, almost—his pimp. That's what's wrong, he thought, that I can think of words like that when I think about it.

He had seen her often since she started on her unrequested campaign; he had been invited to her parties—and introduced to his future clients; he had never been allowed a moment alone with her. He had tried to thank her and to question her. But he could not force a conversation she did not want continued, with a curious mob of guests pressing all around them. So he went on smiling blandly—her hand resting casually on the black sleeve of his dinner jacket, her thigh against his as she stood beside him, her pose possessive and intimate, made flagrantly intimate by her air of not noticing it, while she told an admiring circle what she thought of the Cosmo-Slotnick Building. He heard envious comments from all his friends. He was, he thought bitterly, the only man in New York City who did not think that Dominique Francon was in love with him.

But he knew the dangerous instability of her whims, and this was too valuable a whim to disturb. He stayed away from her and sent her flowers; he rode along and tried not to think of it; the little edge remained—a thin edge of uneasiness.

One day, he met her by chance in a restaurant. He saw her lunching alone and grasped the opportunity. He walked straight to her table, determined to act like an old friend who remembered nothing but her incredible benevolence. After many bright comments on his luck, he asked: "Dominique, why have you been refusing to see me?"

"What should I have wanted to see you for?"

"But good Lord Almighty! . . ." That came out involuntarily, with too sharp a sound of long-suppressed anger, and he corrected it hastily, smiling: "Well, don't you think you owed me a chance to thank you?"

"You've thanked me. Many times."

"Yes, but didn't you think we really had to meet alone? Didn't you think that I'd be a little . . . bewildered?"

"I haven't thought of it. Yes, I suppose you could be."

"Well?"

"Well what?"

"What is it all about?"

"About . . . fifty thousand dollars by now, I think."

"You're being nasty."

"Want me to stop?"

"Oh no! That is, not . . ."

"Not the commissions. Fine. I won't stop them. You see? What was there for us to talk about? I'm doing things for you and you're glad to have me do them—so we're in perfect agreement."

"You do say the funniest things! In perfect agreement. That's sort of a redundancy and an understatement at the same time, isn't it? What else could we be under the circumstances? You wouldn't expect me to object to what you're doing, would you?"

"No. I wouldn't."

"But agreeing is not the word for what I feel. I'm so terribly grateful to you that I'm simply dizzy—I was bowled over—don't let me get silly now—I know you don't like that—but I'm so grateful I don't know what to do with myself."

"Fine, Peter. Now you've thanked me."

"You see, I've never flattered myself by thinking that you thought very much of my work or cared or took any notice. And then you . . . That's what makes me so happy and . . . Dominique," he asked, and his voice jerked a little, because the question was like a hook pulling at a line, long and hidden, and he knew that this was the core of his uneasiness, "do you really think that I'm a great architect?"

She smiled slowly. She said: "Peter, if people heard you asking that, they'd laugh. Particularly, asking that of me."

"Yes, I know, but . . . but do you really mean them, all those things you say about me?"

"They work."

"Yes, but is that why you picked me? Because you think I'm good?"

"You sell like hot cakes. Isn't that the proof?"

"Yes . . . No . . . I mean . . . in a different way . . . I mean . . . Dominique, I'd like to hear you say once, just once, that I . . ."

"Listen, Peter, I'll have to run along in a moment, but before I go I must tell you that you'll probably hear from Mrs. Lonsdale tomorrow or the next day. Now remember that she's a prohibitionist, loves dogs, hates women who smoke, and believes in reincarnation. She wants her house to be better than Mrs. Purdee's—Holcombe did Purdee's—so if you tell her that Mrs. Purdee's house looks ostentatious and that true simplicity costs much more money, you'll get along fine. You might discuss petit point, too. That's her hobby."

He went away, thinking happily about Mrs. Lonsdale's house, and he forgot his question. Later, he remembered it resentfully, and shrugged, and told himself that the best part of Dominique's help was her desire not to see him.

As a compensation, he found pleasure in attending the meetings of Toohey's Council of American Builders. He did not know why he should think of it as compensation, but he did and it was comforting. He listened attentively when Gordon L. Prescott made a speech on the meaning of architecture.

"And thus the intrinsic significance of our craft lies in the philosophical fact that we deal in nothing. We create emptiness through which certain physical bodies are to move—we shall designate them for convenience as humans. By emptiness I mean what is commonly known as rooms. Thus it is only the crass layman who thinks that we put up stone walls. We do nothing of the kind. We put up emptiness, as I have proved. This leads us to a corollary of astronomical importance: to the unconditional acceptance of the premise that 'absence' is superior to 'presence.' That is, to the acceptance of non-acceptance. I shall state this in simpler terms—for the sake of clarity: 'nothing' is superior to 'something.' Thus it is clear that the architect is more than a bricklayer —since the fact of bricks is a secondary illusion anyway. The architect is a metaphysical priest dealing in basic essentials, who has the courage to face the primal conception of reality as nonreality—since there is nothing and he creates nothingness. If this sounds like a contradiction, it is not a proof of bad logic, but of a higher logic, the dialectics of all life and art. Should you wish to make the inevitable deductions from this basic conception, you may come to conclusions of vast sociological importance. You may see that a beautiful woman is inferior to a non-beautiful one, that the literate is inferior to the illiterate, that the rich is inferior to the poor, and the able to the incompetent. The architect is the concrete illustration of a cosmic paradox. Let us be modest in the vast pride of this realization. Everything else is twaddle."

One could not worry about one's value or greatness when listening to this. It made self-respect unnecessary.

Keating listened in thick contentment. He glanced at the others. There was an attentive silence in the audience; they all liked it as he liked it. He saw a boy chewing gum, a man cleaning his fingernails with the corner of a match folder, a youth stretched out loutishly. That, too, pleased Keating; it was as if they said: We are glad to listen to the sublime, but it's not necessary to be too damn reverent about the sublime.

The Council of American Builders met once a month and engaged in no tangible activity, beyond listening to speeches and sipping an inferior brand of root beer. Its membership did not grow fast, either in quantity or in quality. There were no concrete results achieved.

The meetings of the Council were held in a huge, empty room over a garage on the West Side. A long, narrow, unventilated stairway led to a door bearing the Council's name; there were folding chairs inside, a table for the chairman, and a wastebasket. The A.G.A. considered the Council of American Builders a silly joke. "What do you want to waste time on those cranks for?" Francon asked Keating in the rose-lit, satin-stuffed rooms of the A.G.A., wrinkling his nose with fastidious amusement. "Damned if I know," Keating answered gaily. "I like them." Ellsworth Toohey attended every meeting of the Council, but did not speak. He sat in a corner and listened.

One night Keating and Toohey walked home together after the meeting, down the dark, shabby streets of the West Side, and stopped for a cup of coffee at a seedy drugstore. "Why not a drugstore?" Toohey laughed when Keating reminded him of the distinguished restaurants made famous by Toohey's patronage. "At least, no one will recognize us here and bother us."

He sent a jet of smoke from his Egyptian cigarette at a faded Coca-Cola sign over their booth, he ordered a sandwich, he nibbled daintily a slice of pickle which was not flyspecked but looked it, and he talked to Keating. He talked at random. What he said did not matter, at first; it was his voice, the matchless voice of Ellsworth Toohey. Keating felt as if he were standing in the middle of a vast plain, under the stars, held and owned, in assurance, in security.

"Kindness, Peter," said the voice softly, "kindness. That is the first commandment, perhaps the only one. That is why I had to pan that new play, in my column yesterday. That play lacked essential kindness. We must be kind, Peter, to everybody around us. We must accept and forgive—there is so much to be forgiven in each one of us. If you learn to love everything, the humblest, the least, the meanest, then the meanest in you will be loved. Then we'll find the sense of universal equality, the great peace of brotherhood, a new world, Peter, a beautiful new world. . . ."

IX

ELLSWORTH MONKTON TOOHEY WAS SEVEN YEARS OLD WHEN HE turned the hose upon Johnny Stokes, as Johnny was passing by the Toohey lawn, dressed in his best Sunday suit. Johnny had waited for that suit a year and a half, his mother being very poor. Ellsworth did not sneak or hide, but committed his act openly, with systematic deliberation: he walked to the tap, turned it on, stood in the middle of the lawn and directed the hose at Johnny, his aim faultless—with Johnny's mother just a few steps behind him down the street, with his own mother and father and the visiting minister in full view on the Toohey porch. Johnny Stokes was a bright kid with dimples and golden curls; people always turned to look at Johnny Stokes. Nobody had ever turned to look at Ellsworth Toohey.

The shock and amazement of the grownups present were such that nobody rushed to stop Ellsworth for a long moment. He stood, bracing his thin little body against the violence of the nozzle jerking in his hands, never allowing it to leave its objective until he felt satisfied; then he let it drop, the water hissing through the grass, and made two steps toward the porch, and stopped, waiting, his head high, delivering himself for punishment. The punishment would have come from Johnny if Mrs. Stokes had not seized her boy and held him. Ellsworth did not turn to the Stokeses behind him, but said, slowly, distinctly, looking at his mother and the minister: "Johnny is a dirty bully. He beats up all the boys in school." This was true.

The question of punishment became an ethical problem. It was difficult to punish Ellsworth under any circumstances, because of his fragile body and delicate health; besides, it seemed wrong to chastise a boy who had sacrificed himself to avenge injustice, and done it bravely, in the open, ignoring his own physical weakness; somehow, he looked like a martyr. Ellsworth did not say so; he said nothing further; but his mother said it. The minister was inclined to agree with her. Ellsworth was sent to his room without supper. He did not complain. He remained there meekly—refused the food his mother sneaked up to him, late at night, disobeying her husband. Mr. Toohey insisted on paying Mrs. Stokes for Johnny's suit. Mrs. Toohey let him do it, sullenly; she did not like Mrs. Stokes.

Ellsworth's father managed the Boston branch of a national chain of shoe stores. He earned a modest, comfortable salary and owned a modest, comfortable home in an undistinguished suburb of Boston. The secret sorrow of his life was that he did not head a business of his own. But he was a quiet, conscientious, unimaginative man, and an early marriage had ended all his ambition.

Ellsworth's mother was a thin, restless woman who adopted and discarded five religions in nine years. She had delicate features, the kind that made her look beautiful for a few years of her life, at the one period of full flower, never before and never afterward. Ellsworth was her idol. His sister Helen, five years older, was a good-natured, unremarkable girl, not beautiful but pretty and healthy; she presented no problem. Ellsworth, however, had been born puny in health. His mother adored him from the moment the doctor pronounced him unfit to survive; it made her grow in spiritual stature—to know the extent of her own magnanimity in her love for so uninspiring an object; the bluer and uglier baby Ellsworth looked, the more passionate grew her love for him. She was almost disappointed when he survived without becoming an actual cripple. She took little interest in Helen; there was no martyrdom in loving Helen. The girl was so obviously more deserving of love that it seemed just to deny it to her.

Mr. Toohey, for reasons which he could not explain, was not too fond of his son. Ellsworth, however, was the ruler of the household, by a tacit, voluntary submission of both parents, though his father could never understand the cause of his own share in that submission.

In the evenings, under the lamp of the family sitting room, Mrs. Toohey would begin, in a tense, challenging voice, angry and defeated in advance: "Horace, I want a bicycle. A bicycle for Ellsworth. All the boys his age have them, Willie Lovett just got a new one the other day, Horace. Horace, I want a bicycle for Ellsworth."

"Not right now, Mary," Mr. Toohey would answer wearily. "Maybe next summer. . . . Just now we can't afford . . ."

Mrs. Toohey would argue, her voice rising in jerks toward a shriek.

"Mother, what for?" said Ellsworth, his voice soft, rich and clear, lower than the voices of his parents, yet cutting across them, commanding, strangely persuasive. "There's many things we need more than a bicycle. What do you care about Willie Lovett? I don't like Willie. Willie's a dumbbell. Willie can afford it, because his pa's got his own drygoods store. His pa's a show-off. I don't want a bicycle."

Every word of this was true, and Ellsworth did not want a bicycle. But Mr. Toohey looked at him strangely, wondering what had made him say that. He saw his son's eyes looking at him blankly from behind the small glasses; the eyes were not ostentatiously sweet, not reproachful, not malicious; just blank. Mr. Toohey felt that he should be grateful for his son's understanding—and wished to hell the boy had not mentioned that part about the private store.

Ellsworth did not get the bicycle. But he got a polite attention in the house, a respectful solicitude—tender and guilty, from his mother, uneasy and suspicious from his father. Mr. Toohey would do anything rather than be forced into a conversation with Ellsworth—feeling, at the same time, foolish and angry at himself for his fear.

"Horace, I want a new suit. A new suit for Ellsworth. I saw one in a window today and I've . . ."

"Mother, I've got four suits. What do I need another one for? I don't want to look silly like Pat Noonan who changes them every day. That's because his pa's got his own ice-cream parlor. Pat's stuck up like a girl about his clothes. I don't want to be a sissy."

Ellsworth, thought Mrs. Toohey at times, happy and frightened, is going to be a saint; he doesn't care about material things at all; not one bit. This was true. Ellsworth did not care about material things.

He was a thin, pale boy with a bad stomach, and his mother had to watch his diet, as well as his tendency to frequent colds in the head. His sonorous voice was astonishing in his puny frame. He sang in the choir, where he had no rivals. At school he was a model pupil. He always knew his lessons, had the neatest copybooks, the cleanest fingernails, loved Sunday school and preferred reading to athletic games, in which he had no chance. He was not too good at mathematics—which he disliked—but excellent at history, English, civics and penmanship; later, at psychology and sociology.

He studied conscientiously and hard. He was not like Johnny Stokes, who never listened in class, seldom opened a book at home, yet knew everything almost before the teacher had explained it. Learning came to Johnny automatically, as did all things: his able little fists, his healthy body, his startling good looks, his overexuberant vitality. But Johnny did the shocking and the unexpected; Ellsworth did the expected, better than anyone had ever seen it done. When they came to compositions, Johnny would stun the class by some brilliant display of rebellion. Given the theme of "School Days—The Golden Age," Johnny came through with a masterly essay on how he hated school and why. Ellsworth delivered a prose poem on the glory of school days, which was reprinted in a local newspaper.

Besides, Ellsworth had Johnny beaten hollow when it came to names and dates; Ellsworth's memory was like a spread of liquid cement: it held anything that fell upon it. Johnny was a shooting geyser; Ellsworth was a sponge.

The children called him "Elsie Toohey." They usually let him have his way, and avoided him when possible, but not openly; they could not figure him out. He was helpful and dependable when they needed assistance with their lessons; he had a sharp wit and could ruin any child by the apt nickname he coined, the kind that hurt; he drew devastating cartoons on fences; he had all the earmarks of a sissy, but somehow he could not be classified as one; he had too much self-assurance and quiet, disturbingly wise contempt for everybody. He was afraid of nothing.

He would march right up to the strongest boys, in the middle of the street, and state, not yell, in a clear voice that carried for blocks, state without anger—no one had ever seen Ellsworth Toohey angry— "Johnny Stokes's got a patch on his ass. Johnny Stokes lives in a rented flat. Willie Lovett is a dunce. Pat Noonan is a fish eater." Johnny never gave him a beating, and neither did the other boys, because Ellsworth wore glasses.

He could not take part in ball games, and was the only child who boasted about it, instead of feeling frustrated or ashamed like the other boys with substandard bodies. He considered athletics vulgar and said so; the brain, he said, was mightier than the brawn; he meant it.

He had no close personal friends. He was considered impartial and incorruptible. There were two incidents in his childhood of which his mother was very proud.

It happened that the wealthy, popular Willie Lovett gave a birthday party on the same day as Drippy Munn, son of a widowed seamstress, a whining boy whose nose was always running. Nobody accepted Drippy's invitation, except the children who were never invited anywhere. Of those asked for both occasions, Ellsworth Toohey was the only one who snubbed Willie Lovett and went to Drippy Munn's party, a miserable affair from which he expected and received no pleasure. Willie Lovett's enemies howled and taunted Willie for months afterward—about being passed up in favor of Drippy Munn.

It happened that Pat Noonan offered Ellsworth a bag of jelly beans in exchange for a surreptitious peek at his test paper. Ellsworth took the jelly beans and allowed Pat to copy his test. A week later, Ellsworth marched up to the teacher, laid the jelly beans, untouched, upon her desk and confessed his crime, without naming the other culprit. All her efforts to extract that name could not budge him; Ellsworth remained silent; he explained only that the guilty boy was one of the best students, and he could not sacrifice the boy's record to the demands of his own conscience. He was the only one punished—kept after school for two hours. Then the teacher had to drop the matter and let the test marks remain as they were. But it threw suspicion on the grades of Johnny Stokes, Pat Noonan, and all the best pupils of the class, except Ellsworth Toohey.

Ellsworth was eleven years old when his mother died. Aunt Adeline, his father's maiden sister, came to live with them and run the Toohey household. Aunt Adeline was a tall, capable woman to whom the word "horse" clung in conjunction with the words "sense" and "face." The secret sorrow of her life was that she had never inspired romance. Helen became her immediate favorite. She considered Ellsworth an imp out of hell. But Ellsworth never wavered in his manner of grave courtesy toward Aunt Adeline. He leaped to pick up her handkerchief, to move her chair, when they had company, particularly masculine company. He sent her beautiful Valentines on the appropriate day—with paper lace, rosebuds and love poems. He sang "Sweet Adeline" at the top of his town crier's voice. "You're a maggot, Elsie," she told him once. "You feed on sores." "Then I'll never starve," he answered. After a while they reached a state of armed neutrality. Ellsworth was left to grow up as he pleased.

In high school Ellsworth became a local celebrity—the star orator. For years the school did not refer to a promising boy as a good speaker, but as "a Toohey." He won every contest. Afterward, members of the audience spoke about "that beautiful boy"; they did not remember the sorry little figure with the sunken chest, inadequate legs and glasses; they remembered the voice. He won every debate. He could prove anything. Once, after beating Willie Lovett with the affirmative of "The Pen is Mightier than the Sword," he challenged Willie to reverse their positions, took the negative and won again.

Until the age of sixteen Ellsworth felt himself drawn to the career of a minister. He thought a great deal about religion. He talked about God and the spirit. He read extensively on the subject. He read more books on the history of the church than on the substance of faith. He brought his audience to tears in one of his greatest oratorical triumphs with the theme of "The meek shall inherit the earth."

At this period he began to acquire friends. He liked to speak of faith and he found those who liked to listen. Only, he discovered that the bright, the strong, the able boys of his class felt no need of listening, felt no need of him at all. But the suffering and the ill-endowed came to him. Drippy Munn began to follow him about with the silent devotion of a dog. Billy Wilson lost his mother, and came wandering to the Toohey house in the evenings, to sit with Ellsworth on the porch, listening, shivering once in a while, saying nothing, his eyes wide, dry and pleading. Skinny Dix got infantile paralysis—and would lie in bed, watching the street corner beyond the window, waiting for Ellsworth. Rusty Hazelton failed to pass in his grades, and sat for many hours, crying, with Ellsworth's cold, steady hand on his shoulder.

It was never clear whether they all discovered Ellsworth or Ellsworth discovered them. It seemed to work more like a law of nature: as nature allows no vacuum, so pain and Ellsworth Toohey drew each other. His rich, beautiful voice said to them:

"It's good to suffer. Don't complain. Bear, bow, accept—and be grateful that God has made you suffer. For this makes you better than the people who are laughing and happy. If you don't understand this, don't try to understand. Everything bad comes from the mind, because the mind asks too many questions. It is blessed to believe, not to understand. So if you didn't get passing grades, be glad of it. It means that you are better than the smart boys who think too much and too easily."

People said it was touching, the way Ellsworth's friends clung to him. After they had taken him for a while, they could not do without him. It was like a drug habit.

Ellsworth was fifteen, when he astonished the Bible-class teacher by an odd question. The teacher had been elaborating upon the text: "What shall it profit a man, if he shall gain the whole world, and lose his own soul?" Ellsworth asked: "Then, in order to be truly wealthy, a man should collect souls?" The teacher was about to ask him what the hell did he mean, but controlled himself and asked what did he mean. Ellsworth would not eludicate.

At the age of sixteen, Ellsworth lost interest in religion. He discovered socialism.

His transition shocked Aunt Adeline. "In the first place, it is blasphemous and drivel," she said. "In the second place, it doesn't make sense. I'm surprised at you, Elsie. 'The poor in spirit'—that was fine, but just 'the poor'—that doesn't sound respectable at all. Besides, it's not like you. You're not cut out to make big trouble—only little trouble. Something's crazy somewhere, Elsie. It just don't fit. It's not like you at all." "In the first place, my dear aunt," he answered, "don't call me Elsie. In the second place, you're wrong."

The change seemed to be good for Ellsworth. He did not become an aggressive zealot. He became gentler, quieter, milder. He became more attentively considerate of people. It was as if something had taken the nervous edges off his personality and given him new confidence. Those around him began to like him. Aunt Adeline stopped worrying. Nothing actual seemed to come of his preoccupation with revolutionary theories. He joined no political party. He read a great deal and he attended a few dubious meetings, where he spoke once or twice, not too well, but mostly sat in a corner, listening, watching, thinking.

Ellsworth went to Harvard. His mother had willed her life insurance for that specific purpose. At Harvard his scholastic record was superlative. He majored in history. Aunt Adeline had expected to see him go in for economics and sociology; she half feared that he would end up as a social worker. He didn't. He became absorbed in literature and the fine arts. It baffled her a little; it was a new trait in him; he had never shown any particular tendency in that direction. "You're not the arty kind, Elsie," she stated. "It don't fit." "You're wrong, auntie," he said.

Ellsworth's relations with his fellow students were the most unusual of his achievements at Harvard. He made himself accepted. Among the proud young descendants of proud old names, he did not hide the fact of his humble background; he exaggerated it. He did not tell them that his father was the manager of a shoe store; he said that his father was a shoe cobbler. He said it without defiance, bitterness or proletarian arrogance; he said it as if it were a joke on him and—if one looked closely into his smile—on them. He acted like a snob; not a flagrant snob, but a natural, innocent one who tries very hard not to be snobbish. He was polite, not in the manner of one seeking favor, but in the manner of one granting it. His attitude was contagious. People did not question the reasons of his superiority; they took it for granted that such reasons existed. It became amusing, at first, to accept "Monk" Toohey; then it became distinctive and progressive. If this was a victory Ellsworth did not seem conscious of it as such; he did not seem to care. He moved among all these unformed youths, with the assurance of a man who has a plan, a long-range plan set in every detail, and who can spare nothing but amusement for the small incidentals of his way. His smile had a secret, closed quality, the smile of a shopkeeper counting profits—even though nothing in particular seemed to be happening.

He did not talk about God and the nobility of suffering. He talked about the masses. He proved to a rapt audience, at bull sessions lasting till dawn, that religion bred selfishness; because, he stated, religion overemphasized the importance of the individual spirit; religion preached nothing but a single concern—the salvation of one's own soul.

"To achieve virtue in the absolute sense," said Ellsworth Toohey, "a man must be willing to take the foulest crimes upon his soul—for the sake of his brothers. To mortify the flesh is nothing. To mortify the soul is the only act of virtue. So you think you love the broad mass of mankind? You know nothing of love. You give two bucks to a strike fund and you think you've done your duty? You poor fools! No gift is worth a damn, unless it's the most precious thing you've got. Give your soul. To a lie? Yes, if others believe it. To deceit? Yes, if others need it. To treachery, knavery, crime? Yes! To whatever it is that seems lowest and vilest in your eyes. Only when you can feel contempt for your own priceless little ego, only then can you achieve the true, broad peace of selflessness, the merging of your spirit with the vast collective spirit of mankind. There is no room for the love of others within the tight, crowded miser's hole of a private ego. Be empty in order to be filled. 'He that loveth his life shall lose it; and he that hateth his life in this world shall keep it unto life eternal.' The opium peddlers of the church had something there, but they didn't know what they had. Self-abnegation? Yes, my friends, by all means. But one doesn't abnegate by keeping one's self pure and proud of its own purity. The sacrifice that includes the destruction of one's soul—ah, but what am I talking about? This is only for heroes to grasp and to achieve."

He did not have much success among the poor boys working their way through college. He acquired a sizable following among the young heirs, the second and third generation millionaires. He offered them an achievement of which they felt capable.

He graduated with high honors. When he came to New York, he was preceded by a small, private fame; a few trickles of rumor had seeped down from Harvard about an unusual person named Ellsworth Toohey; a few people, among the extreme intellectuals and the extremely wealthy, heard these rumors and promptly forgot what they heard, but remembered the name; it remained in their minds with a vague connotation of such things as brilliance, courage, idealism.

People began to ooze toward Ellsworth Toohey; the right kind of people, those who soon found him to be a spiritual necessity. The other kind did not come; there seemed to be an instinct about it. When someone commented on the loyalty of Toohey's following—he had no title, program or organization, but somehow his circle was called a following from the first—an envious rival remarked: "Toohey draws the sticky kind. You know the two things that stick best: mud and glue." Toohey overheard it and shrugged, smiling, and said: "Oh, come, come, there are many more: adhesive plaster, leeches, taffy, wet socks, rubber girdles, chewing gum and tapioca pudding." Moving away, he added over his shoulder, without smiling: "And cement."

He took his Master's degree from a New York university and wrote a thesis on "Collective Patterns in the City Architecture of the XIVth Century." He earned his living in a busy, varied, scattered way: no one could keep track of all his activities. He held the post of vocational adviser at the university, he reviewed books, plays, art exhibitions, he wrote articles, gave a few lectures to small, obscure audiences. Certain tendencies were apparent in his work. When reviewing books, he leaned toward novels about the soil rather than the city, about the average rather than the gifted, about the sick rather than the healthy; there was a special glow in his writing when he referred to stories about "little people"; "human" was his favorite adjective; he preferred character study to action, and description to character study; he preferred novels without a plot and, above all, novels without a hero.

He was considered outstanding as a vocational adviser. His tiny office at the university became an informal confessional where students brought all their problems, academic as well as personal. He was willing to discuss—with the same gentle, earnest concentration—the choice of classes, or love affairs, or—most particularly—the selection of a future career.

When consulted on love affairs, Toohey counseled surrender, if it concerned a romance with a charming little pushover, good for a few drunken parties—"let us be modern"; and renunciation, if it concerned a deep, emotional passion—"let us be grown-up." When a boy came to confess a feeling of shame after some unsavory sexual experience, Toohey told him to snap out of it: "It was damn good for you. There are two things we must get rid of early in life: a feeling of personal superiority and an exaggerated reverence for the sexual act."

People noticed that Ellsworth Toohey seldom let a boy pursue the career he had chosen. "No, I wouldn't go in for law if I were you. You're much too tense and passionate about it. A hysterical devotion to one's career does not make for happiness or success. It is wiser to select a profession about which you can be calm, sane and matter-of-fact. Yes, even if you hate it. It makes for down-to-earthness." . . . "No, I wouldn't advise you to continue with your music. The fact that it comes to you so easily is a sure sign that your talent is only a superficial one. That's just the trouble—that you love it. Don't you think that sounds like a childish reason? Give it up. Yes, even if it hurts like hell." . . . "No, I'm sorry, I would like so much to say that I approve, but I don't. When you thought of architecture, it was a purely selfish choice, wasn't it? Have you considered anything but your own egotistical satisfaction? Yet a man's career concerns all society. The question of where you could be most useful to your fellow men comes first. It's not what you can get out of society, it's what you can give. And where opportunities for service are concerned, there's no endeavor comparable to that of a surgeon. Think it over."

After leaving college some of his protégés did quite well, others failed. Only one committed suicide. It was said that Ellsworth Toohey had exercised a beneficent influence upon them—for they never forgot him: they came to consult him on many things, years later, they wrote him, they clung to him. They were like machines without a self-starter, that had to be cranked up by an outside hand. He was never too busy to give them his full attention.

His life was crowded, public and impersonal as a city square. The friend of humanity had no single private friend. People came to him; he came close to no one. He accepted all. His affection was golden, smooth and even, like a great expanse of sand; there was no wind of discrimination to raise dunes; the sands lay still and the sun stood high.

Out of his meager income he donated money to many organizations.

He was never known to have loaned a dollar to an individual. He never asked his rich friends to assist a person in need; but he obtained from them large sums and endowments for charitable institutions: for settlement houses, recreation centers, homes for fallen girls, schools for defective children. He served on the boards of all these institutions—without salary. A great many philanthropic undertakings and radical publications, run by all sorts of people, had a single connecting link among them, one common denominator: the name of Ellsworth M. Toohey on their stationery. He was a sort of one-man holding company of altruism.

Women played no part in his life. Sex had never interested him. His furtive, infrequent urges drew him to the young, slim, full-bosomed, brainless girls—the giggling little waitresses, the lisping manicurists, the less efficient stenographers, the kind who wore pink or orchid dresses and little hats on the back of their heads with gobs of blond curls in front. He was indifferent to women of intellect.

He contended that the family was a bourgeois institution; but he made no issue of it and did not crusade for free love. The subject of sex bored him. There was, he felt, too much fuss made over the damn thing; it was of no importance; there were too many weightier problems in the world.

The years passed, with each busy day of his life like a small, neat coin dropped patiently into a gigantic slot machine, without a glance at the combination of symbols, without return. Gradually, one of his many activities began to stand out among the others: he became known as an eminent critic of architecture. He wrote about buildings for three successive magazines that limped on noisily for a few years and failed, one after the other: *New Voices, New Pathways, New Horizons.* The fourth, *New Frontiers,* survived. Ellsworth Toohey was the only thing salvaged from the successive wrecks. Architectural criticism seemed to be a neglected field of endeavor; few people bothered to write about buildings, fewer to read. Toohey acquired a reputation and an unofficial monopoly. The better magazines began calling upon him whenever they needed anything connected with architecture.

In the year 1921 a small change occurred in Toohey's private life; his niece Catherine Halsey, the daughter of his sister Helen, came to live with him. His father had long since died, and Aunt Adeline had vanished into the obscure poverty of some small town; at the death of Catherine's parents there was no one else to take care of her. Toohey had not intended to keep her in his own home. But when she stepped off the train in New York, her plain little face looked beautiful for a moment, as if the future were opening before her and its glow were already upon her forehead, as if she were eager and proud and ready to meet it.

It was one of those rare moments when the humblest person knows suddenly what it means to feel as the center of the universe, and is made beautiful by the knowledge, and the world—in the eyes of witnesses—looks like a better place for having such a center. Ellsworth Toohey saw this—and decided that Catherine would remain with him.

In the year 1925 came *Sermons in Stone*—and fame.

Ellsworth Toohey became a fashion. Intellectual hostesses fought over him. Some people disliked him and laughed at him. But there was little satisfaction in laughing at Ellsworth Toohey, because he was always first to make the most outrageous remarks about himself. Once, at a party, a smug, boorish businessman listened to Toohey's earnest social theories for a while and said complacently: "Well, I wouldn't know much about all that intellectual stuff. I play the stock market." "I," said Toohey, "play the stock market of the spirit. And I sell short."

The most important consequence of *Sermons in Stone* was Toohey's contract to write a daily column for Gail Wynand's New York *Banner*.

The contract came as a surprise to the followers of both sides involved, and, at first, it made everybody angry. Toohey had referred to Wynand frequently and not respectfully; the Wynand papers had called Toohey every name fit to print. But the Wynand papers had no policy, save that of reflecting the greatest prejudices of the greatest number, and this made for an erratic direction, but a recognizable direction, nevertheless: toward the inconsistent, the irresponsible, the trite and the maudlin. The Wynand papers stood against Privilege and for the Common Man, but in a respectable manner that could shock nobody; they exposed monopolies, when they wished; they supported strikes, when they wished, and vice versa. They denounced Wall Street and they denounced socialism and they hollered for clean movies, all with the same gusto. They were strident and blatant—and, in essence, lifelessly mild. Ellsworth Toohey was a phenomenon much too extreme to fit behind the front page of the *Banner*.

But the staff of the *Banner* was as unfastidious as its policy. It included everybody who could please the public or any large section thereof. It was said: "Gail Wynand is not a pig. He'll eat anything." Ellsworth Toohey was a great success and the public was suddenly interested in architecture; the *Banner* had no authority on architecture; the *Banner* would get Ellsworth Toohey. It was a simple syllogism.

Thus "One Small Voice" came into existence.

The *Banner* explained its appearance by announcing: "On Monday the *Banner* will present to you a new friend—ELLSWORTH M. TOOHEY—whose scintillating book *Sermons in Stone* you have all read and loved. The name of Mr. Toohey stands for the great profession of architecture. He will help you to understand everything you want to know about the wonders of modern building. Watch for 'ONE SMALL VOICE' on Monday. To appear exclusively in the *Banner* in New York City." The rest of what Mr. Toohey stood for was ignored.

Ellsworth Toohey made no announcement or explanation to anyone. He disregarded the friends who cried that he had sold himself. He simply went to work. He devoted "One Small Voice" to architecture—once a month. The rest of the time it was the voice of Ellsworth Toohey saying what he wished said—to syndicated millions.

Toohey was the only Wynand employee who had a contract permitting him to write anything he pleased. He had insisted upon it. It was considered a great victory, by everybody except Ellsworth Toohey. He realized that it could mean one of two things: either Wynand had surrendered respectfully to the prestige of his name—or Wynand considered him too contemptible to be worth restraining.

"One Small Voice" never seemed to say anything dangerously revolutionary, and seldom anything political. It merely preached sentiments with which most people felt in agreement: unselfishness, brotherhood, equality. "I'd rather be kind than right." "Mercy is superior to justice, the shallow-hearted to the contrary notwithstanding." "Speaking anatomically—and perhaps otherwise—the heart is our most valuable organ. The brain is a superstition." "In spiritual matters there is a simple, infallible test: everything that proceeds from the ego is evil; everything that proceeds from love for others is good." "Service is the only badge of nobility. I see nothing offensive in the conception of fertilizer as the highest symbol of man's destiny: it is fertilizer that produces wheat and roses." "The worst folk song is superior to the best symphony." "A man braver than his brothers insults them by implication. Let us aspire to no virtue which cannot be shared." "I have yet to see a genius or a hero who, if stuck with a burning match, would feel less pain than his undistinguished average brother." "Genius is an exaggeration of dimension. So is elephantiasis. Both may be only a disease." "We are all brothers under the skin—and I, for one, would be willing to skin humanity to prove it."

In the offices of the *Banner* Ellsworth Toohey was treated respectfully and left alone. It was whispered that Gail Wynand did not like him—because Wynand was always polite to him. Alvah Scarret unbent to the point of cordiality, but kept a wary distance. There was a silent, watchful equilibrium between Toohey and Scarret: they understood each other.

Toohey made no attempt to approach Wynand in any way. Toohey seemed indifferent to all the men who counted on the *Banner*. He concentrated on the others, instead.

He organized a club of Wynand employees. It was not a labor union;

it was just a club. It met once a month in the library of the *Banner*. It did not concern itself with wages, hours or working conditions; it had no concrete program at all. People got acquainted, talked, and listened to speeches. Ellsworth Toohey made most of the speeches. He spoke about new horizons and the press as the voice of the masses. Gail Wynand appeared at a meeting once, entering unexpectedly in the middle of a session. Toohey smiled and invited him to join the club, declaring that he was eligible. Wynand did not join. He sat listening for half an hour, yawned, got up, and left before the meeting was over.

Alvah Scarret appreciated the fact that Toohey did not try to reach into his field, into the important matters of policy. As a kind of return courtesy, Scarret let Toohey recommend new employees, when there was a vacancy to fill, particularly if the position was not an important one; as a rule, Scarret did not care, while Toohey always cared, even when it was only the post of copy boy. Toohey's selections got the jobs. Most of them were young, brash, competent, shifty-eyed and shook hands limply. They had other things in common, but these were not so apparent.

There were several monthly meetings which Toohey attended regularly; the meetings of: the Council of American Builders, the Council of American Writers, the Council of American Artists. He had organized them all.

Lois Cook was chairman of the Council of American Writers. It met in the drawing room of her home on the Bowery. She was the only famous member. The rest included a woman who never used capitals in her books, and a man who never used commas; a youth who had written a thousand-page novel without a single letter o, and another who wrote poems that neither rhymed nor scanned; a man with a beard, who was sophisticated and proved it by using every unprintable four-letter word in every ten pages of his manuscript; a woman who imitated Lois Cook, except that her style was less clear; when asked for explanations she stated that this was the way life sounded to her, when broken by the prism of her subconscious—"You know what a prism does to a ray of light, don't you?" she said. There was also a fierce young man known simply as Ike the Genius, though nobody knew just what he had done, except that he talked about loving all of life.

The council signed a declaration which stated that writers were servants of the proletariat—but the statement did not sound as simple as that; it was more involved and much longer. The declaration was sent to every newspaper in the country. It was never published anywhere, except on page 32 of *New Frontiers*.

The Council of American Artists had, as chairman, a cadaverous youth who painted what he saw in his nightly dreams. There was a boy who used no canvas, but did something with bird cages and metronomes, and another who discovered a new technique of painting: he blackened a sheet of paper and then painted with a rubber eraser. There was a stout middle-aged lady who drew subconsciously, claiming that she never looked at her hand and had no idea of what the hand was doing; her hand, she said, was guided by the spirit of the departed lover whom she had never met on earth. Here they did not talk so much about the proletariat, but merely rebelled against the tyranny of reality and of the objective.

A few friends pointed out to Ellsworth Toohey that he seemed guilty of inconsistency; he was so deeply opposed to individualism, they said, and here were all these writers and artists of his, and every one of them was a rabid individualist. "Do you really think so?" said Toohey, smiling blandly.

Nobody took these Councils seriously. People talked about them, because they thought it made good conversation; it was such a huge joke, they said, certainly there was no harm in any of it. "Do you really think so?" said Toohey.

Ellsworth Toohey was now forty-one years old. He lived in a distinguished apartment that seemed modest when compared to the size of the income he could have commanded if he wished. He liked to apply the adjective "conservative" to himself in one respect only: in his conservative good taste for clothes. No one had ever seen him lose his temper. His manner was immutable; it was the same in a drawing room, at a labor meeting, on a lecture platform, in the bathroom or during sexual intercourse: cool, self-possessed, amused, faintly patronizing.

People admired his sense of humor. He was, they said, a man who could laugh at himself. "I'm a dangerous person. Somebody ought to warn you against me," he said to people, in the tone of uttering the most preposterous thing in the world.

Of all the many titles bestowed upon him, he preferred one: Ellsworth Toohey, the Humanitarian.

X

THE ENRIGHT HOUSE WAS OPENED IN JUNE OF 1929.

There was no formal ceremony. But Roger Enright wanted to mark the moment for his own satisfaction. He invited a few people he liked and he unlocked the great glass entrance door, throwing it open to the sun-filled air. Some press photographers had arrived, because the story concerned Roger Enright and because Roger Enright did not want to have them there. He ignored them. He stood in the middle of the street, looking at the building, then he walked through the lobby, stopping short without reason and resuming his pacing. He said nothing. He frowned fiercely, as if he were about to scream with rage. His friends knew that Roger Enright was happy.

The building stood on the shore of the East River, a structure rapt as raised arms. The rock crystal forms mounted in such eloquent steps that the building did not seem stationary, but moving upward in a continuous flow—until one realized that it was only the movement of one's glance and that one's glance was forced to move in that particular rhythm. The walls of pale gray limestone looked silver against the sky, with the clean, dulled luster of metal, but a metal that had become a warm, living substance, carved by the most cutting of all instruments—a purposeful human will. It made the house alive in a strange, personal way of its own, so that in the minds of spectators five words ran dimly, without object or clear connection: ". . . in His image and likeness . . ."

A young photographer from the *Banner* noticed Howard Roark standing alone across the street, at the parapet of the river. He was leaning back, his hands closed over the parapet, hatless, looking up at the building. It was an accidental, unconscious moment. The young photographer glanced at Roark's face—and thought of something that had puzzled him for a long time: he had always wondered why the sensations one felt in dreams were so much more intense than anything one could experience in waking reality—why the horror was so total and the ecstasy so complete—and what was that extra quality which could never be recaptured afterward; the quality of what he felt when he walked down a path through tangled green leaves in a dream, in an air full of expectation, of causeless, utter rapture—and when he awakened he could not explain it, it had been just a path through some woods. He thought of that because he saw that extra quality for the first time in waking existence, he saw it in Roark's face lifted to the building. The photographer was a young boy, new to his job; he did not know much about it; but he loved his work; he had been an amateur photographer since childhood. So he snapped a picture of Roark in that one moment.

Later the Art Editor of the *Banner* saw the picture and barked: "What the hell's that?" "Howard Roark," said the photographer. "Who's Howard Roark?" "The architect." "Who the hell wants a picture of the architect?" "Well, I only thought . . ." "Besides, it's crazy. What's the matter with the man?" So the picture was thrown into the morgue.

The Enright House rented promptly. The tenants who moved in were people who wanted to live in sane comfort and cared about nothing else. They did not discuss the value of the building; they merely liked living there. They were the sort who lead useful, active private lives in public silence.

But others talked a great deal of the Enright House, for about three weeks. They said that it was preposterous, exhibitionist and phony. They said: "My dear, imagine inviting Mrs. Moreland if you lived in a place like that! And her home is in such good taste!" A few were beginning to appear who said: "You know, I rather like modern architecture, there are some mighty interesting things being done that way nowadays, there's quite a school of it in Germany that's rather remarkable—but this is not like it at all. This is a freak."

Ellsworth Toohey never mentioned the Enright House in his column. A reader of the *Banner* wrote to him: "Dear Mr. Toohey: What do you think of this place they call the Enright House? I have a friend who is an interior decorator and he talks a lot about it and he says it's lousy. Architecture and such various arts being my hobby, I don't know what to think. Will you tell us in your column?" Ellsworth Toohey answered in a private letter: "Dear Friend: There are so many important buildings and great events going on in the world today that I cannot devote my column to trivialities."

But people came to Roark—the few he wanted. That winter, he had received a commission to build the Norris house, a modest country home. In May he signed another contract—for his first office building, a fifty-story skyscraper in the center of Manhattan. Anthony Cord, the owner, had come from nowhere and made a fortune in Wall Street within a few brilliant, violent years. He wanted a building of his own and he went to Roark.

Roark's office had grown to four rooms. His staff loved him. They did not realize it and would have been shocked to apply such a term as love to their cold, unapproachable, inhuman boss. These were the words they used to describe Roark, these were the words they had been trained to use by all the standards and conceptions of their past; only, working with him, they knew that he was none of these things, but they could not explain, neither what he was nor what they felt for him.

He did not smile at his employees, he did not take them out for drinks, he never inquired about their families, their love lives or their church attendance. He responded only to the essence of a man: to his creative capacity. In this office one had to be competent. There were no alternatives, no mitigating considerations. But if a man worked well, he needed nothing else to win his employer's benevolence: it was granted, not as a gift, but as a debt. It was granted, not as affection, but as recognition. It bred an immense feeling of self-respect within every man in that office.

"Oh, but that's not human," said somebody when one of Roark's draftsmen tried to explain this at home, "such a cold, intellectual approach!" One boy, a younger sort of Peter Keating, tried to introduce the human in preference to the intellectual in Roark's office; he did not last two weeks. Roark made mistakes in choosing his employees occasionally, not often; those whom he kept for a month became his friends for life. They did not call themselves friends; they did not praise him to outsiders; they did not talk about him. They knew only, in a dim way, that it was not loyalty to him, but to the best within themselves.

Dominique remained in the city all summer. She remembered, with bitter pleasure, her custom to travel; it made her angry to think that she could not go, could not want to go. She enjoyed the anger; it drove her to his room. On the nights which she did not spend with him she walked through the streets of the city. She walked to the Enright House or to the Fargo Store, and stood looking at the building for a long time. She drove alone out of town—to see the Heller house, the Sanborn house, the Gowan Service Station. She never spoke to him about that.

Once, she took the Staten Island ferry at two o'clock in the morning; she rode to the Island, standing alone at the rail of an empty deck. She watched the city moving away from her. In the vast emptiness of sky and ocean, the city was only a small, jagged solid. It seemed condensed, pressed tight together, not a place of streets and separate buildings, but a single sculptured form. A form of irregular steps that rose and dropped without ordered continuity, long ascensions and sudden drops, like the graph of a stubborn struggle. But it went on mounting—toward a few points, toward the triumphant masts of skyscrapers raised out of the struggle.

The boat went past the Statue of Liberty—a figure in a green light, with an arm raised like the skyscrapers behind it.

She stood at the rail, while the city diminished, and she felt the motion of growing distance as a growing tightness within her, the pull of a living cord that could not be stretched too far. She stood in quiet excitement, when the boat sailed back and she saw the city growing again to meet her. She stretched her arms wide. The city expanded, to her elbows, to her wrists, beyond her finger tips. Then the skyscrapers rose over her head, and she was back.

She came ashore. She knew where she had to go, and wanted to get there fast, but felt she must get there herself, like this, on her own feet. So she walked half the length of Manhattan, through long, empty, echoing streets. It was four-thirty when she knocked at his door. He had been asleep. She shook her head. "No," she said. "Go back to sleep. I just want to be here." She did not touch him. She took off her hat and shoes, huddled into an armchair, and fell asleep, her arm hanging over the chair's side, her head on her arm. In the morning he asked no questions. They fixed breakfast together, then he hurried away to his office. Before leaving, he took her in his arms and kissed her. He walked out, and she stood for a few moments, then left. They had not exchanged twenty words.

There were weekends when they left the city together and drove in her car to some obscure point on the coast. They stretched out in the sun, on the sand of a deserted beach, they swam in the ocean. She liked to watch his body in the water. She would remain behind and stand, the waves hitting her knees, and watch him cutting a straight line through the breakers. She liked to lie with him at the edge of the water; she would lie on her stomach, a few feet away from him, facing the shore, her toes stretched to the waves; she would not touch him, but she would feel the waves coming up behind them, breaking against their bodies, and she would see the backwash running in mingled streams off her body and his.

They spent the night at some country inn, taking a single room. They never spoke of the things left behind them in the city. But it was the unstated that gave meaning to the relaxed simplicity of these hours; their eyes laughed silently at the preposterous contrast whenever they looked at each other.

She tried to demonstrate her power over him. She stayed away from his house; she waited for him to come to her. He spoiled it by coming too soon; by refusing her the satisfaction of knowing that he waited and struggled against his desire; by surrendering at once. She would say: "Kiss my hand, Roark." He would kneel and kiss her ankle. He defeated her by admitting her power; she could not have the gratification of enforcing it. He would lie at her feet, he would say: "Of course I need you. I go insane when I see you. You can do almost anything you wish with me. Is that what you want to hear? Almost, Dominique. And the things you couldn't make me do—you could put me through hell if you demanded them and I had to refuse you, as I would. Through utter hell, Dominique. Does that please you? Why do you want to know whether you own me? It's so simple. Of course you do. All of me that can be owned. You'll never demand anything else. But you want to know whether you could make me suffer. You could. What of it?" The words did not sound like surrender, because they were not torn out of him, but admitted simply and willingly. She felt no thrill of conquest; she felt herself owned more than ever, by a man who could say these things, know them to be true, and still remain controlled and controlling—as she wanted him to remain.

Late in June a man named Kent Lansing came to see Roark. He was forty years old, he was dressed like a fashion plate and looked like a prize fighter, though he was not burly, muscular or tough: he was thin and angular. He merely made one think of a boxer and of other things that did not fit his appearance: of a battering ram, of a tank, of a submarine torpedo. He was a member of a corporation formed for the purpose of erecting a luxurious hotel on Central Park South. There were many wealthy men involved and the corporation was ruled by a numerous board; they had purchased their site; they had not decided on an architect. But Kent Lansing had made up his mind that it would be Roark.

"I won't try to tell you how much I'd like to do it," Roark said to him at the end of their first interview. "But there's not a chance of my getting it. I can get along with people—when they're alone. I can do nothing with them in groups. No board has ever hired me—and I don't think one ever will."

Kent Lansing smiled. "Have you ever known a board to do anything?"

"What do you mean?"

"Just that: have you ever known a board to do anything at all?"

"Well, they seem to exist and function."

"Do they? You know, there was a time when everyone thought it self-evident that the earth was flat. It would be entertaining to speculate upon the nature and causes of humanity's illusions. I'll write a book about it some day. It won't be popular. I'll have a chapter on boards of directors. You see, they don't exist."

"I'd like to believe you, but what's the gag?"

"No, you wouldn't like to believe me. The causes of illusions are not pretty to discover. They're either vicious or tragic. This one is both. Mainly vicious. And it's not a gag. But we won't go into that now. All I mean is that a board of directors is one or two ambitious men—and a lot of ballast. I mean that groups of men are vacuums. Great big empty nothings. They say we can't visualize a total nothing. Hell, sit at any committee meeting. The point is only who chooses to fill that nothing. It's a tough battle. The toughest. It's simple enough to fight any enemy, so long as he's there to be fought. But when he isn't . . . Don't look at me like that, as if I were crazy. You ought to know. You've fought a vacuum all your life."

"I'm looking at you like that because I like you."

"Of course you like me. As I knew I'd like you. Men *are* brothers, you know, and they have a great instinct for brotherhood—except in boards, unions, corporations and other chain gangs. But I talk too much. That's why I'm a good salesman. However, I have nothing to sell *you*. You know. So we'll just say that you're going to build The Aquitania—that's the name of our hotel—and we'll let it go at that."

If the violence of the battles which people never hear about could be measured in material statistics, the battle of Kent Lansing against the board of directors of the Aquitania Corporation would have been listed among the great carnages of history. But the things he fought were not solid enough to leave anything as substantial as corpses on the battlefield.

He had to fight phenomena such as: "Listen, Palmer, Lansing's talking about somebody named Roark, how're you going to vote, do the big boys approve of him or not?" "I'm not going to decide till I know who's voted for or against." "Lansing says . . . but on the other hand, Thorpe tells me . . ." "Talbot's putting up a swank hotel on Fifth up in the sixties—and he's got Francon & Keating." "Harper swears by this young fellow—Gordon Prescott." "Listen, Betsy says we're crazy." "I don't like Roark's face—he doesn't look co-operative." "I know, I *feel* it, Roark's the kind that don't fit in. He's not a regular fellow." "What's a regular fellow?" "Aw hell, you know very well what I mean: *regular.*" "Thompson says that Mrs. Pritchett says that she knows for certain because Mr. Macy told her that if . . ." "Well, boys, I don't give a damn what anybody says, I make up my own mind, and I'm here to tell you that I think this Roark is lousy. I don't like the Enright House." "Why?" "I don't know why. I just don't like it, and that's that. Haven't I got a right to an opinion of my own?"

The battle lasted for weeks. Everybody had his say, except Roark. Lansing told him: "It's all right. Lay off. Don't do anything. Let me do the talking. There's nothing you can do. When facing society, the man most concerned, the man who is to do the most and contribute the most, has the least say. It's taken for granted that he has no voice and the reasons he could offer are rejected in advance as prejudiced—since no speech is ever considered, but only the speaker. It's so much easier to pass judgment on a man than on an idea. Though how in hell one passes judgment on a man without considering the content of his brain is more than I'll ever understand. However, that's how it's done. You see, reasons require scales to weigh them. And scales are not made of cotton. And cotton is what the human spirit is made of—you know, the stuff that keeps no shape and offers no resistance and can be twisted forward and backward and into a pretzel. You could tell them why they should hire you so very much better than I could. But they won't listen to you and they'll listen to me. Because I'm the middleman. The shortest distance between two points is not a straight line—it's a middleman. And the more middlemen, the shorter. Such is the psychology of a pretzel."

"Why are you fighting for me like that?" Roark asked.

"Why are you a good architect? Because you have certain standards of what is good, and they're your own, and you stand by them. I want a good hotel, and I have certain standards of what is good, and they're my own, and you're the one who can give me what I want. And when I fight for you, I'm doing—on my side of it—just what you're doing when you design a building. Do you think integrity is the monopoly of the artist? And what, incidentally, do you think integrity is? The ability not to pick a watch out of your neighbor's pocket? No, it's not as easy as that. If that were all, I'd say ninety-five percent of humanity were honest, upright men. Only, as you can see, they aren't. Integrity is the ability to stand by an idea. That presupposes the ability to think. Thinking is something one doesn't borrow or pawn. And yet, if I were asked to choose a symbol for humanity as we know it, I wouldn't choose a cross nor an eagle nor a lion and unicorn. I'd choose three gilded balls."

And as Roark looked at him, he added: "Don't worry. They're all against me. But I have one advantage: they don't know what they want. I do."

At the end of July, Roark signed a contract to build the Aquitania.

Ellsworth Toohey sat in his office, looking at a newspaper spread out on his desk, at the item announcing the Aquitania contract. He smoked, holding the cigarette propped in the corner of his mouth, supported by two straight fingers; one finger tapped against the cigarette, slowly, rhythmically, for a long time.

He heard the sound of his door thrown open, and he glanced up to see Dominique standing there, leaning against the doorjamb, her arms crossed on her chest. Her face looked interested, nothing more, but it was alarming to see an expression of actual interest on her face.

"My dear," he said, rising, "this is the first time you've taken the trouble to enter my office—in the four years that we've worked in the same building. This is really an occasion."

She said nothing, but smiled gently, which was still more alarming. He added, his voice pleasant: "My little speech, of course, was the equivalent of a question. Or don't we understand each other any longer?"

"I suppose we don't—if you find it necessary to ask what brought me here. But you know it, Ellsworth, you know it; there it is on your desk." She walked to the desk and flipped a corner of the newspaper. She laughed. "Do you wish you had it hidden somewhere? Of course you didn't expect me to come. Not that it makes any difference. But I just like to see you being obvious for once. Right on your desk, like that. Open at the real-estate page, too."

"You sound as if that little piece of news had made you happy."

"It did, Ellsworth. It does."

"I thought you had worked hard to prevent that contract."

"I had."

"If you think this is an act you're putting on right now, Dominique, you're fooling yourself. *This* isn't an act."

"No, Ellsworth. This isn't."

"You're happy that Roark got it?"

"I'm so happy, I could sleep with this Kent Lansing, whoever he is, if I ever met him and if he asked me."

"Then the pact is off?"

"By no means. I shall try to stop any job that comes his way. I shall continue trying. It's not going to be so easy as it was, though. The Enright House, the Cord Building—and this. Not so easy for me—and for you. He's beating you, Ellsworth. Ellsworth, what if we were wrong about the world, you and I?"

"You've always been, my dear. Do forgive me. I should have known better than to be astonished. It would make you happy, of course, that he got it. I don't even mind admitting that it doesn't make me happy at all. There, you see? Now your visit to my office has been a complete success. So we shall just write the Aquitania off as a major defeat, forget all about it and continue as we were."

"Certainly, Ellsworth. Just as we were. I'm cinching a beautiful new hospital for Peter Keating at a dinner party tonight."

Ellsworth Toohey went home and spent the evening thinking about Hopton Stoddard.

Hopton Stoddard was a little man worth twenty million dollars. Three inheritances had contributed to that sum, and seventy-two years of a busy life devoted to the purpose of making money. Hopton Stoddard had a genius for investment; he invested in everything—houses of ill fame, Broadway spectacles on the grand scale, preferably of a religious nature, factories, farm mortgages and contraceptives. He was small and bent. His face was not disfigured; people merely thought it was, because it had a single expression: he smiled. His little mouth was shaped like a v in eternal good cheer; his eyebrows were tiny v's inverted over round, blue eyes; his hair, rich, white and waved, looked like a wig, but was real.

Toohey had known Hopton Stoddard for many years and exercised a strong influence upon him. Hopton Stoddard had never married, had no relatives and no friends; he distrusted people, believing that they were always after his money. But he felt a tremendous respect for Ellsworth Toohey, because Toohey represented the exact opposite of his own life; Toohey had no concern whatever for worldly wealth; by the mere fact of this contrast, he considered Toohey the personification of virtue; what this estimate implied in regard to his own life never quite occurred to him. He was not easy in his mind about his life, and the uneasiness grew with the years, with the certainty of an approaching end. He found relief in religion—in the form of a bribe. He experimented with several different creeds, attended services, donated large sums and switched to another faith. As the years passed, the tempo of his quest accelerated; it had the tone of panic.

Toohey's indifference to religion was the only flaw that disturbed him in the person of his friend and mentor. But everything Toohey preached seemed in line with God's law: charity, sacrifice, help to the poor. Hopton Stoddard felt safe whenever he followed Toohey's advice. He donated handsomely to the institutions recommended by Toohey, without much prompting. In matters of the spirit he regarded Toohey upon earth somewhat as he expected to regard God in heaven.

But this summer Toohey met defeat with Hopton Stoddard for the first time.

Hopton Stoddard decided to realize a dream which he had been planning slyly and cautiously, like all his other investments, for several years: he decided to build a temple. It was not to be the temple of any particular creed, but an interdenominational, non-sectarian monument to religion, a cathedral of faith, open to all. Hopton Stoddard wanted to play safe.

He felt crushed when Ellsworth Toohey advised him against the project. Toohey wanted a building to house a new home for subnormal children; he had an organization set up, a distinguished committee of sponsors, an endowment for operating expenses—but no building and no funds to erect one. If Hopton Stoddard wished a worthy memorial to his name, a grand climax of his generosity, to what nobler purpose could he dedicate his money than to the Hopton Stoddard Home for Subnormal Children, Toohey pointed out to him emphatically; to the poor little blighted ones for whom nobody cared. But Hopton Stoddard could not be aroused to any enthusiasm for a Home nor for any mundane institution. It had to be "The Hopton Stoddard Temple of the Human Spirit."

He could offer no arguments against Toohey's brilliant array; he could say nothing except: "No, Ellsworth, no, it's not right, not right." The matter was left unsettled. Hopton Stoddard would not budge, but Toohey's disapproval made him uncomfortable and he postponed his decision from day to day. He knew only that he would have to decide by the end of summer, because in the fall he was to depart on a long journey, a world tour of the holy shrines of all faiths, from Lourdes to Jerusalem to Mecca to Benares.

A few days after the announcement of the Aquitania contract Toohey came to see Hopton Stoddard, in the evening, in the privacy of Stoddard's vast, overstuffed apartment on Riverside Drive.

"Hopton," he said cheerfully, "I was wrong. You were right about that temple."

"No!" said Hopton Stoddard, aghast.

"Yes," said Toohey, "you were right. Nothing else would be quite fitting. You must build a temple. A Temple of the Human Spirit."

Hopton Stoddard swallowed, and his blue eyes became moist. He felt that he must have progressed far upon the path of righteousness if he had been able to teach a point of virtue to his teacher. After that, nothing else mattered; he sat, like a meek, wrinkled baby, listening to Ellsworth Toohey, nodding, agreeing to everything.

"It's an ambitious undertaking, Hopton, and if you do it, you must do it right. It's a little presumptuous, you know—offering a present to God—and unless you do it in the best way possible, it will be offensive, not reverent."

"Yes, of course. It must be right. It must be right. It must be the best. You'll help me, won't you, Ellsworth? You know all about buildings and art and everything—it must be right."

"I'll be glad to help you, if you really want me to."

"If I want you to! What do you mean—if I want . . . ! Goodness gracious, what would I do without you? I don't know anything about . . . about anything like that. And it must be right."

"If you want it right, will you do exactly as I say?"

"Yes. Yes. Yes, of course."

"First of all, the architect. That's very important."

"Yes, indeed."

"You don't want one of those satin-lined commercial boys with the dollar sign all over them. You want a man who believes in his work as—as you believe in God."

"That's right. That's absolutely right."

"You must take the one I name."

"Certainly. Who's that?"

"Howard Roark."

"Huh?" Hopton Stoddard looked blank. "Who's he?"

"He's the man who's going to build the Temple of the Human Spirit."

"Is he any good?"

Ellsworth Toohey turned and looked straight into his eyes.

"By my immortal soul, Hopton," he said slowly, "he's the best there is."

"Oh! . . ."

"But he's difficult to get. He doesn't work except on certain conditions. You must observe them scrupulously. You must give him complete freedom. Tell him what you want and how much you want to spend, and leave the rest up to him. Let him design it and build it as he wishes. He won't work otherwise. Just tell him frankly that you know nothing about architecture and that you chose him because you felt he was the only one who could be trusted to do it right without advice or interference."

"Okay, if you vouch for him."

"I vouch for him."

"That's fine. And I don't care how much it costs me."

"But you must be careful about approaching him. I think he will refuse to do it, at first. He will tell you that he doesn't believe in God."

"*What!*"

"Don't believe him. He's a profoundly religious man—in his own way. You can see that in his buildings."

"Oh."

"But he doesn't belong to any established church. So you won't appear partial. You won't offend anyone."

"That's good."

"Now, when you deal in matters of faith, you must be the first one to have faith. Is that right?"

"That's right."

"Don't wait to see his drawings. They will take some time—and you mustn't delay your trip. Just hire him—don't sign a contract, it's not necessary—make arrangements for your bank to take care of the financial end and let him do the rest. You don't have to pay him his fee until you return. In a year or so, when you come back after seeing all those great temples, you'll have a better one of your own, waiting here for you."

"That's just what I wanted."

"But you must think of the proper unveiling to the public, the proper dedication, the right publicity."

"Of course . . . That is, publicity?"

"Certainly. Do you know of any great event that's not accompanied by a good publicity campaign? One that isn't, can't be much. If you skimp on that, it will be downright disrespectful."

"That's true."

"Now if you want the proper publicity, you must plan it carefully, well in advance. What you want, when you unveil it, is one grand fanfare, like an opera overture, like a blast on Gabriel's horn."

"That's beautiful, the way you put it."

"Well, to do that you mustn't allow a lot of newspaper punks to dissipate your effect by dribbling out premature stories. Don't release the drawings of the temple. Keep them secret. Tell Roark that you want them kept secret. He won't object to that. Have the contractor put up a solid fence all around the site while it's being built. No one's to know what it's like until you come back and preside at the unveiling in person. Then—pictures in every damn paper in the country!"

"Ellsworth!"

"I beg your pardon."

"The idea's right. That's how we put over *The Legend of the Virgin,* ten years ago that was, with a cast of ninety-seven."

"Yes. But in the meantime, keep the public interested. Get yourself a good press agent and tell him how you want it handled. I'll give you the name of an excellent one. See to it that there's something about the mysterious Stoddard Temple in the papers every other week or so. Keep 'em guessing. Keep 'em waiting. They'll be good and ready when the time comes."

"Right."

"But, above all, don't let Roark know that I recommended him. Don't breathe a word to anyone about my having anything to do with it. Not to a soul. Swear it."

"But why?"

"Because I have too many friends who are architects, and it's such an important commission, and I don't want to hurt anybody's feelings."

"Yes. That's true."

"Swear it."

"Oh, Ellsworth!"

"Swear it. By the salvation of your soul."

"I swear it. By . . . that."

"All right. Now you've never dealt with architects, and he's an unusual kind of architect, and you don't want to muff it. So I'll tell you exactly what you're to say to him."

On the following day Toohey walked into Dominique's office. He stood at her desk, smiled and said, his voice unsmiling:

"Do you remember Hopton Stoddard and that temple of all faith that he's been talking about for six years?"

"Vaguely."

"He's going to build it."

"Is he?"

"He's giving the job to Howard Roark."

"Not really!"

"Really."

"Well, of all the incredible . . . Not Hopton!"

"Hopton."

"Oh, all right. I'll go to work on him."

"No. You'll lay off. I told him to give it to Roark."

She sat still, exactly as the words caught her, the amusement gone from her face. He added:

"I wanted you to know that I did it, so there won't be any tactical contradictions. No one else knows it or is to know it. I trust you to remember that."

"She asked, her lips moving tightly: "What are you after?"

He smiled. He said:

"I'm going to make him famous."

Roark sat in Hopton Stoddard's office and listened, stupefied. Hopton Stoddard spoke slowly; it sounded earnest and impressive, but was due to the fact that he had memorized his speeches almost verbatim. His baby eyes looked at Roark with an ingratiating plea. For once, Roark almost forgot architecture and placed the human element first; he wanted to get up and get out of the office; he could not stand the man. But the words he heard held him; the words did not match the man's face or voice.

"So you see, Mr. Roark, though it is to be a religious edifice, it is also more than that. You notice that we call it the Temple of the Human Spirit. We want to capture—in stone, as others capture in music—not some narrow creed, but the essence of all religion. And what is the essence of religion? The great aspiration of the human spirit toward the highest, the noblest, the best. The human spirit as the creator and the conqueror of the ideal. The great life-giving force of the universe. The heroic human spirit. That is your assignment, Mr. Roark."

Roark rubbed the back of his hand against his eyes, helplessly. It was not possible. It simply was not possible. That could not be what the man wanted; not that man. It seemed horrible to hear him say that.

"Mr. Stoddard, I'm afraid you've made a mistake," he said, his voice slow and tired. "I don't think I'm the man you want. I don't think it would be right for me to undertake it. I don't believe in God."

He was astonished to see Hopton Stoddard's expression of delight and triumph. Hopton Stoddard glowed in appreciation—in appreciation of the clairvoyant wisdom of Ellsworth Toohey who was always right. He drew himself up with new confidence, and he said firmly, for the first time in the tone of an old man addressing a youth, wise and gently patronizing:

"That doesn't matter. You're a profoundly religious man, Mr. Roark —in your own way. I can see that in your buildings."

He wondered why Roark stared at him like that, without moving, for such a long time.

"That's true," said Roark. It was almost a whisper.

That he should learn something about himself, about his buildings, from this man who had seen it and known it before he knew it, that this man should say it with that air of tolerant confidence implying full understanding—removed Roark's doubts. He told himself that he did not really understand people; that an impression could be deceptive; that Hopton Stoddard would be far on another continent anyway; that nothing mattered in the face of such an assignment; that nothing could matter when a human voice—even Hopton Stoddard's—was going on, saying:

"I wish to call it God. You may choose any other name. But what I want in that building is your spirit. Your spirit, Mr. Roark. Give me the best of that—and you will have done your job, as I shall have done mine. Do not worry about the meaning I wish conveyed. Let it be your spirit in the shape of a building—and it will have that meaning, whether you know it or not."

And so Roark agreed to build the Stoddard Temple of the Human Spirit.

XI

IN DECEMBER THE COSMO-SLOTNICK BUILDING WAS OPENED WITH great ceremony. There were celebrities, flower horseshoes, newsreel cameras, revolving searchlights and three hours of speeches, all alike.

I should be happy, Peter Keating told himself—and wasn't. He watched from a window the solid spread of faces filling Broadway from curb to curb. He tried to talk himself into joy. He felt nothing. He had to admit that he was bored. But he smiled and shook hands and let himself be photographed. The Cosmo-Slotnick Building rose ponderously over the street, like a big white bromide.

After the ceremonies Ellsworth Toohey took Keating away to the retreat of a pale-orchid booth in a quiet, expensive restaurant. Many brilliant parties were being given in honor of the opening, but Keating grasped Toohey's offer and declined all the other invitations. Toohey watched him as he seized his drink and slumped in his seat.

"Wasn't it grand?" said Toohey. "That, Peter, is the climax of what you can expect from life." He lifted his glass delicately. "Here's to the hope that you shall have many triumphs such as this. Such as tonight."

"Thanks," said Keating, and reached for his glass hastily, without looking, and lifted it, to find it empty.

"Don't you feel proud, Peter?"

"Yes. Yes, of course."

"That's good. That's how I like to see you. You looked extremely handsome tonight. You'll be splendid in those newsreels."

A flicker of interest snapped in Keating's eyes. "Well, I sure hope so."

"It's too bad you're not married, Peter. A wife would have been most decorative tonight. Goes well with the public. With the movie audiences, too."

"Katie doesn't photograph well."

"Oh, that's right, you're engaged to Katie. So stupid of me. I keep forgetting it. No, Katie doesn't photograph well at all. Also, for the life of me, I can't imagine Katie being very effective at a social function. There are a great many nice adjectives one could use about Katie, but 'poised' and 'distinguished' are not among them. You must forgive me, Peter. I let my imagination run away with me. Dealing with art as much as I do, I'm inclined to see things purely from the viewpoint of artistic fitness. And looking at you tonight, I couldn't help thinking of the woman who would have made such a perfect picture by your side."

"Who?"

"Oh, don't pay attention to me. It's only an esthetic fancy. Life is never as perfect as that. People have too much to envy you for. You couldn't add *that* to your other achievements."

"Who?"

"Drop it, Peter. You can't get her. Nobody can get her. You're good, but you're not good enough for that."

"Who?"

"Dominique Francon, of course."

Keating sat up straight and Toohey saw wariness in his eyes, rebellion, actual hostility. Toohey held his glance calmly. It was Keating who gave in; he slumped again and he said, pleading:

"Oh, God, Ellsworth, I don't love her."

"I never thought you did. But I do keep forgetting the exaggerated importance which the average man attaches to love—sexual love."

"I'm not an average man," said Keating wearily; it was an automatic protest—without fire.

"Sit up, Peter. You don't look like a hero, slumped that way."

Keating jerked himself up—anxious and angry. He said:

"I've always felt that you wanted me to marry Dominique. Why? What's it to you?"

"You've answered your own question, Peter. What could it possibly be to me? But we were speaking of love. Sexual love, Peter, is a profoundly selfish emotion. And selfish emotions are not the ones that lead to happiness. Are they? Take tonight for instance. That was an evening to swell an egotist's heart. Were you happy, Peter? Don't bother, my dear, no answer is required. The point I wish to make is only that one must mistrust one's most personal impulses. What one desires is actually of so little importance! One can't expect to find happiness until one realizes this completely. Think of tonight for a moment. You, my dear Peter, were the least important person there. Which is as it should be. It is not the doer that counts but those for whom things are done. But you were not able to accept that—and so you didn't feel the great elation that should have been yours."

"That's true," whispered Keating. He would not have admitted it to anyone else.

"You missed the beautiful pride of utter selflessness. Only when you learn to deny your ego, completely, only when you learn to be amused by such piddling sentimentalities as your little sex urges—only then will you achieve the greatness which I have always expected of you."

"You . . . you believe that about me, Ellsworth? You really do?"

"I wouldn't be sitting here if I didn't. But to come back to love. Personal love, Peter, is a great evil—as everything personal. And it always leads to misery. Don't you see why? Personal love is an act of discrimination, of preference. It is an act of injustice—to every human being on earth whom you rob of the affection arbitrarily granted to one. You must love all men equally. But you cannot achieve so noble an emotion if you don't kill your selfish little choices. They are vicious and futile—since they contradict the first cosmic law—the basic equality of all men."

"You mean," said Keating, suddenly interested, "that in a . . . in a philosophical way, deep down, I mean, we're all equal? All of us?"

"Of course," said Toohey.

Keating wondered why the thought was so warmly pleasant to him. He did not mind that this made him the equal of every pickpocket in the crowd gathered to celebrate his building tonight; it occurred to him dimly—and left him undisturbed, even though it contradicted the passionate quest for superiority that had driven him all his life. The contradiction did not matter; he was not thinking of tonight nor of the crowd; he was thinking of a man who had not been there tonight.

"You know, Ellsworth," he said, leaning forward, happy in an uneasy kind of way, "I . . . I'd rather talk to you than do anything else, anything at all. I had so many places to go tonight—and I'm so much happier just sitting here with you. Sometimes I wonder how I'd ever go on without you."

"That," said Toohey, "is as it should be. Or else what are friends for?"

That winter the annual costume Arts Ball was an event of greater brilliance and orginality than usual. Athelstan Beasely, the leading spirit of its organization, had had what he called a stroke of genius: all the architects were invited to come dressed as their best buildings. It was a huge success.

Peter Keating was the star of the evening. He looked wonderful as the Cosmo-Slotnick Building. An exact papier-mâché replica of his famous structure covered him from head to knees; one could not see his face, but his bright eyes peered from behind the windows of the top floor, and the crowning pyramid of the roof rose over his head; the colonnade hit him somewhere about the diaphragm, and he wagged a finger through the portals of the great entrance door. His legs were free to move with his usual elegance, in faultless dress trousers and patent-leather pumps.

Guy Francon was very impressive as the Frink National Bank Building, although the structure looked a little squatter than in the original, in order to allow for Francon's stomach; the Hadrian torch over his head had a real electric bulb lit by a miniature battery. Ralston Holcombe was magnificent as a state capitol, and Gordon L. Prescott was very masculine as a grain elevator. Eugene Pettingill waddled about on his skinny, ancient legs, small and bent, an imposing Park Avenue hotel, with horn-rimmed spectacles peering from under the majestic tower. Two wits engaged in a duel, butting each other in the belly with famous spires, great landmarks of the city that greet the ships approaching from across the ocean. Everybody had lots of fun.

Many of the architects, Athelstan Beasely in particular, commented resentfully on Howard Roark who had been invited and did not come. They had expected to see him dressed as the Enright House.

Dominique stopped in the hall and stood looking at the door, at the inscription: "HOWARD ROARK, ARCHITECT."

She had never seen his office. She had fought against coming here for a long time. But she had to see the place where he worked.

The secretary in the reception room was startled when Dominique gave her name, but announced the visitor to Roark. "Go right in, Miss Francon," she said.

Roark smiled when she entered his office; a faint smile without surprise.

"I knew you'd come here some day," he said. "Want me to show you the place?"

"What's that?" she asked.

His hands were smeared with clay; on a long table, among a litter of unfinished sketches, stood the clay model of a building, a rough study of angles and terraces.

"The Aquitania?" she asked.

He nodded.

"Do you always do that?"

"No. Not always. Sometimes. There's a hard problem here. I like to play with it for a while. It will probably be my favorite building—it's so difficult."

"Go ahead. I want to watch you doing that. Do you mind?"

"Not at all."

In a moment, he had forgotten her presence. She sat in a corner and watched his hands. She saw them molding walls. She saw them smash a part of the structure, and begin again, slowly, patiently, with a strange certainty even in his hesitation. She saw the palm of his hand smooth a long, straight plane, she saw an angle jerked across space in the motion of his hand before she saw it in clay.

She rose and walked to the window. The buildings of the city far below looked no bigger than the model on his table. It seemed to her that she could see his hands shaping the setbacks, the corners, the roofs of all the structures below, smashing and molding again. Her hand moved absently, following the form of a distant building in rising steps, feeling a physical sense of possession, feeling it for him.

She turned back to the table. A strand of hair hung down over his face bent attentively to the model; he was not looking at her, he was looking at the shape under his fingers. It was almost as if she were watching his hands moving over the body of another woman. She leaned against the wall, weak with a feeling of violent, physical pleasure.

At the beginning of January, while the first steel columns rose from the excavations that were to become the Cord Building and the Aquitania Hotel, Roark worked on the drawings for the Temple.

When the first sketches were finished, he said to his secretary:

"Get me Steven Mallory."

"Mallory, Mr. Roark? Who . . . Oh, yes, the shooting sculptor."

"The what?"

"He took a shot at Ellsworth Toohey, didn't he?"

"Did he? Yes, that's right."

"Is that the one you want, Mr. Roark?"

"That's the one."

For two days the secretary telephoned art dealers, galleries, architects, newspapers. No one could tell her what had become of Steven Mallory or where he could be found. On the third day she reported to Roark: "I've found an address, in the Village, which I'm told might be his. There's no telephone." Roark dictated a letter asking Mallory to telephone his office.

The letter was not returned, but a week passed without answer. Then Steven Mallory telephoned.

"Hello?" said Roark, when the secretary switched the call to him.

"Steven Mallory speaking," said a young, hard voice, in a way that left an impatient, belligerent silence after the words.

"I should like to see you, Mr. Mallory. Can we make an appointment for you to come to my office?"

"What do you want to see me about?"

"About a commission, of course. I want you to do some work for a building of mine."

There was a long silence.

"All right," said Mallory; his voice sounded dead. He added: "Which building?"

"The Stoddard Temple. You may have heard . . . "

"Yeah, I heard. You're doing it. Who hasn't heard? Will you pay me as much as you're paying your press agent?"

"I'm not paying the press agent. I'll pay you whatever you wish to ask."

"You know that can't be much."

"What time would it be convenient for you to come here?"

"Oh, hell, you name it. You know I'm not busy."

"Two o'clock tomorrow afternoon?"

"All right." He added: "I don't like your voice."

Roark laughed. "I like yours. Cut it out and be here tomorrow at two."

"Okay." Mallory hung up.

Roark dropped the receiver, grinning. But the grin vanished suddenly, and he sat looking at the telephone, his face grave.

Mallory did not keep the appointment. Three days passed without a word from him. Then Roark went to find him in person.

The rooming house where Mallory lived was a dilapidated brownstone in an unlighted street that smelled of a fish market. There was a laundry and a cobbler on the ground floor, at either side of a narrow entrance. A slatternly landlady said: "Mallory? Fifth floor rear," and shuffled away indifferently. Roark climbed sagging wooden stairs lighted by bulbs stuck in a web of pipes. He knocked at a grimy door.

The door opened. A gaunt young man stood on the threshold; he had disheveled hair, a strong mouth with a square lower lip, and the most expressive eyes that Roark had ever seen.

"What do you want?" he snapped.

"Mr. Mallory?"

"Yeah."

"I'm Howard Roark."

Mallory laughed, leaning against the doorjamb, one arm stretched across the opening, with no intention of stepping aside. He was obviously drunk.

"Well, well!" he said. "In person."

"May I come in?"

"What for?"

Roark sat down on the stair banister. "Why didn't you keep your appointment?"

"Oh, the appointment? Oh, yes. Well, I'll tell you," Mallory said gravely. "It was like this: I really intended to keep it, I really did, and started out for your office, but on my way there I passed a movie theater that was showing *Two Heads on a Pillow,* so I went in. I just had to see *Two Heads on a Pillow.*" He grinned, sagging against his stretched arm.

"You'd better let me come in," said Roark quietly.

"Oh what the hell, come in."

The room was a narrow hole. There was an unmade bed in a corner, a litter of newspapers and old clothes, a gas ring, a framed landscape from the five-and-ten, representing some sort of sick brown meadows with sheep; there were no drawings or figures, no hints of the occupant's profession.

Roark pushed some books and a skillet off the only chair, and sat down. Mallory stood before him, grinning, swaying a little.

"You're doing it all wrong," said Mallory. "That's not the way it's done. You must be pretty hard up to come running after a sculptor. The way it's done is like this: You make me come to your office, and the first time I come you mustn't be there. The second time you must keep me waiting for an hour and a half, then come out into the reception room and shake hands and ask me whether I know the Wilsons of Podunk and say how nice that we have mutual friends, but you're in an awful hurry today and you'll call me up for lunch soon and then we'll talk business. Then you keep this up for two months. Then you give me the commission. Then you tell me that I'm no good and wasn't any good in the first place, and you throw the thing into the ash can. Then you hire Valerian Bronson and he does the job. That's the way it's done. Only not this time."

But his eyes were studying Roark intently, and his eyes had the certainty of a professional. As he spoke, his voice kept losing its swaggering gaiety, and it slipped to a dead flatness on the last sentences.

"No," said Roark, "not this time."

The boy stood looking at him silently.

"You're Howard Roark?" he asked. "I like your buildings. That's why I didn't want to meet you. So I wouldn't have to be sick every time I looked at them. I wanted to go on thinking that they had been done by somebody who matched them."

"What if I do?"

"That doesn't happen."

But he sat down on the edge of the crumpled bed and slumped forward, his glance like a sensitive scale weighing Roark's features, impertinent in its open action of appraisal.

"Listen," said Roark, speaking clearly and very carefully, "I want you to do a statue for the Stoddard Temple. Give me a piece of paper and I'll write you a contract right now, stating that I will owe you a million dollars damages if I hire another sculptor or if your work is not used."

"You can speak normal. I'm not drunk. Not all the way. I understand."

"Well?"

"Why did you pick me?"

"Because you're a good sculptor."

"That's not true."

"That you're good?"

"No. That it's your reason. Who asked you to hire me?"

"Nobody."

"Some woman I laid?"

"I don't know any women you laid."

"Stuck on your building budget?"

"No. The budget's unlimited."

"Feel sorry for me?"

"No. Why should I?"

"Want to get publicity out of that shooting-Toohey business?"

"Good God, no!"

"Well, what then?"

"Why do you fish for all that nonsense instead of the simplest reason?"

"Which?"

"That I like your work."

"Sure. That's what they all say. That's what we're all supposed to say and to believe. Imagine what would happen if somebody blew the lid off that one! So, all right, you like my work. What's the real reason?"

"I like your work."

Mallory spoke earnestly, his voice sober.

"You mean you saw the things I've done, and you liked them—you—yourself—alone—without anyone telling you that you should like them or why you should like them—and you decided that you wanted me, for that reason—only for that reason—without knowing anything about me or giving a damn—only because of the things I've done and . . . and what you saw in them—only because of that, you decided to hire me, and you went to the bother of finding me, and coming here, and being insulted—only because you *saw*—and what you saw made me important to you, made you want me? Is that what you mean?"

"Just that," said Roark.

The things that pulled Mallory's eyes wide were frightening to see. Then he shook his head, and said very simply, in the tone of soothing himself:

"No."

He leaned forward. His voice sounded dead and pleading.

"Listen, Mr. Roark. I won't be mad at you. I just want to know. All right, I see that you're set on having me work for you, and you know you can get me, for anything you say, you don't have to sign any million-dollar contract, look at this room, you know you've got me, so why shouldn't you tell me the truth? It won't make any difference to you—and it's very important to me."

"What's very important to you?"

"Not to . . . not to . . . Look. I didn't think anybody'd ever want me again. But you do. All right. I'll go through it again. Only I don't want to think again that I'm working for somebody who . . . who likes my work. That, I couldn't go through any more. I'll feel better if you tell me. I'll . . . I'll feel calmer. Why should you put on an act for me? I'm nothing. I won't think less of you, if that's what you're afraid of. Don't you see? It's much more decent to tell me the truth. Then it will be simple and honest. I'll respect you more. Really, I will."

"What's the matter with you, kid? What have they done to you? Why do you want to say things like that?"

"Because . . ." Mallory roared suddenly, and then his voice broke, and his head dropped, and he finished in a flat whisper: "because I've spent two years"—his hand circled limply indicating the room—"that's how I've spent them—trying to get used to the fact that what you're trying to tell me doesn't exist. . . ."

Roark walked over to him, lifted his chin, knocking it upward, and said:

"You're a God-damn fool. You have no right to care what I think of your work, what I am or why I'm here. You're too good for that. But if you want to know it—I think you're the best sculptor we've got. I think it, because your figures are not what men are, but what men could be—and should be. Because you've gone beyond the probable and made us see what is possible, but possible only through you. Because your figures are more devoid of contempt for humanity than any work I've ever seen. Because you have a magnificent respect for the human being. Because your figures are the heroic in man. And so I didn't come here to do you a favor or because I felt sorry for you or because you need a job pretty badly. I came for a simple, selfish reason—the same reason that makes a man choose the cleanest food he can find. It's a law of survival, isn't it?—to seek the best. I didn't come for your sake. I came for mine."

Mallory jerked himself away from him, and dropped face down on the bed, his two arms stretched out, one on each side of his head, hands closed into two fists. The thin trembling of the shirt cloth on his back showed that he was sobbing; the shirt cloth and the fists that twisted slowly, digging into the pillow. Roark knew that he was looking at a man who had never cried before. He sat down on the side of the bed and could not take his eyes off the twisting wrists, even though the sight was hard to bear.

After a while Mallory sat up. He looked at Roark and saw the calmest, kindest face—a face without a hint of pity. It did not look like the countenance of men who watch the agony of another with a secret pleasure, uplifted by the sight of a beggar who needs their compassion; it did not bear the cast of the hungry soul that feeds upon another's humiliation. Roark's face seemed tired, drawn at the temples, as if he had just taken a beating. But his eyes were serene and they looked at Mallory quietly, a hard, clean glance of understanding—and respect.

"Lie down now," said Roark. "Lie still for a while."

"How did they ever let you survive?"

"Lie down. Rest. We'll talk afterward."

Mallory got up. Roark took him by the shoulders, forced him down, lifted his legs off the floor, lowered his head on the pillow. The boy did not resist.

Stepping back, Roark brushed against a table loaded with junk. Something clattered to the floor. Mallory jerked forward, trying to reach it first. Roark pushed his arm aside and picked up the object.

It was a small plaster plaque, the kind sold in cheap gift shops. It represented a baby sprawled on its stomach, dimpled rear forward, peeking coyly over its shoulder. A few lines, the structure of a few muscles showed a magnificent talent that could not be hidden, that broke fiercely through the rest; the rest was a deliberate attempt to be obvious, vulgar and trite, a clumsy effort, unconvincing and tortured. It was an object that belonged in a chamber of horrors.

Mallory saw Roark's hand begin to shake. Then Roark's arm went back and up, over his head, slowly, as if gathering the weight of air in the crook of his elbow; it was only a flash, but it seemed to last for minutes, the arm stood lifted and still—then it slashed forward, the plaque shot across the room and burst to pieces against the wall. It was the only time anyone had ever seen Roark murderously angry.

"Roark."

"Yes?"

"Roark, I wish I'd met you before you had a job to give me." He spoke without expression, his head lying back on the pillow, his eyes closed. "So that there would be no other reason mixed in. Because, you see, I'm very grateful to you. Not for giving me a job. Not for coming here. Not for anything that you'll ever do for me. Just for what you are."

Then he lay without moving, straight and limp, like a man long past the stage of suffering. Roark stood at the window, looking at the wretched room and at the boy on the bed. He wondered why he felt as if he were waiting. He was waiting for an explosion over their heads. It seemed senseless. Then he understood. He thought, This is how men feel, trapped in a shell hole; this room is not an accident of poverty, it's the footprint of a war; it's the devastation torn by explosives more vicious than any stored in the arsenals of the world. A war . . . against? . . . The enemy had no name and no face. But this boy was a comrade-in-arms, hurt in battle, and Roark stood over him, feeling a strange new thing, a desire to lift him in his arms and carry him to safety . . . Only the hell and the safety had no known designations . . . He kept thinking of Kent Lansing, trying to remember something Kent Lansing had said . . .

Then Mallory opened his eyes, and lifted himself up on one elbow. Roark pulled the chair over to the bed and sat down.

"Now," he said, "talk. Talk about the things you really want said. Don't tell me about your family, your childhood, your friends or your feelings. Tell me about the things you *think*."

Mallory looked at him incredulously and whispered:

"How did you know that?"

Roark smiled and said nothing.

"How did you know what's been killing me? Slowly, for years, driving me to hate people when I don't want to hate. . . . Have you felt it, too? Have you seen how your best friends love everything about you—except the things that count? And your most important is nothing to them, nothing, not even a sound they can recognize. You mean, *you* want to hear? You want to know what I do and why I do it, you want to know what I *think*? It's not boring to you? It's important?"

"Go ahead," said Roark.

Then he sat for hours, listening, while Mallory spoke of his work, of the thoughts behind his work, of the thoughts that shaped his life, spoke gluttonously, like a drowning man flung out to shore, getting drunk on huge, clean snatches of air.

Mallory came to Roark's office on the following morning, and Roark showed him the sketches of the Temple. When he stood at a drafting table, with a problem to consider, Mallory changed; there was no uncertainty in him, no remembrance of pain; the gesture of his hand taking the drawing was sharp and sure, like that of a soldier on duty. The gesture said that nothing ever done to him could alter the function of the thing within him that was now called into action. He had an unyielding, impersonal confidence; he faced Roark as an equal.

He studied the drawings for a long time, then raised his head. Everything about his face was controlled, except his eyes.

"Like it?" Roark asked.

"Don't use stupid words."

He held one of the drawings, walked to the window, stood looking from the sketch to the street to Roark's face and back again.

"It doesn't seem possible," he said. "Not this—and that." He waved the sketch at the street.

There was a poolroom on the corner of the street below; a rooming house with a Corinthian portico; a billboard advertising a Broadway musical; a line of pink-gray underwear fluttering on a roof.

"Not in the same city. Not on the same earth," said Mallory. "But you made it happen. It's possible. . . . I'll never be afraid again."

"Of what?"

Mallory put the sketch down on the table, cautiously. He answered:

"You said something yesterday about a first law. A law demanding that man seek the best. . . . It was funny. . . . The unrecognized genius—that's an old story. Have you ever thought of a much worse one—the genius recognized too well? . . . That a great many men are poor fools who can't see the best—that's nothing. One can't get angry at that. But do you understand about the men who *see* it and *don't want it?*"

"No."

"No. You wouldn't. I spent all night thinking about you. I didn't sleep at all. Do you know what your secret is? It's your terrible innocence."

Roark laughed aloud, looking at the boyish face.

"No," said Mallory, "it's not funny. I know what I'm talking about— and you don't. You can't know. It's because of that absolute health of yours. You're so healthy that you can't conceive of disease. You know of it. But you don't really believe it. I do. I'm wiser than you are about some things, because I'm weaker. I understand—the other side. That's what did it to me . . . what you saw yesterday."

"That's over."

"Probably. But not quite. I'm not afraid any more. But I know that the terror exists. I know the kind of terror it is. You can't conceive of that kind. Listen, what's the most horrible experience you can imagine? To me—it's being left, unarmed, in a sealed cell with a drooling beast of prey or a maniac who's had some disease that's eaten his brain out. You'd have nothing then but your voice—your voice and your thought. You'd scream to that creature why it should not touch you, you'd have the most eloquent words, the unanswerable words, you'd become the vessel of the absolute truth. And you'd see living eyes watching you and you'd know that the thing can't hear you, that it can't be reached, not reached, not in any way, yet it's breathing and moving there before you with a purpose of its own. That's horror. Well, that's what's hanging over the world, prowling somewhere through mankind, that same thing, something closed, mindless, utterly wanton, but something with an aim and a cunning of its own. I don't think I'm a coward, but I'm afraid of it. And that's all I know—only that it exists. I don't know its purpose, I don't know its nature."

"The principle behind the Dean," said Roark.

"What?"

"It's something I wonder about once in a while. . . . Mallory, why did you try to shoot Ellsworth Toohey?" He saw the boy's eyes, and he added: "You don't have to tell me if you don't like to talk about it."

"I don't like to talk about it," said Mallory, his voice tight. "But it was the right question to ask."

"Sit down," said Roark. "We'll talk about your commission."

Then Mallory listened attentively while Roark spoke of the building and of what he wanted from the sculptor. He concluded:

"Just one figure. It will stand here." He pointed to a sketch. "The place is built around it. The statue of a naked woman. If you understand the building, you understand what the figure must be. The human spirit. The heroic in man. The aspiration and the fulfillment, both. Uplifted in its quest—and uplifting by its own essence. Seeking God—and finding itself. Showing that there is no higher reach beyond its own form. . . . You're the only one who can do it for me."

"Yes."

"You'll work as I work for my clients. You know what I want—the rest is up to you. Do it any way you wish. I'd like to suggest the model, but if she doesn't fit your purpose, choose anyone you prefer."

"Who's your choice?"

"Dominique Francon."

"Oh, God!"

"Know her?"

"I've seen her. If I could have her . . . Christ! there's no other woman so right for this. She . . ." He stopped. He added, deflated: "She won't pose. Certainly not for you."

"She will."

Guy Francon tried to object when he heard of it.

"Listen, Dominique," he said angrily, "there is a limit. There really is a limit—even for you. *Why* are you doing it? Why—for a building of Roark's, of all things? After everything you've said and done against him—do you wonder people are talking? Nobody'd care or notice if it were anyone else. But you—and Roark! I can't go anywhere without having somebody ask me about it. What am I to do?"

"Order yourself a reproduction of the statue, Father. It's going to be beautiful."

Peter Keating refused to discuss it. But he met Dominique at a party and he asked, having intended not to ask it:

"Is it true that you're posing for a statue for Roark's temple?"

"Yes."

"Dominique, I don't like it."

"No?"

"Oh, I'm sorry. I know I have no right . . . It's only . . . It's only that of all people, I don't want to see you being friendly with Roark. Not Roark. Anybody but Roark."

She looked interested: "Why?"

"I don't know."

Her glance of curious study worried him.

"Maybe," he muttered, "maybe it's because it has never seemed right that you should have such contempt for his work. It made me very happy that you had, but . . . but it never seemed right—for you."

"It didn't, Peter?"

"No. But you don't like him as a person, do you?"

"No, I don't like him as a person."

Ellsworth Toohey was displeased. "It was most unwise of you, Dominique," he said in the privacy of her office. His voice did not sound smooth.

"I know it was."

"Can't you change your mind and refuse?"

"I won't change my mind, Ellsworth."

He sat down, and shrugged; after a while he smiled. "All right, my dear, have it your own way."

She ran a pencil through a line of copy and said nothing.

Toohey lighted a cigarette. "So he's chosen Steven Mallory for the job," he said.

"Yes. A funny coincidence, wasn't it?"

"It's no coincidence at all, my dear. Things like that are never a coincidence. There's a basic law behind it. Though I'm sure he doesn't know it and nobody helped him to choose."

"I believe you approve?"

"Wholeheartedly. It makes everything just right. Better than ever."

"Ellsworth, why did Mallory try to kill you?"

"I haven't the faintest idea. I don't know. I think Mr. Roark does. Or should. Incidentally, who selected you to pose for that statue? Roark or Mallory?"

"That's none of your business, Ellsworth."

"I see. Roark."

"Incidentally, I've told Roark that it was you who made Hopton Stoddard hire him."

He stopped his cigarette in mid-air; then moved again and placed it in his mouth.

"You did? Why?"

"I saw the drawings of the temple."

"That good?"

"Better, Ellsworth."

"What did he say when you told him?"

"Nothing. He laughed."

"He did? Nice of him. I daresay many people will join him after a while."

Through the months of that winter Roark seldom slept more than three hours a night. There was a swinging sharpness in his movements, as if his body fed energy to all those around him. The energy ran through the walls of his office to three points of the city: to the Cord Building, in the center of Manhattan, a tower of copper and glass; to the Aquitania Hotel on Central Park South; and to the Temple on a rock over the Hudson, far north on Riverside Drive.

When they had time to meet, Austen Heller watched him, amused and pleased. "When these three are finished, Howard," he said, "nobody will be able to stop you. Not ever again. I speculate occasionally upon how far you'll go. You see, I've always had a weakness for astronomy."

On an evening in March Roark stood within the tall enclosure that had been erected around the site of the Temple, according to Stoddard's orders. The first blocks of stone, the base of future walls, rose above the ground. It was late and the workers had left. The place lay deserted, cut off from the world, dissolved in darkness; but the sky glowed, too luminous for the night below, as if the light had remained past the normal hour, in announcement of the coming spring. A ship's siren cried out once, somewhere on the river, and the sound seemed to come from a distant countryside, through miles of silence. A light still burned in the wooden shack built as a studio for Steven Mallory, where Dominique posed for him.

The Temple was to be a small building of gray limestone. Its lines were horizontal, not the lines reaching to heaven, but the lines of the earth. It seemed to spread over the ground like arms outstretched at shoulder-height, palms down, in great, silent acceptance. It did not cling to the soil and it did not crouch under the sky. It seemed to lift the earth, and its few vertical shafts pulled the sky down. It was scaled to human height in such a manner that it did not dwarf man, but stood as a setting that made his figure the only absolute, the gauge of perfection by which all dimensions were to be judged. When a man entered this temple, he would feel space molded around him, for him, as if it had waited for his entrance, to be completed. It was a joyous place, with the joy of exaltation that must be quiet. It was a place where one would come to feel sinless and strong, to find the peace of spirit never granted save by one's own glory.

There was no ornamentation inside, except the graded projections of the walls, and the vast windows. The place was not sealed under vaults, but thrown open to the earth around it, to the trees, the river, the sun—and to the skyline of the city in the distance, the skyscrapers, the shapes of man's achievement on earth. At the end of the room, facing the entrance, with the city as background, stood the figure of a naked human body.

There was nothing before him now in the darkness except the first stones, but Roark thought of the finished building, feeling it in the joints of his fingers, still remembering the movements of his pencil that had drawn it. He stood thinking of it. Then he walked across the rough, torn earth to the studio shack.

"Just a moment," said Mallory's voice when he knocked.

Inside the shack Dominique stepped down from the stand and pulled a robe on. Then Mallory opened the door.

"Oh, it's you?" he said. "We thought it was the watchman. What are you doing here so late?"

"Good evening, Miss Francon," said Roark, and she nodded curtly. "Sorry to interrupt, Steve."

"It's all right. We haven't been doing so well. Dominique can't get quite what I want tonight. Sit down, Howard. What the hell time is it?"

"Nine-thirty. If you're going to stay longer, want me to have some dinner sent up?"

"I don't know. Let's have a cigarette."

The place had an unpainted wooden floor, bare wooden rafters, a cast-iron stove glowing in a corner. Mallory moved about like a feudal host, with smudges of clay on his forehead. He smoked nervously, pacing up and down.

"Want to get dressed, Dominique?" he asked. "I don't think we'll do much more tonight." She didn't answer. She stood looking at Roark. Mallory reached the end of the room, whirled around, smiled at Roark: "Why haven't you ever come in before, Howard? Of course, if I'd been really busy, I'd have thrown you out. What, by the way, are you doing here at this hour?"

"I just wanted to see the place tonight. Couldn't get here earlier."

"Is this what you want, Steve?" Dominique asked suddenly. She took her robe off and walked naked to the stand. Mallory looked from her to Roark and back again. Then he saw what he had been struggling to see all day. He saw her body standing before him, straight and tense, her head thrown back, her arms at her sides, palms out, as she had stood for many days; but now her body was alive, so still that it seemed to tremble, saying what he had wanted to hear: a proud, reverent, enraptured surrender to a vision of her own, the right moment, the moment before the figure would sway and break, the moment touched by the reflection of what she saw.

Mallory's cigarette went flying across the room.

"Hold it, Dominique!" he cried. "Hold it! Hold it!"

He was at his stand before the cigarette hit the ground.

He worked, and Dominique stood without moving, and Roark stood facing her, leaning against the wall.

In April the walls of the Temple rose in broken lines over the ground. On moonlit nights they had a soft, smeared, underwater glow. The tall fence stood on guard around them.

After the day's work, four people would often remain at the site— Roark, Mallory, Dominique and Mike Donnigan. Mike had not missed employment on a single building of Roark's.

The four of them sat together in Mallory's shack, after all the others had left. A wet cloth covered the unfinished statue. The door of the shack stood open to the first warmth of a spring night. A tree branch hung outside, with three new leaves against the black sky, stars trembling like drops of water on the edges of the leaves. There were no chairs in the shack. Mallory stood at the cast-iron stove, fixing hot dogs and coffee. Mike sat on the model's stand, smoking a pipe. Roark lay stretched out on the floor, propped up on his elbows. Dominique sat on a kitchen stool, a thin silk robe wrapped about her, her bare feet on the planks of the floor.

They did not speak about their work. Mallory told outrageous stories and Dominique laughed like a child. They talked about nothing in particular, sentences that had meaning only in the sound of the voices, in the warm gaiety, in the ease of complete relaxation. They were simply four people who liked being there together. The walls rising in the darkness beyond the open door gave sanction to their rest, gave them the right to lightness, the building on which they had all worked together, the building that was like a low, audible harmony to the sound of their voices. Roark laughed as Dominique had never seen him laugh anywhere else, his mouth loose and young.

They stayed there late into the night. Mallory poured coffee into a mongrel assortment of cracked cups. The odor of coffee met the odor of the new leaves outside.

In May work was stopped on the construction of the Aquitania Hotel.

Two of the owners had been cleaned out in the stock market; a third got his funds attached by a lawsuit over an inheritance disputed by someone; a fourth embezzled somebody else's shares. The corporation blew up in a tangle of court cases that were to require years of untangling. The building had to wait, unfinished.

"I'll straighten it out, if I have to murder a few of them," Kent Lansing told Roark. "I'll get it out of their hands. We'll finish it some day, you and I. But it will take time. Probably a long time. I won't tell you to be patient. Men like you and me would not survive beyond their first fifteen years if they did not acquire the patience of a Chinese executioner. And the hide of a battleship."

Ellsworth Toohey laughed, sitting on the edge of Dominique's desk. "The Unfinished Symphony—thank God," he said.

Dominique used that in her column. "The Unfinished Symphony on Central Park South," she wrote. She did not say, "thank God." The nickname was repeated. Strangers noticed the odd sight of an expensive structure on an important street, left gaping with empty windows, half-covered walls, naked beams; when they asked what it was, people who had never heard of Roark or of the story behind the building, snickered and answered: "Oh, that's the Unfinished Symphony."

Late at night Roark would stand across the street, under the trees of the Park, and look at the black, dead shape among the glowing structures of the city's skyline. His hands would move as they had moved over the clay model; at that distance, a broken projection could be covered by the palm of his hand; but the instinctive completing motion met nothing but air.

He forced himself sometimes to walk through the building. He walked on shivering planks hung over emptiness, through rooms without ceilings and rooms without floors, to the open edges where girders stuck out like bones through a broken skin.

An old watchman lived in a cubbyhole at the back of the ground floor. He knew Roark and let him wander around. Once, he stopped Roark on the way out and said suddenly: "I had a son once—almost. He was born dead." Something had made him say that, and he looked at Roark, not quite certain of what he had wanted to say. But Roark smiled, his eyes closed, and his hand covered the old man's shoulder, like a handshake, and then he walked away.

It was only the first few weeks. Then he made himself forget the Aquitania.

On an evening in October Roark and Dominique walked together through the completed Temple. It was to be opened publicly in a week, the day after Stoddard's return. No one had seen it except those who had worked on its construction.

It was a clear, quiet evening. The site of the Temple lay empty and silent. The red of the sunset on the limestone walls was like the first light of morning.

They stood looking at the Temple, and then stood inside, before the marble figure, saying nothing to each other. The shadows in the molded space around them seemed shaped by the same hand that had shaped the walls. The ebbing motion of light flowed in controlled discipline, like the sentences of a speech giving voice to the changing facets of the walls.

"Roark . . ."

"Yes, my dearest?"

"No . . . nothing . . ."

They walked back to the car together, his hand clasping her wrist.

XII

THE OPENING OF THE STODDARD TEMPLE WAS ANNOUNCED FOR THE afternoon of November first.

The press agent had done a good job. People talked about the event, about Howard Roark, about the architectural masterpiece which the city was to expect.

On the morning of October 31 Hopton Stoddard returned from his journey around the world. Ellsworth Toohey met him at the pier.

On the morning of November 1 Hopton Stoddard issued a brief statement announcing that there would be no opening. No explanation was given.

On the morning of November 2 the New York *Banner* came out with the column "One Small Voice" by Ellsworth M. Toohey subtitled "Sacrilege." It read as follows:

> "The time has come, the walrus said,
> To talk of many things:
> Of ships—and shoes—and Howard Roark—
> And cabbages—and kings—
> And why the sea is boiling hot—
> And whether Roark has wings.

"It is not our function—paraphrasing a philosopher whom we do not like—to be a fly swatter, but when a fly acquires delusions of grandeur, the best of us must stoop to do a little job of extermination.

"There has been a great deal of talk lately about somebody named Howard Roark. Since freedom of speech is our sacred heritage and includes the freedom to waste one's time, there would have been no harm in such talk—beyond the fact that one could find so many endeavors more profitable than discussions of a man who seems to have nothing to his credit except a building that was begun and could not be completed. There would have been no harm, if the ludicrous had not become the tragic—and the fraudulent.

"Howard Roark—as most of you have not heard and are not likely to hear again—is an architect. A year ago he was entrusted with an assignment of extraordinary responsibility. He was commissioned to erect a great monument in the absence of the owner who believed in him and gave him complete freedom of action. If the terminology of our criminal law could be applied to the realm of art, we would have to say that what Mr. Roark delivered constitutes the equivalent of spiritual embezzlement.

348

"Mr. Hopton Stoddard, the noted philanthropist, had intended to present the City of New York with a Temple of Religion, a non-sectarian cathedral symbolizing the spirit of human faith. What Mr. Roark has built for him might be a warehouse—though it does not seem practical. It might be a brothel—which is more likely, if we consider some of its sculptural ornamentation. It is certainly not a temple.

"It seems as if a deliberate malice had reversed in this building every conception proper to a religious structure. Instead of being austerely enclosed, this alleged temple is wide open, like a western saloon. Instead of a mood of deferential sorrow, befitting a place where one contemplates eternity and realizes the insignificance of man, this building has a quality of loose, orgiastic elation. Instead of the soaring lines reaching for heaven, demanded by the very nature of a temple, as a symbol of man's quest for something higher than his little ego, this building is flauntingly horizontal, its belly in the mud, thus declaring its allegiance to the carnal, glorifying the gross pleasures of the flesh above those of the spirit. The statue of a nude female in a place where men come to be uplifted speaks for itself and requires no further comment.

"A person entering a temple seeks release from himself. He wishes to humble his pride, to confess his unworthiness, to beg forgiveness. He finds fulfillment in a sense of abject humility. Man's proper posture in a house of God is on his knees. Nobody in his right mind would kneel within Mr. Roark's temple. The place forbids it. The emotions it suggests are of a different nature: arrogance, audacity, defiance, self-exaltation. It is not a house of God, but the cell of a megalomaniac. It is not a temple, but its perfect antithesis, an insolent mockery of all religion. We would call it pagan but for the fact that the pagans were notoriously good architects.

"This column is not the supporter of any particular creed, but simple decency demands that we respect the religious convictions of our fellow men. We felt we must explain to the public the nature of this deliberate attack on religion. We cannot condone an outrageous sacrilege.

"If we seem to have forgotten our function as a critic of purely architectural values, we can say only that the occasion does not call for it. It is a mistake to glorify mediocrity by an effort at serious criticism. We seem to recall something or other that this Howard Roark has built before, and it had the same ineptitude, the same pedestrian quality of an overambitious amateur. All God's chillun may have wings, but, unfortunately, this is not true of all God's geniuses.

"And that, my friends, is that. We are glad today's chore is over. We really do not enjoy writing obituaries."

*   *   *   *   *

On November 3 Hopton Stoddard filed suit against Howard Roark for breach of contract and malpractice, asking damages; he asked a sum sufficient to have the temple altered by another architect.

It had been easy to persuade Hopton Stoddard. He had returned from his journey, crushed by the universal spectacle of religion, most particularly by the various forms in which the promise of hell confronted him all over the earth. He had been driven to the conclusion that his life qualified him for the worst possible hereafter under any system of faith. It had shaken what remained of his mind. The ship stewards, on his return trip, had felt certain that the old gentleman was senile.

On the afternoon of his return Ellsworth Toohey took him to see the temple. Toohey said nothing. Hopton Stoddard stared, and Toohey heard Stoddard's false teeth clicking spasmodically. The place did not resemble anything Stoddard had seen anywhere in the world; nor anything he had expected. He did not know what to think. When he turned a glance of desperate appeal upon Toohey, Stoddard's eyes looked like Jello. He waited. In that moment, Toohey could have convinced him of anything. Toohey spoke and said what he said later in his column.

"But you told me this Roark was good!" Stoddard moaned in panic.

"I had expected him to be good," Toohey answered coldly.

"But then—why?"

"I don't know," said Toohey—and his accusing glance gave Stoddard to understand that there was an ominous guilt behind it all, and that the guilt was Stoddard's.

Toohey said nothing in the limousine, on their way back to Stoddard's apartment, while Stoddard begged him to speak. He would not answer. The silence drove Stoddard to terror. In the apartment, Toohey led him to an armchair and stood before him, somber as a judge.

"Hopton, I know why it happened."

"Oh, why?"

"Can you think of any reason why I should have lied to you?"

"No, of course not, you're the greatest expert and the most honest man living, and I don't understand, I just simply don't understand at all!"

"I do. When I recommended Roark, I had every reason to expect—to the best of my honest judgment—that he would give you a masterpiece. But he didn't. Hopton, do you know what power can upset all the calculations of men?"

"W-what power?"

"God has chosen this way to reject your offering. He did not consider you worthy of presenting Him with a shrine. I guess you can fool me,

Hopton, and all men, but you can't fool God. He knows that your record is blacker than anything I suspected."

He went on speaking for a long time, calmly, severely, to a silent huddle of terror. At the end, he said:

"It seems obvious, Hopton, that you cannot buy forgiveness by starting at the top. Only the pure in heart can erect a shrine. You must go through many humbler steps of expiation before you reach that stage. You must atone to your fellow men before you can atone to God. This building was not meant to be a temple, but an institution of human charity. Such as a home for subnormal children."

Hopton Stoddard would not commit himself to that. "Afterward, Ellsworth, afterward," he moaned. "Give me time." He agreed to sue Roark, as Toohey suggested, for recovery of the costs of alterations, and later to decide what these alterations would be.

"Don't be shocked by anything I will say or write about this," Toohey told him in parting. "I shall be forced to state a few things which are not quite true. I must protect my own reputation from a disgrace which is your fault, not mine. Just remember that you have sworn never to reveal who advised you to hire Roark."

On the following day "Sacrilege" appeared in the *Banner* and set the fuse. The announcement of Stoddard's suit lighted it.

Nobody would have felt an urge to crusade about a building; but religion had been attacked; the press agent had prepared the ground too well, the spring of public attention was wound, a great many people could make use of it.

The clamor of indignation that rose against Howard Roark and his temple astonished everyone, except Ellsworth Toohey. Ministers damned the building in sermons. Women's clubs passed resolutions of protest. A Committee of Mothers made page eight of the newspapers, with a petition that shrieked something about the protection of their children. A famous actress wrote an article on the essential unity of all the arts, explained that the Stoddard Temple had no sense of structural diction, and spoke of the time when she had played Mary Magdalene in a great Biblical drama. A society woman wrote an article on the exotic shrines she had seen in her dangerous jungle travels, praised the touching faith of the savages and reproached modern man for cynicism; the Stoddard Temple, she said, was a symptom of softness and decadence; the illustration showed her in breeches, one slim foot on the neck of a dead lion. A college professor wrote a letter to the editor about his spiritual experiences and stated that he could not have experienced them in a place like the Stoddard Temple. Kiki Holcombe wrote a letter to the editor about her views on life and death.

The A.G.A. issued a dignified statement denouncing the Stoddard Temple as a spiritual and artistic fraud. Similar statements, with less dignity and more slang, were issued by the Councils of American Builders, Writers and Artists. Nobody had ever heard of them, but they were Councils and this gave weight to their voice. One man would say to another: "Do you know that the Council of American Builders has said this temple is a piece of architectural tripe?" in a tone suggesting intimacy with the best of the art world. The other wouldn't want to reply that he had not heard of such a group, but would answer: "I expected them to say it. Didn't you?"

Hopton Stoddard received so many letters of sympathy that he began to feel quite happy. He had never been popular before. Ellsworth, he thought, was right; his brother men were forgiving him; Ellsworth was always right.

The better newspapers dropped the story after a while. But the *Banner* kept it going. It had been a boon to the *Banner*. Gail Wynand was away, sailing his yacht through the Indian Ocean, and Alvah Scarret was stuck for a crusade. This suited him. Ellsworth Toohey needed to make no suggestions; Scarret rose to the occasion all by himself.

He wrote about the decline of civilization and deplored the loss of the simple faith. He sponsored an essay contest for high-school students on "Why I Go to Church." He ran a series of illustrated articles on "The Churches of Our Childhood." He ran photographs of religious sculpture through the ages—the Sphinx, gargoyles, totem poles—and gave great prominence to pictures of Dominique's statue, with proper captions of indignation, but omitting the model's name. He ran cartoons of Roark as a barbarian with bearskin and club. He wrote many clever things about the Tower of Babel that could not reach heaven and about Icarus who flopped on his wax wings.

Ellsworth Toohey sat back and watched. He made two minor suggestions: he found, in the *Banner's* morgue, the photograph of Roark at the opening of the Enright House, the photograph of a man's face in a moment of exaltation, and he had it printed in the *Banner,* over the caption: "Are you happy, Mr. Superman?" He made Stoddard open the Temple to the public while awaiting the trial of his suit. The Temple attracted crowds of people who left obscene drawings and inscriptions on the pedestal of Dominique's statue.

There were a few who came, and saw, and admired the building in silence. But they were the kind who do not take part in public issues. Austen Heller wrote a furious article in defense of Roark and of the Temple. But he was not an authority on architecture or religion, and the article was drowned in the storm.

Howard Roark did nothing.

He was asked for a statement, and he received a group of reporters in his office. He spoke without anger. He said: "I can't tell anyone anything about my building. If I prepared a hash of words to stuff into other people's brains, it would be an insult to them and to me. But I am glad you came here. I do have something to say. I want to ask every man who is interested in this to go and see the building, to look at it and then to use the words of his own mind, if he cares to speak."

The *Banner* printed the interview as follows: "Mr. Roark, who seems to be a publicity hound, received reporters with an air of swaggering insolence and stated that the public mind was hash. He did not choose to talk, but he seemed well aware of the advertising angles in the situation. All he cared about, he explained, was to have his building seen by as many people as possible."

Roark refused to hire an attorney to represent him at the coming trial. He said he would handle his own defense and refused to explain how he intended to handle it, in spite of Austen Heller's angry protests.

"Austen, there are some rules I'm perfectly willing to obey. I'm willing to wear the kind of clothes everybody wears, to eat the same food and use the same subways. But there are some things which I can't do their way—and this is one of them."

"What do you know about courtrooms and law? He's going to win."

"To win what?"

"His case."

"Is the case of any importance? There's nothing I can do to stop him from touching the building. He owns it. He can blast if off the face of the earth or make a glue factory out of it. He can do it whether I win that suit or lose it."

"But he'll take your money to do it with."

"Yes. He might take my money."

Steven Mallory made no comment on anything. But his face looked as it had looked on the night Roark met him for the first time.

"Steve, talk about if, if it will make it easier for you," Roark said to him one evening.

"There's nothing to talk about," Mallory answered indifferently. "I told you I didn't think they'd let you survive."

"Rubbish. You have no right to be afraid for me."

"I'm not afraid for you. What would be the use? It's something else."

Days later, sitting on the window sill in Roark's room, looking out at the street, Mallory said suddenly:

"Howard, do you remember what I told you about the beast I'm afraid of? I know nothing about Ellsworth Toohey. l had never seen him before I shot at him. I had only read what he writes. Howard, I shot at him because I think he knows everything about that beast."

Dominique came to Roark's room on the evening when Stoddard announced his lawsuit. She said nothing. She put her bag down on a table and stood removing her gloves, slowly, as if she wished to prolong the intimacy of performing a routine gesture here, in his room; she looked down at her fingers. Then she raised her head. Her face looked as if she knew his worst suffering and it was hers and she wished to bear it like this, coldly, asking no words of mitigation.

"You're wrong," he said. They could always speak like this to each other, continuing a conversation they had not begun. His voice was gentle. "I don't feel that."

"I don't want to know."

"I want you to know. What you're thinking is much worse than the truth. I don't believe it matters to me—that they're going to destroy it. Maybe it hurts so much that I don't even know I'm hurt. But I don't think so. If you want to carry it for my sake, don't carry more than I do. I'm not capable of suffering completely. I never have. It goes only down to a certain point and then it stops. As long as there is that untouched point, it's not really pain. You mustn't look like that."

"Where does it stop?"

"Where I can think of nothing and feel nothing except that I designed that temple. I built it. Nothing else can seem very important."

"You shouldn't have built it. You shouldn't have delivered it to the sort of thing they're doing."

"That doesn't matter. Not even that they'll destroy it. Only that it had existed."

She shook her head. "Do you see what I was saving you from when I took commissions away from you? . . . To give them no right to do this to you. . . . No right to live in a building of yours . . . No right to touch you . . . not in any way. . . ."

When Dominique walked into Toohey's office, he smiled, an eager smile of welcome, unexpectedly sincere. He forgot to control it while his eyebrows moved into a frown of disappointment; the frown and the smile remained ludicrously together for a moment. He was disappointed, because it was not her usual dramatic entrance; he saw no anger, no mockery; she entered like a bookkeeper on a business errand. She asked:

"What do you intend to accomplish by it?"

He tried to recapture the exhilaration of their usual feud. He said:

"Sit down, my dear. I'm delighted to see you. Quite frankly and helplessly delighted. It really took you too long. I expected you here much sooner. I've had so many compliments on that little article of mine, but, honestly, it was no fun at all, I wanted to hear what you'd say."

"What do you intend to accomplish by it?"

"Look, darling, I do hope you didn't mind what I said about that uplifting statue of yours. I thought you'd understand I just couldn't pass up that one."

"What is the purpose of that lawsuit?"

"Oh well, you want to make me talk. And I did so want to hear you. But half a pleasure is better than none. I want to talk. I've waited for you so impatiently. But I do wish you'd sit down, I'll be more comfortable. . . . No? Well, as you prefer, so long as you don't run away. The lawsuit? Well, isn't it obvious?"

"How is it going to stop him?" she asked in the tone one would use to recite a list of statistics. "It will prove nothing, whether he wins or loses. The whole thing is just a spree for great numbers of louts, filthy but pointless. I did not think you wasted your time on stink bombs. All of it will be forgotten before next Christmas."

"My God, but I must be a failure! I never thought of myself as such a poor teacher. That you should have learned so little in two years of close association with me! It's really discouraging. Since you are the most intelligent woman I know, the fault must be mine. Well, let's see, you did learn one thing: that I don't waste my time. Quite correct. I don't. Right, my dear, everything will be forgotten by next Christmas. And *that*, you see, will be the achievement. You can fight a live issue. You can't fight a dead one. Dead issues, like all dead things, don't just vanish, but leave some decomposing matter behind. A most unpleasant thing to carry on your name. Mr. Hopton Stoddard will be thoroughly forgotten. The Temple will be forgotten. The lawsuit will be forgotten. But here's what will remain: 'Howard Roark? Why, how could you trust a man like that? He's an enemy of religion. He's completely immoral. First thing you know, he'll gyp you on your construction costs.' 'Roark? He's no good—why, a client had to sue him because he made such a botch of a building.' 'Roark? Roark? Wait a moment, isn't that the guy who got into all the papers over some sort of mess? Now what was it? Some rotten kind of scandal, the owner of the building—I think the place was a disorderly house—anyway the owner had to sue him. You don't want to get involved with a notorious character like that. What for, when there are so many decent architects to choose from?' Fight that, my dear. Tell me a way to fight it. Particularly when you have no weapons except your genius, which is not a weapon but a great liability."

Her eyes were disappointing; they listened patiently, an unmoving glance that would not become anger. She stood before his desk, straight, controlled, like a sentry in a storm who knows that he has to take it and has to remain there even when he can take it no longer.

"I believe you want me to continue," said Toohey. "Now you see the peculiar effectiveness of a dead issue. You can't talk your way out of it, you can't explain, you can't defend yourself. Nobody wants to listen. It is difficult enough to acquire fame. It is impossible to change its nature once you've acquired it. No, you can never ruin an architect by proving that he's a bad architect. But you can ruin him because he's an atheist, or because somebody sued him, or because he slept with some woman, or because he pulls wings off bottleflies. You'll say it doesn't make sense? Of course it doesn't. That's why it works. Reason can be fought with reason. How are you going to fight the unreasonable? The trouble with you, my dear, and with most people, is that you don't have sufficient respect for the senseless. The senseless is the major factor in our lives. You have no chance if it is your enemy. But if you can make it become your ally—ah, my dear! . . . Look, Dominique, I will stop talking the moment you show a sign of being frightened."

"Go on," she said.

"I think you should now ask me a question. Or perhaps you don't like to be obvious and feel that I must guess the question myself? I think you're right. The question is, why did I choose Howard Roark? Because —to quote my own article—it is not my function to be a fly swatter. I quote this now with a somewhat different meaning, but we'll let that pass. Also, this has helped me to get something I wanted from Hopton Stoddard, but that's only a minor side-issue, an incidental, just pure gravy. Principally, however, the whole thing was an experiment. Just a test skirmish, shall we say? The results are most gratifying. If you were not involved as you are, you'd be the one person who'd appreciate the spectacle. Really, you know, I've done very little when you consider the extent of what followed. Don't you find it interesting to see a huge, complicated piece of machinery, such as our society, all levers and belts and interlocking gears, the kind that looks as if one would need an army to operate it—and you find that by pressing your little finger against one spot, the one vital spot, the center of all its gravity, you can make the thing crumble into a worthless heap of scrap iron? It can be done, my dear. But it takes a long time. It takes centuries. I have the advantage of many experts who came before me. I think I shall be the last and the successful one of the line, because—though not abler than they were— I see more clearly what we're after. However, that's abstraction. Speaking of concrete reality, don't you find anything amusing in my little experiment? I do. For instance, do you notice that all the wrong people are on the wrong sides? Mr. Alvah Scarret, the college professors, the newspaper editors, the respectable mothers and the Chambers of Commerce should have come flying to the defense of Howard Roark—if they value their own lives. But they didn't. They are upholding Hopton Stoddard. On the other hand I heard that some screwy bunch of cafeteria radicals called 'The New League of Proletarian Art' tried to enlist in support of Howard Roark—they said he was a victim of capitalism—when they should have known that Hopton Stoddard is their champion. Roark, by the way, had the good sense to decline. He understands. You do. I do. Not many others. Oh, well. Scrap iron has its uses."

She turned to leave the room.

"Dominique, you're not going?" He sounded hurt. "You won't say anything? Not anything at all?"

"No."

"Dominique, you're letting me down. And how I waited for you! I'm a very self-sufficient person, as a rule, but I do need an audience once in a while. You're the only person with whom I can be myself. I suppose it's because you have such contempt for me that nothing I say can make any difference. You see, I know that, but I don't care. Also, the methods I use on other people would never work on you. Strangely enough, only my honesty will. Hell, what's the use of accomplishing a skillful piece of work if nobody knows that you've accomplished it? Had you been your old self, you'd tell me, at this point, that that is the psychology of a murderer who's committed the perfect crime and then confesses because he can't bear the idea that nobody knows it's a perfect crime. And I'd answer that you're right. I want an audience. That's the trouble with victims—they don't even know they're victims, which is as it should be, but it does become monotonous and takes half the fun away. You're such a rare treat—a victim who can appreciate the artistry of its own execution. . . . For God's sake, Dominique, are you leaving when I'm practically begging you to remain?"

She put her hand on the doorknob. He shrugged and settled back in his chair.

"All right," he said. "Incidentally, don't try to buy Hopton Stoddard out. He's eating out of my hand just now. He won't sell." She had opened the door, but she stopped and pulled it shut again. "Oh, yes, of course I know that you've tried. It's no use. You're not that rich. You haven't enough to buy that temple and you couldn't raise enough. Also, Hopton won't accept any money from you to pay for the alterations. I know you've offered that, too. He wants it from Roark. By the way, I don't think Roark would like it if I let him know that you've tried."

He smiled in a manner that demanded a protest. Her face gave no answer. She turned to the door again.

"Just one more question, Dominique. Mr. Stoddard's attorney wants to know whether he can call you as a witness. An expert on architecture. You will testify for the plaintiff, of course?"

"Yes. I will testify for the plaintiff."

The case of Hopton Stoddard versus Howard Roark opened in February of 1931.

The courtroom was so full that mass reactions could be expressed only by a slow motion running across the spread of heads, a sluggish wave like the ripple under the tight-packed skin of a sea lion.

The crowd, brown and streaked with subdued color, looked like a fruitcake of all the arts, with the cream of the A.G.A. rich and heavy on top. There were distinguished men and well-dressed, tight-lipped women; each woman seemed to feel an exclusive proprietorship of the art practiced by her escort, a monopoly guarded by resentful glances at the others. Almost everybody knew almost everybody else. The room had the atmosphere of a convention, an opening night and a family picnic. There was a feeling of "our bunch," "our boys," "our show."

Steven Mallory, Austen Heller, Roger Enright, Kent Lansing and Mike sat together in one corner. They tried not to look around them. Mike was worried about Steven Mallory. He kept close to Mallory, insisted on sitting next to him and glanced at him whenever a particularly offensive bit of conversation reached them. Mallory noticed it at last, and said:

"Don't worry, Mike. I won't scream. I won't shoot anyone."

"Watch your stomach, kid," said Mike, "just watch your stomach. A man can't get sick just because he oughta."

"Mike, do you remember the night when we stayed so late that it was almost daylight, and Dominique's car was out of gas, and there were no busses, and we all decided to walk home, and there was sun on the rooftops by the time the first one of us got to his house?"

"That's right. You think about that, and I'll think about the granite quarry."

"What granite quarry?"

"It's something made me very sick once, but then it turned out it made no difference at all, in the long run."

Beyond the windows the sky was white and flat like frosted glass. The light seemed to come from the banks of snow on roofs and ledges, an unnatural light that made everything in the room look naked.

The judge sat hunched on his high bench as if he were roosting. He had a small face, wizened into virtue. He kept his hands upright in front of his chest, the finger tips pressed together. Hopton Stoddard was not present. He was represented by his attorney, a handsome gentleman, tall and grave as an ambassador.

Roark sat alone at the defense table. The crowd had stared at him and given up angrily, finding no satisfaction. He did not look crushed and he did not look defiant. He looked impersonal and calm. He was not like a public figure in a public place; he was like a man alone in his own room, listening to the radio. He took no notes; there were no papers on the table before him, only a large brown envelope. The crowd would have forgiven anything, except a man who could remain normal under the vibrations of its enormous collective sneer. Some of them had come prepared to pity him; all of them hated him after the first few minutes.

The plaintiff's attorney stated his case in a simple opening address: it was true, he admitted, that Hopton Stoddard had given Roark full freedom to design and build the Temple; the point was, however, that Mr. Stoddard had clearly specified and expected *a temple;* the building in question could not be considered a temple by any known standards; as the plaintiff proposed to prove with the help of the best authorities in the field.

Roark waived his privilege to make an opening statement to the jury.

Ellsworth Monkton Toohey was the first witness called by the plaintiff. He sat on the edge of the witness chair and leaned back, resting on the end of his spine: he lifted one leg and placed it horizontally across the other. He looked amused—but managed to suggest that his amusement was a well-bred protection against looking bored.

The attorney went through a long list of questions about Mr. Toohey's professional qualifications, including the number of copies sold of his book *Sermons in Stone.* Then he read aloud Toohey's column "Sacrilege" and asked him to state whether he had written it. Toohey replied that he had. There followed a list of questions in erudite terms on the architectural merits of the Temple. Toohey proved that it had none. There followed an historical review. Toohey, speaking easily and casually, gave a brief sketch of all known civilizations and of their outstanding religious monuments—from the Incas to the Phoenicians to the Easter Islanders—including, whenever possible, the dates when these monuments were begun and the dates when they were completed, the number of workers employed in the construction and the approximate cost in modern American dollars. The audience listened punch-drunk.

Toohey proved that the Stoddard Temple contradicted every brick, stone and precept of history. "I have endeavored to show," he said in conclusion, "that the two essentials of the conception of a temple are a sense of awe and a sense of man's humility. We have noted the gigantic proportions of religious edifices, the soaring lines, the horrible grotesques of monsterlike gods, or, later, gargoyles. All of it tends to impress upon man his essential insignificance, to crush him by sheer magnitude, to imbue him with that sacred terror which leads to the meekness of virtue. The Stoddard Temple is a brazen denial of our entire past, an insolent 'No' flung in the face of history. I may venture a guess as to the reason why this case has aroused such public interest. All of us have recognized instinctively that it involves a moral issue much beyond its legal aspects. This building is a monument to a profound hatred of humanity. It is one man's ego defying the most sacred impulses of all mankind, of every man on the street, of every man in this courtroom!"

This was not a witness in court, but Ellsworth Toohey addressing a meeting—and the reaction was inevitable: the audience burst into applause. The judge struck his gavel and made a threat to have the courtroom cleared. Order was restored, but not to the faces of the crowd: the faces remained lecherously self-righteous. It was pleasant to be singled out and brought into the case as an injured party. Three-fourths of them had never seen the Stoddard Temple.

"Thank you, Mr. Toohey," said the attorney, faintly suggesting a bow. Then he turned to Roark and said with delicate courtesy: "Your witness."

"No questions," said Roark.

Ellsworth Toohey raised one eyebrow and left the stand regretfully.

"Mr. Peter Keating!" called the attorney.

Peter Keating's face looked attractive and fresh, as if he had had a good night's sleep. He mounted the witness stand with a collegiate sort of gusto, swinging his shoulders and arms unnecessarily. He took the oath and answered the first questions gaily. His pose in the witness chair was strange: his torso slumped to one side with swaggering ease, an elbow on the chair's arm; but his feet were planted awkwardly straight, and his knees were pressed tight together. He never looked at Roark.

"Will you please name some of the outstanding buildings which you have designed, Mr. Keating?" the attorney asked.

Keating began a list of impressive names; the first few came fast, the rest slower and slower, as if he wished to be stopped; the last one died in the air, unfinished.

"Aren't you forgetting the most important one, Mr. Keating?" the attorney asked. "Didn't you design the Cosmo-Slotnick Building?"

"Yes," whispered Keating.

"Now, Mr. Keating, you attended the Stanton Institute of Technology at the same period as Mr. Roark?"

"Yes."

"What can you tell us about Mr. Roark's record there?"

"He was expelled."

"He was expelled because he was unable to live up to the Institute's high standard of requirements?"

"Yes. Yes, that was it."

The judge glanced at Roark. A lawyer would have objected to this testimony as irrelevant. Roark made no objection.

"At that time, did you think he showed any talent for the profession of architecture?"

"No."

"Will you please speak a little louder, Mr. Keating?"

"I didn't . . . think he had any talent."

Queer things were happening to Keating's verbal punctuation: some words came out crisply, as if he dropped an exclamation point after each; others ran together, as if he would not stop to let himself hear them. He did not look at the attorney. He kept his eyes on the audience. At times, he looked like a boy out on a lark, a boy who has just drawn a mustache on the face of a beautiful girl on a subway tooth-paste ad. Then he looked as if he were begging the crowd for support—as if he were on trial before them.

"At one time you employed Mr. Roark in your office?"

"Yes."

"And you found yourself forced to fire him?"

"Yes . . . we did."

"For incompetence?"

"Yes."

"What can you tell us about Mr. Roark's subsequent career?"

"Well, you know, 'career' is a relative term. In volume of achievement any draftsman in our office has done more than Mr. Roark. We don't call one or two buildings a career. We put up that many every month or so."

"Will you give us your professional opinion of his work?"

"Well, I think it's immature. Very startling, even quite interesting at times, but essentially—adolescent."

"Then Mr. Roark cannot be called a full-fledged architect?"

"Not in the sense in which we speak of Mr. Ralston Holcombe, Mr. Guy Francon, Mr. Gordon Prescott—no. But, of course, I want to be fair. I think Mr. Roark had definite potentialities, particularly in problems of pure engineering. He could have made something of himself. I've tried to talk to him about it—I've tried to help him—I honestly did. But it was like talking to one of his pet pieces of reinforced concrete. I knew that he'd come to something like this. I wasn't surprised when I heard that a client had had to sue him at last."

"What can you tell us about Mr. Roark's attitude toward clients?"

"Well, that's the point. That's the whole point. He didn't care what the clients thought or wished, what anyone in the world thought or wished. He didn't even understand how other architects could care. He wouldn't even give you that, not even understanding, not even enough to ... respect you a little just the same. I don't see what's so wrong with trying to please people. I don't see what's wrong with wanting to be friendly and liked and popular. Why is that a crime? Why should anyone sneer at you for that, sneer all the time, all the time, day and night, not giving you a moment's peace, like the Chinese water torture, you know where they drop water on your skull drop by drop?"

People in the audience began to realize that Peter Keating was drunk. The attorney frowned; the testimony had been rehearsed; but it was getting off the rails.

"Well, now, Mr. Keating, perhaps you'd better tell us about Mr. Roark's views on architecture."

"I'll tell you, if you want to know. He thinks you should take your shoes off and kneel, when you speak of architecture. That's what he thinks. Now why should you? Why? It's a business like any other, isn't it? What's so damn sacred about it? Why do we have to be all keyed up? We're only human. We want to make a living. Why can't things be simple and easy? Why do we have to be some sort of God-damn heroes?"

"Now, now, Mr. Keating, I think we're straying slightly from the subject. We're ..."

"No, we're not. I know what I'm talking about. You do, too. They all do. Every one of them here. I'm talking about the temple. Don't you see? Why pick a fiend to build a temple? Only a very human sort of man should be chosen to do that. A man who understands ... and forgives. A man who forgives ... That's what you go to church for—to be ... forgiven ..."

"Yes, Mr. Keating, but speaking of Mr. Roark ..."

"Well, what about Mr. Roark? He's no architect. He's no good. Why should I be afraid to say that he's no good? Why are you all afraid of him?"

"Mr. Keating, if you're not well and wish to be dismissed ..."

Keating looked at him, as if awakening. He tried to control himself. After a while he said, his voice flat, resigned:

"No. I'm all right. I'll tell you anything you want. What is it you want me to say?"

"Will you tell us—in professional terms—your opinion of the structure known as the Stoddard Temple?"

"Yes. Sure. The Stoddard Temple ... The Stoddard Temple has an improperly articulated plan, which leads to spatial confusion. There is no balance of masses. It lacks a sense of symmetry. Its proportions are inept." He spoke in a monotone. His neck was stiff; he was making an effort not to let it drop forward. "It's out of scale. It contradicts the elementary principles of composition. The total effect is that of . . ."

"Louder please, Mr. Keating."

"The total effect is that of crudeness and architectural illiteracy. It shows . . . it shows no sense of structure, no instinct for beauty, no creative imagination, no . . ." he closed his eyes, ". . . artistic integrity . . ."

"Thank you, Mr. Keating. That is all."

The attorney turned to Roark and said nervously:

"Your witness."

"No questions," said Roark.

This concluded the first day of the trial.

That evening Mallory, Heller, Mike, Enright and Lansing gathered in Roark's room. They had not consulted one another, but they all came, prompted by the same feeling. They did not talk about the trial, but there was no strain and no conscious avoidance of the subject. Roark sat on his drafting table and talked to them about the future of the plastics industry. Mallory laughed aloud suddenly, without apparent reason. "What's the matter, Steve?" Roark asked. "I just thought . . . Howard, we all came here to help you, to cheer you up. But it's *you* who're helping *us,* instead. You're supporting your supporters, Howard."

That evening, Peter Keating lay half-stretched across a table in a speakeasy, one arm extended along the table top, his face on his arm.

In the next two days a succession of witnesses testified for the plaintiff. Every examination began with questions that brought out the professional achievements of the witness. The attorney gave them leads like an expert press agent. Austen Heller remarked that architects must have fought for the privilege of being called to the witness stand, since it was the grandest spree of publicity in a usually silent profession.

None of the witnesses looked at Roark. He looked at them. He listened to the testimony. He said: "No questions," to each one.

Ralston Holcombe on the stand, with flowing tie and gold-headed cane, had the appearance of a Grand Duke or a beer-garden composer. His testimony was long and scholarly, but it came down to:

"It's all nonsense. It's all a lot of childish nonsense. I can't say that I feel much sympathy for Mr. Hopton Stoddard. He should have known better. It is a scientific fact that the architectural style of the Renaissance is the only one appropriate to our age. If our best people, like Mr. Stoddard, refuse to recognize this, what can you expect from all sorts of parvenus, would-be architects and the rabble in general? It has been proved that Renaissance is the only permissible style for all churches, temples and cathedrals. What about Sir Christopher Wren? Just laugh that off. And remember the greatest religious monument of all time—St. Peter's in Rome. Are you going to improve upon St. Peter's? And if Mr. Stoddard did not specifically insist on Renaissance, he got just exactly what he deserved. It serves him jolly well right."

Gordon L. Prescott wore a turtle-neck sweater under a plaid coat, tweed trousers and heavy golf shoes.

"The correlation of the transcendental to the purely spatial in the building under discussion is entirely screwy," he said. "If we take the horizontal as the one-dimensional, the vertical as the two-dimensional, the diagonal as the three-dimensional, and the interpenetration of spaces as the fourth-dimensional—architecture being a fourth-dimensional art—we can see quite simply that this building is homaloidal, or—in the language of the layman—flat. The flowing life which comes from the sense of order in chaos, or, if you prefer, from unity in diversity, as well as vice versa, which is the realization of the contradiction inherent in architecture, is here absolutely absent. I am really trying to express myself as clearly as I can, but it is impossible to present a dialectic state by covering it up with an old fig leaf of logic just for the sake of the mentally lazy layman."

John Erik Snyte testified modestly and unobtrusively that he had employed Roark in his office, that Roark had been an unreliable, disloyal and unscrupulous employee, and that Roark had started his career by stealing a client from him.

On the fourth day of the trial the plaintiff's attorney called his last witness.

"Miss Dominique Francon," he announced solemnly.

Mallory gasped, but no one heard it; Mike's hand clamped down on his wrist and made him keep still.

The attorney had reserved Dominique for his climax, partly because he expected a great deal from her, and partly because he was worried: she was the only unrehearsed witness; she had refused to be coached. She had never mentioned the Stoddard Temple in her column; but he had looked up her earlier writings on Roark; and Ellsworth Toohey had advised him to call her.

Dominique stood for a moment on the elevation of the witness stand, looking slowly over the crowd. Her beauty was startling but too impersonal, as if it did not belong to her; it seemed present in the room as a separate entity. People thought of a vision that had not quite appeared, of a victim on a scaffold, of a person standing at night at the rail of an ocean liner.

"What is your name?"

"Dominique Francon."

"And your occupation, Miss Francon?"

"Newspaper woman."

"You are the author of the brilliant column 'Your House' appearing in the New York *Banner?*"

"I am the author of 'Your House.' "

"Your father is Guy Francon, the eminent architect?"

"Yes. My father was asked to come here to testify. He refused. He said he did not care for a building such as the Stoddard Temple, but he did not think that we were behaving like gentlemen."

"Well, now, Miss Francon, shall we confine our answers to our questions? We are indeed fortunate to have you with us, since you are our only woman witness, and women have always had the purest sense of religious faith. Being, in addition, an outstanding authority on architecture, you are eminently qualified to give us what I shall call, with all deference, the feminine angle on this case. Will you tell us in your own words what you think of the Stoddard Temple?"

"I think that Mr. Stoddard has made a mistake. There would have been no doubt about the justice of his case if he had sued, not for alteration costs, but for demolition costs."

The attorney looked relieved. "Will you explain your reasons, Miss Francon?"

"You have heard them from every witness at this trial."

"Then I take it that you agree with the preceding testimony?"

"Completely. Even more completely than the persons who testified. They were very convincing witnesses."

"Will you . . . clarify that, Miss Francon? Just what do you mean?"

"What Mr. Toohey said: that this temple is a threat to all of us."

"Oh, I see."

"Mr. Toohey understood the issue so well. Shall I clarify it—in my own words?"

"By all means."

"Howard Roark built a temple to the human spirit. He saw man as strong, proud, clean, wise and fearless. He saw man as a heroic being. And he built a temple to that. A temple is a place where man is to experience exaltation. He thought that exaltation comes from the consciousness of being guiltless, of seeing the truth and achieving it, of living up to one's highest possibility, of knowing no shame and having no cause for shame, of being able to stand naked in full sunlight. He thought that exaltation means joy and that joy is man's birthright. He thought that a place built as a setting for man is a sacred place. That is what Howard Roark thought of man and of exaltation. But Ellsworth Toohey said that this temple was a monument to a profound hatred of humanity. Ellsworth Toohey said that the essence of exaltation was to be scared out of your wits, to fall down and to grovel. Ellsworth Toohey said that man's highest act was to realize his own worthlessness and to beg forgiveness. Ellsworth Toohey said it was depraved not to take for granted that man is something which needs to be forgiven. Ellsworth Toohey saw that this building was of man and of the earth—and Ellsworth Toohey said that this building had its belly in the mud. To glorify man, said Ellsworth Toohey, was to glorify the gross pleasures of the flesh, for the realm of the spirit is beyond the grasp of man. To enter that realm, said Ellsworth Toohey, man must come as a beggar, on his knees. Ellsworth Toohey is a lover of mankind."

"Miss Francon, we are not really discussing Mr. Toohey, so if you will confine yourself to . . ."

"I do not condemn Ellsworth Toohey. I condemn Howard Roark. A building, they say, must be part of its site. In what kind of world did Roark build his temple? For what kind of men? Look around you. Can you see a shrine becoming sacred by serving as a setting for Mr. Hopton Stoddard? For Mr. Ralston Holcombe? For Mr. Peter Keating? When you look at them all, do you hate Ellsworth Toohey—or do you damn Howard Roark for the unspeakable indignity which he did commit? Ellsworth Toohey is right, that temple *is* a sacrilege, though not in the sense he meant. I think Mr. Toohey knows that, however. When you see a man casting pearls without getting even a pork chop in return—it is not against the swine that you feel indignation. It is against the man who valued his pearls so little that he was willing to fling them into the muck and to let them become the occasion for a whole concert of grunting, transcribed by the court stenographer."

"Miss Francon, I hardly think that this line of testimony is relevant or admissible . . ."

"The witness must be allowed to testify," the judge declared unexpectedly. He had been bored and he liked to watch Dominique's figure. Besides, he knew that the audience was enjoying it, in the sheer excitement of scandal, even though their sympathies were with Hopton Stoddard.

"Your Honor, some misunderstanding seems to have occurred," said the attorney. "Miss Francon, for whom are you testifying? For Mr. Roark or Mr. Stoddard?"

"For Mr. Stoddard, of course. I am stating the reasons why Mr. Stoddard should win this case. I have sworn to tell the truth."

"Proceed," said the judge.

"All the witnesses have told the truth. But not the whole truth. I am merely filling in the omissions. They spoke of a threat and of hatred. They were right. The Stoddard Temple is a threat to many things. If it were allowed to exist, nobody would dare to look at himself in the mirror. And that is a cruel thing to do to men. Ask anything of men. Ask them to achieve wealth, fame, love, brutality, murder, self-sacrifice. But don't ask them to achieve self-respect. They will hate your soul. Well, they know best. They must have their reasons. They won't say, of course, that they hate you. They will say that you hate them. It's near enough, I suppose. They know the emotion involved. Such are men as they are. So what is the use of being a martyr to the impossible? What is the use of building for a world that does not exist?"

"Your Honor, I don't see what possible bearing this can have on . . ."

"I am proving your case for you. I am proving why you must go with Ellsworth Toohey, as you will anyway. The Stoddard Temple must be destroyed. Not to save men from it, but to save it from men. What's the difference, however? Mr. Stoddard wins. I am in full agreement with everything that's being done here, except for one point. I didn't think we should be allowed to get away with that point. Let us destroy, but don't let us pretend that we are committing an act of virtue. Let us say that we are moles and we object to mountain peaks. Or, perhaps, that we are lemmings, the animals who cannot help swimming out to self-destruction. I realize fully that at this moment I am as futile as Howard Roark. *This* is my Stoddard Temple—my first and my last." She inclined her head to the judge. "That is all, Your Honor."

"Your witness," the attorney snapped to Roark.

"No questions," said Roark.

Dominique left the stand.

The attorney bowed to the bench and said: "The plaintiff rests."

The judge turned to Roark and made a vague gesture, inviting him to proceed.

Roark got up and walked to the bench, the brown envelope in hand. He took out of the envelope ten photographs of the Stoddard Temple and laid them on the judge's desk. He said:

"The defense rests."

XIII

HOPTON STODDARD WON THE SUIT.

Ellsworth Toohey wrote in his column: "Mr. Roark pulled a Phryne in court and didn't get away with it. We never believed that story in the first place."

Roark was instructed to pay the costs of the Temple's alterations. He said that he would not appeal the case. Hopton Stoddard announced that the Temple would be remodeled into the Hopton Stoddard Home for Subnormal Children.

On the day after the end of the trial Alvah Scarret gasped when he glanced at the proofs of "Your House" delivered to his desk: the column contained most of Dominique's testimony in court. Her testimony had been quoted in the newspaper accounts of the case but only in harmless excerpts. Alvah Scarret hurried to Dominique's office.

"Darling, darling, darling," he said, "we can't print that."

She looked at him blankly and said nothing.

"Dominique, sweetheart, be reasonable. Quite apart from some of the language you use and some of your utterly unprintable ideas, you know very well the stand this paper has taken on the case. You know the campaign we've conducted. You've read my editorial this morning—'A Victory for Decency.' We can't have one writer running against our whole policy."

"You'll have to print it."

"But, sweetheart . . ."

"Or I'll have to quit."

"Oh, go on, go on, go on, don't be silly. Now don't get ridiculous. You know better than that. We can't get along without you. We can't . . ."

"You'll have to choose, Alvah."

Scarret knew that he would get hell from Gail Wynand if he printed the thing, and might get hell if he lost Dominique Francon whose column was popular. Wynand had not returned from his cruise. Scarret cabled him in Bali, explaining the situation.

Within a few hours Scarret received an answer. It was in Wynand's private code. Translated it read: FIRE THE BITCH. G. W.

Scarret stared at the cable, crushed. It was an order that allowed no alternative, even if Dominique surrendered. He hoped she would resign. He could not face the thought of having to fire her.

Through an office boy whom he had recommended for the job, Toohey obtained the decoded copy of Wynand's cable. He put it in his

368

pocket and went to Dominique's office. He had not seen her since the trial. He found her engaged in emptying the drawers of her desk.

"Hello," he said curtly. "What are you doing?"

"Waiting to hear from Alvah Scarret."

"Meaning?"

"Waiting to hear whether I'll have to resign."

"Feel like talking about the trial?"

"No."

"I do. I think I owe you the courtesy of admitting that you've done what no one has ever done before: you proved me wrong." He spoke coldly; his face looked flat; his eyes had no trace of kindness. "I had not expected you to do what you did on the stand. It was a scurvy trick. Though up to your usual standard. I simply miscalculated the direction of your malice. However, you did have the good sense to admit that your act was futile. Of course, you made your point. And mine. As a token of appreciation, I have a present for you."

He laid the cable on her desk.

She read it and stood holding it in her hand.

"You can't even resign, my dear," he said. "You can't make that sacrifice to your pearl-casting hero. Remembering that you attach such great importance to not being beaten except by your own hand, I thought you would enjoy this."

She folded the cable and slipped it into her purse.

"Thank you, Ellsworth."

"If you're going to fight me, my dear, it will take more than speeches."

"Haven't I always?"

"Yes. Yes, of course you have. Quite right. You're correcting me again. You have always fought me—and the only time you broke down and screamed for mercy was on that witness stand."

"That's right."

"That's where I miscalculated."

"Yes."

He bowed formally and left the room.

She made a package of the things she wanted to take home. Then she went to Scarret's office. She showed him the cable in her hand, but she did not give it to him.

"Okay, Alvah," she said.

"Dominique, I couldn't help it, I couldn't help it, it was— How the hell did you get that?"

"It's all right, Alvah. No, I won't give it back to you. I want to keep it." She put the cable back in her bag. "Mail me my check and anything else that has to be discussed."

"You . . . you *were* going to resign anyway, weren't you?"

"Yes, I was. But I like it better—being fired."

"Dominique, if you knew how awful I feel about it. I can't believe it. I simply can't believe it."

"So you people made a martyr out of me, after all. And that is the one thing I've tried all my life not to be. It's so graceless, being a martyr. It's honoring your adversaries too much. But I'll tell you this, Alvah— I'll tell it to you, because I couldn't find a less appropriate person to hear it: nothing that you do to me—or to him—will be worse than what I'll do myself. If you think I can't take the Stoddard Temple, wait till you see what I can take."

On an evening three days after the trial Ellsworth Toohey sat in his room, listening to the radio. He did not feel like working and he allowed himself a rest, relaxing luxuriously in an armchair, letting his fingers follow the rhythm of a complicated symphony. He heard a knock at his door. "Co-ome in," he drawled.

Catherine came in. She glanced at the radio by way of apology for her entrance.

"I knew you weren't working, Uncle Ellsworth. I want to speak to you."

She stood slumped, her body thin and curveless. She wore a skirt of expensive tweed, unpressed. She had smeared some make-up on her face; the skin showed lifeless under the patches of powder. At twenty-six she looked like a woman trying to hide the fact of being over thirty.

In the last few years, with her uncle's help, she had become an able social worker. She held a paid job in a settlement house, she had a small bank account of her own; she took her friends out to lunch, older women of her profession, and they talked about the problems of unwed mothers, self-expression for the children of the poor and the evils of industrial corporations.

In the last few years Toohey seemed to have forgotten her existence. But he knew that she was enormously aware of him in her silent, self-effacing way. He was seldom first to speak to her. But she came to him continuously for minor advice. She was like a small motor running on his energy, and she had to stop for refueling once in a while. She would not go to the theater without consulting him about the play. She would not attend a lecture course without asking his opinion. Once she developed a friendship with a girl who was intelligent, capable, gay and loved the poor, though a social worker. Toohey did not approve of the girl. Catherine dropped her.

When she needed advice, she asked for it briefly, in passing, anxious not to delay him: between the courses of a meal, at the elevator door on his way out, in the living room when some important broadcast stopped for station identification. She made it a point to show that she would presume to claim nothing but the waste scraps of his time.

So Toohey looked at her, surprised, when she entered his study. He said:

"Certainly, pet. I'm not busy. I'm never too busy for you, anyway. Turn the thing down a bit, will you?"

She softened the volume of the radio, and she slumped down in an armchair facing him. Her movements were awkward and contradictory, like an adolescent's: she had lost the habit of moving with assurance, and yet, at times, a gesture, a jerk of her head, would show a dry, over-bearing impatience which she was beginning to develop.

She looked at her uncle. Behind her glasses, her eyes were still and tense, but unrevealing. She said:

"What have you been doing, Uncle Ellsworth? I saw something in the papers about winning some big lawsuit that you were connected with. I was glad. I haven't read the papers for months. I've been so busy . . . No, that's not quite true. I've had the time, but when I came home I just couldn't make myself do anything, I just fell in bed and went to sleep. Uncle Ellsworth, do people sleep a lot because they're tired or because they want to escape from something?"

"Now, my dear, this doesn't sound like you at all. None of it."

She shook her head helplessly: "I know."

"What is the matter?"

She said, looking at the toes of her shoes, her lips moving with effort:

"I guess I'm no good, Uncle Ellsworth." She raised her eyes to him. "I'm so terribly unhappy."

He looked at her silently, his face earnest, his eyes gentle. She whispered:

"You understand?" He nodded. "You're not angry at me? You don't despise me?"

"My dear, how could I?"

"I didn't want to say it. Not even to myself. It's not just tonight, it's for a long time back. Just let me say everything, don't be shocked, I've got to tell it. It's like going to confession as I used to—oh, don't think I'm returning to that, I know religion is only a . . . a device of class exploitation, don't think I'd let you down after you explained it all so well. I don't miss going to church. But it's just—it's just that I've got to have somebody listen."

"Katie, darling, first of all, why are you so frightened? You mustn't be. Certainly not of speaking to me. Just relax, be yourself and tell me what happened."

She looked at him gratefully. "You're . . . so sensitive, Uncle Ellsworth. That's one thing I didn't want to say, but you guessed. I *am* frightened. Because—well, you see, you just said, be yourself. And what I'm afraid of most is of being myself. Because I'm vicious."

He laughed, not offensively, but warmly, the sound destroying her statement. But she did not smile.

"No, Uncle Ellsworth, it's true. I'll try to explain. You see, always, since I was a child, I wanted to do right. I used to think everybody did, but now I don't think so. Some people try their best, even if they do make mistakes, and others just don't care. I've always cared. I took it very seriously. Of course I knew that I'm not a brilliant person and that it's a very big subject, good and evil. But I felt that whatever is the good—as much as it would be possible for me to know—I would do my honest best to live up to it. Which is all anybody can try, isn't it? This probably sounds terribly childish to you."

"No, Katie, it doesn't. Go on, my dear."

"Well, to begin with, I knew that it was evil to be selfish. That much I was sure of. So I tried never to demand anything for myself. When Peter would disappear for months . . . No, I don't think you approve of that."

"Of what, my dear?"

"Of Peter and me. So I won't talk about that. It's not important anyway. Well, you can see why I was so happy when I came to live with you. You're as close to the ideal of unselfishness as anyone can be. I tried to follow you the best I could. That's how I chose the work I'm doing. You never actually said that I should choose it, but I came to feel that you thought so. Don't ask me how I came to feel it—it was nothing tangible, just little things you said. I felt very confident when I started. I knew that unhappiness comes from selfishness, and that one can find true happiness only in dedicating oneself to others. You said that. So many people have said that. Why, all the greatest men in history have been saying that for centuries."

"And?"

"Well, look at me."

His face remained motionless for a moment, then he smiled gaily and said:

"What's wrong with you, pet? Apart from the fact that your stockings don't match and that you could be more careful about your make-up?"

"Don't laugh, Uncle Ellsworth. Please don't laugh. I know you say we must be able to laugh at everything, particularly at ourselves. Only—I can't."

"I won't laugh, Katie. But what *is* the matter?"

"I'm unhappy. I'm unhappy in such a horrible, nasty, undignified way. In a way that seems . . . unclean. And dishonest. I go for days, afraid to think, to look at myself. And that's wrong. It's . . . becoming a hypocrite.

I always wanted to be honest with myself. But I'm not, I'm not, I'm not!"

"Hold on, my dear. Don't shout. The neighbors will hear you."

She brushed the back of her hand against her forehead. She shook her head. She whispered:

"I'm sorry. . . . I'll be all right. . . ."

"Just why are you unhappy, my dear?"

"I don't know. I can't understand it. For instance, it was I who arranged to have the classes in prenatal care down at the Clifford House —it was my idea—I raised the money—I found the teacher. The classes are doing very well. I tell myself that I should be happy about it. But I'm not. It doesn't seem to make any difference to me. I sit down and I tell myself: It was you who arranged to have Marie Gonzales' baby adopted into a nice family—now, be happy. But I'm not. I feel nothing. When I'm honest with myself, I know that the only emotion I've felt for years is being tired. Not physically tired. Just tired. It's as if . . . as if there were nobody there to feel any more."

She took off her glasses, as if the double barrier of her glasses and his prevented her from reaching him. She spoke, her voice lower, the words coming with greater effort:

"But that's not all. There's something much worse. It's doing something horrible to me. I'm beginning to hate people, Uncle Ellsworth. I'm beginning to be cruel and mean and petty in a way I've never been before. I expect people to be grateful to me. I . . . I *demand* gratitude. I find myself pleased when slum people bow and scrape and fawn over me. I find myself liking only those who are servile. Once . . . once I told a woman that she didn't appreciate what people like us did for trash like her. I cried for hours afterward, I was so ashamed. I begin to resent it when people argue with me. I feel that they have no right to minds of their own, that I know best, that I'm the final authority for them. There was a girl we were worried about, because she was running around with a very handsome boy who had a bad reputation. I tortured her for weeks about it, telling her how he'd get her in trouble and that she should drop him. Well, they got married and they're the happiest couple in the district. Do you think I'm glad? No, I'm furious and I'm barely civil to the girl when I meet her. Then there was a girl who needed a job desperately—it was really a ghastly situation in her home, and I promised that I'd get her one. Before I could find it, she got a good job all by herself. I wasn't pleased. I was sore as hell that somebody got out of a bad hole without *my* help. Yesterday, I was speaking to a boy who wanted to go to college and I was discouraging him, telling him to get a good job, instead. I was quite angry, too. And suddenly I realized that it was because I had wanted so much to go to college—you remember, you wouldn't let me—and so I wasn't going to let that kid do it either. . . . Uncle Ellsworth, don't you see? I'm becoming *selfish*. I'm becoming selfish in a way that's much more horrible than if I were some petty chiseler pinching pennies off these people's wages in a sweatshop!"

He asked quietly:

"Is that all?"

She closed her eyes, and then she said, looking down at her hands:

"Yes . . . except that I'm not the only one who's like that. A lot of them are, most of the women I work with. . . . I don't know how they got that way. . . . I don't know how it happened to me. . . . I used to feel happy when I helped somebody. I remember once—I had lunch with Peter that day—and on my way back I saw an old organ-grinder and I gave him five dollars I had in my bag. It was all the money I had; I'd saved it to buy a bottle of 'Christmas Night,' I wanted 'Christmas Night' very badly, but afterward every time I thought of that organ-grinder I was happy. . . . I saw Peter often in those days. . . . I'd come home after seeing him and I'd want to kiss every ragged kid on our block. . . . I think I hate the poor now. . . . I think all the other women do, too. . . . But the poor don't hate us, as they should. They only despise us. . . . You know, it's funny: it's the masters who despise the slaves, and the slaves who hate the masters. I don't know who is which. Maybe it doesn't fit here. Maybe it does. I don't know . . ."

She raised her head with a last spurt of rebellion.

"Don't you see what it is that I must understand? Why is it that I set out honestly to do what I thought was right and it's making me rotten? I think it's probably because I'm vicious by nature and incapable of leading a good life. That seems to be the only explanation. But . . . but sometimes I think it doesn't make sense that a human being is completely sincere in good will and yet the good is not for him to achieve. I can't be as rotten as that. But . . . but I've given up everything, I have no selfish desire left, I have nothing of my own—and I'm miserable. And so are the other women like me. And I don't know a single selfless person in the world who's happy—except you."

She dropped her head and she did not raise it again; she seemed indifferent even to the answer she was seeking.

"Katie," he said softly, reproachfully, "Katie darling."

She waited silently.

"Do you really want me to tell you the answer?" She nodded. "Because, you know, you've given the answer yourself, in the things you said." She lifted her eyes blankly. "What have you been talking about? What have you been complaining about? About the fact that *you* are unhappy. About Katie Halsey and nothing else. It was the most egotistical speech I've ever heard in my life."

She blinked attentively, like a schoolchild disturbed by a difficult lesson.

"Don't you see how selfish you have been? You chose a noble career, not for the good you could accomplish, but for the personal happiness you expected to find in it."

"But I really wanted to help people."

"Because you thought you'd be good and virtuous doing it."

"Why—yes. Because I thought it was right. Is it vicious to want to do right?"

"Yes, if it's your chief concern. Don't you see how egotistical it is? To hell with everybody so long as I'm virtuous."

"But if you have no . . . no self-respect, how can you be anything?"

"Why must you be anything?"

She spread her hands out, bewildered.

"If your first concern is for what you are or think or feel or have or haven't got—you're still a common egotist."

"But I can't jump out of my own body."

"No. But you can jump out of your narrow soul."

"You mean, I must *want* to be unhappy?"

"No. You must stop wanting *anything*. You must forget how important Miss Catherine Halsey is. Because, you see, she isn't. Men are important only in relation to other men, in their usefulness, in the service they render. Unless you understand that completely, you can expect nothing but one form of misery or another. Why make such a cosmic tragedy out of the fact that you've found yourself feeling cruel toward people? So what? It's just growing pains. One can't jump from a state of animal brutality into a state of spiritual living without certain transitions. And some of them may seem evil. A beautiful woman is usually a gawky adolescent first. All growth demands destruction. You can't make an omelet without breaking eggs. You must be willing to suffer, to be cruel, to be dishonest, to be unclean—anything, my dear, anything to kill the most stubborn of roots, the ego. And only when it is dead, when you care no longer, when you have lost your identity and forgotten the name of your soul—only then will you know the kind of happiness I spoke about, and the gates of spiritual grandeur will fall open before you."

"But, Uncle Ellsworth," she whispered, "when the gates fall open, who is it that's going to enter?"

He laughed aloud, crisply. It sounded like a laugh of appreciation. "My dear," he said, "I never thought you could surprise me."

Then his face became earnest again.

"It was a smart crack, Katie, but you know, I hope, that it was only a smart crack?"

"Yes," she said uncertainly, "I suppose so. Still . . ."

"We can't be too literal when we deal in abstractions. Of course it's you who'll enter. You won't have lost your identity—you will merely have acquired a broader one, an identity that will be part of everybody else and of the whole universe."

"How? In what way? Part of what?"

"Now you see how difficult it is to discuss these things when our entire language is the language of individualism, with all its terms and superstitions. 'Identity'—it's an illusion, you know. But you can't build a new house out of crumbling old bricks. You can't expect to understand me completely through the medium of present-day conceptions. We are poisoned by the superstition of the ego. We cannot know what will be right or wrong in a selfless society, nor what we'll feel, nor in what manner. We must destroy the ego first. That is why the mind is so unreliable. We must not think. We must *believe*. Believe, Katie, even if your mind objects. Don't think. Believe. Trust your heart, not your brain. Don't think. Feel. Believe."

She sat still, composed, but somehow she looked like something run over by a tank. She whispered obediently:

"Yes, Uncle Ellsworth . . . I . . . I didn't think of it that way. I mean, I always thought that I must think . . . But you're right, that is, if right is the word I mean, if there is a word . . . Yes, I will believe. . . . I'll try to understand. . . . No, not to understand. To feel. To believe, I mean. . . . Only I'm so weak. . . . I always feel so small after talking to you. . . . I suppose I was right in a way—I *am* worthless . . . but it doesn't matter . . . it doesn't matter. . . ."

When the doorbell rang on the following evening Toohey went to open the door himself.

He smiled when he admitted Peter Keating. After the trial he had expected Keating to come to him; he knew that Keating would need to come. But he had expected him sooner.

Keating walked in uncertainly. His hands seemed too heavy for his wrists. His eyes were puffed, and the skin of his face looked slack.

"Hello, Peter," said Toohey brightly. "Want to see me? Come right in. Just your luck. I have the whole evening free."

"No," said Keating. "I want to see Katie."

He was not looking at Toohey and he did not see the expression behind Toohey's glasses.

"Katie? But of course!" said Toohey gaily. "You know, you've never come here to call on Katie, so it didn't occur to me, but . . . Go right in, I believe she's home. This way—you don't know her room?—second door."

Keating shuffled heavily down the hall, knocked on Catherine's door and went in when she answered. Toohey stood looking after him, his face thoughtful.

Catherine jumped to her feet when she saw her guest. She stood stupidly, incredulously for a moment, then she dashed to her bed to snatch a girdle she had left lying there and stuff it hurriedly under the pillow. Then she jerked off her glasses, closed her whole fist over them, and slipped them into her pocket. She wondered which would be worse: to remain as she was or to sit down at her dressing table and make up her face in his presence.

She had not seen Keating for six months. In the last three years, they had met occasionally, at long intervals, they had had a few luncheons together, a few dinners, they had gone to the movies twice. They had always met in a public place. Since the beginning of his acquaintance with Toohey, Keating would not come to see her at her home. When they met, they talked as if nothing had changed. But they had not spoken of marriage for a long time.

"Hello, Katie," said Keating softly. "I didn't know you wore glasses now."

"It's just . . . it's only for reading. . . . I . . . Hello, Peter. . . . I guess I look terrible tonight. . . . I'm glad to see you, Peter. . . ."

He sat down heavily, his hat in his hand, his overcoat on. She stood smiling helplessly. Then she made a vague, circular motion with her hands and asked:

"Is it just for a little while or . . . or do you want to take your coat off?"

"No, it's not just for a little while." He got up, threw his coat and hat on the bed, then he smiled for the first time and asked: "Or are you busy and want to throw me out?"

She pressed the heels of her hands against her eye sockets, and dropped her hands again quickly; she had to meet him as she had always met him, she had to sound light and normal: "No, no, I'm not busy at all."

He sat down and stretched out his arm in silent invitation. She came to him promptly, she put her hand in his, and he pulled her down to the arm of his chair.

The lamplight fell on him, and she had recovered enough to notice the appearance of his face.

"Peter," she gasped, "what have you been doing to yourself? You look awful."

"Drinking."

"Not . . . like that!"

"Like that. But it's over now."

"What was it?"

"I wanted to see you, Katie. I wanted to see you."

"Darling . . . what have they done to you?"

"Nobody's done anything to me. I'm all right now. I'm all right. Because I came here . . . Katie, have you ever heard of Hopton Stoddard?"

"Stoddard? . . . I don't know. I've seen the name somewhere."

"Well, never mind, it doesn't matter. I was only thinking how strange it is. You see, Stoddard's an old bastard who just couldn't take his own rottenness any more, so to make up for it he built a big present to the city. But when I . . . when I couldn't take it any more, I felt that the only way I could make up for it was by doing the thing I really wanted to do most—by coming here."

"When you couldn't take—what, Peter?"

"I've done something very dirty, Katie. I'll tell you about it some day, but not now. . . . Look, will you say that you forgive me—without asking what it is? I'll think . . . I'll think that I've been forgiven by someone who can never forgive me. Someone who can't be hurt and so can't forgive—but that makes it worse for me."

She did not seem perplexed. She said earnestly:

"I forgive you, Peter."

He nodded his head slowly several times and said:

"Thank you."

Then she pressed her head to his and she whispered:

"You've gone through hell, haven't you?"

"Yes. But it's all right now."

He pulled her into his arms and kissed her. Then he did not think of the Stoddard Temple any longer, and she did not think of good and evil. They did not need to; they felt too clean.

"Katie, why haven't we married?"

"I don't know," she said. And added hastily, saying it only because her heart was pounding, because she could not remain silent and because she felt called upon not to take advantage of him: "I guess it's because we know we don't have to hurry."

"But we do. If we're not too late already."

"Peter, you . . . you're not proposing to me again?"

"Don't look so stunned, Katie. If you do, I'll know that you've doubted it all these years. And I couldn't stand to think that just now. That's what I came here to tell you tonight. We're going to get married. We're going to get married right away."

"Yes, Peter."

"We don't need announcements, dates, preparations, guests, any of it. We've let one of those things or another stop us every time. I honestly don't know just how it happened that we've let it all drift like that. . . . We won't say anything to anyone. We'll just slip out of town and get married. We'll announce and explain afterward, if anyone wants explanations. And that means your uncle, and my mother, and everybody."

"Yes, Peter."

"Quit your damn job tomorrow. I'll make arrangements at the office to take a month off. Guy will be sore as hell—I'll enjoy that. Get your things ready—you won't need much—don't bother about the make-up, by the way—did you say you looked terrible tonight?—you've never looked lovelier. I'll be here at nine o'clock in the morning, day after tomorrow. You must be ready to start then."

"Yes, Peter."

After he had gone, she lay on her bed, sobbing aloud, without restraint, without dignity, without a care in the world.

Ellsworth Toohey had left the door of his study open. He had seen Keating pass by the door without noticing it and go out. Then he heard the sound of Catherine's sobs. He walked to her room and entered without knocking. He asked:

"What's the matter, my dear? Has Peter done something to hurt you?"

She half lifted herself on the bed, she looked at him, throwing her hair back off her face, sobbing exultantly. She said without thinking the first thing she felt like saying. She said something which she did not understand, but he did: "I'm not afraid of you, Uncle Ellsworth!"

XIV

"WHO?" GASPED KEATING.

"Miss Dominique Francon," the maid repeated.

"You're drunk, you damn fool!"

"Mr. Keating! . . ."

He was on his feet, he shoved her out of the way, he flew into the living room, and saw Dominique Francon standing there, in his apartment.

"Hello, Peter."

"Dominique! . . . Dominique, how come?" In his anger, apprehension, curiosity and flattered pleasure, his first conscious thought was gratitude to God that his mother was not at home.

"I phoned your office. They said you had gone home."

"I'm so delighted, so pleasantly sur . . . Oh, hell, Dominique, what's the use? I always try to be correct with you and you always see through it so well that it's perfectly pointless. So I won't play the poised host. You know that I'm knocked silly and that your coming here isn't natural and anything I say will probably be wrong."

"Yes, that's better, Peter."

He noticed that he still held a key in his hand and he slipped it into his pocket; he had been packing a suitcase for his wedding trip of tomorrow. He glanced at the room and noted angrily how vulgar his Victorian furniture looked beside the elegance of Dominique's figure. She wore a gray suit, a black fur jacket with a collar raised to her cheeks, and a hat slanting down. She did not look as she had looked on the witness stand, nor as he remembered her at dinner parties. He thought suddenly of that moment, years ago, when he stood on the stair landing outside Guy Francon's office and wished never to see Dominique again. She was what she had been then: a stranger who frightened him by the crystal emptiness of her face.

"Well, sit down, Dominique. Take your coat off."

"No, I shan't stay long. Since we're not pretending anything today, shall I tell you what I came for—or do you want some polite conversation first?"

"No, I don't want polite conversation."

"All right. Will you marry me, Peter?"

He stood very still; then he sat down heavily—because he knew she meant it.

"If you want to marry me," she went on in the same precise, impersonal voice, "you must do it right now. My car is downstairs. We drive to Connecticut and we come back. It will take about three hours."

"Dominique . . ." He didn't want to move his lips beyond the effort of her name. He wanted to think that he was paralyzed. He knew that he was violently alive, that he was forcing the stupor into his muscles and into his mind, because he wished to escape the responsibility of consciousness.

"We're not pretending, Peter. Usually, people discuss their reasons and their feelings first, then make the practical arrangements. With us, this is the only way. If I offered it to you in any other form, I'd be cheating you. It must be like this. No questions, no conditions, no explanations. What we don't say answers itself. By not being said. There is nothing for you to ponder—only whether you want to do it or not."

"Dominique," he spoke with the concentration he used when he walked down a naked girder in an unfinished building, "I understand only this much: I understand that I must try to imitate you, not to discuss it, not to talk, just answer."

"Yes."

"Only—I can't—quite."

"This is one time, Peter, when there are no protections. Nothing to hide behind. Not even words."

"If you'd just say one thing . . ."

"No."

"If you'd give me time . . ."

"No. Either we go downstairs together now or we forget it."

"You mustn't resent it if I . . . You've never allowed me to hope that you could . . . that you . . . no, no, I won't say it . . . but what can you expect me to think? I'm here, alone, and . . ."

"And I'm the only one present to give you advice. My advice is to refuse. I'm honest with you, Peter. But I won't help you by withdrawing the offer. You would prefer not to have had the chance of marrying me. But you have the chance. Now. The choice will be yours."

Then he could not hold on to his dignity any longer; he let his head drop, he pressed his fist to his forehead.

"Dominique—*Why?*"

"You know the reasons. I told them to you once, long ago. If you haven't the courage to think of them, don't expect me to repeat them."

He sat still, his head down. Then he said:

"Dominique, two people like you and me getting married, it's almost a front-page event."

"Yes."

"Wouldn't it be better to do it properly, with an announcement and a real wedding ceremony?"

"I'm strong, Peter, but I'm not that strong. You can have your receptions and your publicity afterward."

"You don't want me to say anything now, except yes or no?"

"That's all."

He sat looking up at her for a long time. Her glance was on his eyes, but it had no more reality than the glance of a portrait. He felt alone in the room. She stood, patient, waiting, granting him nothing, not even the kindness of prompting him to hurry.

"All right, Dominique. Yes," he said at last.

She inclined her head gravely in acquiescence.

He stood up. "I'll get my coat," he said. "Do you want to take your car?"

"Yes."

"It's an open car, isn't it? Should I wear my fur coat?"

"No. Take a warm muffler, though. There's a little wind."

"No luggage? We're coming right back to the city?"

"We're coming right back."

He left the door to the hall open, and she saw him putting on his coat, throwing a muffler around his throat, with the gesture of flinging a cape over his shoulder. He stepped to the door of the living room, hat in hand, and invited her to go, with a silent movement of his head. In the hall outside he pressed the button of the elevator and he stepped back to let her enter first. He was precise, sure of himself, without joy, without emotion. He seemed more coldly masculine than he had ever been before.

He took her elbow firmly, protectively, to cross the street where she had left her car. He opened the car's door, let her slide behind the wheel and got in silently beside her. She leaned over across him and adjusted the glass wind screen on his side. She said: "If it's not right, fix it any way you want when we start moving, so it won't be too cold for you." He said: "Get to the Grand Concourse, fewer lights there." She put her handbag down on his lap while she took the wheel and started the car. There was suddenly no antagonism between them, but a quiet, hopeless feeling of comradeship, as if they were victims of the same impersonal disaster, who had to help each other.

She drove fast, as a matter of habit, an even speed without a sense of haste. They sat silently to the level drone of the motor, and they sat patiently, without shifting the positions of their bodies, when the car stopped for a light. They seemed caught in a single streak of motion, an imperative direction like the flight of a bullet that could not be stopped on its course. There was a first hint of twilight in the streets of the city. The pavements looked yellow. The shops were still open. A movie theater had lighted its sign, and the red bulbs whirled jerkily, sucking the last daylight out of the air, making the street look darker.

Peter Keating felt no need of speech. He did not seem to be Peter Keating any longer. He did not ask for warmth and he did not ask for pity. He asked nothing. She thought of that once, and she glanced at him, a glance of appreciation that was almost gentle. He met her eyes steadily; she saw understanding, but no comment. It was as if his glance said: "Of course," nothing else.

They were out of the city, with a cold brown road flying to meet them, when he said:

"The traffic cops are bad around here. Got your press card with you, just in case?"

"I'm not the press any longer."

"You're not what?"

"I'm not a newspaper woman any more."

"You quit your job?"

"No, I was fired."

"What are you talking about?"

"Where have you been the last few days? I thought everybody knew it."

"Sorry. I didn't follow things very well the last few days."

Miles later, she said: "Give me a cigarette. In my bag."

He opened her bag, and he saw her cigarette case, her compact, her lipstick, her comb, a folded handkerchief too white to touch, smelling faintly of her perfume. Somewhere within him he thought that this was almost like unbuttoning her blouse. But most of him was not conscious of the thought nor of the intimate proprietorship with which he opened the bag. He took a cigarette from her case, lighted it and put it from his lips to hers. "Thanks," she said. He lighted one for himself and closed the bag.

When they reached Greenwich, it was he who made the inquiries, told her where to drive, at what block to turn, and said, "Here it is," when they pulled up in front of the judge's house. He got out first and helped her out of the car. He pressed the button of the doorbell.

They were married in a living room that displayed armchairs of faded tapestry, blue and purple, and a lamp with a fringe of glass beads. The witnesses were the judge's wife and someone from next door named Chuck, who had been interrupted at some household task and smelled faintly of Clorox.

Then they came back to their car and Keating asked: "Want me to drive if you're tired?" She said: "No, I'll drive."

The road to the city cut through brown fields where every rise in the ground had a shade of tired red on the side facing west. There was a purple haze eating away the edges of the fields, and a motionless streak of fire in the sky. A few cars came toward them as brown shapes, still visible; others had their lights on, two disquieting spots of yellow.

Keating watched the road; it looked narrow, a small dash in the middle of the windshield, framed by earth and hills, all of it held within the rectangle of glass before him. But the road spread as the windshield flew forward. The road filled the glass, it ran over the edges, it tore apart to let them pass, streaming in two gray bands on either side of the car. He thought it was a race and he waited to see the windshield win, to see the car hurtle into that small dash before it had time to stretch.

"Where are we going to live now, at first?" he asked. "Your place or mine?"

"Yours, of course."

"I'd rather move to yours."

"No. I'm closing my place."

"You can't possibly like my apartment."

"Why not?"

"I don't know. It doesn't fit you."

"I'll like it."

They were silent for a while, then he asked: "How are we going to announce this now?"

"In any way you wish. I'll leave it up to you."

It was growing darker and she switched on the car's headlights. He watched the small blurs of traffic signs, low by the side of the road, springing suddenly into life as they approached, spelling out: "Left turn," "Crossing ahead," in dots of light that seemed conscious, malevolent, winking.

They drove silently, but there was no bond in their silence now; they were not walking together toward disaster; the disaster had come; their courage did not matter any longer. He felt disturbed and uncertain as he always felt in the presence of Dominique Francon.

He half turned to look at her. She kept her eyes on the road. Her profile in the cold wind was serene and remote and lovely in a way that was hard to bear. He looked at her gloved hands resting firmly, one on each side of the wheel. He looked down at her slender foot on the accelerator, then his eyes rose up the line of her leg. His glance remained on the narrow triangle of her tight gray skirt. He realized suddenly that he had a right to think what he was thinking.

For the first time this implication of marriage occurred to him fully and consciously. Then he knew that he had always wanted this woman, that it was the kind of feeling he would have for a whore, only lasting and hopeless and vicious. My wife, he thought for the first time, without a trace of respect in the word. He felt so violent a desire that had it been summer he would have ordered her to drive into the first side lane and he would have taken her there.

He slipped his arm along the back of the seat and encircled her shoulders, his fingers barely touching her. She did not move, resist or turn to look at him. He pulled his arm away, and he sat staring straight ahead.

"Mrs. Keating," he said flatly, not addressing her, just as a statement of fact.

"Mrs. Peter Keating," she said.

When they stopped in front of his apartment house, he got out and held the door for her, but she remained sitting behind the wheel.

"Good night, Peter," she said. "I'll see you tomorrow."

She added, before the expression of his face had turned into an obscene swearword: "I'll send my things over tomorrow and we'll discuss everything then. Everything will begin tomorrow, Peter."

"Where are you going?"

"I have things to settle."

"But what will I tell people tonight?"

"Anything you wish, if at all."

She swung the car into the traffic and drove away.

When she entered Roark's room, that evening, he smiled, not his usual faint smile of acknowledging the expected, but a smile that spoke of waiting and pain.

He had not seen her since the trial. She had left the courtroom after her testimony and he had heard nothing from her since. He had come to her house, but her maid had told him that Miss Francon could not see him.

She looked at him now and she smiled. It was, for the first time, like a gesture of complete acceptance, as if the sight of him solved everything, answered all questions, and her meaning was only to be a woman who looked at him.

They stood silently before each other for a moment, and she thought that the most beautiful words were those which were not needed.

When he moved, she said: "Don't say anything about the trial. Afterward."

When he took her in his arms, she turned her body to meet his straight on, to feel the width of his chest with the width of hers, the length of his legs with the length of hers, as if she were lying against him, and her feet felt no weight, and she was held upright by the pressure of his body.

They lay in bed together that night, and they did not know when they slept, the intervals of exhausted unconsciousness as intense an act of union as the convulsed meetings of their bodies.

In the morning, when they were dressed, she watched him move about the room. She saw the drained relaxation of his movements; she thought of what she had taken from him, and the heaviness of her wrists told her that her own strength was now in his nerves, as if they had exchanged their energy.

He was at the other end of the room, his back turned to her for a moment, when she said, "Roark," her voice quiet and low.

He turned to her, as if he had expected it and, perhaps, guessed the rest.

She stood in the middle of the floor, as she had stood on her first night in this room, solemnly composed to the performance of a rite.

"I love you, Roark."

She had said it for the first time.

She saw the reflection of her next words on his face before she had pronounced them.

"I was married yesterday. To Peter Keating."

It would have been easy, if she had seen a man distorting his mouth to bite off sound, closing his fists and twisting them in defense against himself. But it was not easy, because she did not see him doing this, yet knew that this was being done, without the relief of a physical gesture.

"Roark . . ." she whispered, gently, frightened.

He said: "I'm all right." Then he said: "Please wait a moment . . . All right. Go on."

"Roark, before I met you, I had always been afraid of seeing someone like you, because I knew that I'd also have to see what I saw on the witness stand and I'd have to do what I did in that courtroom. I hated doing it, because it was an insult to you to defend you—and it was an insult to myself that you had to be defended. . . . Roark, I can accept anything, except what seems to be the easiest for most people: the halfway, the almost, the just-about, the in-between. They may have their justifications. I don't know. I don't care to inquire. I know that it is the one thing not given me to understand. When I think of what you are, I can't accept any reality except a world of your kind. Or at least a world in which you have a fighting chance and a fight on your own terms. That does not exist. And I can't live a life torn between that which exists— and you. It would mean to struggle against things and men who don't deserve to be your opponents. Your fight, using their methods—and that's too horrible a desecration. It would mean doing for you what I did for Peter Keating: lie, flatter, evade, compromise, pander to every ineptitude—in order to beg of them a chance for you, beg them to let you live, to let you function, to beg them, Roark, not to laugh at them, but to tremble because they hold the power to hurt you. Am I too weak because I can't do this? I don't know which is the greater strength: to accept all this for you—or to love you so much that the rest is beyond acceptance. I don't know. I love you too much."

He looked at her, waiting. She knew that he had understood this long ago, but that it had to be said.

"You're not aware of them. I am. I can't help it. I love you. The contrast is too great. Roark, you won't win, they'll destroy you, but I won't be there to see it happen. I will have destroyed myself first. That's the only gesture of protest open to me. What else could I offer you? The things people sacrifice are so little. I'll give you my marriage to Peter Keating. I'll refuse to permit myself happiness in their world. I'll take suffering. That will be my answer to them, and my gift to you. I shall probably never see you again. I shall try not to. But I will live for you, through every minute and every shameful act I take, I will live for you in my own way, in the only way I can."

He made a movement to speak, and she said:

"Wait. Let me finish. You could ask, why not kill myself then. Because I love you. Because you exist. That alone is so much that it won't allow me to die. And since I must be alive in order to know that you are, I will live in the world as it is, in the manner of life it demands. Not halfway, but completely. Not pleading and running from it, but walking out to meet it, beating it to the pain and the ugliness, being first to choose the worst it can do to me. Not as the wife of some half-decent human being, but as the wife of Peter Keating. And only within my own mind, only where nothing can touch it, kept sacred by the protecting wall of my own degradation, there will be the thought of you and the knowledge of you, and I shall say 'Howard Roark' to myself once in a while, and I shall feel that I have deserved to say it."

She stood before him, her face raised; her lips were not drawn, but closed softly, yet the shape of her mouth was too definite on her face, a shape of pain and tenderness, and resignation.

In his face she saw suffering that was made old, as if it had been part of him for a long time, because it was accepted, and it looked not like a wound, but like a scar.

"Dominique, if I told you now to have that marriage annulled at once—to forget the world and my struggle—to feel no anger, no concern, no hope—just to exist for me, for my need of you—as my wife—as my property . . . ?"

He saw in her face what she had seen in his when she told him of her marriage; but he was not frightened and he watched it calmly. After a while, she answered and the words did not come from her lips, but as if her lips were forced to gather the sounds from the outside:

"I'd obey you."

"Now you see why I won't do it. I won't try to stop you. I love you, Dominique."

She closed her eyes, and he said:

"You'd rather not hear it now? But I want you to hear it. We never need to say anything to each other when we're together. This is—for the time when we won't be together. I love you, Dominique. As selfishly as the fact that I exist. As selfishly as my lungs breathe air. I breathe for my own necessity, for the fuel of my body, for my survival. I've given you, not my sacrifice or my pity, but my ego and my naked need. This is the only way you can wish to be loved. This is the only way I can want you to love me. If you married me now, I would become your whole existence. But I would not want you then. You would not want yourself—and so you would not love me long. To say 'I love you' one must know first how to say the 'I.' The kind of surrender I could have from you now would give me nothing but an empty hulk. If I demanded it, I'd destroy you. That's why I won't stop you. I'll let you go to your husband. I don't know how I'll live through tonight, but I will. I want you whole, as I am, as you'll remain in the battle you've chosen. A battle is never selfless."

She heard, in the measured tension of his words, that it was harder for him to speak them than for her to listen. So she listened.

"You must learn not to be afraid of the world. Not to be held by it as you are now. Never to be hurt by it as you were in that courtroom. I must let you learn it. I can't help you. You must find your own way. When you have, you'll come back to me. They won't destroy me, Dominique. And they won't destroy you. You'll win, because you've chosen the hardest way of fighting for your freedom from the world. I'll wait for you. I love you. I'm saying this now for all the years we'll have to wait. I love you, Dominique."

Then he kissed her and he let her go.

XV

A T NINE O'CLOCK THAT MORNING PETER KEATING WAS PACING
the floor of his room, his door locked. He forgot that it was
nine o'clock and that Catherine was waiting for him. He had made
himself forget her and everything she implied.

The door of his room was locked to protect him from his mother.
Last night, seeing his furious restlessness, she had forced him to tell her
the truth. He had snapped that he was married to Dominique Francon,
and he had added some sort of explanation about Dominique going out
of town to announce the marriage to some old relative. His mother had
been so busy with gasps of delight and questions, that he had been able
to answer nothing and to hide his panic; he was not certain that he had a
wife and that she would come back to him in the morning.

He had forbidden his mother to announce the news, but she had made
a few telephone calls last night, and she was making a few more this
morning, and now their telephone was ringing constantly, with eager
voices asking: "Is it true?" pouring out sounds of amazement and congratulations. Keating could see the news spreading through the city in
widening circles, by the names and social positions of the people who
called. He refused to answer the telephone. It seemed to him that every
corner of New York was flooded with celebration and that he alone,
hidden in the watertight caisson of his room, was cold and lost and
horrified.

It was almost noon when the doorbell rang, and he pressed his hands
to his ears, not to know who it was and what they wanted. Then he
heard his mother's voice, so shrill with joy that it sounded embarrass-
ingly silly: "Petey darling, don't you want to come out and kiss your
wife?" He flew out into the hall, and there was Dominique, removing her
soft mink coat, the fur throwing to his nostrils a wave of the street's cold
air touched by her perfume. She was smiling correctly, looking straight
at him, saying: "Good morning, Peter."

He stood drawn up, for one instant, and in that instant he relived all
the telephone calls and felt the triumph to which they entitled him. He
moved as a man in the arena of a crowded stadium, he smiled as if he
felt the ray of an arc light playing in the creases of his smile, and he
said: "Dominique my dear, this is like a dream come true!"

The dignity of their doomed understanding was gone and their marriage was what it had been intended to be.

389

She seemed glad of it. She said: "Sorry you didn't carry me over the threshold, Peter." He did not kiss her, but took her hand and kissed her arm above the wrist, in casual, intimate tenderness.

He saw his mother standing there, and he said with a dashing gesture of triumph: "Mother—Dominique Keating."

He saw his mother kissing her. Dominique returned the kiss gravely. Mrs. Keating was gulping: "My dear, I'm so happy, so happy, God bless you, I had no idea you were so beautiful!"

He did not know what to do next, but Dominique took charge, simply, leaving them no time for wonder. She walked into the living room and she said: "Let's have lunch first, and then you'll show me the place, Peter. My things will be here in an hour or so."

Mrs. Keating beamed: "Lunch is all ready for three, Miss Fran . . ." She stopped. "Oh, dear, what am I to call you, honey? Mrs. Keating or . . ."

"Dominique, of course," Dominique answered without smiling.

"Aren't we going to announce, to invite anyone, to . . . ?" Keating began, but Dominique said:

"Afterward, Peter. It will announce itself."

Later, when her luggage arrived, he saw her walking into his bedroom without hesitation. She instructed the maid how to hang up her clothes, she asked him to help her rearrange the contents of the closets.

Mrs. Keating looked puzzled. "But aren't you children going to go away at all? It's all so sudden and romantic, but—no honeymoon of any kind?"

"No," said Dominique, "I don't want to take Peter away from his work."

He said: "This is temporary of course, Dominique. We'll have to move to another apartment, a bigger one. I want you to choose it."

"Why, no," she said. "I don't think that's necessary. We'll remain here."

"I'll move out," Mrs. Keating offered generously, without thinking, prompted by an overwhelming fear of Dominique. "I'll take a little place for myself."

"No," said Dominique. "I'd rather you wouldn't. I want to change nothing. I want to fit myself into Peter's life just as it is."

"That's sweet of you!" Mrs. Keating smiled, while Keating thought numbly that it was not sweet of her at all.

Mrs. Keating knew that when she had recovered she would hate her daughter-in-law. She could have accepted snubbing. She could not forgive Dominique's grave politeness.

The telephone rang. Keating's chief designer at the office delivered his congratulations and said: "We just heard it, Peter, and Guy's pretty stunned. I really think you ought to call him up or come over here or something."

Keating hurried to the office, glad to escape from his house for a while. He entered the office like a perfect figure of a radiant young lover. He laughed and shook hands in the drafting room, through noisy congratulations, gay shouts of envy and a few smutty references. Then he hastened to Francon's office.

For an instant he felt oddly guilty when he entered and saw the smile on Francon's face, a smile like a blessing. He tugged affectionately at Francon's shoulders and he muttered: "I'm so happy, Guy, I'm so happy . . ."

"I've always expected it," said Francon quietly, "but now I feel right. Now it's right that it should be all yours, Peter, all of it, this room, everything, soon."

"What are you talking about?"

"Come, you always understand. I'm tired, Peter. You know, there comes a time when you get tired in a way that's final and then . . . No, you wouldn't know, you're too young. But hell, Peter, of what use am I around here? The funny part of it is that I don't care any more even about pretending to be of any use. . . . I like to be honest sometimes. It's a nice sort of feeling. . . . Well, anyway, it might be another year or two, but then I'm going to retire. Then it's all yours. It might amuse me to hang on around here just a little longer—you know, I actually love the place—it's so busy, it's done so well, people respect us—it was a good firm, Francon & Heyer, wasn't it?—What the hell am I saying? Francon & Keating. Then it will be just Keating. . . . Peter," he asked softly, "why don't you look happy?"

"Of course I'm happy, I'm very grateful and all that, but why in blazes should you think of retiring now?"

"I don't mean that. I mean—why don't you look happy when I say that it will be yours? I . . . I'd like you to be happy about that, Peter."

"For God's sake, Guy, you're being morbid, you're . . ."

"Peter, it's very important to me—that you should be happy at what I'm leaving you. That you should be proud of it. And you are, aren't you, Peter? You are?"

"Well, who wouldn't be?" He did not look at Francon. He could not stand the sound of pleading in Francon's voice.

"Yes, who wouldn't be? Of course. . . . And you are, Peter?"

"What do you want?" snapped Keating angrily.

"I want you to feel proud of me, Peter," said Francon humbly, simply, desperately. "I want to know that I've accomplished something. I want to feel that it had some meaning. At the last summing up, I want to be sure that it wasn't all—for nothing."

"You're not sure of that? You're not sure?" Keating's eyes were murderous, as if Francon were a sudden danger to him.

"What's the matter, Peter?" Francon asked gently, almost indifferently.

"God damn you, you have no right—not to be sure! At your age, with your name, with your prestige, with your . . ."

"I want to be sure, Peter. I've worked very hard."

"But you're not sure!" He was furious and frightened, and so he wanted to hurt, and he flung out the one thing that could hurt most, forgetting that it hurt him, not Francon, that Francon wouldn't know, had never known, wouldn't even guess: "Well, I know somebody who'll be sure, at the end of *his* life, who'll be so God-damn sure I'd like to cut his damn throat for it!"

"Who?" asked Francon quietly, without interest.

"Guy! Guy, what's the matter with us? What are we talking about?"

"I don't know," said Francon. He looked tired.

That evening Francon came to Keating's house for dinner. He was dressed jauntily, and he twinkled with his old gallantry as he kissed Mrs. Keating's hand. But he looked grave when he congratulated Dominique and he found little to say to her; there was a pleading look in his eyes when he glanced up at her face. Instead of the bright, cutting mockery he had expected from her, he saw a sudden understanding. She said nothing, but bent down and kissed him on the forehead and held her lips pressed gently to his head a second longer than formality required. He felt a warm flood of gratitude—and then he felt frightened. "Dominique," he whispered—the others could not hear him—"how terribly unhappy you must be. . . ." She laughed gaily, taking his arm: "Why, no, Father, how can you say that!" "Forgive me," he muttered, "I'm just stupid. . . . This is really wonderful. . . ."

Guests kept coming in all evening, uninvited and unannounced, anyone who had heard the news and felt privileged to drop in. Keating did not know whether he was glad to see them or not. It seemed all right, so long as the gay confusion lasted. Dominique behaved exquisitely. He did not catch a single hint of sarcasm in her manner.

It was late when the last guest departed and they were left alone among the filled ash trays and empty glasses. They sat at opposite ends of the living room, and Keating tried to postpone the moment of thinking what he had to think now.

"All right, Peter," said Dominique, rising, "let's get it over with."

When he lay in the darkness beside her, his desire satisfied and left hungrier than ever by the unmoving body that had not responded, not even in revulsion, when he felt defeated in the one act of mastery he had hoped to impose upon her, his first whispered words were: "God damn you!"

He heard no movement from her.

Then he remembered the discovery which the moments of passion had wiped off his mind.

"Who was he?" he asked.

"Howard Roark," she answered.

"All right," he snapped, "you don't have to tell me if you don't want to!"

He switched on the light. He saw her lying still, naked, her head thrown back. Her face looked peaceful, innocent, clean. She said to the ceiling, her voice gentle: "Peter, if I could do this . . . I can do anything now. . . ."

"If you think I'm going to bother you often, if that's your idea of . . ."

"As often or as seldom as you wish, Peter."

Next morning, entering the dining room for breakfast, Dominique found a florist's box, long and white, resting across her plate.

"What's that?" she asked the maid.

"It was brought this morning, madam, with instructions to be put on the breakfast table."

The box was addressed to Mrs. Peter Keating. Dominique opened it. It contained a few branches of white lilac, more extravagantly luxurious than orchids at this time of the year. There was a small card with a name written upon it in large letters that still held the quality of a hand's dashing movement, as if the letters were laughing on the pasteboard: "Ellsworth M. Toohey."

"How nice!" said Keating. "I wondered why we hadn't heard from him at all yesterday."

"Please put them in water, Mary," said Dominique, handing the box to the maid.

In the afternoon Dominique telephoned Toohey and invited him for dinner.

The dinner took place a few days later. Keating's mother had pleaded some previous engagement and escaped for the evening; she explained it to herself by believing that she merely needed time to get used to things. So there were only three places set on the dining-room table, candles in crystal holders, a centerpiece of blue flowers and glass bubbles.

When Toohey entered he bowed to his hosts in a manner proper to a court reception. Dominique looked like a society hostess who had always been a society hostess and could not possibly be imagined as anything else.

"Well, Ellsworth? Well?" Keating asked, with a gesture that included the hall, the air and Dominique.

"My dear Peter," said Toohey, "let's skip the obvious."

Dominique led the way into the living room. She wore a dinner dress—a white satin blouse tailored like a man's, and a long black skirt, straight and simple as the polished planes of her hair. The narrow band of the skirt about her waistline seemed to state that two hands could encircle her waist completely or snap her figure in half without much effort. The short sleeves left her arms bare, and she wore a plain gold bracelet, too large and heavy for her thin wrist. She had an appearance of elegance become perversion, an appearance of wise, dangerous maturity achieved by looking like a very young girl.

"Ellsworth, isn't it wonderful?" said Keating, watching Dominique as one watches a fat bank account.

"No less than I expected," said Toohey. "And no more."

At the dinner table Keating did most of the talking. He seemed possessed by a talking jag. He turned over in words with the sensuous abandon of a cat rolling in catnip.

"Actually, Ellsworth, it was Dominique who invited you. I didn't ask her to. You're our first formal guest. I think that's wonderful. My wife and my best friend. I've always had the silly idea that you two didn't like each other. God knows where I get those notions. But this is what makes me so damn happy—the three of us, together."

"Then you don't believe in mathematics, do you, Peter?" said Toohey. "Why the surprise? Certain figures in combination have to give certain results. Granting three entities such as Dominique, you and I—this had to be the inevitable sum."

"They say three's a crowd," laughed Keating. "But that's bosh. Two are better than one, and sometimes three are better than two, it all depends."

"The only thing wrong with that old cliché," said Toohey, "is the erroneous implication that 'a crowd' is a term of opprobrium. It is quite the opposite. As you are so merrily discovering. Three, I might add, is a mystic key number. As for instance, the Holy Trinity. Or the triangle, without which we would have no movie industry. There are so many variations upon the triangle, not necessarily unhappy. Like the three of us—with me serving as understudy for the hypotenuse, quite an appropriate substitution, since I'm replacing my antipode, don't you think so, Dominique?"

They were finishing dessert when Keating was called to the telephone. They could hear his impatient voice in the next room, snapping instructions to a draftsman who was working late on a rush job and needed help. Toohey turned, looked at Dominique and smiled. The smile said everything her manner had not allowed to be said earlier. There was no visible movement on her face, as she held his glance, but there was a change of expression, as if she were acknowledging his meaning instead of refusing to understand it. He would have preferred the closed look of refusal. The acceptance was infinitely more scornful.

"So you've come back to the fold, Dominique?"

"Yes, Ellsworth."

"No more pleas for mercy?"

"Does it appear as if they will be necessary?"

"No. I admire you, Dominique. . . . How do you like it? I should imagine Peter is not bad, though not as good as the man we're both thinking of, who's probably superlative, but you'll never have a chance to learn."

She did not look disgusted; she looked genuinely puzzled.

"What are you talking about, Ellsworth?"

"Oh, come, my dear, we're past pretending now, aren't we? You've been in love with Roark from that first moment you saw him in Kiki Holcombe's drawing room—or shall I be honest?—you wanted to sleep with him—but he wouldn't spit at you—hence all your subsequent behavior."

"Is that what you thought?" she asked quietly.

"Wasn't it obvious? The woman scorned. As obvious as the fact that Roark had to be the man you'd want. That you'd want him in the most primitive way. And that he'd never know you existed."

"I overestimated you, Ellsworth," she said. She had lost all interest in his presence, even the need of caution. She looked bored. He frowned, puzzled.

Keating came back. Toohey slapped his shoulder as he passed by on the way to his seat.

"Before I go, Peter, we must have a chat about the rebuilding of the Stoddard Temple. I want you to bitch that up, too."

"Ellsworth . . . !" he gasped.

Toohey laughed. "Don't be stuffy, Peter. Just a little professional vulgarity. Dominique won't mind. She's an ex-newspaper woman."

"What's the matter, Ellsworth?" Dominique asked. "Feeling pretty desperate? The weapons aren't up to your usual standard." She rose. "Shall we have coffee in the drawing room?"

Hopton Stoddard added a generous sum to the award he had won from Roark, and the Stoddard Temple was rebuilt for its new purpose by a group of architects chosen by Ellsworth Toohey: Peter Keating, Gordon L. Prescott, John Erik Snyte and somebody named Gus Webb, a boy of twenty-four who liked to utter obscenities when passing well-bred women on the street, and who had never handled an architectural commission of his own. Three of these men had social and professional standing; Gus Webb had none; Toohey included him for that reason. Of the four Gus Webb had the loudest voice and the greatest self-assurance. Gus Webb said he was afraid of nothing; he meant it. They were all members of the Council of American Builders.

The Council of American Builders had grown. After the Stoddard trial many earnest discussions were held informally in the club rooms of the A.G.A. The attitude of the A.G.A. toward Ellsworth Toohey had not been cordial, particularly since the establishment of his Council. But the trial brought a subtle change; many members pointed out that the article in "One Small Voice" had actually brought about the Stoddard lawsuit; and that a man who could force clients to sue was a man to be treated with caution. So it was suggested that Ellsworth Toohey should be invited to address the A.G.A. at one of its luncheons. Some members objected, Guy Francon among them. The most passionate objector was a young architect who made an eloquent speech, his voice trembling with the embarrassment of speaking in public for the first time; he said that he admired Ellsworth Toohey and had always agreed with Toohey's social ideals, but if a group of people felt that some person was acquiring power over them, that was the time to fight such person. The majority overruled him. Ellsworth Toohey was asked to speak at the luncheon, the attendance was enormous and Toohey made a witty, gracious speech. Many members of the A.G.A. joined the Council of American Builders, John Erik Snyte among the first.

The four architects in charge of the Stoddard reconstruction met in Keating's office, around a table on which they spread blueprints of the temple, photographs of Roark's original drawings, obtained from the contractor, and a clay model which Keating had ordered made. They talked about the depression and its disastrous effect on the building industry; they talked about women, and Gordon L. Prescott told a few jokes of a bathroom nature. Then Gus Webb raised his fist and smacked it plump upon the roof of the model which was not quite dry and spread into a flat mess. "Well, boys," he said, "let's go to work." "Gus, you son of a bitch," said Keating, "the thing cost money." "Balls!" said Gus, "we're not paying for it."

Each of them had a set of photographs of the original sketches with the signature "Howard Roark" visible in the corner. They spent many evenings and many weeks, drawing their own versions right on the originals, remaking and improving. They took longer than necessary. They made more changes than required. They seemed to find pleasure in doing it. Afterward, they put the four versions together and made a co-operative combination. None of them had ever enjoyed a job quite so much. They had long, friendly conferences. There were minor dissensions, such as Gus Webb saying: "Hell, Gordon, if the kitchen's going to be yours, then the johns've got to be mine," but these were only surface ripples. They felt a sense of unity and an anxious affection for one another, the kind of brotherhood that makes a man withstand the third degree rather than squeal on the gang.

The Stoddard Temple was not torn down, but its framework was carved into five floors, containing dormitories, schoolrooms, infirmary, kitchen, laundry. The entrance hall was paved with colored marble, the stairways had railings of hand-wrought aluminum, the shower stalls were glass-enclosed, the recreation rooms had gold-leafed Corinthian pilasters. The huge windows were left untouched, merely crossed by floorlines.

The four architects had decided to achieve an effect of harmony and therefore not to use any historical style in its pure form. Peter Keating designed the white marble semi-Doric portico that rose over the main entrance, and the Venetian balconies for which new doors were cut. John Erik Snyte designed the small semi-Gothic spire surmounted by a cross, and the bandcourses of stylized acanthus leaves which were cut into the limestone of the walls. Gordon L. Prescott designed the semi-Renaissance cornice, and the glass-enclosed terrace projecting from the third floor. Gus Webb designed a cubistic ornament to frame the original windows, and the modern neon sign on the roof, which read: "The Hopton Stoddard Home for Subnormal Children."

"Comes the revolution," said Gus Webb, looking at the completed structure, "and every kid in the country will have a home like that!"

The original shape of the building remained discernible. It was not like a corpse whose fragments had been mercifully scattered; it was like a corpse hacked to pieces and reassembled.

In September the tenants of the Home moved in. A small, expert staff was chosen by Toohey. It had been harder to find the children who qualified as inmates. Most of them had to be taken from other institutions. Sixty-five children, their ages ranging from three to fifteen, were picked out by zealous ladies who were full of kindness and so made a point of rejecting those who could be cured and selecting only the hopeless cases. There was a fifteen-year-old boy who had never learned to speak; a grinning child who could not be taught to read or write; a girl born without a nose, whose father was also her grandfather; a person called "Jackie" of whose age or sex nobody could be certain. They marched into their new home, their eyes staring vacantly, the stare of death before which no world existed.

On warm evenings children from the slums nearby would sneak into the park of the Stoddard Home and gaze wistfully at the playrooms, the gymnasium, the kitchen beyond the big windows. These children had filthy clothes and smudged faces, agile little bodies, impertinent grins, and eyes bright with a roaring, imperious, demanding intelligence. The ladies in charge of the Home chased them away with angry exclamations about "little gangsters."

Once a month a delegation from the sponsors came to visit the Home. It was a distinguished group whose names were in many exclusive registers, though no personal achievement had ever put them there. It was a group of mink coats and diamond clips; occasionally, there was a dollar cigar and a glossy derby from a British shop among them. Ellsworth Toohey was always present to show them through the Home. The inspection made the mink coats seem warmer and their wearers' rights to them incontestable, since it established superiority and altruistic virtue together, in a demonstration more potent than a visit to a morgue. On the way back from such an inspection Ellsworth Toohey received humbled compliments on the wonderful work he was doing, and had no trouble in obtaining checks for his other humanitarian activities, such as publications, lecture courses, radio forums and the Workshop of Social Study.

Catherine Halsey was put in charge of the children's occupational therapy, and she moved into the Home as a permanent resident. She took up her work with a fierce zeal. She spoke about it insistently to anyone who would listen. Her voice was dry and arbitrary. When she spoke, the movements of her mouth hid the two lines that had appeared recently, cut from her nostrils to her chin; people preferred her not to remove her glasses; her eyes were not good to see. She spoke belligerently about her work not being charity, but "human reclamation."

The most important time of her day was the hour assigned to the children's art activities, known as the "Creative Period." There was a special room for the purpose—a room with a view of the distant city skyline—where the children were given materials and encouraged to create freely, under the guidance of Catherine who stood watch over them like an angel presiding at a birth.

She was elated on the day when Jackie, the least promising one of the lot, achieved a completed work of imagination. Jackie picked up fistfuls of colored felt scraps and a pot of glue, and carried them to a corner of the room. There was, in the corner, a slanting ledge projecting from the wall—plastered over and painted green—left from Roark's modeling of the Temple interior that had once controlled the recession of the light at sunset. Catherine walked over to Jackie and saw, spread out on the ledge, the recognizable shape of a dog, brown, with blue spots and five legs. Jackie wore an expression of pride. "Now you see, you see?" Catherine said to her colleagues. "Isn't it wonderful and moving! There's no telling how far the child will go with proper encouragement. Think of what happens to their little souls if they are frustrated in their creative instincts! It's so important not to deny them a chance for self-expression. Did you see Jackie's face?"

* * * * *

Dominique's statue had been sold. No one knew who bought it. It had been bought by Ellsworth Toohey.

Roark's office had shrunk back to one room. After the completion of the Cord Building he found no work. The depression had wrecked the building trade; there was little work for anyone; it was said that the skyscraper was finished; architects were closing their offices.

A few commissions still dribbled out occasionally, and a group of architects hovered about them with the dignity of a bread line. There were men like Ralston Holcombe among them, men who had never begged, but had demanded references before they accepted a client. When Roark tried to get a commission, he was rejected in a manner implying that if he had no more sense than that, politeness would be a wasted effort. "Roark?" cautious businessmen said. "The tabloid hero? Money's too scarce nowadays to waste it on lawsuits afterwards."

He got a few jobs, remodeling rooming houses, an assignment that involved no more than erecting partitions and rearranging the plumbing. "Don't take it, Howard," Austen Heller said angrily. "The infernal gall of offering you that kind of work! After a skyscraper like the Cord Building. After the Enright House." "I'll take anything," said Roark.

The Stoddard award had taken more than the amount of his fee for the Cord Building. But he had saved enough to exist on for a while. He paid Mallory's rent and he paid for most of their frequent meals together.

Mallory had tried to object. "Shut up, Steve," Roark had said. "I'm not doing it for you. At a time like this I owe myself a few luxuries. So I'm simply buying the most valuable thing that can be bought—your time. I'm competing with a whole country—and that's quite a luxury, isn't it? They want you to do baby plaques and I don't, and I like having my way against theirs."

"What do you want me to work on, Howard?"

"I want you to work without asking anyone what he wants you to work on."

Austen Heller heard about it from Mallory, and spoke of it to Roark in private.

"If you're helping him, why don't you let me help you?"

"I'd let you if you could," said Roark. "But you can't. All he needs is his time. He can work without clients. I can't."

"It's amusing, Howard, to see you in the role of an altruist."

"You don't have to insult me. It's not altruism. But I'll tell you this: most people say they're concerned with the suffering of others. I'm not. And yet there's one thing I can't understand. Most of them would not pass by if they saw a man bleeding in the road, mangled by a hit-and-run driver. And most of them would not turn their heads to look at Steven Mallory. But don't they know that if suffering could be measured, there's more suffering in Steven Mallory when he can't do the work he wants to do, than in a whole field of victims mowed down by a tank? If one must relieve the pain of this world, isn't Mallory the place to begin? ... However, that's not why I'm doing it."

Roark had never seen the reconstructed Stoddard Temple. On an evening in November he went to see it. He did not know whether it was surrender to pain or victory over the fear of seeing it.

It was late and the garden of the Stoddard Home was deserted. The building was dark, a single light showed in a back window upstairs. Roark stood looking at the building for a long time.

The door under the Greek portico opened and a slight masculine figure came out. It hurried casually down the steps—and then stopped.

"Hello, Mr. Roark," said Ellsworth Toohey quietly.

Roark looked at him without curiosity. "Hello," said Roark.

"Please don't run away." The voice was not mocking, but earnest.

"I wasn't going to."

"I think I knew that you'd come here some day and I think I wanted to be here when you came. I've kept inventing excuses for myself to hang about this place." There was no gloating in the voice; it sounded drained and simple.

"Well?"

"You shouldn't mind speaking to me. You see, I understand your work. What I do about it is another matter."

"You are free to do what you wish about it."

"I understand your work better than any living person—with the possible exception of Dominique Francon. And, perhaps, better than she does. That's a great deal, isn't it, Mr. Roark? You haven't many people around you who can say that. It's a greater bond than if I were your devoted, but blind supporter."

"I knew you understood."

"Then you won't mind talking to me."

"About what?"

In the darkness it sounded almost as if Toohey had sighed. After a while he pointed to the building and asked:

"Do you understand this?"

Roark did not answer.

Toohey went on softly: "What does it look like to you? Like a senseless mess? Like a chance collection of driftwood? Like an imbecile chaos? But is it, Mr. Roark? Do you see no method? You who know the language of structure and the meaning of form. Do you see no purpose here?"

"I see none in discussing it."

"Mr. Roark, we're alone here. Why don't you tell me what you think of me? In any words you wish. No one will hear us."

"But I don't think of you."

Toohey's face had an expression of attentiveness, of listening quietly to something as simple as fate. He remained silent, and Roark asked:

"What did you want to say to me?"

Toohey looked at him, and then at the bare trees around them, at the river far below, at the great rise of the sky beyond the river.

"Nothing," said Toohey.

He walked away, his steps creaking on the gravel in the silence, sharp and even, like the cracks of an engine's pistons.

Roark stood alone in the empty driveway, looking at the building.

Part 3

GAIL WYNAND

I

GAIL WYNAND RAISED A GUN TO HIS TEMPLE.
He felt the pressure of a metal ring against his skin—and nothing else. He might have been holding a lead pipe or a piece of jewelry; it was just a small circle without significance. "I am going to die," he said aloud—and yawned.

He felt no relief, no despair, no fear. The moment of his end would not grant him even the dignity of seriousness. It was an anonymous moment; a few minutes ago, he had held a toothbrush in that hand; now he held a gun with the same casual indifference.

One does not die like this, he thought. One must feel a great joy or a healthy terror. One must salute one's own end. Let me feel a spasm of dread and I'll pull the trigger. He felt nothing.

He shrugged and lowered the gun. He stood tapping it against the palm of his left hand. People always speak of a black death or a red death, he thought; yours, Gail Wynand, will be a gray death. Why hasn't anyone ever said that *this* is the ultimate horror? Not screams, pleas or convulsions. Not the indifference of a clean emptiness, disinfected by the fire of some great disaster. But this—a mean, smutty little horror, impotent even to frighten. You can't do it like that, he told himself, smiling coldly; it would be in such bad taste.

He walked to the wall of his bedroom. His penthouse was built above the fifty-seventh floor of a great residential hotel which he owned, in the center of Manhattan; he could see the whole city below him. The bedroom was a glass cage on the roof of the penthouse, its walls and ceiling made of huge glass sheets. There were dust-blue suede curtains to be pulled across the walls and enclose the room when he wished; there was nothing to cover the ceiling. Lying in bed, he could study the stars over his head, or see flashes of lightning, or watch the rain smashed into furious, glittering sunburst in mid-air above him, against the unseen protection. He liked to extinguish the lights and pull all the curtains open when he lay in bed with a woman. "We are fornicating in the sight of six million people," he would tell her.

He was alone now. The curtains were open. He stood looking at the city. It was late and the great riot of lights below him was beginning to die down. He thought that he did not mind having to look at the city for many more years and he did not mind never seeing it again.

He leaned against the wall and felt the cold glass through the thin, dark silk of his pyjamas. A monogram was embroidered in white on his breast pocket: GW, reproduced from his handwriting, exactly as he signed his initials with a single imperial motion.

People said that Gail Wynand's greatest deception, among many, was his appearance. He looked like the decadent, overperfected end product of a long line of exquisite breeding—and everybody knew that he came from the gutter. He was tall, too slender for physical beauty, as if all his flesh and muscle had been bred away. It was not necessary for him to stand erect in order to convey an impression of hardness. Like a piece of expensive steel, he bent, slouched and made people conscious, not of his pose, but of the ferocious spring that could snap him straight at any moment. This hint was all he needed; he seldom stood quite straight; he lounged about. Under any clothes he wore, it gave him an air of consummate elegance.

His face did not belong to modern civilization, but to ancient Rome; the face of an eternal patrician. His hair, streaked with gray, was swept smoothly back from a high forehead. His skin was pulled tight over the sharp bones of his face; his mouth was long and thin; his eyes, under slanting eyebrows, were pale blue and photographed like two sardonic white ovals. An artist had asked him once to sit for a painting of Mephistopheles; Wynand had laughed, refusing, and the artist had watched sadly, because the laughter made the face perfect for his purpose.

He slouched casually against the glass pane of his bedroom, the weight of a gun on his palm. Today, he thought; what was today? Did anything happen that would help me now and give meaning to this moment?

Today had been like so many other days behind him that particular features were hard to recognize. He was fifty-one years old, and it was the middle of October in the year 1932; he was certain of this much; the rest took an effort of memory.

He had awakened and dressed at six o'clock this morning; he had never slept more than four hours on any night of his adult life. He descended to his dining room where breakfast was served to him. His penthouse, a small structure, stood on the edge of a vast roof landscaped as a garden. The rooms were a superlative artistic achievement; their simplicity and beauty would have aroused gasps of admiration had this house belonged to anyone else; but people were shocked into silence when they thought that this was the home of the publisher of the New York *Banner,* the most vulgar newspaper in the country.

After breakfast he went to his study. His desk was piled with every important newspaper, book and magazine received that morning from all over the country. He worked alone at his desk for three hours, reading and making brief notes with a large blue pencil across the printed pages. The notes looked like a spy's shorthand; nobody could decipher them except the dry, middle-aged secretary who entered the study when Wynand left it. He had not heard her voice in five years, but no communication between them was necessary. When he returned to his study in the evening, the secretary and the pile of papers were gone; on his desk he found neatly typed pages containing the things he had wished to be recorded from his morning's work.

At ten o'clock he arrived at the Banner Building, a plain, grimy structure in an undistinguished neighborhood of lower Manhattan. When he walked through the narrow halls of the building, the employees he met wished him a good morning. The greeting was correct and he answered courteously; but his passage had the effect of a death ray that stopped the motor of living organisms.

Among the many hard rules imposed upon the employees of all Wynand enterprises, the hardest was the one demanding that no man pause in his work if Mr. Wynand entered the room, or notice his entrance. Nobody could predict what department he would choose to visit or when. He could appear at any moment in any part of the building— and his presence was as unobtrusive as an electric shock. The employees tried to obey the rule as best they could; but they preferred three hours of overtime to ten minutes of working under his silent observation.

This morning, in his office, he went over the proofs of the *Banner's* Sunday editorials. He slashed blue lines across the spreads he wished eliminated. He did not sign his initials; everybody knew that only Gail Wynand could make quite that kind of blue slashes, lines that seemed to rip the authors of the copy out of existence.

He finished the proofs, then asked to be connected with the editor of the Wynand *Herald*, in Springville, Kansas. When he telephoned his provinces, Wynand's name was never announced to the victim. He expected his voice to be known to every key citizen of his empire.

"Good morning, Cummings," he said when the editor answered.

"My God!" gasped the editor. "It isn't . . ."

"It is," said Wynand. "Listen, Cummings. One more piece of crap like yesterday's yarn on the Last Rose of Summer and you can go back to the high school *Bugle*."

"Yes, Mr. Wynand."

Wynand hung up. He asked to be connected with an eminent Senator in Washington.

"Good morning, Senator," he said when the gentleman came on the wire within two minutes. "It is so kind of you to answer this call. I appreciate it. I do not wish to impose on your time. But I felt I owed you an expression of my deepest gratitude. I called to thank you for your work in passing the Hayes-Langston Bill."

"But . . . Mr. Wynand!" The Senator's voice seemed to squirm. "It's so nice of you, but . . . the Bill hasn't been passed."

"Oh, that's right. My mistake. It will be passed tomorrow."

A meeting of the board of directors of the Wynand Enterprises, Inc., had been scheduled for eleven-thirty that morning. The Wynand Enterprises consisted of twenty-two newspapers, seven magazines, three news services and two newsreels. Wynand owned seventy-five percent of the stock. The directors were not certain of their functions or purpose. Wynand had ordered meetings of the board always to start on time, whether he was present or not. Today he entered the board room at twelve twenty-five. A distinguished old gentleman was making a speech. The directors were not allowed to stop or notice Wynand's presence. He walked to the empty chair at the head of the long mahogany table and sat down. No one turned to him; it was as if the chair had just been occupied by a ghost whose existence they dared not admit. He listened silently for fifteen minutes. He got up in the middle of a sentence and left the room as he had entered.

On a large table in his office he spread out maps of Stoneridge, his new real-estate venture, and spent half an hour discussing it with two of his agents. He had purchased a vast tract of land on Long Island, which was to be converted into the Stoneridge Development, a new community of small home owners, every curbstone, street and house to be built by Gail Wynand. The few people who knew of his real-estate activities had told him that he was crazy. It was a year when no one thought of building. But Gail Wynand had made his fortune on decisions which people called crazy.

The architect to design Stoneridge had not been chosen. News of the project had seeped into the starved profession. For weeks Wynand had refused to read letters or answer calls from the best architects of the country and their friends. He refused once more when, at the end of his conference, his secretary informed him that Mr. Ralston Holcombe most urgently requested two minutes of his time on the telephone.

When the agents were gone, Wynand pressed a button on his desk, summoning Alvah Scarret. Scarret entered the office, smiling happily. He always answered that buzzer with the flattered eagerness of an office boy.

"Alvah, what in hell is the Gallant Gallstone?"

Scarret laughed. "Oh, that? It's the title of a novel. By Lois Cook."

"What kind of a novel?"

"Oh, just a lot of drivel. It's supposed to be a sort of prose poem. It's all about a gallstone that thinks that it's an independent entity, a sort of a rugged individualist of the gall bladder, if you see what I mean, and then the man takes a big dose of castor oil—there's a graphic description of the consequences—I'm not sure it's correct medically, but anyway that's the end of the gallant gallstone. It's all supposed to prove that there's no such thing as free will."

"How many copies has it sold?"

"I don't know. Not very many, I think. Just among the intelligentsia. But I hear it's picked up some, lately, and . . ."

"Precisely. What's going on around here, Alvah?"

"What? Oh, you mean you noticed the few mentions which . . ."

"I mean I've noticed it all over the *Banner* in the last few weeks. Very nicely done, too, if it took me that long to discover that it wasn't accidental."

"What do you mean?"

"What do you think I mean? Why should that particular title appear continuously, in the most inappropriate places? One day it's in a police story about the execution of some murderer who 'died bravely like the Gallant Gallstone.' Two days later it's on page sixteen, in a state yarn from Albany. 'Senator Hazleton thinks he's an independent entity, but it might turn out that he's only a Gallant Gallstone.' Then it's in the obituaries. Yesterday it was on the women's page. Today, it's in the comics. Snooxy calls his rich landlord a Gallant Gallstone."

Scarret chortled peacefully. "Yes, isn't it silly?"

"I thought it was silly. At first. Now I don't."

"But what the hell, Gail! It's not as if it were a major issue and our by-liners plugged it. It's just the small fry, the forty-dollar-a-week ones."

"That's the point. One of them. The other is that the book's not a famous best-seller. If it were, I could understand the title popping into their heads automatically. But it isn't. So someone's doing the popping. Why?"

"Oh, come, Gail! Why would anyone want to bother? And what do we care? If it were a political issue . . . But hell, who can get any gravy out of plugging for free will or against free will?"

"Did anyone consult you about this plugging?"

"No. I tell you, nobody's behind it. It's just spontaneous. Just a lot of people who thought it was a funny gag."

"Who was the first one that you heard it from?"

"I don't know. . . . Let me see. . . . It was . . . yes, I think it was Ellsworth Toohey."

"Have it stopped. Be sure to tell Mr. Toohey."

"Okay, if you say so. But it's really nothing. Just a lot of people amusing themselves."

"I don't like to have anyone amusing himself on my paper."

"Yes, Gail."

At two o'clock Wynand arrived, as guest of honor, at a luncheon given by a National Convention of Women's Clubs. He sat at the right of the chairwoman, in an echoing banquet hall filled with the odors of corsages—gardenias and sweet peas—and of fried chicken. After luncheon Wynand spoke. The Convention advocated careers for married women; the Wynand papers had fought against the employment of married women for many years. Wynand spoke for twenty minutes and said nothing at all; but he conveyed the impression that he supported every sentiment expressed at the meeting. Nobody had ever been able to explain the effect of Gail Wynand on an audience, particularly an audience of women. He did nothing spectacular; his voice was low, metallic, inclined to sound monotonous; he was too correct, in a manner that was almost deliberate satire on correctness. Yet he conquered all listeners. People said it was his subtle, enormous virility; it made the courteous voice speaking about school, home and family sound as if he were making love to every old hag present.

Returning to his office, Wynand stopped in the city room. Standing at a tall desk, a big blue pencil in his hand, he wrote on a huge sheet of plain print stock, in letters an inch high, a brilliant, ruthless editorial denouncing all advocates of careers for women. The GW at the end stood like a streak of blue flame. He did not read the piece over—he never needed to—but threw it on the desk of the first editor in sight and walked out of the room.

Late in the afternoon, when Wynand was ready to leave his office, his secretary announced that Ellsworth Toohey requested the privilege of seeing him. "Let him in," said Wynand.

Toohey entered, a cautious half-smile on his face, a smile mocking himself and his boss, but with a delicate sense of balance, sixty percent of the mockery directed at himself. He knew that Wynand did not want to see him, and being received was not in his favor.

Wynand sat behind his desk, his face courteously blank. Two diagonal ridges stood out faintly on his forehead, parallel with his slanting eyebrows. It was a disconcerting peculiarity which his face assumed at times; it gave the effect of a double exposure, an ominous emphasis.

"Sit down, Mr. Toohey. Of what service can I be to you?"

"Oh, I'm much more presumptuous than that, Mr. Wynand," said Toohey gaily. "I didn't come to ask for your services, but to offer you mine."

"In what matter?"

"Stoneridge."

The diagonal lines stood out sharper on Wynand's forehead.

"Of what use can a newspaper columnist be to Stoneridge?"

"A newspaper columnist—none, Mr. Wynand. But an architectural expert . . ." Toohey let his voice trail into a mocking question mark.

If Toohey's eyes had not been fixed insolently on Wynand's, he would have been ordered out of the office at once. But the glance told Wynand that Toohey knew to what extent he had been plagued by people recommending architects and how hard he had tried to avoid them; and that Toohey had outwitted him by obtaining this interview for a purpose Wynand had not expected. The impertinence of it amused Wynand, as Toohey had known it would.

"All right, M. Toohey. Whom are you selling?"

"Peter Keating."

"Well?"

"I beg your pardon?"

"Well, sell him to me."

Toohey was stopped, then shrugged brightly and plunged in:

"You understand, of course, that I'm not connected with Mr. Keating in any way. I'm acting only as his friend—and yours." The voice sounded pleasantly informal, but it had lost some of its certainty. "Honestly, I know it does sound trite, but what else can I say? It just happens to be the truth." Wynand would not help him out. "I presumed to come here because I felt it was my duty to give you my opinion. No, not a moral duty. Call it an esthetic one. I know that you demand the best in anything you do. For a project of the size you have in mind there's not another architect living who can equal Peter Keating in efficiency, taste, originality, imagination. That, Mr. Wynand, is my sincere opinion."

"I quite believe you."

"You do?"

"Of course. But, Mr. Toohey, why should I consider your opinion?"

"Well, after all, I *am* your architectural expert!" He could not keep the edge of anger out of his voice.

"My dear Mr. Toohey, don't confuse me with my readers."

After a moment, Toohey leaned back and spread his hands out in laughing helplessness.

"Frankly, Mr. Wynand, I didn't think my word would carry much weight with you. So I didn't intend trying to sell you Peter Keating."

"No? What did you intend?"

"Only to ask that you give half an hour of your time to someone who can convince you of Peter Keating's ability much better than I can."

"Who is that?"

"Mrs. Peter Keating."

"Why should I wish to discuss this matter with Mrs. Peter Keating?"

"Because she is an exceedingly beautiful woman and an extremely difficult one."

Wynand threw his head back and laughed aloud.

"Good God, Toohey, am I as obvious as that?"

Toohey blinked, unprepared.

"Really, Mr. Toohey, I owe you an apology, if, by allowing my tastes to become so well known, I caused you to be so crude. But I had no idea that among your many other humanitarian activities you were also a pimp."

Toohey rose to his feet.

"Sorry to disappoint you, Mr. Toohey. I have no desire whatever to meet Mrs. Peter Keating."

"I didn't think you would have, Mr. Wynand. Not on my unsupported suggestion. I foresaw that several hours ago. In fact, as early as this morning. So I took the liberty of preparing for myself another chance to discuss this with you. I took the liberty of sending you a present. When you get home tonight, you will find my gift there. Then, if you feel that I was justified in expecting you to do so, you can telephone me and I shall come over at once so that you will be able to tell me whether you wish to meet Mrs. Peter Keating or not."

"Toohey, this is unbelievable, but I believe you're offering me a bribe."

"I am."

"You know, that's the sort of stunt you should be allowed to get away with completely—or lose your job for."

"I shall rest upon your opinion of my present tonight."

"All right, Mr. Toohey, I'll look at your present."

Toohey bowed and turned to go. He was at the door when Wynand added:

"You know, Toohey, one of these days you'll bore me."

"I shall endeavor not to do so until the right time," said Toohey, bowed again and went out.

When Wynand returned to his home, he had forgotten all about Ellsworth Toohey.

That evening, in his penthouse, Wynand had dinner with a woman who had a white face, soft brown hair and, behind her, three centuries of fathers and brothers who would have killed a man for a hint of the things which Gail Wynand had experienced with her.

The line of her arm, when she raised a crystal goblet of water to her lips, was as perfect as the lines of the silver candelabra produced by a matchless talent—and Wynand observed it with the same appreciation. The candlelight flickering on the planes of her face made a sight of such beauty that he wished she were not alive, so that he could look, say nothing and think what he pleased.

"In a month or two, Gail," she said, smiling lazily, "when it gets really cold and nasty, let's take the *I Do* and sail somewhere straight into the sun, as we did last winter."

I Do was the name of Wynand's yacht. He had never explained that name to anyone. Many women had questioned him about it. This woman had questioned him before. Now, as he remained silent, she asked it again:

"By the way, darling, what does it mean—the name of that wonderful mud-scow of yours?"

"It's a question I don't answer," he said. "One of them."

"Well, shall I get my wardrobe ready for the cruise?"

"Green is your best color. It looks well at sea. I love to watch what it does to your hair and your arms. I shall miss the sight of your naked arms against green silk. Because tonight is the last time."

Her fingers lay still on the stem of the glass. Nothing had given her a hint that tonight was to be the last time. But she knew that these words were all he needed to end it. All of Wynand's women had known that they were to expect an end like this and that it was not to be discussed. After a while, she asked, her voice low:

"What reason, Gail?"

"The obvious one."

He reached into his pocket and took out a diamond bracelet; it flashed a cold, brilliant fire in the candlelight; its heavy links hung limply in his fingers. It had no case, no wrapper. He tossed it across the table.

"A memorial, my dear," he said. "Much more valuable than that which it commemorates."

The bracelet hit the goblet and made it ring, a thin, sharp cry, as if the glass had screamed for the woman. The woman made no sound. He knew that it was horrible, because she was the kind to whom one did not offer such gifts at such moments, just as all those other women had been; and because she would not refuse, as all the others had not refused.

"Thank you, Gail," she said, clasping the bracelet about her wrist, not looking at him across the candles.

Later, when they had walked into the drawing room, she stopped and the glance between her long eyelashes moved toward the darkness where the stairway to his bedroom began.

"To let me earn the memorial, Gail?" she asked, her voice flat.

He shook his head.

"I had really intended that," he said. "But I'm tired."

When she had gone, he stood in the hall and thought that she suffered, that the suffering was real, but after a while none of it would be real to her, except the bracelet. He could no longer remember the time when such a thought had the power to give him bitterness. When he recalled that he, too, was concerned in the event of this evening, he felt nothing, except wonder why he had not done this long ago.

He went to his library. He sat reading for a few hours. Then he stopped. He stopped short, without reason, in the middle of an important sentence. He had no desire to read on. He had no desire ever to make another effort.

Nothing had happened to him—a happening is a positive reality, and no reality could ever make him helpless; this was some enormous negative—as if everything had been wiped out, leaving a senseless emptiness, faintly indecent because it seemed so ordinary, so unexciting, like murder wearing a homey smile.

Nothing was gone—except desire; no, more than that—the root, the desire to desire. He thought that a man who loses his eyes still retains the concept of sight; but he had heard of a ghastlier blindness—if the brain centers controlling vision are destroyed, one loses even the memory of visual perception.

He dropped the book and stood up. He had no wish to remain on that spot; he had no wish to move from it. He thought that he should go to sleep. It was much too early for him, but he could get up earlier tomorrow. He went to his bedroom, he took a shower, he put on his pyjamas.

Then he opened a drawer of his dresser and saw the gun he always kept there. It was the immediate recognition, the sudden stab of interest, that made him pick it up.

It was the lack of shock, when he thought he would kill himself, that convinced him he should. The thought seemed so simple, like an argument not worth contesting. Like a bromide.

Now he stood at the glass wall, stopped by that very simplicity. One could make a bromide of one's life, he thought; but not of one's death.

He walked to the bed and sat down, the gun hanging in his hand. A man about to die, he thought, is supposed to see his whole life in a last flash. I see nothing. But I could make myself see it. I could go over it again, by force. Let me find in it either the will to live on or the reason to end it now.

Gail Wynand, aged twelve, stood in the darkness under a broken piece of wall on the shore of the Hudson, one arm swung back, the fist closed, ready to strike, waiting.

The stones under his feet rose to the remnant of a corner; one side of it hid him from the street; there was nothing behind the other side but a sheer drop to the river. An unlighted, unpaved stretch of waterfront lay before him, sagging structures and empty spaces of sky, warehouses, a crooked cornice hanging somewhere over a window with a malignant light.

In a moment he would have to fight—and he knew it would be for his life. He stood still. His closed fist, held down and back, seemed to clutch invisible wires that stretched to every key spot of his lanky, fleshless body, under the ragged pants and shirt, to the long, swollen tendon of his bare arm, to the taut cords of his neck. The wires seemed to quiver; the body was motionless. He was like a new sort of lethal instrument; if a finger were to touch any part of him, it would release the trigger.

He knew that the leader of the boys' gang was looking for him and that the leader would not come alone. Two of the boys he expected fought with knives; one had a killing to his credit. He waited for them, his own pockets empty. He was the youngest member of the gang and the last to join. The leader had said that he needed a lesson.

It had started over the looting of the barges on the river, which the gang was planning. The leader had decided that the job would be done at night. The gang had agreed; all but Gail Wynand. Gail Wynand had explained, in a slow, contemptuous voice, that the Little Plug-Uglies, farther down the river, had tried the same stunt last week and had left six members in the hands of the cops, plus two in the cemetery; the job had to be done at daybreak, when no one would expect it. The gang hooted him. It made no difference. Gail Wynand was not good at taking orders. He recognized nothing but the accuracy of his own judgment. So the leader wished to settle the issue once and for all.

The three boys walked so softly that the people behind the thin walls they passed could not hear their steps. Gail Wynand heard them a block away. He did not move in his corner; only his wrist stiffened a little.

When the moment was right, he leaped. He leaped straight into space, without thought of landing, as if a catapult had sent him on a flight of miles. His chest struck the head of one enemy, his stomach another, his feet smashed into the chest of the third. The four of them went down. When the three lifted their faces, Gail Wynand was unrecognizable; they saw a whirl suspended in the air above them, and something darted at them out of the whirl with a scalding touch.

He had nothing but his two fists; they had five fists and a knife on their side; it did not seem to count. They heard their blows landing with a thud as on hard rubber; they felt the break in the thrust of their knife, which told that it had been stopped and had cut its way out. But the thing they were fighting was invulnerable. He had no time to feel; he was too fast; pain could not catch up with him; he seemed to leave it hanging in the air over the spot where it had hit him and where he was no longer in the next second.

He seemed to have a motor between his shoulder blades to propel his arms in two circles; only the circles were visible; the arms had vanished like the spokes of a speeding wheel. The circle landed each time, and stopped whatever it had landed upon, without a break in its spin. One boy saw his knife disappear in Wynand's shoulder; he saw the jerk of the shoulder that sent the knife slicing down through Wynand's side and flung it out at the belt. It was the last thing the boy saw. Something happened to his chin and he did not feel it when the back of his head struck against a pile of old bricks.

For a long time the two others fought the centrifuge that was now spattering red drops against the walls around them. But it was no use. They were not fighting a man. They were fighting a bodiless human will.

When they gave up, groaning among the bricks, Gail Wynand said in a normal voice: "We'll pull it off at daybreak," and walked away. From that moment on, he was the leader of the gang.

The looting of the barges was done at daybreak, two days later, and came off with brilliant success.

Gail Wynand lived with his father in the basement of an old house in the heart of Hell's Kitchen. His father was a longshoreman, a tall, silent, illiterate man who had never gone to school. His own father and his grandfather were of the same kind, and they knew of nothing but poverty in their family. But somewhere far back in the line there had been a root of aristocracy, the glory of some noble ancestor and then some tragedy, long since forgotten, that had brought the descendants to the gutter. Something about all the Wynands—in tenement, saloon and jail —did not fit their surroundings. Gail's father was known on the water-front as the Duke.

Gail's mother had died of consumption when he was two years old. He was an only son. He knew vaguely that there had been some great drama in his father's marriage; he had seen a picture of his mother; she did not look and she was not dressed like the women of their neighbor-hood; she was very beautiful. All life had gone out of his father when she died. He loved Gail; but it was the kind of devotion that did not require two sentences a week.

Gail did not look like his mother or father. He was a throwback to something no one could quite figure out; the distance had to be reck-oned, not in generations, but in centuries. He was always too tall for his age, and too thin. The boys called him Stretch Wynand. Nobody knew what he used for muscles; they knew only that he used it.

He had worked at one job after another since early childhood. For a long while he sold newspapers on street corners. One day he walked up to the press-room boss and stated that they should start a new service— delivering the paper to the reader's door in the morning; he explained how and why it would boost circulation. "Yeah?" said the boss. "I know it will work," said Wynand. "Well, you don't run things around here," said the boss. "You're a fool," said Wynand. He lost the job.

He worked in a grocery store. He ran errands, he swept the soggy wooden floor, he sorted out barrels of rotting vegetables, he helped to wait on customers, patiently weighing a pound of flour or filling a pitcher with milk from a huge can. It was like using a steamroller to press handkerchiefs. But he set his teeth and stuck to it. One day, he explained to the grocer what a good idea it would be to put milk up in bottles, like whisky. "You shut your trap and go wait on Mrs. Sullivan there," said the grocer, "don't you tell me nothing I don't know about my business. You don't run things around here." He waited on Mrs. Sullivan and said nothing.

He worked in a poolroom. He cleaned spittoons and washed up after drunks. He heard and saw things that gave him immunity from astonish-ment for the rest of his life. He made his greatest effort and learned to keep silent, to keep the place others described as his place, to accept ineptitude as his master—and to wait. No one had ever heard him speak of what he felt. He felt many emotions toward his fellow men, but respect was not one of them.

He worked as bootlack on a ferryboat. He was shoved and ordered around by every bloated horse trader, by every drunken deck hand aboard. If he spoke, he heard some thick voice answering: "You don't run things around here." But he liked this job. When he had no customers, he stood at the rail and looked at Manhattan. He looked at the yellow boards of new houses, at the vacant lots, at the cranes and derricks, at the few towers rising in the distance. He thought of what should be built and what should be destroyed, of the space, the promise and what could be made of it. A hoarse shout—"Hey, boy!"—interrupted him. He went back to his bench and bent obediently over some muddy shoe. The customer saw only a small head of light brown hair and two thin, capable hands.

On foggy evenings, under a gas lantern on a street corner, nobody noticed the slender figure leaning against a lamppost, the aristocrat of the Middle Ages, the timeless patrician whose every instinct cried that he should command, whose swift brain told him why he had the right to do so, the feudal baron created to rule—but born to sweep floors and take orders.

He had taught himself to read and write at the age of five, by asking questions. He read everything he found. He could not tolerate the inexplicable. He had to understand anything known to anyone. The emblem of his childhood—the coat-of-arms he devised for himself in place of the one lost for him centuries ago—was the question mark. No one ever needed to explain anything to him twice. He learned his first mathematics from the engineers laying sewer pipes. He learned geography from the sailors on the waterfront. He learned civics from the politicians at a local club that was a gangsters' hang-out. He had never gone to church or to school. He was twelve when he walked into a church. He listened to a sermon on patience and humility. He never came back. He was thirteen when he decided to see what education was like and enrolled at a public school. His father said nothing about this decision, as he said nothing whenever Gail came home battered after a gang fight.

During his first week at school the teacher called on Gail Wynand constantly—it was sheer pleasure to her, because he always knew the answers. When he trusted his superiors and their purpose, he obeyed like a Spartan, imposing on himself the kind of discipline he demanded of his own subjects in the gang. But the force of his will was wasted: within a week he saw that he needed no effort to be first in the class. After a month the teacher stopped noticing his presence; it seemed pointless, he always knew his lesson and she had to concentrate on the slower, duller children. He sat, unflinching, through hours that dragged like chains, while the teacher repeated and chewed and rechewed, sweating to force some spark of intellect from vacant eyes and mumbling voices. At the end of two months, reviewing the rudiments of history which she had tried to pound into her class, the teacher asked: "And how many original states were there in the Union?" No hands were raised. Then Gail Wynand's arm went up. The teacher nodded to him. He rose. "Why," he asked, "should I swill everything down ten times? I know all that." "You are not the only one in the class," said the teacher. He uttered an expression that struck her white and made her blush fifteen minutes later, when she grasped it fully. He walked to the door. On the threshold he turned to add: "Oh yes. There were thirteen original states."

That was the last of his formal education.

There were people in Hell's Kitchen who never ventured beyond its boundaries, and others who seldom stepped out of the tenement in which they were born. But Gail Wynand often went for a walk through the best streets of the city. He felt no bitterness against the world of wealth, no envy and no fear. He was simply curious and he felt at home on Fifth Avenue, just as anywhere else. He walked past the stately mansions, his hands in his pockets, his toes sticking out of flat-soled shoes. People glared at him, but it had no effect. He passed by and left behind him the feeling that he belonged on this street and they didn't. He wanted nothing, for the time being, except to understand.

He wanted to know what made these people different from those in his neighborhood. It was not the clothes, the carriages or the banks that caught his notice; it was the books. People in his neighborhood had clothes, horse wagons and money; degrees were inessential; but they did not read books. He decided to learn what was read by the people on Fifth Avenue. One day, he saw a lady waiting in a carriage at the curb; he knew she was a lady—his judgment on such matters was more acute than the discrimination of the *Social Register;* she was reading a book. He leaped to the steps of the carriage, snatched the book and ran away. It would have taken swifter, slimmer men than the cops to catch him.

It was a volume of Herbert Spencer. He went through a quiet agony trying to read it to the end. He read it to the end. He understood one quarter of what he had read. But this started him on a process which he pursued with a systematic, fist-clenched determination. Without advice, assistance or plan, he began reading an incongruous assortment of books; he would find some passage which he could not understand in one book, and he would get another on that subject. He branched out erratically in all directions; he read volumes of specialized erudition first, and high-school primers afterward. There was no order in his reading; but there was order in what remained of it in his mind.

He discovered the reading room of the Public Library and he went there for a while—to study the layout. Then, one day, at various times, a succession of young boys, painfully combed and unconvincingly washed, came to visit the reading room. They were thin when they came, but not when they left. That evening Gail Wynand had a small library of his own in the corner of his basement. His gang had executed his orders without protest. It was a scandalous assignment; no self-respecting gang had ever looted anything as pointless as books. But Stretch Wynand had given the orders—and one did not argue with Stretch Wynand.

He was fifteen when he was found, one morning, in the gutter, a mass of bleeding pulp, both legs broken, beaten by some drunken longshoreman. He was unconsious when found. But he had been conscious that night, after the beating. He had been left alone in a dark alley. He had seen a light around the corner. Nobody knew how he could have managed to drag himself around that corner; but he had; they saw the long smear of blood on the pavement afterward. He had crawled, able to move nothing but his arms. He had knocked against the bottom of a door. It was a saloon, still open. The saloonkeeper came out. It was the only time in his life that Gail Wynand asked for help. The saloonkeeper looked at him with a flat, heavy glance, a glance that showed full consciousness of agony, of injustice—and a stolid, bovine indifference. The saloonkeeper went inside and slammed the door. He had no desire to get mixed up with gang fights.

Years later, Gail Wynand, publisher of the New York *Banner,* still knew the names of the longshoreman and the saloonkeeper, and where to find them. He never did anything to the longshoreman. But he caused the saloonkeeper's business to be ruined, his home and savings to be lost, and drove the man to suicide.

Gail Wynand was sixteen when his father died. He was alone, jobless at the moment, with sixty-five cents in his pocket, an unpaid rent bill and a chaotic erudition. He decided that the time had come to decide what he would make of his life. He went, that night, to the roof of his tenement and looked at the lights of the city, the city where he did not run things. He let his eyes move slowly from the windows of the sagging hovels around him to the windows of the mansions in the distance. There were only lighted squares hanging in space, but he could tell from them the quality of the structures to which they belonged; the lights around him looked muddy, discouraged; those in the distance were clean and tight. He asked himself a single question: what was there that entered all those houses, the dim and the brilliant alike, what reached into every room, into every person? They all had bread. Could one rule men through the bread they bought? They had shoes, they had coffee, they had . . . The course of his life was set.

Next morning, he walked into the office of the editor of the *Gazette,* a fourth-rate newspaper in a run-down building, and asked for a job in the city room. The editor looked at his clothes and inquired, "Can you spell cat?" "Can you spell anthropomorphology?" asked Wynand. "We have no jobs here," said the editor. "I'll hang around," said Wynand. "Use me when you want to. You don't have to pay me. You'll put me on salary when you'll feel you'd better."

He remained in the building, sitting on the stairs outside the city room. He sat there every day for a week. No one paid any attention to him. At night he slept in doorways. When most of his money was gone, he stole food, from counters or from garbage pails, before returning to his post on the stairs.

One day a reporter felt sorry for him and, walking down the stairs, threw a nickel into Wynand's lap, saying: "Go buy yourself a bowl of stew, kid." Wynand had a dime left in his pocket. He took the dime and threw it at the reporter, saying: "Go buy yourself a screw." The man swore and went on down. The nickel and the dime remained lying on the steps. Wynand would not touch them. The story was repeated in the city room. A pimply-faced clerk shrugged and took the two coins.

At the end of the week, in a rush hour, a man from the city room called Wynand to run an errand. Other small chores followed. He obeyed with military precision. In ten days he was on salary. In six months he was a reporter. In two years he was an associate editor.

Gail Wynand was twenty when he fell in love. He had known everything there was to know about sex since the age of thirteen. He had had many girls. He never spoke of love, created no romantic illusion and treated the whole matter as a simple animal transaction; but at this he was an expert—and women could tell it, just by looking at him. The girl with whom he fell in love had an exquisite beauty, a beauty to be worshiped, not desired. She was fragile and silent. Her face told of the lovely mysteries within her, left unexpressed.

She became Gail Wynand's mistress. He allowed himself the weakness of being happy. He would have married her at once, had she mentioned it. But they said little to each other. He felt that everything was understood between them.

One evening he spoke. Sitting at her feet, his face raised to her, he allowed his soul to be heard. "My darling, anything you wish, anything I am, anything I can ever be . . . That's what I want to offer you—not the things I'll get for you, but the thing in me that will make me able to get them. That thing—a man can't renounce it—but I want to renounce it—so that it will be yours—so that it will be in your service—only for you." The girl smiled and asked: "Do you think I'm prettier than Maggy Kelly?"

He got up. He said nothing and walked out of the house. He never saw that girl again. Gail Wynand, who prided himself on never needing a lesson twice, did not fall in love again in the years that followed.

He was twenty-one when his career on the *Gazette* was threatened, for the first and only time. Politics and corruption had never disturbed him; he knew all about it; his gang had been paid to help stage beatings at the polls on election days. But when Pat Mulligan, police captain of his precinct, was framed, Wynand could not take it; because Pat Mulligan was the only honest man he had ever met in his life.

The *Gazette* was controlled by the powers that had framed Mulligan. Wynand said nothing. He merely put in order in his mind such items of information he possessed as would blow the *Gazette* into hell. His job would be blown with it, but that did not matter. His decision contradicted every rule he had laid down for his career. But he did not think. It was one of the rare explosions that hit him at times, throwing him beyond caution, making of him a creature possessed by the single impulse to have his way, because the rightness of his way was so blindingly total. But he knew that the destruction of the *Gazette* would be only a first step. It was not enough to save Mulligan.

For three years Wynand had kept one small clipping, an editorial on corruption, by the famous editor of a great newspaper. He had kept it, because it was the most beautiful tribute to integrity he had ever read. He took the clipping and went to see the great editor. He would tell him about Mulligan and together they would beat the machine.

He walked far across town, to the building of the famous paper. He had to walk. It helped to control the fury within him. He was admitted into the office of the editor—he had a way of getting admitted into places against all rules. He saw a fat man at a desk, with thin slits of eyes set close together. He did not introduce himself, but laid the clipping down on the desk and asked: "Do you remember this?" The editor glanced at the clipping, then at Wynand. It was a glance Wynand had seen before: in the eyes of the saloonkeeper who had slammed the door. "How do you expect me to remember every piece of swill I write?" asked the editor.

After a moment, Wynand said : "Thanks." It was the only time in his life that he felt gratitude to anyone. The gratitude was genuine—a payment for a lesson he would never need again. But even the editor knew there was something very wrong in that short "Thanks," and very frightening. He did not know that it had been an obituary on Gail Wynand.

Wynand walked back to the *Gazette,* feeling no anger toward the editor or the political machine. He felt only a furious contempt for himself, for Pat Mulligan, for all integrity; he felt shame when he thought of those whose victims he and Mulligan had been willing to become. He did not think "victims"—he thought "suckers." He got back to the office and wrote a brilliant editorial blasting Captain Mulligan. "Why, I thought you kinda felt sorry for the poor bastard," said his editor, pleased. "I don't feel sorry for anyone," said Wynand.

Grocers and deck hands had not appreciated Gail Wynand; politicians did. In his years on the paper he had learned how to get along with people. His face had assumed the expression it was to wear for the rest of his life: not quite a smile, but a motionless look of irony directed at the whole world. People could presume that his mockery was intended for the particular things they wished to mock. Besides, it was pleasant to deal with a man untroubled by passion or sanctity.

He was twenty-three when a rival political gang, intent on winning a municipal election and needing a newspaper to plug a certain issue, bought the *Gazette*. They bought it in the name of Gail Wynand, who was to serve as a respectable front for the machine. Gail Wynand became editor-in-chief. He plugged the issue, he won the election for his bosses. Two years later, he smashed the gang, sent its leaders to the penitentiary, and remained as sole owner of the *Gazette*.

His first act was to tear down the sign over the door of the building and to throw out the paper's old masthead. The *Gazette* became the New York *Banner*. His friends objected. "Publishers don't change the name of a paper," they told him. "This one does," he said.

The first campaign of the *Banner* was an appeal for money for a charitable cause. Displayed side by side, with an equal amount of space, the *Banner* ran two stories: one about a struggling young scientist, starving in a garret, working on a great invention; the other about a chambermaid, the sweetheart of an executed murderer, awaiting the birth of her illegitimate child. One story was illustrated with scientific diagrams; the other—with the picture of a loose-mouth girl wearing a tragic expression and disarranged clothes. The *Banner* asked its readers to help both these unfortunates. It received nine dollars and forty-five cents for the young scientist; it received one thousand and seventy-seven dollars for the unwed mother. Gail Wynand called a meeting of his staff. He put down on the table the paper carrying both stories and the money collected for both funds. "Is there anyone here who doesn't understand?" he asked. No one answered. He said: "Now you all know the kind of paper the *Banner* is to be."

The publishers of his time took pride in stamping their individual personalities upon their newspapers. Gail Wynand delivered his paper, body and soul, to the mob. The *Banner* assumed the appearance of a circus poster in body, of a circus performance in soul. It accepted the same goal—to stun, to amuse and to collect admission. It bore the imprint, not of one, but of a million men. "Men differ in their virtues, if any," said Gail Wynand, explaining his policy, "but they are alike in their vices." He added, looking straight into the questioner's eyes: "I am serving that which exists on this earth in greatest quantity. I am representing the majority—surely an act of virtue?"

The public asked for crime, scandal and sentiment. Gail Wynand provided it. He gave people what they wanted, plus a justification for indulging the tastes of which they had been ashamed. The *Banner* presented murder, arson, rape, corruption—with an appropriate moral against each. There were three columns of details to one stick of moral. "If you make people perform a noble duty, it bores them," said Wynand. "If you make them indulge themselves, it shames them. But combine the two—and you've got them." He ran stories about fallen girls, society divorces, foundling asylums, red-light districts, charity hospitals. "Sex first," said Wynand. "Tears second. Make them itch and make them cry—and you've got them."

The *Banner* led great, brave crusades—on issues that had no opposition. It exposed politicians—one step ahead of the Grand Jury; it attacked monopolies—in the name of the downtrodden; it mocked the rich and the successful—in the manner of those who could never be either. It overstressed the glamour of society—and presented society news with a subtle sneer. This gave the man on the street two satisfactions: that of entering illustrious drawing rooms and that of not wiping his feet on the threshold.

The *Banner* was permitted to strain truth, taste and credibility, but not its readers' brain power. Its enormous headlines, glaring pictures and oversimplified text hit the senses and entered men's consciousness without any necessity for an intermediary process of reason, like food shot through the rectum, requiring no digestion.

"News," Gail Wynand told his staff, "is that which will create the greatest excitement among the greatest number. The thing that will knock them silly. The sillier the better, provided there's enough of them."

One day he brought into the office a man he had picked off the street. It was an ordinary man, neither well-dressed nor shabby, neither tall nor short, neither dark nor quite blond; he had the kind of face one could not remember even while looking at it. He was frightening by being so totally undifferentiated; he lacked even the positive distinction of a half-wit. Wynand took him through the building, introduced him to every member of the staff and let him go. Then Wynand called his staff together and told them: "When in doubt about your work, remember that man's face. You're writing for him." "But, Mr. Wynand," said a young editor, "one can't remember his face." "That's the point," said Wynand.

When the name of Gail Wynand became a threat in the publishing world, a group of newspaper owners took him aside—at a city charity affair which all had to attend—and reproached him for what they called his debasement of the public taste. "It is not my function," said Wynand, "to help people preserve a self-respect they haven't got. You give them what they profess to like in public. I give them what they really like. Honesty is the best policy, gentlemen, though not quite in the sense you were taught to believe."

It was impossible for Wynand not to do a job well. Whatever his aim, his means were superlative. All the drive, the force, the will barred from the pages of his paper went into its making. An exceptional talent was burned prodigally to achieve perfection in the unexceptional. A new religious faith could have been founded on the energy of spirit which he spent upon collecting lurid stories and smearing them across sheets of paper.

The *Banner* was always first with the news. When an earthquake occurred in South America and no communications came from the stricken area, Wynand chartered a liner, sent a crew down to the scene and had extras on the streets of New York days ahead of his competitors, extras with drawings that represented flames, chasms and crushed bodies. When an S.O.S. was received from a ship sinking in a storm off the Atlantic coast, Wynand himself sped to the scene with his crew, ahead of the Coast Guard; Wynand directed the rescue and brought back an exclusive story with photographs of himself climbing a ladder over raging waves, a baby in his arms. When a Canadian village was cut off from the world by an avalanche, it was the *Banner* that sent a balloon to drop food and Bibles to the inhabitants. When a coal-mining community was paralyzed by a strike, the *Banner* opened soup-kitchens and printed tragic stories on the perils confronting the miners' pretty daughters under the pressure of poverty. When a kitten got trapped on the top of a pole, it was rescued by a *Banner* photographer.

"When there's no news, make it," was Wynand's order. A lunatic escaped from a state institution for the insane. After days of terror for miles around—terror fed by the *Banner's* dire predictions and its indignation at the inefficiency of the local police—he was captured by a reporter of the *Banner*. The lunatic recovered miraculously two weeks after his capture, was released, and sold to the *Banner* an exposé of the ill-treatment he had suffered at the institution. It led to sweeping reforms. Afterward, some people said that the lunatic had worked on the *Banner* before his commitment. It could never be proved.

A fire broke out in a sweatshop employing thirty young girls. Two of them perished in the disaster. Mary Watson, one of the survivors, gave the *Banner* an exclusive story about the exploitation they had suffered. It led to a crusade against sweatshops, headed by the best women of the city. The origin of the fire was never discovered. It was whispered that Mary Watson had once been Evelyn Drake who wrote for the *Banner*. It could not be proved.

In the first years of the *Banner's* existence Gail Wynand spent more nights on his office couch than in his bedroom. The effort he demanded of his employees was hard to perform; the effort of himself was hard to believe. He drove them like an army; he drove himself like a slave. He paid them well; he got nothing but his rent and meals. He lived in a furnished room at the time when his best reporters lived in suites at expensive hotels. He spent money faster than it came in—and he spent it all on the *Banner*. The paper was like a luxurious mistress whose every need was satisfied without inquiry about the price.

The *Banner* was first to get the newest typographical equipment. The *Banner* was last to get the best newspapermen—last, because it kept them. Wynand raided his competitors' city rooms; nobody could meet the salaries he offered. His procedure evolved into a simple formula. When a newspaperman received an invitation to call on Wynand, he took it as an insult to his journalistic integrity, but he came to the appointment. He came, prepared to deliver a set of offensive conditions on which he would accept the job, if at all. Wynand began the interview by stating the salary he would pay. Then he added: "You might wish, of course, to discuss other conditions——" and seeing the swallowing movement in the man's throat, concluded: "No? Fine. Report to me on Monday."

When Wynand opened his second paper—in Philadelphia—the local publishers met him like European chieftains united against the invasion of Attila. The war that followed was as savage. Wynand laughed over it. No one could teach him anything about hiring thugs to highjack a paper's delivery wagons and beat up news vendors. Two of his competitors perished in the battle. The Wynand *Philadelphia Star* survived.

The rest was swift and simple like an epidemic. By the time he reached the age of thirty-five there were Wynand papers in all the key cities of the United States. By the time he was forty there were Wynand magazines, Wynand newsreels and most of the Wynand Enterprises, Inc.

A great many activities, not publicized, helped to build his fortune. He had forgotten nothing of his childhood. He remembered the things he had thought, standing as a bootblack at the rail of a ferryboat—the chances offered by a growing city. He bought real estate where no one expected it to become valuable, he built against all advice—and he ran hundreds into thousands. He bought his way into a great many enterprises of all kinds. Sometimes they crashed, ruining everybody concerned, save Gail Wynand. He staged a crusade against a shady streetcar monopoly and caused it to lose its franchise; the franchise was granted to a shadier group, controlled by Gail Wynand. He exposed a vicious attempt to corner the beef market in the Middle West—and left the field clear for another gang, operating under his orders.

He was helped by a great many people who discovered that young Wynand was a bright fellow, worth using. He exhibited a charming complaisance about being used. In each case, the people found that they had been used instead—like the men who bought the *Gazette* for Gail Wynand.

Sometimes he lost money on his investments, coldly and with full intention. Through a series of untraceable steps he ruined many powerful men: the president of a bank, the head of an insurance company, the owner of a steamship line, and others. No one could discover his motives. The men were not his competitors and he gained nothing from their destruction.

"Whatever that bastard Wynand is after," people said, "it's not after money."

Those who denounced him too persistently were run out of their professions: some in a few weeks, others many years later. There were occasions when he let insults pass unnoticed; there were occasions when he broke a man for an innocuous remark. One could never tell what he would avenge and what he would forgive.

One day he noticed the brilliant work of a young reporter on another paper and sent for him. The boy came, but the salary Wynand mentioned had no effect on him. "I can't work for you, Mr. Wynand," he said with desperate earnestness, "because you . . . you have no ideals." Wynand's thin lips smiled. "You can't escape human depravity, kid," he said gently. "The boss you work for may have ideals, but he has to beg money and take orders from many contemptible people. I have no ideals —but I don't beg. Take your choice. There's no other." The boy went back to his paper. A year later he came to Wynand and asked if his offer were still open. Wynand said that it was. The boy had remained on the *Banner* ever since. He was the only one on the staff who loved Gail Wynand.

Alvah Scarret, sole survivor of the original *Gazette*, had risen with Wynand. But one could not say that he loved Wynand—he merely clung to his boss with the automatic devotion of a rug under Wynand's feet. Alvah Scarret had never hated anything, and so was incapable of love. He was shrewd, competent and unscrupulous in the innocent manner of one unable to grasp the conception of a scruple. He believed everything he wrote and everything written in the *Banner*. He could hold a belief for all of two weeks. He was invaluable to Wynand—as a barometer of public reaction.

No one could say whether Gail Wynand had a private life. His hours away from the office had assumed the style of the *Banner*'s front page— but a style raised to a grand plane, as if he were still playing circus, only to a gallery of kings. He bought out the entire house for a great opera performance—and sat alone in the empty auditorium with his current mistress. He discovered a beautiful play by an unknown playwright and paid him a huge sum to have the play performed once and never again; Wynand was the sole spectator at the single performance; the script was burned next morning. When a distinguished society woman asked him to contribute to a worthy charity cause, Wynand handed her a signed blank check—and laughed, confessing that the amount she dared to fill in was less than he would have given otherwise. He bought some kind of Balkan throne for a penniless pretender whom he met in a speak-easy and never bothered to see afterward; he often referred to "my valet, my chauffeur and my king."

At night, dressed in a shabby suit bought for nine dollars, Wynand would often ride the subways and wander through the dives of slum districts, listening to his public. Once, in a basement beer joint, he heard a truck driver denouncing Gail Wynand as the worst exponent of capitalistic evils, in a language of colorful accuracy. Wynand agreed with him and helped him out with a few expressions of his own, from his Hell's Kitchen vocabulary. Then Wynand picked up a copy of the *Banner* left by someone on a table, tore his own photograph from page 3, clipped it to a hundred-dollar bill, handed it to the truck driver and walked out before anyone could utter a word.

The succession of his mistresses was so rapid that it ceased to be gossip. It was said that he never enjoyed a woman unless he had bought her—and that she had to be the kind who could not be bought.

He kept the details of his life secret by making it glaringly public as a whole. He had delivered himself to the crowd; he was anyone's property, like a monument in a park, like a bus stop sign, like the pages of the *Banner*. His photographs appeared in his papers more often than pictures of movie stars. He had been photographed in all kinds of clothes, on every imaginable occasion. He had never been photographed naked, but his readers felt as if he had. He derived no pleasure from personal publicity; it was merely a matter of policy to which he submitted. Every corner of his penthouse had been reproduced in his papers and magazines. "Every bastard in the country knows the inside of my icebox and bathtub," he said.

One phase of his life, however, was little known and never mentioned. The top floor of the building under his penthouse was his private art gallery. It was locked. He had never admitted anyone, except the caretaker. A few people knew about it. Once a French ambassador asked him for permission to visit it. Wynand refused. Occasionally, not often, he would descend to his gallery and remain there for hours. The things he collected were chosen by standards of his own. He had famous masterpieces; he had canvases by unknown artists; he rejected the works of immortal names for which he did not care. The estimates set by collectors and the matter of great signatures were of no concern to him. The art dealers whom he patronized reported that his judgment was that of a master.

One night his valet saw Wynand returning from the art gallery below and was shocked by the expression of his face; it was a look of suffering, yet the face seemed ten years younger. "Are you ill, sir?" he asked. Wynand looked at him indifferently and said: "Go to bed."

"We could make a swell spread for the Sunday scandal sheet out of your art gallery," said Alvah Scarret wistfully. "No," said Wynand. "But why, Gail?" "Look, Alvah. Every man on earth has a soul of his own that nobody can stare at. Even the convicts in a penitentiary and the freaks in a side show. Everybody but me. My soul is spread in your Sunday scandal sheet—in three-color process. So I must have a substitute—even if it's only a locked room and a few objects not to be pawed."

It was a long process and there had been premonitory signs, but Scarret did not notice a certain new trait in Gail Wynand's character until Wynand was forty-five. Then it became apparent to many. Wynand lost interest in breaking industrialists and financiers. He found a new kind of victim. People could not tell whether it was a sport, a mania or a systematic pursuit. They thought it was horrible, because it seemed so vicious and pointless.

It began with the case of Dwight Carson. Dwight Carson was a talented young writer who had achieved the spotless reputation of a man passionately devoted to his convictions. He upheld the cause of the individual against the masses. He wrote for magazines of great prestige and small circulation, which were no threat to Wynand. Wynand bought Dwight Carson. He forced Carson to write a column on the *Banner,* dedicated to preaching the superiority of the masses over the man of genius. It was a bad column, dull and unconvincing; it made many people angry. It was a waste of space and of a big salary. Wynand insisted on continuing it.

Even Alvah Scarret was shocked by Carson's apostasy. "Anybody else, Gail," he said, "but, honest, I didn't expect it of Carson." Wynand laughed; he laughed too long, as if he could not stop it; his laughter had an edge of hysteria. Scarret frowned; he did not like the sight of Wynand being unable to control an emotion; it contradicted everything he knew of Wynand; it gave Scarret a funny feeling of apprehension, like the sight of a tiny crack in a solid wall; the crack could not possibly endanger the wall—except that it had no business being there.

A few months later Wynand bought a young writer from a radical magazine, a man known for his honesty, and put him to work on a series of articles glorifying exceptional men and damning the masses. That, too, made a great many of his readers angry. He continued it. He seemed not to care any longer about the delicate signs of effect on circulation.

He hired a sensitive poet to cover baseball games. He hired an art expert to handle financial news. He got a socialist to defend factory owners and a conservative to champion labor. He forced an atheist to write on the glories of religion. He made a disciplined scientist proclaim the superiority of mystical intuition over the scientific method. He gave a great symphony conductor a munificent yearly income, for no work at all, on the sole condition that he never conduct an orchestra again.

Some of these men had refused, at first. But they surrendered when they found themselves on the edge of bankruptcy through a series of untraceable circumstances within a few years. Some of the men were famous, others obscure. Wynand showed no interest in the previous standing of his prey. He showed no interest in men of glittering success who had commercialized their careers and held no particular beliefs of any kind. His victims had a single attribute in common: their immaculate integrity.

Once they were broken, Wynand continued to pay them scrupulously. But he felt no further concern for them and no desire to see them again. Dwight Carson became a dipsomaniac. Two men became drug addicts. One committed suicide. This last was too much for Scarret. "Isn't it going too far, Gail?" he asked. "That was practically murder." "Not at all," said Wynand, "I was merely an outside circumstance. The cause was in him. If lightning strikes a rotten tree and it collapses, it's not the fault of the lightning." "But what do you call a healthy tree?" "They don't exist, Alvah," said Wynand cheerfully, "they don't exist."

Alvah Scarret never asked Wynand for an explanation of this new pursuit. By some dim instinct Scarret guessed a little of the reason behind it. Scarret shrugged and laughed, telling people that it was nothing to worry about, it was just "a safety valve." Only two men understood Gail Wynand: Alvah Scarret—partially; Ellsworth Toohey—completely.

Ellsworth Toohey—who wished, above all, to avoid a quarrel with Wynand at that time—could not refrain from a feeling of resentment, because Wynand had not chosen him as a victim. He almost wished Wynand would try to corrupt him, no matter what the consequences. But Wynand seldom noticed his existence.

Wynand had never been afraid of death. Through the years the thought of suicide had occurred to him, not as an intention, but as one of the many possibilities among the chances of life. He examined it indifferently, with polite curiosity, as he examined any possibility—and then forgot it. He had known moments of blank exhaustion when his will deserted him. He had always cured himself by a few hours in his art gallery.

Thus he reached the age of fifty-one, and a day when nothing of consequence happened to him, yet the evening found him without desire to make a step farther.

Gail Wynand sat on the edge of the bed, slumped forward, his elbows on his knees, the gun on the palm of his hand.

Yes, he told himself, there's an answer there somewhere. But I don't want to know it. I don't want to know it.

And because he felt a pang of dread at the root of this desire not to examine his life further, he knew that he would not die tonight. As long as he still feared something, he had a foothold on living; even if it meant only moving forward to an unknown disaster. The thought of death gave him nothing. The thought of living gave him a slender alms—the hint of fear.

He moved his hand, weighing the gun. He smiled, a faint smile of derision. No, he thought, that's not for you. Not yet. You still have the sense of not wanting to die senselessly. You were stopped by that. Even that is a remnant—of something.

He tossed the gun aside on the bed, knowing that the moment was past and the thing was of no danger to him any longer. He got up. He felt no elation; he felt tired; but he was back in his normal course. There were no problems, except to finish this day quickly and go to sleep.

He went down to his study to get a drink.

When he switched on the light in the study, he saw Toohey's present. It was a huge, vertical crate, standing by his desk. He had seen it earlier in the evening. He had thought "What the hell," and forgotten all about it.

He poured himself a drink and stood sipping it slowly. The crate was too large to escape his field of vision, and as he drank he tried to guess what it could possibly contain. It was too tall and slender for a piece of furniture. He could not imagine what material property Toohey could wish to send him; he had expected something less tangible—a small envelope containing a hint at some sort of blackmail; so many people had tried to blackmail him so unsuccessfully; he did think Toohey would have more sense than that.

By the time he finished his drink, he had found no plausible explanation for the crate. It annoyed him, like a stubborn crossword puzzle. He had a kit of tools somewhere in a drawer of his desk. He found it and broke the crate open.

It was Steven Mallory's statue of Dominique Francon.

Gail Wynand walked to his desk and put down the pliers he held as if they were of fragile crystal. Then he turned and looked at the statue again. He stood looking at it for an hour.

Then he went to the telephone and dialed Toohey's number.

"Hello?" said Toohey's voice, its hoarse impatience confessing that he had been awakened out of sound sleep.

"All right. Come over," said Wynand and hung up.

Toohey arrived half an hour later. It was his first visit to Wynand's home. Wynand himself answered the door bell, still dressed in his pyjamas. He said nothing and walked into the study, Toohey following.

The naked marble body, its head thrown back in exaltation, made the room look like a place that did not exist any longer: like the Stoddard Temple. Wynand's eyes rested on Toohey expectantly, a heavy glance of suppressed anger.

"You want, of course, to know the name of the model?" Toohey asked, with just a hint of triumph in his voice.

"Hell, no," said Wynand. "I want to know the name of the sculptor."

He wondered why Toohey did not like the question; there was something more than disappointment in Toohey's face.

"The sculptor?" said Toohey. "Wait . . . let me see . . . I think I did know it. . . . It's Steven . . . or Stanley . . . Stanley something or other. . . . Honestly, I don't remember."

"If you knew enough to buy this, you knew enough to ask the name and never forget it."

"I'll look it up, Mr. Wynand."

"Where did you get this?"

"In some art shop, you know, one of those places on Second Avenue."

"How did it get there?"

"I don't know. I didn't ask. I bought it because I knew the model."

"You're lying about that. If that were all you saw in it, you wouldn't have taken the chance you took. You know that I've never let anyone see my gallery. Did you think I'd allow you the presumption of contributing to it? Nobody has ever dared offer me a gift of that kind. You wouldn't have risked it, unless you were sure, terribly sure, of how great a work of art this is. Sure that I'd have to accept it. That you'd beat me. And you have."

"I'm glad to hear it, Mr. Wynand."

"If you wish to enjoy that, I'll tell you also that I hate seeing this come from you. I hate your having been able to appreciate it. It doesn't fit you. Though I was obviously wrong about you: you're a greater art expert than I thought you were."

"Such as it is, I'll have to accept this as a compliment and thank you, Mr. Wynand."

"Now what was it you wanted? You intended me to understand that you won't let me have this unless I grant an interview to Mrs. Peter Keating?"

"Why, no, Mr. Wynand. I've made you a present of it. I intended you only to understand that this is Mrs. Peter Keating."

Wynand looked at the statue, then back at Toohey.

"Oh you damn fool!" said Wynand softly.

Toohey stared at him, bewildered.

"So you really did use *this* as a red lamp in a window?" Wynand seemed relieved; he did not find it necessary to hold Toohey's glance now. "That's better, Toohey. You're not as smart as I thought for a moment."

"But, Mr. Wynand, what . . .?"

"Didn't you realize that this statue would be the surest way to kill any possible appetite I might have for your Mrs. Keating?"

"You haven't seen her, Mr. Wynand."

"Oh, she's probably beautiful. She might be more beautiful than this. But she can't have what that sculptor has given her. And to see that same face, but without any meaning, like a dead caricature—don't you think one would hate the woman for that?"

"You haven't seen her."

"Oh, all right, I'll see her. I told you you should be allowed to get away with your stunt completely or not at all. I didn't promise you to lay her, did I? Only to see her."

"That is all I wanted, Mr. Wynand."

"Have her telephone my office and make an appointment."

"Thank you, Mr. Wynand."

"Besides, you're lying about not knowing the name of that sculptor. But it's too much bother to make you tell me. She'll tell me."

"I'm sure she'll tell you. Though why should I lie?"

"God knows. By the way, if it had been a lesser sculptor, you'd have lost your job over this."

"But, after all, Mr. Wynand, I have a contract."

"Oh, save that for your labor unions, Elsie! And now I think you should wish me a good night and get out of here."

"Yes, Mr. Wynand. I wish you a good night."

Wynand accompanied him to the hall. At the door Wynand said:

"You're a poor businessman, Toohey. I don't know why you're so anxious to have me meet Mrs. Keating. I don't know what your racket is in trying to get a commission for that Keating of yours. But whatever it is, it can't be so valuable that you should have been willing to part with a thing like this in exchange."

II

"WHY DIDN'T YOU WEAR YOUR EMERALD BRACELET?" ASKED Peter Keating. "Gordon Prescott's so-called fiancée had everybody gaping at her star sapphire."

"I'm sorry, Peter. I shall wear it next time," said Dominique.

"It was a nice party. Did you have a good time?"

"I always have a good time."

"So did I . . . Only . . . Oh God, do you want to know the truth?"

"No."

"Dominique, I was bored to death. Vincent Knowlton is a pain in the neck. He's such a damn snob. I can't stand him." He added, cautiously: "I didn't show it, did I?"

"No. You behaved very well. You laughed at all his jokes—even when no one else did."

"Oh, you noticed that? It always works."

"Yes, I noticed that."

"You think I shouldn't, don't you?"

"I haven't said that."

"You think it's . . . low, don't you?"

"I don't think anything is low."

He slumped farther in his armchair; it made his chin press uncomfortably against his chest; but he did not care to move again. A fire crackled in the fireplace of his living room. He had turned out all the lights, save one lamp with a yellow silk shade; but it created no air of intimate relaxation, it only made the place look deserted, like a vacant apartment with the utilities shut off. Dominique sat at the other end of the room, her thin body fitted obediently to the contours of a straight-backed chair; she did not look stiff, only too poised for comfort. They were alone, but she sat like a lady at a public function; like a lovely dress dummy in a public show window—a window facing a busy intersection.

They had come home from a tea party at the house of Vincent Knowlton, a prominent young society man, Keating's new friend. They had had a quiet dinner together, and now their evening was free. There were no other social engagements till tomorrow.

"You shouldn't have laughed at theosophy when you spoke to Mrs. Marsh," he said. "She believes in it."

"I'm sorry. I shall be more careful."

434

He waited to have her open a subject of conversation. She said nothing. He thought suddenly that she had never spoken to him first—in the twenty months of their marriage. He told himself that that was ridiculous and impossible; he tried to recall an occasion when she had addressed him. Of course he had; he remembered her asking him: "What time will you be back tonight?" and "Do you wish to include the Dixons for Tuesday's dinner?" and many things like that.

He glanced at her. She did not look bored or anxious to ignore him. She sat there, alert and ready, as if his company held her full interest; she did not reach for a book, she did not stare at some distant thought of her own. She looked straight at him, not past him, as if she were waiting for a conversation. He realized that she had always looked straight at him, like this; and now he wondered whether he liked it. Yes, he did, it allowed him no cause to be jealous, not even of her hidden thoughts. No, he didn't, not quite, it allowed no escape, for either one of them.

"I've just finished *The Gallant Gallstone*," he said. "It's a swell book. It's the product of a scintillating brain, a Puck with tears streaming down his face, a golden-hearted clown holding for a moment the throne of God."

"I read the same book review. In the Sunday *Banner*."

"I read the book itself. You know I did."

"That was nice of you."

"Huh?" He heard approval and it pleased him.

"It was considerate toward the author. I'm sure she likes to have people read her book. So it was kind to take the time—when you knew in advance what you'd think of it."

"I didn't know. But I happen to agree with the reviewer."

"The *Banner* has the best reviewers."

"That's true. Of course. So there's nothing wrong in agreeing with them, is there?"

"Nothing whatever. I always agree."

"With whom?"

"With everybody."

"Are you making fun of me, Dominique?"

"Have you given me reason to?"

"No. I don't see how. No, of course I haven't."

"Then I'm not."

He waited. He heard a truck rumbling past, in the street below, and that filled a few seconds; but when the sound died, he had to speak again:

"Dominique, I'd like to know what you think."

"Of what?"

"Of . . . of . . ." He searched for an important subject and ended with: ". . . of Vincent Knowlton."

"I think he's a man worth kissing the backside of."

"For Christ's sake, Dominique!"

"I'm sorry. That's bad English and bad manners. It's wrong, of course. Well, let's see: Vincent Knowlton is a man whom it's pleasant to know. Old families deserve a great deal of consideration, and we must have tolerance for the opinions of others, because tolerance is the greatest virtue, therefore it would be unfair to force your views on Vincent Knowlton, and if you just let him believe what he pleases, he will be glad to help you too, because he's a very human person."

"Now, that's sensible," said Keating; he felt at home in recognizable language. "I think tolerance is very important, because . . ." He stopped. He finished, in an empty voice: "You said exactly the same thing as before."

"Did you notice that," she said. She said it without question mark, indifferently, as a simple fact. It was not sarcasm; he wished it were; sarcasm would have granted him a personal recognition—the desire to hurt him. But her voice had never carried any personal relation to him—not for twenty months.

He stared into the fire. That was what made a man happy—to sit looking dreamily into a fire, at his own hearth, in his own home; that's what he had always heard and read. He stared at the flames, unblinking, to force himself into a complete obedience to an established truth. Just one more minute of it and I will feel happy, he thought, concentrating. Nothing happened.

He thought of how convincingly he could describe this scene to friends and make them envy the fullness of his contentment. Why couldn't he convince himself? He had everything he'd ever wanted. He had wanted superiority—and for the last year he had been the undisputed leader of his profession. He had wanted fame—and he had five thick albums of clippings. He had wanted wealth—and he had enough to insure luxury for the rest of his life. He had everything anyone ever wanted. How many people struggled and suffered to achieve what he had achieved? How many dreamed and bled and died for this, without reaching it? "Peter Keating is the luckiest fellow on earth." How often had he heard that?

This last year had been the best of his life. He had added the impossible to his possessions—Dominique Francon. It had been such a joy to laugh casually when friends repeated to him: "Peter, how did you ever do it?" It had been such a pleasure to introduce her to strangers, to say lightly: "My wife," and to watch the stupid, uncontrolled look of envy in their eyes. Once at a large party an elegant drunk had asked him, with a wink declaring unmistakable intentions: "Say, do you know that gorgeous creature over there?" "Slightly," Keating had answered, gratified, "she's my wife."

He often told himself gratefully that their marriage had turned out much better than he had expected. Dominique had become an ideal wife. She devoted herself completely to his interests: pleasing his clients, entertaining his friends, running his home. She changed nothing in his existence: not his hours, not his favorite menus, not even the arrangement of his furniture. She had brought nothing with her, except her clothes; she had not added a single book or ash tray to his house. When he expressed his views on any subject, she did not argue—she agreed with him. Graciously, as a matter of natural course, she took second place, vanishing in his background.

He had expected a torrent that would lift him and smash him against some unknown rocks. He had not found even a brook joining his peaceful river. It was more as if the river went on and someone came to swim quietly in his wake; no, not even to swim—that was a cutting, forceful action—but just to float behind him with the current. Had he been offered the power to determine Dominique's attitude after their marriage, he would have asked that she behave exactly as she did.

Only their nights left him miserably unsatisfied. She submitted whenever he wanted her. But it was always as on their first night: an indifferent body in his arms, without revulsion, without answer. As far as he was concerned, she was still a virgin: he had never made her experience anything. Each time, burning with humiliation, he decided never to touch her again. But his desire returned, aroused by the constant presence of her beauty. He surrendered to it, when he could resist no longer; not often.

It was his mother who stated the thing he had not admitted to himself about his marriage. "I can't stand it," his mother said, six months after the wedding. "If she'd just get angry at me once, call me names, throw things at me, it would be all right. But I can't stand this." "What, Mother?" he asked, feeling a cold hint of panic. "It's no use, Peter," she answered. His mother, whose arguments, opinions, reproaches he had never been able to stop, would not say another word about his marriage. She took a small apartment of her own and moved out of his house. She came to visit him often and she was always polite to Dominique, with a strange, beaten air of resignation. He told himself that he should be glad to be free of his mother; but he was not glad.

Yet he could not grasp what Dominique had done to inspire that mounting dread within him. He could find no word or gesture for which to reproach her. But for twenty months it had been like tonight: he could not bear to remain alone with her—yet he did not want to escape her and she did not want to avoid him.

"Nobody's coming tonight?" he asked tonelessly, turning away from the fire.

"No," she said, and smiled, the smile serving as connection to her next words: "Shall I leave you alone, Peter?"

"No!" It was almost a cry. I must not sound so desperate, he thought, while he was saying aloud: "Of course not. I'm glad to have an evening with my wife all to myself."

He felt a dim instinct telling him that he must solve this problem, must learn to make their moments together endurable, that he dare not run from it, for his own sake more than hers.

"What would you like to do tonight, Dominique?"

"Anything you wish."

"Want to go to a movie?"

"Do you?"

"Oh, I don't know. It kills time."

"All right. Let's kill time."

"No. Why should we? That sounds awful."

"Does it?"

"Why should we run from our own home? Let's stay here."

"Yes, Peter."

He waited. But the silence, he thought, is a flight too, a worse kind of flight.

"Want to play a hand of Russian Bank?" he asked.

"Do you like Russian Bank?"

"Oh, it kills ti——" He stopped. She smiled.

"Dominique," he said, looking at her, "you're so beautiful. You're always so . . . so utterly beautiful. I always want to tell you how I feel about it."

"I'd like to hear how you feel about it, Peter."

"I love to look at you. I always think of what Gordon Prescott said. He said that you are God's perfect exercise in structural mathematics. And Vincent Knowlton said you're a spring morning. And Ellsworth—Ellsworth said you're a reproach to every other female shape on earth."

"And Ralston Holcombe?" she asked.

"Oh, never mind!" he snapped, and turned back to the fire.

I know why I can't stand the silence, he thought. It's because it makes no difference to her at all whether I speak or not; as if I didn't exist and never had existed . . . the thing more inconceivable than one's death—never to have been born. . . . He felt a sudden, desperate desire which he could identify—a desire to be real to her.

"Dominique, do you know what I've been thinking?" he asked eagerly.

"No. What have you been thinking?"

"I've thought of it for some time—all by *myself*—I haven't mentioned it to anyone. And nobody suggested it. It's my own idea."

"Why, that's fine. What is it?"

"I think I'd like to move to the country and build a house of our own. Would you like that?"

"I'd like it very much. Just as much as you would. You want to design a home for yourself?"

"Hell, no. Bennett will dash one off for me. He does all our country homes. He's a whiz at it."

"Will you like commuting?"

"No, I think that will be quite an awful nuisance. But you know, everybody that's anybody commutes nowadays. I always feel like a damn proletarian when I have to admit that I live in the city."

"Will you like to see trees and a garden and the earth around you?"

"Oh, that's a lot of nonsense. When will I have the time? A tree's a tree. When you've seen a newsreel of the woods in spring, you've seen it all."

"Will you like to do some gardening? People say it's very nice, working the soil yourself."

"Good God, no! What kind of grounds do you think we'd have? We can afford a gardener, and a good one—so the place will be something for the neighbors to admire."

"Will you like to take up some sport?"

"Yes, I'll like that."

"Which one?"

"I think I'll do better with my golf. You know, belonging to a country club right where you're one of the leading citizens in the community is different from occasional week ends. And the people you meet are different. Much higher class. And the contacts you make . . ." He caught himself, and added angrily: "Also, I'll take up horseback riding."

"I like horseback riding. Do you?"

"I've never had much time for it. Well, it does shake your insides unmercifully. But who the hell is Gordon Prescott to think he's the only he-man on earth and plaster his photo in riding clothes right in his reception room?"

"I suppose you will want to find some privacy?"

"Well, I don't believe in that desert-island stuff. I think the house should stand in sight of a major highway, so people would point it out, you know, the Keating estate. Who the hell is Claude Stengel to have a country home while I live in a rented flat? He started out about the same time I did, and look where he is and where I am, why, he's lucky if two and a half men ever heard of him, so why should he park himself in Westchester and . . ."

And he stopped. She sat looking at him, her face serene.

"Oh God damn it!" he cried. "If you don't want to move to the country, why don't you just say so?"

"I want very much to do anything you want, Peter. To follow any idea you get all by yourself."

He remained silent for a long time.

"What do we do tomorrow night?" he asked, before he could stop himself.

She rose, walked to a desk and picked up her calendar.

"We have the Palmers for dinner tomorrow night," she said.

"Oh, Christ!" he moaned. "They're such awful bores! Why do we have to have them?"

She stood holding the calendar forward between the tips of her fingers, as if she were a photograph with the focus on the calendar and her own figure blurred in its background.

"We have to have the Palmers," she said, "so that we can get the commission for their new store building. We have to get that commission so that we can entertain the Eddingtons for dinner on Saturday. The Eddingtons have no commissions to give, but they're in the Social Register. The Palmers bore you and the Eddingtons snub you. But you have to flatter people whom you despise in order to impress other people who despise you."

"Why do you have to say things like that?"

"Would you like to look at this calendar, Peter?"

"Well, that's what everybody does. That's what everybody lives for."

"Yes, Peter. Almost everybody."

"If you don't approve, why don't you say so?"

"Have I said anything about not approving?"

He thought back carefully. "No," he admitted. "No, you haven't. . . . But it's the way you put things."

"Would you rather I put it in a more involved way—as I did about Vincent Knowlton?"

"I'd rather . . ." Then he cried: "I'd rather you'd express an opinion, God damn it, just once!"

She asked, in the same level monotone: "Whose opinion, Peter? Gordon Prescott's? Ralston Holcombe's? Ellsworth Toohey's?"

He turned to her, leaning on the arm of his chair, half rising, suddenly tense. The thing between them was beginning to take shape. He had a first hint of words that would name it.

"Dominique," he said, softly, reasonably, "that's it. Now I know. I know what's been the matter all the time."

"Has anything been the matter?"

"Wait. This is terribly important. Dominique, you've never said, not once, what you thought. Not about anything. You've never expressed a desire. Not of any kind."

"What's wrong about that?"

"But it's . . . it's like death. You're not real. You're only a body. Look, Dominique, you don't know it, I'll try to explain. You understand what death is? When a body can't move any more, when it has no . . . no will, no meaning. You understand? Nothing. The absolute nothing. Well, your body moves—but that's all. The other, the thing inside you, your—oh, don't misunderstand me, I'm not talking religion, but there's no other word for it, so I'll say: your soul—your soul doesn't exist. No will, no meaning. There's no real *you* any more."

"What's the real me?" she asked. For the first time, she looked attentive; not compassionate; but, at least, attentive.

"What's the real anyone?" he said, encouraged. "It's not just the body. It's . . . it's the soul."

"What is the soul?"

"It's—you. The thing inside you."

"The thing that thinks and values and makes decisions?"

"Yes! Yes, that's it. And the thing that feels. You've—you've given it up."

"So there are two things that one can't give up: one's thoughts and one's desires?"

"Yes! Oh, you do understand! So you see, you're like a corpse to everybody around you. A kind of walking death. That's worse than any active crime. It's . . . ."

"Negation?"

"Yes. Just blank negation. You're not here. You've never been here. If you'd tell me that the curtains in this room are ghastly and if you'd rip them off and put up some you like—something of you would be real, here, in this room. But you never have. You've never told the cook what dessert you liked for dinner. You're not here, Dominique. You're not alive. Where's your I?"

"Where's yours, Peter?" she asked quietly.

He sat still, his eyes wide. She knew that his thoughts, in this moment, were clear and immediate like visual perception, that the act of thinking was an act of seeing a procession of years behind him.

"It's not true," he said at last, his voice hollow. "It's not true."

"What is not true?"

"What you said."

"I've said nothing. I asked you a question."

His eyes were begging her to speak, to deny. She rose, stood before him, and the taut erectness of her body was a sign of life, the life he had missed and begged for, a positive quality of purpose, but the quality of a judge.

"You're beginning to see, aren't you, Peter? Shall I make it clearer? You never wanted me to be real. You never wanted anyone to be. But you didn't want me to show it. You wanted an act to help your act—a beautiful, complicated act, all twists, trimmings and words. All words. You didn't like what I said about Vincent Knowlton. You liked it when I said the same thing under cover of virtuous sentiments. You didn't want me to believe. You only wanted me to convince you that I believed. My real soul, Peter? It's real only when it's independent—you've discovered that, haven't you? It's real only when it chooses curtains and desserts—you're right about that—curtains, desserts and religions, Peter, and the shapes of buildings. But you've never wanted that. You wanted a mirror. People want nothing but mirrors around them. To reflect them while they're reflecting too. You know, like the senseless infinity you get from two mirrors facing each other across a narrow passage. Usually in the more vulgar kind of hotels. Reflections of reflections and echoes of echoes. No beginning and no end. No center and no purpose. I gave you what you wanted. I became what you are, what your friends are, what most of humanity is so busy being—only without the trimmings. I didn't go around spouting book reviews to hide my emptiness of judgment—I said I had no judgment. I didn't borrow designs to hide my creative impotence—I created nothing. I didn't say that equality is a noble conception and unity the chief goal of mankind—I just agreed with everybody. You call it death, Peter? That kind of death—I've imposed it on you and on everyone around us. But you—you haven't done that. People are comfortable with you, they like you, they enjoy your presence. You've spared them the blank death. Because you've imposed it—on yourself."

He said nothing. She walked away from him, and sat down again, waiting.

He got up. He made a few steps toward her. He said: "Dominique . . ."

Then he was on his knees before her, clutching her, his head buried against her legs.

"Dominique, it's not true—that I never loved you. I love you, I always have, it was not . . . just to show the others—that was not all—I loved you. There were two people—you and another person, a man, who always made me feel the same thing—not fear exactly, but like a wall, a steep wall to climb—like a command to rise—I don't know where—but a feeling going up—I've always hated that man—but you, I wanted you—always—that's why I married you—when I knew you despised me—so you should have forgiven me that marriage—you shouldn't have taken your revenge like this—not like this, Dominique—Dominique, I can't fight back, I——"

"Who is the man you hated, Peter?"

"It doesn't matter."

"Who is he?"

"Nobody. I . . ."

"Name him."

"Howard Roark."

She said nothing for a long time. Then she put her hand on his hair. The gesture had the form of gentleness.

"I never wanted to take a revenge on you, Peter," she said softly.

"Then—why?"

"I married you for my own reasons. I acted as the world demands one should act. Only I can do nothing halfway. Those who can, have a fissure somewhere inside. Most people have many. They lie to themselves—not to know that. I've never lied to myself. So I had to do what you all do—only consistently and completely. I've probably destroyed you. If I could care, I'd say I'm sorry. That was not my purpose."

"Dominique, I love you. But I'm afraid. Because you've changed something in me, ever since our wedding, since I said yes to you—even if I were to lose you now, I couldn't go back to what I was before—you took something I had . . ."

"No. I took something you never had. I grant you that's worse."

"What?"

"It's said that the worst thing one can do to a man is to kill his self-respect. But that's not true. Self-respect is something that can't be killed. The worst thing is to kill a man's pretense at it."

"Dominique, I . . . I don't want to talk."

She looked down at his face resting against her knees, and he saw pity in her eyes, and for one moment he knew what a dreadful thing true pity is, but he kept no knowledge of it, because he slammed his mind shut before the words in which he was about to preserve it.

She bent down and kissed his forehead. It was the first kiss she had ever given him.

"I don't want you to suffer, Peter," she said gently. "This, now, is real—it's I—it's my own words—I don't want you to suffer—I can't feel anything else—but I feel that much."

He pressed his lips to her hand.

When he raised his head, she looked at him as if, for a moment, he was her husband. She said: "Peter, if you could hold on to it—to what you are now——"

"I love you," he said.

They sat silently together for a long time. He felt no strain in the silence.

The telephone rang.

It was not the sound that destroyed the moment; it was the eagerness with which Keating jumped up and ran to answer it. She heard his voice through the open door, a voice indecent in its relief:

"Hello? . . . Oh, *hello*, Ellsworth! . . . No, not a thing. . . . Free as a lark. . . . Sure, come over, come *right* over! . . . Okey-doke!"

"It's Ellsworth," he said, returning to the living room. His voice was gay and it had a touch of insolence. "He wants to drop in."

She said nothing.

He busied himself emptying ash trays that contained a single match or one butt, gathering newspapers, adding a log to the fire that did not need it, lighting more lamps. He whistled a tune from a screen operetta.

He ran to open the door when he heard the bell.

"How nice," said Toohey, coming in. "A fire and just the two of you. Hello, Dominique. Hope I'm not intruding."

"Hello, Ellsworth," she said.

"You're never intruding," said Keating. "I can't tell you how glad I am to see you." He pushed a chair to the fire. "Sit down here, Ellsworth. What'll you have? You know, when I heard your voice on the phone . . . well, I wanted to jump and yelp like a pup."

"Don't wag your tail, though," said Toohey. "No, no drinks, thanks. How have you been, Dominique?"

"Just as I was a year ago," she said.

"But not as you were two years ago?"

"No."

"What did we do two years ago this time?" Keating asked idly.

"You weren't married," said Toohey. "Prehistorical period. Let me see—what happened then? I think the Stoddard Temple was just being completed."

"Oh that," said Keating.

Toohey asked: "Hear anything about your friend Roark . . . Peter?"

"No. I don't think he's worked for a year or more. He's finished, this time."

"Yes, I think so. . . . What have you been doing, Peter?"

"Nothing much. . . . Oh, I've just read *The Gallant Gallstone*."

"Liked it?"

"Yes! You know, I think it's a very important book. Because it's true that there's no such thing as free will. We can't help what we are or what we do. It's not our fault. Nobody's to blame for anything. It's all in your background and . . . and your glands. If you're good, that's no achievement of yours—you were just lucky in your glands. If you're rotten, nobody should punish you—you were unlucky, that's all." He was saying it defiantly, with a violence inappropriate to a literary discussion. He was not looking at Toohey nor at Dominique, but speaking to the room and to what that room had witnessed.

"Substantially correct," said Toohey. "To be logical, however, we should not think of punishment for those who are rotten. Since they suffered through no fault of their own, since they were unlucky and underendowed, they should deserve a compensation of some sort—more like a reward."

"Why—yes!" cried Keating. "That's . . . that's logical."

"And just," said Toohey.

"Got the *Banner* pretty much where you want it, Ellsworth?" asked Dominique.

"What's that in reference to?"

"The Gallant Gallstone."

"Oh. No, I can't say I have. Not quite. There are always the—imponderables."

"What are you talking about?" asked Keating.

"Professional gossip," said Toohey. He stretched his hands to the fire and flexed his fingers playfully. "By the way, Peter, are you doing anything about Stoneridge?"

"God damn it," said Keating.

"What's the matter?"

"You know what's the matter. You know the bastard better than I do. To have a project like that going up, now, when its manna in the desert, and of all people to have that son of a bitch Wynand doing it!"

"What's the matter with Mr. Wynand?"

"Oh come, Ellsworth! You know very well if it were anyone else, I'd get that commission just like that"—he snapped his fingers—"I wouldn't even have to ask, the owner'd come to me. Particularly when he knows that an architect like me is practically sitting on his fanny now, compared to the work our office could handle. But Mr. Gail Wynand! You'd think he was a holy Lama who's just allergic to the air breathed by architects!"

"I gather you've tried?"

"Oh, don't talk about it. It makes me sick. I think I've spent three hundred dollars feeding lunches and pouring liquor into all sorts of crappy people who said they could get me to meet him. All I got is hangovers. I think it'd be easier to meet the Pope."

"I gather you do want to get Stoneridge?"

"Are you baiting me, Ellsworth? I'd give my right arm for it."

"That wouldn't be advisable. You couldn't make any drawings then—or pretend to. It would be preferable to give up something less tangible."

"I'd give my soul."

"Would you, Peter?" asked Dominique.

"What's on your mind, Ellsworth?" Keating snapped.

"Just a practical suggestion," said Toohey. "Who has been your most effective salesman in the past and got you some of your best commissions?"

"Why—Dominique I guess."

"That's right. And since you can't get to Wynand and it wouldn't do you any good if you did, don't you think Dominique is the one who'll be able to persuade him?"

Keating stared at him. "Are you crazy, Ellsworth?"

Dominique leaned forward. She seemed interested.

"From what I've heard," she said, "Gail Wynand does not do favors for a woman, unless she's beautiful. And if she's beautiful, he doesn't do it as a favor."

Toohey looked at her, underscoring the fact that he offered no denial.

"It's silly," snapped Keating angrily. "How would Dominique ever get to see him?"

"By telephoning his office and making an appointment," said Toohey.

"Who ever told you he'd grant it?"

"He did."

"When?!"

"Late last night. Or early this morning, to be exact."

"Ellsworth!" gasped Keating. He added: "I don't believe it."

"I do," said Dominique, "or Ellsworth wouldn't have started this conversation." She smiled at Toohey. "So Wynand promised you to see me?"

"Yes, my dear."

"How did you work that?"

"Oh, I offered him a convincing argument. However, it would be advisable not to delay it. You should telephone him tomorrow—if you wish to do it."

"Why can't she telephone now?" said Keating. "Oh, I guess it's too late. You'll telephone first thing in the morning."

She looked at him, her eyes half closed, and said nothing.

"It's a long time since you've taken any active interest in Peter's career," said Toohey. "Wouldn't you like to undertake a difficult feat like that—for Peter's sake?"

"If Peter wants me to."

"If I want you to?" cried Keating. "Are you both crazy? It's the chance of a lifetime, the . . ." He saw them both looking at him curiously. He snapped: "Oh, rubbish!"

"What is rubbish, Peter?" asked Dominique.

"Are you going to be stopped by a lot of fool gossip? Why, any other architect's wife'd crawl on her hands and knees for a chance like that to . . ."

"No other architect's wife would be offered the chance," said Toohey. "No other architect has a wife like Dominique. You've always been so proud of that, Peter."

"Dominique can take care of herself in any circumstances."

"There's no doubt about that."

"All right, Ellsworth," said Dominique. "I'll telephone Wynand tomorrow."

"Ellsworth, you're wonderful!" said Keating, not looking at her.

"I believe I'd like a drink now," said Toohey. "We should celebrate."

When Keating hurried out to the kitchen, Toohey and Dominique looked at each other. He smiled. He glanced at the door through which Keating had gone, then nodded to her faintly, amused.

"You expected it," said Dominique.

"Of course."

"Now what's the real purpose, Ellsworth?"

"Why, I want to help you get Stoneridge for Peter. It's really a terrific commission."

"Why are you so anxious to have me sleep with Wynand?"

"Don't you think it would be an interesting experience for all concerned?"

"You're not satisfied with the way my marriage has turned out, are you, Ellsworth?"

"Not entirely. Just about fifty percent. Well, nothing's perfect in this world. One gathers what one can and then one tries further."

"You were very anxious to have Peter marry me. You knew what the result would be, better than Peter or I."

"Peter didn't know it at all."

"Well, it worked—fifty percent. You got Peter Keating where you wanted him—the leading architect of the country who's now mud clinging to your galoshes."

"I've never liked your style of expression, but it's always been accurate. I should have said: who's now a soul wagging its tail. Your style is gentler."

"But the other fifty percent, Ellsworth? A failure?"

"Approximately total. My fault. I should have known better than to expect anyone like Peter Keating, even in the role of husband, to destroy you."

"Well, you're frank."

"I told you once it's the only method that will work with you. Besides, surely it didn't take you two years to discover what I wanted of that marriage?"

"So you think Gail Wynand will finish the job?"

"Might. What do you think?"

"I think I'm only a side issue again. Didn't you call it 'gravy' once? What have you got against Wynand?"

He laughed; the sound betrayed that he had not expected the question. She said contemptuously: "Don't show that you're shocked, Ellsworth."

"All right. We're taking it straight. I have nothing specific against Mr. Gail Wynand. I've been planning to have him meet you, for a long time. If you want minor details, he did something that annoyed me yesterday morning. He's too observant. So I decided the time was right."

"And there was Stoneridge."

"And there was Stoneridge. I knew that part of it would appeal to you. You'd never sell yourself to save your country, your soul or the life of a man you loved. But you'll sell yourself to get a commission he doesn't deserve for Peter Keating. See what will be left of you afterward. Or of Gail Wynand. I'll be interested to see it, too."

"Quite correct, Ellsworth."

"All of it? Even the part about a man you loved—if you did?"

"Yes."

"You wouldn't sell yourself for Roark? Though, of course, you don't like to hear that name pronounced."

"Howard Roark," she said evenly.

"You have a great deal of courage, Dominique."

Keating returned, carrying a tray of cocktails. His eyes were feverish and he made too many gestures.

Toohey raised his glass. He said:

"To Gail Wynand and the New York *Banner!*"

III

GAIL WYNAND ROSE AND MET HER HALFWAY ACROSS HIS OFFICE.
"How do you do, Mrs. Keating," he said.

"How do you do, Mr. Wynand," said Dominique.

He moved a chair for her, but when she sat down he did not cross to sit behind his desk, he stood studying her professionally, appraisingly. His manner implied a self-evident necessity, as if his reason were known to her and there could be nothing improper in this behavior.

"You look like a stylized version of your own stylized version," he said. "As a rule seeing the models of art works tends to make one atheistic. But this time it's a close one between that sculptor and God."

"What sculptor?"

"The one who did that statue of you."

He had felt that there was some story behind that statue and he became certain of it now, by something in her face, a tightening that contradicted, for a second, the trim indifference of her self-control.

"Where and when did you see that statue, Mr. Wynand?"

"In my art gallery, this morning."

"Where did you get it?"

It was his turn to show perplexity. "But don't you know that?"

"No."

"Your friend Ellsworth Toohey sent it to me. As a present."

"To get this appointment for me?"

"Not through as direct a motivation as I believe you're thinking. But in substance—yes."

"He hasn't told me that."

"Do you mind my having that statue?"

"Not particularly."

"I expected you to say that you were delighted."

"I'm not."

He sat down, informally, on the outer edge of his desk, his legs stretched out, his ankles crossed. He asked:

"I gather you lost track of that statue and have been trying to find it?"

"For two years."

"You can't have it." He added, watching her: "You might have Stoneridge."

"I shall change my mind. I'm delighted that Toohey gave it to you."

He felt a bitter little stab of triumph—and of disappointment, in

449

thinking that he could read her mind and that her mind was obvious, after all. He asked:

"Because it gave you this interview?"

"No. Because you're the person before last in the world whom I'd like to have that statue. But Toohey is last."

He lost the triumph; it was not a thing which a woman intent on Stoneridge should have said or thought. He asked:

"You didn't know that Toohey had it?"

"No."

"We should get together on our mutual friend, Mr. Ellsworth Toohey. I don't like being a pawn and I don't think you do or could ever be made to. There are too many things Mr. Toohey chose not to tell. The name of that sculptor, for instance."

"He didn't tell you that?"

"No."

"Steven Mallory."

"Mallory? . . . Not the one who tried to . . ." He laughed aloud.

"What's the matter?"

"Toohey told me he couldn't remember the name. *That* name."

"Does Mr. Toohey still astonish you?"

"He has, several times, in the last few days. There's a special kind of subtlety in being as blatant as he's been. A very difficult kind. I almost like his artistry."

"I don't share your taste."

"Not in any field? Not in sculpture—or architecture?"

"I'm sure not in architecture."

"Isn't that the utterly wrong thing for you to say?"

"Probably."

He looked at her. He said: "You're interesting."

"I didn't intend to be."

"That's your third mistake."

"Third?"

"The first was about Mr. Toohey. In the circumstances, one would expect you to praise him to me. To quote him. To lean on his great prestige in matters of architecture."

"But one would expect you to know Ellsworth Toohey. That should disqualify any quotations."

"I intended to say that to you—had you given me the chance you won't give me."

"That should make it more entertaining."

"You expected to be entertained?"

"I am."

"About the statue?" It was the only point of weakness he had discovered.

"No." Her voice was hard. "Not about the statue."

"Tell me, when was it made and for whom?"

"Is that another thing Mr. Toohey forgot?"

"Apparently."

"Do you remember a scandal about a building called the Stoddard Temple? Two years ago. You were away at the time."

"The Stoddard Temple. . . . How do you happen to know where I was two years ago? . . . Wait, the Stoddard Temple. I remember: a sacrilegious church or some such object that gave the Bible brigade a howling spree."

"Yes."

"There was . . ." He stopped. His voice sounded hard and reluctant—like hers. "There was the statue of a naked woman involved."

"Yes."

"I see."

He was silent for a moment. Then he said, his voice harsh, as if he were holding back some anger whose object she could not guess:

"I was somewhere around Bali at the time. I'm sorry all New York saw that statue before I did. But I don't read newspapers when I'm sailing. There's a standing order to fire any man who brings a Wynand paper aboard the yacht."

"Have you ever seen pictures of the Stoddard Temple?"

"No. Was the building worth the statue?"

"The statue was almost worthy of the building."

"It has been destroyed, hasn't it?"

"Yes. With the help of the Wynand papers."

He shrugged. "I remember Alvah Scarret had a good time with it. A big story. Sorry I missed it. But Alvah did very well. Incidentally, how did you know that I was away and why has the fact of my absence remained in your memory?"

"It was the story that cost me my job with you."

"*Your* job? With *me?*"

"Didn't you know my name was Dominique Francon?"

Under the trim jacket his shoulders made a sagging movement forward; it was surprise—and helplessness. He stared at her, quite simply. After a while, he said:

"No."

She smiled indifferently. She said: "It appears that Toohey wanted to make it as difficult for both of us as he could."

"To hell with Toohey. This has to be understood. It doesn't make sense. You're Dominique Francon?"

"I was."

"You worked here, in this building, for years?"

"For six years."

"Why haven't I met you before?"

"I'm sure you don't meet every one of your employees."

"I think you understand what I mean."

"Do you wish me to state it for you?"

"Yes."

"Why haven't I tried to meet you before?"

"Yes."

"I had no desire to."

"That, precisely, doesn't make sense."

"Shall I let this go by or understand it?"

"I'll spare you the choice. With the kind of beauty you possess and with knowledge of the kind of reputation I am said to possess—why didn't you attempt to make a real career for yourself on the *Banner?*"

"I never wanted a real career on the *Banner.*"

"Why?"

"Perhaps for the same reason that makes you forbid Wynand papers on your yacht."

"It's a good reason," he said quietly. Then he asked, his voice casual again: "Let's see, what was it you did to get fired? You went against our policy, I believe?"

"I tried to defend the Stoddard Temple."

"Didn't you know better than to attempt sincerity on the *Banner?*"

"I intended to say that to you—if you'd given me the chance."

"Are you being entertained?"

"I wasn't, then. I liked working here."

"You're the only one who's ever said that in this building."

"I must be one of two."

"Who's the other?"

"Yourself, Mr. Wynand."

"Don't be too sure of that." Lifting his head, he saw the hint of amusement in her eyes and asked: "You said it just to trap me into that kind of a statement?"

"Yes, I think so," she answered placidly.

"Dominique Francon . . ." he repeated, not addressing her. "I used to like your stuff. I almost wish you were here to ask for your old job."

"I'm here to discuss Stoneridge."

"Ah, yes, of course." He settled back, to enjoy a long speech of persuasion. He thought it would be interesting to hear what arguments she'd choose and how she'd act in the role of petitioner. "Well, what do you wish to tell me about that?"

"I should like you to give that commission to my husband. I understand, of course, that there's no reason why you should do so—unless I agree to sleep with you in exchange. If you consider that a sufficient reason—I am willing to do it."

He looked at her silently, allowing no hint of personal reaction in his face. She sat looking up at him, faintly astonished by his scrutiny, as if her words had deserved no special attention. He could not force on himself, though he was seeking it fiercely, any other impression of her face than the incongruous one of undisturbed purity.

He said:

"That is what I was to suggest. But not so crudely and not on our first meeting."

"I have saved you time and lies."

"You love your husband very much?"

"I despise him."

"You have a great faith in his artistic genius?"

"I think he's a third-rate architect."

"Then why are you doing this?"

"It amuses me."

"I thought I was the only one who acted on such motives."

"You shouldn't mind. I don't believe you've ever found originality a desirable virtue, Mr. Wynand."

"Actually, you don't care whether your husband gets Stoneridge or not?"

"No."

"And you have no desire to sleep with me?"

"None at all."

"I could admire a woman who'd put on an act like that. Only it's not an act."

"It's not. Please don't begin admiring me. I have tried to avoid it."

Whenever he smiled no obvious movement was required of his facial muscles; the hint of mockery was always there and it merely came into sharper focus for a moment, to recede imperceptibly again. The focus was sharper now.

"As a matter of fact," he said, "your chief motive is I, after all. The desire to give yourself to me." He saw the glance she could not control and added: "No, don't enjoy the thought that I have fallen into so gross an error. I didn't mean it in the usual sense. But in its exact opposite. Didn't you say you considered me the person before last in the world? You don't want Stoneridge. You want to sell yourself for the lowest motive to the lowest person you can find."

"I didn't expect you to understand that," she said simply.

"You want—men do that sometimes, not women—to express through the sexual act your utter contempt for me."

"No, Mr. Wynand. For myself."

The thin line of his mouth moved faintly, as if his lips had caught the first hint of a personal revelation—an involuntary one and, therefore, a weakness—and were holding it tight while he spoke:

"Most people go to very great length in order to convince themselves of their self-respect."

"Yes."

"And, of course, a quest for self-respect is proof of its lack."

"Yes."

"Do you see the meaning of a quest for self-contempt?"

"That I lack it?"

"And that you'll never achieve it."

"I didn't expect you to understand that either."

"I won't say anything else—or I'll stop being the person before last in the world and I'll become unsuitable to your purpose." He rose. "Shall I tell you formally that I accept your offer?"

She inclined her head in agreement.

"As a matter of fact," he said, "I don't care whom I choose to build Stoneridge. I've never hired a good architect for any of the things I've built. I give the public what it wants. I was stuck for a choice this time, because I'm tired of the bunglers who've worked for me, and it's hard to decide without standards or reason. I'm sure you don't mind my saying this. I'm really grateful to you for giving me a much better motive than any I could hope to find."

"I'm glad you didn't say that you've always admired the work of Peter Keating."

"You didn't tell me how glad you were to join the distinguished list of Gail Wynand's mistresses."

"You may enjoy my admitting it, if you wish, but I think we'll get along very well together."

"Quite likely. At least, you've given me a new experience: to do what I've always done—but honestly. Shall I now begin to give you my orders? I won't pretend they're anything else."

"If you wish."

"You'll go with me for a two months' cruise on my yacht. We'll sail in ten days. When we come back, you'll be free to return to your husband —with the contract for Stoneridge."

"Very well."

"I should like to meet your husband. Will you both have dinner with me Monday night?"

"Yes, if you wish."

When she rose to leave, he asked:

"Shall I tell you the difference between you and your statue?"

"No."

"But I want to. It's startling to see the same elements used in two compositions with opposite themes. Everything about you in that statue is the theme of exaltation. But your own theme is suffering."

"Suffering? I'm not conscious of having shown that."

"You haven't. That's what I meant. No happy person can be quite so impervious to pain."

Wynand telephoned his art dealer and asked him to arrange a private showing of Steven Mallory's work. He refused to meet Mallory in person; he never met those whose work he liked. The art dealer executed the order in great haste. Wynand bought five of the pieces he saw—and paid more than the dealer had hoped to ask. "Mr. Mallory would like to know," said the dealer, "what brought him to your attention." "I saw one of his works." "Which one?" "It doesn't matter."

Toohey had expected Wynand to call for him after the interview with Dominique. Wynand had not called. But a few days later, meeting Toohey by chance in the city room, Wynand asked aloud:

"Mr. Toohey, have so many people tried to kill you that you can't remember their names?"

Toohey smiled and said: "I'm sure quite so many would like to."

"You flatter your fellow men," said Wynand, walking away.

Peter Keating stared at the brilliant room of the restaurant. It was the most exclusive place in town, and the most expensive. Keating gloated, chewing the thought that he was here as the guest of Gail Wynand.

He tried not to stare at the gracious elegance of Wynand's figure across the table. He blessed Wynand for having chosen to give this dinner in a public place. People were gaping at Wynand—discreetly and with practiced camouflage, but gaping nevertheless—and their attention included the two guests at Wynand's table.

Dominique sat between the two men. She wore a white silk dress with long sleeves and a cowl neck, a nun's garment that acquired the startling effect of an evening gown only by being so flagrantly unsuited to that purpose. She wore no jewelry. Her gold hair looked like a hood. The dull white silk moved in angular planes with the movements of her body, revealing it in a manner of cold innocence, the body of a sacrificial object publicly offered, beyond the need of concealment or desire. Keating found it unattractive. He noticed that Wynand seemed to admire it.

Someone at a distant table stared in their direction insistently, someone tall and bulky. Then the big shape rose to its feet—and Keating recognized Ralston Holcombe hurrying toward them.

"Peter, my boy, so glad to see you," boomed Holcombe, shaking his hand, bowing to Dominique, conspicuously ignoring Wynand. "Where have you been hiding? Why don't we see you around any more?" They had had luncheon together three days ago.

Wynand had risen and stood leaning forward a little, courteously. Keating hesitated; then, with obvious reluctance, said:

"Mr. Wynand—Mr. Holcombe."

"Not Mr. Gail Wynand?" said Holcombe, with splendid innocence.

"Mr. Holcombe, if you saw one of the cough-drop Smith brothers in real life, would you recognize him?" asked Wynand.

"Why—I guess so," said Holcombe, blinking.

"My face, Mr. Holcombe, is just as much of a public bromide."

Holcombe muttered a few benevolent generalities and escaped.

Wynand smiled affectionately. "You didn't have to be afraid of introducing Mr. Holcombe to me, Mr. Keating, even though he is an architect."

"Afraid, Mr. Wynand?"

"Unnecessarily, since it's all settled. Hasn't Mrs. Keating told you that Stoneridge is yours?"

"I . . . no, she hasn't told me . . . I didn't know. . . ." Wynand was smiling, but the smile remained fixed, and Keating felt compelled to go on talking until some sign stopped him. "I hadn't quite hoped . . . not so soon . . . of course, I thought this dinner might be a sign . . . help you to decide . . ." He blurted out involuntarily: "Do you always throw surprises like that—just like that?"

"Whenever I can," said Wynand gravely.

"I shall do my best to deserve this honor and live up to your expectations, Mr. Wynand."

"I have no doubt about that," said Wynand.

He had said little to Dominique tonight. His full attention seemed centered on Keating.

"The public has been kind to my past endeavors," said Keating, "but I shall make Stoneridge my best achievement."

"That is quite a promise, considering the distinguished list of your works."

"I had not hoped that my works were of sufficient importance to attract your attention, Mr. Wynand."

"But I know them quite well. The Cosmo-Slotnick Building, which is pure Michelangelo." Keating's face spread in incredulous pleasure; he knew that Wynand was a great authority on art and would not make such comparisons lightly. "The Prudential Bank Building, which is genuine Palladio. The Slottern Department Store, which is snitched Christopher Wren." Keating's face had changed. "Look what an illustrious company I get for the price of one. Isn't it quite a bargain?"

Keating smiled, his face tight, and said:

"I've heard about your brilliant sense of humor, Mr. Wynand."

"Have you heard about my descriptive style?"

"What do you mean?"

Wynand half turned in his chair and looked at Dominique, as if he were inspecting an inanimate object.

"Your wife has a lovely body, Mr. Keating. Her shoulders are too thin, but admirably in scale with the rest of her. Her legs are too long, but that gives her the elegance of line you'll find in a good yacht. Her breasts are beautiful, don't you think?"

"Architecture is a crude profession, Mr. Wynand," Keating tried to laugh. "It doesn't prepare one for the superior sort of sophistication."

"You don't understand me, Mr. Keating?"

"If I didn't know you were a perfect gentleman, I might misunderstand it, but you can't fool me."

"That is just what I am trying not to do."

"I appreciate compliments, Mr. Wynand, but I'm not conceited enough to think that we must talk about my wife."

"Why not, Mr. Keating? It is considered good form to talk of the things one has—or will have—in common."

"Mr. Wynand, I . . . I don't understand."

"Shall I be more explicit?"

"No, I . . ."

"No? Shall we drop the subject of Stoneridge?"

"Oh, let's talk about Stoneridge! I . . ."

"But we are, Mr. Keating."

Keating looked at the room about them. He thought that things like this could not be done in such a place; the fastidious magnificence made it monstrous; he wished it were a dank cellar. He thought: blood on paving stones—all right, but not blood on a drawing-room rug. . . .

"Now I know this is a joke, Mr. Wynand," he said.

"It is my turn to admire your sense of humor, Mr. Keating."

"Things like . . . like this aren't being done . . ."

"That's not what you mean at all, Mr. Keating. You mean, they're being done all the time, but not talked about."

"I didn't think . . ."

"You thought it before you came here. You didn't mind. I grant you I'm behaving abominably. I'm breaking all the rules of charity. It's extremely cruel to be honest."

"Please, Mr. Wynand, let's . . . drop it. I don't know what . . . I'm supposed to do."

"That's simple. You're supposed to slap my face." Keating giggled. "You were supposed to do that several minutes ago."

Keating noticed that his palms were wet and that he was trying to support his weight by holding on to the napkin on his lap. Wynand and Dominique were eating, slowly and graciously, as if they were at another table. Keating thought that they were not human bodies, either one of them; something had vanished; the light of the crystal fixtures in the room was the radiance of X-rays that ate through, not to the bones, but deeper; they were souls, he thought, sitting at a dinner table, souls held within evening clothes, lacking the intermediate shape of flesh, terrifying in naked revelation—terrifying, because he expected to see torturers, but saw a great innocence. He wondered what they saw, what his own clothes contained if his physical shape had gone.

"No?" said Wynand. "You don't want to do that, Mr. Keating? But of course you don't have to. Just say that you don't want any of it. I won't mind. There's Mr. Ralston Holcombe across the room. He can build Stoneridge as well as you could."

"I don't know what you mean, Mr. Wynand," whispered Keating. His eyes were fixed upon the tomato aspic on his salad plate; it was soft and shivering; it made him sick.

Wynand turned to Dominique.

"Do you remember our conversation about a certain quest, Mrs. Keating? I said it was a quest at which you would never succeed. Look at your husband. He's an expert—without effort. That is the way to go about it. Match that, sometime. Don't bother to tell me that you can't. I know it. You're an amateur, my dear."

Keating thought that he must speak again, but he couldn't, not as long as that salad was there before him. The terror came from that plate, not from the fastidious monster across the table; the rest of the room was warm and safe. He lurched forward and his elbow swept the plate off the table.

He made a kind of sound expressing regrets. Somebody's shape came up, there were polite voices of apology, and the mess vanished from the carpet.

Keating heard a voice saying: "Why are you doing this?" saw two faces turned to him and knew that he had said it.

"Mr. Wynand is not doing it to torture you, Peter," said Dominique calmly. "He's doing it for me. To see how much I can take."

"That's true, Mrs. Keating," said Wynand. "Partly true. The other part is: to justify myself."

"In whose eyes?"

"Yours. And my own, perhaps."

"Do you need to?"

"Sometimes. The *Banner* is a contemptible paper, isn't it? Well, I have paid with my honor for the privilege of holding a position where I can amuse myself by observing how honor operates in other men."

His own clothes, thought Keating, contained nothing now, because the two faces did not notice him any longer. He was safe; his place at that table was empty. He wondered, from a great, indifferent distance, why the two were looking at each other quietly, not like enemies, not like fellow executioners, but like comrades.

Two days before they were to sail, Wynand telephoned Dominique late in the evening.

"Could you come over right now?" he asked, and hearing a moment's silence, added: "Oh, not what you're thinking. I live up to my agreements. You'll be quite safe. I just would like to see you tonight."

"All right," she said, and was astonished to hear a quiet: "Thank you."

When the elevator door slid open in the private lobby of his penthouse, he was waiting there, but did not let her step out. He joined her in the elevator.

"I don't want you to enter my house," he said. "We're going to the floor below."

The elevator operator looked at him, amazed.

The car stopped and opened before a locked door. Wynand unlocked it and let her step out first, following her into the art gallery. She remembered that this was the place no outsider ever entered. She said nothing. He offered no explanation.

For hours she walked silently through the vast rooms, looking at the incredible treasures of beauty. There was a deep carpet and no sound of steps, no sounds from the city outside, no windows. He followed her, stopping when she stopped. His eyes went with hers from object to object. At times his glance moved to her face. She passed, without stopping, by the statue from the Stoddard Temple.

He did not urge her to stay nor to hurry, as if he had turned the place over to her. She decided when she wished to leave, and he followed her to the door. Then she asked:

"Why did you want me to see this? It won't make me think better of you. Worse, perhaps."

"Yes, I'd expect that," he said quietly, "if I had thought of it that way. But I didn't. I just wanted you to see it."

IV

THE SUN HAD SET WHEN THEY STEPPED OUT OF THE CAR. IN THE spread of sky and sea, a green sky over a sheet of mercury, tracings of fire remained at the edges of the clouds and in the brass fittings of the yacht. The yacht was like a white streak of motion, a sensitive body strained against the curb of stillness.

Dominique looked at the gold letters—*I Do*—on the delicate white bow.

"What does that name mean?" she asked.

"It's an answer," said Wynand, "to people long since dead. Though perhaps they are the only immortal ones. You see, the sentence I heard most often in my childhood was 'You don't run things around here.' "

She remembered hearing that he had never answered this question before. He had answered her at once; he had not seemed conscious of making an exception. She felt a sense of calm in his manner, strange and new to him, an air of quiet finality.

When they went aboard, the yacht started moving, almost as if Wynand's steps on deck had served as contact. He stood at the rail, not touching her, he looked at the long, brown shore that rose and fell against the sky, moving away from them. Then he turned to her. She saw no new recognition in his eyes, no beginning, but only the continuation of a glance—as if he had been looking at her all the time.

When they went below he walked with her into her cabin. He said: "Please let me know if there's anything you wish," and walked out through an inside door. She saw that it led to his bedroom. He closed the door and did not return.

She moved idly across the cabin. A smear of reflection followed her on the lustrous surfaces of the pale satinwood paneling. She stretched out in a low armchair, her ankles crossed, her arms thrown behind her head, and watched the porthole turning from green to a dark blue. She moved her hand, switched on a light; the blue vanished and became a glazed black circle.

The steward announced dinner. Wynand knocked at her door and accompanied her to the dining salon. His manner puzzled her: it was gay, but the sense of calm in the gaiety suggested a peculiar earnestness.

She asked, when they were seated at the table:

"Why did you leave me alone?"

"I thought you might want to be alone."

"To get used to the idea?"

"If you wish to put it that way."

"I was used to it before I came to your office."

"Yes, of course. Forgive me for implying any weakness in you. I know better. By the way, you haven't asked me where we're going."

"That, too, would be weakness."

"True. I'm glad you don't care. Because I never have any definite destination. This ship is not for going to places, but for getting away from them. When I stop at a port, it's only for the sheer pleasure of leaving it. I always think: Here's one more spot that can't hold me."

"I used to travel a great deal. I always felt just like that. I've been told it's because I'm a hater of mankind."

"You're not foolish enough to believe that, are you?"

"I don't know."

"Surely you've seen through that particular stupidity. I mean the one that claims the pig is the symbol of love for humanity—the creature that accepts anything. As a matter of fact, the person who loves everybody and feels at home everywhere is the true hater of mankind. He expects nothing of men, so no form of depravity can outrage him."

"You mean the person who says that there's some good in the worst of us?"

"I mean the person who has the filthy insolence to claim that he loves equally the man who made that statue of you and the man who makes a Mickey Mouse balloon to sell on street corners. I mean the person who loves the men who prefer the Mickey Mouse to your statue—and there are many of that kind. I mean the person who loves Joan of Arc and the salesgirls in dress shops on Broadway—with an equal fervor. I mean the person who loves your beauty and the women he sees in a subway—the kind that can't cross their knees and show flesh hanging publicly over their garters—with the same sense of exaltation. I mean the person who loves the clean, steady, unfrightened eyes of man looking through a telescope and the white stare of an imbecile—equally. I mean quite a large, generous, magnanimous company. Is it you who hate mankind, Mrs. Keating?"

"You're saying all the things that—since I can remember—since I began to see and think—have been . . ." She stopped.

"Have been torturing you. Of course. One can't love man without hating most of the creatures who pretend to bear his name. It's one or the other. One doesn't love God and sacrilege impartially. Except when one doesn't know that sacrilege has been committed. Because one doesn't know God."

"What will you say if I give you the answer people usually give me—that love is forgiveness?"

"I'll say it's an indecency of which you're not capable—even though you think you're an expert in such matters."

"Or that love is pity."

"Oh, keep still. It's bad enough to hear things like that. To hear them from you is revolting—even as a joke."

"What's your answer?"

"That love is reverence, and worship, and glory, and the upward glance. Not a bandage for dirty sores. But they don't know it. Those who speak of love most promiscuously are the ones who've never felt it. They make some sort of feeble stew out of sympathy, compassion, contempt and general indifference, and they call it love. Once you've felt what it means to love as you and I know it—the total passion for the total height—you're incapable of anything less."

"As—you and I—know it?"

"It's what we feel when we look at a thing like your statue. There's no forgiveness in that, and no pity. And I'd want to kill the man who claims that there should be. But, you see, when he looks at your statue—he feels nothing. That—or a dog with a broken paw—it's all the same to him. He even feels that he's done something nobler by bandaging the dog's paw than by looking at your statue. So if you seek a glimpse of greatness, if you want exaltation, if you ask for God and refuse to accept the washing of wounds as substitute—you're called a hater of humanity, Mrs. Keating, because you've committed the crime of knowing a love humanity has not learned to deserve."

"Mr. Wynand, have you read what I got fired for?"

"No. I didn't then. I don't dare to now."

"Why?"

He ignored the question. He said, smiling: "And so, you came to me and said 'You're the vilest person on earth—take me so that I'll learn self-contempt. I lack that which most people live by. They find life endurable, while I can't.' Do you see now what you've shown?"

"I didn't expect it to be seen."

"No. Not by the publisher of the New York *Banner,* of course. That's all right. I expected a beautiful slut who was a friend of Ellsworth Toohey."

They laughed together. She thought it was strange that they could talk without strain—as if he had forgotten the purpose of this journey. His calm had become a contagious sense of peace between them.

She watched the unobtrusively gracious way their dinner was served, she looked at the white tablecloth against the deep red of the mahogany walls. Everything on the yacht had an air that made her think it was the first truly luxurious place she had ever entered: the luxury was secondary, a background so proper to him that it could be ignored. The man humbled his own wealth. She had seen people of wealth, stiff and awed before that which represented their ultimate goal. The splendor of this place was not the aim, not the final achievement of the man who leaned casually across the table. She wondered what his aim had been.

"This ship is becoming to you," she said.

She saw a look of pleasure in his eyes—and of gratitude.

"Thank you. . . . Is the art gallery?"

"Yes. Only that's less excusable."

"I don't want you to make excuses for me." He said it simply, without reproach.

They had finished dinner. She waited for the inevitable invitation. It did not come. He sat smoking, talking about the yacht and the ocean.

Her hand came to rest accidentally on the tablecloth, close to his. She saw him looking at it. She wanted to jerk her hand away, but forced herself to let it lie still. Now, she thought.

He got up. "Let's go on deck," he said.

They stood at the rail and looked at a black void. Space was not to be seen, only felt by the quality of the air against their faces. A few stars gave reality to the empty sky. A few sparks of white fire in the water gave life to the ocean.

He stood, slouched carelessly, one arm raised, grasping a stanchion. She saw the sparks flowing, forming the edges of waves, framed by the curve of his body. That, too, was becoming to him.

She said:

"May I name another vicious bromide you've never felt?"

"Which one?"

"You've never felt how small you were when looking at the ocean."

He laughed. "Never. Nor looking at the planets. Nor at mountain peaks. Nor at the Grand Canyon. Why should I? When I look at the ocean, I feel the greatness of man. I think of man's magnificent capacity that created this ship to conquer all that senseless space. When I look at mountain peaks, I think of tunnels and dynamite. When I look at the planets, I think of airplanes."

"Yes. And that particular sense of sacred rapture men say they experience in contemplating nature—I've never received it from nature, only from . . ." She stopped.

"From what?"

"Buildings," she whispered. "Skyscrapers."

"Why didn't you want to say that?"

"I . . . don't know."

"I would give the greatest sunset in the world for one sight of New York's skyline. Particularly when one can't see the details. Just the shapes. The shapes and the thought that made them. The sky over New York and the will of man made visible. What other religion do we need? And then people tell me about pilgrimages to some dank pesthole in a jungle where they go to do homage to a crumbling temple, to a leering stone monster with a pot belly, created by some leprous savage. Is it beauty and genius they want to see? Do they seek a sense of the sublime? Let them come to New York, stand on the shore of the Hudson, look and kneel. When I see the city from my window—no, I don't feel how small I am—but I feel that if a war came to threaten this, I would like to throw myself into space, over the city, and protect these buildings with my body."

"Gail, I don't know whether I'm listening to you or to myself."

"Did you hear yourself just now?"

She smiled. "Actually not. But I won't take it back, Gail."

"Thank you—Dominique." His voice was soft and amused. "But we weren't talking about you or me. We were talking about other people." He leaned with both forearms on the rail, he spoke watching the sparks in the water. "It's interesting to speculate on the reasons that make men so anxious to debase themselves. As in that idea of feeling small before nature. It's not a bromide, it's practically an institution. Have you noticed how self-righteous a man sounds when he tells you about it? Look, he seems to say, I'm so glad to be a pigmy, that's how virtuous I am. Have you heard with what delight people quote some great celebrity who's proclaimed that he's not so great when he looks at Niagara Falls? It's as if they were smacking their lips in sheer glee that their best is dust before the brute force of an earthquake. As if they were sprawling on all fours, rubbing their foreheads in the mud to the majesty of a hurricane. But that's not the spirit that leashed fire, steam, electricity, that crossed oceans in sailing sloops, that built airplanes and dams . . . and skyscrapers. What is it they fear? What is it they hate so much, those who love to crawl? And why?"

"When I find the answer to that," she said, "I'll make my peace with the world."

He went on talking—of his travels, of the continents beyond the darkness around them, the darkness that made of space a soft curtain pressed against their eyelids. She waited. She stopped answering. She gave him a chance to use the brief silences for ending this, for saying the words she expected. He would not say them.

"Are you tired, my dear?" he asked.

"No."

"I'll get you a deck chair, if you want to sit down."

"No, I like standing here."

"It's a little cold. But by tomorrow we'll be far south and then you'll see the ocean on fire, at night. It's very beautiful."

He was silent. She heard the ship's speed in the sound of the water, the rustling moan of protest against the thing that cut a long wound across the water's surface.

"When are we going below?" she asked.

"We're not going below."

He had said it quietly, with an odd kind of simplicity, as if he were standing helpless before a fact he could not alter.

"Will you marry me?" he asked.

She could not hide the shock; he had seen it in advance, he was smiling quietly, understanding.

"It would be best to say nothing else." He spoke carefully. "But you prefer to hear it stated—because that kind of silence between us is more than I have a right to expect. You don't want to tell me much, but I've spoken for you tonight, so let me speak for you again. You've chosen me as the symbol of your contempt for men. You don't love me. You wish to grant me nothing. I'm only your tool of self-destruction. I know all that, I accept it and I want you to marry me. If you wish to commit an unspeakable act as your revenge against the world, such an act is not to sell yourself to your enemy, but to marry him. Not to match your worst against his worst, but your worst against his best. You've tried that once, but your victim wasn't worthy of your purpose. You see, I'm pleading my case in your own terms. What mine are, what I want to find in that marriage is of no importance to you and I shall regard it in that manner. You don't have to know about it. You don't have to consider it. I exact no promises and impose no obligations on you. You'll be free to leave me whenever you wish. Incidentally—since it is of no concern to you—I love you."

She stood, one arm stretched behind her, finger tips pressed to the rail. She said:

"I did not want that."

"I know. But if you're curious about it, I'll tell you that you've made a mistake. You let me see the cleanest person I've ever seen."

"Isn't that ridiculous, after the way we met?"

"Dominique, I've spent my life pulling the strings of the world. I've seen all of it. Do you think I could believe any purity—unless it came to me twisted in some such dreadful shape as the one you chose? But what I feel must not affect your decision."

She stood looking at him, looking incredulously at all the hours past. Her mouth had the shape of gentleness. He saw it. She thought that every word he said today had been of her language, that this offer and the form he gave it were of her own world—and that he had destroyed his purpose by it, taken away from her the motive he suggested, made it impossible to seek degradation with a man who spoke as he did. She wanted suddenly to reach for him, to tell him everything, to find a moment's release in his understanding, then ask him never to see her again.

Then she remembered.

He noticed the movement of her hand. Her fingers were not leaning tensely against the rail, betraying a need of support, giving importance to the moment; they relaxed and closed about the rail; as if she had taken hold of some reins, carelessly, because the occasion required no earnest effort any longer.

She remembered the Stoddard Temple. She thought of the man before her, who spoke about the total passion for the total height and about protecting skyscrapers with his body—and she saw a picture on a page of the New York *Banner,* the picture of Howard Roark looking up at the Enright House, and the caption: "Are you happy, Mr. Superman?"

She raised her face to him. She asked:

"To marry you? To become Mrs. Wynand-Papers?"

She heard the effort in his voice as he answered: "If you wish to call it that—yes."

"I will marry you."

"Thank you, Dominique."

She waited indifferently.

When he turned to her, he spoke as he had spoken all day, a calm voice with an edge of gaiety.

"We'll cut the cruise short. We'll take just a week—I want to have you here for a while. You'll leave for Reno the day after we return. I'll take care of your husband. He can have Stoneridge and anything else he wants and may God damn him. We'll be married the day you come back."

"Yes, Gail. Now let's go below."

"Do you want it?"

"No. But I don't want our marriage to be important."

"I want it to be important, Dominique. That's why I won't touch you tonight. Not until we're married. I know it's a senseless gesture. I know that a wedding ceremony has no significance for either one of us. But to be conventional is the only abnormality possible between us. That's why I want it. I have no other way of making an exception."

"As you wish, Gail."

Then he pulled her to him and he kissed her mouth. It was the completion of his words, the finished statement, a statement of such intensity that she tried to stiffen her body, not to respond, and felt her body responding, forced to forget everything but the physical fact of a man who held her.

He let her go. She knew he had noticed. He smiled and said:

"You're tired, Dominique. Shall I say good night? I want to remain here for a while."

She turned obediently and walked alone down to her cabin.

V

"WHAT'S THE MATTER? DON'T I GET STONERIDGE?" SNAPPED Peter Keating.

Dominique walked into the living room. He followed, waiting in the open door. The elevator boy brought in her luggage, and left. She said, removing her gloves:

"You'll get Stoneridge, Peter. Mr. Wynand will tell you the rest himself. He wants to see you tonight. At eight-thirty. At his home."

"Why in hell?"

"He'll tell you."

She slapped her gloves softly against her palm, a small gesture of finality, like a period at the end of a sentence. She turned to leave the room. He stood in her way.

"I don't care," he said. "I don't give a damn. I can play it your way. You're great, aren't you?—because you act like truck drivers, you and Mr. Gail Wynand? To hell with decency, to hell with the other fellow's feelings? Well, I can do that too. I'll use you both and I'll get what I can out of it—and that's all I care. How do you like it? No point when the worm refuses to be hurt? Spoils the fun?"

"I think that's much better, Peter. I'm glad."

He found himself unable to preserve this attitude when he entered Wynand's study that evening. He could not escape the awe of being admitted into Gail Wynand's home. By the time he crossed the room to the seat facing the desk he felt nothing but a sense of weight, and he wondered whether his feet had left prints on the soft carpet; like the leaded feet of a deep-sea diver.

"What I have to tell you, Mr. Keating, should never have needed to be said or done," said Wynand. Keating had never heard a man speak in a manner so consciously controlled. He thought crazily that it sounded as if Wynand held his fist closed over his voice and directed each syllable. "Any extra word I speak will be offensive, so I shall be brief. I am going to marry your wife. She is leaving for Reno tomorrow. Here is the contract for Stoneridge. I have signed it. Attached is a check for two hundred and fifty thousand dollars. It is in addition to what you will receive for your work under the contract. I'll appreciate it if you will now make no comment of any kind. I realize that I could have had your consent for less, but I wish no discussion. It would be intolerable if we were to bargain about it. Therefore, will you please take this and consider the matter settled?"

467

He extended the contract across the desk. Keating saw the pale blue rectangle of the check held to the top of the page by a paper clip. The clip flashed silver in the light of the desk lamp.

Keating's hand did not reach to meet the paper. He said, his chin moving awkwardly to frame the words:

"I don't want it. You can have my consent for nothing."

He saw a look of astonishment—and almost of kindness—on Wynand's face.

"You don't want it? You don't want Stoneridge either?"

"I want Stoneridge!" Keating's hand rose and snatched the paper. "I want it all! Why should you get away with it? Why should I care?"

Wynand got up. He said, relief and regret in his voice:

"Right, Mr. Keating. For a moment, you had almost justified your marriage. Let it remain what it was. Good night."

Keating did not go home. He walked to the apartment of Neil Dumont, his new designer and best friend. Neil Dumont was a lanky, anemic society youth, with shoulders stooped under the burden of too many illustrious ancestors. He was not a good designer, but he had connections; he was obsequious to Keating in the office, and Keating was obsequious to him after office hours.

He found Dumont at home. Together, they got Gordon Prescott and Vincent Knowlton, and started out to make a wild night of it. Keating did not drink much. He paid for everything. He paid more than necessary. He seemed anxious to find things to pay for. He gave exorbitant tips. He kept asking: "We're friends—aren't we friends?—aren't we?" He looked at the glasses around him and he watched the lights dancing in the liquid. He looked at the three pairs of eyes; they were blurred, but they turned upon him occasionally with contentment. They were soft and comforting.

That evening, her bags packed and ready in her room, Dominique went to see Steven Mallory.

She had not seen Roark for twenty months. She had called on Mallory once in a while. Mallory knew that these visits were breakdowns in a struggle she would not name; he knew that she did not want to come, that her rare evenings with him were time torn out of her life. He never asked any questions and he was always glad to see her. They talked quietly, with a feeling of companionship such as that of an old married couple; as if he had possessed her body, and the wonder of it had long since been consumed, and nothing remained but an untroubled intimacy. He had never touched her body, but he had possessed it in a deeper kind of ownership when he had done her statue, and they could not lose the special sense of each other it had given them.

He smiled when he opened the door and saw her.

"Hello, Dominique."

"Hello, Steve. Interrupting you?"

"No. Come in."

He had a studio, a huge, sloppy place in an old building. She noticed the change since her last visit. The room had an air of laughter, like a breath held too long and released. She saw second-hand furniture, an Oriental rug of rare texture and sensuous color, jade ash trays, pieces of sculpture that came from historical excavations, anything he had wished to seize, helped by the sudden fortune of Wynand's patronage. The walls looked strangely bare above the gay clutter. He had bought no paintings. A single sketch hung over his studio—Roark's original drawing of the Stoddard Temple.

She looked slowly about her, noting every object and the reason for its presence. He kicked two chairs toward the fireplace and they sat down, one at each side of the fire.

He said, quite simply:

"Clayton, Ohio."

"Doing what?"

"A new building for Janer's Department Store. Five stories. On Main Street."

"How long has he been there?"

"About a month."

It was the first question he answered whenever she came here, without making her ask it. His simple ease spared her the necessity of explanation or pretense; his manner included no comment.

"I'm going away tomorrow, Steve."

"For long?"

"Six weeks. Reno."

"I'm glad."

"I'd rather not tell you now what I'll do when I come back. You won't be glad."

"I'll try to be—if it's what you want to do."

"It's what I want to do."

One log still kept its shape on the pile of coals in the fireplace; it was checkered into small squares and it glowed without flame, like a solid string of lighted windows. He reached down and threw a fresh log on the coals. It cracked the string of windows in half and sent sparks shooting up against the sooted bricks.

He talked about his own work. She listened, as if she were an emigrant hearing her homeland's language for a brief while.

In a pause, she asked:

"How is he, Steve?"

"As he's always been. He doesn't change, you know."

He kicked the log. A few coals rolled out. He pushed them back. He said:

"I often think that he's the only one of us who's achieved immortality. I don't mean in the sense of fame and I don't mean that he won't die some day. But he's living it. I think he is what the conception really means. You know how people long to be eternal. But they die with every day that passes. When you meet them, they're not what you met last. In any given hour, they kill some part of themselves. They change, they deny, they contradict—and they call it growth. At the end there's nothing left, nothing unreversed or unbetrayed; as if there had never been any entity, only a succession of adjectives fading in and out on an unformed mass. How do they expect a permanence which they have never held for a single moment? But Howard—one can imagine him existing forever."

She sat looking at the fire. It gave a deceptive semblance of life to her face. After a while he asked:

"How do you like all the new things I got?"

"I like them. I like your having them."

"I didn't tell you what happened to me since I saw you last. The completely incredible. Gail Wynand . . ."

"Yes, I know about that."

"You do? Wynand, of all people—what on earth made him discover me?"

"I know that too. I'll tell you when I come back."

"He has an amazing judgment. Amazing for him. He bought the best."

"Yes, he would."

Then she asked, without transition, yet he knew that she was not speaking of Wynand:

"Steve, has he ever asked you about me?"

"No."

"Have you told him about my coming here?"

"No."

"Is that—for my sake, Steve?"

"No. For his."

He knew he had told her everything she wanted to know.

She said, rising:

"Let's have some tea. Show me where you keep your stuff. I'll fix it."

Dominique left for Reno early in the morning. Keating was still asleep and she did not awaken him to say good-by.

When he opened his eyes, he knew that she was gone, before he looked at the clock, by the quality of the silence in the house. He thought he should say "Good riddance," but he did not say it and he did not feel it. What he felt was a vast, flat sentence without subject—"It's no use"—related neither to himself nor to Dominique. He was alone and there was no necessity to pretend anything. He lay in bed, on his back, his arms flung out helplessly. His face looked humble and his eyes bewildered. He felt that it was an end and a death, but he did not mean the loss of Dominique.

He got up and dressed. In the bathroom he found a hand towel she had used and discarded. He picked it up, he pressed his face to it and held it for a long time, not in sorrow, but in nameless emotion, not understanding, knowing only that he had loved her twice—on that evening when Toohey telephoned, and now. Then he opened his fingers and let the towel slip down to the floor, like a liquid running between his fingers.

He went to his office and worked as usual. Nobody knew of his divorce and he felt no desire to inform anyone. Neil Dumont winked at him and drawled: "I say, Pete, you look peaked." He shrugged and turned his back. The sight of Dumont made him sick today.

He left the office early. A vague instinct kept pulling at him, like hunger, at first, then taking shape. He had to see Ellsworth Toohey. He had to reach Toohey. He felt like the survivor of a shipwreck swimming toward a distant light.

That evening he dragged himself to Ellsworth Toohey's apartment. When he entered, he felt dimly glad of his self-control, because Toohey seemed to notice nothing in his face,

"Oh, hello, Peter," said Toohey airily. "Your sense of timing leaves much to be desired. You catch me on the worst possible evening. Busy as all hell. But don't let that bother you. What are friends for but to inconvenience one? Sit down, sit down, I'll be with you in a minute."

"I'm sorry, Ellsworth. But . . . I had to."

"Make yourself at home. Just ignore me for a minute, will you?"

Keating sat down and waited. Toohey worked, making notes on sheets of typewritten copy. He sharpened a pencil, the sound grating like a saw across Keating's nerves. He bent over his copy again, rustling the pages once in a while.

Half an hour later he pushed the papers aside and smiled at Keating. "That's that," he said. Keating made a small movement forward. "Sit tight," said Toohey, "just one telephone call I've got to make."

He dialed the number of Gus Webb. "Hello, Gus," he said gaily. "How are you, you walking advertisement for contraceptives?" Keating had never heard that tone of loose intimacy from Toohey, a special tone of brotherhood that permitted sloppiness. He heard Webb's piercing voice say something and laugh in the receiver. The receiver went on spitting out rapid sounds from deep down in its tube, like a throat being cleared. The words could not be recognized, only their quality; the quality of abandon and insolence, with high shrieks of mirth once in a while.

Toohey leaned back in his chair, listening, half smiling. "Yes," he said occasionally, "uh-huh. . . . You said it, boy. . . . Surer'n hell. . . ." He leaned back farther and put one foot in a shining, pointed shoe on the edge of the desk. "Listen, boy, what I wanted to tell you is go easy on old Bassett for a while. Sure he liked your work, but don't shock hell out of him for the time being. No rough-house, see? Keep that big facial cavity of yours buttoned up. . . . You know damn well who I am to tell you. . . . That's right. . . . That's the stuff, kid. . . . Oh, he did? Good, angel-face. . . . Well, bye-bye—oh, say, Gus, have you heard the one about the British lady and the plumber?" There followed a story. The receiver yelled raucously at the end. "Well, watch your step and your digestion, angel-face. Nighty-night."

Toohey dropped the receiver, said: "Now, Peter," stretched, got up, walked to Keating and stood before him, rocking a little on his small feet, his eyes bright and kindly.

"Now, Peter, what's the matter? Has the world crashed about your nose?"

Keating reached into his inside pocket and produced a yellow check, crumpled, much handled. It bore his signature and the sum of ten thousand dollars, made out to Ellsworth M. Toohey. The gesture with which he handed it to Toohey was not that of a donor, but of a beggar.

"Please, Ellsworth . . . here . . . take this . . . for a good cause . . . for the Workshop of Social Study . . . or for anything you wish . . . you know best . . . for a good cause . . ."

Toohey held the check with the tips of his fingers, like a soiled penny, bent his head to one side, pursing his lips in appreciation, and tossed the check on his desk.

"Very handsome of you, Peter. Very handsome indeed. What's the occasion?"

"Ellsworth, you remember what you said once—that it doesn't matter what we are or do, if we help others? That's all that counts? That's good, isn't it? That's clean?"

"I haven't said it once. I've said it a million times."

"And it's really true?"

"Of course it's true. If you have the courage to accept it."

"You're my friend, aren't you? You're the only friend I've got. I . . . I'm not even friendly with myself, but you are. With me, I mean, aren't you, Ellsworth?"

"But of course. Which is of more value than your own friendship with yourself—a rather queer conception, but quite valid."

"You understand. Nobody else does. And you like me."

"Devotedly. Whenever I have the time."

"Ah?"

"Your sense of humor, Peter, where's your sense of humor? What's the matter? A bellyache? Or a soul-indigestion?"

"Ellsworth, I . . ."

"Yes?"

"I can't tell you. Even you."

"You're a coward, Peter."

Keating stared helplessly: the voice had been severe and gentle, he did not know whether he should feel pain, insult or confidence.

"You come here to tell me that it doesn't matter what you do—and then you go to pieces over something or other you've done. Come on, be a man and say it doesn't matter. Say you're not important. Mean it. Show some guts. Forget your little ego."

"I'm not important, Ellsworth. I'm not important. Oh God, if only everybody'd say it like you do! I'm not important. I don't want to be important."

"Where did that money come from?"

"I sold Dominique."

"What are you talking about? The cruise?"

"Only it seems as if it's not Dominique that I sold."

"What do you care if . . ."

"She's gone to Reno."

"What?"

He could not understand the violence of Toohey's reaction, but he was too tired to wonder. He told everything, as it had happened to him; it had not taken long to happen or to tell.

"You damn fool! You shouldn't have allowed it!"

"What could I do? Against Wynand?"

"But to let him *marry* her!"

"Why not, Ellsworth? It's better than . . ."

"I didn't think he'd ever . . . but . . . Oh, God damn it, I'm a bigger fool than you are!"

"But it's better for Dominique if . . ."

"To hell with your Dominique! It's Wynand I'm thinking about!"

"Ellsworth, what's the matter with you? . . . Why should you care?"

"Keep still, will you? Let me think."

In a moment, Toohey shrugged, sat down beside Keating and slipped his arm about his shoulders.

"I'm sorry, Peter," he said. "I apologize. I've been inexcusably rude to you. It was just the shock. But I understand how you feel. Only you mustn't take it too seriously. It doesn't matter." He spoke automatically. His mind was far away. Keating did not notice that. He heard the words. They were the spring in the desert. "It doesn't matter. You're only human. That's all you want to be. Who's any better? Who has the right to cast the first stone? We're all human. It doesn't matter."

"My God!" said Alvah Scarret. "He can't! Not Dominique Francon!"

"He will," said Toohey. "As soon as she returns."

Scarret had been surprised that Toohey should invite him to lunch, but the news he heard wiped out the surprise in a greater and more painful one.

"I'm fond of Dominique," said Scarret, pushing his plate aside, his appetite gone. "I've always been very fond of her. But to have her as Mrs. Gail Wynand!"

"These, exactly, are my own sentiments," said Toohey.

"I've always advised him to marry. It helps. Lends an air. An insurance of respectability, sort of, and he could do with one. He's always skated on pretty thin ice. Got away with it, so far. But Dominique!"

"Why do you find such a marriage unsuitable?"

"Well . . . well, it's not . . . Damn it, you know it's not right!"

"I know it. Do you?"

"Look, she's a dangerous kind of woman."

"She is. That's your minor premise. Your major premise, however, is: he's a dangerous kind of man."

"Well . . . in some ways . . . yes."

"My esteemed editor, you understand me quite well. But there are times when it's helpful to formulate things. It tends toward future—co-operation. You and I have a great deal in common—though you have been somewhat reluctant to admit it. We are two variations on the same theme, shall we say? Or we play two ends against the same middle, if you prefer your own literary style. But our dear boss is quite another tune. A different leitmotif entirely—don't you think so, Alvah? Our dear boss is an accident in our midst. Accidents are unreliable phenomena. You've been sitting on the edge of your seat for years—haven't you? —watching Mr. Gail Wynand. So you know exactly what I'm talking about. You know also that Miss Dominique Francon is not our tune either. And you do not wish to see that particular influence enter the life of our boss. Do I have to state the issue any plainer?"

"You're a smart man, Ellsworth," said Scarret heavily.

"That's been obvious for years."

"I'll talk to him. You'd better not—he hates your guts, if you'll excuse me. But I don't think I'd do much good either. Not if he's made up his mind."

"I don't expect you to. You may try, if you wish, though it's useless. We can't stop that marriage. One of my good points is the fact that I admit defeat when it has to be admitted."

"But then, why did you——"

"Tell you this? In the nature of a scoop, Alvah. Advance information."

"I appreciate it, Ellsworth. I sure do."

"It would be wise to go on appreciating it. The Wynand papers, Alvah, are not to be given up easily. In unity there is strength. Your style."

"What do you mean?"

"Only that we're in for a difficult time, my friend. So we'd do better to stick together."

"Why, I'm with you, Ellsworth. I've always been."

"Inaccurate, but we'll let it pass. We're concerned only with the present. And the future. As a token of mutual understanding, how about getting rid of Jimmy Kearns at the first opportunity?"

"I *thought* you've been driving at that for months! What's the matter with Jimmy Kearns? He's a bright kid. The best drama critic in town. He's got a mind. Smart as a whip. Most promising."

"He's got a mind—of his own. I don't think you want any whips around the place—except the one you hold. I think you want to be careful about what the promise promises."

"Whom'll I stick in his spot?"

"Jules Fougler."

"Oh, hell, Ellsworth!"

"Why not?"

"That old son of a . . . We can't afford him."

"You can if you want to. And look at the name he's got."

"But he's the most impossible old . . ."

"Well, you don't have to take him. We'll discuss it some other time. Just get rid of Jimmy Kearns."

"Look, Ellsworth, I don't play favorites; it's all the same to me. I'll give Jimmy the boot if you say so. Only I don't see what difference it makes and what it's got to do with what we were talking about."

"You don't," said Toohey. "You will."

"Gail, you know that I want you to be happy," said Alvah Scarret, sitting in a comfortable armchair in the study of Wynand's penthouse that evening. "You know that. I'm thinking of nothing else."

Wynand lay stretched out on a couch, one leg bent, with the foot resting on the knee of the other. He smoked and listened silently.

"I've known Dominique for years," said Scarret. "Long before you even heard of her. I love her. I love her, you might say, like a father.

But you've got to admit that she's not the kind of woman your public would expect to see as Mrs. Gail Wynand."

Wynand said nothing.

"Your wife is a public figure, Gail. Just automatically. A public property. Your readers have a right to demand and expect certain things of her. A symbol value, if you know what I mean. Like the Queen of England, sort of. How do you expect Dominique to live up to that? How do you expect her to preserve any appearances at all? She's the wildest person I know. She has a terrible reputation. But worst of all—think, Gail!—a divorcee! And here we spend tons of good print, standing for the sanctity of the home and the purity of womanhood! How are you going to make your public swallow that one? How am I going to sell your wife to them?"

"Don't you think this conversation had better be stopped, Alvah?"

"Yes, Gail," said Scarret meekly.

Scarret waited, with a heavy sense of aftermath, as if after a violent quarrel, anxious to make up.

"I know, Gail!" he cried happily. "I know what we can do. We'll put Dominique back on the paper and we'll have her write a column—a different one—a syndicated column on the home. You know, household hints, kitchen, babies and all that. It'll take the curse off. Show what a good little homebody she really is, her youthful mistakes notwithstanding. Make the women forgive her. We'll have a special department—'Mrs. Gail Wynand's recipes.' A few pictures of her will help—you know, gingham dresses and aprons and her hair done up in a more conventional way."

"Shut up, Alvah, before I slap your face," said Wynand without raising his voice.

"Yes, Gail."

Scarret made a move to get up.

"Sit still. I haven't finished."

Scarret waited obediently.

"Tomorrow morning," said Wynand, "you will send a memo to every one of our papers. You will tell them to look through their files and find any pictures of Dominique Francon they might have in connection with her old column. You will tell them to destroy the pictures. You will tell them that henceforward any mention of her name or the use of her picture in any of my papers will cost the job of the entire editorial staff responsible. When the proper time comes, you will have an announcement of my marriage appear in all our papers. That cannot be avoided. The briefest announcement you can compose. No commentaries. No stories. No pictures. Pass the word around and make sure it's understood. It's any man's job, yours included, if this is disobeyed."

"No stories—when you marry her?"

"No stories, Alvah."

"But good God! That's news! The other papers . . ."

"I don't care what the other papers do about it."

"But—*why*, Gail?"

"You wouldn't understand."

Dominique sat at the window, listening to the train wheels under the floor. She looked at the countryside of Ohio flying past in the fading daylight. Her head lay back against the seat and her hands lay limply at each side of her on the seat cushion. She was one with the structure of the car, she was carried forward just as the window frame, the floor, the walls of the compartment were carried forward. The corners blurred, gathering darkness; the window remained luminous, evening light rising from the earth. She let herself rest in that faint illumination; it entered the car and ruled it, so long as she did not turn on the light to shut it out.

She had no consciousness of purpose. There was no goal to this journey, only the journey itself, only the motion and the metal sound of motion around her. She felt slack and empty, losing her identity in a painless ebb, content to vanish and let nothing remain defined save that particular earth in the window.

When she saw, in the slowing movement beyond the glass, the name "Clayton" on a faded board under the eaves of a station building, she knew what she had been expecting. She knew why she had taken this train, not a faster one, why she had looked carefully at the timetable of its stops—although it had been just a column of meaningless names to her then. She seized her suitcase, coat and hat. She ran. She could not take time to dress, afraid that the floor under her feet would carry her away from here. She ran down the narrow corridor of the car, down the steps. She leaped to the station platform, feeling the shock of winter cold on her bare throat. She stood looking at the station building. She heard the train moving behind her, clattering away.

Then she put on her coat and hat. She walked across the platform, into the waiting room, across a wooden floor studded with lumps of dry chewing gum, through the heavy billows of heat from an iron stove, to the square beyond the station.

She saw a last band of yellow in the sky above the low roof lines. She saw a pitted stretch of paving bricks, and small houses leaning against one another; a bare tree with twisted branches, skeletons of weeds at the doorless opening of an abandoned garage, dark shop fronts, a drugstore still open on a corner, its lighted window dim, low over the ground.

She had never been here before, but she felt this place proclaiming its ownership of her, closing in about her with ominous intimacy. It was as if every dark mass exercised a suction like the pull of the planets in space, prescribing her orbit. She put her hand on a fire hydrant and felt the cold seeping through her glove into her skin. This was the way the town held her, a direct penetration which neither her clothes nor her mind could stop. The peace of the inevitable remained. Only now she had to act, but the actions were simple, set in advance. She asked a passer-by: "Where is the site of the new building of Janer's Department Store?"

She walked patiently through the dark streets. She walked past desolate winter lawns and sagging porches; past vacant lots where weeds rustled against tin cans; past closed grocery stores and a steaming laundry; past an uncurtained window where a man in shirtsleeves sat by a fire, reading a paper. She turned corners and crossed streets, with the feel of cobblestones under the thin soles of her pumps. Rare passers-by looked, astonished, at her air of foreign elegance. She noticed it; she felt an answering wonder. She wanted to say: But don't you understand?—I belong here more than you do. She stopped, once in a while, closing her eyes; she found it difficult to breathe.

She came to Main Street and walked slower. There were a few lights, cars parked diagonally at the curb, a movie theater, a store window displaying pink underwear among kitchen utensils. She walked stiffly, looking ahead.

She saw a glare of light on the side of an old building, on a blind wall of yellow bricks showing the sooted floor lines of a neighboring structure that had been torn down. The light came from an excavation pit. She knew this was the site. She hoped it was not. If they worked late, he would be here. She did not want to see him tonight. She had wanted only to see the place and the building; she was not ready for more; she had wanted to see him tomorrow. But she could not stop now. She walked to the excavation. It lay on a corner, open to the street, without fence. She heard the grinding clatter of iron, she saw the arm of a derrick, the shadows of men on the slanting sides of fresh earth, yellow in the light. She could not see the planks that led up to the sidewalk, but she heard the sound of steps and then she saw Roark coming up to the street. He was hatless, he had a loose coat hanging open.

He stopped. He looked at her. She thought that she was standing straight; that it was simple and normal, she was seeing the gray eyes and the orange hair as she had always seen them. She was astonished that he moved toward her with a kind of urgent haste, that his hand closed over her elbow too firmly and he said: "You'd better sit down."

Then she knew she could not have stood up without that hand on her elbow. He took her suitcase. He led her across the dark side street and made her sit down on the steps of a vacant house. She leaned back against a closed door. He sat down beside her. He kept his hand tight on her elbow, not a caress, but an impersonal hold of control over both of them.

After a while he dropped his hand. She knew that she was safe now. She could speak.

"That's your new building?"

"Yes. You walked here from the station?"

"Yes."

"It's a long walk."

"I think it was."

She thought that they had not greeted each other and that it was right. This was not a reunion, but just one moment out of something that had never been interrupted. She thought how strange it would be if she ever said "Hello" to him; one did not greet oneself each morning.

"What time did you get up today?" she asked.

"At seven."

"I was in New York then. In a cab, going to Grand Central. Where did you have breakfast?"

"In a lunch wagon."

"The kind that stays open all night?"

"Yes. Mostly for truck drivers."

"Do you go there often?"

"Whenever I want a cup of coffee."

"And you sit at a counter? And there are people around, looking at you?"

"I sit at a counter when I have the time. There are people around. I don't think they look at me much."

"And afterward? You walk to work?"

"Yes."

"You walk every day? Down any of these streets? Past any window? So that if one just wanted to reach and open the window . . ."

"People don't stare out of windows here."

From the vantage of the high stoop they could see the excavation across the street, the earth, the workmen, the rising steel columns in a glare of harsh light. She thought it was strange to see fresh earth in the midst of pavements and cobblestones; as if a piece had been torn from the clothing of a town, showing naked flesh. She said:

"You've done two country homes in the last two years."

"Yes. One in Pennsylvania and one near Boston."

"They were unimportant houses."

"Inexpensive, if that's what you mean. But very interesting to do."

"How long will you remain here?"

"Another month."

"Why do you work at night?"

"It's a rush job."

Across the street the derrick was moving, balancing a long girder in the air. She saw him watching it, and she knew he was not thinking of it, but there was the instinctive response in his eyes, something physically personal, intimacy with any action taken for his building.

"Roark . . ."

They had not pronounced each other's names. It had the sensuous pleasure of a surrender long delayed—to pronounce the name and to have him hear it.

"Roark, it's the quarry again."

He smiled. "If you wish. Only it isn't."

"After the Enright House? After the Cord Building?"

"I don't think of it that way."

"How do you think of it?"

"I love doing it. Every building is like a person. Single and unrepeatable."

He was looking across the street. He had not changed. There was the old sense of lightness in him, of ease in motion, in action, in thought. She said, her sentence without beginning or end:

". . . doing five-story buildings for the rest of your life . . ."

"If necessary. But I don't think it will be like that."

"What are you waiting for?"

"I'm not waiting."

She closed her eyes, but she could not hide her mouth; her mouth held bitterness, anger and pain.

"Roark, if you'd been in the city, I wouldn't have come to see you."

"I know it."

"But it was you—in another place—in some nameless hole of a place like this. I had to see it. I had to see the place."

"When are you going back?"

"You know I haven't come to remain?"

"Yes."

"Why?"

"You're still afraid of lunch wagons and windows."

"I'm not going back to New York. Not at once."

"No?"

"You haven't asked me anything, Roark. Only whether I walked from the station."

"What do you want me to ask you?"

"I got off the train when I saw the name of the station," she said, her voice dull. "I didn't intend coming here. I was on my way to Reno."

"And after that?"

"I will marry again."

"Do I know your fiancé?"

"You've heard of him. His name is Gail Wynand."

She saw his eyes. She thought she should want to laugh; she had brought him at last to a shock she had never expected to achieve. But she did not laugh. He thought of Henry Cameron; of Cameron saying: "I have no answer to give them, Howard. I'm leaving you to face them. You'll answer them. All of them, the Wynand papers and what makes the Wynand papers possible and what lies behind that."

"Roark."

He didn't answer.

"That's worse than Peter Keating, isn't it?" she asked.

"Much worse."

"Do you want to stop me?"

"No."

He had not touched her since he had released her elbow, and that had been only a touch proper in an ambulance. She moved her hand and let it rest against his. He did not withdraw his fingers and he did not pretend indifference. She bent over, holding his hand, not raising it from his knee, and she pressed her lips to his hand. Her hat fell off, he saw the blond head at his knees, he felt her mouth kissing his hand again and again. His fingers held hers, answering, but that was the only answer.

She raised her head and looked at the street. A lighted window hung in the distance, behind a grillwork of bare branches. Small houses stretched off into the darkness, and trees stood by the narrow sidewalks.

She noticed her hat on the steps below and bent to pick it up. She leaned with her bare hand flat against the steps. The stone was old, worn smooth, icy. She felt comfort in the touch. She sat for a moment, bent over, palm pressed to the stone; to feel these steps—no matter how many feet had used them—to feel them as she had felt the fire hydrant.

"Roark, where do you live?"

"In a rooming house."

"What kind of room?"

"Just a room."

"What's in it? What kind of walls?"

"Some sort of wallpaper. Faded."

"What furniture?"

"A table, chairs, a bed."

"No, tell me in detail."

"There's a clothes closet, then a chest of drawers, the bed in the corner by the window, a large table at the other side——"

"By the wall?"

"No, I put it across the corner, to the window—I work there. Then there's a straight chair, an armchair with a bridge lamp and a magazine rack I never use. I think that's all."

"No rugs? Or curtains?"

"I think there's something at the window and some kind of rug. The floor is nicely polished, it's beautiful old wood."

"I want to think of your room tonight—on the train."

He sat looking across the street. She said:

"Roark, let me stay with you tonight."

"No."

She let her glance follow his to the grinding machinery below. After a while she asked:

"How did you get this store to design?"

"The owner saw my buildings in New York and liked them."

A man in overalls stepped out of the excavation pit, peered into the darkness at them and called: "Is that you up there, boss?"

"Yes," Roark called back.

"Come here a minute, will you?"

Roark walked to him across the street. She could not hear their conversation, but she heard Roark saying gaily: "That's easy," and then they both walked down the planks to the bottom. The man stood talking, pointing up, explaining. Roark threw his head back, to glance up at the rising steel frame; the light was full on his face, and she saw his look of concentration, not a smile, but an expression that gave her a joyous feeling of competence, of disciplined reason in action. He bent, picked up a piece of board, took a pencil from his pocket. He stood with one foot on a pile of planks, the board propped on his knee, and drew rapidly, explaining something to the man who nodded, pleased. She could not hear the words, but she felt the quality of Roark's relation to that man, to all the other men in that pit, an odd sense of loyalty and of brotherhood, but not the kind she had ever heard named by these words. He finished, handed the board to the man, and they both laughed at something. Then he came back and sat down on the steps beside her.

"Roark," she said, "I want to remain here with you for all the years we might have."

He looked at her, attentively, waiting.

"I want to live here." Her voice had the sound of pressure against a dam. "I want to live as you live. Not to touch my money—I'll give it away, to anyone, to Steve Mallory, if you wish, or to one of Toohey's organizations, it doesn't matter. We'll take a house here—like one of these—and I'll keep it for you—don't laugh, I can—I'll cook, I'll wash your clothes, I'll scrub the floor. And you'll give up architecture."

He had not laughed. She saw nothing but an unmoving attention prepared to listen on.

"Roark, try to understand, please try to understand. I can't bear to see what they're doing to you, what they're going to do. It's too great—you and building and what you feel about it. You can't go on like that for long. It won't last. They won't let you. You're moving to some terrible kind of disaster. It can't end any other way. Give it up. Take some meaningless job—like the quarry. We'll live here. We'll have little and we'll give nothing. We'll live only for what we are and for what we know."

He laughed. She heard, in the sound of it, a surprising touch of consideration for her—the attempt not to laugh; but he couldn't stop it.

"Dominique." The way he pronounced the name remained with her and made it easier to hear the words that followed: "I wish I could tell you that it was a temptation, at least for a moment. But it wasn't." He added: "If I were very cruel, I'd accept it. Just to see how soon you'd beg me to go back to building."

"Yes . . . Probably . . ."

"Marry Wynand and stay married to him. It will be better than what you're doing to yourself right now."

"Do you mind . . . if we just sit here for a little while longer . . . and not talk about that . . . but just talk, as if everything were right . . . just an armistice for half an hour out of years. . . . Tell me what you've done every day you've been here, everything you can remember. . . ."

Then they talked, as if the stoop of the vacant house were an airplane hanging in space, without sight of earth or sky; he did not look across the street.

Then he glanced at his wrist watch and said:

"There's a train for the West in an hour. Shall I go with you to the station?"

"Do you mind if we walk there?"

"All right."

She stood up. She asked:

"Until—when, Roark?"

His hand moved over the streets. "Until you stop hating all this, stop being afraid of it, learn not to notice it."

They walked together to the station. She listened to the sound of his steps with hers in the empty streets. She let her glance drag along the walls they passed, like a clinging touch. She loved this place, this town and everything that was part of it.

They were walking past a vacant lot. The wind blew an old sheet of newspaper against her legs. It clung to her with a tight insistence that seemed conscious, like the peremptory caress of a cat. She thought, anything of this town had that intimate right to her. She bent, picked up the paper and began folding it, to keep it.

"What are you doing?" he asked.

"Something to read on the train," she said stupidly.

He snatched the paper from her, crumpled it and flung it away into the weeds. She said nothing and they walked on.

A single light bulb hung over the empty station platform. They waited. He stood looking up the tracks, where the train was to appear. When the tracks rang, shuddering, when the white ball of a headlight spurted out of the distance and stood still in the sky, not approaching, only widening, growing in furious speed, he did not move or turn to her. The rushing beam flung his shadow across the platform, made it sweep over the planks and vanish. For an instant she saw the tall, straight line of his body against the glare. The engine passed them and the cars rattled, slowing down. He looked at the windows rolling past. She could not see his face, only the outline of his cheekbone.

When the train stopped, he turned to her. They did not shake hands, they did not speak. They stood straight, facing each other for a moment, as if at attention; it was almost like a military salute. Then she picked up her suitcase and went aboard the train. The train started moving a minute later.

VI

C HUCK: AND WHY NOT A MUSKRAT? WHY SHOULD MAN IMAGINE himself superior to a muskrat? Life beats in all the small creatures of field and wood. Life singing of eternal sorrow. An old sorrow. The Song of Songs. We don't understand—but who cares about understanding? Only public accountants and chiropodists. Also mailmen. We only love. The Sweet Mystery of Love. That's all there is to it. Give me love and shove all your philosophers up your stovepipe. When Mary took the homeless muskrat, her heart broke open and life and love rushed in. Muskrats make good imitation mink coats, but that's not the point. Life is the point.

"Jake: (rushing in) Say, folks, who's got a stamp with a picture of George Washington on it?

"Curtain."

Ike slammed his manuscript shut and took a long swig of air. His voice was hoarse after two hours of reading aloud and he had read the climax of his play on a single long breath. He looked at his audience, his mouth smiling in self-mockery, his eyebrows raised insolently, but his eyes pleading.

Ellsworth Toohey, sitting on the floor, scratched his spine against a chair leg and yawned. Gus Webb, stretched out on his stomach in the middle of the room, rolled over on his back. Lancelot Clokey, the foreign correspondent, reached for his highball glass and finished it off. Jules Fougler, the new drama critic of the *Banner*, sat without moving; he had not moved for two hours. Lois Cook, hostess, raised her arms, twisting them, stretching, and said:

"Jesus, Ike, it's awful."

Lancelot Clokey drawled, "Lois, my girl, where do you keep your gin? Don't be such a damn miser. You're the worst hostess I know."

Gus Webb said, "I don't understand literature. It's nonproductive and a waste of time. Authors will be liquidated."

Ike laughed shrilly. "A stinker, huh?" He waved his script. "A real super-stinker. What do you think I wrote it for? Just show me anyone who can write a bigger flop. Worst play you'll ever hear in your life."

It was not a formal meeting of the Council of American Writers, but an unofficial gathering. Ike had asked a few of his friends to listen to his latest work. At twenty-six he had written eleven plays, but had never had one produced.

"You'd better give up the theater, Ike," said Lancelot Clokey. "Writ-

485

ing is a serious business and not for any stray bastard that wants to try it." Lancelot Clokey's first book—an account of his personal adventures in foreign countries—was in its tenth week on the best-seller list.

"Why, isn't it, Lance?" Toohey drawled sweetly.

"All right," snapped Clokey, "all right. Give me a drink."

"It's awful," said Lois Cook, her head lolling wearily from side to side. "It's perfectly awful. It's so awful it's wonderful."

"Balls," said Gus Webb. "Why do I ever come here?"

Ike flung his script at the fireplace, it struck against the wire screen and landed, face down, open, the thin pages crushed.

"If Ibsen can write plays, why can't I?" he asked. "He's good and I'm lousy, but that's not a sufficient reason."

"Not in the cosmic sense," said Lancelot Clokey. "Still, you're lousy."

"You don't have to say it. I said so first."

"This is a great play," said a voice.

The voice was slow, nasal and bored. It had spoken for the first time that evening, and they all turned to Jules Fougler. A cartoonist had once drawn a famous picture of him; it consisted of two sagging circles, a large one and a small one: the large one was his stomach, the small one—his lower lip. He wore a suit, beautifully tailored, of a color to which he referred as *"merde d'oie."* He kept his gloves on at all times and he carried a cane. He was an eminent drama critic.

Jules Fougler stretched out his cane, caught the playscript with the hook of the handle and dragged it across the floor to his feet. He did not pick it up, but he repeated, looking at it:

"This is a great play."

"Why?" asked Lancelot Clokey.

"Because I say so," said Jules Fougler.

"Is that a gag, Jules?" asked Lois Cook.

"I never gag," said Jules Fougler. "It is vulgar."

"Send me a coupla seats to the opening," sneered Lancelot Clokey.

"Eight-eighty for two seats to the opening," said Jules Fougler. "It will be the biggest hit of the season."

Jules Fougler turned and saw Toohey looking at him. Toohey smiled but the smile was not light or careless; it was an approving commentary upon something he considered as very serious indeed. Fougler's glance was contemptuous when turned to the others, but it relaxed for a moment of understanding when it rested on Toohey.

"Why don't you join the Council of American Writers, Jules?" asked Toohey.

"I am an individualist," said Fougler. "I don't believe in organizations. Besides, is it necessary?"

"No, not necessary at all," said Toohey cheerfully. "Not for you, Jules. There's nothing I can teach you."

"What I like about you, Ellsworth, is that it's never necessary to explain myself to you."

"Hell, why explain anything here? We're six of a kind."

"Five," said Fougler. "I don't like Gus Webb."

"Why don't you?" asked Gus. He was not offended.

"Because he doesn't wash his ears," answered Fougler, as if the question had been asked by a third party.

"Oh, that," said Gus.

Ike had risen and stood staring at Fougler, not quite certain whether he should breathe.

"You like my play, Mr. Fougler?" he asked at last, his voice small.

"I haven't said I like it," Fougler answered coldly. "I think it smells. That is why it's great."

"Oh," said Ike. He laughed. He seemed relieved. His glance went around the faces in the room, a glance of sly triumph.

"Yes," said Fougler, "my approach to its criticism is the same as your approach to its writing. Our motives are identical."

"You're a grand guy, Jules."

"Mr. Fougler, please."

"You're a grand guy and the swellest bastard on earth, Mr. Fougler."

Fougler turned the pages of the script at his feet with the tip of his cane.

"Your typing is atrocious, Ike," he said.

"Hell, I'm not a stenographer. I'm a creative artist."

"You will be able to afford a secretary after this show opens. I shall be obliged to praise it—if for no other reason than to prevent any further abuse of a typewriter, such as this. The typewriter is a splendid instrument, not to be outraged."

"All right, Jules," said Lancelot Clokey, "it's all very witty and smart and you're sophisticated and brilliant as all get-out—but what do you actually want to praise that crap for?"

"Because it is—as you put it—crap."

"You're not logical, Lance," said Ike. "Not in the cosmic sense you aren't. To write a good play and to have it praised is nothing. Anybody can do that. Anybody with talent—and talent is only a glandular accident. But to write a piece of crap and have it praised—well, you match that."

"He has," said Toohey.

"That's a matter of opinion," said Lancelot Clokey. He upturned his empty glass over his mouth and sucked at a last piece of ice.

"Ike understands things much better than you do, Lance," said Jules Fougler. "He has just proved himself to be a real thinker—in that little speech of his. Which, incidentally, was better than his whole play."

"I'll write my next play about that," said Ike.

"Ike has stated his reasons," Fougler continued. "And mine. And also yours, Lance. Examine my case, if you wish. What achievement is there for a critic in praising a good play? None whatever. The critic is then nothing but a kind of glorified messenger boy between author and public. What's there in that for me? I'm sick of it. I have a right to wish to impress my own personality upon people. Otherwise I shall become frustrated—and I do not believe in frustration. But if a critic is able to put over a perfectly worthless play—ah, you do perceive the difference! Therefore, I shall make a hit out of—what's the name of your play, Ike?"

"No skin off your ass," said Ike.

"I beg your pardon?"

"That's the title."

"Oh, I see. Therefore, I shall make a hit out of *No Skin Off Your Ass*."

Lois Cook laughed loudly.

"You all make too damn much fuss about everything," said Gus Webb, lying flat, his hands entwined under his head.

"Now if you wish to consider your own case, Lance," Fougler went on. "What satisfaction is there for a correspondent in reporting on world events? The public reads about all sorts of international crises and you're lucky if they even notice your by-line. But you're every bit as good as any general, admiral or ambassador. You have a right to make people conscious of yourself. So you've done the wise thing. You've written a remarkable collection of bilge—yes, bilge—but morally justified. A clever book. World catastrophes used as a backdrop for your own nasty little personality. How Lancelot Clokey got drunk at an international conference. What beauties slept with Lancelot Clokey during an invasion. How Lancelot Clokey got dysentery in a land of famine. Well, why not, Lance? It went over, didn't it? Ellsworth put it over, didn't he?"

"The public appreciates good human-interest stuff," said Lancelot Clokey, looking angrily into his glass.

"Oh, can the crap, Lance!" cried Lois Cook. "Who're you acting for here? You know damn well it wasn't any kind of a human interest, but plain Ellsworth Toohey."

"I don't forget what I owe Ellsworth," said Clokey sullenly. "Ellsworth's my best friend. Still, he couldn't have done it if he didn't have a good book to do it with."

Eight months ago Lancelot Clokey had stood with a manuscript in his hand before Ellsworth Toohey, as Ike stood before Fougler now, not believing it when Toohey told him that his book would top the best-seller list. But two hundred thousand copies sold had made it impossible for Clokey ever to recognize any truth again in any form.

"Well, he did it with *The Gallant Gallstone*," said Lois Cook placidly, "and a worse piece of trash never was put down on paper. I ought to know. But he did it."

"And almost lost my job doing it," said Toohey indifferently.

"What do you do with your liquor, Lois?" snapped Clokey. "Save it to take a bath in?"

"All right, blotter," said Lois Cook, rising lazily.

She shuffled across the room, picked somebody's unfinished drink off the floor, drank the remnant, walked out and came back with an assortment of expensive bottles. Clokey and Ike hurried to help themselves.

"I think you're unfair to Lance, Lois," said Toohey. "Why shouldn't he write an autobiography?"

"Because his life wasn't worth living, let alone recording."

"Ah, but that is precisely why I made it a best-seller."

"You're telling me?"

"I like to tell someone."

There were many comfortable chairs around him, but Toohey preferred to remain on the floor. He rolled over to his stomach, propping his torso upright on his elbows, and he lolled pleasurably, switching his weight from elbow to elbow, his legs spread out in a wide fork on the carpet. He seemed to enjoy unrestraint.

"I like to tell someone. Next month I'm pushing the autobiography of a small-town dentist who's really a remarkable person—because there's not a single remarkable day in his life nor sentence in his book. You'll like it, Lois. Can you imagine a solid bromide undressing his soul as if it were a revelation?"

"The little people," said Ike tenderly. "I love the little people. We must love the little people of this earth."

"Save that for your next play," said Toohey.

"I can't," said Ike. "It's in this one."

"What's the big idea, Ellsworth?" snapped Clokey.

"Why, it's simple, Lance. When the fact that one is a total nonentity who's done nothing more outstanding than eating, sleeping and chatting with neighbors becomes a fact worthy of pride, of announcement to the world and of diligent study by millions of readers—the fact that one has built a cathedral becomes unrecordable and unannounceable. A matter of perspectives and relativity. The distance permissible between the extremes of any particular capacity is limited. The sound perception of an ant does not include thunder."

"You talk like a decadent bourgeois, Ellsworth," said Gus Webb.

"Pipe down, Sweetie-pie," said Toohey without resentment.

"It's all very wonderful," said Lois Cook, "except that you're doing too well, Ellsworth. You'll run me out of business. Pretty soon if I still want to be noticed, I'll have to write something that's actually good."

"Not in this century, Lois," said Toohey. "And perhaps not in the next. It's later than you think."

"But you haven't said . . . !" Ike cried suddenly, worried.

"What haven't I said?"

"You haven't said who's going to produce my play!"

"Leave that to me," said Jules Fougler.

"I forgot to thank you, Ellsworth," said Ike solemnly. "So now I thank you. There are lots of bum plays, but you picked mine. You and Mr. Fougler."

"Your bumness is serviceable, Ike."

"Well, that's something."

"It's a great deal."

"How—for instance?"

"Don't talk too much, Ellsworth," said Gus Webb. "You've got a talking jag."

"Shut your face, Kewpie-doll. I like to talk. For instance, Ike? Well, for instance, suppose I didn't like Ibsen——"

"Ibsen is good," said Ike.

"Sure he's good, but suppose I didn't like him. Suppose I wanted to stop people from seeing his plays. It would do me no good whatever to tell them so. But if I sold them the idea that you're just as great as Ibsen—pretty soon they wouldn't be able to tell the difference."

"Jesus, can you?"

"It's only an example, Ike."

"But it would be wonderful!"

"Yes. It would be wonderful. And then it wouldn't matter what they went to see at all. Then nothing would matter—neither the writers nor those for whom they wrote."

"How's that, Ellsworth?"

"Look, Ike, there's no room in the theater for both Ibsen and you. You do understand that, don't you?"

"In a manner of speaking—yes."

"Well, you do want me to make room for you, don't you?"

"All of this useless discussion has been covered before and much better," said Gus Webb. "Shorter. I believe in functional economy."

"Where's it covered, Gus?" asked Lois Cook.

" 'Who had been nothing shall be all,' sister."

"Gus is crude, but deep," said Ike. "I like him."

"Go to hell," said Gus.

Lois Cook's butler entered the room. He was a stately, elderly man and he wore full-dress evening clothes. He announced Peter Keating.

"Pete?" said Lois Cook gaily. "Why, sure, shove him in, shove him right in."

Keating entered and stopped, startled, when he saw the gathering.

"Oh . . . hello, everybody," he said bleakly. "I didn't know you had company, Lois."

"That's not company. Come in, Pete, sit down, grab yourself a drink, you know everybody."

"Hello, Ellsworth," said Keating, his eyes resting on Toohey for support.

Toohey waved his hand, scrambled to his feet and settled down in an armchair, crossing his legs gracefully. Everybody in the room adjusted himself automatically to a sudden control: to sit straighter, to bring knees together, to pull in a relaxed mouth. Only Gus Webb remained stretched as before.

Keating looked cool and handsome, bringing into the unventilated room the freshness of a walk through cold streets. But he was pale and his movements were slow, tired.

"Sorry if I intrude, Lois," he said. "Had nothing to do and felt so damn lonely, thought I'd drop in." He slurred over the word "lonely," throwing it away with a self-deprecatory smile. "Damn tired of Neil Dumont and the bunch. Wanted more uplifting company—sort of spiritual food, huh?"

"I'm a genius," said Ike. "I'll have a play on Broadway. Me and Ibsen. Ellsworth said so."

"Ike has just read his new play to us," said Toohey. "A magnificent piece of work."

"You'll love it, Peter," said Lancelot Clokey. "It's really great."

"It is a masterpiece," said Jules Fougler. "I hope you will prove yourself worthy of it, Peter. It is the kind of play that depends upon what the members of the audience are capable of bringing with them into the theater. If you are one of those literal-minded people, with a dry soul and a limited imagination, it is not for you. But if you are a real human being with a big, big heart full of laughter, who has preserved the uncorrupted capacity of his childhood for pure emotion—you will find it an unforgettable experience."

"Except as ye become as little children ye shall not enter the Kingdom of Heaven," said Ellsworth Toohey.

"Thanks, Ellsworth," said Jules Fougler. "That will be the lead of my review."

Keating looked at Ike, at the others, his eyes eager. They all seemed remote and pure, far above him in the safety of their knowledge, but their faces had hints of smiling warmth, a benevolent invitation extended downward.

Keating drank the sense of their greatness, the spiritual food he sought in coming here, and felt himself rising through them. They saw their greatness made real by him. A circuit was established in the room and the circle closed. Everybody was conscious of that, except Peter Keating.

Ellsworth Toohey came out in support of the cause of modern architecture.

In the past ten years, while most of the new residences continued to be built as faithful historical copies, the principles of Henry Cameron had won the field of commercial structures: the factories, the office buildings, the skyscrapers. It was a pale, distorted victory; a reluctant compromise that consisted of omitting columns and pediments, allowing a few stretches of wall to remain naked, apologizing for a shape—good through accident—by finishing it off with an edge of simplified Grecian volutes. Many stole Cameron's forms; few understood his thinking. The sole part of his argument irresistible to the owners of new structures was financial economy; he won to that extent.

In the countries of Europe, most prominently in Germany, a new school of building had been growing for a long time: it consisted of putting up four walls and a flat top over them, with a few openings. This was called new architecture. The freedom from arbitrary rules, for which Cameron had fought, the freedom that imposed a great new responsibility on the creative builder, became a mere elimination of all effort, even the effort of mastering historical styles. It became a rigid set of new rules—the discipline of conscious incompetence, creative poverty made into a system, mediocrity boastfully confessed.

"A building creates its own beauty, and its ornament is derived from the rules of its theme and its structure," Cameron had said. "A building needs no beauty, no ornament and no theme," said the new architects. It was safe to say it. Cameron and a few men had broken the path and paved it with their lives. Other men, of whom there were greater numbers, the men who had been safe in copying the Parthenon, saw the danger and found a way to security: to walk Cameron's path and make it lead them to a new Parthenon, an easier Parthenon in the shape of a packing crate of glass and concrete. The palm tree had broken through; the fungus came to feed on it, to deform it, to hide, to pull it back into the common jungle.

The jungle found its words.

In "One Small Voice," sub-titled "I Swim with the Current," Ellsworth Toohey wrote:

"We have hesitated for a long time to acknowledge the powerful phenomenon known as Modern Architecture. Such caution is requisite in anyone who stands in the position of mentor to the public taste. Too often, isolated manifestations of anomaly can be mistaken for a broad popular movement, and one should be careful not to ascribe to them a significance they do not deserve. But Modern Architecture has stood the test of time, has answered a demand of the masses, and we are glad to salute it.

"It is not amiss to offer a measure of recognition to the pioneers of this movement, such as the late Henry Cameron. Premonitory echoes of the new grandeur can be found in some of his work. But like all pioneers he was still bound by the inherited prejudices of the past, by the sentimentality of the middle class from which he came. He succumbed to the superstition of beauty and ornament, even though the ornament was of his own devising, and, consequently, inferior to that of established historical forms.

"It remained for the power of a broad, collective movement to bring Modern Architecture to its full and true expression. Now it can be seen—growing throughout the world—not as a chaos of individual fancies, but as a cohesive, organized discipline which makes severe demands upon the artist, among them the demand to subordinate himself to the collective nature of his craft.

"The rules of this new architecture have been formulated by the vast process of popular creation. They are as strict as the rules of Classicism. They demand unadorned simplicity—like the honesty of the unspoiled common man. Just as in the passing age of international bankers every building had to have an ostentatious cornice, so now the coming age ordains that every building have a flat roof. Just as the imperialist era required a Roman portico on every house, so the era of humanity requires that every house have corner windows—symbol of the sunshine distributed equally to all.

"The discriminating will see the social significance eloquent in the forms of this new architecture. Under the old system of exploitation, the most useful social elements—the workers—were never permitted to realize their importance; their practical functions were kept hidden and disguised; thus a master had his servants dressed up in fancy gold-braided livery. This was reflected in the architecture of the period; the functional elements of a building—its doors, windows, stairways—were hidden under the scrolls of pointless ornamentation. But in a modern building, it is precisely these useful elements—symbols of toil—that come starkly in the open. Do we not hear in this the voice of a new world where the worker shall come into his own?

"As the best example of Modern Architecture in America, we call to your attention the new plant of the Bassett Brush Company, soon to be completed. It is a small building, but in its modest proportions it embodies all the grim simplicity of the new discipline and presents an invigorating example of the Grandeur of the Little. It was designed by Augustus Webb, a young architect of great promise."

Meeting Toohey a few days later, Peter Keating asked, disturbed: "Say, Ellsworth, did you mean it?"
"What?"
"About modern architecture."
"Of course I meant it. How did you like my little piece?"
"Oh, I thought it was very beautiful. Very convincing. But say, Ellsworth, why . . . why did you pick Gus Webb? After all, I've done some modernistic things in the last few years. The Palmer Building was quite bare, and the Mowry Building was nothing but roof and windows, and the Sheldon Warehouse was . . ."
"Now, Peter, don't be a hog. I've done pretty well by you, haven't I? Let me give somebody else a boost once in a while."
At a luncheon where he had to speak on architecture, Peter Keating stated:
"In reviewing my career to date, I came to the conclusion that I have worked on a true principle: the principle that constant change is a necessity of life. Since buildings are an indispensable part of life, it follows that architecture must change constantly. I have never developed any architectural prejudices for myself, but insisted on keeping my mind open to all the voices of the times. The fanatics who went around preaching that all structures must be modern were just as narrow-minded as the hidebound conservatives who demanded that we employ nothing but historical styles. I do not apologize for those of my buildings which were designed in the Classical tradition. They were an answer to the need of their era. Neither do I apologize for the buildings which I designed in the modern style. They represent the coming better world. It is my opinion that in the humble realization of this principle lies the reward and the joy of being an architect."

There was gratifying publicity, and many flattering comments of envy in professional circles, when the news of Peter Keating's selection to build Stoneridge was made public. He tried to recapture his old pleasure in such manifestations. He failed. He still felt something that resembled gladness, but it was faded and thin.

The effort of designing Stoneridge seemed a load too vast to lift. He did not mind the circumstances through which he had obtained it; that, too, had become pale and weightless in his mind, accepted and almost forgotten. He simply could not face the task of designing the great number of houses that Stoneridge required. He felt very tired. He felt tired when he awakened in the morning, and he found himself waiting all day for the time when he would be able to go back to bed.

He turned Stoneridge over to Neil Dumont and Bennett. "Go ahead," he said wearily, "do what you want." "What style, Pete?" Dumont asked. "Oh, make it some sort of period—the small home owners won't go for it otherwise. But trim it down a little—for the press comments. Give it historical touches and a modern feeling. Any way you wish. I don't care."

Dumont and Bennett went ahead. Keating changed a few roof lines on their sketches, a few windows. The preliminary drawings were approved by Wynand's office. Keating did not know whether Wynand had approved in person. He did not see Wynand again.

Dominique had been away a month, when Guy Francon announced his retirement. Keating had told him about the divorce, offering no explanation. Francon had taken the news calmly. He had said: "I expected it. It's all right, Peter. It's probably not your fault nor hers." He had not mentioned it since. Now he gave no explanation of his retirement, only: "I told you it was coming, long ago. I'm tired. Good luck, Peter."

The responsibility of the firm on his lonely shoulders and the prospect of his solitary name on the office door left Keating uneasy. He needed a partner. He chose Neil Dumont. Neil had grace and distinction. He was another Lucius Heyer. The firm became Peter Keating & Cornelius Dumont. Some sort of drunken celebration of the event was held by a few friends, but Keating did not attend it. He had promised to attend, but he forgot about it, went for a solitary weekend in the snowbound country, and did not remember the celebration until the morning after it was held, when he was walking alone down a frozen country road.

Stoneridge was the last contract signed by the firm of Francon & Keating.

VII

WHEN DOMINIQUE STEPPED OFF THE TRAIN IN NEW YORK, Wynand was there to meet her. She had not written to him nor heard from him during the weeks of her residence in Reno; she had notified no one of her return. But his figure standing on the platform, standing calmly, with an air of finality, told her that he had kept in touch with her lawyers, had followed every step of the divorce proceedings, had known the date when the decree was granted, the hour when she took the train and the number of her compartment.

He did not move forward when he saw her. It was she who walked to him, because she knew that he wanted to see her walking, if only the short space between them. She did not smile, but her face had the lovely serenity that can become a smile without transition.

"Hello, Gail."

"Hello, Dominique."

She had not thought of him in his absence, not sharply, not with a personal feeling of his reality, but now she felt an immediate recognition, a sense of reunion with someone known and needed.

He said: "Give me your baggage checks, I'll have it attended to later; my car is outside."

She handed him the checks and he slipped them into his pocket. They knew they must turn and walk up the platform to the exit, but the decisions both had made in advance broke down in the same instant, because they did not turn, but remained standing, looking at each other.

He made the first effort to correct the breach. He smiled lightly.

"If I had the right to say it, I'd say that I couldn't have endured the waiting had I known that you'd look as you do. But since I have no such right, I'm not going to say it."

She laughed. "All right, Gail. That was a form of pretense, too—our being too casual. It makes things more important, not less, doesn't it? Let's say whatever we wish."

"I love you," he said, his voice expressionless, as if the words were a statement of pain and not addressed to her.

"I'm glad to be back with you, Gail. I didn't know I would be, but I'm glad."

"In what way, Dominique?"

"I don't know. In a way of contagion from you, I think. In a way of finality and peace."

496

Then they noticed that this was said in the middle of a crowded platform, with people and baggage racks hurrying past.

They walked out to the street, to his car. She did not ask where they were going; and did not care. She sat silently beside him. She felt divided, most of her swept by a wish not to resist, and a small part of her left to wonder about it. She felt a desire to let him carry her—a feeling of confidence without appraisal, not a happy confidence, but confidence. After a while, she noticed that her hand lay in his, the length of her gloved fingers held to the length of his, only the spot of her bare wrist pressed to his skin. She had not noticed him take her hand; it seemed so natural and what she had wanted from the moment of seeing him. But she would not allow herself to want it.

"Where are we going, Gail?" she asked.

"To get the license. Then to the judge's office. To be married."

She sat up slowly, turning to face him. She did not withdraw her hand, but her fingers became rigid, conscious, taken away from him.

"No," she said.

She smiled and held the smile too long, in deliberate, fixed precision. He looked at her calmly.

"I want a real wedding, Gail. I want it at the most ostentatious hotel in town. I want engraved invitations, guests, mobs of guests, celebrities, flowers, flash bulbs and newsreel cameras. I want the kind of wedding the public expects of Gail Wynand."

He released her fingers, simply, without resentment. He looked abstracted for a moment, as if he were calculating a problem in arithmetic, not too difficult. Then he said:

"All right. That will take a week to arrange. I could have it done tonight, but if it's engraved invitations, we must give the guests a week's notice at the least. Otherwise it would look abnormal and you want a normal Gail Wynand wedding. I'll have to take you to a hotel now, where you can live for a week. I had not planned for this, so I've made no reservations. Where would you like to stay?"

"At your penthouse."

"No."

"The Nordland, then."

He leaned forward and said to the chauffeur:

"The Nordland, John."

In the lobby of the hotel, he said to her:

"I will see you a week from today, Tuesday, at the Noyes-Belmont, at four o'clock in the afternoon. The invitations will have to be in the name of your father. Let him know that I'll get in touch with him. I'll attend to the rest."

He bowed, his manner unchanged, his calm still holding the same peculiar quality made of two things: the mature control of a man so certain of his capacity for control that it could seem casual, and a childlike simplicity of accepting events as if they were subject to no possible change.

She did not see him during that week. She found herself waiting impatiently.

She saw him again when she stood beside him, facing the judge who pronounced the words of the marriage ceremony over the silence of six hundred people in the floodlighted ballroom of the Noyes-Belmont Hotel.

The background she had wished was set so perfectly that it became its own caricature, not a specific society wedding, but an impersonal proto-type of lavish, exquisite vulgarity. He had understood her wish and obeyed scrupulously; he had refused himself the relief of exaggeration, he had not staged the event crudely, but made it beautiful in the exact manner Gail Wynand, the publisher, would have chosen had he wished to be married in public. But Gail Wynand did not wish to be married in public.

He made himself fit the setting, as if he were part of the bargain, subject to the same style. When he entered, she saw him looking at the mob of guests as if he did not realize that such a mob was appropriate to a Grand Opera premiere or a royal rummage sale, not to the solemn climax of his life. He looked correct, incomparably distinguished.

Then she stood with him, the mob becoming a heavy silence and a gluttonous stare behind him, and they faced the judge together. She wore a long, black dress with a bouquet of fresh jasmine, his present, attached by a black band to her wrist. Her face in the halo of a black lace hat was raised to the judge who spoke slowly, letting his words hang one by one in the air.

She glanced at Wynand. He was not looking at her nor at the judge. Then she knew that he was alone in that room. He held this moment and he made of it, of the glare, of the vulgarity, a silent height of his own. He had not wished a religious ceremony, which he did not respect, and he could have less respect for the state's functionary reciting a formula before him—but he made the rite an act of pure religion. She thought, if she were being married to Roark in such a setting, Roark would stand like this.

Afterward, the mockery of the monster reception that followed, left him immune. He posed with her for the battery of press cameras and he complied gracefully with all the demands of the reporters, a special, noisier mob within the mob. He stood with her in the receiving line, shaking an assembly belt of hands that unrolled past them for hours. He looked untouched by the lights, the haystacks of Easter lilies, the sounds of a string orchestra, the river of people flowing on and breaking into a delta when it reached the champagne; untouched by these guests who had come here driven by boredom, by an envious hatred, a reluctant submission to an invitation bearing his dangerous name, a scandal-hungry curiosity. He looked as if he did not know that they took his public immolation as their rightful due, that they considered their presence as the indispensable seal of sacrament upon the occasion, that of all the hundreds he and his bride were the only ones to whom the performance was hideous.

She watched him intently. She wanted to see him take pleasure in all this, if only for a moment. Let him accept and join, just once, she thought, let him show the soul of the New York *Banner* in its proper element. She saw no acceptance. She saw a hint of pain, at times; even the pain did not reach him completely. And she thought of the only other man she knew who had spoken about suffering that went down only to a certain point.

When the last congratulations had drifted past them, they were free to leave by the rules of the occasion. But he made no move to leave. She knew he was waiting for her decision. She walked away from him into the currents of guests; she smiled, bowed and listened to offensive nonsense, a glass of champagne in her hand.

She saw her father in the throng. He looked proud and wistful; he seemed bewildered. He had taken the announcement of her marriage quietly; he had said: "I want you to be happy, Dominique. I want it very much. I hope he's the right man." His tone had said that he was not certain.

She saw Ellsworth Toohey in the crowd. He noticed her looking at him and turned away quickly. She wanted to laugh aloud; but the matter of Ellsworth Toohey caught off guard did not seem important enough to laugh about now.

Alvah Scarret pushed his way toward her. He was making a poor effort at a suitable expression, but his face looked hurt and sullen. He muttered something rapid about his wishes for her happiness, but then he said distinctly and with a lively anger:

"But why, Dominique? *Why?*"

She could not quite believe that Alvah Scarret would permit himself the crudeness of what the question seemed to mean. She asked coldly:

"What are you talking about, Alvah?"

"The veto, of course."

"What veto?"

"You know very well what veto. Now I ask you, with every sheet in the city here, every damn one of them, the lousiest tabloid included, and the wire services too—everything but the *Banner!* Everything but the Wynand papers! What am I to tell people? How am I to explain? Is that a thing for you to do to a former comrade of the trade?"

"You'd better repeat that, Alvah."

"You mean you didn't know that Gail wouldn't allow a single one of our boys here? That we won't have any stories tomorrow, not a spread, not a picture, nothing but two lines on page eighteen?"

"No," she said, "I didn't know it."

He wondered at the sudden jerk of her movement as she turned away from him. She handed the champagne glass to the first stranger in sight, whom she mistook for a waiter. She made her way through the crowd to Wynand.

"Let's go, Gail."

"Yes, my dear."

She stood, incredulously, in the middle of the drawing room of his penthouse, thinking that this place was now her home and how right it looked to be her home.

He watched her. He showed no desire to speak or touch her, only to observe her here, in his house, brought here, lifted high over the city; as if the significance of the moment were not to be shared, not even with her.

She moved slowly across the room, took off her hat, leaned against the edge of a table. She wondered why her normal desire to say little, to hold things closed, broke down before him, why she felt compelled to simple frankness, such as she could offer no one else.

"You've had your way after all, Gail. You were married as you wanted to be married.

"Yes, I think so."

"It was useless to try to torture you."

"Actually, yes. But I didn't mind it too much."

"You didn't?"

"No. If that's what you wanted it was only a matter of keeping my promise."

"But you hated it, Gail."

"Utterly. What of it? Only the first moment was hard—when you said it in the car. Afterward, I was rather glad of it." He spoke quietly, matching her frankness; she knew he would leave her the choice—he would follow her manner—he would keep silent or admit anything she wished to be admitted.

"Why?"

"Didn't you notice your own mistake—if it was a mistake? You wouldn't have wanted to make me suffer if you were completely indifferent to me."

"No. It was not a mistake."

"You're a good loser, Dominique."

"I think that's also contagion from you, Gail. And there's something I want to thank you for."

"What?"

"That you barred our wedding from the Wynand papers."

He looked at her, his eyes alert in a special way for a moment, then he smiled.

"It's out of character—your thanking me for that."

"It was out of character for you to do it."

"I had to. But I thought you'd be angry."

"I should have been. But I wasn't. I'm not. I thank you."

"Can one feel gratitude for gratitude? It's a little hard to express, but that's what I feel, Dominique."

She looked at the soft light on the walls around her. That lighting was part of the room, giving the walls a special texture of more than material or color. She thought that there were other rooms beyond these walls, rooms she had never seen which were hers now. And she found that she wanted them to be hers.

"Gail, I haven't asked what we are to do now. Are we going away? Are we having a honeymoon? Funny, I haven't even wondered about it. I thought of the wedding and nothing beyond. As if it stopped there and you took over from then on. Also out of character, Gail."

"But not in my favor, this time. Passivity is not a good sign. Not for you."

"It might be—if I'm glad of it."

"Might. Though it won't last. No, we're not going anywhere. Unless you wish to go."

"No."

"Then we stay here. Another peculiar manner of making an exception. The proper manner for you and me. Going away has always been running—for both of us. This time, we don't run."

"Yes, Gail."

When he held her and kissed her, her arm lay bent, pressed between her body and his, her hand at her shoulder—and she felt her cheek touching the faded jasmine bouquet on her wrist, its perfume still intact, still a delicate suggestion of spring.

When she entered his bedroom, she found that it was not the place she had seen photographed in countless magazines. The glass cage had been demolished. The room built in its place was a solid vault without a single window. It was lighted and air-conditioned, but neither light nor air came from the outside.

She lay in his bed and she pressed her palms to the cold, smooth sheet at her sides, not to let her arms move and touch him. But her rigid indifference did not drive him to helpless anger. He understood. He laughed. She heard him say—his voice rough, without consideration, amused—"It won't do, Dominique." And she knew that this barrier would not be held between them, that she had no power to hold it. She felt the answer in her body, an answer of hunger, of acceptance, of pleasure. She thought that it was not a matter of desire, not even a matter of the sexual act, but only that man was the life force and woman could respond to nothing else; that this man had the will of life, the prime power, and this act was only its simplest statement, and she was responding not to the act nor to the man, but to that force within him.

"Well?" asked Ellsworth Toohey. "Now do you get the point?"

He stood leaning informally against the back of Scarret's chair, and Scarret sat staring down at a hamper full of mail by the side of his desk.

"Thousands," sighed Scarret, "thousands, Ellsworth. You ought to see what they call him. Why didn't he print the story of his wedding? What's he ashamed of? What's he got to hide? Why didn't he get married in church, like any decent man. How could he marry a divorcee? That's what they're all asking. Thousands. And he won't even look at the letters. Gail Wynand, the man they called the seismograph of public opinion."

"That's right," said Toohey. "That kind of a man."

"Here's a sample," Scarret picked up a letter from his desk and read aloud: " 'I'm a respectable woman and mother of five children and I certainly don't think I want to bring up my children with your newspaper. Have taken same for fourteen years, but now that you show that you're the kind of man that has no decency and making a mockery of the holy institution of marriage which is to commit adultery with a fallen woman also another man's wife who gets married in a black dress as she jolly well ought to, I won't read your newspaper any more as you're not a man fit for children, and I'm certainly disappointed in you. Very truly yours. Mrs. Thomas Parker.' I read it to him. He just laughed."

"Uh-huh," said Toohey.

"What's got into him?"

"It's nothing that got into him, Alvah. It's something that got out at last."

"By the way, did you know that many papers dug up their old pictures of Dominique's nude statue from that goddamn temple and ran it right with the wedding story—to show Mrs. Wynand's interest in art, the bastards! Are they glad to get back at Gail! Are they giving it to him, the lice! Wonder who reminded them of that one."

"I wouldn't know."

"Well, of course, it's just one of those storms in a teacup. They'll forget all about it in a few weeks. I don't think it will do much harm."

"No. Not this incident alone. Not by itself."

"Huh? Are you predicting something?"

"Those letters predict it, Alvah. Not the letters as such. But that he wouldn't read them."

"Oh, it's no use getting too silly either. Gail knows where to stop and when. Don't make a mountain out of a mo——" He glanced up at Toohey and his voice switched to: "Christ, yes, Ellsworth, you're right. What are we going to do?"

"Nothing, my friend, nothing. Not for a long time yet."

Toohey sat down on the edge of Scarret's desk and let the tip of his pointed shoe play among the envelopes in the hamper, tossing them up, making them rustle. He had acquired a pleasant habit of dropping in and out of Scarret's office at all hours. Scarret had come to depend on him.

"Say, Ellsworth," Scarret asked suddenly, "are you really loyal to the *Banner?*"

"Alvah, don't talk in dialect. Nobody's really that stuffy."

"No, I mean it. . . . Well, you know what I mean."

"Haven't the faintest idea. Who's ever disloyal to his bread and butter?"

"Yeah, that's so. . . . Still, you know, Ellsworth, I like you a lot, only I'm never sure when you're just talking my language or when it's really yours."

"Don't go getting yourself into psychological complexities. You'll get all tangled up. What's on your mind?"

"Why do you still write for the *New Frontiers?*"

"For money."

"Oh, come, that's chicken feed to you."

"Well, it's a prestige magazine. Why shouldn't I write for them? You haven't got an exclusive on me."

"No, and I don't care who you write for on the side. But the *New Frontiers* has been damn funny lately."

"About what?"

"About Gail Wynand."

"Oh, rubbish, Alvah!"

"No sir, this isn't rubbish. You just haven't noticed, guess you don't read it close enough, but I've got an instinct about things like that and I know. I know when it's just some smart young punk taking pot-shots or when a magazine means business."

"You're nervous, Alvah, and you're exaggerating. The *New Frontiers* is a liberal magazine and they've always sniped at Gail Wynand. Everybody has. He's never been any too popular in the trade, you know. Hasn't hurt him, though, has it?"

"This is different. I don't like it when there's a system behind it, a kind of special purpose, like a lot of little trickles dribbling along, all innocently, and pretty soon they make a little stream, and it all fits pat, and pretty soon . . ."

"Getting a persecution mania, Alvah?"

"I don't like it. It was all right when people took cracks at his yachts and women and a few municipal election scandals—which were never proved," he added hastily. "But I don't like it when it's that new intelligentsia slang that people seem to be going for nowadays: Gail Wynand, the exploiter, Gail Wynand, the pirate of capitalism, Gail Wynand, the disease of an era. It's still crap, Ellsworth, only there's dynamite in that kind of crap."

"It's just the modern way of saying the same old things, nothing more. Besides, I can't be responsible for the policy of a magazine just because I sell them an article once in a while."

"Yeah, but . . . That's not what I hear."

"What do you hear?"

"I hear you're financing the damn thing."

"Who, *me?* With what?"

"Well, not you yourself exactly. But I hear it was you who got young Ronny Pickering, the booze hound, to give them a shot in the arm to the tune of one hundred thousand smackers, just about when *New Frontiers* was going the way of all frontiers."

"Hell, that was just to save Ronny from the town's more expensive gutters. The kid was going to the dogs. Gave him a sort of higher purpose in life. And put one hundred thousand smackers to better use than the chorus cuties who'd have got it out of him anyway."

"Yeah, but you could've attached a little string to the gift, slipped word to the editors that they'd better lay off Gail or else."

"The *New Frontiers* is not the *Banner,* Alvah. It's a magazine of principles. One doesn't attach strings to its editors and one doesn't tell them 'or else.' "

"In this game, Ellsworth? Whom are you kidding?"

"Well, if it will set your mind at rest, I'll tell you something you haven't heard. It's not supposed to be known—it was done through a lot of proxies. Did you know that I got Mitchell Layton to buy a nice fat chunk of the *Banner?*"

"No!"

"Yes."

"Christ, Ellsworth, that's great! Mitchell Layton? We can use a reservoir like that and . . . Wait a minute. Mitchell Layton?"

"Yes. What's wrong with Mitchell Layton?"

"Isn't he the little boy who couldn't digest grandpaw's money?"

"Grandpaw left him an awful lot of money."

"Yeah, but he's a crackpot. He's the one who's been a Yogi, then a vegetarian, then a Unitarian, then a nudist—and now he's gone to build a palace of the proletariat in Moscow."

"So what?"

"But Jesus!—a Red among our stockholders?"

"Mitch isn't a Red. How can one be a Red with a quarter of a billion dollars? He's just a pale tea-rose. Mostly yellow. But a nice kid at heart."

"But—on the *Banner!*"

"Alvah, you're an ass. Don't you see? I've made him put some dough into a good, solid, conservative paper. That'll cure him of his pink notions and set him in the right direction. Besides, what harm can he do? Your dear Gail controls his papers, doesn't he?"

"Does Gail know about this?"

"No. Dear Gail hasn't been as watchful in the last five years as he used to be. And you'd better not tell him. You see the way Gail's going. He'll need a little pressure. And you'll need the dough. Be nice to Mitch Layton. He can come in handy."

"That's so."

"It is. You see? My heart's in the right place. I've helped a puny little liberal mag like the *New Frontiers,* but I've also brought a much more substantial hunk of cash to a big stronghold of arch-conservatism such as the New York *Banner.*"

"So you have. Damn decent of you, too, considering that you're a kind of radical yourself."

"Now are you going to talk about any disloyalty?"

"Guess not. Guess you'll stand by the old *Banner.*"

"Of course I will. Why, I love the *Banner.* I'd do anything for it. Why, I'd give my life for the New York *Banner.*"

VIII

WALKING THE SOIL OF A DESERT ISLAND HOLDS ONE ANCHORED to the rest of the earth; but in their penthouse, with the telephone disconnected, Wynand and Dominique had no feeling of the fifty-seven floors below them, of steel shafts braced against granite—and it seemed to them that their home was anchored in space, not an island, but a planet. The city became a friendly sight, an abstraction with which no possible communication could be established, like the sky, a spectacle to be admired, but of no direct concern in their lives.

For two weeks after their wedding they never left the penthouse. She could have pressed the button of the elevator and broken these weeks any time she wished; she did not wish it. She had no desire to resist, to wonder, to question. It was enchantment and peace.

He sat talking to her for hours when she wanted. He was content to sit silently, when she preferred, and look at her as he looked at the objects in his art gallery, with the same distant, undisturbing glance. He answered any question she put to him. He never asked questions. He never spoke of what he felt. When she wished to be alone, he did not call for her. One evening she sat reading in her room and saw him standing at the frozen parapet of the dark roof garden outside, not looking back at the house, only standing in the streak of light from her window.

When the two weeks ended, he went back to his work, to the office of the *Banner*. But the sense of isolation remained, like a theme declared and to be preserved through all their future days. He came home in the evening and the city ceased to exist. He had no desire to go anywhere. He invited no guests.

He never mentioned it, but she knew that he did not want her to step out of the house, neither with him nor alone. It was a quiet obsession which he did not expect to enforce. When he came home, he asked: "Have you been out?"—never: "Where have you been?" It was not jealousy—the "where" did not matter. When she wanted to buy a pair of shoes, he had three stores send a collection of shoes for her choice—it prevented her visit to a store. When she said she wanted to see a certain picture, he had a projection room built on the roof.

She obeyed, for the first few months. When she realized that she loved their isolation, she broke it at once. She made him accept invitations and she invited guests to their home. He complied without protest.

506

But he maintained a wall she could not break—the wall he had erected between his wife and his newspapers. Her name never appeared in their pages. He stopped every attempt to draw Mrs. Gail Wynand into public life—to head committees, sponsor charity drives, endorse crusades. He did not hesitate to open her mail—if it bore an official letterhead that betrayed its purpose—to destroy it without answer and to tell her that he had destroyed it. She shrugged and said nothing.

Yet he did not seem to share her contempt for his papers. He did not allow her to discuss them. She could not discover what he thought of them, nor what he felt. Once, when she commented on an offensive editorial, he said coldly:

"I've never apologized for the *Banner*. I never will."

"But this is really awful, Gail."

"I thought you married me as the publisher of the *Banner*."

"I thought you didn't like to think of that."

"What I like or dislike doesn't concern you. Don't expect me to change the *Banner* or sacrifice it. I wouldn't do that for anyone on earth."

She laughed. "I wouldn't ask it, Gail."

He did not laugh in answer.

In his office in the Banner Building, he worked with a new energy, a kind of elated, ferocious drive that surprised the men who had known him in his most ambitious years. He stayed in the office all night when necessary, as he had not done for a long time. Nothing changed in his methods and policy. Alvah Scarret watched him with satisfaction. "We were wrong about him, Ellsworth," said Scarret to his constant companion, "it's the same old Gail, God bless him. Better than ever." "My dear Alvah," said Toohey, "nothing is ever as simple as you think—nor as fast." "But he's happy. Don't you see that he's happy?" "To be happy is the most dangerous thing that could have happened to him. And, as a humanitarian for once, I mean this for his own sake."

Sally Brent decided to outwit her boss. Sally Brent was one of the proudest possessions of the *Banner*, a stout, middle-aged woman who dressed like a model for a style show of the twenty-first century and wrote like a chambermaid. She had a large personal following among the readers of the *Banner*. Her popularity made her overconfident.

Sally Brent decided to do a story on Mrs. Gail Wynand. It was just her type of story and there it was, simply going to waste. She gained admittance to Wynand's penthouse, using the tactics of gaining admittance to places where one is not wanted which she had been taught as a well-trained Wynand employee. She made her usual dramatic entrance, wearing a black dress with a fresh sunflower on her shoulder —her constant ornament that had become a personal trade-mark—and she said to Dominique breathlessly: "Mrs. Wynand, I've come here to help you deceive your husband!"

Then she winked at her own naughtiness and explained: "Our dear Mr. Wynand has been unfair to you, my dear, depriving you of your rightful fame, for some reason which I just simply can't understand. But we'll fix him, you and I. What can a man do when we girls get together? He simply doesn't know what good copy you are. So just give me your story, and I'll write it, and it will be so good that he just simply won't be able not to run it."

Dominique was alone at home, and she smiled in a manner which Sally Brent had never seen before, so the right adjectives did not occur to Sally's usually observant mind. Dominique gave her the story. She gave the exact kind of story Sally had dreamed about.

"Yes, of course I cook his breakfast," said Dominique. "Ham and eggs is his favorite dish, just plain ham and eggs . . . Oh yes, Miss Brent, I'm very happy. I open my eyes in the morning and I say to myself, it can't be true, it's not poor little me who's become the wife of the great Gail Wynand who had all the glamorous beauties of the world to choose from. You see, I've been in love with him for years. He was just a dream to me, a beautiful, impossible dream. And now it's like a dream come true. . . . Please, Miss Brent, take this message from me to the women of America: Patience is always rewarded and romance is just around the corner. I think it's a beautiful thought and perhaps it will help other girls as it has helped me. . . . Yes, all I want of life is to make Gail happy, to share his joys and sorrows, to be a good wife and mother."

Alvah Scarret read the story and liked it so much that he lost all caution. "Run it off, Alvah," Sally Brent urged him, "just have a proof run off and leave it on his desk. He'll okay it, see if he won't." That evening Sally Brent was fired. Her costly contract was bought off—it had three more years to run—and she was told never to enter the Banner Building again for any purpose whatsoever.

Scarret protested in panic: "Gail, you can't fire Sally! Not *Sally!*"

"When I can't fire anyone I wish on my paper, I'll close it and blow up the God-damn building," said Wynand calmly.

"But her public! We'll lose her public!"

"To hell with her public."

That night, at dinner, Wynand took from his pocket a crumpled wad of paper—the proof cut of the story—and threw it, without a word, at Dominique's face across the table. It hit her cheek and fell to the floor. She picked it up, unrolled it, saw what it was and laughed aloud.

Sally Brent wrote an article on Gail Wynand's love life. In a gay, intellectual manner, in the terms of a sociological study, the article presented material such as no pulp magazine would have accepted. It was published in the *New Frontiers*.

* * * * *

Wynand brought Dominique a necklace designed at his special order. It was made of diamonds without visible settings, spaced wide apart in an irregular pattern, like a handful scattered accidentally, held together by platinum chains made under a microscope, barely noticeable. When he clasped it about her neck, it looked like drops of water fallen at random.

She stood before a mirror. She slipped her dressing gown off her shoulders and let the raindrops glitter on her skin. She said:

"That life story of the Bronx housewife who murdered her husband's young mistress is pretty sordid, Gail. But I think there's something dirtier—the curiosity of the people who pander to that curiosity. Actually, it was that housewife—she has piano legs and such a baggy neck in her pictures—who made this necklace possible. It's a beautiful necklace. I shall be proud to wear it."

He smiled; the sudden brightness of his eyes had an odd quality of courage.

"That's one way of looking at it," he said. "There's another. I like to think that I took the worst refuse of the human spirit—the mind of that housewife and the minds of the people who like to read about her—and I made of it this necklace on your shoulders. I like to think that I was an alchemist capable of performing so great a purification."

She saw no apology, no regret, no resentment as he looked at her. It was a strange glance; she had noticed it before; a glance of simple worship. And it made her realize that there is a stage of worship which makes the worshiper himself an object of reverence.

She was sitting before her mirror when he entered her dressing room on the following night. He bent down, he pressed his lips to the back of her neck—and he saw a square of paper attached to the corner of her mirror. It was the decoded copy of the cablegram that had ended her career on the *Banner*. FIRE THE BITCH. G W

He lifted his shoulders, to stand erect behind her. He asked:

"How did you get that?"

"Ellsworth Toohey gave it to me. I thought it was worth preserving. Of course, I didn't know it would ever become so appropriate."

He inclined his head gravely, acknowledging the authorship, and said nothing else.

She expected to find the cablegram gone next morning. But he had not touched it. She would not remove it. It remained displayed on the corner of her mirror. When he held her in his arms, she often saw his eyes move to that square of paper. She could not tell what he thought.

* * * * *

In the spring, a publishers' convention took him away from New York for a week. It was their first separation. Dominique surprised him by coming to meet him at the airport when he returned. She was gay and gentle; her manner held a promise he had never expected, could not trust, and found himself trusting completely.

When he entered the drawing room of their penthouse and slumped down, half stretching on the couch, she knew that he wanted to lie still here, to feel the recaptured safety of his own world. She saw his eyes, open, delivered to her, without defense. She stood straight, ready. She said:

"You'd better dress, Gail. We're going to the theater tonight."

He lifted himself to a sitting posture. He smiled, the slanting ridges standing out on his forehead. She had a cold feeling of admiration for him: the control was perfect, all but these ridges. He said:

"Fine. Black tie or white?"

"White. I have tickets for *No Skin Off Your Nose*. They were very hard to get."

It was too much; it seemed too ludicrous to be part of this moment's contest between them. He broke down by laughing frankly, in helpless disgust.

"Good God, Dominique, not that one!"

"Why, Gail, it's the biggest hit in town. Your own critic, Jules Fougler"—he stopped laughing. He understood—"said it was the greatest play of our age. Ellsworth Toohey said it was the fresh voice of the coming new world. Alvah Scarret said it was not written in ink, but in the milk of human kindness. Sally Brent—before you fired her—said it made her laugh with a lump in her throat. Why, it's the godchild of the *Banner*. I thought you would certainly want to see it."

"Yes, of course," he said.

He got up and went to dress.

No Skin Off Your Nose had been running for many months. Ellsworth Toohey had mentioned regretfully in his column that the title of the play had had to be changed slightly—"as a concession to the stuffy prudery of the middle class which still controls our theater. It is a crying example of interference with the freedom of the artist. Now don't let's hear any more of that old twaddle about ours being a free society. Originally, the title of this beautiful play was an authentic line drawn from the language of the people, with the brave, simple eloquence of folk expression."

Wynand and Dominique sat in the center of the fourth row, not looking at each other, listening to the play. The things being done on the stage were merely trite and crass; but the undercurrent made them frightening. There was an air about the ponderous inanities spoken, which the actors had absorbed like an infection; it was in their smirking faces, in the slyness of their voices, in their untidy gestures. It was an air of inanities uttered as revelations and insolently demanding acceptance as such; an air, not of innocent presumption, but of conscious effrontery; as if the author knew the nature of his work and boasted of his power to make it appear sublime in the minds of his audience and thus destroy the capacity for the sublime within them. The work justified the verdict of its sponsors: it brought laughs, it was amusing; it was an indecent joke, acted out not on the stage but in the audience. It was a pedestal from which a god had been torn, and in his place there stood, not Satan with a sword, but a corner lout sipping a bottle of Coca-Cola.

There was silence in the audience, puzzled and humble. When someone laughed, the rest joined in, with relief, glad to learn that they were enjoying themselves. Jules Fougler had not tried to influence anybody; he had merely made clear—well in advance and through many channels—that anyone unable to enjoy this play was, basically, a worthless human being. "It's no use asking for explanations," he had said. "Either you're fine enough to like it or you aren't."

In the intermission Wynand heard a stout woman saying: "It's wonderful. I don't understand it, but I have the *feeling* that it's something very important." Dominique asked him: "Do you wish to go, Gail?" He said: "No. We'll stay to the end."

He was silent in the car on their way home. When they entered their drawing room, he stood waiting, ready to hear and accept anything. For a moment she felt the desire to spare him. She felt empty and very tired. She did not want to hurt him; she wanted to seek his help.

Then she thought again what she had thought in the theater. She thought that this play was the creation of the *Banner,* this was what the *Banner* had forced into life, had fed, upheld, made to triumph. And it was the *Banner* that had begun and ended the destruction of the Stoddard Temple. . . . The New York *Banner,* November 2, 1930—"One Small Voice"—"Sacrilege" by Ellsworth M. Toohey—"The Churches of our Childhood" by Alvah Scarret—"Are you happy, Mr. Superman?" . . . And now that destruction was not an event long since past—this was not a comparison between two mutually unmeasurable entities, a building and a play—it was not an accident, nor a matter of persons, of Ike, Fougler, Toohey, herself . . . and Roark. It was a contest without time, a struggle of two abstractions, the thing that had created the building against the things that made the play possible—two forces, suddenly naked to her in their simple statement—two forces that had fought since the world began—and every religion had known of them—and there had always been a God and a Devil—only men had been so mistaken about the shapes of their Devil—he was not single and big, he was many and smutty and small. The *Banner* had destroyed the Stoddard Temple in order to make room for this play—it could not do otherwise—there was no middle choice, no escape, no neutrality—it was one or the other—it had always been—and the contest had many symbols, but no name and no statement. . . . Roark, she heard herself screaming inside, Roark . . . Roark . . . Roark . . .

"Dominique . . . what's the matter?"

She heard Wynand's voice. It was soft and anxious. He had never allowed himself to betray anxiety. She grasped the sound as a reflection of her own face, of what he had seen in her face.

She stood straight, and sure of herself, and very silent inside.

"I'm thinking of you, Gail," she said.

He waited.

"Well, Gail? The total passion for the total height?" She laughed, letting her arms swing sloppily in the manner of the actors they had seen. "Say, Gail, have you got a two-cent stamp with a picture of George Washington on it? . . . How old are you, Gail? How hard have you worked? Your life is more than half over, but you've seen your reward tonight. Your crowning achievement. Of course, no man is ever quite equal to his highest passion. Now if you strive and make a great effort, some day you'll rise to the level of that play!"

He stood quietly, hearing it, accepting.

"I think you should take a manuscript of that play and place it on a stand in the center of your gallery downstairs. I think you should re-christen your yacht and call her *No Skin Off Your Nose.* I think you should take me——"

"Keep still."

"—and put me in the cast and make me play the role of Mary every evening, Mary who adopts the homeless muskrat and . . ."

"Dominique, keep still."

"Then talk. I want to hear you talk."

"I never justified myself to anyone."

"Well, boast then. That would do just as well."

"If you want to hear it, it made me sick, that play. As you knew it would. That was worse than the Bronx housewife."

"Much worse."

"But I can think of something worse still. Writing a great play and offering it for tonight's audience to laugh at. Letting oneself be martyred by the kind of people we saw frolicking tonight."

He saw that something had reached her; he could not tell whether it was an answer of surprise or of anger. He did not know how well she recognized these words. He went on:

"It did make me sick. But so have a great many things which

the *Banner* has done. It was worse tonight, because there was a quality about it that went beyond the usual. A special kind of malice. But if this is popular with fools, it's the *Banner's* legitimate province. The *Banner* was created for the benefit of fools. What else do you want me to admit?"

"What you felt tonight."

"A minor kind of hell. Because you sat there with me. That's what you wanted, wasn't it? To make me feel the contrast. Still, you miscalculated. I looked at the stage and I thought, this is what people are like, such are their spirits, but I—I've found you, I have you—and the contrast was worth the pain. I did suffer tonight, as you wanted, but it was a pain that went only down to a certain point and then . . ."

"Shut up!" she screamed. "Shut up, God damn you!"

They stood for a moment, both astonished. He moved first; he knew she needed his help; he grasped her shoulders. She tore herself away. She walked across the room, to the window; she stood looking at the city, at the great buildings spread in black and fire below her.

After a while she said, her voice toneless:

"I'm sorry, Gail."

He did not answer.

"I had no right to say those things to you." She did not turn, her arms raised, holding the frame of the window. "We're even, Gail. I'm paid back, if that will make it better for you. I broke first."

"I don't want you to be paid back." He spoke quietly. "Dominique, what was it?"

"Nothing."

"What did I make you think of? It wasn't what I said. It was something else. What did the words mean to you?"

"Nothing."

"A pain that went only down to a certain point. It was that sentence. Why?" She was looking at the city. In the distance she could see the shaft of the Cord Building. "Dominique, I've seen what you can take. It must be something very terrible if it could do that to you. I must know. There's nothing impossible. I can help you against it, whatever it is." She did not answer. "At the theater, it was not just that fool play. There was something else for you tonight. I saw your face. And then it was the same thing again here. What is it?"

"Gail," she said softly, "will you forgive me?"

He let a moment pass; he had not been prepared for that.

"What have I to forgive you?"

"Everything. And tonight."

"That was your privilege. The condition on which you married me. To make me pay for the *Banner*."

"I don't want to make you pay for it."

"Why don't you want it any more?"

"It can't be paid for."

In the silence she listened to his steps pacing the room behind her.

"Dominique. What was it?"

"The pain that stops at a certain point? Nothing. Only that you had no right to say it. The men who have, pay for that right, a price you can't afford. But it doesn't matter now. Say it if you wish. I have no right to say it either."

"That wasn't all."

"I think we have a great deal in common, you and I. We've committed the same treason somewhere. No, that's a bad word. . . . Yes, I think it's the right word. It's the only one that has the feeling of what I mean."

"Dominique, you can't feel that." His voice sounded strange. She turned to him.

"Why?"

"Because that's what I felt tonight. Treason."

"Toward whom?"

"I don't know. If I were religious, I'd say 'God.' But I'm not religious."

"That's what I meant, Gail."

"Why should you feel it? The *Banner* is not your child."

"There are other forms of the same guilt."

Then he walked to her across the long room, he held her in his arms, he said:

"You don't know the meaning of the kind of words you use. We have a great deal in common, but not that. I'd rather you went on spitting at me than trying to share my offenses."

She let her hand rest against the length of his cheek, her finger tips at his temple.

He asked:

"Will you tell me—now—what it was?"

"Nothing. I undertook more than I could carry. You're tired, Gail. Why don't you go on upstairs? Leave me here for a little while. I just want to look at the city. Then I'll join you and I'll be all right."

IX

DOMINIQUE STOOD AT THE RAIL OF THE YACHT, THE DECK WARM under her flat sandals, the sun on her bare legs, the wind blowing her thin white dress. She looked at Wynand stretched in a deck chair before her.

She thought of the change she noticed in him again aboard ship. She had watched him through the months of their summer cruise. She had seen him once running down a companionway; the picture remained in her mind; a tall white figure thrown forward in a streak of speed and confidence; his hand grasped a railing, risking deliberately the danger of a sudden break, gaining a new propulsion. He was not the corrupt publisher of a popular empire. He was an aristocrat aboard a yacht. He looked, she thought, like what one believes aristocracy to be when one is young: a brilliant kind of gaiety without guilt.

She looked at him in the deck chair. She thought that relaxation was attractive only in those for whom it was an unnatural state; then even limpness acquired purpose. She wondered about him; Gail Wynand, famous for his extraordinary capacity; but this was not merely the force of an ambitious adventurer who had created a chain of newspapers; this—the quality she saw in him here—the thing stretched out under the sun, like an answer—this was greater, a first cause, a faculty out of universal dynamics.

"Gail," she said suddenly, involuntarily.

He opened his eyes to look at her.

"I wish I had taken a recording of that," he said lazily. "You'd be startled to hear what it sounded like. Quite wasted here. I'd like to play it back in a bedroom."

"I'll repeat it there if you wish."

"Thank you, dearest. And I promise not to exaggerate or presume too much. You're not in love with me. You've never loved anyone."

"Why do you think that?"

"If you loved a man, it wouldn't be just a matter of a circus wedding and an atrocious evening in the theater. You'd put him through total hell."

"How do you know that, Gail?"

"Why have you been staring at me ever since we met? Because I'm not the Gail Wynand you'd heard about. You see, I love you. And love is exception-making. If you were in love you'd want to be broken, trampled, ordered, dominated, because that's the impossible, the incon-

515

ceivable for you in your relations with people. That would be the one gift, the great exception you'd want to offer the man you loved. But it wouldn't be easy for you."

"If that's true, then you . . ."

"Then I become gentle and humble—to your great astonishment—because I'm the worst scoundrel living."

"I don't believe that, Gail."

"No? I'm not the person before last any more?"

"Not any more."

"Well, dearest, as a matter of fact, I am."

"Why do you want to think that?"

"I don't want to. But I like to be honest. That has been my only private luxury. Don't change your mind about me. Go on seeing me as you saw me before we met."

"Gail, that's not what you want."

"It doesn't matter what I want. I don't want anything—except to own you. Without answer from you. It has to be without answer. If you begin to look at me too closely, you'll see things you won't like at all."

"What things?"

"You're so beautiful, Dominique. Its such a lovely accident on God's part that there's one person who matches inside and out."

"What things, Gail?"

"Do you know what you're actually in love with? Integrity. The impossible. The clean, consistent, reasonable, self-faithful, the all-of-one-style, like a work of art. That's the only field where it can be found—art. But you want it in the flesh. You're in love with it. Well, you see, I've never had any integrity."

"How sure are you of that, Gail?"

"Have you forgotten the *Banner?*"

"To hell with the *Banner.*"

"All right, to hell with the *Banner*. It's nice to hear you say that. But the *Banner's* not the major symptom. That I've never practiced any sort of integrity is not so important. What's important is that I've never felt any need for it. I hate the conception of it. I hate the presumptuousness of the idea."

"Dwight Carson . . ." she said. He heard the sound of disgust in her voice.

He laughed. "Yes, Dwight Carson. The man I bought. The individualist who's become a mob-glorifier and, incidentally, a dipsomaniac. I did that. That was worse than the *Banner*, wasn't it? You don't like to be reminded of that?"

"No."

"But surely you've heard enough screaming about it. All the giants of the spirit whom I've broken. I don't think anybody ever realized how much I enjoyed doing it. It's a kind of lust. I'm perfectly indifferent to slugs like Ellsworth Toohey or my friend Alvah, and quite willing to leave them in peace. But just let me see a man of a slightly higher dimension—and I've got to make a sort of Toohey out of him. I've got to. It's like a sex urge."

"Why?"

"I don't know."

"Incidentally, you misunderstand Ellsworth Toohey."

"Possibly. You don't expect me to waste mental effort to untangle that snail's shell?"

"And you contradict yourself."

"Where?"

"Why didn't you set out to destroy me?"

"The exception-making, Dominique. I love you. I had to love you. God help you if you were a man."

"Gail—why?"

"Why have I done all that?"

"Yes."

"Power, Dominique. The only thing I ever wanted. To know that there's not a man living whom I can't force to do—anything. Anything I choose. The man I couldn't break would destroy me. But I've spent years finding out how safe I am. They say I have no sense of honor, I've missed something in life. Well, I haven't missed very much, have I? The thing I've missed—it doesn't exist."

He spoke in a normal tone of voice, but he noticed suddenly that she was listening with the intent concentration needed to hear a whisper of which one can afford to lose no syllable.

"What's the matter, Dominique? What are you thinking about?"

"I'm listening to you, Gail."

She did not say she was listening to his words and to the reason behind them. It was suddenly so clear to her that she heard it as an added clause to each sentence, even though he had no knowledge of what he was confessing.

"The worst thing about dishonest people is what they think of as honesty," he said. "I know a woman who's never held to one conviction for three days running, but when I told her she had no integrity, she got very tight-lipped and said her idea of integrity wasn't mine; it seems she'd never stolen any money. Well, she's one that's in no danger from me whatever. I don't hate her. I hate the impossible conception you love so passionately, Dominique."

"Do you?"

"I've had a lot of fun proving it."

She walked to him and sat down on the deck beside his chair, the planks smooth and hot under her bare legs. He wondered why she looked at him so gently. He frowned. She knew that some reflection of what she had understood remained in her eyes—and she looked away from him.

"Gail, why tell me all that? It's not what you want me to think of you."

"No. It isn't. Why tell you now? Want the truth? Because it has to be told. Because I wanted to be honest with you. Only with you and with myself. But I wouldn't have the courage to tell you anywhere else. Not at home. Not ashore. Only here—because here it doesn't seem quite real. Does it?"

"No."

"I think I hoped that here you'd accept it—and still think of me as you did when you spoke my name in that way I wanted to record."

She put her head against his chair, her face pressed to his knees, her hands dropped, fingers half-curled, on the glistening planks of the deck. She did not want to show what she had actually heard him saying about himself today.

On a night of late fall they stood together at the roof-garden parapet, looking at the city. The long shafts made of lighted windows were like streams breaking out of the black sky, flowing down in single drops to feed the great pools of fire below.

"There they are, Dominique—the great buildings. The skyscrapers. Do you remember? They were the first link between us. We're both in love with them, you and I."

She thought she should resent his right to say it. But she felt no resentment."

"Yes, Gail. I'm in love with them."

She looked at the vertical threads of light that were the Cord Building, she raised her fingers off the parapet, just enough to touch the place of its unseen form on the distant sky. She felt no reproach from it.

"I like to see a man standing at the foot of a skyscraper," he said. "It makes him no bigger than an ant—isn't that the correct bromide for the occasion? The God-damn fools! It's man who made it—the whole incredible mass of stone and steel. It doesn't dwarf him, it makes him greater than the structure. It reveals his true dimensions to the world. What we love about these buildings, Dominique, is the creative faculty, the heroic in man."

"Do you love the heroic in man, Gail?"

"I love to think of it. I don't believe it."

She leaned against the parapet and watched the green lights stretched in a long straight line far below. She said:

"I wish I could understand you."

"I thought I should be quite obvious. I've never hidden anything from you."

He watched the electric signs that flashed in disciplined spasms over the black river. Then he pointed to a blurred light, far to the south, a faint reflection of blue.

"That's the Banner Building. See, over there?—that blue light. I've done so many things, but I've missed one, the most important. There's no Wynand Building in New York. Some day I'll build a new home for the *Banner*. It will be the greatest structure of the city and it will bear my name. I started in a miserable dump, and the paper was called the *Gazette*. I was only a stooge for some very filthy people. But I thought, then, of the Wynand Building that would rise some day. I've thought of it all the years since."

"Why haven't you built it?"

"I wasn't ready for it."

"Why?"

"I'm not ready for it now. I don't know why. I know only that it's very important to me. It will be the final symbol. I'll know the right time when it comes."

He turned to look out to the west, to a patch of dim scattered lights. He pointed:

"That's where I was born. Hell's Kitchen." She listened attentively; he seldom spoke of his beginning. "I was sixteen when I stood on a roof and looked at the city, like tonight. And decided what I would be."

The quality of his voice became a line underscoring the moment, saying: Take notice, *this* is important. Not looking at him, she thought this was what she had waited for, this should give her the answer, the key to him. Years ago, thinking of Gail Wynand, she had wondered how such a man faced his life and his work; she expected boasting and a hidden sense of shame, or impertinence flaunting its own guilt. She looked at him. His head lifted, his eyes level on the sky before him, he conveyed none of the things she had expected; he conveyed a quality incredible in this connection: a sense of gallantry.

She knew it was a key, but it made the puzzle greater. Yet something within her understood, knew the use of that key and made her speak.

"Gail, fire Ellsworth Toohey."

He turned to her, bewildered.

"Why?"

"Gail, listen." Her voice had an urgency she had never shown in speaking to him. "I've never wanted to stop Toohey. I've even helped him. I thought he was what the world deserved. I haven't tried to save anything from him . . . or anyone. I never thought it would be the *Banner*—the *Banner* which he fits best—that I'd want to save from him."

"What on earth are you talking about?"

"Gail, when I married you, I didn't know I'd come to feel this kind of loyalty to you. It contradicts everything I've done, it contradicts so much more than I can tell you—it's a sort of catastrophe for me, a turning point—don't ask me why—it will take me years to understand —I know only that this is what I owe you. Fire Ellsworth Toohey. Get him out before it's too late. You've broken many much less vicious men and much less dangerous. Fire Toohey, go after him and don't rest until you've destroyed every last bit of him."

"Why? Why should you think of him just now?"

"Because I know what he's after."

"What is he after?"

"Control of the Wynand papers."

He laughed aloud; it was not derision or indignation; just pure gaiety greeting the point of a silly joke.

"Gail . . ." she said helplessly.

"Oh for God's sake, Dominique! And here I've always respected your judgment."

"You've never understood Toohey."

"And I don't care to. Can you see me going to Ellsworth Toohey? A tank to eliminate a bedbug? Why should I fire Elsie? He's the kind that makes money for me. People love to read his twaddle. I don't fire good booby-traps like that. He's as valuable to me as a piece of flypaper."

"That's the danger. Part of it."

"His wonderful following? I've had bigger and better sob-sisters on my payroll. When a few of them had to be kicked out, that was the end of them. Their popularity stopped at the door of the *Banner*. But the *Banner* went on."

"It's not his popularity. It's the special nature of it. You can't fight him on his terms. You're only a tank—and that's a very clean, innocent weapon. An honest weapon that goes first, out in front, and mows everything down or takes every counterblow. He's a corrosive gas. The kind that eats lungs out. I think there really is a secret to the core of evil and he has it. I don't know what it is. I know how he uses it and what he's after."

"Control of the Wynand papers?"

"Control of the Wynand papers—as one of the means to an end."

"What end?"

"Control of the world."

He said with patient disgust: "What is this, Dominique? What sort of gag and what for?"

"I'm serious, Gail. I'm terribly serious."

"Control of the world, my dear, belongs to men like me. The Tooheys of this earth wouldn't know how to dream about it."

"I'll try to explain. It's very difficult. The hardest thing to explain is the glaringly evident which everybody has decided not to see. But if you'll listen . . ."

"I won't listen. You'll forgive me, but discussing the idea of Ellsworth Toohey as a threat to me is ridiculous. Discussing it seriously is offensive."

"Gail, I . . ."

"No. Darling, I don't think you really understand much about the *Banner*. And I don't want you to. I don't want you to take any part in it. Forget it. Leave the *Banner* to me."

"Is it a demand, Gail?"

"It's an ultimatum."

"All right."

"Forget it. Don't go acquiring horror complexes about anyone as big as Ellsworth Toohey. It's not like you."

"All right, Gail. Let's go in. It's too cold for you here without an overcoat."

He chuckled softly—it was the kind of concern she had never shown for him before. He took her hand and kissed her palm, holding it against his face.

For many weeks, when left alone together, they spoke little and never about each other. But it was not a silence of resentment; it was the silence of an understanding too delicate to limit by words. They would be in a room together in the evening, saying nothing, content to feel each other's presence. They would look at each other suddenly—and both would smile, the smile like hands clasped.

Then, one evening, she knew he would speak. She sat at her dressing-table. He came in and leaned against the wall beside her. He looked at her hands, at her naked shoulders, but she felt as if he did not see her; he was looking at something greater than the beauty of her body, greater than his love for her; he was looking at himself—and this, she knew, was the one incomparable tribute.

"I breathe for my own necessity, for the fuel of my body, for my survival . . . I've given you, not my sacrifice or my pity, but my ego and my naked need . . ." She heard Roark's words, Roark's voice speaking for Gail Wynand—and she felt no sense of treason to Roark in using the words of his love for the love of another man.

"Gail," she said gently, "some day I'll have to ask your forgiveness for having married you."

He shook his head slowly, smiling. She said:

"I wanted you to be my chain to the world. You've become my defense, instead. And that makes my marriage dishonest."

"No. I told you I would accept any reason you chose."

"But you've changed everything for me. Or was it I that changed it? I don't know. We've done something strange to each other. I've given you what I wanted to lose. That special sense of living I thought this marriage would destroy for me. The sense of life as exaltation. And you—you've done all the things I would have done. Do you know how much alike we are?"

"I knew that from the first."

"But it should have been impossible. Gail, I want to remain with you now—for another reason. To wait for an answer. I think when I learn to understand what you are, I'll understand myself. There is an answer. There is a name for the thing we have in common. I don't know it. I know it's very important."

"Probably. I suppose I should want to understand it. But I don't. I can't care about anything now. I can't even be afraid."

She looked up at him and said very calmly:

"I am afraid, Gail."

"Of what, dearest?"

"Of what I'm doing to you."

"Why?"

"I don't love you, Gail."

"I can't care even about that."

She dropped her head and he looked down at the hair that was like a pale helmet of polished metal.

"Dominique."

She raised her face to him obediently.

"I love you, Dominique. I love you so much that nothing can matter to me—not even you. Can you understand that? Only my love—not your answer. Not even your indifference. I've never taken much from the world. I haven't wanted much. I've never really wanted anything. Not in the total, undivided way, not with the kind of desire that becomes an ultimatum, 'yes' or 'no,' and one can't accept the 'no' without ceasing to exist. That's what you are to me. But when one reaches that stage, it's not the object that matters, it's the desire. Not you, but I. The ability to desire like that. Nothing less is worth feeling or honoring. And I've never felt that before. Dominique, I've never known how to say 'mine' about anything. Not in the sense I say it about you. Mine. Did you call it a sense of life as exaltation? You said that. You understand. I can't be afraid. I love you, Dominique—I love you—you're letting me say it now—I love you."

She reached over and took the cablegram off the mirror. She crumpled it, her fingers twisting slowly in a grinding motion against her palm. He stood listening to the crackle of the paper. She leaned forward, opened her hand over the wastebasket, and let the paper drop. Her hand remained still for a moment, the fingers extended, slanting down, as they had opened.

Part 4

HOWARD ROARK

I

THE LEAVES STREAMED DOWN, TREMBLING IN THE SUN. THEY were not green; only a few, scattered through the torrent, stood out in single drops of a green so bright and pure that it hurt the eyes; the rest were not a color, but a light, the substance of fire on metal, living sparks without edges. And it looked as if the forest were a spread of light boiling slowly to produce this color, this green rising in small bubbles, the condensed essence of spring. The trees met, bending over the road, and the spots of sun on the ground moved with the shifting of the branches, like a conscious caress. The young man hoped he would not have to die.

Not if the earth could look like this, he thought. Not if he could hear the hope and the promise like a voice, with leaves, tree trunks and rocks instead of words. But he knew that the earth looked like this only because he had seen no sign of men for hours; he was alone, riding his bicycle down a forgotten trail through the hills of Pennsylvania where he had never been before, where he could feel the fresh wonder of an untouched world.

He was a very young man. He had just graduated from college—in the spring of the year 1935—and he wanted to decide whether life was worth living. He did not know that this was the question in his mind. He did not think of dying. He thought only that he wished to find joy and reason and meaning in life—and that none had been offered to him anywhere.

527

He had not liked the things taught to him in college. He had been taught a great deal about social responsibility, about a life of service and self-sacrifice. Everybody had said it was beautiful and inspiring. Only he had not felt inspired. He had felt nothing at all.

He could not name the thing he wanted of life. He felt it here, in this wild loneliness. But he did not face nature with the joy of a healthy animal—as a proper and final setting; he faced it with the joy of a healthy man—as a challenge; as tools, means and material. So he felt anger that he should find exaltation only in the wilderness, that this great sense of hope had to be lost when he would return to men and men's work. He thought that this was not right; that man's work should be a higher step, an improvement on nature, not a degradation. He did not want to despise men; he wanted to love and admire them. But he dreaded the sight of the first house, poolroom and movie poster he would encounter on his way.

He had always wanted to write music, and he could give no other identity to the thing he sought. If you want to know what it is, he told himself, listen to the first phrases of Tchaikovsky's *First Concerto*—or the last movement of Rachmaninoff's *Second*. Men have not found the words for it nor the deed nor the thought, but they have found the music. Let me see that in one single act of man on earth. Let me see it made real. Let me see the answer to the promise of that music. Not servants nor those served; not altars and immolations; but the final, the fulfilled, innocent of pain. Don't help me or serve me, but let me see it once, because I need it. Don't work for my happiness, my brothers— show me yours—show me that it is possible—show me your achievement—and the knowledge will give me courage for mine.

He saw a blue hole ahead, where the road ended on the crest of a ridge. The blue looked cool and clean like a film of water stretched in the frame of green branches. It would be funny, he thought, if I came to the edge and found nothing but that blue beyond; nothing but the sky ahead, above and below. He closed his eyes and went on, suspending the possible for a moment, granting himself a dream, a few instants of believing that he would reach the crest, open his eyes and see the blue radiance of the sky below.

His foot touched the ground, breaking his motion; he stopped and opened his eyes. He stood still.

In the broad valley, far below him, in the first sunlight of early morning, he saw a town. Only it was not a town. Towns did not look like that. He had to suspend the possible for a while longer, to seek no questions or explanations, only to look.

There were small houses on the ledges of the hill before him, flowing down to the bottom. He knew that the ledges had not been touched, that no artifice had altered the unplanned beauty of the graded steps. Yet some power had known how to build on these ledges in such a way that the houses became inevitable, and one could no longer imagine the hills as beautiful without them—as if the centuries and the series of chances that produced these ledges in the struggle of great blind forces had waited for their final expression, had been only a road to a goal—and the goal was these buildings, part of the hills, shaped by the hills, yet ruling them by giving them meaning.

The houses were of plain field stone—like the rocks jutting from the green hillsides—and of glass, great sheets of glass used as if the sun were invited to complete the structures, sunlight becoming part of the masonry. There were many houses, they were small, they were cut off from one another, and no two of them were alike. But they were like variations on a single theme, like a symphony played by an inexhaustible imagination, and one could still hear the laughter of the force that had been let loose on them, as if that force had run, unrestrained, challenging itself to be spent, but had never reached its end. Music, he thought, the promise of the music he had invoked, the sense of it made real—there it was before his eyes—he did not see it—he heard it in chords—he thought that there was a common language of thought, sight and sound—was it mathematics?—the discipline of reason—music was mathematics—and architecture was music in stone—he knew he was dizzy because this place below him could not be real.

He saw trees, lawns, walks twisting up the hillsides, steps cut in the stone, he saw fountains, swimming pools, tennis courts—and not a sign of life. The place was uninhabited.

It did not shock him, not as the sight of it had shocked him. In a way, it seemed proper; this was not part of known existence. For the moment he had no desire to know what it was.

After a long time he glanced about him—and then he saw that he was not alone. Some steps away from him a man sat on a boulder, looking down at the valley. The man seemed absorbed in the sight and had not heard his approach. The man was tall and gaunt and had orange hair.

He walked straight to the man, who turned his eyes to him; the eyes were gray and calm; the boy knew suddenly that they felt the same thing, and he could speak as he would not speak to a stranger anywhere else.

"That isn't real, is it?" the boy asked, pointing down.

"Why, yes, it is, now," the man answered.

"It's not a movie set or a trick of some kind?"

"No. It's a summer resort. It's just been completed. It will be opened in a few weeks."

"Who built it?"

"I did."

"What's your name?"

"Howard Roark."

"Thank you," said the boy. He knew that the steady eyes looking at him understood everything these two words had to cover. Howard Roark inclined his head, in acknowledgment.

Wheeling his bicycle by his side, the boy took the narrow path down the slope of the hill to the valley and the houses below. Roark looked after him. He had never seen the boy before and he would never see him again. He did not know that he had given someone the courage to face a lifetime.

Roark had never understood why he was chosen to build the summer resort at Monadnock Valley.

It had happened a year and a half ago, in the fall of 1933. He had heard of the project and gone to see Mr. Caleb Bradley, the head of some vast company that had purchased the valley and was doing a great deal of loud promotion. He went to see Bradley as a matter of duty, without hope, merely to add another refusal to his long list of refusals. He had built nothing in New York since the Stoddard Temple.

When he entered Bradley's office, he knew that he must forget Monadnock Valley because this man would never give it to him. Caleb Bradley was a short, pudgy person with a handsome face between rounded shoulders. The face looked wise and boyish, unpleasantly ageless; he could have been fifty or twenty; he had blank blue eyes, sly and bored.

But it was difficult for Roark to forget Monadnock Valley. So he spoke of it, forgetting that speech was useless here. Mr. Bradley listened, obviously interested, but obviously not in what Roark was saying. Roark could almost feel some third entity present in the room. Mr. Bradley said little, beyond promising to consider it and to get in touch with him. But then he said a strange thing. He asked, in a voice devoid of all clue to the purpose of the question, neither in approval nor scorn: "You're the architect who built the Stoddard Temple, aren't you, Mr. Roark?" "Yes," said Roark. "Funny that I hadn't thought of you myself," said Mr. Bradley. Roark went away, thinking that it would have been funny if Mr. Bradley had thought of him.

Three days later, Bradley telephoned and invited him to his office. Roark came and met four other men—the Board of the Monadnock Valley Company. They were well-dressed men, and their faces were as closed as Mr. Bradley's. "Please tell these gentlemen what you told me, Mr. Roark," Bradley said pleasantly.

Roark explained his plan. If what they wished to build was an unusual summer resort for people of moderate incomes—as they had announced—then they should realize that the worst curse of poverty was the lack of privacy; only the very rich or the very poor of the city could enjoy their summer vacations; the very rich, because they had private estates; the very poor, because they did not mind the feel and smell of one another's flesh on public beaches and public dance floors; the people of good taste and small income had no place to go, if they found no rest or pleasure in herds. Why was it assumed that poverty gave one the instincts of cattle? Why not offer these people a place where, for a week or a month, at small cost, they could have what they wanted and needed? He had seen Monadnock Valley. It could be done. Don't touch those hillsides, don't blast and level them down. Not one huge ant pile of a hotel—but small houses hidden from one another, each a private estate, where people could meet or not, as they pleased. Not one fish-market tank of a swimming-pool—but many private swimming pools, as many as the company wished to afford—he could show them how it could be done cheaply. Not one stock-farm corral of tennis courts for exhibitionists—but many private tennis courts. Not a place where one went to meet "refined company" and land a husband in two weeks—but a resort for people who enjoyed their own presence well enough and sought only a place where they would be left free to enjoy it.

The men listened to him silently. He saw them exchanging glances once in a while. He felt certain that they were the kind of glances people exchange when they cannot laugh at the speaker aloud. But it could not have been that—because he signed a contract to build the Monadnock Valley summer resort, two days later.

He demanded Mr. Bradley's initials on every drawing that came out of his drafting room; he remembered the Stoddard Temple. Mr. Bradley initialed, signed, okayed; he agreed to everything; he approved everything. He seemed delighted to let Roark have his way. But this eager complaisance had a peculiar undertone—as if Mr. Bradley were humoring a child.

He could learn little about Mr. Bradley. It was said that the man had made a fortune in real estate, in the Florida boom. His present company seemed to command unlimited funds, and the names of many wealthy backers were mentioned as shareholders. Roark never met them. The four gentlemen of the Board did not appear again, except on short visits to the construction site, where they exhibited little interest. Mr. Bradley was in full charge of everything—but beyond a close watch over the budget he seemed to like nothing better than to leave Roark in full charge.

In the eighteen months that followed, Roark had no time to wonder about Mr. Bradley. Roark was building his greatest assignment.

For the last year he lived at the construction site, in a shanty hastily thrown together on a bare hillside, a wooden enclosure with a bed, a stove and a large table. His old draftsmen came to work for him again, some abandoning better jobs in the city, to live in shacks and tents, to work in naked plank barracks that served as architect's office. There was so much to build that none of them thought of wasting structural effort on their own shelters. They did not realize, until much later, that they had lacked comforts; and then they did not believe it—because the year at Monadnock Valley remained in their minds as the strange time when the earth stopped turning and they lived through twelve months of spring. They did not think of the snow, the frozen clots of earth, wind whistling through the cracks of planking, thin blankets over army cots, stiff fingers stretched over coal stoves in the morning, before a pencil could be held steadily. They remembered only the feeling which is the meaning of spring—one's answer to the first blades of grass, the first buds on tree branches, the first blue of the sky—the singing answer, not to grass, trees and sky, but to the great sense of beginning, of triumphant progression, of certainty in an achievement that nothing will stop. Not from leaves and flowers, but from wooden scaffoldings, from steam shovels, from blocks of stone and sheets of glass rising out of the earth they received the sense of youth, motion, purpose, fulfillment.

They were an army and it was a crusade. But none of them thought of it in these words, except Steven Mallory. Steven Mallory did the fountains and all the sculpture work of Monadnock Valley. But he came to live at the site long before he was needed. Battle, thought Steven Mallory, is a vicious concept. There is no glory in war, and no beauty in crusades of men. But this was a battle, this was an army and a war—and the highest experience in the life of every man who took part in it. Why? Where was the root of the difference and the law to explain it?

He did not speak of it to anyone. But he saw the same feeling in Mike's face, when Mike arrived with the gang of electricians. Mike said nothing, but he winked at Mallory in cheerful understanding. "I told you not to worry," Mike said to him once, without preamble, "at the trial that was. He can't lose, quarries or no quarries, trials or no trials. They can't beat him, Steve, they just can't, not the whole goddamn world."

But they had really forgotten the world, thought Mallory. This was a new earth, their own. The hills rose to the sky around them, as a wall of protection. And they had another protection—the architect who walked among them, down the snow or the grass of the hillsides, over the boulders and the piled planks, to the drafting tables, to the derricks, to the tops of rising walls—the man who had made this possible—the thought in the mind of that man—and not the content of that thought, nor the result, not the vision that had created Monadnock Valley, nor the will that had made it real—but the method of his thought, the rule of its function—the method and rule which were not like those of the world beyond the hills. That stood on guard over the valley and over the crusaders within it.

And then he saw Mr. Bradley come to visit the site, to smile blandly and depart again. Then Mallory felt anger without reason—and fear.

"Howard," Mallory said one night, when they sat together at a fire of dry branches on the hillside over the camp, "it's the Stoddard Temple again."

"Yes," said Roark, "I think so. But I can't figure out in just what way or what they're after."

He rolled over on his stomach and looked down at the panes of glass scattered through the darkness below; they caught reflections from somewhere and looked like phosphorescent, self-generated springs of light rising out of the ground. He said:

"It doesn't matter, Steve, does it? Not what they do about it nor who comes to live here. Only that we've made it. Would you have missed this, no matter what price they make you pay for it afterward?"

"No," said Mallory.

Roark had wanted to rent one of the houses for himself and spend the summer there, the first summer of Monadnock Valley's existence. But before the resort was open, he received a wire from New York:

"I told you I would, didn't I? It took five years to get rid of my friends and brothers, but the Aquitania is now mine—and yours. Come to finish it. Kent Lansing."

So he went back to New York—to see the rubble and cement dust cleared away from the hulk of the Unfinished Symphony, to see derricks swing girders high over Central Park, to see the gaps of windows filled, the broad decks spread over the roofs of the city, the Aquitania Hotel completed, glowing at night in the Park's skyline.

He had been very busy in the last two years. Monadnock Valley had not been his only commission. From different states, from unexpected parts of the country, calls had come for him: private homes, small office buildings, modest shops. He had built them—snatching a few hours of sleep on trains and planes that carried him from Monadnock Valley to distant small towns. The story of every commission he received was the same: "I was in New York and I liked the Enright House." "I saw the Cord Building." "I saw a picture of that temple they tore down." It was as if an underground stream flowed through the country and broke out in sudden springs that shot to the surface at random, in unpredictable places. They were small, inexpensive jobs—but he was kept working.

That summer, with Monadnock Valley completed, he had no time to worry about its future fate. But Steven Mallory worried about it. "Why don't they advertise it, Howard? Why the sudden silence? Have you noticed? There was so much talk about their grand project, so many little items in print—before they started. There was less and less while we were doing it. And now? Mr. Bradley and company have gone deaf-mute. Now, when you'd expect them to stage a press agent's orgy. Why?"

"I wouldn't know," said Roark. "I'm an architect, not a rental agent. Why should you worry? We've done our job, let them do theirs in their own way."

"It's a damn queer way. Did you see their ads—the few they've let dribble out? They say all the things you told them, about rest, peace and privacy—but how they say it! Do you know what those ads amount to in effect? 'Come to Monadnock Valley and be bored to death.' It sounds— it actually sounds as if they were trying to keep people away."

"I don't read ads, Steve."

But within a month of its opening every house in Monadnock Valley was rented. The people who came were a strange mixture: society men and women who could have afforded more fashionable resorts, young writers and unknown artists, engineers and newspapermen and factory workers. Suddenly, spontaneously, people were talking about Monadnock Valley. There was a need for that kind of a resort, a need no one had tried to satisfy. The place became news, but it was private news; the papers had not discovered it. Mr. Bradley had no press agents; Mr. Bradley and his company had vanished from public life. One magazine, unsolicited, printed four pages of photographs of Monadnock Valley, and sent a man to interview Howard Roark. By the end of summer the houses were leased in advance for the following year.

In October, early one morning, the door of Roark's reception room flew open and Steven Mallory rushed in, making straight for Roark's office. The secretary tried to stop him; Roark was working and no interruptions were allowed. But Mallory shoved her aside and tore into the office, slamming the door behind. She noticed that he held a newspaper in his hand.

Roark glanced up at him, from the drafting table, and dropped his pencil. He knew that this was the way Mallory's face had looked when he shot at Ellsworth Toohey.

"Well, Howard? Do you want to know why you got Monadnock Valley?"

He threw the newspaper down on the table. Roark saw the heading of a story on the third page: "Caleb Bradley arrested."

"It's all there," said Mallory. "Don't read it. It will make you sick."

"All right, Steve, what is it?"

"They sold two hundred percent of it."

"Who did? Of what?"

"Bradley and his gang. Of Monadnock Valley." Mallory spoke with a forced, vicious, self-torturing precision. "They thought it was worthless —from the first. They got the land practically for nothing—they thought it was no place for a resort at all—out of the way, with no bus lines or movie theaters around—they thought the time wasn't right and the public wouldn't go for it. They made a lot of noise and sold shares to a lot of wealthy suckers—it was just a huge fraud. They sold two hundred percent of the place. They got twice what it cost them to build it. They were certain it would fail. They *wanted* it to fail. They expected no profits to distribute. They had a nice scheme ready for how to get out of it when the place went bankrupt. They were prepared for anything—except for seeing it turn into the kind of success it is. And they couldn't go on—because now they'd have to pay their backers twice the amount the place earned each year. And it's earning plenty. And they thought they had arranged for certain failure. Howard, don't you understand? They chose you as the worst architect they could find!"

Roark threw his head back and laughed.

"God damn you, Howard! It's not funny!"

"Sit down, Steve. Stop shaking. You look as if you'd just seen a whole field of butchered bodies."

"I have. I've seen worse. I've seen the root. I've seen what makes such fields possible. What do the damn fools think of as horror? Wars, murders, fires, earthquakes? To hell with that! *This* is horror—that story in the paper. That's what men should dread and fight and scream about and call the worst shame on their record. Howard, I'm thinking of all the explanations of evil and all the remedies offered for it through the centuries. None of them worked. None of them explained or cured anything. But the root of evil—my drooling beast—it's there, Howard, in that story. In that—and in the souls of the smug bastards who'll read it and say: 'Oh well, genius must always struggle, it's good for 'em'—and then go and look for some village idiot to help, to teach him how to weave baskets. That's the drooling beast in action. Howard, think of Monadnock. Close your eyes and see it. And then think that the men who ordered it, believed it was the worst thing they could build! Howard, there's something wrong, something very terribly wrong in the world if you were given your greatest job—as a filthy joke!"

"When will you stop thinking about that? About the world and me? When will you learn to forget it? When will Dominique . . ."

He stopped. They had not mentioned that name in each other's presence for five years. He saw Mallory's eyes, intent and shocked. Mallory realized that his words had hurt Roark, hurt him enough to force this admission. But Roark turned to him and said deliberately:

"Dominique used to think just as you do."

Mallory had never spoken of what he guessed about Roark's past. Their silence had always implied that Mallory understood, that Roark knew it, and that it was not to be discussed. But now Mallory asked:

"Are you still waiting for her to come back? Mrs. Gail Wynand—God damn her!"

Roark said without emphasis:

"Shut up, Steve."

Mallory whispered: "I'm sorry."

Roark walked to his table and said, his voice normal again:

"Go home, Steve, and forget about Bradley. They'll all be suing one another now, but we won't be dragged in and they won't destroy Monadnock. Forget it, and get out, I have to work."

He brushed the newspaper off the table, with his elbow, and bent over the sheets of drafting paper.

There was a scandal over the revelations of the financing methods behind Monadnock Valley, there was a trial, a few gentlemen sentenced to the penitentiary, and a new management taking Monadnock over for the shareholders. Roark was not involved. He was busy, and he forgot to read the accounts of the trial in the papers. Mr. Bradley admitted—in apology to his partners—that he would be damned if he could have expected a resort built on a crazy, unsociable plan ever to become successful. "I did all I could—I chose the worst fool I could find."

Then Austen Heller wrote an article about Howard Roark and Monadnock Valley. He spoke of all the buildings Roark had designed, and he put into words the things Roark had said in structure. Only they were not Austen Heller's usual quiet words—they were a ferocious cry of admiration and of anger. "And may we be damned if greatness must reach us through fraud!"

The article started a violent controversy in art circles.

"Howard," Mallory said one day, some months later, "you're famous."

"Yes," said Roark, "I suppose so."

"Three-quarters of them don't know what it's all about, but they've heard the other one-quarter fighting over your name and so now they feel they must pronounce it with respect. Of the fighting quarter, four-tenths are those who hate you, three-tenths are those who feel they must express an opinion in any controversy, two-tenths are those who play safe and herald any 'discovery,' and one-tenth are those who understand. But they've all found out suddenly that there is a Howard Roark and that he's an architect. The *A.G.A. Bulletin* refers to you as a great but unruly talent—and the Museum of the Future has hung up photographs of Monadnock, the Enright House, the Cord Building and the Aquitania, under beautiful glass—next to the room where they've got Gordon L. Prescott. And still—I'm glad."

Kent Lansing said, one evening: "Heller did a grand job. Do you remember, Howard, what I told you once about the psychology of a pretzel? Don't despise the middleman. He's necessary. Someone had to tell them. It takes two to make every great career: the man who is great, and the man—almost rarer—who is great enough to see greatness and say so."

Ellsworth Toohey wrote: "The paradox in all this preposterous noise is the fact that Mr. Caleb Bradley is the victim of a grave injustice. His ethics are open to censure, but his esthetics were unimpeachable. He exhibited sounder judgment in matters of architectural merit than Mr. Austen Heller, the outmoded reactionary who has suddenly turned art critic. Mr. Caleb Bradley was martyred by the bad taste of his tenants. In the opinion of this column his sentence should have been commuted in recognition of his artistic discrimination. Monadnock Valley is a fraud —but not merely a financial one."

There was little response to Roark's fame among the solid gentlemen of wealth who were the steadiest source of architectural commissions. The men who had said: "Roark? Never heard of him," now said: "Roark? He's too sensational."

But there were men who were impressed by the simple fact that Roark had built a place which made money for owners who didn't want to make money; this was more convincing than abstract artistic discussions. And there was the one-tenth who understood. In the year after Monadnock Valley Roark built two private homes in Connecticut, a movie theater in Chicago, a hotel in Philadelphia.

In the spring of 1936 a western city completed plans for a World's Fair to be held next year, an international exposition to be known as "The March of the Centuries." The committee of distinguished civic leaders in charge of the project chose a council of the country's best architects to design the fair. The civic leaders wished to be conspicuously progressive. Howard Roark was one of the eight architects chosen.

When he received the invitation, Roark appeared before the committee and explained that he would be glad to design the fair—alone.

"But you can't be serious, Mr. Roark," the chairman declared. "After all, with a stupendous undertaking of this nature, we want the best that can be had. I mean, two heads are better than one, you know, and eight heads . . . why, you can see for yourself—the best talents of the country, the brightest names—you know, friendly consultation, co-operation and collaboration—you know what makes great achievements."

"I do."

"Then you realize . . ."

"If you want me, you'll have to let me do it all, alone. I don't work with councils."

"You wish to reject an opportunity like this, a spot in history, a chance of world fame, practically a chance of immortality . . ."

"I don't work with collectives. I don't consult, I don't co-operate, I don't collaborate."

There was a great deal of angry comment on Roark's refusal, in architectural circles. People said: "The conceited bastard!" The indignation was too sharp and raw for a mere piece of professional gossip; each man took it as a personal insult; each felt himself qualified to alter, advise and improve the work of any man living.

"The incident illustrates to perfection," wrote Ellsworth Toohey, "the antisocial nature of Mr. Howard Roark's egotism, the arrogance of the unbridled individualism which he has always personified."

Among the eight chosen to design "The March of the Centuries" were Peter Keating, Gordon L. Prescott, Ralston Holcombe. "I won't work with Howard Roark," said Peter Keating, when he saw the list of the council, "you'll have to choose. It's he or I." He was informed that Mr. Roark had declined. Keating assumed leadership over the council. The press stories about the progress of the fair's construction referred to "Peter Keating and his associates."

Keating had acquired a sharp, intractable manner in the last few years. He snapped orders and lost his patience before the smallest difficulty; when he lost his patience, he screamed at people; he had a vocabulary of insults that carried a caustic, insidious, almost feminine malice; his face was sullen.

In the fall of 1936 Roark moved his office to the top floor of the Cord Building. He had thought, when he designed that building, that it would be the place of his office some day. When he saw the inscription: "Howard Roark, Architect," on his new door, he stopped for a moment; then he walked into the office. His own room, at the end of a long suite, had three walls of glass, high over the city. He stopped in the middle of the room. Through the broad panes, he could see the Fargo Store, the Enright House, the Aquitania Hotel. He walked to the windows facing south and stood there for a long time. At the tip of Manhattan, far in the distance, he could see the Dana Building by Henry Cameron.

On an afternoon of November, returning to his office after a visit to the site of a house under construction on Long Island, Roark entered the reception room, shaking his drenched raincoat, and saw a look of suppressed excitement on the face of his secretary; she had been waiting impatiently for his return.

"Mr. Roark, this is probably something very big," she said. "I made an appointment for you for three o'clock tomorrow afternoon. At his office."

"Whose office?"

"He telephoned half an hour ago. Mr. Gail Wynand."

II

A SIGN HUNG OVER THE ENTRANCE DOOR, A REPRODUCTION OF THE paper's masthead:

THE NEW YORK BANNER

The sign was small, a statement of fame and power that needed no emphasis; it was like a fine, mocking smile that justified the building's bare ugliness; the building was a factory scornful of all ornament save the implications of that masthead.

The entrance lobby looked like the mouth of a furnace; elevators drew a stream of human fuel and spat it out. The men did not hurry, but they moved with subdued haste, the propulsion of purpose; nobody loitered in that lobby. The elevator doors clicked like valves, a pulsating rhythm in their sound. Drops of red and green light flashed on a wall board, signaling the progress of cars high in space.

It looked as if everything in that building were run by such control boards in the hands of an authority aware of every motion, as if the building were flowing with channeled energy, functioning smoothly, soundlessly, a magnificent machine that nothing could destroy. Nobody paid any attention to the redheaded man who stopped in the lobby for a moment.

Howard Roark looked up at the tiled vault. He had never hated anyone. Somewhere in this building was its owner, the man who had made him feel his nearest approach to hatred.

Gail Wynand glanced at the small clock on his desk. In a few minutes he had an appointment with an architect. The interview, he thought, would not be difficult; he had held many such interviews in his life; he merely had to speak, he knew what he wanted to say, and nothing was required of the architect except a few sounds signifying understanding.

His glance went from the clock back to the sheets of proofs on his desk. He read an editorial by Alvah Scarret on the public feeding of squirrels in Central Park, and a column by Ellsworth Toohey on the great merits of an exhibition of paintings done by the workers of the City Department of Sanitation. A buzzer rang on his desk, and his secretary's voice said: "Mr. Howard Roark, Mr. Wynand."

"Okay," said Wynand, flicking the switch off. As his hand moved back, he noticed the row of buttons at the edge of his desk, bright little knobs with a color code of their own, each representing the end of a

539

wire that stretched to some part of the building, each wire controlling some man, each man controlling many men under his orders, each group of men contributing to the final shape of words on paper to go into millions of homes, into millions of human brains—these little knobs of colored plastic, there under his fingers. But he had no time to let the thought amuse him, the door of his office was opening, he moved his hand away from the buttons.

Wynand was not certain that he missed a moment, that he did not rise at once as courtesy demanded, but remained seated, looking at the man who entered; perhaps he had risen immediately and it only seemed to him that a long time preceded his movement. Roark was not certain that he stopped when he entered the office, that he did not walk forward, but stood looking at the man behind the desk; perhaps there had been no break in his steps and it only seemed to him that he had stopped. But there had been a moment when both forgot the terms of immediate reality, when Wynand forgot his purpose in summoning this man, when Roark forgot that this man was Dominique's husband, when no door, desk or stretch of carpet existed, only the total awareness, for each, of the man before him, only two thoughts meeting in the middle of the room—"This is Gail Wynand"—"This is Howard Roark."

Then Wynand rose, his hand motioned in simple invitation to the chair beside his desk, Roark approached and sat down, and they did not notice that they had not greeted each other.

Wynand smiled, and said what he had never intended to say. He said very simply:

"I don't think you'll want to work for me."

"I want to work for you," said Roark, who had come here prepared to refuse.

"Have you seen the kind of things I've built?"

"Yes."

Wynand smiled. "This is different. It's not for my public. It's for me."

"You've never built anything for yourself before?"

"No—if one doesn't count the cage I have up on a roof and this old printing factory here. Can you tell me why I've never built a structure of my own, with the means of erecting a city if I wished? I don't know. I think you'd know." He forgot that he did not allow men he hired the presumption of personal speculation upon him.

"Because you've been unhappy," said Roark.

He said it simply, without insolence; as if nothing but total honesty were possible to him here. This was not the beginning of an interview, but the middle; it was like a continuation of something begun long ago. Wynand said:

"Make that clear."

"I think you understand."

"I want to hear you explain it."

"Most people build as they live—as a matter of routine and senseless accident. But a few understand that building is a great symbol. We live in our minds, and existence is the attempt to bring that life into physical reality, to state it in gesture and form. For the man who understands this, a house he owns is a statement of his life. If he doesn't build, when he has the means, it's because his life has not been what he wanted."

"You don't think it's preposterous to say that to me of all people?"

"No."

"I don't either." Roark smiled. "But you and I are the only two who'd say it. Either part of it: that I didn't have what I wanted or that I could be included among the few expected to understand any sort of great symbols. You don't want to retract that either?"

"No."

"How old are you?"

"Thirty-six."

"I owned most of the papers I have now—when I was thirty-six." He added: "I didn't mean that as any kind of a personal remark. I don't know why I said that. I just happened to think of it."

"What do you wish me to build for you?"

"My home."

Wynand felt that the two words had some impact on Roark apart from any normal meaning they could convey; he sensed it without reason; he wanted to ask: "What's the matter?" but couldn't, since Roark had really shown nothing.

"You were right in your diagnosis," said Wynand, "because you see, now I do want to build a house of my own. Now I'm not afraid of a visible shape for my life. If you want it said directly, as you did, now I'm happy."

"What kind of a house?"

"In the country. I've purchased the site. An estate in Connecticut, five hundred acres. What kind of a house? You'll decide that."

"Did Mrs. Wynand choose me for the job?"

"No. Mrs. Wynand knows nothing about this. It was I who wanted to move out of the city, and she agreed. I did ask her to select the architect —my wife is the former Dominique Francon; she was once a writer on architecture. But she preferred to leave the choice to me. You want to know why I picked you? I took a long time to decide. I felt rather lost, at first. I had never heard of you. I didn't know any architects at all. I mean this literally—and I'm not forgetting the years I've spent in real estate, the things I've built and the imbeciles who built them for me. This is not a Stoneridge, this is—what did you call it?—a statement of my life? Then I saw Monadnock. It was the first thing that made me remember your name. But I gave myself a long test. I went around the country, looking at homes, hotels, all sort of buildings. Every time I saw one I liked and asked who had designed it, the answer was always the same: Howard Roark. So I called you." He added: "Shall I tell you how much I admire your work?"

"Thank you," said Roark. He closed his eyes for an instant.

"You know, I didn't want to meet you."

"Why?"

"Have you heard about my art gallery?"

"Yes."

"I never meet the men whose work I love. The work means too much to me. I don't want the men to spoil it. They usually do. They're an anticlimax to their own talent. You're not. I don't mind talking to you. I told you this only because I want you to know that I respect very little in life, but I respect the things in my gallery, and your buildings, and man's capacity to produce work like that. Maybe it's the only religion I've ever had." He shrugged. "I think I've destroyed, perverted, corrupted just about everything that exists. But I've never touched that. Why are you looking at me like this?"

"I'm sorry. Please tell me about the house you want."

"I want it to be a palace—only I don't think palaces are very luxurious. They're so big, so promiscuously public. A small house is the true luxury. A residence for two people only—for my wife and me. It won't be necessary to allow for a family, we don't intend to have children. Nor for visitors, we don't intend to entertain. One guest room—in case we should need it—but not more than that. Living room, dining room, library, two studies, one bedroom. Servants' quarters, garage. That's the general idea. I'll give you the details later. The cost—whatever you need. The appearance—" he smiled, shrugging. "I've seen your buildings. The man who wants to tell you what a house should look like must either be able to design it better—or shut up. I'll say only that I want my house to have the Roark quality."

"What is that?"

"I think you understand."

"I want to hear you explain it."

"I think some buildings are cheap show-offs, all front, and some are cowards, apologizing for themselves in every brick, and some are the eternal unfit, botched, malicious and false. Your buildings have one sense above all—a sense of joy. Not a placid joy. A difficult, demanding kind of joy. The kind that makes one feel as if it were an achievement to experience it. One looks and thinks: I'm a better person if I can feel that."

Roark said slowly, not in the tone of an answer:

"I suppose it was inevitable."

"What?"

"That you would see that."

"Why do you say it as if you . . . regretted my being able to see it?"

"I don't regret it."

"Listen, don't hold it against me—the things I've built before."

"I don't."

"It's all those Stoneridges and Noyes-Belmont Hotels—and Wynand papers—that made it possible for me to have a house by you. Isn't that a luxury worth achieving? Does it matter how? They were the means. You're the end."

"You don't have to justify yourself to me."

"I wasn't jus . . . Yes, I think that's what I was doing."

"You don't need to. I wasn't thinking of what you've built."

"What were you thinking?"

"That I'm helpless against anyone who sees what you saw in my buildings."

"You felt you wanted help against me?"

"No. Only I don't feel helpless as a rule."

"I'm not prompted to justify myself as a rule, either. Then—it's all right, isn't it?"

"Yes."

"I must tell you much more about the house I want. I suppose an architect is like a father confessor—he must know everything about the people who are to live in his house, since what he gives them is more personal than their clothes or food. Please consider it in that spirit—and forgive me if you notice that this is difficult for me to say—I've never gone to confession. You see, I want this house because I'm very desperately in love with my wife. . . . What's the matter? Do you think it's an irrelevant statement?"

"No. Go on."

"I can't stand to see my wife among other people. It's not jealousy. It's much more and much worse. I can't stand to see her walking down the streets of a city. I can't share her, not even with shops, theaters, taxicabs or sidewalks. I must take her away. I must put her out of reach—where nothing can touch her, not in any sense. This house is to be a fortress. My architect is to be my guard."

Roark sat looking straight at him. He had to keep his eyes on Wynand in order to be able to listen. Wynand felt the effort in that glance; he did not recognize it as effort, only as strength; he felt himself supported by the glance; he found that nothing was hard to confess.

"This house is to be a prison. No, not quite that. A treasury—a vault to guard things too precious for sight. But it must be more. It must be a separate world, so beautiful that we'll never miss the one we left. A prison only by the power of its own perfection. Not bars and ramparts —but your talent standing as a wall between us and the world. That's what I want of you. And more. Have you ever built a temple?"

For a moment, Roark had no strength to answer; but he saw that the question was genuine; Wynand didn't know.

"Yes," said Roark.

"Then think of this commission as you would think of a temple. A temple to Dominique Wynand. . . . I want you to meet her before you design it."

"I met Mrs. Wynand some years ago."

"You have? Then you understand."

"I do."

Wynand saw Roark's hand lying on the edge of his desk, the long fingers pressed to the glass, next to the proofs of the *Banner*. The proofs were folded carelessly; he saw the heading "One Small Voice" inside the page. He looked at Roark's hand. He thought he would like to have a bronze paperweight made of it and how beautiful it would look on his desk.

"Now you know what I want. Go ahead. Start at once. Drop anything else you're doing. I'll pay whatever you wish. I want that house by summer. . . . Oh, forgive me. Too much association with bad architects. I haven't asked whether you want to do it."

Roark's hand moved first; he took it off the desk.

"Yes," said Roark. "I'll do it."

Wynand saw the prints of the fingers left on the glass, distinct as if the skin had cut grooves in the surface and the grooves were wet.

"How long will it take you?" Wynand asked.

"You'll have it by July."

"Of course you must see the site. I want to show it to you myself. Shall I drive you down there tomorrow morning?"

"If you wish."

"Be here at nine."

"Yes."

"Do you want me to draw up a contract? I have no idea how you prefer to work. As a rule, before I deal with a man in any matter, I make it a point to know everything about him from the day of his birth or earlier. I've never checked up on you. I simply forgot. It didn't seem necessary."

"I can answer any question you wish."

Wynand smiled and shook his head:

"No. There's nothing I need to ask you. Except about the business arrangements."

"I never make any conditions, except one: if you accept the preliminary drawings of the house, it is to be built as I designed it, without any alterations of any kind."

"Certainly. That's understood. I've heard you don't work otherwise. But will you mind if I don't give you any publicity on this house? I know it would help you professionally, but I want this building kept out of the newspapers."

"I won't mind that."

"Will you promise not to release pictures of it for publication?"

"I promise."

"Thank you. I'll make up for it. You may consider the Wynand papers as your personal press service. I'll give you all the plugging you wish on any other work of yours."

"I don't want any plugging."

Wynand laughed aloud. "What a thing to say in what a place! I don't think you have any idea how your fellow architects would have conducted this interview. I don't believe you were actually conscious at any time that you were speaking to Gail Wynand."

"I was," said Roark.

"This was my way of thanking you. I don't always like being Gail Wynand."

"I know that."

"I'm going to change my mind and ask you a personal question. You said you'd answer anything."

"I will."

"Have you always liked being Howard Roark?"

Roark smiled. The smile was amused, astonished, involuntarily contemptuous.

"You've answered," said Wynand.

Then he rose and said: "Nine o'clock tomorrow morning," extending his hand.

When Roark had gone, Wynand sat behind his desk, smiling. He moved his hand toward one of the plastic buttons—and stopped. He realized that he had to assume a different manner, his usual manner, that he could not speak as he had spoken in the last half-hour. Then he understood what had been strange about the interview: for the first time in his life he had spoken to a man without feeling the reluctance, the sense of pressure, the need of disguise he had always experienced when he spoke to people; there had been no strain and no need of strain; as if he had spoken to himself.

He pressed the button and said to his secretary:

"Tell the morgue to send me everything they have on Howard Roark."

"Guess what," said Alvah Scarret, his voice begging to be begged for his information.

Ellsworth Toohey waved a hand impatiently in a brushing-off motion, not raising his eyes from his desk.

"Go 'way, Alvah. I'm busy."

"No, but this is interesting, Ellsworth. Really, it's interesting. I know you'll want to know."

Toohey lifted his head and looked at him, the faint contraction of boredom in the corners of his eyes letting Scarret understand that this moment of attention was a favor; he drawled in a tone of emphasized patience:

"All right. What is it?"

Scarret saw nothing to resent in Toohey's manner. Toohey had treated him like that for the last year or longer. Scarret had not noticed the transition in their relationship; by the time he noticed the change, it was too late to resent it—it had become normal to them both.

Scarret smiled like a bright pupil who expects the teacher to praise him for discovering an error in the teacher's own textbook.

"Ellsworth, your private F.B.I. is slipping."

"What are you talking about?"

"Bet you don't know what Gail's been doing—and you always make such a point of keeping yourself informed."

"What don't I know?"

"Guess who was in his office today."

"My dear Alvah, I have no time for quiz games."

"You wouldn't guess in a thousand years."

"Very well, since the only way to get rid of you is to play the vaudeville stooge, I shall ask the proper question: Who was in dear Gail's office today?"

"Howard Roark."

Toohey turned to him full face, forgetting to dole out his attention, and said incredulously:

"No!"

"Yes!" said Scarret, proud of the effect.

"Well!" said Toohey and burst out laughing.

Scarret half smiled tentatively, puzzled, anxious to join in, but not quite certain of the cause for amusement.

"Yes, it's funny. But . . . just exactly why, Ellsworth?"

"Oh, Alvah, it would take so long to tell you."

"I had an idea it might . . ."

"Haven't you any sense of the spectacular, Alvah? Don't you like fireworks? If you want to know what to expect, just think that the worst wars are religious wars between sects of the same religion or civil wars between brothers of the same race."

"I don't quite follow you."

"Oh, dear, I have so many followers. I brush them out of my hair."

"Well, I'm glad you're so cheerful about it, but I thought it's bad."

"Of course it's bad. But not for us."

"But look: you know how we've gone out on a limb, you particularly, on how this Roark is just about the worst architect in town, and if now our own boss hires him—isn't it going to be embarrassing?"

"Oh that? . . . Oh, maybe . . ."

"Well, I'm glad you take it that way."

"What was he doing in Wynand's office? Is it a commission?"

"That's what I don't know. Can't find out. Nobody knows."

"Have you heard of Mr. Wynand planning to build anything lately?"

"No. Have you?"

"No. I guess my F.B.I. is slipping. Oh, well, one does the best one can."

"But you know, Ellsworth, I had an idea. I had an idea where this might be very helpful to us indeed."

"What idea?"

"Ellsworth, Gail's been impossible lately."

Scarret uttered it solemnly, with the air of imparting a discovery. Toohey sat half smiling.

"Well, of course, you predicted it, Ellsworth. You were right. You're always right. I'll be damned if I can figure out just what's happening to him, whether it's Dominique or some sort of a change of life or what, but something's happening. Why does he get fits suddenly and start reading every damn line of every damn edition and raise hell for the silliest reasons? He's killed three of my best editorials lately—and he's never done that to me before. Never. You know what he said to me? He said: 'Motherhood is wonderful, Alvah, but for God's sake go easy on the bilge. There's a limit even for intellectual depravity.' What depravity? That was the sweetest Mother's Day editorial I ever put together. Honest, I was touched myself. Since when has he learned to talk about depravity? The other day, he called Jules Fougler a bargain-basement mind, right to his face, and threw his Sunday piece into the wastebasket. A swell piece, too—on the Workers' theater. Jules Fougler, our best writer! No wonder Gail hasn't got a friend left in the place. If they hated his guts before, you ought to hear them now!"

"I've heard them."

"He's losing his grip, Ellsworth. I don't know what I'd do if it weren't for you and the swell bunch of people you picked. They're practically our whole actual working staff, those youngsters of yours, not our old sacred cows who're writing themselves out anyway. Those bright kids will keep the *Banner* going. But Gail . . . Listen, last week he fired Dwight Carson. Now you know, I think that was significant. Of course

Dwight was just a deadweight and a damn nuisance, but he was the first one of those special pets of Gail's, the boys who sold their souls. So, in a way, you see, I liked having Dwight around, it was all right, it was healthy, it was a relic of Gail's best days. I always said it was Gail's safety valve. And when he suddenly let Carson go—I didn't like it, Ellsworth. I didn't like it at all."

"What is this, Alvah? Are you telling me things I don't know, or is this just in the nature of letting off steam—do forgive the mixed metaphor—on my shoulder?"

"I guess so. I don't like to knock Gail, but I've been so damn mad for so long I'm fit to be tied. But here's what I'm driving at: This Howard Roark, what does he make you think of?"

"I could write a volume on that, Alvah. This is hardly the time to launch into such an undertaking."

"No, but I mean, what's the one thing we know about him? That he's a crank and a freak and a fool, all right, but what else? That he's one of those fools you can't budge with love or money or a sixteen-inch gun. He's worse than Dwight Carson, worse than the whole lot of Gail's pets put together. Well? Get my point? What's Gail going to do when he comes up against that kind of a man?"

"One of several possible things."

"One thing only, if I know Gail, and I know Gail. That's why I feel kind of hopeful. This is what he's needed for a long time. A swig of his old medicine. The safety valve. He'll go out to break that guy's spine—and it will be good for Gail. The best thing in the world. Bring him back to normal. . . . That was my idea, Ellsworth." He waited, saw no complimentary enthusiasm on Toohey's face and finished lamely: "Well, I might be wrong. . . . I don't know. . . . It might mean nothing at all. . . . I just thought that was psychology. . . ."

"That's what it was, Alvah."

"Then you think it'll work that way?"

"It might. Or it might be much worse than anything you imagine. But it's of no importance to us any more. Because you see, Alvah, as far as the *Banner* is concerned, if it came to a showdown between us and our boss, we don't have to be afraid of Mr. Gail Wynand any longer."

When the boy from the morgue entered, carrying a thick envelope of clippings, Wynand looked up from his desk and said:

"That much? I didn't know he was so famous."

"Well, it's the Stoddard trial, Mr. Wynand."

The boy stopped. There was nothing wrong—only the ridges on Wynand's forehead, and he did not know Wynand well enough to know what these meant. He wondered what made him feel as if he should be afraid. After a moment, Wynand said:

"All right. Thank you."

The boy deposited the envelope on the glass surface of the desk, and walked out.

Wynand sat looking at the bulging shape of yellow paper. He saw it reflected in the glass, as if the bulk had eaten through the surface and grown roots to his desk. He looked at the walls of his office and he wondered whether they contained a power which could save him from opening that envelope.

Then he pulled himself erect, he put both forearms in a straight line along the edge of the desk, his fingers stretched and meeting, he looked down, past his nostrils, at the surface of the desk, he sat for a moment, grave, proud, collected, like the angular mummy of a Pharaoh, then he moved one hand, pulled the envelope forward, opened it and began to read.

"Sacrilege" by Ellsworth M. Toohey—"The Churches of our Childhood" by Alvah Scarret—editorials, sermons, speeches, statements, letters to the editor, the *Banner* unleashed full-blast, photographs, cartoons, interviews, resolutions of protest, letters to the editor.

He read every word, methodically, his hands on the edge of the desk, fingers meeting, not lifting the clippings, not touching them, reading them as they lay on top of the pile, moving a hand only to turn a clipping over and read the one beneath, moving the hand with a mechanical perfection of timing, the fingers rising as his eyes took the last word, not allowing the clipping to remain in sight a second longer than necessary. But he stopped for a long time to look at the photographs of the Stoddard Temple. He stopped longer to look at one of Roark's pictures, the picture of exultation captioned "Are you happy, Mr. Superman?" He tore it from the story it illustrated, and slipped it into his desk drawer. Then he continued reading.

The trial—the testimony of Ellsworth M. Toohey—of Peter Keating —of Ralston Holcombe—of Gordon L. Prescott—no quotations from the testimony of Dominique Francon, only a brief report. "The defense rests." A few mentions in "One Small Voice"—then a gap—the next clipping dated three years later—Monadnock Valley.

It was late when he finished reading. His secretaries had left. He felt the sense of empty rooms and halls around him. But he heard the sound of the presses: a low, rumbling vibration that went through every room. He had always liked that—the sound of the building's heart, beating. He listened. They were running off tomorrow's *Banner*. He sat without moving for a long time.

III

ROARK AND WYNAND STOOD ON THE TOP OF A HILL, LOOKING OVER a spread of land that sloped away in a long gradual curve. Bare trees rose on the hilltop and descended to the shore of a lake, their branches geometrical compositions cut through the air. The color of the sky, a clear, fragile blue-green, made the air colder. The cold washed the colors of the earth, revealing that they were not colors but only the elements from which color was to come, the dead brown not a full brown but a future green, the tired purple an overture to flame, the gray a prelude to gold. The earth was like the outline of a great story, like the steel frame of a building—to be filled and finished, holding all the splendor of the future in naked simplification.

"Where do you think the house should stand?" asked Wynand.

"Here," said Roark.

"I hoped you'd choose this."

Wynand had driven his car from the city, and they had walked for two hours down the paths of his new estate, through deserted lanes, through a forest, past the lake, to the hill. Now Wynand waited, while Roark stood looking at the countryside spread under his feet. Wynand wondered what reins this man was gathering from all the points of the landscape into his hand.

When Roark turned to him, Wynand asked:

"May I speak to you now?"

"Of course." Roark smiled, amused by the deference which he had not requested.

Wynand's voice sounded clear and brittle, like the color of the sky above them, with the same quality of ice-green radiance:

"Why did you accept this commission?"

"Because I'm an architect for hire."

"You know what I mean."

"I'm not sure I do."

"Don't you hate my guts?"

"No. Why should I?"

"You want me to speak of it first?"

"Of what?"

"The Stoddard Temple."

Roark smiled. "So you did check up on me since yesterday."

"I read our clippings." He waited, but Roark said nothing. "All of them." His voice was harsh, half defiance, half plea. "Everything we said about you." The calm of Roark's face drove him to fury. He went on, giving slow, full value to each word: "We called you an incompetent fool, a tyro, a charlatan, a swindler, an egomaniac . . ."

"Stop torturing yourself."

Wynand closed his eyes, as if Roark had struck him. In a moment, he said:

"Mr. Roark, you don't know me very well. You might as well learn this: I don't apologize. I never apologize for any of my actions."

"What made you think of apology? I haven't asked for it."

"I stand by every one of those descriptive terms. I stand by every word printed in the *Banner*."

"I haven't asked you to repudiate it."

"I know what you think. You understood that I didn't know about the Stoddard Temple yesterday. I had forgotten the name of the architect involved. You concluded it wasn't I who led that campaign against you. You're right, it wasn't I, I was away at the time. But you don't understand that the campaign was in the true and proper spirit of the *Banner*. It was in strict accordance with the *Banner's* function. No one is responsible for it but me. Alvah Scarret was doing only what I taught him. Had I been in town, I would have done the same."

"That's your privilege."

"You don't believe I would have done it?"

"No."

"I haven't asked you for compliments and I haven't asked you for pity."

"I can't do what you're asking for."

"What do you think I'm asking?"

"That I slap your face."

"Why don't you?"

"I can't pretend an anger I don't feel," said Roark. "It's not pity. It's much more cruel than anything I could do. Only I'm not doing it in order to be cruel. If I slapped your face, you'd forgive me for the Stoddard Temple."

"Is it you who should seek forgiveness?"

"No. You wish I did. You know that there's an act of forgiveness involved. You're not clear about the actors. You wish I would forgive you—or demand payment, which is the same thing—and you believe that that would close the record. But, you see, I have nothing to do with it. I'm not one of the actors. It doesn't matter what I do or feel about it now. You're not thinking of me. I can't help you. I'm not the person you're afraid of just now."

"Who is?"

"Yourself."

"Who gave you the right to say all this?"

"You did."

"Well, go on."

"Do you wish the rest?"

"Go on."

"I think it hurts you to know that you've made me suffer. You wish you hadn't. And yet there's something that frightens you more. The knowledge that I haven't suffered at all."

"Go on."

"The knowledge that I'm neither kind nor generous now, but simply indifferent. It frightens you, because you know that things like the Stoddard Temple always require payment—and you see that I'm not paying for it. You were astonished that I accepted this commission. Do you think my acceptance required courage? You needed far greater courage to hire me. You see, this is what I think of the Stoddard Temple. I'm through with it. You're not."

Wynand let his fingers fall open, palms out. His shoulders sagged a little, relaxing. He said very simply:

"All right. It's true. All of it."

Then he stood straight, but with a kind of quiet resignation, as if his body were consciously made vulnerable.

"I hope you know you've given me a beating in your own way," he said.

"Yes. And you've taken it. So you've accomplished what you wanted. Shall we say we're even and forget the Stoddard Temple?"

"You're very wise or I've been very obvious. Either is your achievement. Nobody's ever caused me to become obvious before."

"Shall I still do what you want?"

"What do you think I want now?"

"Personal recognition from me. It's my turn to give in, isn't it?"

"You're appallingly honest, aren't you?"

"Why shouldn't I be? I can't give you the recognition of having made me suffer. But you'll take the substitute of having given me pleasure, won't you? All right, then. I'm glad you like me. I think you know this is as much an exception for me as your taking a beating. I don't usually care whether I'm liked or not. I do care this time. I'm glad."

Wynand laughed aloud. "You're as innocent and presumptuous as an emperor. When you confer honors you merely exalt yourself. What in hell made you think I liked you?"

"Now you don't want any explanations of that. You've reproached me once for causing you to be obvious."

Wynand sat down on a fallen tree trunk. He said nothing; but his movement was an invitation and a demand. Roark sat down beside him;

Roark's face was sober, but the trace of a smile remained, amused and watchful, as if every word he heard were not a disclosure but a confirmation.

"You've come up from nothing, haven't you?" Wynand asked. "You came from a poor family."

"Yes. How did you know that?"

"Just because it feels like a presumption—the thought of handing you anything: a compliment, an idea or a fortune. I started at the bottom, too. Who was your father?"

"A steel puddler."

"Mine was a longshoreman. Did you hold all sorts of funny jobs when you were a child?"

"All sorts. Mostly in the building trades."

"I did worse than that. I did just about everything. What job did you like best?"

"Catching rivets, on steel structures."

"I liked being a bootblack on a Hudson ferry. I should have hated that, but I didn't. I don't remember the people at all. I remember the city. The city—always there, on the shore, spread out, waiting, as if I were tied to it by a rubber band. The band would stretch and carry me away, to the other shore, but it would always snap back and I would return. It gave me the feeling that I'd never escape from that city—and it would never escape from me."

Roark knew that Wynand seldom spoke of his childhood, by the quality of his words: they were bright and hesitant, untarnished by usage, like coins that had not passed through many hands.

"Were you ever actually homeless and starving?" Wynand asked.

"A few times."

"Did you mind that?"

"No."

"I didn't either. I minded something else. Did you want to scream, when you were a child, seeing nothing but fat ineptitude around you, knowing how many things could be done and done so well, but having no power to do them? Having no power to blast the empty skulls around you? Having to take orders—and that's bad enough—but to take orders from your inferiors! Have you felt that?"

"Yes."

"Did you drive the anger back inside of you, and store it, and decide to let yourself be torn to pieces if necessary, but reach the day when you'd rule those people and all people and everything around you?"

"No."

"You didn't? You let yourself forget?"

"No. I hate incompetence. I think it's probably the only thing I do hate. But it didn't make me want to rule people. Nor to teach them anything. It made me want to do my own work in my own way and let myself be torn to pieces if necessary."

"And you were?"

"No. Not in any way that counts."

"You don't mind looking back? At anything?"

"No."

"I do. There was one night. I was beaten and I crawled to a door—I remember the pavement—it was right under my nostrils—I can still see it—there were veins in the stone and white spots—I had to make sure that that pavement moved—I couldn't feel whether I was moving or not—but I could tell by the pavement—I had to see that those veins and spots changed—I had to reach the next pattern or the crack six inches away—it took a long time—and I knew it was blood under my stomach . . ."

His voice had no tone of self-pity; it was simple, impersonal, with a faint sound of wonder.

Roark said: "I'd like to help you."

Wynand smiled slowly, not gaily. "I believe you could. I even believe that it would be proper. Two days ago I would have murdered anyone who'd think of me as an object for help. . . . You know, of course, that that night's not what I hate in my past. Not what I dread to look back on. It was only the least offensive to mention. The other things can't be talked about."

"I know. I meant the other things."

"What are they? You name them."

"The Stoddard Temple."

"You want to help me with that?"

"Yes."

"You're a damn fool. Don't you realize . . ."

"Don't you realize I'm doing it already?"

"How?"

"By building this house for you."

Roark saw the slanting ridges on Wynand's forehead. Wynand's eyes seemed whiter than usual, as if the blue had ebbed from the iris, two white ovals, luminous on his face. He said:

"And getting a fat commission check for it."

He saw Roark's smile, suppressed before it appeared fully. The smile would have said that this sudden insult was a declaration of surrender, more eloquent than the speeches of confidence; the suppression said that Roark would not help him over this particular moment.

"Why, of course," said Roark calmly.

Wynand got up. "Let's go. We're wasting time. I have more important things to do at the office."

They did not speak on their way back to the city. Wynand drove his car at ninety miles an hour. The speed made two solid walls of blurred motion on the sides of the road; as if they were flying down a long, closed, silent corridor.

He stopped at the entrance to the Cord Building and let Roark out. He said:

"You're free to go back to that site as often as you wish, Mr. Roark. I don't have to go with you. You can get the surveys and all the information you need from my office. Please do not call on me again until it is necessary. I shall be very busy. Let me know when the first drawings are ready."

When the drawings were ready, Roark telephoned Wynand's office. He had not spoken to Wynand for a month. "Please hold the wire, Mr. Roark," said Wynand's secretary. He waited. The secretary's voice came back and informed him that Mr. Wynand wished the drawings brought to his office that afternoon; she gave the hour; Wynand would not answer in person.

When Roark entered the office, Wynand said: "How do you do, Mr. Roark," his voice gracious and formal. No memory of intimacy remained on his blank, courteous face.

Roark handed him the plans of the house and a large perspective drawing. Wynand studied each sheet. He held the drawing for a long time. Then he looked up.

"I am very much impressed, Mr. Roark." The voice was offensively correct. "I have been quite impressed by you from the first. I have thought it over and I want to make a special deal with you."

His glance was directed at Roark with a soft emphasis, almost with tenderness; as if he were showing that he wished to treat Roark cautiously, to spare him intact for a purpose of his own.

He lifted the sketch and held it up between two fingers, letting the light hit it straight on; the white sheet glowed as a reflector for a moment, pushing the black pencil lines eloquently forward.

"You want to see this house erected?" Wynand asked softly. "You want it very much?"

"Yes," said Roark.

Wynand did not move his hand, only parted his fingers and let the cardboard drop face down on the desk.

"It will be erected, Mr. Roark. Just as you designed it. Just as it stands on this sketch. On one condition."

Roark sat leaning back, his hands in his pockets, attentive, waiting.

"You don't want to ask me what condition, Mr. Roark? Very well, I'll tell you. I shall accept this house on condition that you accept the deal I offer you. I wish to sign a contract whereby you will be sole architect for any building I undertake to erect in the future. As you realize, this would be quite an assignment. I venture to say I control more structural work than any other single person in the country. Every man in your profession has wanted to be known as my exclusive architect. I am offering it to you. In exchange, you will have to submit yourself to certain conditions. Before I name them, I'd like to point out some of the consequences, should you refuse. As you may have heard, I do not like to be refused. The power I hold can work two ways. It would be easy for me to arrange that no commission be available to you anywhere in this country. You have a small following of your own, but no prospective employer can withstand the kind of pressure I am in a position to exert. You have gone through wasted periods of your life before. They were nothing, compared to the blockade I can impose. You might have to go back to a granite quarry—oh yes, I know about that, summer of 1928, the Francon quarry in Connecticut—how?—private detectives, Mr. Roark—you might have to go back to a granite quarry, only I shall see to it that the quarries also will be closed to you. Now I'll tell you what I want of you."

In all the gossip about Gail Wynand, no one had ever mentioned the expression of his face as it was in this moment. The few men who had seen it did not talk about it. Of these men, Dwight Carson had been the first. Wynand's lips were parted, his eyes brilliant. It was an expression of sensual pleasure derived from agony—the agony of his victim or his own, or both.

"I want you to design all my future commercial structures—as the public wishes commercial structures to be designed. You'll build Colonial houses, Rococo hotels and semi-Grecian office buildings. You'll exercise your matchless ingenuity within forms chosen by the taste of the people —and you'll make money for me. You'll take your spectacular talent and make it obedient. Originality and subservience together. They call it harmony. You'll create in your sphere what the *Banner* is in mine. Do you think it took no talent to create the *Banner?* Such will be your future career. But the house you've designed for me shall be erected as you designed it. It will be the last Roark building to rise on earth. Nobody will have one after mine. You've read about ancient rulers who put to death the architect of their palace, that no others might equal the glory he had given them. They killed the architect or cut his eyes out. Modern methods are different. For the rest of your life you'll obey the will of the majority. I shan't attempt to offer you any arguments. I am merely stating an alternative. You're the kind of man who can understand plain language. You have a simple choice: if you refuse, you'll never build anything again; if you accept, you'll build this house which you want so much to see erected, and a great many other houses which you won't like, but which will make money for both of us. For the rest of your life you'll design rental developments, such as Stoneridge. That is what I want."

He leaned forward, waiting for one of the reactions he knew well and enjoyed: a look of anger, or indignation, or ferocious pride.

"Why, of course," said Roark gaily. "I'll be glad to do it. That's easy."

He reached over, took a pencil and the first piece of paper he saw on Wynand's desk—a letter with an imposing letterhead. He drew rapidly on the back of the letter. The motion of his hand was smooth and confident. Wynand looked at his face bent over the paper; he saw the unwrinkled forehead, the straight line of the eyebrows, attentive, but untroubled by effort.

Roark raised his head and threw the paper to Wynand across the desk.

"Is this what you want?"

Wynand's house stood drawn on the paper—with Colonial porches, a gambrel roof, two massive chimneys, a few little pilasters, a few porthole windows. It was not a parody, it was a serious job of adaptation in what any professor would have called excellent taste.

"Good God, no!" The gasp was instinctive and immediate.

"Then shut up," said Roark, "and don't ever let me hear any architectural suggestions."

Wynand slumped down in his chair and laughed. He laughed for a long time, unable to stop. It was not a happy sound.

Roark shook his head wearily. "You knew better than that. And it's such an old one to me. My antisocial stubbornness is so well-known that I didn't think anyone would waste time trying to tempt me again."

"Howard. I meant it. Until I saw this."

"I knew you meant it. I didn't think you could be such a fool."

"You knew you were taking a terrible kind of chance?"

"None at all. I had an ally I could trust."

"What? Your integrity?"

"Yours, Gail."

Wynand sat looking down at the surface of his desk. After a while he said:

"You're wrong about that."

"I don't think so."

Wynand lifted his head; he looked tired; he sounded indifferent.

"It was your method of the Stoddard trial again, wasn't it? 'The defense rests.' . . . I wish I had been in the courtroom to hear that sentence. . . . You did throw the trial back at me again, didn't you?"

"Call it that."

"But this time, you won. I suppose you know I'm not glad that you won."

"I know you're not."

"Don't think it was one of those temptations when you tempt just to test your victim and are happy to be beaten, and smile and say, well, at last, here's the kind of man I want. Don't imagine that. Don't make that excuse for me."

"I'm not. I know what you wanted."

"I wouldn't have lost so easily before. This would have been only the beginning. I know I can try further. I don't want to try. Not because you'd probably hold out to the end. But because I wouldn't hold out. No, I'm not glad and I'm not grateful to you for this. . . . But it doesn't matter. . . ."

"Gail, how much lying to yourself are you actually capable of?"

"I'm not lying. Everything I just told you is true. I thought you understood it."

"Everything you just told me—yes. I wasn't thinking of that."

"You're wrong in what you're thinking. You're wrong in remaining here."

"Do you wish to throw me out?"

"You know I can't."

Wynand's glance moved from Roark to the drawing of the house lying face down on his desk. He hesitated for a moment, looking at the blank cardboard, then turned it over. He asked softly:

"Shall I tell you now what I think of this?"

"You've told me."

"Howard, you spoke about a house as a statement of my life. Do you think my life deserves a statement like this?"

"Yes."

"Is this your honest judgment?"

"My honest judgment, Gail. My most sincere one. My final one. No matter what might happen between us in the future."

Wynand put the drawing down and sat studying the plans for a long time. When he raised his head, he looked calm and normal.

"Why did you stay away from here?" he asked.

"You were busy with private detectives."

Wynand laughed. "Oh that? I couldn't resist my old bad habits and I was curious. Now I know everything about you—except the women in your life. Either you've been very discreet or there haven't been many. No information available on that anywhere."

"There haven't been many."

"I think I missed you. It was a kind of substitute—gathering the details of your past. Why did you actually stay away?"

"You told me to."

"Are you always so meek about taking orders?"

"When I find it advisable."

"Well, here's an order—hope you place it among the advisable ones: come to have dinner with us tonight. I'll take this drawing home to show my wife. I've told her nothing about the house so far."

"You haven't told her?"

"No. I want her to see this. And I want you to meet her. I know she hasn't been kind to you in the past—I read what she wrote about you. But it's so long ago. I hope it doesn't matter now."

"No, it doesn't matter."

"Then will you come?"

"Yes."

IV

DOMINIQUE STOOD AT THE GLASS DOOR OF HER ROOM. WYNAND saw the starlight on the ice sheets of the roof garden outside. He saw its reflection touching the outline of her profile, a faint radiance on her eyelids, on the planes of her cheeks. He thought that this was the illumination proper to her face. She turned to him slowly, and the light became an edge around the pale straight mass of her hair. She smiled as she had always smiled at him, a quiet greeting of understanding.

"What's the matter, Gail?"

"Good evening, dear. Why?"

"You look happy. That's not the word. But it's the nearest."

" 'Light' is nearer. I feel light, thirty years lighter. Not that I'd want to be what I was thirty years ago. One never does. What the feeling means is only a sense of being carried back intact, as one is now, back to the beginning. It's quite illogical and impossible and wonderful."

"What the feeling usually means is that you've met someone. A woman as a rule."

"I have. Not a woman. A man. Dominique, you're very beautiful tonight. But I always say that. It's not what I wanted to say. It's this: I am very happy tonight that you're so beautiful."

"What is it, Gail?"

"Nothing. Only a feeling of how much is unimportant and how easy it is to live."

He took her hand and held it to his lips.

"Dominique, I've never stopped thinking it's a miracle that our marriage has lasted. Now I believe that it won't be broken. By anything or anyone." She leaned back against the glass pane. "I have a present for you—don't remind me it's the sentence I use more often than any other. I will have a present for you by the end of this summer. Our house."

"The house? You haven't spoken of it for so long, I thought you had forgotten."

"I've thought of nothing else for the last six months. You haven't changed your mind? You do want to move out of the city?"

"Yes, Gail, if you want it so much. Have you decided on an architect?"

"I've done more than that. I have the drawing of the house to show you."

"Oh, I'd like to see it."

"It's in my study. Come on. I want you to see it."

She smiled and closed her fingers over his wrist, a brief pressure, like a caress of encouragement, then she followed him. He threw the door of his study open and let her enter first. The light was on and the drawing stood propped on his desk, facing the door.

She stopped, her hands behind her, palms flattened against the door-jamb. She was too far away to see the signature, but she knew the work and the only man who could have designed that house.

Her shoulders moved, describing a circle, twisting slowly, as if she were tied to a pole, had abandoned hope of escape, and only her body made a last, instinctive gesture of protest.

She thought, were she lying in bed in Roark's arms in the sight of Gail Wynand, the violation would be less terrible; this drawing, more personal than Roark's body, created in answer to a matching force that came from Gail Wynand, was a violation of her, of Roark, of Wynand —and yet, she knew suddenly that it was the inevitable.

"No," she whispered, "things like that are never a coincidence."

"What?"

But she held up her hand, softly pushing back all conversation, and she walked to the drawing, her steps soundless on the carpet. She saw the sharp signature in the corner—"Howard Roark." It was less terrifying than the shape of the house; it was a thin point of support, almost a greeting.

"Dominique?"

She turned her face to him. He saw her answer. He said:

"I knew you'd like it. Forgive the inadequacy. We're stuck for words tonight."

She walked to the davenport and sat down; she let her back press against the cushions; it helped to sit straight. She kept her eyes on Wynand. He stood before her, leaning on the mantelpiece, half turned away, looking at the drawing. She could not escape that drawing; Wynand's face was like a mirror of it.

"You've seen him, Gail?"

"Whom?"

"The architect."

"Of course I've seen him. Not an hour ago."

"When did you first meet him?"

"Last month."

"You knew him all this time? . . . Every evening . . . when you came home . . . at the dinner table . . ."

"You mean, why didn't I tell you? I wanted to have the sketch to show you. I saw the house like this, but I couldn't explain it. I didn't think anyone would ever understand what I wanted and design it. He did."

"Who?"

"Howard Roark."

She had wanted to hear the name pronounced by Gail Wynand.

"How did you happen to choose him, Gail?"

"I looked all over the country. Every building I liked had been done by him."

She nodded slowly.

"Dominique, I take it for granted you don't care about it any more, but I know that I picked the one architect you spent all your time denouncing when you were on the *Banner*."

"You read that?"

"I read it. You had an odd way of doing it. It was obvious that you admired his work and hated him personally. But you defended him at the Stoddard trial."

"Yes."

"You even worked for him once. That statue, Dominique, it was made for his temple."

"Yes."

"It's strange. You lost your job on the *Banner* for defending him. I didn't know it when I chose him. I didn't know about that trial. I had forgotten his name. Dominique, in a way, it's he who gave you to me. That statue—from his temple. And now he's going to give me this house. Dominique, why did you hate him?"

"I didn't hate him. . . . It was so long ago . . ."

"I suppose none of that matters now, does it?" He pointed to the drawing.

"I haven't seen him for years."

"You're going to see him in about an hour. He's coming here for dinner."

She moved her hand, tracing a spiral on the arm of the davenport, to convince herself that she could.

"Here?"

"Yes."

"You've asked him for dinner?"

He smiled; he remembered his resentment against the presence of guests in their house. He said: "This is different. I want him here. I don't think you remember him well—or you wouldn't be astonished."

She got up.

"All right, Gail. I'll give the orders. Then I'll get dressed."

They faced each other across the drawing room of Gail Wynand's penthouse. She thought how simple it was. He had always been here. He had been the motive power of every step she had taken in these rooms.

He had brought her here and now he had come to claim this place. She was looking at him. She was seeing him as she had seen him on the morning when she awakened in his bed for the last time. She knew that neither his clothes nor the years stood between her and the living intactness of that memory. She thought this had been inevitable from the first, from the instant when she had looked down at him on the ledge of a quarry—it had to come like this, in Gail Wynand's house—and now she felt the peace of finality, knowing that her share of decision had ended; she had been the one who acted, but he would act from now on.

She stood straight, her head level; the planes of her face had a military cleanliness of precision and a feminine fragility; her hands hung still, composed by her sides, parallel with the long straight lines of her black dress.

"How do you do, Mr. Roark."

"How do you do, Mrs. Wynand."

"May I thank you for the house you have designed for us? It is the most beautiful of your buildings."

"It had to be, by the nature of the assignment, Mrs. Wynand."

She turned her head slowly.

"How did you present the assignment to Mr. Roark, Gail?"

"Just as I spoke of it to you."

She thought of what Roark had heard from Wynand, and had accepted. She moved to sit down; the two men followed her example. Roark said:

"If you like the house, the first achievement was Mr. Wynand's conception of it."

She asked: "Are you sharing the credit with a client?"

"Yes, in a way."

"I believe this contradicts what I remember of your professional convictions."

"But supports my personal ones."

"I'm not sure I ever understood that."

"I believe in conflict, Mrs. Wynand."

"Was there a conflict involved in designing this house?"

"The desire not to be influenced by my client."

"In what way?"

"I have liked working for some people and did not like working for others. But neither mattered. This time, I knew that the house would be what it became only because it was being done for Mr. Wynand. I had to overcome this. Or rather, I had to work with it and against it. It was the best way of working. The house had to surpass the architect, the client and the future tenant. It did."

"But the house—it's you, Howard," said Wynand. "It's still you."

It was the first sign of emotion on her face, a quiet shock, when she heard the "Howard." Wynand did not notice it. Roark did. He glanced at her—his first glance of personal contact. She could read no comment in it—only a conscious affirmation of the thought that had shocked her.

"Thank you for understanding that, Gail," he answered.

She was not certain whether she had heard him stressing the name.

"It's strange," said Wynand. "I am the most offensively possessive man on earth. I do something to things. Let me pick up an ash tray from a dime-store counter, pay for it and put it in my pocket—and it becomes a special kind of ash tray, unlike any on earth, because it's *mine*. It's an extra quality in the thing, like a sort of halo. I feel that about everything I own. From my overcoat—to the oldest linotype in the composing room—to the copies of the *Banner* on newsstands—to this penthouse— to my wife. And I've never wanted to own anything as much as I want this house you're going to build for me, Howard. I will probably be jealous of Dominique living in it—I can be quite insane about things like that. And yet—I don't feel that I'll own it, because no matter what I do or pay, it's still yours. It will always be yours."

"It has to be mine," said Roark. "But in another sense, Gail, you own that house and everything else I've built. You own every structure you've stopped before and heard yourself answering."

"In what sense?"

"In the sense of that personal answer. What you feel in the presence of a thing you admire is just one word—'Yes.' The affirmation, the acceptance, the sign of admittance. And that 'Yes' is more than an answer to one thing, it's a kind of 'Amen' to life, to the earth that holds this thing, to the thought that created it, to yourself for being able to see it. But the ability to say 'Yes' or 'No' is the essence of all ownership. It's your ownership of your own ego. Your soul, if you wish. Your soul has a single basic function—the act of valuing. 'Yes' or 'No,' 'I wish' or 'I do not wish.' You can't say 'Yes' without saying 'I.' There's no affirmation without the one who affirms. In this sense, everything to which you grant your love is yours."

"In this sense, you share things with others?"

"No. It's not sharing. When I listen to a symphony I love, I don't get from it what the composer got. His 'Yes' was different from mine. He could have no concern for mine and no exact conception of it. That answer is too personal to each man. But in giving himself what he wanted, he gave me a great experience. I'm alone when I design a house, Gail, and you can never know the way in which I own it. But if you said your own 'Amen' to it—it's also yours. And I'm glad it's yours."

Wynand said, smiling:

"I like to think that. That I own Monadnock and the Enright House and the Cord Building . . ."

"And the Stoddard Temple," said Dominique.

She had listened to them. She felt numb. Wynand had never spoken like this to any guest in their house; Roark had never spoken like this to any client. She knew that the numbness would break into anger, denial, indignation later; now it was only a cutting sound in her voice, a sound to destroy what she had heard.

She thought that she succeeded. Wynand answered, the word dropping heavily:

"Yes."

"Forget the Stoddard Temple, Gail," said Roark. There was such a simple, careless gaiety in his voice that no solemn dispensation could have been more effective.

"Yes, Howard," said Wynand, smiling.

She saw Roark's eyes turned to her.

"I have not thanked you, Mrs. Wynand, for accepting me as your architect. I know that Mr. Wynand chose me and you could have refused my services. I wanted to tell you that I'm glad you didn't."

She thought, I believe it because none of this can be believed; I'll accept anything tonight; I'm looking at him.

She said, courteously indifferent: "Wouldn't it be a reflection on my judgment to suppose that I would wish to reject a house you had designed, Mr. Roark?" She thought that nothing she said aloud could matter tonight.

Wynand asked:

"Howard, that 'Yes'—once granted, can it be withdrawn?"

She wanted to laugh in incredulous anger. It was Wynand's voice that had asked this; it should have been hers. He must look at me when he answers, she thought; he must look at me.

"Never," Roark answered, looking at Wynand.

"There's so much nonsense about human inconstancy and the transience of all emotions," said Wynand. "I've always thought that a feeling which changes never existed in the first place. There are books I liked at the age of sixteen. I still like them."

The butler entered, carrying a tray of cocktails. Holding her glass, she watched Roark take his off the tray. She thought: At this moment the glass stem between his fingers feels just like the one between mine; we have this much in common. . . . Wynand stood, holding a glass, looking at Roark with a strange kind of incredulous wonder, not like a host, like an owner who cannot quite believe his ownership of his prize possession. . . . She thought: I'm not insane, I'm only hysterical, but it's quite all right, I'm saying something, I don't know what it is, but it must be all right, they are both listening and answering, Gail is smiling, I must be saying the proper things. . . .

Dinner was announced and she rose obediently; she led the way to the dining room, like a graceful animal given poise by conditioned reflexes. She sat at the head of the table, between the two men facing each other at her sides. She watched the silverware in Roark's fingers, the pieces of polished metal with the initials "D. W." She thought: I have done this so many times—I am the gracious Mrs. Gail Wynand—they were Senators, judges, presidents of insurance companies, sitting at dinner in that place at my right—and this is what I was being trained for, this is why Gail has been rising through tortured years to the position of entertaining Senators and judges at dinner—for the purpose of reaching an evening when the guest facing him would be Howard Roark.

Wynand spoke about the newspaper business; he showed no reluctance to discuss it with Roark, and she pronounced a few sentences when it seemed necessary. Her voice had a luminous simplicity; she was being carried along, unresisting, any personal reaction would be superfluous, even pain or fear. She thought, if in the flow of conversation Wynand's next sentence should be: "You've slept with him," she would answer: "Yes, Gail, of course," just as simply. But Wynand seldom looked at her; when he did, she knew by his face that hers was normal.

Afterward, they were in the drawing room again, and she saw Roark standing at the window, against the lights of the city. She thought: Gail built this place as a token of his own victory—to have the city always before him—the city where he did run things at last. But this is what it had really been built for—to have Roark stand at that window—and I think Gail knows it tonight—Roark's body blocking miles out of that perspective, with only a few dots of fire and a few cubes of lighted glass left visible around the outline of his figure. He was smoking and she watched his cigarette moving slowly against the black sky, as he put it between his lips, then held it extended in his fingers, and she thought: they are only sparks from his cigarette, those points glittering in space behind him.

She said softly: "Gail always liked to look at the city at night. He was in love with skyscrapers."

Then she noticed she had used the past tense, and wondered why.

She did not remember what she said when they spoke about the new house. Wynand brought the drawings from his study, spread the plans on a table, and the three of them stood bent over the plans together. Roark's pencil moved, pointing, across the hard geometrical patterns of thin black lines on white sheets. She heard his voice, close to her, explaining. They did not speak of beauty and affirmation, but of closets, stairways, pantries, bathrooms. Roark asked her whether she found the arrangements convenient. She thought it was strange that they all spoke as if they really believed she would ever live in this house.

When Roark had gone, she heard Wynand asking her:

"What do you think of him?"

She felt something angry and dangerous, like a single, sudden twist within her, and she said, half in fear, half in deliberate invitation:

"Doesn't he remind you of Dwight Carson?"

"Oh, forget Dwight Carson!"

Wynand's voice, refusing earnestness, refusing guilt, had sounded exactly like the voice that had said: "Forget the Stoddard Temple."

The secretary in the reception room looked, startled, at the patrician gentleman whose face she had seen so often in the papers.

"Gail Wynand," he said, inclining his head in self-introduction. "I should like to see Mr. Roark. If he is not busy. Please do not disturb him if he is. I had no appointment."

She had never expected Wynand to come to an office unannounced and to ask admittance in that tone of grave deference.

She announced the visitor. Roark came out into the reception room, smiling, as if he found nothing unusual in this call.

"Hello, Gail. Come in."

"Hello, Howard."

He followed Roark to the office. Beyond the broad windows, the darkness of late afternoon dissolved the city; it was snowing; black specks whirled furiously across the lights.

"I don't want to interrupt if you're busy, Howard. This is not important." He had not seen Roark for five days, since the dinner.

"I'm not busy. Take your coat off. Shall I have the drawings brought in?"

"No. I don't want to talk about the house. Actually, I came without any reason at all. I was down at my office all day, got slightly sick of it, and felt like coming here. What are you grinning about?"

"Nothing. Only you said that it wasn't important."

Wynand looked at him, smiled and nodded.

He sat down on the edge of Roark's desk, with an ease which he had never felt in his own office, his hands in his pockets, one leg swinging.

"It's almost useless to talk to you, Howard. I always feel as if I were reading to you a carbon copy of myself and you've already seen the original. You seem to hear everything I say a minute in advance. We're unsynchronized."

"You call that unsynchronized?"

"All right. Too well synchronized." His eyes were moving slowly over the room. "If we own the things to which we say 'Yes,' then I own this office?"

"Then you own it."

"You know what I feel here? No, I won't say I feel at home—I don't think I've ever felt at home anywhere. And I won't say I feel as I did in the palaces I've visited or in the great European cathedrals. I feel as I did when I was still in Hell's Kitchen—in the best days I had there—there weren't many. But sometimes—when I sat like this—only it was some piece of broken wall by the wharf—and there were a lot of stars above and dump heaps around me and the river smelt of rotting shells. . . . Howard, when you look back, does it seem to you as if all your days had rolled forward evenly, like a sort of typing exercise, all alike? Or were there stops—points reached—and then the typing rolled on again?"

"There were stops."

"Did you know them at the time—did you know that that's what they were?"

"Yes."

"I didn't. I knew afterward. But I never knew the reasons. There was one moment—I was twelve and I stood behind a wall, waiting to be killed. Only I knew I wouldn't be killed. Not what I did afterward, not the fight I had, but just that one moment when I waited. I don't know why that was a stop to be remembered or why I feel proud of it. I don't know why I have to think of it here."

"Don't look for the reason."

"Do you know it?"

"I said don't look for it."

"I have been thinking about my past—ever since I met you. And I had gone for years without thinking of it. No, no secret conclusions for you to draw from that. It doesn't hurt me to look back this way, and it doesn't give me pleasure. It's just looking. Not a quest, not even a journey. Just a kind of walk at random, like wandering through the countryside in the evening, when one's a little tired. . . . If there's any connection to you at all, it's only one thought that keeps coming back to me. I keep thinking that you and I started in the same way. From the same point. From nothing. I just think that. Without any comment. I don't seem to find any particular meaning in it at all. Just 'we started in the same way' . . . Want to tell me what it means?"

"No."

Wynand glanced about the room—and noticed a newspaper on top of a filing cabinet.

"Who the hell reads the *Banner* around here?"

"I do."

"Since when?"

"Since about a month ago."

"Sadism?"

"No. Just curiosity."

Wynand rose, picked up the paper and glanced through the pages. He stopped at one and chuckled. He held it up: the page bore photographed drawings of the buildings for "The March of the Centuries" exposition.

"Awful, isn't it?" said Wynand. "It's disgusting that we have to plug that stuff. But I feel better about it when I think of what you did to those eminent civic leaders." He chuckled happily. "You told them you don't co-operate or collaborate."

"But it wasn't a gesture, Gail. It was plain common sense. One can't collaborate on one's own job. I can co-operate, if that's what they call it, with the workers who erect my buildings. But I can't help them to lay bricks and they can't help me to design the house."

"It was the kind of gesture I'd like to make. I'm forced to give those civic leaders free space in my papers. But it's all right. You've slapped their faces for me." He tossed the paper aside, without anger. "It's like that luncheon I had to attend today. A national convention of advertisers. I must give them publicity—all wiggling, wriggling and drooling. I got so sick of it I thought I'd run amuck and bash somebody's skull. And then I thought of you. I thought that you weren't touched by any of it. Not in any way. The national convention of advertisers doesn't exist as far as you're concerned. It's in some sort of fourth dimension that can never establish any communication with you at all. I thought of that—and I felt a peculiar kind of relief."

He leaned against the filing cabinet, letting his feet slide forward, his arms crossed, and he spoke softly:

"Howard, I had a kitten once. The damn thing attached itself to me—a flea-bitten little beast from the gutter, just fur, mud and bones—followed me home, I fed it and kicked it out, but the next day there it was again, and finally I kept it. I was seventeen then, working for the *Gazette*, just learning to work in the special way I had to learn for life. I could take it all right, but not all of it. There were times when it was pretty bad. Evenings, usually. Once I wanted to kill myself. Not anger—anger made me work harder. Not fear. But disgust, Howard. The kind of disgust that made it seem as if the whole world were under water and the water stood still, water that had backed up out of the sewers and ate into everything, even the sky, even my brain. And then I looked at that kitten. And I thought that it didn't know the things I loathed, it could never know. It was clean—clean in the absolute sense, because it had no capacity to conceive of the world's ugliness. I can't tell you what relief there was in trying to imagine the state of consciousness inside that little brain, trying to share it, a living consciousness, but clean and free. I would lie down on the floor and put my face on that cat's belly, and hear the beast purring. And then I would feel better. . . . There, Howard. I've called your office a rotting wharf and yourself an alley cat. That's my way of paying homage."

Roark smiled. Wynand saw that the smile was grateful.

"Keep still," Wynand said sharply. "Don't say anything." He walked to a window and stood looking out. "I don't know why in hell I should speak like that. These are the first happy years of my life. I met you because I wanted to build a monument to my happiness. I come here to find rest, and I find it, and yet these are the things I talk about. . . . Well, never mind. . . . Look at the filthy weather. Are you through with your work here? Can you call it a day?"

"Yes. Just about."

"Let's go and have dinner together somewhere close by."

"All right."

"May I use your phone? I'll tell Dominique not to expect me for dinner."

He dialed the number. Roark moved to the door of the drafting room—he had orders to give before leaving. But he stopped at the door. He had to stop and hear it.

"Hello, Dominique? . . . Yes. . . . Tired? . . . No, you just sounded like it. . . . I won't be home for dinner, will you excuse me, dearest? . . . I don't know, it might be late. . . . I'm eating downtown. . . . No. I'm having dinner with Howard Roark. . . . Hello, Dominique? . . . Yes. . . . What? . . . I'm calling from his office. . . . So long, dear." He replaced the receiver.

In the library of the penthouse Dominique stood with her hand on the telephone, as if some connection still remained.

For five days and nights, she had fought a single desire—to go to him. To see him alone—anywhere—his home or his office or the street—for one word or only one glance—but alone. She could not go. Her share of action was ended. He would come to her when he wished. She knew he would come, and that he wanted her to wait. She had waited, but she had held on to one thought—of an address, an office in the Cord Building.

She stood, her hand closed over the stem of the telephone receiver. She had no right to go to that office. But Gail Wynand had.

When Ellsworth Toohey entered Wynand's office, as summoned, he made a few steps, then stopped. The walls of Wynand's office—the only luxurious room in the Banner Building—were made of cork and copper paneling and had never borne any pictures. Now, on the wall facing Wynand's desk, he saw an enlarged photograph under glass: the picture of Roark at the opening of the Enright House; Roark standing at the parapet of the river, his head thrown back.

Toohey turned to Wynand. They looked at each other.

Wynand indicated a chair and Toohey sat down. Wynand spoke, smiling:

"I never thought I would come to agree with some of your social theories, Mr. Toohey, but I find myself forced to do so. You have always denounced the hypocrisy of the upper caste and preached the virtue of the masses. And now I find that I regret the advantages I enjoyed in my former proletarian state. Were I still in Hell's Kitchen, I would have begun this interview by saying: Listen, louse!—but since I am an inhibited capitalist, I shall not do so."

Toohey waited; he looked curious.

"I shall begin by saying: Listen, Mr. Toohey. I do not know what makes you tick. I do not care to dissect your motives. I do not have the stomach required of medical students. So I shall ask no questions and I wish to hear no explanations. I shall merely tell you that from now on there is a name you will never mention in your column again." He pointed to the photograph. "I could make you reverse yourself publicly and I would enjoy it, but I prefer to forbid the subject to you entirely. Not a word, Mr. Toohey. Not ever again. Now don't mention your contract or any particular clause of it. It would not be advisable. Go on writing your column, but remember its title and devote it to commensurate subjects. Keep it small, Mr. Toohey. Very small."

"Yes, Mr. Wynand," said Toohey easily. "I don't have to write about Mr. Roark at present."

"That's all."

Toohey rose. "Yes, Mr. Wynand."

V

GAIL WYNAND SAT AT HIS DESK IN HIS OFFICE AND READ THE proofs of an editorial on the moral value of raising large families. Sentences like used chewing gum, chewed and rechewed, spat out and picked up again, passing from mouth to mouth to pavement to shoe sole to mouth to brain. . . . He thought of Howard Roark and went on reading the *Banner;* it made things easier.

"Daintiness is a girl's greatest asset. Be sure to launder your undies every night, and learn to talk on some cultured subject, and you will have all the dates you want." "Your horoscope for tomorrow shows a beneficent aspect. Application and sincerity will bring rewards in the fields of engineering, public accounting and romance." "Mrs. Huntington-Cole's hobbies are gardening, the opera and early American sugar bowls. She divides her time between her little son 'Kit' and her numerous charitable activities." "I'm jus' Millie, I'm jus' a orphan." "For the complete diet send ten cents and a self-addressed, stamped envelope." . . . He turned the pages, thinking of Howard Roark.

He signed the advertising contract with Kream-O Pudding—for five years, on the entire Wynand chain, two full pages in every paper every Sunday. The men before his desk sat like triumphal arches in flesh, monuments to victory, to evenings of patience and calculation, restaurant tables, glasses emptied into throats, months of thought, his energy, his living energy flowing like the liquid in the glasses into the opening of heavy lips, into stubby fingers, across a desk, into two full pages every Sunday, into drawings of yellow molds trimmed with strawberries and yellow molds trimmed with butterscotch sauce. He looked, over the heads of the men, at the photograph on the wall of his office: the sky, the river and a man's face, lifted.

But it hurts me, he thought. It hurts me every time I think of him. It makes everything easier—the people, the editorials, the contracts—but easier because it hurts so much. Pain is a stimulant also. I think I hate that name. I will go on repeating it. It is a pain I wish to bear.

Then he sat facing Roark in the study of his penthouse—and he felt no pain; only a desire to laugh without malice.

"Howard, everything you've done in your life is wrong according to the stated ideals of mankind. And here you are. And somehow it seems a huge joke on the whole world."

Roark sat in an armchair by the fireplace. The glow of the fire moved over the study; the light seemed to curve with conscious pleasure about every object in the room, proud to stress its beauty, stamping approval upon the taste of the man who had achieved this setting for himself. They were alone. Dominique had excused herself after dinner. She had known that they wanted to be alone.

"A joke on all of us," said Wynand. "On every man in the street. I always look at the men in the street. I used to ride in the subways just to see how many of them carried the *Banner*. I used to hate them and, sometimes, to be afraid. But now I look at every one of them and I want to say: 'Why, you poor fool!' That's all."

He telephoned Roark's office one morning.

"Can you have lunch with me, Howard? . . . Meet me at the Nordland in half an hour."

He shrugged, smiling, when he faced Roark across the restaurant table.

"Nothing at all, Howard. No special reason. Just spent a revolting half-hour and wanted to take the taste of it out of my mouth."

"What revolting half-hour?"

"Had my picture taken with Lancelot Clokey."

"Who's Lancelot Clokey?"

Wynand laughed aloud, forgetting his controlled elegance, forgetting the startled glance of the waiter.

"That's it, Howard. That's why I had to have lunch with you. Because you can say things like that."

"Now what's the matter?"

"Don't you read books? Don't you know that Lancelot Clokey is 'our most sensitive observer of the international scene'? That's what the critic said—in my own *Banner*. Lancelot Clokey has just been chosen author of the year or something by some organization or other. We're running his biography in the Sunday supplement, and I had to pose with my arm around his shoulders. He wears silk shirts and smells of gin. His second book is about his childhood and how it helped him to understand the international scene. It sold a hundred thousand copies. But you've never heard of him. Go on, eat your lunch, Howard. I like to see you eating. I wish you were broke, so that I could feed you this lunch and know you really needed it."

At the end of a day, he would come, unannounced, to Roark's office or to his home. Roark had an apartment in the Enright House, one of the crystal-shaped units over the East River: a workroom, a library, a bedroom. He had designed the furniture himself. Wynand could not understand for a long time why the place gave him an impression of luxury, until he saw that one did not notice the furniture at all: only a clean sweep of space and the luxury of an austerity that had not been simple to achieve. In financial value it was the most modest home that Wynand had entered as a guest in twenty-five years.

"We started in the same way, Howard," he said, glancing about

Roark's room. "According to my judgment and experience, you should have remained in the gutter. But you haven't. I like this room. I like to sit here."

"I like to see you here."

"Howard, have you ever held power over a single human being?"

"No. And I wouldn't take it if it were offered to me."

"I can't believe that."

"It was offered to me once, Gail. I refused it."

Wynand looked at him with curiosity; it was the first time that he heard effort in Roark's voice.

"Why?"

"I had to."

"Out of respect for the man?"

"It was a woman."

"Oh, you damn fool! Out of respect for a woman?"

"Out of respect for myself."

"Don't expect me to understand. We're as opposite as two men can be."

"I thought that once. I wanted to think that."

"And now you don't?"

"No."

"Don't you despise every act I've ever committed?"

"Just about every one I know of."

"And you still like to see me here?"

"Yes. Gail, there was a man who considered you the symbol of the special evil that destroyed him and would destroy me. He left me his hatred. And there was another reason. I think I hated you, before I saw you."

"I knew you did. What made you change your mind?"

"I can't explain that to you."

They drove together to the estate in Connecticut where the walls of the house were rising out of the frozen ground. Wynand followed Roark through the future rooms, he stood aside and watched Roark giving instructions. Sometimes, Wynand came alone. The workers saw the black roadster twisting up the road to the top of the hill, saw Wynand's figure standing at a distance, looking at the structure. His figure always carried with it all the implications of his position; the quiet elegance of his overcoat, the angle of his hat, the confidence of his posture, tense and casual together, made one think of the Wynand empire; of the presses thundering from ocean to ocean, of the papers, the lustrous magazine covers, the light rays trembling through newsreels, the wires coiling over the world, the power flowing into every palace, every capital, every secret, crucial room, day and night, through every costly minute of this man's life. He stood still against a sky gray as laundry water, and snowflakes fluttered lazily past the brim of his hat.

On a day in April he drove alone to Connecticut after an absence of many weeks. The roadster flew across the countryside, not an object, but a long streak of speed. He felt no jolting motion inside his small cube of glass and leather; it seemed to him that his car stood still, suspended over the ground, while the control of his hands on the wheel made the earth fly past him, and he merely had to wait until the place he desired came rolling to him. He loved the wheel of a car as he loved his desk in the office of the *Banner:* both gave him the same sense of a dangerous monster let loose under the expert direction of his fingers.

Something tore past across his vision, and he was a mile away before he thought how strange it was that he should have noticed it, because it had been only a clump of weeds by the road; a mile later he realized that it was stranger still: the weeds were green. Not in the middle of winter, he thought, and then he understood, surprised, that it was not winter any longer. He had been very busy in the last few weeks; he had not had time to notice. Now he saw it, hanging over the fields around him, a hint of green, like a whisper. He heard three statements in his mind, in precise succession, like interlocking gears: It's spring—I wonder if I have many left to see—I am fifty-five years old.

They were statements, not emotions; he felt nothing, neither eagerness nor fear. But he knew it was strange that he should experience a sense of time; he had never thought of his age in relation to any measure, he had never defined his position on a limited course, he had not thought of a course nor of limits. He had been Gail Wynand and he had stood still, like this car, and the years had sped past him, like this earth, and the motor within him had controlled the flight of the years.

No, he thought, I regret nothing. There have been things I missed, but I ask no questions, because I have loved it, such as it has been, even the moments of emptiness, even the unanswered—and that I loved it, *that* is the unanswered in my life. But I loved it.

If it were true, that old legend about appearing before a supreme judge and naming one's record, I would offer, with all my pride, not any act I committed, but one thing I have never done on this earth: that I never sought an outside sanction. I would stand and say: I am Gail Wynand, the man who has committed every crime except the foremost one: that of ascribing futility to the wonderful fact of existence and seeking justification beyond myself. This is my pride: that now, thinking of the end, I do not cry like all the men of my age: but what was the use and the meaning? *I* was the use and the meaning, I, Gail Wynand. That I lived and that I acted.

He drove to the foot of the hill and slammed the brakes on, startled, looking up. In his absence the house had taken shape; it could be recognized now—it looked like the drawing. He felt a moment of childish wonder that it had really come out just as on the sketch, as if he had never quite believed it. Rising against the pale blue sky, it still looked like a drawing, unfinished, the planes of masonry like spreads of watercolor filled in, the naked scaffolding like pencil lines; a huge drawing on a pale blue sheet of paper.

He left the car and walked to the top of the hill. He saw Roark among the men. He stood outside and watched the way Roark walked through the structure, the way he turned his head or raised his hand, pointing. He noticed Roark's manner of stopping: his legs apart, his arms straight at his sides, his head lifted; an instinctive pose of confidence, of energy held under effortless control, a moment that gave to his body the structural cleanliness of his own building. Structure, thought Wynand, is a solved problem of tension, of balance, of security in counterthrusts.

He thought: There's no emotional significance in the act of erecting a building; it's just a mechanical job, like laying sewers or making an automobile. And he wondered why he watched Roark, feeling what he felt in his art gallery. He belongs in an unfinished building, thought Wynand, more than in a completed one, more than at a drafting table, it's his right setting, it's becoming to him—as Dominique said a yacht was becoming to me.

Afterward Roark came out and they walked together along the crest of the hill, among the trees. They sat down on a fallen tree trunk, they saw the structure in the distance through the stems of the brushwood. The stems were dry and naked, but there was a quality of spring in the cheerful insolence of their upward thrust, the stirring of a self-assertive purpose.

Wynand asked:

"Howard, have you ever been in love?"

Roark turned to look straight at him and answer quietly:

"I still am."

"But when you walk through a building, what you feel is greater than that?"

"Much greater, Gail."

"I was thinking of people who say that happiness is impossible on earth. Look how hard they all try to find some joy in life. Look how they struggle for it. Why should any living creature exist in pain? By what conceivable right can anyone demand that a human being exist for anything but for his own joy? Every one of them wants it. Every part of him wants it. But they never find it. I wonder why. They whine and say they don't understand the meaning of life. There's a particular kind of people that I despise. Those who seek some sort of a higher purpose or 'universal goal,' who don't know what to live for, who moan that they must 'find themselves.' You hear it all around us. That seems to be the official bromide of our century. Every book you open. Every drooling self-confession. It seems to be the noble thing to confess. I'd think it would be the most shameful one."

"Look, Gail." Roark got up, reached out, tore a thick branch off a tree, held it in both hands, one fist closed at each end; then, his wrists and knuckles tensed against the resistance, he bent the branch slowly into an arc. "Now I can make what I want of it: a bow, a spear, a cane, a railing. That's the meaning of life."

"Your strength?"

"Your work." He tossed the branch aside. "The material the earth offers you and what you make of it . . . What are you thinking of, Gail?"

"The photograph on the wall of my office."

To remain controlled, as he wished, to be patient, to make of patience an active duty executed consciously each day, to stand before Roark and let her serenity tell him: "This is the hardest you could have demanded of me, but I'm glad, if it's what you want"—such was the discipline of Dominique's existence.

She stood by, as a quiet spectator of Roark and Wynand. She watched them silently. She had wanted to understand Wynand. This was the answer.

She accepted Roark's visits to their house and the knowledge that in the hours of these evenings he was Wynand's property, not hers. She met him as a gracious hostess, indifferent and smiling, not a person but an exquisite fixture of Wynand's home, she presided at the dinner table, she left them in the study afterward.

She sat alone in the drawing room, with the lights turned off and the door open; she sat erect and quiet, her eyes on the slit of light under the door of the study across the hall. She thought: This is my task, even when alone, even in the darkness, within no knowledge but my own, to look at that door as I looked at him here, without complaint. . . . Roark, if it's the punishment you chose for me, I'll carry it completely, not as a part to play in your presence, but as a duty to perform alone—you know that violence is not hard for me to bear, only patience is, you chose the hardest, and I must perform it and offer it to you . . . my . . . dearest one . . .

When Roark looked at her, there was no denial of memory in his eyes. The glance said simply that nothing had changed and nothing was needed to state it. She felt as if she heard him saying: Why are you shocked? Have we ever been parted? Your drawing room, your husband

and the city you dread beyond the windows, are they real now, Dominique? Do you understand? Are you beginning to understand? "Yes," she would say suddenly, aloud, trusting that the word would fit the conversation of the moment, knowing that Roark would hear it as his answer.

It was not a punishment he had chosen for her. It was a discipline imposed on both of them, the last test. She understood his purpose when she found that she could feel her love for him proved by the room, by Wynand, even by his love for Wynand and hers, by the impossible situation, by her enforced silence—the barriers proving to her that no barriers could exist.

She did not see him alone. She waited.

She would not visit the site of construction. She had said to Wynand: "I'll see the house when it's finished." She never questioned him about Roark. She let her hands lie in sight on the arms of her chair, so that the relief of any violent motion would be denied her, her hands as her private barometer of endurance, when Wynand came home late at night and told her that he had spent the evening at Roark's apartment, the apartment she had never seen.

Once she broke enough to ask:

"What is this, Gail? An obsession?"

"I suppose so." He added: "It's strange that you don't like him."

"I haven't said that."

"I can see it. I'm not really surprised. It's your way. You would dislike him—precisely because he's the type of man you should like. . . . Don't resent my obsession."

"I don't resent it."

"Dominique, would you understand it if I told you that I love you more since I've met him? Even—I want to say this—even when you lie in my arms, it's more than it was. I feel a greater right to you."

He spoke with the simple confidence they had given each other in the last three years. She sat looking at him as she always did; her glance had tenderness without scorn and sadness without pity.

"I understand, Gail."

After a moment she asked:

"What is he to you, Gail? In the nature of a shrine?"

"In the nature of a hair shirt," said Wynand.

When she had gone upstairs, he walked to a window and stood looking up at the sky. His head thrown back, he felt the pull of his throat muscles and he wondered whether the peculiar solemnity of looking at the sky comes, not from what one contemplates, but from that uplift of one's head.

VI

"THE BASIC TROUBLE WITH THE MODERN WORLD," SAID ELLS-worth Toohey, "is the intellectual fallacy that freedom and compulsion are opposites. To solve the gigantic problems crushing the world today, we must clarify our mental confusion. We must acquire a philosophical perspective. In essence, freedom and compulsion are one. Let me give you a simple illustration. Traffic lights restrain your freedom to cross a street whenever you wish. But this restraint gives you the freedom from being run over by a truck. If you were assigned to a job and prohibited from leaving it, it would restrain the freedom of your career. But it would give you freedom from the fear of unemployment. Whenever a new compulsion is imposed upon us, we automatically gain a new freedom. The two are inseparable. Only by accepting total compulsion can we achieve total freedom."

"That's right!" shrieked Mitchell Layton.

It was an actual shriek, thin and high. It had come with the startling suddenness of a fire siren. His guests looked at Mitchell Layton.

He sat in a tapestry armchair of his drawing room, half lying, legs and stomach forward, like an obnoxious child flaunting his bad posture. Everything about the person of Mitchell Layton was almost and not quite, just short of succeeding: his body had started out to be tall, but changed its mind, leaving him with a long torso above short, stocky legs; his face had delicate bones, but the flesh had played a joke on them, puffing out, not enough to achieve obesity, just enough to suggest permanent mumps. Mitchell Layton pouted. It was not a temporary expression nor a matter of facial arrangement. It was a chronic attribute, pervading his entire person. He pouted with his whole body.

Mitchell Layton had inherited a quarter of a billion dollars and had spent the thirty-three years of his life trying to make amends for it.

Ellsworth Toohey, in dinner clothes, stood lounging against a cabinet. His nonchalance had an air of gracious informality and a touch of impertinence, as if the people around him did not deserve the preservation of rigid good manners.

His eyes moved about the room. The room was not exactly modern, not quite Colonial and just a little short of French Empire; the furnishings presented straight planes and swan-neck supports, black mirrors and electric hurricane lamps, chromium and tapestry; there was unity in a single attribute: in the expensiveness of everything.

"That's right," said Mitchell Layton belligerently, as if he expected

579

everyone to disagree and was insulting them in advance. "People make too damn much fuss about freedom. What I mean is it's a vague, over-abused word. I'm not even sure it's such a God-damn blessing. *I* think people would be much happier in a regulated society that had a definite pattern and a unified form—like a folk dance. You know how beautiful a folk dance is. And rhythmic too. That's because it took generations to work it out and they don't let just any chance fool come along to change it. That's what we need. Pattern, I mean, and rhythm. Also beauty."

"That's an apt comparison, Mitch," said Ellsworth Toohey. "I've always told you that you had a creative mind."

"What I mean is, what makes people unhappy is not too little choice, but too much," said Mitchell Layton. "Having to decide, always to decide, torn every which way all of the time. Now in a society of pattern, a man could feel safe. Nobody would come to him all the time pestering him to do something. Nobody would have to do anything. What I mean is, of course, except working for the common good."

"It's spiritual values that count," said Homer Slottern. "Got to be up to date and keep up with the world. This is a spiritual century."

Homer Slottern had a big face with drowsy eyes. His shirt studs were made of rubies and emeralds combined, like gobs of salad dripping down his starched white shirt front. He owned three department stores.

"There ought to be a law to make everybody study the mystical secrets of the ages," said Mitchell Layton. "It's all been written out in the pyramids in Egypt."

"That's true, Mitch," Homer Slottern agreed. "There's a lot to be said for mysticism. On the one hand. On the other hand, dialectic material-ism . . ."

"It's not a contradiction," Mitchell Layton drawled contemptuously. "The world of the future will combine both."

"As a matter of fact," said Ellsworth Toohey, "the two are superfi-cially varied manifestations of the same thing. Of the same intention." His eyeglasses gave a spark, as if lighted from within; he seemed to relish this particular statement in his own way.

"All I know is, unselfishness is the only moral principle," said Jessica Pratt, "the noblest principle and a sacred duty and much more impor-tant than freedom. Unselfishness is the only way to happiness. I would have everybody who refused to be unselfish shot. To put them out of their misery. They can't be happy anyway."

Jessica Pratt spoke wistfully. She had a gentle, aging face; her pow-dery skin, innocent of make-up, gave the impression that a finger touching it would be left with a spot of white dust.

Jessica Pratt had an old family name, no money, and a great passion: her love for her younger sister Renée. They had been left orphaned at an early age, and she had dedicated her life to Renée's upbringing. She had sacrificed everything; she had never married; she had struggled, plotted, schemed, defrauded through the years—and achieved the triumph of Renée's marriage to Homer Slottern.

Renée Slottern sat curled up on a footstool, munching peanuts. Once in a while she reached up to the crystal dish on a side table and took another. She exhibited no further exertion. Her pale eyes stared placidly out of her pale face.

"That's going too far, Jess," said Homer Slottern. "You can't expect everybody to be a saint."

"I don't expect anything," said Jessica Pratt meekly. "I've given up expecting long ago. But it's education that we all need. Now I think Mr. Toohey understands. If everybody were compelled to have the proper kind of education, we'd have a better world. If we force people to do good, they will be free to be happy."

"This is a perfectly useless discussion," said Eve Layton. "No intelligent person believes in freedom nowadays. It's dated. The future belongs to social planning. Compulsion is a law of nature. That's that. It's self-evident."

Eve Layton was beautiful. She stood under the light of a chandelier, her smooth black hair clinging to her skull, the pale green satin of her gown alive like water about to stream off and expose the rest of her soft, tanned skin. She had the special faculty of making satin and perfume appear as modern as an aluminum table top. She was Venus rising out of a submarine hatch.

Eve Layton believed that her mission in life was to be the vanguard—it did not matter of what. Her method had always been to take a careless leap and land triumphantly far ahead of all others. Her philosophy consisted of one sentence—"I can get away with anything." In conversation she paraphrased it to her favorite line: "I? I'm the day after tomorrow." She was an expert horsewoman, a racing driver, a stunt pilot, a swimming champion. When she saw that the emphasis of the day had switched to the realm of ideas, she took another leap, as she did over any ditch. She landed well in front, in the latest. Having landed, she was amazed to find that there were people who questioned her feat. Nobody had ever questioned her other achievements. She acquired an impatient anger against all those who disagreed with her political views. It was a personal issue. She had to be right, since she was the day after tomorrow.

Her husband, Mitchell Layton, hated her.

"It's a perfectly valid discussion," he snapped. "Everybody can't be as competent as you, my dear. We must help the others. It's the moral duty of intellectual leaders. What I mean is we ought to lose that bugaboo of being scared of the word compulsion. It's not compulsion when it's for a good cause. What I mean is in the name of love. But I don't know how we can make this country understand it. Americans are so stuffy."

He could not forgive his country because it had given him a quarter of a billion dollars and then refused to grant him an equal amount of reverence. People would not take his views on art, literature, history, biology, sociology and metaphysics as they took his checks. He complained that people identified him with his money too much; he hated them because they did not identify him enough.

"There's a great deal to be said for compulsion," stated Homer Slottern. "Provided it's democratically planned. The common good must always come first, whether we like it or not."

Translated into language, Homer Slottern's attitude consisted of two parts; they were contradictory parts, but this did not trouble him, since they remained untranslated in his mind. First, he felt that abstract theories were nonsense, and if the customers wanted this particular kind, it was perfectly safe to give it to them, and good business, besides. Second, he felt uneasy that he had neglected whatever it was people called spiritual life, in the rush of making money; maybe men like Toohey had something there. And what if his stores were taken away from him? Wouldn't it really be easier to live as manager of a State-owned Department Store? Wouldn't a manager's salary give him all the prestige and comfort he now enjoyed, without the responsibility of ownership?

"Is it true that in the future society any woman will sleep with any man she wants," asked Renée Slottern. It had started as a question, but it petered out. She did not really want to know. She merely felt a vapid wonder about how it felt to have a man one really wanted and how one went about wanting.

"It's stupid to talk about personal choice," said Eve Layton. "It's old-fashioned. There's no such thing as a person. There's only a collective entity. It's self-evident."

Ellsworth Toohey smiled and said nothing.

"Something's got to be done about the masses," Mitchell Layton declared. "They've got to be led. They don't know what's good for them. What I mean is, I can't understand why people of culture and position like us understand the great ideal of collectivism so well and are willing to sacrifice our personal advantages, while the working man who has everything to gain from it remains so stupidly indifferent. I can't understand why the workers in this country have so little sympathy with collectivism."

"Can't you?" said Ellsworth Toohey. His glasses sparkled.

"I'm bored with this," snapped Eve Layton, pacing the room, light streaming off her shoulders.

The conversation switched to art and its acknowledged leaders of the day in every field.

"Lois Cook said that words must be freed from the oppression of reason. She said the stranglehold of reason upon words is like the exploitation of the masses by the capitalists. Words must be permitted to negotiate with reason through collective bargaining. That's what she said. She's so amusing and refreshing."

"Ike—what's his name again?—says that the theater is an instrument of love. It's all wrong, he says, about a play taking place on the stage—it takes place in the hearts of the audience."

"Jules Fougler said in last Sunday's *Banner* that in the world of the future the theater will not be necessary at all. He says that the daily life of the common man is as much a work of art in itself as the best Shakespearean tragedy. In the future there will be no need for a dramatist. The critic will simply observe the life of the masses and evaluate its artistic points for the public. That's what Jules Fougler said. Now I don't know whether I agree with him, but he's got an interesting fresh angle there."

"Lancelot Clokey says the British Empire is doomed. He says there will be no war, because the workers of the world won't allow it, it's international bankers and munition makers who start wars and they've been kicked out of the saddle. Lancelot Clokey says that the universe is a mystery and that his mother is his best friend. He says the Premier of Bulgaria eats herring for breakfast."

"Gordon Prescott says that four walls and a ceiling is all there is to architecture. The floor is optional. All the rest is capitalistic ostentation. He says nobody should be allowed to build anything anywhere until every inhabitant of the globe has a roof over his head . . . Well, what about the Patagonians? It's *our* job to teach them to *want* a roof. Prescott calls it dialectic trans-spatial interdependence."

Ellsworth Toohey said nothing. He stood smiling at the vision of a huge typewriter. Each famous name he heard was a key of its keyboard, each controlling a special field, each hitting, leaving its mark, and the whole making connected sentences on a vast blank sheet. A typewriter, he thought, presupposes the hand that punches its keys.

He snapped to attention when he heard Mitchell Layton's sulking voice say:

"Oh, yes, the *Banner*, God damn it!"

"I know," said Homer Slottern.

"It's slipping," said Mitchell Layton. "It's definitely slipping. A swell investment it turned out to be for me. It's the only time Ellsworth's been wrong."

"Ellsworth is never wrong," said Eve Layton.

"Well, he was, that time. It was he who advised me to buy a piece of that lousy sheet." He saw Toohey's eyes, patient as velvet, and he added hastily: "What I mean is, I'm not complaining, Ellsworth. It's all right. It may even help me to slice something off my damned income tax. But that filthy reactionary rag is sure going downhill."

"Have a little patience, Mitch," said Toohey.

"You don't think I should sell and get out from under?"

"No, Mitch, I don't."

"Okay, if you say so. I can afford it. I can afford anything."

"But I jolly well can't!" Homer Slottern cried with surprising vehemence. "It's coming to where one can't afford to advertise in the *Banner*. It's not their circulation—that's okay—but there's a feeling around—a funny kind of feeling. . . . Ellsworth, I've been thinking of dropping my contract."

"Why?"

"Do you know about the 'We Don't Read Wynand' movement?"

"I've heard about it."

"It's run by somebody named Gus Webb. They paste stickers on parked windshields and in public privies. They hiss Wynand newsreels in theaters. I don't think it's a large group, but . . . Last week an unappetizing female threw a fit in my store—the one on Fifth Avenue—calling us enemies of labor because we advertised in the *Banner*. You can ignore that, but it becomes serious when one of our oldest customers, a mild little old lady from Connecticut and a Republican for three generations, calls us to say that perhaps maybe she should cancel her charge account, because somebody told her that Wynand is a dictator."

"Gail Wynand knows nothing about politics, except of the most primitive kind," said Toohey. "He still thinks in terms of the Democratic Club of Hell's Kitchen. There was a certain innocence about the political corruption of those days, don't you think so?"

"I don't care. That's not what I'm talking about. I mean, the *Banner* is becoming a kind of liability. It hurts business. One's got to be so careful nowadays. You get tied up with the wrong people and first thing you know there's a smear campaign going on and you get splashed too. I can't afford that sort of thing."

"It's not entirely an unjustified smear."

"I don't care. I don't give a damn whether it's true or not. Who am I to stick my neck out for Gail Wynand? If there's a public sentiment against him, my job is to get as far away as I can, pronto. And I'm not the only one. There's a bunch of us who're thinking the same. Jim Ferris of Ferris & Symes, Billy Shultz of Vimo Flakes, Bud Harper of Toddler Togs, and . . . hell, you know them all, they're all your friends, our bunch, the liberal businessmen. We all want to yank our ads out of the *Banner*."

"Have a little patience, Homer. I wouldn't hurry. There's a proper time for everything. There's such a thing as a psychological moment."

"Okay, I'll take your word for it. But there's—there's a kind of feeling in the air. It will become dangerous some day."

"It might. I'll tell you when it will."

"I thought Ellsworth worked on the *Banner*," said Renée Slottern vacantly, puzzled.

The others turned to her with indignation and pity.

"You're naïve, Renée," shrugged Eve Layton.

"But what's the matter with the *Banner?*"

"Now, child, don't you bother with dirty politics," said Jessica Pratt. "The *Banner* is a wicked paper. Mr. Wynand is a very evil man. He represents the selfish interests of the rich."

"I think he's good-looking," said Renée. "I think he has sex appeal."

"Oh, for Christ's sake!" cried Eve Layton.

"Now, after all, Renée is entitled to express her opinion," Jessica Pratt said with immediate rage.

"Somebody told me Ellsworth is the president of the Union of Wynand Employees," drawled Renée.

"Oh dear me, no, Renée. I'm never president of anything. I'm just a rank-and-file member. Like any copy boy."

"Do they have a Union of Wynand Employees?" asked Homer Slottern.

"It was just a club, at first," said Toohey. "It became a union last year."

"Who organized it?"

"How can one tell? It was more or less spontaneous. Like all mass movements."

"*I* think Wynand is a bastard," declared Mitchell Layton. "Who does he think he is anyway? I come to a meeting of stockholders and he treats us like flunkies. Isn't my money as good as his? Don't I own a hunk of his damn paper? I could teach him a thing or two about journalism. I have ideas. What's he so damn arrogant about? Just because he made that fortune himself? Does he have to be such a damn snob just because he came from Hell's Kitchen? It isn't other people's fault if they weren't lucky enough to be born in Hell's Kitchen to rise out of! Nobody understands what a terrible handicap it is to be born rich. Because people just take for granted that because you were born that way you'd just be no good if you weren't. What I mean is if I'd had Gail Wynand's breaks, I'd be twice as rich as he is by now and three times as famous. But he's so conceited he doesn't realize this at all!"

Nobody said a word. They heard the rising inflection of hysteria in

Mitchell Layton's voice. Eve Layton looked at Toohey, silently appealing for help. Toohey smiled and made a step forward.

"I'm ashamed of you, Mitch," he said.

Homer Slottern gasped. One did not rebuke Mitchell Layton on this subject; one did not rebuke Mitchell Layton on any subject.

Mitchell Layton's lower lip vanished.

"I'm ashamed of you, Mitch," Toohey repeated sternly, "for comparing yourself to a man as contemptible as Gail Wynand."

Mitchell Layton's mouth relaxed in the equivalent of something almost as gentle as a smile.

"That's true," he said humbly.

"No, you would never be able to match Gail Wynand's career. Not with your sensitive spirit and humanitarian instincts. That's what's holding you down, Mitch, not your money. Who cares about money? The age of money is past. It's your nature that's too fine for the brute competition of our capitalistic system. But that, too, is passing."

"It's self-evident," said Eve Layton.

It was late when Toohey left. He felt exhilarated and he decided to walk home. The streets of the city lay gravely empty around him, and the dark masses of the buildings rose to the sky, confident and unprotected. He remembered what he had said to Dominique once: "A complicated piece of machinery, such as our society . . . and by pressing your little finger against one spot . . . the center of all its gravity . . . you can make the thing crumble into a worthless heap of scrap iron . . ." He missed Dominique. He wished she could have been with him to hear this evening's conversation.

The unshared was boiling up within him. He stopped in the middle of a silent street, threw his head back and laughed aloud, looking at the tops of skyscrapers.

A policeman tapped him on the shoulder, asking: "Well, Mister?"

Toohey saw buttons and blue cloth tight over a broad chest, a stolid face, hard and patient; a man as set and dependable as the buildings around them.

"Doing your duty, officer?" Toohey asked, the echoes of laughter like jerks in his voice. "Protecting law and order and decency and human lives?" The policeman scratched the back of his head. "You ought to arrest me, officer."

"Okay, pal, okay," said the policeman. "Run along. We all take one too many once in a while."

VII

I T WAS ONLY WHEN THE LAST PAINTER HAD DEPARTED THAT PETER Keating felt a sense of desolation and a numb weakness in the crook of his elbows. He stood in the hall, looking up at the ceiling. Under the harsh gloss of paint he could still see the outline of the square where the stairway had been removed and the opening closed over. Guy Francon's old office was gone. The firm of Keating & Dumont had a single floor left now.

He thought of the stairway and how he had walked up its red-plushed steps for the first time, carrying a drawing on the tips of his fingers. He thought of Guy Francon's office with the glittering butterfly reflections. He thought of the four years when that office had been his own.

He had known what was happening to his firm, in these last years; he had known it quite well while men in overalls removed the stairway and closed the gap in the ceiling. But it was that square under the white paint that made it real to him, and final.

He had resigned himself to the process of going down, long ago. He had not chosen to resign himself—that would have been a positive decision—it had merely happened and he had let it happen. It had been simple and almost painless, like drowsiness carrying one down to nothing more sinister than a welcome sleep. The dull pain came from wishing to understand why it had happened.

There was "The March of the Centuries" exposition, but that alone could not have mattered. "The March of the Centuries" had opened in May. It was a flop. What's the use, thought Keating, why not say the right word? Flop. It was a ghastly flop. "The title of this venture would be most appropriate," Ellsworth Toohey had written, "if we assume that the centuries had passed by on horseback." Everything else written about the architectural merits of the exposition had been of the same order.

Keating thought, with wistful bitterness, of how conscientiously they had worked, he and the seven other architects, designing those buildings. It was true that he had pushed himself forward and hogged the publicity, but he certainly had not done that as far as designing was concerned. They had worked in harmony, through conference after conference, each giving in to the others, in true collective spirit, none trying to impose his personal prejudices or selfish ideas. Even Ralston Holcombe had forgotten Renaissance. They had made the buildings modern, more modern than anything ever seen, more modern than the show windows

587

of Slottern's Department Store. He did not think that the buildings looked like "coils of toothpaste when somebody steps on the tube or stylized versions of the lower intestine," as one critic had said.

But the public seemed to think it, if the public thought at all. He couldn't tell. He knew only that tickets to "The March of the Centuries" were being palmed off at Screeno games in theaters, and that the sensation of the exposition, the financial savior, was somebody named Juanita Fay who danced with a live peacock as sole garment.

But what if the Fair did flop? It had not hurt the other architects of its council. Gordon L. Prescott was going stronger than ever. It wasn't that, thought Keating. It had begun before the Fair. He could not say when.

There could be so many explanations. The depression had hit them all; others had recovered to some extent, Keating & Dumont had not. Something had gone out of the firm and out of the circles from which it drew its clients, with the retirement of Guy Francon. Keating realized that there had been art and skill and its own kind of illogical energy in the career of Guy Francon, even if the art consisted only of his social charm and the energy was directed at snaring bewildered millionaires. There had been a twisted sort of sense in people's response to Guy Francon.

He could see no hint of rationality in the things to which people responded now. The leader of the profession—on a mean scale, there was no grand scale left in anything—was Gordon L. Prescott, Chairman of the Council of American Builders; Gordon L. Prescott who lectured on the transcendental pragmatism of architecture and social planning, who put his feet on tables in drawing rooms, attended formal dinners in knickerbockers and criticized the soup aloud. Society people said they liked an architect who was a liberal. The A.G.A. still existed, in stiff, hurt dignity, but people referred to it as the Old Folks' Home. The Council of American Builders ruled the profession and talked about a closed shop, though no one had yet devised a way of achieving that. Whenever an architect's name appeared in Ellsworth Toohey's column, it was always that of Augustus Webb. At thirty-nine, Keating heard himself described as old-fashioned.

He had given up trying to understand. He knew dimly that the explanation of the change swallowing the world was of a nature he preferred not to know. In his youth he had felt an amicable contempt for the works of Guy Francon or Ralston Holcombe, and emulating them had seemed no more than innocent quackery. But he knew that Gordon L. Prescott and Gus Webb represented so impertinent, so vicious a fraud that to suspend the evidence of his eyes was beyond his elastic capacity. He had believed that people found greatness in Holcombe and there had been a reasonable satisfaction in borrowing his borrowed greatness. He knew that no one saw anything whatever in Prescott. He felt something dark and leering in the manner with which people spoke of Prescott's genius; as if they were not doing homage to Prescott, but spitting upon genius. For once, Keating could not follow people; it was too clear, even to him, that public favor had ceased being a recognition of merit, that it had become almost a brand of shame.

He went on, driven by inertia. He could not afford his large floor of offices and he did not use half the rooms, but he kept them and paid the deficit out of his own pocket. He had to go on. He had lost a large part of his personal fortune in careless stock speculation; but he had enough left to insure some comfort for the rest of his life. This did not disturb him; money had ceased to hold his attention as a major concern. It was inactivity he dreaded; it was the question mark looming beyond, if the routine of his work were to be taken away from him.

He walked slowly, his arms pressed to his body, his shoulders hunched, as if drawn against a permanent chill. He was gaining weight. His face was swollen; he kept it down, and the pleat of a second chin was flattened against the knot of his necktie. A hint of his beauty remained and made him look worse; as if the lines of his face had been drawn on a blotter and had spread, blurring. The gray threads on his temples were becoming noticeable. He drank often, without joy.

He had asked his mother to come back to live with him. She had come back. They sat through long evenings together in the living room, saying nothing; not in resentment, but seeking reassurance from each other. Mrs. Keating offered no suggestions, no reproaches. There was, instead, a new, panic-shaped tenderness in her manner toward her son. She would cook his breakfast, even though they had a maid; she would prepare his favorite dish—French pancakes, the kind he had liked so much when he was nine years old and sick with the measles. If he noticed her efforts and made some comment of pleasure, she nodded, blinking, turning away, asking herself why it should make her so happy and if it did, why should her eyes fill with tears.

She would ask suddenly, after a silence: "It will be all right, Petey? Won't it?" And he would not ask what she meant, but answer quietly: "Yes, Mother, it will be all right," putting the last of his capacity for pity into an effort to make his voice sound convincing.

Once, she asked him: "You're happy, Petey? Aren't you?" He looked at her and saw that she was not laughing at him; her eyes were wide and frightened. And as he could not answer, she cried: "But you've got to be happy! Petey, you've got to! Else what have I lived for?" He wanted to get up, gather her in his arms and tell her that it was all right—and then he remembered Guy Francon saying to him on his wedding day: "I want you to feel proud of me, Peter. . . . I want to feel that it had some meaning." Then he could not move. He felt himself in the presence of something he must not grasp, must never allow into his mind. He turned away from his mother.

One evening, she said without preamble: "Petey, I think you should get married. I think it would be much better if you were married." He found no answer, and while he groped for something gay to utter, she added: "Petey, why don't you . . . why don't you marry Catherine Halsey?" He felt anger filling his eyes, he felt pressure on his swollen lids, while he was turning slowly to his mother; then he saw her squat little figure before him, stiff and defenseless, with a kind of desperate pride, offering to take any blow he wished to deliver, absolving him in advance—and he knew that it had been the bravest gesture she had ever attempted. The anger went, because he felt her pain more sharply than the shock of his own, and he lifted one hand, to let it fall limply, to let the gesture cover everything, saying only: "Mother, don't let's . . ."

On weekends, not often, but once or twice a month, he vanished out of town. No one knew where he went. Mrs. Keating worried about it, but asked no questions. She suspected that there was a woman somewhere, and not a nice one, or he would not be so glumly silent on the subject. Mrs. Keating found herself hoping that he had fallen into the clutches of the worst, greediest slut who would have sense enough to make him marry her.

He went to a shack he had rented in the hills of an obscure village. He kept paints, brushes and canvas in the shack. He spent his days in the hills, painting. He could not tell why he had remembered that unborn ambition of his youth, which his mother had drained and switched into the channel of architecture. He could not tell by what process the impulse had become irresistible; but he had found the shack and he liked going there.

He could not say that he liked to paint. It was neither pleasure nor relief, it was self-torture, but, somehow, that didn't matter. He sat on a canvas stool before a small easel and he looked at an empty sweep of hills, at the woods and the sky. He had a quiet pain as sole conception of what he wanted to express, a humble, unbearable tenderness for the sight of the earth around him—and something tight, paralyzed, as sole means to express it. He went on. He tried. He looked at his canvases and knew that nothing was captured in their childish crudeness. It did not matter. No one was to see them. He stacked them carefully in a corner of the shack, and he locked the door before he returned to town. There was no pleasure in it, no pride, no solution; only—while he sat alone before the easel—a sense of peace.

He tried not to think of Ellsworth Toohey. A dim instinct told him that he could preserve a precarious security of spirit so long as he did not touch upon that subject. There could be but one explanation of Toohey's behavior toward him—and he preferred not to formulate it.

Toohey had drifted away from him. The intervals between their meetings had grown longer each year. He accepted it and told himself that Toohey was busy. Toohey's public silence about him was baffling. He told himself that Toohey had more important things to write about. Toohey's criticism of "The March of the Centuries" had been a blow. He told himself that his work had deserved it. He accepted any blame. He could afford to doubt himself. He could not afford to doubt Ellsworth Toohey.

It was Neil Dumont who forced him to think of Toohey again. Neil spoke petulantly about the state of the world, about crying over spilt milk, change as a law of existence, adaptability, and the importance of getting in on the ground floor. Keating gathered, from a long, confused speech, that business, as they had known it, was finished, that government would take over whether they liked it or not, that the building trade was dying and the government would soon be the sole builder and they might as well get in now, if they wanted to get in at all. "Look at Gordon Prescott," said Neil Dumont, "and what a sweet little monopoly he's got himself in housing projects and post offices. Look at Gus Webb muscling in on the racket."

Keating did not answer. Neil Dumont was throwing his own unconfessed thoughts at him; he had known that he would have to face this soon and he had tried to postpone the moment.

He did not want to think of Cortlandt Homes.

Cortlandt Homes was a government housing project to be built in Astoria, on the shore of the East River. It was planned as a gigantic experiment in low-rent housing, to serve as model for the whole country; for the whole world. Keating had heard architects talking about it for over a year. The appropriation had been approved and the site chosen; but not the architect. Keating would not admit to himself how desperately he wanted to get Cortlandt and how little chance he had of getting it.

"Listen, Pete, we might as well call a spade a spade," said Neil Dumont. "We're on the skids, pal, and you know it. All right, we'll last another year or two, coasting on your reputation. And then? It's not our fault. It's just that private enterprise is dead and getting deader. It's a historical process. The wave of the future. So we might as well get our surfboard while we can. There's a good, sturdy one waiting for the boy who's smart enough to grab it. Cortlandt Homes."

Now he had heard it pronounced. Keating wondered why the name had sounded like the muffled stroke of a bell; as if the sound had opened and closed a sequence which he would not be able to stop.

"What do you mean, Neil?"

"Cortlandt Homes. Ellsworth Toohey. Now you know what I mean."

"Neil, I . . ."

"What's the matter with you, Pete? Listen, everybody's laughing about it. Everybody's saying that if they were Toohey's special pet, like you are, they'd get Cortlandt Homes like that"—he snapped his manicured fingers—"just like that, and nobody can understand what you're waiting for. You know it's friend Ellsworth who's running this particular housing show."

"It's not true. He is not. He has no official position. He never has any official position."

"Whom are you kidding? Most of the boys that count in every office are *his* boys. Damned if I know how he got them in, but he did. What's the matter, Pete? Are you afraid of asking Ellsworth Toohey for a favor?"

This was it, thought Keating; now there was no retreat. He could not admit to himself that he was afraid of asking Ellsworth Toohey.

"No," he said, his voice dull, "I'm not afraid, Neil. I'll . . . All right, Neil. I'll speak to Ellsworth."

Ellsworth Toohey sat spread out on a couch, wearing a dressing gown. His body had the shape of a sloppy letter X—arms stretched over his head, along the edge of the back pillows, legs open in a wide fork. The dressing gown was made of silk bearing the trademarked pattern of Coty's face powder, white puffs on an orange background; it looked daring and gay, supremely elegant through sheer silliness. Under the gown, Toohey wore sleeping pyjamas of pistachio-green linen, crumpled. The trousers floated about the thin sticks of his ankles.

This was just like Toohey, thought Keating; this pose amidst the severe fastidiousness of his living room; a single canvas by a famous artist on the wall behind him—and the rest of the room unobtrusive like a monk's cell; no, thought Keating, like the retreat of a king in exile, scornful of material display.

Toohey's eyes were warm, amused, encouraging. Toohey had answered the telephone in person; Toohey had granted him the appointment at once. Keating thought: It's good to be received like this, informally. What was I afraid of? What did I doubt? We're old friends.

"Oh dear me," said Toohey, yawning, "one gets so tired! There comes a moment into every man's day when he gets the urge to relax like a stumble bum. I got home and just felt I couldn't keep my clothes on another minute. Felt like a damn peasant—just plain itchy—and had to get out. You don't mind, do you, Peter? With some people it's necessary to be stiff and formal, but with you it's not necessary at all."

"No, of course not."

"Think I'll take a bath after a while. There's nothing like a good hot bath to make one feel like a parasite. Do you like hot baths, Peter?"

"Why ... yes ... I guess so ..."

"You're gaining weight, Peter. Pretty soon you'll look revolting in a bathtub. You're gaining weight and you look peaked. That's a bad combination. Absolutely wrong esthetically. Fat people should be happy and jolly."

"I ... I'm all right, Ellsworth. It's only that ..."

"You used to have a nice disposition. You mustn't lose that. People will get bored with you."

"I haven't changed, Ellsworth." Suddenly he stressed the words. "I haven't really changed at all. I'm just what I was when I designed the Cosmo-Slotnick Building."

He looked at Toohey hopefully. He thought this was a hint crude enough for Toohey to understand; Toohey understood things much more delicate than that. He waited to be helped out. Toohey went on looking at him, his eyes sweet and blank.

"Why, Peter, that's an unphilosophical statement. Change is the basic principle of the universe. Everything changes. Seasons, leaves, flowers, birds, morals, men and buildings. The dialectic process, Peter."

"Yes, of course. Things change, so fast, in such a funny way. You don't even notice how, and suddenly one morning there it is. Remember, just a few years ago, Lois Cook and Gordon Prescott and Ike and Lance—they were nobody at all. And now—why, Ellsworth, they're on top and they're all yours. Anywhere I look, any big name I hear—it's one of your boys. You're amazing, Ellsworth. How anybody can do that—in just a few years—"

"It's much simpler than it appears to you, Peter. That's because you think in terms of personalities. You think it's done piecemeal. But dear me, the lifetimes of a hundred press agents wouldn't be enough. It can be done much faster. This is the age of time-saving devices. If you want something to grow, you don't nurture each seed separately. You just spread a certain fertilizer. Nature will do the rest. I believe you think I'm the only one responsible. But I'm not. Goodness, no. I'm just one figure out of many, one lever in a very vast movement. Very vast and very ancient. It just so happened that I chose the field that interests you—the field of art—because I thought that it focused the decisive factors in the task we had to accomplish."

"Yes, of course, but I mean, I think you were so clever. I mean, that you could pick young people who had talent, who had a future. Damned if I know how you guessed in advance. Remember the awful loft we had for the Council of American Builders? And nobody took us seriously. And people used to laugh at you for wasting time on all kinds of silly organizations."

"My dear Peter, people go by so many erroneous assumptions. For instance, that old one—divide and conquer. Well, it has its applications. But it remained for our century to discover a much more potent formula. Unite and rule."

"What do you mean?"

"Nothing that you could possibly grasp. And I must not overtax your strength. You don't look as if you had much to spare."

"Oh, I'm all right. I might look a little worried, because . . ."

"Worry is a waste of emotional reserves. Very foolish. Unworthy of an enlightened person. Since we are merely the creatures of our chemical metabolism and of the economic factors of our background, there's not a damn thing we can do about anything whatever. So why worry? There are, of course, apparent exceptions. Merely apparent. When circumstances delude us into thinking that free action is indicated. Such, for instance, as your coming here to talk about Cortlandt Homes."

Keating blinked, then smiled gratefully. He thought it was just like Toohey to guess and spare him the embarrassing preliminaries.

"That's right, Ellsworth. That's just what I wanted to talk to you about. You're wonderful. You know me like a book."

"What kind of a book, Peter? A dime novel? A love story? A crime thriller? Or just a plagiarized manuscript? No, let's say: like a serial. A good, long, exciting serial—with the last installment missing. The last installment got mislaid somewhere. There won't be any last installment. Unless, of course, it's Cortlandt Homes. Yes, that would be a fitting closing chapter." Keating waited, eyes intent and naked, forgetting to think of shame, of pleading that should be concealed. "A tremendous project, Cortlandt Homes. Bigger than Stoneridge. Do you remember Stoneridge, Peter?"

He's just relaxed with me, thought Keating, he's tired, he can't be tactful all the time, he doesn't realize what he . . .

"Stoneridge. The great residential development by Gail Wynand. Have you ever thought of Gail Wynand's career, Peter? From wharf rat to Stoneridge—do you know what a step like that means? Would you care to compute the effort, the energy, the suffering with which Gail Wynand has paid for every step of his way? And here I am, and I hold a project much bigger than Stoneridge in the palm of my hand, without any effort at all." He dropped his hand and added: "If I do hold it. Might be only a figure of speech. Don't take me literally, Peter."

"I hate Wynand," said Keating, looking down at the floor, his voice thick. "I hate him more than any man living."

"Wynand? He's a very naïve person. He's naïve enough to think that men are motivated primarily by money."

"You aren't, Ellsworth. You're a man of integrity. That's why I believe in you. It's all I've got. If I stopped believing in you, there would be nothing . . . anywhere."

"Thank you, Peter. That's sweet of you. Hysterical, but sweet."

"Ellsworth . . . you know how I feel about you."

"I have a fair idea."

"You see, that's why I can't understand."

"What?"

He had to say it. He had decided, above all, never to say it, but he had to.

"Ellsworth, why have you dropped me? Why don't you ever write anything about me any more? Why is it always—in your column and everywhere—and on any commission you have a chance to swing—why is it always Gus Webb?"

"But, Peter, why shouldn't it be?"

"But . . . I . . ."

"I'm sorry to see that you haven't understood me at all. In all these years, you've learned nothing of my principles. I don't believe in individualism, Peter. I don't believe that any one man is any one thing which everybody else can't be. I believe we're all equal and interchangeable. A position you hold today can be held by anybody and everybody tomorrow. Equalitarian rotation. Haven't I always preached that to you? Why do you suppose I chose you? Why did I put you where you were? To protect the field from men who would become irreplaceable. To leave a chance for the Gus Webbs of this world. Why do you suppose I fought against—for instance—Howard Roark?"

Keating's mind was a bruise. He thought it would be a bruise, because it felt as if something flat and heavy had smashed against it, and it would be black and blue and swollen later; now he felt nothing, except a sweetish numbness. Such chips of thought as he could distinguish told him that the ideas he heard were of a high moral order, the ones he had always accepted, and therefore no evil could come to him from that, no evil could be intended. Toohey's eyes looked straight at him, dark, gentle, benevolent. Maybe later . . . he would know later . . . But one thing had pierced through and remained caught on some fragment of his brain. He had understood that. The name.

And while his sole hope of grace rested in Toohey, something inexplicable twisted within him, he leaned forward, knowing that this would hurt, wishing it to hurt Toohey, and his lips curled incredibly into a smile, baring his teeth and gums:

"You failed there, didn't you, Ellsworth? Look where he is now—Howard Roark."

"Oh dear me, how dull it is to discuss things with minds devoted to the obvious. You are utterly incapable of grasping principles, Peter. You think only in terms of persons. Do you really suppose that I have no mission in life save to worry over the specific fate of your Howard Roark? Mr. Roark is merely one detail out of many. I have dealt with him when it was convenient. I am still dealing with him—though not directly. I do grant you, however, that Mr. Howard Roark is a great temptation to me. At times I feel it would be a shame if I never came up against him personally again. But it might not be necessary at all. When you deal in principles, Peter, it saves you the trouble of individual encounters."

"What do you mean?"

"I mean that you can follow one of two procedures. You can devote your life to pulling out each single weed as it comes up—and then ten lifetimes won't be enough for the job. Or you can prepare your soil in such a manner—by spreading a certain chemical, let us say—that it will be impossible for weeds to grow. This last is faster. I say 'weed' because it is the conventional symbolism and will not frighten you. The same technique, of course, holds true in the case of any other living plant you may wish to eliminate: buckwheat, potatoes, oranges, orchids or morning glories."

"Ellsworth, I don't know what you're talking about."

"But of course you don't. That's my advantage. I say these things publicly every single day—and nobody knows what I'm talking about."

"Have you heard that Howard Roark is doing a house, his own home, for Gail Wynand?"

"My dear Peter, did you think I had to wait to learn it from you?"

"Well, how do you like that?"

"Why should it concern me one way or another?"

"Have you heard that Roark and Wynand are the best of friends? And what friendship, from what I hear! Well? You know what Wynand can do. You know what he can make of Roark. Try and stop Roark now! Try and stop him! Try . . ."

He choked on a gulp and kept still. He found himself staring at Toohey's bare ankle between the pyjama trouser and the rich fur of a sheepskin-lined slipper. He had never visualized Toohey's nudity; somehow, he had never thought of Toohey as possessing a physical body. There was something faintly indecent about that ankle: just skin, too bluish-white, stretched over bones that looked too brittle. It made him think of chicken bones left on a plate after dinner, dried out; if one touches them, it takes no effort at all, they just snap. He found himself wishing to reach out, to take that ankle between thumb and forefinger, and just twist the pads of his fingertips.

"Ellsworth, I came here to talk about Cortlandt Homes!" He could not take his eyes off the ankle. He hoped the words would release him.

"Don't shout like that. What's the matter? . . . Cortlandt Homes? Well, what did you want to say about it?"

He had to lift his eyes now, in astonishment. Toohey waited innocently.

"I want to design Cortlandt Homes," he said, his voice coming like a paste strained through a cloth. "I want you to give it to me."

"Why should I give it to you?"

There was no answer. If he were to say now: Because you've written that I'm the greatest architect living, the reminder would prove that Toohey believed it no longer. He dared not face such proof, nor Toohey's possible reply. He was staring at two long black hairs on the bluish knob of Toohey's ankle; he could see them quite clearly: one straight, the other twisted into a curlicue. After a long time, he answered:

"Because I need it very badly, Ellsworth."

"I know you do."

There was nothing further to say. Toohey shifted his ankle, raised his foot and put it flat upon the arm of the couch, spreading his legs comfortably.

"Sit up, Peter. You look like a gargoyle."

Keating did not move.

"What made you assume that the selection of an architect for Cortlandt Homes was up to me?"

Keating raised his head; it was a stab of relief. He had presumed too much and offended Toohey; that was the reason; that was the only reason.

"Why, I understand . . . it's being said . . . I was told that you have a great deal of influence on this particular project . . . with those people . . . and in Washington . . . and places . . ."

"Strictly in an unofficial capacity. As something of an expert in architectural matters. Nothing else."

"Yes, of course. . . . That's . . . what I meant."

"I can recommend an architect. That's all. I can guarantee nothing. My word is not final."

"That's all I wanted, Ellsworth. A word of recommendation from you . . ."

"But, Peter, if I recommend someone, I must give a reason. I can't use such influence as I might have, just to push a friend, can I?"

Keating stared at the dressing gown, thinking: powder puffs, why powder puffs? That's what's wrong with me, if he'd only take the thing off.

"Your professional standing is not what it used to be, Peter."

"You said 'to push a friend,' Ellsworth . . ." It was a whisper.

"Well, of course I'm your friend. I've always been your friend. You're not doubting that, are you?"

"No . . . I can't, Ellsworth. . . ."

"Well, cheer up, then. Look, I'll tell you the truth. We're stuck on that damn Cortlandt. There's a nasty little sticker involved. I've tried to get it for Gordon Prescott and Gus Webb—I thought it was more in their line, I didn't think you'd be so interested. But neither of them could make the grade. Do you know the big problem in housing? Economy, Peter. How to design a decent modern unit that could rent for fifteen dollars a month. Ever tried to figure out that one? Well, that's what's expected of the architect who'll do Cortlandt—if they ever find him. Of course, tenant selection helps, they stagger the rents, the families who make twelve hundred a year pay more for the same apartment to help carry the families who make six hundred a year—you know, underdog milked to help somebody underdoggier—but still, the cost of the building and the upkeep must be as low as humanly possible. The boys in Washington don't want another one of those—you heard about it, a little government development where the homes cost ten thousand dollars apiece, while a private builder could have put them up for two thousand. Cortlandt is to be a model project. An example for the whole world. It must be the most brilliant, the most efficient exhibit of planning ingenuity and structural economy ever achieved anywhere. That's what the big boys demand. Gordon and Gus couldn't do it. They tried and were turned down. You'd be surprised to know how many people have tried. Peter, I couldn't sell you to them even at the height of your career. What can I tell them about you? All you stand for is plush, gilt and marble, old Guy Francon, the Cosmo-Slotnick Building, the Frink National Bank, and that little abortion of the Centuries that will never pay for itself. What they want is a millionaire's kitchen for a sharecropper's income. Think you can do it?"

"I . . . I have ideas, Ellsworth. I've watched the field . . . I've . . . studied new methods. . . . I could . . ."

"If you can, it's yours. If you can't, all my friendship won't help you. And God knows I'd like to help you. You look like an old hen in the rain. Here's what I'll do for you, Peter: come to my office tomorrow, I'll give you all the dope, take it home and see if you wish to break your head over it. Take a chance, if you care to. Work me out a preliminary scheme. I can't promise anything. But if you come anywhere near it, I'll submit it to the right people and I'll push it for all I'm worth. That's all I can do for you. It's not up to me. It's really up to you."

Keating sat looking at him. Keating's eyes were anxious, eager and hopeless.

"Care to try, Peter?"

"Will you let me try?"

"Of course I'll let you. Why shouldn't I? I'd be delighted if you, of all people, turned out to be the one to turn the trick."

"About the way I look, Ellsworth," he said suddenly, "about the way I look . . . it's not because I mind so much that I'm a failure . . . it's because I can't understand why I slipped like that . . . from the top . . . without any reason at all . . ."

"Well, Peter, that could be terrifying to contemplate. The inexplicable is always terrifying. But it wouldn't be so frightening if you stopped to ask yourself whether there's ever been any reason why you should have been at the top. . . . Oh, come, Peter, smile, I'm only kidding. One loses everything when one loses one's sense of humor."

On the following morning Keating came to his office after a visit to Ellsworth Toohey's cubbyhole in the Banner Building. He brought with him a briefcase containing the data on the Cortlandt Homes project. He spread the papers on a large table in his office and locked the door. He asked a draftsman to bring him a sandwich at noon, and he ordered another sandwich at dinner time. "Want me to help, Pete?" asked Neil Dumont. "We could consult and discuss it and . . ." Keating shook his head.

He sat at his table all night. After a while he stopped looking at the papers; he sat still, thinking. He was not thinking of the charts and figures spread before him. He had studied them. He had understood what he could not do.

When he noticed that it was daylight, when he heard steps behind his locked door, the movement of men returning to work, and knew that office hours had begun, here and everywhere else in the city—he rose, walked to his desk and reached for the telephone book. He dialed the number.

"This is Peter Keating speaking. I should like to make an appointment to see Mr. Roark."

Dear God, he thought while waiting, don't let him see me. Make him refuse. Dear God, make him refuse and I will have the right to hate him to the end of my days. Don't let him see me.

"Will four o'clock tomorrow afternoon be convenient for you, Mr. Keating?" said the calm, gentle voice of the secretary. "Mr. Roark will see you then."

VIII

ROARK KNEW THAT HE MUST NOT SHOW THE SHOCK OF HIS FIRST glance at Peter Keating—and that it was too late: he saw a faint smile on Keating's lips, terrible in its resigned acknowledgment of disintegration.

"Are you only two years younger than I am, Howard?" was the first thing Keating asked, looking at the face of the man he had not seen for six years.

"I don't know, Peter, I think so. I'm thirty-seven."

"I'm thirty-nine—that's all."

He moved to the chair in front of Roark's desk, groping for it with his hand. He was blinded by the band of glass that made three walls of Roark's office. He stared at the sky and the city. He had no feeling of height here, and the buildings seemed to lie under his toes, not a real city, but miniatures of famous landmarks, incongruously close and small; he felt he could bend and pick any one of them up in his hand. He saw the black dashes which were automobiles and they seemed to crawl, it took them so long to cover a block the size of his finger. He saw the stone and plaster of the city as a substance that had soaked light and was throwing it back, row upon row of flat, vertical planes grilled with dots of windows, each plane a reflector, rose-colored, gold and purple—and jagged streaks of smoke-blue running among them, giving them shape, angles and distance. Light streamed from the buildings into the sky and made of the clear summer blue a humble second thought, a spread of pale water over living fire. My God, thought Keating, who are the men that made all this?—and then remembered that he had been one of them.

He saw Roark's figure for an instant, straight and gaunt against the angle of two glass panes behind the desk, then Roark sat down facing him.

Keating thought of men lost in the desert and of men perishing at sea, when, in the presence of the silent eternity of the sky, they have to speak the truth. And now he had to speak the truth, because he was in the presence of the earth's greatest city.

"Howard, is this the terrible thing they meant by turning the other cheek—your letting me come here?"

He did not think of his voice. He did not know that it had dignity.

Roark looked at him silently for a moment; this was a greater change than the swollen face.

"I don't know, Peter. No, if they meant actual forgiveness. Had I been hurt, I'd never forgive it. Yes, if they meant what I'm doing. I don't

600

think a man can hurt another, not in any important way. Neither hurt him nor help him. I have really nothing to forgive you."

"It would be better if you felt you had. It would be less cruel."

"I suppose so."

"You haven't changed, Howard."

"I guess not."

"If this is the punishment I must take—I want you to know that I'm taking it and that I understand. At one time I would have thought I was getting off easy."

"You have changed, Peter."

"I know I have."

"I'm sorry if it has to be punishment."

"I know you are. I believe you. But it's all right. It's only the last of it. I really took it night before last."

"When you decided to come here?"

"Yes."

"Then don't be afraid now. What is it?"

Keating sat straight, calm, not as he had sat facing a man in a dressing gown three days ago, but almost in confident repose. He spoke slowly and without pity:

"Howard, I'm a parasite. I've been a parasite all my life. You designed my best projects at Stanton. You designed the first house I ever built. You designed the Cosmo-Slotnick Building. I have fed on you and on all the men like you who lived before we were born. The men who designed the Parthenon, the Gothic cathedrals, the first skyscrapers. If they hadn't existed, I wouldn't have known how to put stone on stone. In the whole of my life, I haven't added a new doorknob to what men have done before me. I have taken that which was not mine and given nothing in return. I had nothing to give. This is not an act, Howard, and I'm very conscious of what I'm saying. And I came here to ask you to save me again. If you wish to throw me out, do it now."

Roark shook his head slowly, and moved one hand in silent permission to continue.

"I suppose you know that I'm finished as an architect. Oh, not actually finished, but near enough. Others could go on like this for quite a few years, but I can't, because of what I've been. Or was thought to have been. People don't forgive a man who's slipping. I must live up to what they thought. I can do it only in the same way I've done everything else in my life. I need a prestige I don't deserve for an achievement I didn't accomplish to save a name I haven't earned the right to bear. I've been given a last chance. I know it's my last chance. I know I can't do it. I won't try to bring you a mess and ask you to correct it. I'm asking you to design it and let me put my name on it."

"What's the job?"

"Cortlandt Homes."

"The housing project?"

"Yes. You've heard about it?"

"I know everything about it."

"You're interested in housing projects, Howard?"

"Who offered it to you? On what conditions?"

Keating explained, precisely, dispassionately, relating his conversation with Toohey as if it were the summary of a court transcript he had read long ago. He pulled the papers out of his briefcase, put them down on the desk and went on speaking, while Roark looked at them. Roark interrupted him once: "Wait a moment, Peter. Keep still." He waited for a long time. He saw Roark's hand moving the papers idly, but he knew that Roark was not looking at the papers. Roark said: "Go on," and Keating continued obediently, allowing himself no questions.

"I suppose there's no reason why you should do it for me," he concluded. "If you can solve their problem, you can go to them and do it on your own."

Roark smiled. "Do you think I could get past Toohey?"

"No. No, I don't think you could."

"Who told you I was interested in housing projects?"

"What architect isn't?"

"Well, I am. But not in the way you think."

He got up. It was a swift movement, impatient and tense. Keating allowed himself his first opinion: he thought it was strange to see suppressed excitement in Roark.

"Let me think this over, Peter. Leave that here. Come to my house tomorrow night. I'll tell you then."

"You're not . . . turning me down?"

"Not yet."

"You might . . . after everything that's happened . . . ?"

"To hell with that."

"You're going to consider . . ."

"I can't say anything now, Peter. I must think it over. Don't count on it. I might want to demand something impossible of you."

"Anything you ask, Howard. Anything."

"We'll talk about it tomorrow."

"Howard, I . . . how can I try to thank you, even for . . ."

"Don't thank me. If I do it, I'll have my own purpose. I'll expect to gain as much as you will. Probably more. Just remember that I don't do things on any other terms."

*　*　*　*　*

Keating came to Roark's house on the following evening. He could not say whether he had waited impatiently or not. The bruise had spread. He could act; he could weigh nothing.

He stood in the middle of Roark's room and looked about slowly. He had been grateful for all the things Roark had not said to him. But he gave voice to the things himself when he asked:

"This is the Enright House, isn't it?"

"Yes."

"You built it?"

Roark nodded, and said: "Sit down, Peter," understanding too well.

Keating had brought his briefcase; he put it down on the floor, propping it against his chair. The briefcase bulged and looked heavy; he handled it cautiously. Then he spread his hands out and forgot the gesture, holding it, asking:

"Well?"

"Peter, can you think for a moment that you're alone in the world?"

"I've been thinking that for three days."

"No. That's not what I mean. Can you forget what you've been taught to repeat, and think, think hard, with your own brain? There are things I'll want you to understand. It's my first condition. I'm going to tell you what I want. If you think of it as most people do, you'll say it's nothing. But if you say that, I won't be able to do it. Not unless you understand completely, with your whole mind, how important it is."

"I'll try, Howard. I was . . . honest with you yesterday."

"Yes. If you hadn't been, I would have turned you down yesterday. Now I think you might be able to understand and do your part of it."

"You want to do it?"

"I might. If you offer me enough."

"Howard—anything you ask. Anything. I'd sell my soul . . ."

"That's the sort of thing I want you to understand. To sell your soul is the easiest thing in the world. That's what everybody does every hour of his life. If I asked you to keep your soul—would you understand why that's much harder?"

"Yes . . . Yes, I think so."

"Well? Go on. I want you to give me a reason why I should wish to design Cortlandt. I want you to make me an offer."

"You can have all the money they pay me. I don't need it. You can have twice the money. I'll double their fee."

"You know better than that, Peter. Is that what you wish to tempt me with?"

"You would save my life."

"Can you think of any reason why I should want to save your life?"

"No."

"Well?"

"It's a great public project, Howard. A humanitarian undertaking. Think of the poor people who live in slums. If you can give them decent comfort within their means, you'll have the satisfaction of performing a noble deed."

"Peter, you were more honest than that yesterday."

His eyes dropped, his voice low, Keating said:

"You will love designing it."

"Yes, Peter. Now you're speaking my language."

"What do you want?"

"Now listen to me. I've been working on the problem of low-rent housing for years. I never thought of the poor people in slums. I thought of the potentialities of our modern world. The new materials, the means, the chances to take and use. There are so many products of man's genius around us today. There are such great possibilities to exploit. To build cheaply, simply, intelligently. I've had a lot of time to study. I didn't have much to do after the Stoddard Temple. I didn't expect results. I worked because I can't look at any material without thinking: What could be done with it? And the moment I think that, I've got to do it. To find the answer, to break the thing. I've worked on it for years. I loved it. I worked because it was a problem I wanted to solve. You wish to know how to build a unit to rent for fifteen dollars a month? I'll show you how to build it for ten."

Keating made an involuntary movement forward.

"But first, I want you to think and tell me what made me give years to this work. Money? Fame? Charity? Altruism?" Keating shook his head slowly. "All right. You're beginning to understand. So whatever we do, don't let's talk about the poor people in the slums. They have nothing to do with it, though I wouldn't envy anyone the job of trying to explain that to fools. You see, I'm never concerned with my clients, only with their architectural requirements. I consider these as part of my building's theme and problem, as my building's material—just as I consider bricks and steel. Bricks and steel are not my motive. Neither are the clients. Both are only the means of my work. Peter, before you can do things for people, you must be the kind of man who can get things done. But to get things done, you must love the doing, not the secondary consequences. The work, not the people. Your own action, not any possible object of your charity. I'll be glad if people who need it find a better manner of living in a house I designed. But that's not the motive of my work. Nor my reason. Nor my reward."

He walked to a window and stood looking out at the lights of the city trembling in the dark river.

"You said yesterday: 'What architect isn't interested in housing?' I hate the whole blasted idea of it. I think it's a worthy undertaking—to provide a decent apartment for a man who earns fifteen dollars a week. But not at the expense of other men. Not if it raises the taxes, raises all the other rents and makes the man who earns forty live in a rat hole. That's what's happening in New York. Nobody can afford a modern apartment—except the very rich and the paupers. Have you seen the converted brownstones in which the average self-supporting couple has to live? Have you seen their closet kitchens and their plumbing? They're forced to live like that—because they're not incompetent enough. They make forty dollars a week and wouldn't be allowed into a housing project. But they're the ones who provide the money for the damn project. They pay the taxes. And the taxes raise their own rent. And they have to move from a converted brownstone into an unconverted one and from that into a railroad flat. I'd have no desire to penalize a man because he's worth only fifteen dollars a week. But I'll be damned if I can see why a man worth forty must be penalized—and penalized in favor of the one who's less competent. Sure, there are a lot of theories on the subject and volumes of discussion. But just look at the results. Still, architects are all for government housing. And have you ever seen an architect who wasn't screaming for planned cities? I'd like to ask him how he can be so sure that the plan adopted will be his own. And if it is, what right has he to impose it on the others? And if it isn't, what happens to his work? I suppose he'll say that he wants neither. He wants a council, a conference, co-operation and collaboration. And the result will be 'The March of the Centuries.' Peter, every single one of you on that committee has done better work alone than the eight of you produced collectively. Ask yourself why, sometime."

"I think I know it . . . But Cortlandt . . ."

"Yes. Cortlandt. Well, I've told you all the things in which I don't believe, so that you'll understand what I want and what right I have to want it. I don't believe in government housing. I don't want to hear anything about its noble purposes. I don't think they're noble. But that, too, doesn't matter. That's not my first concern. Not who lives in the house nor who orders it built. Only the house itself. If it has to be built, it might as well be built right."

"You . . . want to build it?"

"In all the years I've worked on this problem, I never hoped to see the results in practical application. I forced myself not to hope. I knew I couldn't expect a chance to show what could be done on a large scale. Your government housing, among other things, has made all building so expensive that private owners can't afford such projects, nor any type of low-rent construction. And I will never be given any job by any government. You've understood that much yourself. You said I couldn't get past Toohey. He's not the only one. I've never been given a job by any group, board, council or committee, public or private, unless some man fought for me, like Kent Lansing. There's a reason for that, but we don't have to discuss it now. I want you to know only that I realize in what manner I need you, so that what we'll do will be a fair exchange."

"*You* need me?"

"Peter, I love this work. I want to see it erected. I want to make it real, living, functioning, built. But every living thing is integrated. Do you know what that means? Whole, pure, complete, unbroken. Do you know what constitutes an integrating principle? A thought. The one thought, the single thought that created the thing and every part of it. The thought which no one can change or touch. I want to design Cortlandt. I want to see it built. I want to see it built exactly as I design it."

"Howard . . . I won't say 'it's nothing.' "

"You understand?"

"Yes."

"I like to receive money for my work. But I can pass that up this time. I like to have people know my work is done by me. But I can pass that up. I like to have tenants made happy by my work. But that doesn't matter too much. The only thing that matters, my goal, my reward, my beginning, my end is the work itself. My work done my way. Peter, there's nothing in the world that you can offer me, except this. Offer me this and you can have anything I've got to give. My work done my way. A private, personal, selfish, egotistical motivation. That's the only way I function. That's all I am."

"Yes, Howard. I understand. With my whole mind."

"Then here's what I'm offering you: I'll design Cortlandt. You'll put your name on it. You'll keep all the fees. But you'll guarantee that it will be built exactly as I design it."

Keating looked at him and held the glance deliberately, quietly, for a moment.

"All right, Howard." He added: "I waited, to show you that I know exactly what you're asking and what I'm promising."

"You know it won't be easy?"

"I know it will be very terribly difficult."

"It will. Because it's such a large project. Most particularly because it's a government project. There will be so many people involved, each with authority, each wanting to exercise it in some way or another. You'll have a hard battle. You will have to have the courage of my convictions."

"I'll try to live up to that, Howard."

"You won't be able to, unless you understand that I'm giving you a trust which is more sacred—and nobler, if you like the word—than any altruistic purpose you could name. Unless you understand that this is not a favor, that I'm not doing it for you nor for the future tenants, but for myself, and that you have no right to it except on these terms."

"Yes, Howard."

"You'll have to devise your own way of accomplishing it. You'll have to get yourself an ironclad contract with your bosses and then fight every bureaucrat that comes along every five minutes for the next year or more. I will have no guarantee except your word. Wish to give it to me?"

"I give you my word."

Roark took two typewritten sheets of paper from his pocket and handed them to him.

"Sign it."

"What's that?"

"A contract between us, stating the terms of our agreement. A copy for each of us. It would probably have no legal validity whatever. But I can hold it over your head. I couldn't sue you. But I could make this public. If it's prestige you want, you can't allow this to become known. If your courage fails you at any point, remember that you'll lose everything by giving in. But if you'll keep your word—I give you mine—it's written there—that I'll never betray this to anyone. Cortlandt will be yours. On the day when it's finished, I'll send this paper back to you and you can burn it if you wish."

"All right, Howard."

Keating signed, handed the pen to him, and Roark signed.

Keating sat looking at him for a moment, then said slowly, as if trying to distinguish the dim form of some thought of his own:

"Everybody would say you're a fool. . . . Everybody would say I'm getting everything. . . ."

"You'll get everything society can give a man. You'll keep all the money. You'll take any fame or honor anyone might want to grant. You'll accept such gratitude as the tenants might feel. And I—I'll take what nobody can give a man, except himself. I will have built Cortlandt."

"You're getting more than I am, Howard."

"Peter!" The voice was triumphant. "You understand that?"

"Yes. . . ."

Roark leaned back against a table, and laughed softly; it was the happiest sound Keating had ever heard.

"This will work, Peter. It will work. It will be all right. You've done something wonderful. You haven't spoiled everything by thanking me."

Keating nodded silently.

"Now relax, Peter. Want a drink? We won't discuss any details to-night. Just sit here and get used to me. Stop being afraid of me. Forget everything you said yesterday. This wipes it off. We're starting from the beginning. We're partners now. You have your share to do. It's a legitimate share. This is my idea of co-operation, by the way. You'll handle people. I'll do the building. We'll each do the job we know best, as honestly as we can."

He walked to Keating and extended his hand.

Sitting still, not raising his head, Keating took the hand. His fingers tightened on it for a moment.

When Roark brought him a drink, Keating swallowed three long gulps and sat looking at the room. His fingers were closed firmly about the glass, his arm steady; but the ice tinkled in the liquid once in a while, without apparent motion.

His eyes moved heavily over the room, over Roark's body. He thought, it's not intentional, not just to hurt me, he can't help it, he doesn't even know it—but it's in his whole body, that look of a creature glad to be alive. And he realized he had never actually believed that any living thing could be glad of the gift of existence.

"You're . . . so young, Howard. . . . You're so young . . . Once I reproached you for being too old and serious . . . Do you remember when you worked for me at Francon's?"

"Drop it, Peter. We've done so well without remembering."

"That's because you're kind. Wait, don't frown. Let me talk. I've got to talk about something. I know, this is what you didn't want to mention. God, I didn't want you to mention it! I had to steel myself against it, that night—against all the things you could throw at me. But you didn't. If it were reversed now and this were my home—can you imagine what I'd do or say? You're not conceited enough."

"Why, no. I'm too conceited. If you want to call it that. I don't make comparisons. I never think of myself in relation to anyone else. I just refuse to measure myself as part of anything. I'm an utter egotist."

"Yes. You are. But egotists are not kind. And you are. You're the most egotistical and the kindest man I know. And that doesn't make sense."

"Maybe the concepts don't make sense. Maybe they don't mean what people have been taught to think they mean. But let's drop that now. If you've got to talk of something, let's talk of what we're going to do." He leaned out to look through the open window. "It will stand down there. That dark stretch—that's the site of Cortlandt. When it's done, I'll be able to see it from my window. Then it will be part of the city. Peter, have I ever told you how much I love this city?"

Keating swallowed the rest of the liquid in his glass.

"I think I'd rather go now, Howard. I'm . . . no good tonight."

"I'll call you in a few days. We'd better meet here. Don't come to my office. You don't want to be seen there—somebody might guess. By the way, later, when my sketches are done, you'll have to copy them yourself, in your own manner. Some people would recognize my way of drawing."

"Yes. . . . All right. . . ."

Keating rose and stood looking uncertainly at his briefcase for a moment, then picked it up. He mumbled some vague words of parting, he took his hat, he walked to the door, then stopped and looked down at his briefcase.

"Howard . . . I brought something I wanted to show you."

He walked back into the room and put the briefcase on the table.

"I haven't shown it to anyone." His fingers fumbled, opening the straps. "Not to mother or Ellsworth Toohey . . . I just want you to tell me if there's any . . . ."

He handed to Roark six of his canvases.

Roark looked at them, one after another. He took a longer time than he needed. When he could trust himself to lift his eyes, he shook his head in silent answer to the word Keating had not pronounced.

"It's too late, Peter," he said gently.

Keating nodded. "Guess I . . . knew that."

When Keating had gone, Roark leaned against the door, closing his eyes. He was sick with pity.

He had never felt this before—not when Henry Cameron collapsed in the office at his feet, not when he saw Steven Mallory sobbing on a bed before him. Those moments had been clean. But this was pity—this complete awareness of a man without worth or hope, this sense of finality, of the not to be redeemed. There was shame in this feeling—his own shame that he should have to pronounce such judgment upon a man, that he should know an emotion which contained no shred of respect.

This is pity, he thought, and then he lifted his head in wonder. He thought that there must be something terribly wrong with a world in which this monstrous feeling is called a virtue.

IX

THEY SAT ON THE SHORE OF THE LAKE—WYNAND SLOUCHED ON A boulder—Roark stretched out on the ground—Dominique sitting straight, her body rising stiffly from the pale blue circle of her skirt on the grass.

The Wynand house stood on the hill above them. The earth spread out in terraced fields and rose gradually to make the elevation of the hill. The house was a shape of horizontal rectangles rising toward a slashing vertical projection; a group of diminishing setbacks, each a separate room, its size and form making the successive steps in a series of interlocking floor lines. It was as if from the wide living room on the first level a hand had moved slowly, shaping the next steps by a sustained touch, then had stopped, had continued in separate movements, each shorter, brusquer, and had ended, torn off, remaining somewhere in the sky. So that it seemed as if the slow rhythm of the rising fields had been picked up, stressed, accelerated and broken into the staccato chords of the finale.

"I like to look at it from here," said Wynand. "I spent all day here yesterday, watching the light change on it. When you design a building, Howard, do you know exactly what the sun will do to it at any moment of the day from any angle? Do you control the sun?"

"Sure," said Roark without raising his head. "Unfortunately, I can't control it here. Move over, Gail. You're in my way. I like the sun on my back."

Wynand let himself flop down into the grass. Roark lay stretched on his stomach, his face buried on his arm, the orange hair on the white shirt sleeve, one hand extended before him, palm pressed to the ground. Dominique looked at the blades of grass between his fingers. The fingers moved once in a while, crushing the grass with lazy, sensuous pleasure.

The lake spread behind them, a flat sheet darkening at the edges, as if the distant trees were moving in to enclose it for the evening. The sun cut a glittering band across the water. Dominique looked up at the house and thought that she would like to stand there at a window and look down and see this one white figure stretched on a deserted shore, his hand on the ground, spent, emptied, at the foot of that hill.

She had lived in the house for a month. She had never thought she would. Then Roark had said: "The house will be ready for you in ten days, Mrs. Wynand," and she had answered: "Yes, Mr. Roark."

610

She accepted the house, the touch of the stair railings under her hand, the walls that enclosed the air she breathed. She accepted the light switches she pressed in the evening, and the light firm wires he had laid out through the walls; the water that ran when she turned a tap, from conduits he had planned; the warmth of an open fire on August evenings, before a fireplace built stone by stone from his drawing. She thought: Every moment . . . every need of my existence . . . She thought: Why not? It's the same with my body—lungs, blood vessels, nerves, brain—under the same control. She felt one with the house.

She accepted the nights when she lay in Wynand's arms and opened her eyes to see the shape of the bedroom Roark had designed, and she set her teeth against a racking pleasure that was part answer, part mockery of the unsatisfied hunger in her body, and surrendered to it, not knowing what man gave her this, which one of them, or both.

Wynand watched her as she walked across a room, as she descended the stairs, as she stood at a window. She had heard him saying to her: "I didn't know a house could be designed for a woman, like a dress. You can't see yourself here as I do, you can't see how completely this house is yours. Every angle, every part of every room is a setting for you. It's scaled to your height, to your body. Even the texture of the walls goes with the texture of your skin in an odd way. It's the Stoddard Temple, but built for a single person, and it's mine. This is what I wanted. The city can't touch you here. I've always felt that the city would take you away from me. It gave me everything I have. I don't know why I feel at times that it will demand payment some day. But here you're safe and you're mine." She wanted to cry: Gail, I belong to him here as I've never belonged to him.

Roark was the only guest Wynand allowed in their new home. She accepted Roark's visits to them on weekends. That was the hardest to accept. She knew he did not come to torture her, but simply because Wynand asked him and he liked being with Wynand. She remembered saying to him in the evening, her hand on the stair railing, on the steps of the stairs leading up to her bedroom: "Come down to breakfast whenever you wish, Mr. Roark. Just press the button in the dining room." "Thank you, Mrs. Wynand. Good night."

Once, she saw him alone, for a moment. It was early morning; she had not slept all night, thinking of him in a room across the hall; she had come out before the house was awake. She walked down the hill and she found relief in the unnatural stillness of the earth around her, the stillness of full light without sun, of leaves without motion, of a luminous, waiting silence. She heard steps behind her, she stopped, she leaned against a tree trunk. He had a bathing suit thrown over his shoulder, he was going down to swim in the lake. He stopped before her, and they stood still with the rest of the earth, looking at each other. He said nothing, turned, and went on. She remained leaning against the tree, and after a while she walked back to the house.

Now, sitting by the lake, she heard Wynand saying to him:

"You look like the laziest creature in the world, Howard."

"I am."

"I've never seen anyone relax like that."

"Try staying awake for three nights in succession."

"I told you to get here yesterday."

"Couldn't."

"Are you going to pass out right here?"

"I'd like to. This is wonderful." He lifted his head, his eyes laughing, as if he had not seen the building on the hill, as if he were not speaking of it. "This is the way I'd like to die, stretched out on some shore like this, just close my eyes and never come back."

She thought: He thinks what I'm thinking—we still have that together —Gail wouldn't understand—not he and Gail, for this once—he and I.

Wynand said: "You damn fool. This is not like you, not even as a joke. You're killing yourself over something. What?"

"Ventilator shafts, at the moment. Very stubborn ventilator shafts."

"For whom?"

"Clients. . . . I have all sorts of clients right now."

"Do you have to work nights?"

"Yes—for these particular people. Very special work. Can't even bring it into the office."

"What are you talking about?"

"Nothing. Don't pay any attention. I'm half asleep."

She thought: This is the tribute to Gail, the confidence of surrender— he relaxes like a cat—and cats don't relax except with people they like.

"I'll kick you upstairs after dinner and lock the door," said Wynand, "and leave you there to sleep twelve hours."

"All right."

"Want to get up early? Let's go for a swim before sunrise."

"Mr. Roark is tired, Gail," said Dominique, her voice sharp.

Roark raised himself on an elbow to look at her. She saw his eyes, direct, understanding.

"You're acquiring the bad habits of all commuters, Gail," she said, "imposing your country hours on guests from the city who are not used to them." She thought: Let it be mine—that one moment when you were walking to the lake—don't let Gail take that also, like everything else. "You can't order Mr. Roark around as if he were an employee of the *Banner*."

"I don't know anyone on earth I'd rather order around than Mr. Roark," said Wynand gaily, "whenever I can get away with it."

"You're getting away with it."

"I don't mind taking orders, Mrs. Wynand," said Roark. "Not from a man as capable as Gail."

Let me win this time, she thought, please let me win this time—it means nothing to you—it's senseless and it means nothing at all—but refuse him, refuse him for the sake of the memory of a moment's pause that had not belonged to him.

"I think you should rest, Mr. Roark. You should sleep late tomorrow. I'll tell the servants not to disturb you."

"Why, no, thanks, I'll be all right in a few hours, Mrs. Wynand. I like to swim before breakfast. Knock at the door when you're ready, Gail, and we'll go down together."

She looked over the spread of lake and hills, with not a sign of men, not another house anywhere, just water, trees and sun, a world of their own, and she thought he was right—they belonged together—the three of them.

The drawings of Cortlandt Homes presented six buildings, fifteen stories high, each made in the shape of an irregular star with arms extending from a central shaft. The shafts contained elevators, stairways, heating systems and all the utilities. The apartments radiated from the center in the form of extended triangles. The space between the arms allowed light and air from three sides. The ceilings were pre-cast; the inner walls were of plastic tile that required no painting or plastering; all pipes and wires were laid out in metal ducts at the edge of the floors, to be opened and replaced, when necessary, without costly demolition; the kitchens and bathrooms were prefabricated as complete units; the inner partitions were of light metal that could be folded into the walls to provide one large room or pulled out to divide it; there were few halls or lobbies to clean, a minimum of cost and labor required for the maintenance of the place. The entire plan was a composition in triangles. The buildings, of poured concrete, were a complex modeling of simple structural features; there was no ornament; none was needed; the shapes had the beauty of sculpture.

Ellsworth Toohey did not look at the plans which Keating had spread out on his desk. He stared at the perspective drawing. He stared, his mouth open.

Then he threw his head back and howled with laughter.

"Peter," he said, "you're a genius."

He added: "I think you know exactly what I mean." Keating looked at him blankly, without curiosity. "You've succeeded in what I've spent a lifetime trying to achieve, in what centuries of men and bloody battles behind us have tried to achieve. I take my hat off to you, Peter, in awe and admiration."

"Look at the plans," said Keating listlessly. "It will rent for ten dollars a unit."

"I haven't the slightest doubt that it will. I don't have to look. Oh yes, Peter, this will go through. Don't worry. This will be accepted. My congratulations, Peter."

"You God-damn fool!" said Gail Wynand. "What are you up to?"

He threw to Roark a copy of the *Banner*, folded at an inside page. The page bore a photograph captioned: "Architects' drawing of Cortlandt Homes, the $15,000,000 Federal Housing Project to be built in Astoria, L. I., Keating & Dumont, architects."

Roark glanced at the photograph and asked: "What do you mean?"

"You know damn well what I mean. Do you think I picked the things in my art gallery by their signatures? If Peter Keating designed this, I'll eat every copy of today's *Banner.*"

"Peter Keating designed this, Gail."

"You fool. What are you after?"

"If I don't want to understand what you're talking about, I won't understand it, no matter what you say."

"Oh, you might, if I run a story to the effect that a certain housing project was designed by Howard Roark, which would make a swell exclusive story and a joke on one Mr. Toohey who's the boy behind the boys on most of those damn projects."

"You publish that and I'll sue hell out of you."

"You really would?"

"I would. Drop it, Gail. Don't you see I don't want to discuss it?"

Later, Wynand showed the picture to Dominique and asked:

"Who designed this?"

She looked at it. "Of course," was all she answered.

"What kind of 'changing world,' Alvah? Changing to what? From what? Who's doing the changing?"

Parts of Alvah Scarret's face looked anxious, but most of it was impatient, as he glanced at the proofs of his editorial on "Motherhood in a Changing World," which lay on Wynand's desk.

"What the hell, Gail," he muttered indifferently.

"That's what I want to know—what the hell?" He picked up the proof and read aloud: " 'The world we have known is gone and done for and it's no use kidding ourselves about it. We cannot go back, we must go forward. The mothers of today must set the example by broadening their own emotional view and raising their selfish love for their own children to a higher plane, to include everybody's little children. Mothers must love every kid in their block, in their street, in their city, county, state, nation and the whole wide, wide world—just exactly as much as their own little Mary or Johnny.' " Wynand wrinkled his nose fastidiously. "Alvah? . . . It's all right to dish out crap. But—this kind of crap?"

Alvah Scarret would not look at him.

"You're out of step with the times, Gail," he said. His voice was low; it had a tone of warning—as of something baring its teeth, tentatively, just for future reference.

This was so odd a behavior for Alvah Scarret that Wynand lost all desire to pursue the conversation. He drew a line across the editorial, but the blue pencil stroke seemed tired and ended in a blur. He said: "Go and bat out something else, Alvah."

Scarret rose, picked up the strip of paper, turned and left the room without a word.

Wynand looked after him, puzzled, amused and slightly sick.

He had known for several years the trend which his paper had embraced gradually, imperceptibly, without any directive from him. He had noticed the cautious "slanting" of news stories, the half-hints, the vague allusions, the peculiar adjectives peculiarly placed, the stressing of certain themes, the insertion of political conclusions where none was needed. If a story concerned a dispute between employer and employee, the employer was made to appear guilty, simply through wording, no matter what the facts presented. If a sentence referred to the past, it was always "our dark past" or "our dead past." If a statement involved someone's personal motive, it was always "goaded by selfishness" or "egged by greed." A crossword puzzle gave the definition of "obsolescent individuals" and the word came out as "capitalists."

Wynand had shrugged about it, contemptuously amused. His staff, he thought, was well trained: if this was the popular slang of the day, his boys assumed it automatically. It meant nothing at all. He kept it off the editorial page and the rest did not matter. It was no more than a fashion of the moment—and he had survived many changing fashions.

He felt no concern over the "We Don't Read Wynand" campaign. He obtained one of their men's-room stickers, pasted it on the windshield of his own Lincoln, added the words: "We don't either," and kept it there long enough to be discovered and snapped by a photographer from a neutral paper. In the course of his career he had been fought, damned, denounced by the greatest publishers of his time, by the shrewdest coalitions of financial power. He could not summon any apprehension over the activities of somebody named Gus Webb.

He knew that the *Banner* was losing some of its popularity. "A temporary fad," he told Scarret, shrugging. He would run a limerick contest, or a series of coupons for victrola records, see a slight spurt of circulation and promptly forget the matter.

He could not rouse himself to full action. He had never felt a greater desire to work. He entered his office each morning with impatient eagerness. But within an hour he found himself studying the joints of the paneling on the walls and reciting nursery rhymes in his mind. It was not boredom, not the satisfaction of a yawn, but more like the gnawing pull of wishing to yawn and not quite making it. He could not say that he disliked his work. It had merely become distasteful; not enough to force a decision; not enough to make him clench his fists; just enough to contract his nostrils.

He thought dimly that the cause lay in that new trend of the public taste. He saw no reason why he should not follow it and play on it as expertly as he had played on all other fads. But he could not follow. He felt no moral scruples. It was not a positive stand rationally taken; not defiance in the name of a cause of importance; just a fastidious feeling, something pertaining almost to chastity: the hesitation one feels before putting one's foot down into muck. He thought: It doesn't matter—it will not last—I'll be back when the wave swings on to another theme—I think I'd just rather sit this one out.

He could not say why the encounter with Alvah Scarret gave him a feeling of uneasiness, sharper than usual. He thought it was funny that Alvah should have switched to that line of tripe. But there had been something else; there had been a personal quality in Alvah's exit; almost a declaration that he saw no necessity to consider the boss's opinion any longer.

I ought to fire Alvah, he thought—and then laughed at himself, aghast: fire Alvah Scarret?—one might as well think of stopping the earth—or—of the unthinkable—of closing the *Banner*.

But through the months of that summer and fall, there were days when he loved the *Banner*. Then he sat at his desk, with his hand on the pages spread before him, fresh ink smearing his palm, and he smiled as he saw the name of Howard Roark in the pages of the *Banner*.

The word had come down from his office to every department concerned: Plug Howard Roark. In the art section, the real-estate section, the editorials, the columns, mentions of Roark and his buildings began to appear regularly. There were not many occasions when one could give publicity to an architect, and buildings had little news value, but the *Banner* managed to throw Roark's name at the public under every kind of ingenious pretext. Wynand edited every word of it. The material was startling on the pages of the *Banner:* it was written in good taste. There were no sensational stories, no photographs of Roark at breakfast, no human interest, no attempt to sell a man; only a considered, gracious tribute to the greatness of an artist.

He never spoke of it to Roark, and Roark never mentioned it. They did not discuss the *Banner.*

Coming home to his new house in the evening, Wynand saw the *Banner* on the living-room table every night. He had not allowed it in his home since his marriage. He smiled, when he saw it for the first time, and said nothing.

Then he spoke of it, one evening. He turned the pages until he came to an article on the general theme of summer resorts, most of which was a description of Monadnock Valley. He raised his head to glance at Dominique across the room; she sat on the floor by the fireplace. He said:

"Thank you, dear."

"For what, Gail?"

"For understanding when I would be glad to see the *Banner* in my house."

He walked to her and sat down on the floor beside her. He held her thin shoulders in the curve of his arm. He said:

"Think of all the politicians, movie stars, visiting grand dukes and sashweight murderers whom the *Banner* has trumpeted all these years. Think of my great crusades about streetcar companies, red-light districts and home-grown vegetables. For once, Dominique, I can say what I believe."

"Yes, Gail . . ."

"All this power I wanted, reached and never used . . . Now they'll see what I can do. I'll force them to recognize him as he should be recognized. I'll give him the fame he deserves. Public opinion? Public opinion is what I make it."

"Do you think he wants this?"

"Probably not. I don't care. He needs it and he's going to get it. I want him to have it. As an architect, he's public property. He can't stop a newspaper from writing about him if it wants to."

"All that copy on him—do you write it yourself?"

"Most of it."

"Gail, what a great journalist you could have been."

The campaign brought results, of a kind he had not expected. The general public remained blankly indifferent. But in the intellectual circles, in the art world, in the profession, people were laughing at Roark. Comments were reported to Wynand: "Roark? Oh yes, Wynand's pet." "The *Banner's* glamour boy." "The genius of the yellow press." "The *Banner* is now selling art—send two box tops or a reasonable facsimile." "Wouldn't you know it? That's what I've always thought of Roark—the kind of talent fit for the Wynand papers."

"We'll see," said Wynand contemptuously—and continued his private crusade.

He gave Roark every commission of importance whose owners were open to pressure. Since spring, he had brought to Roark's office the contracts for a yacht club on the Hudson, an office building, two private residences. "I'll get you more than you can handle," he said. "I'll make you catch up with all the years they've made you waste."

Austen Heller said to Roark one evening: "If I may be so presumptuous, I think you need advice, Howard. Yes, of course, I mean this preposterous business of Mr. Gail Wynand. You and he as inseparable friends upsets every rational concept I've ever held. After all, there are distinct classes of humanity—no, I'm not talking Toohey's language—but there are certain boundary lines among men which cannot be crossed."

"Yes, there are. But nobody has ever given the proper statement of where they must be drawn."

'Well, the friendship is your own business. But there's one aspect of it that must be stopped—and you're going to listen to me for once."

"I'm listening."

"I think it's fine, all those commissions he's dumping on you. I'm sure he'll be rewarded for that and lifted several rungs in hell, where he's certain to go. But he must stop that publicity he's splashing you with in the *Banner.* You've got to make him stop. Don't you know that the support of the Wynand papers is enough to discredit anyone?" Roark said nothing. "It's hurting you professionally, Howard."

"I know it is."

"Are you going to make him stop?"

"No."

"But why in blazes?"

"I said I'd listen, Austen. I didn't say I'd speak about him."

Late one afternoon in the fall Wynand came to Roark's office, as he often did at the end of a day, and when they walked out together, he said: "It's a nice evening. Let's go for a walk, Howard. There's a piece of property I want you to see."

He led the way to Hell's Kitchen. They walked around a great rectangle—two blocks between Ninth Avenue and Eleventh, five blocks from north to south. Roark saw a grimy desolation of tenements, sagging hulks of what had been red brick, crooked doorways, rotting boards, strings of gray underclothing in narrow air shafts, not as a sign of life, but as a malignant growth of decomposition.

"You own that?" Roark asked.

"All of it."

"Why show it to me? Don't you know that making an architect look at that is worse than showing him a field of unburied corpses?"

Wynand pointed to the white-tiled front of a new diner across the street: "Let's go in there."

They sat by the window, at a clean metal table, and Wynand ordered coffee. He seemed as graciously at home as in the best restaurants of the city; his elegance had an odd quality here—it did not insult the place, but seemed to transform it, like the presence of a king who never alters his manner, yet makes a palace of any house he enters. He leaned forward with his elbows on the table, watching Roark through the steam of the coffee, his eyes narrowed, amused. He moved one finger to point across the street.

"That's the first piece of property I ever bought, Howard. It was a long time ago. I haven't touched it since."

"What were you saving it for?"

"You."

Roark raised the heavy white mug of coffee to his lips, his eyes holding Wynand's, narrowed and mocking in answer. He knew that Wynand wanted eager questions and he waited patiently instead.

"You stubborn bastard," Wynand chuckled, surrendering. "All right. Listen. This is where I was born. When I could begin to think of buying real estate, I bought this piece. House by house. Block by block. It took a long time. I could have bought better property and made money fast, as I did later, but I waited until I had this. Even though I knew I would make no use of it for years. You see, I had decided then that this is where the Wynand Building would stand some day. . . . All right, keep still all you want—I've seen what your face looked like just now."

"Oh, God, Gail! . . ."

"What's the matter? Want to do it? Want it pretty badly?"

"I think I'd almost give my life for it—only then I couldn't build it. Is that what you wanted to hear?"

"Something like that. I won't demand your life. But it's nice to shock the breath out of you for once. Thank you for being shocked. It means you understood what the Wynand Building implies. The highest structure in the city. And the greatest."

"I know that's what you'd want."

"I won't build it yet. But I've waited for it all these years. And now you'll wait with me. Do you know that I really like to torture you, in a way? That I always want to?"

"I know."

"I brought you here only to tell you that it will be yours when I build it. I have waited, because I felt I was not ready for it. Since I met you, I knew I was ready—and I don't mean because you're an architect. But we'll have to wait a little longer, just another year or two, till the country gets back on its feet. This is the wrong time for building. Of course, everybody says that the day of the skyscraper is past. That it's obsolete. I don't give a damn about that. I'll make it pay for itself. The Wynand Enterprises have offices scattered all over town. I want them all in one building. And I hold enough over the heads of enough important people to force them to rent all the rest of the space. Perhaps, it will be the last skyscraper built in New York. So much the better. The greatest and the last."

Roark sat looking across the street, at the streaked ruins.

"To be torn down, Howard. All of it. Razed off. The place where I did not run things. To be supplanted by a park and the Wynand Building. . . . The best structures of New York are wasted because they can't be seen, squeezed against one another in blocks. My building will be seen. It will reclaim the whole neighborhood. Let the others follow. Not the right location, they'll say? Who makes right locations? They'll see. This might become the new center of the city—when the city starts living again. I planned it when the *Banner* was nothing but a fourth-rate rag. I haven't miscalculated, have I? I knew what I would become . . . A monument to my life, Howard. Remember what you said when you came to my office for the first time? A statement of my life. There were things in my past which I have not liked. But all the things of which I was proud will remain. After I am gone that building will be Gail Wynand. . . . I knew I'd find the right architect when the time came. I didn't know he would be much more than just an architect I hired. I'm glad it happened this way. It's a kind of reward. It's as if I had been forgiven. My last and greatest achievement will also be your greatest. It will be not only my monument but the best gift I could offer to the man who means most to me on earth. Don't frown, you know that's what you are to me. Look at that horror across the street. I want to sit here and watch you looking at it. That's what we're going to destroy—you and I. That's what it will rise from—the Wynand Building by Howard Roark. I've waited for it from the day I was born. From the day you were born, you've waited for your one great chance. There it is, Howard, across the street. Yours—from me."

X

I T HAD STOPPED RAINING, BUT PETER KEATING WISHED IT WOULD
start again. The pavements glistened, there were dark blotches on
the walls of buildings, and since it did not come from the sky, it looked
as if the city were bathed in cold sweat. The air was heavy with un-
timely darkness, disquieting like premature old age, and there were
yellow puddles of light in windows. Keating had missed the rain, but
he felt wet, from his bones out.

He had left his office early, and he walked home. The office seemed
unreal to him, as it had for a long time. He could find reality only in the
evenings, when he slipped furtively up to Roark's apartment. He did not
slip and it was not furtive, he told himself angrily—and knew that it
was; even though he walked through the lobby of the Enright House and
rode up in an elevator, like any man on a legitimate errand. It was the
vague anxiety, the impulse to glance around at every face, the fear of
being recognized; it was a load of anonymous guilt, not toward any
person, but the more frightening sense of guilt without a victim.

He took from Roark rough sketches for every detail of Cortlandt—to
have them translated into working drawings by his own staff. He listened
to Roark's instructions. He memorized arguments to offer his employers
against every possible objection. He absorbed like a recording machine.
Afterward, when he gave explanations to his draftsmen, his voice
sounded like a disk being played. He did not mind. He questioned
nothing.

Now he walked slowly, through the streets full of rain that would not
come. He looked up and saw empty space where the towers of familiar
buildings had been; it did not look like fog or clouds, but like a solid
spread of gray sky that had worked a gigantic, soundless destruction.
That sight of buildings vanishing through the sky had always made him
uneasy. He walked on, looking down.

It was the shoes that he noticed first. He knew that he must have seen
the woman's face, that the instinct of self-preservation had jerked his
glance away from it and let his conscious perception begin with the
shoes. They were flat, brown oxfords, offensively competent, too well
shined on the muddy pavement, contemptuous of rain and of beauty.
His eyes went to the brown skirt, to the tailored jacket, costly and cold
like a uniform, to the hand with a hole in the finger of an expensive
glove, to the lapel that bore a preposterous ornament—a bow-legged

Mexican with red-enameled pants—stuck there in a clumsy attempt at pertness; to the thin lips, to the glasses, to the eyes.

"Katie," he said.

She stood by the window of a bookstore; her glance hesitated halfway between recognition and a book title she had been examining; then, with recognition evident in the beginning of a smile, the glance went back to the book title, to finish and make an efficient note of it. Then her eyes returned to Keating. Her smile was pleasant; not as an effort over bitterness, and not as welcome; just pleasant.

"Why, Peter Keating," she said. "Hello, Peter."

"Katie . . ." He could not extend his hand or move closer to her.

"Yes, imagine running into you like this, why, New York is just like any small town, though I suppose without the better features." There was no strain in her voice.

"What are you doing here? I thought . . . I heard . . ." He knew she had a good job in Washington and had moved there two years ago.

"Just a business trip. Have to dash right back tomorrow. Can't say that I mind it, either. New York seems so dead, so *slow*."

"Well, I'm glad you like your job . . . if you mean . . . isn't that what you mean?"

"Like my job? What a silly thing to say. Washington is the only grown-up place in the country. I don't see how people can live anywhere else. What have you been doing, Peter? I saw your name in the paper the other day, it was something important."

"I . . . I'm working. . . . You haven't changed much, Katie, not really, have you?—I mean, your face—you look like you used to—in a way . . ."

"It's the only face I've got. Why do people always have to talk about changes if they haven't seen each other for a year or two? I ran into Grace Parker yesterday and she had to go into an inventory of my appearance. I could just hear every word before she said it—'You look so nice—not a day older, really, Catherine.' People are provincial."

"But . . . you do look nice. . . . It's . . . nice to see you . . ."

"I'm glad to see you, too. How is the building industry?"

"I don't know. . . . What you read about must have been Cortlandt . . . I'm doing Cortlandt Homes, a housing . . ."

"Yes, of course. That was it. I think it's very good for you, Peter. To do a job, not just for private profit and a fat fee, but with a social purpose. I think architects should stop money grubbing and give a little time to government work and broader objectives."

"Why, most of them would grab it if they could get it, it's one of the hardest rackets to break into, it's a closed . . ."

"Yes, yes, I know. It's simply impossible to make the laymen understand our methods of working, and that's why all we hear are all those stupid, boring complaints. You mustn't read the Wynand papers, Peter."

"I never read the Wynand papers. What on earth has it got to do with . . . Oh, I . . . I don't know what we're talking about, Katie."

He thought that she owed him nothing, or every kind of anger and scorn she could command; and yet there was a human obligation she still had toward him: she owed him an evidence of strain in this meeting. There was none.

"We really should have a great deal to talk about, Peter." The words would have lifted him, had they not been pronounced so easily. "But we can't stand here all day." She glanced at her wrist watch. "I've got an hour or so, suppose you take me somewhere for a cup of tea, you could use some hot tea, you look frozen."

That was her first comment on his appearance; that, and a glance without reaction. He thought, even Roark had been shocked, had acknowledged the change.

"Yes, Katie. That will be wonderful. I . . ." He wished she had not been the one to suggest it; it was the right thing for them to do; he wished she had not been able to think of the right thing; not so quickly. "Let's find a nice, quiet place. . . ."

"We'll go to Thorpe's. There's one around the corner. They have the nicest watercress sandwiches."

It was she who took his arm to cross the street, and dropped it again on the other side. The gesture had been automatic. She had not noticed it.

There was a counter of pastry and candy inside the door of Thorpe's. A large bowl of sugar-coated almonds, green and white, glared at Keating. The place smelled of orange icing. The lights were dim, a stuffy orange haze; the odor made the light seem sticky. The tables were too small, set close together.

He sat, looking down at a paper lace doily on a black glass table top. But when he lifted his eyes to Catherine, he knew that no caution was necessary: she did not react to his scrutiny; her expression remained the same, whether he studied her face or that of the woman at the next table; she seemed to have no consciousness of her own person.

It was her mouth that had changed most, he thought; the lips were drawn in, with only a pale edge of flesh left around the imperious line of their opening; a mouth to issue orders, he thought, but not big orders or cruel orders; just mean little ones—about plumbing and disinfectants. He saw the fine wrinkles at the corners of her eyes—a skin like paper that had been crumpled and then smoothed out.

She was telling him about her work in Washington, and he listened bleakly. He did not hear the words, only the tone of her voice, dry and crackling.

A waitress in a starched orchid uniform came to take their orders. Catherine snapped:

"The tea sandwiches special. Please."

Keating said:

"A cup of coffee." He saw Catherine's eyes on him, and in a sudden panic of embarrassment, feeling he must not confess that he couldn't swallow a bite of food now, feeling that the confession would anger her, he added: "A ham and swiss on rye, I guess."

"Peter, what ghastly food habits! Wait a minute, waitress. You don't want that, Peter. It's very bad for you. You should have a fresh salad. And coffee is bad at this time of the day. Americans drink too much coffee."

"All right," said Keating.

"Tea and a combination salad, waitress. . . . And—oh, waitress!—no bread with the salad—you're gaining weight, Peter—some diet crackers. Please."

Keating waited until the orchid uniform had moved away, and then he said, hopefully:

"I have changed, haven't I, Katie? I do look pretty awful?" Even a disparaging comment would be a personal link.

"What? Oh, I guess so. It isn't healthy. But Americans know nothing whatever about the proper nutritional balance. Of course, men do make too much fuss over mere appearance. They're much vainer than women. It's really women who're taking charge of all productive work now, and women will build a better world."

"How does one build a better world, Katie?"

"Well, if you consider the determining factor, which is, of course, economic . . ."

"No, I . . . I didn't ask it that way. . . . Katie, I've been very unhappy."

"I'm sorry to hear that. One hears so many people say that nowadays. That's because it's a transition period and people feel rootless. But you've always had a bright disposition, Peter."

"Do you . . . do you remember what I was like?"

"Goodness, Peter, you talk as if it had been sixty-five years ago."

"But so many things happened. I . . . ." He took the plunge; he had to take it; the crudest way seemed the easiest. "I was married. And divorced."

"Yes, I read about that. I was glad when you were divorced." She leaned forward. "If your wife was the kind of woman who could marry Gail Wynand, you were lucky to get rid of her."

The tone of chronic impatience that ran words together had not altered to pronounce this. He had to believe it: this was all the subject meant to her.

"Katie, you're very tactful and kind . . . but drop the act," he said, knowing in dread that it was not an act. "Drop it. . . . Tell me what you thought of me then. . . . Say everything. . . . I don't mind. . . . I want to hear it. . . . Don't you understand? I'll feel better if I hear it."

"Surely, Peter, you don't want me to start some sort of recriminations? I'd say it was conceited of you, if it weren't so childish."

"What did you feel—that day—when I didn't come—and then you heard I was married?" He did not know what instinct drove him, through numbness, to be brutal as the only means left to him. "Katie, you suffered then?"

"Yes, of course I suffered. All young people do in such situations. It seems foolish afterward. I cried, and I screamed some dreadful things at Uncle Ellsworth, and he had to call a doctor to give me a sedative, and then weeks afterward I fainted on the street one day without any reason, which was really disgraceful. All the conventional things, I suppose, everybody goes through them, like measles. Why should I have expected to be exempt?—as Uncle Ellsworth said." He thought that he had not known there was something worse than a living memory of pain: a dead one. "And of course we knew it was for the best. I can't imagine myself married to you."

"You can't imagine it, Katie?"

"That is, nor to anyone else. It wouldn't have worked, Peter. I'm temperamentally unsuited to domesticity. It's too selfish and narrow. Of course, I understand what you feel just now and I appreciate it. It's only human that you should feel something like remorse, since you did what is known as jilted me." He winced. "You see how stupid those things sound. It's natural for you to be a little contrite—a normal reflex—but we must look at it objectively, we're grown-up, rational people, nothing is too serious, we can't really help what we do, we're conditioned that way, we just charge it off to experience and go on from there."

"Katie! You're not talking some fallen girl out of her problem. You're speaking about yourself."

"Is there any essential difference? Everybody's problems are the same, just like everybody's emotions."

He saw her nibbling a thin strip of bread with a smear of green, and noticed that his order had been served. He moved his fork about in his salad bowl, and he made himself bite into a gray piece of diet cracker. Then he discovered how strange it was when one lost the knack of eating automatically and had to do it by full conscious effort; the cracker seemed inexhaustible; he could not finish the process of chewing; he moved his jaws without reducing the amount of gritty pulp in his mouth.

"Katie . . . for six years . . . I thought of how I'd ask your forgiveness some day. And now I have the chance, but I won't ask it. It seems . . . it seems beside the point. I know it's horrible to say that, but that's how it seems to me. It was the worst thing I ever did in my life—but not because I hurt you. I did hurt you, Katie, and maybe more than you know yourself. But that's not my worst guilt. . . . Katie, I wanted to marry you. It was the only thing I ever really wanted. And that's the sin that can't be forgiven—that I hadn't done what I wanted. It feels so dirty and pointless and monstrous, as one feels about insanity, because there's no sense to it, no dignity, nothing but pain—and wasted pain. . . . Katie, why do they always teach us that it's easy and evil to do what we want and that we need discipline to restrain ourselves? It's the hardest thing in the world—to do what we want. And it takes the greatest kind of courage. I mean, what we really want. As I wanted to marry you. Not as I want to sleep with some woman or get drunk or get my name in the papers. Those things—they're not even desires—they're things people do to escape from desires—because it's such a big responsibility, really to want something."

"Peter, what you're saying is very ugly and selfish."

"Maybe. I don't know. I've always had to tell you the truth. About everything. Even if you didn't ask. I had to."

"Yes. You did. It was a commendable trait. You were a charming boy, Peter."

It was the bowl of sugar-coated almonds on the counter that hurt him, he thought in dull anger. The almonds were green and white; they had no business being green and white at this time of the year; the colors of St. Patrick's Day—then there was always candy like that in all the store windows—and St. Patrick's Day meant spring—no, better than spring, that moment of wonderful anticipation just before spring is to begin.

"Katie, I won't say that I'm still in love with you. I don't know whether I am or not. I've never asked myself. It wouldn't matter now. I'm not saying this because I hope for anything or think of trying or . . . I know only that I loved you, Katie, I loved you, whatever I made of it, even if this is how I've got to say it for the last time, I loved you, Katie."

She looked at him—and she seemed pleased. Not stirred, not happy, not pitying; but pleased in a casual way. He thought: If she were completely the spinster, the frustrated social worker, as people think of those women, the kind who would scorn sex in the haughty conceit of her own virtue, that would still be recognition, if only in hostility. But this—this amused tolerance seemed to admit that romance was only human, one had to take it, like everybody else, it was a popular weakness of no great consequence—she was gratified as she would have been gratified by the same words from any other man—it was like that red-enamel Mexican on her lapel, a contemptuous concession to people's demand of vanity.

"Katie . . . Katie, let's say that this doesn't count—this, now—it's past counting anyway, isn't it? This can't touch what it was like, can it, Katie? . . . People always regret that the past is so final, that nothing can change it—but I'm glad it's so. We can't spoil it. We can think of the past, can't we? Why shouldn't we? I mean, as you said, like grown-up people, not fooling ourselves, not trying to hope, but only to look back at it. . . . Do you remember when I came to your house in New York for the first time? You looked so thin and small, and your hair hung every which way. I told you I would never love anyone else. I held you on my lap, you didn't weigh anything at all, and I told you I would never love anyone else. And you said you knew it."

"I remember."

"When we were together . . . Katie, I'm ashamed of so many things, but not of one moment when we were together. When I asked you to marry me—no, I never asked you to marry me—I just said we were engaged—and you said 'yes'—it was on a park bench—it was snowing . . ."

"Yes."

"You had funny woolen gloves. Like mittens. I remember—there were drops of water in the fuzz—round—like crystal—they flashed—it was because a car passed by."

"Yes, I think it's agreeable to look back occasionally. But one's perspective widens. One grows richer spiritually with the years."

He kept silent for a long time. Then he said, his voice flat:

"I'm sorry."

"Why? You're very sweet, Peter. I've always said men are the sentimentalists."

He thought: It's not an act—one can't put on an act like that—unless it's an act inside, for oneself, and then there is no limit, no way out, no reality. . . .

She went on talking to him, and after a while it was about Washington again. He answered when it was necessary.

He thought that he had believed it was a simple sequence, the past and the present, and if there was loss in the past one was compensated by pain in the present, and pain gave it a form of immortality—but he had not known that one could destroy like this, kill retroactively—so that to her it had never existed.

She glanced at her wrist watch and gave a little gasp of impatience.

"I'm late already. I must run along."

He said heavily:

"Do you mind if I don't go with you, Katie? It's not rudeness. I just think it's better."

"But of course. Not at all. I'm quite able to find my way in the streets and there's no need for formalities among old friends." She added, gathering her bag and gloves, crumpling a paper napkin into a ball, dropping it neatly into her teacup: "I'll give you a ring next time I'm in town and we'll have a bite together again. Though I can't promise when that will be. I'm so busy, I have to go so many places, last month it was Detroit and next week I'm flying to St. Louis, but when they shoot me out to New York again, I'll ring you up, so long, Peter, it was ever so nice."

XI

GAIL WYNAND LOOKED AT THE SHINING WOOD OF THE YACHT DECK. The wood and a brass doorknob that had become a smear of fire gave him a sense of everything around him: the miles of space filled with sun, between the burning spreads of sky and ocean. It was February, and the yacht lay still, her engines idle, in the southern Pacific.

He leaned on the rail and looked down at Roark in the water. Roark floated on his back, his body stretched into a straight line, arms spread, eyes closed. The tan of his skin implied a month of days such as this. Wynand thought that this was the way he liked to apprehend space and time: through the power of his yacht, through the tan of Roark's skin or the sunbrown of his own arms folded before him on the rail.

He had not sailed his yacht for several years. This time he had wanted Roark to be his only guest. Dominique was left behind.

Wynand had said: "You're killing yourself, Howard. You've been going at a pace nobody can stand for long. Ever since Monadnock, isn't it? Think you'd have the courage to perform the feat most difficult for you—to rest?"

He was astonished when Roark accepted without argument. Roark laughed:

"I'm not running away from my work, if that's what surprises you. I know when to stop—and I can't stop, unless it's completely. I know I've overdone it. I've been wasting too much paper lately and doing awful stuff."

"Do you ever do awful stuff?"

"Probably more of it than any other architect and with less excuse. The only distinction I can claim is that my botches end up in my own wastebasket."

"I warn you, we'll be away for months. If you begin to regret it and cry for your drafting table in a week, like all men who've never learned to loaf, I won't take you back. I'm the worst kind of dictator aboard my yacht. You'll have everything you can imagine, except paper or pencils. I won't even leave you any freedom of speech. No mention of girders, plastics or reinforced concrete once you step on board. I'll teach you to eat, sleep and exist like the most worthless millionaire."

"I'd like to try that."

The work in the office did not require Roark's presence for the next few months. His current jobs were being completed. Two new commissions were not to be started until spring.

629

He had made all the sketches Keating needed for Cortlandt. The construction was about to begin. Before sailing, on a day in late December, Roark went to take a last look at the site of Cortlandt. An anonymous spectator in a group of the idle curious, he stood and watched the steam shovels biting the earth, breaking the way for future foundations. The East River was a broad band of sluggish black water; and beyond, in a sparse haze of snowflakes, the towers of the city stood softened, half suggested in watercolors of orchid and blue.

Dominique did not protest when Wynand told her that he wanted to sail on a long cruise with Roark. "Dearest, you understand that it's not running away from you? I just need some time taken out of everything. Being with Howard is like being alone with myself, only more at peace."

"Of course, Gail. I don't mind."

But he looked at her, and suddenly he laughed, incredulously pleased. "Dominique, I believe you're jealous. It's wonderful, I'm more grateful to him than ever—if it could make you jealous of me."

She could not tell him that she was jealous or of whom.

The yacht sailed at the end of December. Roark watched, grinning, Wynand's disappointment when Wynand found that he needed to enforce no discipline. Roark did not speak of buildings, lay for hours stretched out on deck in the sun, and loafed like an expert. They spoke little. There were days when Wynand could not remember what sentences they had exchanged. It would have seemed possible to him that they had not spoken at all. Their serenity was their best means of communication.

Today they had dived together to swim and Wynand had climbed back first. As he stood at the rail, watching Roark in the water, he thought of the power he held in this moment: he could order the yacht to start moving, sail away and leave that redheaded body to sun and ocean. The thought gave him pleasure: the sense of power and the sense of surrender to Roark in the knowledge that no conceivable force could make him exercise that power. Every physical instrumentality was on his side: a few contractions of his vocal chords giving the order and someone's hand opening a valve—and the obedient machine would move away. He thought: It's not just a moral issue, not the mere horror of the act, one could conceivably abandon a man if the fate of a continent depended on it. But nothing would enable him to abandon this man. He, Gail Wynand, was the helpless one in this moment, with the solid planking of the deck under his feet. Roark, floating like a piece of driftwood, held a power greater than that of the engine in the belly of the yacht. Wynand thought: Because that is the power from which the engine has come.

Roark climbed back on deck; Wynand looked at Roark's body, at the threads of water running down the angular planes. He said:

"You made a mistake on the Stoddard Temple, Howard. That statue should have been, not of Dominique, but of you."

"No. I'm too egotistical for that."

"Egotistical? An egotist would have loved it. You use words in the strangest way."

"In the exact way. I don't wish to be the symbol of anything. I'm only myself."

Stretched in a deck chair, Wynand glanced up with satisfaction at the lantern, a disk of frosted glass on the bulkhead behind him: it cut off the black void of the ocean and gave him privacy within solid walls of light. He heard the sound of the yacht's motion, he felt the warm night air on his face, he saw nothing but the stretch of deck around him, enclosed and final.

Roark stood before him at the rail; a tall white figure leaning back against black space, his head lifted as Wynand had seen it lifted in an unfinished building. His hands clasped the rail. The short shirt sleeves left his arms in the light; vertical ridges of shadow stressed the tensed muscles of his arms and the tendons of his neck. Wynand thought of the yacht's engine, of skyscrapers, of transatlantic cables, of everything man had made.

"Howard, this is what I wanted. To have you here with me."

"I know."

"Do you know what it really is? Avarice. I'm a miser about two things on earth: you and Dominique. I'm a millionaire who's never owned anything. Do you remember what you said about ownership? I'm like a savage who's discovered the idea of private property and run amuck on it. It's funny. Think of Ellsworth Toohey."

"Why Ellsworth Toohey?"

"I mean, the things he preaches. I've been wondering lately whether he really understands what he's advocating. Selflessness in the absolute sense? Why, that's what I've been. Does he know that I'm the embodiment of his ideal? Of course, he wouldn't approve of my motive, but motives never alter facts. If it's true selflessness he's after, in the philosophical sense—and Mr. Toohey is a philosopher—in a sense much beyond matters of money, why, let him look at me. I've never owned anything. I've never wanted anything. I didn't give a damn—in the most cosmic way Toohey could ever hope for. I made myself into a barometer subject to the pressure of the whole world. The voice of his masses pushed me up and down. Of course, I collected a fortune in the process. Does that change the intrinsic reality of the picture? Suppose I gave away every penny of it. Suppose I had never wished to take any money at all, but had set out in pure altruism to serve the people. What would I have to do? Exactly what I've done. Give the greatest pleasure to the greatest number. Express the opinions, the desires, the tastes of the majority. The majority that voted me its approval and support freely, in the shape of a three-cent ballot dropped at the corner newsstand every morning. The Wynand papers? For thirty-one years they have represented everybody except Gail Wynand. I erased my ego out of existence in a way never achieved by any saint in a cloister. Yet people call me corrupt. Why? The saint in a cloister sacrifices only material things. It's a small price to pay for the glory of his soul. He hoards his soul and gives up the world. But I—I took automobiles, silk pyjamas, a penthouse, and gave the world my soul in exchange. Who's sacrificed more —if sacrifice is the test of virtue? Who's the actual saint?"

"Gail . . . I didn't think you'd ever admit that to yourself."

"Why not? I knew what I was doing. I wanted power over a collective soul and I got it. A collective soul. It's a messy kind of concept, but if anyone wishes to visualize it concretely, let him pick up a copy of the New York *Banner*."

"Yes . . ."

"Of course, Toohey would tell me that this is not what he means by altruism. He means I shouldn't leave it up to the people to decide what they want. I should decide it. I should determine, not what I like nor what they like, but what I think they should like, and then ram it down their throats. It would have to be rammed, since their voluntary choice is the *Banner*. Well, there are several such altruists in the world today."

"You realize that?"

"Of course. What else can one do if one must serve the people? If one must live for others? Either pander to everybody's wishes and be called corrupt; or impose on everybody by force your own idea of everybody's good. Can you think of any other way?"

"No."

"What's left then? Where does decency start? What begins where altruism ends? Do you see what I'm in love with?"

"Yes, Gail." Wynand had noticed that Roark's voice had a reluctance that sounded almost like sadness.

"What's the matter with you? Why do you sound like that?"

"I'm sorry. Forgive me. It's just something I thought. I've been thinking of this for a long time. And particularly all these days when you've made me lie on deck and loaf."

"Thinking about me?"

"About you—among many other things."

"What have you decided?"

"I'm not an altruist, Gail. I don't decide for others."

"You don't have to worry about me. I've sold myself, but I've held no illusions about it. I've never become an Alvah Scarret. He really believes whatever the public believes. I despise the public. That's my only vindication. I've sold my life, but I got a good price. Power. I've never used it. I couldn't afford a personal desire. But now I'm free. Now I can use it for what I want. For what I believe. For Dominique. For you."

Roark turned away. When he looked back at Wynand, he said only: "I hope so, Gail."

"What have you been thinking about, these past weeks?"

"The principle behind the dean who fired me from Stanton."

"What principle?"

"The thing that is destroying the world. The thing you were talking about. Actual selflessness."

"The ideal which they say does not exist?"

"They're wrong. It does exist—though not in the way they imagine. It's what I couldn't understand about people for a long time. They have no self. They live within others. They live second-hand. Look at Peter Keating."

"You look at him. I hate his guts."

"I've looked at him—at what's left of him—and it's helped me to understand. He's paying the price and wondering for what sin and telling himself that he's been too selfish. In what act or thought of his has there ever been a self? What was his aim in life? Greatness—in other people's eyes. Fame, admiration, envy—all that which comes from others. Others dictated his convictions, which he did not hold, but he was satisfied that others believed he held them. Others were his motive power and his prime concern. He didn't want to be great, but to be thought great. He didn't want to build, but to be admired as a builder. He borrowed from others in order to make an impression on others. There's your actual selflessness. It's his ego that he's betrayed and given up. But everybody calls him selfish."

"That's the pattern most people follow."

"Yes! And isn't that the root of every despicable action? Not selfishness, but precisely the absence of a self. Look at them. The man who cheats and lies, but preserves a respectable front. He knows himself to be dishonest, but others think he's honest and he derives his self-respect from that, second-hand. The man who takes credit for an achievement which is not his own. He knows himself to be mediocre, but he's great in the eyes of others. The frustrated wretch who professes love for the inferior and clings to those less endowed, in order to establish his own superiority by comparison. The man whose sole aim is to make money. Now I don't see anything evil in a desire to make money. But money is only a means to some end. If a man wants it for a personal purpose—to invest in his industry, to create, to study, to travel, to enjoy luxury—he's completely moral. But the men who place money first go much beyond that. Personal luxury is a limited endeavor. What they want is ostentation: to show, to stun, to entertain, to impress others. They're second-handers. Look at our so-called cultural endeavors. A lecturer who spouts some borrowed rehash of nothing at all that means nothing at all to him—and the people who listen and don't give a damn, but sit there in order to tell their friends that they have attended a lecture by a famous name. All second-handers."

"If I were Ellsworth Toohey, I'd say: aren't you making out a case against selfishness? Aren't they all acting on a selfish motive—to be noticed, liked, admired?"

"—by others. At the price of their own self-respect. In the realm of greatest importance—the realm of values, of judgment, of spirit, of thought—they place others above self, in the exact manner which altruism demands. A truly selfish man cannot be affected by the approval of others. He doesn't need it."

"I think Toohey understands that. That's what helps him spread his vicious nonsense. Just weakness and cowardice. It's so easy to run to others. It's so hard to stand on one's own record. You can fake virtue for an audience. You can't fake it in your own eyes. Your ego is your strictest judge. They run from it. They spend their lives running. It's easier to donate a few thousands to charity and think oneself noble than to base self-respect on personal standards of personal achievement. It's simple to seek substitutes for competence—such easy substitutes: love, charm, kindness, charity. But there is no substitute for competence."

"That, precisely, is the deadliness of second-handers. They have no concern for facts, ideas, work. They're concerned only with people. They don't ask: 'Is this true?' They ask: 'Is this what others think is true?' Not to judge, but to repeat. Not to do, but to give the impression of doing. Not creation, but show. Not ability, but friendship. Not merit, but pull. What would happen to the world without those who do, think, work, produce? Those are the egotists. You don't think through another's brain and you don't work through another's hands. When you suspend your faculty of independent judgment, you suspend consciousness. To stop consciousness is to stop life. Second-handers have no sense of reality. Their reality is not within them, but somewhere in that space which divides one human body from another. Not an entity, but a relation—anchored to nothing. That's the emptiness I couldn't understand in people. That's what stopped me whenever I faced a committee. Men without an ego. Opinion without a rational process. Motion without brakes or motor. Power without responsibility. The second-hander acts, but the source of his actions is scattered in every other living person. It's everywhere and nowhere and you can't reason with him.

He's not open to reason. You can't speak to him—he can't hear. You're tried by an empty bench. A blind mass running amuck, to crush you without sense or purpose. Steve Mallory couldn't define the monster, but he knew. That's the drooling beast he fears. The second-hander."

"I think your second-handers understand this, try as they might not to admit it to themselves. Notice how they'll accept anything except a man who stands alone. They recognize him at once. By instinct. There's a special, insidious kind of hatred for him. They forgive criminals. They admire dictators. Crime and violence are a tie. A form of mutual dependence. They need ties. They've got to force their miserable little personalities on every single person they meet. The independent man kills them—because they don't exist within him and that's the only form of existence they know. Notice the malignant kind of resentment against any idea that propounds independence. Notice the malice toward an independent man. Look back at your own life, Howard, and at the people you've met. They know. They're afraid. You're a reproach."

"That's because some sense of dignity always remains in them. They're still human beings. But they've been taught to seek themselves in others. Yet no man can achieve the kind of absolute humility that would need no self-esteem in any form. He wouldn't survive. So after centuries of being pounded with the doctrine that altruism is the ultimate ideal, men have accepted it in the only way it could be accepted. By seeking self-esteem through others. By living second-hand. And it has opened the way for every kind of horror. It has become the dreadful form of selfishness which a truly selfish man couldn't have conceived. And now, to cure a world perishing from selflessness, we're asked to destroy the self. Listen to what is being preached today. Look at everyone around us. You've wondered why they suffer, why they seek happiness and never find it. If any man stopped and asked himself whether he's ever held a truly personal desire, he'd find the answer. He'd see that all his wishes, his efforts, his dreams, his ambitions are motivated by other men. He's not really struggling even for material wealth, but for the second-hander's delusion—prestige. A stamp of approval, not his own. He can find no joy in the struggle and no joy when he has succeeded. He can't say about a single thing: 'This is what I wanted because *I* wanted it, not because it made my neighbors gape at me.' Then he wonders why he's unhappy. Every form of happiness is private. Our greatest moments are personal, self-motivated, not to be touched. The things which are sacred or precious to us are the things we withdraw from promiscuous sharing. But now we are taught to throw everything within us into public light and common pawing. To seek joy in meeting halls. We haven't even got a word for the quality I mean—for the self-sufficiency of man's spirit. It's difficult to call it selfishness or egotism, the words have been perverted, they've come to mean Peter Keating. Gail, I think the only cardinal evil on earth is that of placing your prime concern within other men. I've always demanded a certain quality in the people I liked. I've always recognized it at once—and it's the only quality I respect in men. I chose my friends by that. Now I know what it is. A self-sufficient ego. Nothing else matters."

"I'm glad you admit that you have friends."

"I even admit that I love them. But I couldn't love them if they were my chief reason for living. Do you notice that Peter Keating hasn't a single friend left? Do you see why? If one doesn't respect oneself one can have neither love nor respect for others."

"To hell with Peter Keating. I'm thinking of you—and your friends."

Roark smiled. "Gail, if this boat were sinking, I'd give my life to save you. Not because it's any kind of duty. Only because I like you, for reasons and standards of my own. I could die for you. But I couldn't and wouldn't live for you."

"Howard, what were the reasons and standards?"

Roark looked at him and realized that he had said all the things he had tried not to say to Wynand. He answered:

"That you weren't born to be a second-hander."

Wynand smiled. He heard the sentence—and nothing else.

Afterward, when Wynand had gone below to his cabin, Roark remained alone on deck. He stood at the rail, staring out at the ocean, at nothing.

He thought: I haven't mentioned to him the worst second-hander of all—the man who goes after power.

XII

I T WAS APRIL WHEN ROARK AND WYNAND RETURNED TO THE CITY. The skyscrapers looked pink against the blue sky, an incongruous shade of porcelain on masses of stone. There were small tufts of green on the trees in the streets.

Roark went to his office. His staff shook hands with him and he saw the strain of smiles self-consciously repressed, until a young boy burst out: "What the hell! Why can't we say how glad we are to see you back, boss?" Roark laughed. "Go ahead. I can't tell you how damn glad I am to be back." Then he sat on a table in the drafting room, while they all reported to him on the past three months, interrupting one another; he played with a ruler in his hands, not noticing it, like a man with the feel of his farm's soil under his fingers, after an absence.

In the afternoon, alone at his desk, he opened a newspaper. He had not seen a newspaper for three months. He noticed an item about the construction of Cortlandt Homes. He saw the line: "Peter Keating, architect. Gordon L. Prescott and Augustus Webb, associate designers."

He sat very still.

That evening, he went to see Cortlandt.

The first building was almost completed. It stood alone on the large, empty tract. The workers had left for the day; a small light showed in the shack of the night watchman. The building had the skeleton of what Roark had designed, with the remnants of ten different breeds piled on the lovely symmetry of the bones. He saw the economy of plan preserved, but the expense of incomprehensible features added; the variety of modeled masses gone, replaced by the monotony of brutish cubes; a new wing added, with a vaulted roof, bulging out of a wall like a tumor, containing a gymnasium; strings of balconies added, made of metal stripes painted a violent blue; corner windows without purpose; an angle cut off for a useless door, with a round metal awning supported by a pole, like a haberdashery in the Broadway district; three vertical bands of brick, leading from nowhere to nowhere; the general style of what the profession called "Bronx Modern"; a panel of bas-relief over the main entrance, representing a mass of muscle which could be discerned as either three or four bodies, one of them with an arm raised, holding a screwdriver.

There were white crosses on the fresh panes of glass in the windows, and it looked appropriate, like an error x'ed out of existence. There was a band of red in the sky, to the west, beyond Manhattan, and the buildings of the city rose straight and black against it.

637

Roark stood across the space of the future road before the first house of Cortlandt. He stood straight, the muscles of his throat pulled, his wrists held down and away from his body, as he would have stood before a firing squad.

No one could tell how it had happened. There had been no deliberate intention behind it. It had just happened.

First, Toohey told Keating one morning that Gordon L. Prescott and Gus Webb would be put on the payroll as associate designers. "What do you care, Peter? It won't come out of your fee. It won't cut your prestige at all, since you're the big boss. They won't be much more than your draftsmen. All I want is to give the boys a boost. It will help their reputation, to be tagged with this project in some way. I'm very interested in building up their reputation."

"But what for? There's nothing for them to do. It's all done."

"Oh, any kind of last-minute drafting. Save time for your own staff. You can share the expense with them. Don't be a hog."

Toohey had told the truth; he had no other purpose in mind.

Keating could not discover what connections Prescott and Webb possessed, with whom, in what office, on what terms—among the dozens of officials involved in the project. The entanglement of responsibility was such that no one could be quite certain of anyone's authority. It was clear only that Prescott and Webb had friends, and that Keating could not keep them off the job.

The changes began with the gymnasium. The lady in charge of tenant selection demanded a gymnasium. She was a social worker and her task was to end with the opening of the project. She acquired a permanent job by getting herself appointed Director of Social Recreation for Cortlandt. No gymnasium had been provided in the original plans; there were two schools and a Y.M.C.A. within walking distance. She declared that this was an outrage against the children of the poor. Prescott and Webb supplied the gymnasium. Other changes followed, of a purely esthetic nature. Extras piled on the cost of construction so carefully devised for economy. The Director of Social Recreation departed for Washington to discuss the matter of a Little Theater and a Meeting Hall she wished added to the next two buildings of Cortlandt.

The changes in the drawings came gradually, a few at a time. The orders okaying the changes came from headquarters. "But we're ready to start!" cried Keating. "What the hell," drawled Gus Webb, "set 'em back just a coupla thousand bucks more, that's all." "Now as to the balconies," said Gordon L. Prescott, "they lend a certain modern style. You don't want the damn thing to look so bare. It's depressing. Besides, you don't understand psychology. The people who'll live here are used to sitting out on fire-escapes. They love it. They'll miss it. You gotta give 'em a place to sit on in the fresh air. . . . The cost? Hell, if you're so damn worried about the cost, I've got an idea where we can save plenty. We'll do without closet doors. What do they need doors for on closets? It's old-fashioned." All the closet doors were omitted.

Keating fought. It was the kind of battle he had never entered, but he tried everything possible to him, to the honest limit of his exhausted strength. He went from office to office, arguing, threatening, pleading. But he had no influence, while his associate designers seemed to control an underground river with interlocking tributaries. The officials shrugged and referred him to someone else. No one cared about an issue of esthetics. "What's the difference?" "It doesn't come out of *your* pocket, does it?" "Who are you to have it all your way? Let the boys contribute something."

He appealed to Ellsworth Toohey, but Toohey was not interested. He was busy with other matters and he had no desire to provoke a bureaucratic quarrel. In all truth, he had not prompted his protégés to their artistic endeavor, but he saw no reason for attempting to stop them. He was amused by the whole thing. "But it's awful, Ellsworth! You know it's awful!" "Oh, I suppose so. What do you care, Peter? Your poor but unwashed tenants won't be able to appreciate the finer points of architectural art. See that the plumbing works."

"But what for? What for? What for?" Keating cried to his associate designers. "Well, why shouldn't we have any say at all?" asked Gordon L. Prescott. "We want to express our individuality too."

When Keating invoked his contract, he was told: "All right, go ahead, try to sue the government. Try it." At times, he felt a desire to kill. There was no one to kill. Had he been granted the privilege, he could not have chosen a victim. Nobody was responsible. There was no purpose and no cause. It had just happened.

Keating came to Roark's house on the evening after Roark's return. He had not been summoned. Roark opened the door and said: "Good evening, Peter," but Keating could not answer. They walked silently into the work room. Roark sat down, but Keating remained standing in the middle of the floor and asked, his voice dull:

"What are you going to do?"

"You must leave that up to me now."

"I couldn't help it, Howard. . . . I couldn't help it!"

"I suppose not."

"What can you do now? You can't sue the government."

"No."

Keating thought that he should sit down, but the distance to a chair seemed too great. He felt he would be too conspicuous if he moved.

"What are you going to do to me, Howard?"

"Nothing."

"Want me to confess the truth to them? To everybody?"

"No."

After a while Keating whispered:

"Will you let me give you the fee . . . everything . . . and . . ."

Roark smiled.

"I'm sorry . . ." Keating whispered, looking away.

He waited, and then the plea he knew he must not utter came out as:

"I'm scared, Howard . . ."

Roark shook his head.

"Whatever I do, it won't be to hurt you, Peter. I'm guilty, too. We both are."

"You're guilty?"

"It's I who've destroyed you, Peter. From the beginning. By helping you. There are matters in which one must not ask for help nor give it. I shouldn't have done your projects at Stanton. I shouldn't have done the Cosmo-Slotnick Building. Nor Cortlandt. I loaded you with more than you could carry. It's like an electric current too strong for the circuit. It blows the fuse. Now we'll both pay for it. It will be hard on you, but it will be harder on me."

"You'd rather . . . I went home now, Howard?"

"Yes."

At the door Keating said:

"Howard! They didn't do it on purpose."

"That's what makes it worse."

Dominique heard the sound of the car rising up the hill road. She thought it was Wynand coming home. He had worked late in the city every night of the two weeks since his return.

The motor filled the spring silence of the countryside. There was no sound in the house; only the small rustle of her hair as she leaned her head back against a chair cushion. In a moment she was not conscious of hearing the car's approach, it was so familiar at this hour, part of the loneliness and privacy outside.

She heard the car stop at the door. The door was never locked; there were no neighbors or guests to expect. She heard the door opening, and steps in the hall downstairs. The steps did not pause, but walked with familiar certainty up the stairs. A hand turned the knob of her door.

It was Roark. She thought, while she was rising to her feet, that he had never entered her room before; but he knew every part of this house; as he knew everything about her body. She felt no moment of shock, only the memory of one, a shock in the past tense, the thought: I must have been shocked when I saw him, but not now. Now, by the time she was standing before him, it seemed very simple.

She thought: The most important never has to be said between us. It has always been said like this. He did not want to see me alone. Now he's here. I waited and I'm ready.

"Good evening, Dominique."

She heard the name pronounced to fill the space of five years. She said quietly:

"Good evening, Roark."

"I want you to help me."

She was standing on the station platform of Clayton, Ohio, on the witness stand of the Stoddard trial, on the ledge of a quarry, to let herself—as she had been then—share this sentence she heard now.

"Yes, Roark."

He walked across the room he had designed for her, he sat down, facing her, the width of the room between them. She found herself seated too, not conscious of her own movements, only of his, as if his body contained two sets of nerves, his own and hers.

"Next Monday night, Dominique, exactly at eleven-thirty, I want you to drive up to the site of Cortlandt Homes."

She noticed that she was conscious of her eyelids; not painfully, but just conscious; as if they had tightened and would not move again. She had seen the first building of Cortlandt. She knew what she was about to hear.

"You must be alone in your car and you must be on your way home from some place where you had an appointment to visit, made in advance. A place that can be reached from here only by driving past Cortlandt. You must be able to prove that afterward. I want your car to run out of gas in front of Cortlandt, at eleven-thirty. Honk your horn. There's an old night watchman there. He will come out. Ask him to help you and send him to the nearest garage, which is a mile away."

She said steadily, "Yes, Roark."

"When he's gone, get out of your car. There's a big stretch of vacant land by the road, across from the building, and a kind of trench beyond. Walk to that trench as fast as you can, get to the bottom and lie down on the ground. Lie flat. After a while, you can come back to the car. You will know when to come back. See that you're found in the car and that your condition matches its condition—approximately."

"Yes, Roark."

"Have you understood?"

"Yes."

"Everything?"

"Yes. Everything."

They were standing. She saw only his eyes and that he was smiling.

She heard him say: "Good night, Dominique," he walked out and she heard his car driving away. She thought of his smile.

She knew that he did not need her help for the thing he was going to do, he could find other means to get rid of the watchman; that he had let her have a part in this, because she would not survive what was to follow if he hadn't; that this had been the test.

He had not wanted to name it; he had wanted her to understand and show no fear. She had not been able to accept the Stoddard trial, she had run from the dread of seeing him hurt by the world, but she had agreed to help him in this. Had agreed in complete serenity. She was free and he knew it.

The road ran flat across the dark stretches of Long Island, but Dominique felt as if she were driving uphill. That was the only abnormal sensation: the sensation of rising, as if her car were speeding vertically. She kept her eyes on the road, but the dashboard on the rim of her vision looked like the panel of an airplane. The clock on the dashboard said 11:10.

She was amused, thinking: I've never learned to fly a plane and now I know how it feels; just like this, the unobstructed space and no effort. And no weight. That's supposed to happen in the stratosphere—or is it the interplanetary space?—where one begins to float and there's no law of gravity. No law of any kind of gravity at all. She heard herself laughing aloud.

Just that sense of rising. . . . Otherwise, she felt normal. She had never driven a car so well. She thought: It's a dry, mechanical job, to drive a car, so I know I'm very clearheaded; because driving seemed easy, like breathing or swallowing, an immediate function requiring no attention. She stopped for red lights that hung in the air over crossings of anonymous streets in unknown suburbs, she turned corners, she passed other cars, and she was certain that no accident could happen to her tonight; her car was directed by remote control—one of those automatic rays she'd read about—was it a beacon or a radio beam?—and she only sat at the wheel.

It left her free to be conscious of nothing but small matters, and to feel careless and . . . unserious, she thought; so completely unserious. It was a kind of clarity, being more normal than normal, as crystal is more transparent than empty air. Just small matters: the thin silk of her short, black dress and the way it was pulled over her knee, the flexing of her toes inside her pump when she moved her foot, "Danny's Diner" in gold letters on a dark window that flashed past.

She had been very gay at the dinner given by the wife of some banker, important friends of Gail's, whose names she could not quite remember now. It had been a wonderful dinner in a huge Long Island mansion. They had been so glad to see her and so sorry that Gail could not come. She had eaten everything she had seen placed before her. She had had a splendid appetite—as on rare occasions of her childhood when she came running home after a day spent in the woods and her mother was so pleased, because her mother was afraid that she might grow up to be anemic.

She had entertained the guests at the dinner table with stories of her childhood, she had made them laugh, and it had been the gayest dinner party her hosts could remember. Afterward, in the drawing room, with the windows open wide to a dark sky—a moonless sky that stretched out beyond the trees, beyond the towns, all the way to the banks of the East River—she had laughed and talked, she had smiled at the people around her with a warmth that made them all speak freely of the things dearest to them, she had loved those people, and they had known they were loved, she had loved every person anywhere on earth, and some woman had said: "Dominique, I didn't know you could be so wonderful!" and she had answered: "I haven't a care in the world."

But she had really noticed nothing except the watch on her wrist and that she must be out of that house by 10:50. She had no idea of what she would say to take her leave, but by 10:45 it had been said, correctly and convincingly, and by 10:50 her foot was on the accelerator.

It was a closed roadster, black with red leather upholstery. She thought how nicely John, the chauffeur, had kept that red leather polished. There would be nothing left of the car, and it was proper that it should look its best for its last ride. Like a woman on her first night. I never dressed for my first night—I had no first night—only something ripped off me and the taste of quarry dust in my teeth.

When she saw black vertical strips with dots of light filling the glass of the car's side window, she wondered what had happened to the glass. Then she realized that she was driving along the East River and that this was New York, on the other side. She laughed and thought: No, this is not New York, this is a private picture pasted to the window of my car, all of it, here, on one small pane, under my hand, I own it, it's mine now—she ran one hand across the buildings from the Battery to Queensborough Bridge—Roark, it's mine and I'm giving it to you.

The figure of the night watchman was now fifteen inches tall in the distance. When it gets to be ten inches, I'll start, thought Dominique. She stood by the side of her car and wished the watchman would walk faster.

The building was a black mass that propped the sky in one spot. The rest of the sky sagged, intimately low over a flat stretch of ground. The closest streets and houses were years away, far on the rim of space, irregular little dents, like the teeth of a broken saw.

She felt a large pebble under the sole of her pump; it was uncomfortable, but she would not move her foot; it would make a sound. She was not alone. She knew that he was somewhere in that building, the width of a street away from her. There was no sound and no light in the building; only white crosses on black windows. He would need no light; he knew every hall, every stairwell.

The watchman had shrunk away. She jerked the door of her car open. She threw her hat and bag inside, and flung the door shut. She heard the slam of sound when she was across the road, running over the empty tract, away from the building.

She felt the silk of her dress clinging to her legs, and it served as a tangible purpose of flight, to push against that, to tear past that barrier as fast as she could. There were pits and dry stubble on the ground. She fell once, but she noticed it only when she was running again.

She saw the trench in the darkness. Then she was on her knees, at the bottom, and then stretched flat on her stomach, face down, her mouth pressed to the earth.

She felt the pounding in her thighs and she twisted her body once in a long convulsion, to feel the earth with her legs, her breasts, the skin of her arms. It was like lying in Roark's bed.

The sound was the crack of a fist on the back of her head. She felt the thrust of the earth against her, flinging her up, to her feet, to the edge of the trench. The upper part of the Cortlandt building had tilted and hung still while a broken streak of sky grew slowly across it. As if the sky were slicing the building in half. Then the streak became turquoise blue light. Then there was no upper part, but only window frames and girders flying through the air, the building spreading over the sky, a long, thin tongue of red shooting from the center, another blow of a fist, and then another, a blinding flash and the glass panes of the skyscrapers across the river glittering like spangles.

She did not remember that he had ordered her to lie flat, that she was standing, that glass and twisted iron were raining around her. In the flash when the walls rose outward and a building opened like a sunburst, she thought of him there, somewhere beyond, the builder who had to destroy, who knew every crucial point of that structure, who had made the delicate balance of stress and support; she thought of him selecting these key spots, placing the blast, a doctor turned murderer, expertly cracking heart, brain and lungs at once. He was there, he saw it and what it did to him was worse than what it did to the building. But he was there and he welcomed it.

She saw the city enveloped in the light for half a second, she could see window ledges and cornices miles away, she thought of dark rooms and ceilings licked by this fire, she saw the peaks of towers lighted against the sky, her city now and his. "Roark!" she screamed. "Roark! Roark!" She did not know she screamed. She could not hear her voice in the blast.

Then she was running across the field to the smoking ruin, running over broken glass, planting her feet down full with each step, because she enjoyed the pain. There was no pain left ever to be felt by her again. A spread of dust stood over the field like an awning. She heard the shriek of sirens starting far away.

It was still a car, though the rear wheels were crushed under a piece of furnace machinery, and an elevator door lay over the hood. She crawled to the seat. She had to look as if she had not moved from here. She gathered handfuls of glass off the floor and poured it over her lap, over her hair. She took a sharp splinter and slashed the skin of her neck, her legs, her arms. What she felt was not pain. She saw blood shooting out of her arm, running down on her lap, soaking the black silk, trickling between her thighs. Her head fell back, mouth open, panting. She did not want to stop. She was free. She was invulnerable. She did not know she had cut an artery. She felt so light. She was laughing at the law of gravity.

When she was found by the men of the first police car to reach the scene, she was unconscious, a few minutes' worth of life left in her body.

XIII

DOMINIQUE GLANCED ABOUT THE BEDROOM OF THE PENTHOUSE. IT was her first contact with surroundings she was ready to recognize. She knew she had been brought here after many days in a hospital. The bedroom seemed lacquered with light. It's that clarity of crystal over everything, she thought; that has remained; it will remain forever. She saw Wynand standing by her bed. He was watching her. He looked amused.

She remembered seeing him at the hospital. He had not looked amused then. She knew the doctor had told him she would not survive, that first night. She had wanted to tell them all that she would, that she had no choice now but to live; only it did not seem important to tell people anything, ever.

Now she was back. She could feel bandages on her throat, her legs, her left arm. But her hands lay before her on the blanket, and the gauze had been removed; there were only a few thin red scars left.

"You blasted little fool!" said Wynand happily. "Why did you have to make such a good job of it?"

Lying on the white pillow, with her smooth gold hair and a white, high-necked hospital gown, she looked younger than she had ever looked as a child. She had the quiet radiance presumed and never found in childhood: the full consciousness of certainty, of innocence, of peace.

"I ran out of gas," she said, "and I was waiting there in my car when suddenly . . ."

"I've already told that story to the police. So has the night watchman. But didn't you know that glass must be handled with discretion?"

Gail looks rested, she thought, and very confident. It has changed everything for him, too; in the same way.

"It didn't hurt," she said.

"Next time you want to play the innocent bystander, let me coach you."

"They believe it though, don't they?"

"Oh yes, they believe it. They have to. You almost died. I don't see why he had to save the watchman's life and almost take yours."

"Who?"

"Howard, my dear. Howard Roark."

"What has he to do with it?"

"Darling, you're not being questioned by the police. You will be, though, and you'll have to be more convincing than that. However, I'm sure you'll succeed. They won't think of the Stoddard trial."

"Oh."

"You did it then and you'll always do it. Whatever you think of him, you'll always feel what I feel about his work."

"Gail, you're glad I did it?"

"Yes."

She saw him looking down at her hand that lay on the edge of the bed. Then he was on his knees, his lips pressed to her hand, not raising it, not touching it with his fingers, only with his mouth. That was the sole confession he would permit himself of what her days in the hospital had cost him. She lifted her other hand and moved it over his hair. She thought: It will be worse for you than if I had died, Gail, but it will be all right, it won't hurt you, there's no pain left in the world, nothing to compare with the fact that we exist: he, you and I—you've understood all that matters, though you don't know you've lost me.

He lifted his head and got up.

"I didn't intend to reproach you in any way. Forgive me."

"I won't die, Gail. I feel wonderful."

"You look it."

"Have they arrested him?"

"He's out on bail."

"You're happy?"

"I'm glad you did it and that it was for him. I'm glad he did it. He had to."

"Yes. And it will be the Stoddard trial again."

"Not quite."

"You've wanted another chance, Gail? All these years?"

"Yes."

"May I see the papers?"

"No. Not until you're up."

"Not even the *Banner?*"

"Particularly not the *Banner.*"

"I love you, Gail. If you stick to the end . . ."

"Don't offer me any bribes. This is not between you and me. Not even between him and me."

"But between you and God?"

"If you want to call it that. But we won't discuss it. Not until after it's over. You have a visitor waiting for you downstairs. He's been here every day."

"Who?"

"Your lover. Howard Roark. Want to let him thank you now?"

The gay mockery, the tone of uttering the most preposterous thing he could think of, told her how far he was from guessing the rest. She said:

"Yes. I want to see him. Gail, if I decide to make him my lover?"

"I'll kill you both. Now don't move, lie flat, the doctor said you must take it easy, you've got twenty-six assorted stitches all over you."

He walked out and she heard him descending the stairs.

When the first policeman had reached the scene of the explosion, he had found, behind the building, on the shore of the river, the plunger that had set off the dynamite. Roark stood by the plunger, his hands in his pockets, looking at the remnants of Cortlandt.

"What do you know about this, buddy?" the policeman asked.

"You'd better arrest me," said Roark. "I'll talk at the trial."

He had not added another word in reply to all the official questions that followed.

It was Wynand who got him released on bail, in the early hours of the morning. Wynand had been calm at the emergency hospital where he had seen Dominique's wounds and had been told she would not live. He had been calm while he telephoned, got a county judge out of bed and arranged Roark's bail. But when he stood in the warden's office of a small county jail, he began to shake suddenly. "You bloody fools!" he said through his teeth and there followed every obscenity he had learned on the waterfront. He forgot all the aspects of the situation save one: Roark being held behind bars. He was Stretch Wynand of Hell's Kitchen again and this was the kind of fury that had shattered him in sudden flashes in those days, the fury he had felt when standing behind a crumbling wall, waiting to be killed. Only now he knew that he was also Gail Wynand, the owner of an empire, and he couldn't understand why some sort of legal procedure was necessary, why he didn't smash this jail, with his fists or through his papers, it was all one to him at the moment, he wanted to kill, he had to kill, as that night behind the wall, in defense of his life.

He managed to sign papers, he managed to wait until Roark was brought out to him. They walked out together, Roark leading him by the wrist, and by the time they reached the car, Wynand was calm. In the car, Wynand asked:

"You did it, of course?"

"Of course."

"We'll fight it out together."

"If you want to make it your battle."

"At the present estimate, my personal fortune amounts to forty million dollars. That should be enough to hire any lawyer you wish or the whole profession."

"I won't use a lawyer."

"Howard! You're not going to submit photographs again?"

"No. Not this time."

Roark entered the bedroom and sat down on a chair by the bed. Dominique lay still, looking at him. They smiled at each other. Nothing has to be said, not this time either, she thought.

She asked:

"You were in jail?"

"For a few hours."

"What was it like?"

"Don't start acting about it as Gail did."

"Gail took it very badly?"

"Very."

"I won't."

"I might have to go back to a cell for years. You knew that when you agreed to help me."

"Yes. I knew that."

"I'm counting on you to save Gail, if I go."

"Counting on me?"

He looked at her and shook his head. "Dearest . . ." It sounded like a reproach.

"Yes?" she whispered.

"Don't you know by now that it was a trap I set for you?"

"How?"

"What would you do if I hadn't asked you to help me?"

"I'd be with you, in your apartment, at the Enright House, right now, publicly and openly."

"Yes. But now you can't. You're Mrs. Gail Wynand, you're above suspicion, and everyone believes you were at the scene by accident. Just let it be known what we are to each other—and it will be a confession that I did it."

"I see."

"I want you to keep quiet. If you had any thoughts of wanting to share my fate, drop them. I won't tell you what I intend to do, because that's the only way I have of controlling you until the trial. Dominique, if I'm convicted, I want you to remain with Gail. I'm counting on that. I want you to remain with him, and never tell him about us, because he and you will need each other."

"And if you're acquitted?"

"Then . . ." He glanced about the room, Wynand's bedroom. "I don't want to say it here. But you know it."

"You love him very much?"

"Yes."

"Enough to sacrifice . . ."

He smiled. "You've been afraid of that ever since I came here for the first time?"

"Yes."

He looked straight at her. "Did you think that possible?"

"No."

"Not my work nor you, Dominique. Not ever. But I can do this much for him: I can leave it to him if I have to go."

"You'll be acquitted."

"That's not what I want to hear you say."

"If they convict you—if they lock you in jail or put you in a chain gang—if they smear your name in every filthy headline—if they never let you design another building—if they never let me see you again—it will not matter. Not too much. Only down to a certain point."

"That's what I've waited to hear for seven years, Dominique."

He took her hand, he raised it and held it to his lips, and she felt his lips where Wynand's had been. Then he got up.

"I'll wait," she said. "I'll keep quiet. I won't come near you. I promise."

He smiled and nodded. Then he left.

"It happens, upon rare occasions, that world forces too great to comprehend become focused in a single event, like rays gathered by a lens to one point of superlative brightness, for all of us to see. Such an event is the outrage of Cortlandt. Here, in a microcosm, we can observe the evil that has crushed our poor planet from the day of its birth in cosmic ooze. One man's Ego against all the concepts of mercy, humanity and brotherhood. One man destroying the future home of the disinherited. One man condemning thousands to the horror of the slums, to filth, disease and death. When an awakening society, with a new sense of humanitarian duty, made a mighty effort to rescue the underprivileged, when the best talents of society united to create a decent home for them—the egotism of one man blew the achievement of others to pieces. And for what? For some vague matter of personal vanity, for some empty conceit. I regret that the laws of our state allow nothing more than a prison sentence for this crime. That man should forfeit his life. Society needs the right to rid itself of men such as Howard Roark."

Thus spoke Ellsworth M. Toohey in the pages of the *New Frontiers*.

Echoes answered him from all over the country. The explosion of Cortlandt had lasted half a minute. The explosion of public fury went on and on, with a cloud of powdered plaster filling the air, with glass, rust and refuse raining out of the cloud.

Roark had been indicted by a grand jury, had pleaded "Not guilty" and had refused to make any other statement. He had been released on a bond furnished by Gail Wynand, and he awaited trial.

There were many speculations on his motive. Some said it was professional jealousy. Others declared that there was a certain similarity between the design of Cortlandt and Roark's style of building, that Keating, Prescott and Webb might have borrowed a little from Roark—"a legitimate adaptation"—"there's no property rights on ideas"—"in a democracy, art belongs to all the people"—and that Roark had been prompted by the vengeance lust of an artist who had believed himself plagiarized.

None of it was too clear, but nobody cared too much about the motive. The issue was simple: one man against many. He had no right to a motive.

A home, built in charity, for the poor. Built upon ten thousand years in which men had been taught that charity and self-sacrifice are an absolute not to be questioned, the touchstone of virtue, the ultimate ideal. Ten thousand years of voices speaking of service and sacrifice— sacrifice is the prime rule of life—serve or be served—crush or get crushed—sacrifice is noble—make what you can of it, at the one end or the other—serve and sacrifice—serve and serve and serve . . .

Against that—one man who wished neither to serve nor to rule. And had thereby committed the only unforgivable crime.

It was a sensational scandal, and there was the usual noise and the usual lust of righteous anger, such as is proper to all lynchings. But there was a fierce, personal quality in the indignation of every person who spoke about it.

"He's just an egomaniac devoid of all moral sense"—

—said the society woman dressing for a charity bazaar, who dared not contemplate what means of self-expression would be left to her and how she could impose her ostentation on her friends, if charity were not the all-excusing virtue—

—said the social worker who had found no aim in life and could generate no aim from within the sterility of his soul, but basked in virtue and held an unearned respect from all, by grace of his fingers on the wounds of others—

—said the novelist who had nothing to say if the subject of service and sacrifice were to be taken away from him, who sobbed in the hearing of attentive thousands that he loved them and loved them and would they please love him a little in return—

—said the lady columnist who had just bought a country mansion because she wrote so tenderly about the little people—

—said all the little people who wanted to hear of love, the great love, the unfastidious love, the love that embraced everything, forgave everything and permitted them everything—

—said every second-hander who could not exist except as a leech on the souls of others.

Ellsworth Toohey sat back, watched, listened and smiled.

Gordon L. Prescott and Gus Webb were entertained at dinners and cocktail parties; they were treated with tender, curious solicitude, like survivors of disaster. They said that they could not understand what possible motive Roark could have had, and they demanded justice.

Peter Keating went nowhere. He refused to see the press. He refused to see anyone. But he issued a written statement that he believed Roark was not guilty. His statement contained one curious sentence, the last. It said: "Leave him alone, please can't you leave him alone?"

Pickets from the Council of American Builders paced in front of the Cord Building. It served no purpose, because there was no work in Roark's office. The commissions he was to start had been canceled.

This was solidarity. The debutante having her toenails pedicured—the housewife buying carrots from a pushcart—the bookkeeper who had wanted to be a pianist, but had the excuse of a sister to support—the businessman who hated his business—the worker who hated his work—the intellectual who hated everybody—all were united as brothers in the luxury of common anger that cured boredom and took them out of themselves, and they knew well enough what a blessing it was to be taken out of themselves. The readers were unanimous. The press was unanimous.

Gail Wynand went against the current.

"Gail!" Alvah Scarret had gasped. "We can't defend a dynamiter!"

"Keep still, Alvah," Wynand had said, "before I bash your teeth in."

Gail Wynand stood alone in the middle of his office, his head thrown back, glad to be living, as he had stood on a wharf on a dark night facing the lights of a city.

"In the filthy howling now going on all around us," said an editorial in the *Banner,* signed "Gail Wynand" in big letters, "nobody seems to remember that Howard Roark surrendered himself of his own free will. If he blew up that building—did he have to remain at the scene to be arrested? But we don't wait to discover his reasons. We have convicted him without a hearing. We want him to be guilty. We are delighted with this case. What you hear is not indignation—it's gloating. Any illiterate maniac, any worthless moron who commits some revolting murder, gets shrieks of sympathy from us and marshals an army of humanitarian defenders. But a man of genius is guilty by definition. Granted that it is a vicious injustice to condemn a man simply because he is weak and small. To what level of depravity has a society descended when it condemns a man simply because he is strong and great? Such, however, is the whole moral atmosphere of our century—the century of the second-rater."

"We hear it shouted," said another Wynand editorial, "that Howard Roark spends his career in and out of courtrooms. Well, that is true. A man like Roark is on trial before society all his life. Whom does that indict—Roark or society?"

"We have never made an effort to understand what is greatness in man and how to recognize it," said another Wynand editorial. "We have come to hold, in a kind of mawkish stupor, that greatness is to be gauged by self-sacrifice. Self-sacrifice, we drool, is the ultimate virtue. Let's stop and think for a moment. Is sacrifice a virtue? Can a man sacrifice his integrity? His honor? His freedom? His ideal? His convictions? The honesty of his feeling? The independence of his thought? But these are a man's supreme possessions. Anything he gives up for them is not a sacrifice but an easy bargain. They, however, are above sacrificing to any cause or consideration whatsoever. Should we not, then, stop preaching dangerous and vicious nonsense? *Self*-sacrifice? But it is precisely the self that cannot and must not be sacrificed. It is the unsacrificed self that we must respect in man above all."

This editorial was quoted in the *New Frontiers* and in many newspapers, reprinted in a box under the heading: "Look who's talking!"

Gail Wynand laughed. Resistance fed him and made him stronger. This was a war, and he had not engaged in a real war for years, not since the time when he laid the foundations of his empire amid cries of protest from the whole profession. He was granted the impossible, the dream of every man: the chance and intensity of youth, to be used with the wisdom of experience. A new beginning and a climax, together. I have waited and lived, he thought, for this.

His twenty-two newspapers, his magazines, his newsreels were given the order: Defend Roark. Sell Roark to the public. Stem the lynching.

"Whatever the facts," Wynand explained to his staff, "this is not going to be a trial by facts. It's a trial by public opinion. We've always made public opinion. Let's make it. Sell Roark. I don't care how you do it. I've trained you. You're experts at selling. Now show me how good you are."

He was greeted by silence, and his employees glanced at one another. Alvah Scarret mopped his forehead. But they obeyed.

The *Banner* printed a picture of the Enright House, with the caption:

"Is this the man you want to destroy?" A picture of Wynand's home: "Match this, if you can." A picture of Monadnock Valley: "Is this the man who has contributed nothing to society?"

The *Banner* ran Roark's biography, under the byline of a writer nobody had ever heard of; it was written by Gail Wynand. The *Banner* ran a series on famous trials in which innocent men had been convicted by the majority prejudice of the moment. The *Banner* ran articles on men martyred by society: Socrates, Galileo, Pasteur, the thinkers, the scientists, a long, heroic line—each a man who stood alone, the man who defied men.

"But, Gail, for God's sake, Gail, it was a *housing project!*" wailed Alvah Scarret.

Wynand looked at him helplessly: "I suppose it's impossible to make you fools understand that that has nothing to do with it. All right. We'll talk about housing projects."

The *Banner* ran an exposé of the housing racket: the graft, the incompetence, the structures erected at five times the cost a private builder would have needed, the settlements built and abandoned, the horrible performance accepted, admired, forgiven, protected by the sacred cow of altruism. "Hell is said to be paved with good intentions," said the *Banner.* "Could it be because we've never learned to distinguish what intentions constitute the good? Is it not time to learn? Never have there been so many good intentions so loudly proclaimed in the world. And look at it."

The *Banner* editorials were written by Gail Wynand as he stood at a table in the composing room, written as always on a huge piece of print stock, with a blue pencil, in letters an inch high. He slammed the G W at the end, and the famous initials had never carried such an air of reckless pride.

Dominique had recovered and returned to their country house. Wynand drove home late in the evening. He brought Roark along as often as he could. They sat together in the living room, with the windows open to the spring night. The dark stretches of the hill rolled gently down to the lake from under the walls of the house, and the lake glittered through the trees far below. They did not talk of the case or of the coming trial. But Wynand spoke of his crusade, impersonally, almost as if it did not concern Roark at all. Wynand stood in the middle of the room, saying:

"All right, it was contemptible—the whole career of the *Banner.* But this will vindicate everything. Dominique, I know you've never been able to understand why I've felt no shame in my past. Why I love the *Banner.* Now you'll see the answer. Power. I hold a power I've never tested. Now you'll see the test. They'll think what I want them to think.

They'll do as I say. Because it is *my* city and I *do* run things around here. Howard, by the time you come to trial, I'll have them all twisted in such a way there won't be a jury who'll dare convict you."

He could not sleep at night. He felt no desire to sleep. "Go on to bed," he would say to Roark and Dominique, "I'll come up in a few minutes." Then, Dominique from the bedroom, Roark from the guest room across the hall, would hear Wynand's steps pacing the terrace for hours, a kind of joyous restlessness in the sound, each step like a sentence anchored, a statement pounded into the floor.

Once, when Wynand dismissed them, late at night, Roark and Dominique went up the stairs together and stopped on the first landing; they heard the violent snap of a match in the living room below, a sound that carried the picture of a hand jerked recklessly, lighting the first of the cigarettes that would last till dawn, a small dot of fire crossing and recrossing the terrace to the pounding of steps.

They looked down the stairs and then looked at each other.

"It's horrible," said Dominique.

"It's great," said Roark.

"He can't help you, no matter what he does."

"I know he can't. That's not the point."

"He's risking everything he has to save you. He doesn't know he'll lose me if you're saved."

"Dominique, which will be worse for him—to lose you or to lose his crusade?" She nodded, understanding. He added: "You know that it's not me he wants to save. I'm only the excuse."

She lifted her hand. She touched his cheekbone, a faint pressure of her finger tips. She could allow herself nothing else. She turned and went on to her bedroom, and heard him closing the guest-room door.

"Is it not appropriate," wrote Lancelot Clokey in a syndicated article, "that Howard Roark is being defended by the Wynand papers? If anyone doubts the moral issues involved in this appalling case, here is the proof of what's what and who stands where. The Wynand papers—that stronghold of yellow journalism, vulgarity, corruption and muckraking, that organized insult to public taste and decency, that intellectual underworld ruled by a man who has less conception of principles than a cannibal—the Wynand papers are the proper champions of Howard Roark, and Howard Roark is their rightful hero. After a lifetime devoted to blasting the integrity of the press, it is only fit that Gail Wynand should now support a cruder fellow dynamiter."

"All this fancy talk going 'round," said Gus Webb in a public speech, "is a lot of bull. Here's the plain dope. That guy Wynand's salted away plenty, and I mean plenty, by skinning suckers in the real-estate racket all these years. Does he like it when the government muscles in and shoves him out, so's the little fellows can get a clean roof over their heads and a modern john for their kids? You bet your boots he don't like it, not one bit. It's a put-up job between the two of them, Wynand and that redheaded boy friend of his, and if you ask me the boy friend got a good hunk of cash out of Mr. Wynand for pulling the job."

"We have it from an unimpeachable source," wrote a radical newspaper, "that Cortlandt was only the first step in a gigantic plot to blow up every housing project, every public power plant, post office and school house in the U.S.A. The conspiracy is headed by Gail Wynand—as we can see—and by other bloated capitalists of his kind, including some of our biggest moneybags."

"Too little attention has been paid to the feminine angle of this case," wrote Sally Brent in the *New Frontiers*. "The part played by Mrs. Gail Wynand is certainly highly dubious, to say the least. Isn't it just the cutest coincidence that it was Mrs. Wynand who just so conveniently sent the watchman away at just the right time? And that her husband is now raising the roof to defend Mr. Roark? If we weren't blinded by a stupid, senseless, old-fashioned sense of gallantry where a so-called beautiful woman is concerned, we wouldn't allow that part of the case to be hushed up. If we weren't overawed by Mrs. Wynand's social position and the so-called prestige of her husband—who's making an utter fool of himself—we'd ask a few questions about the story that she almost lost her life in the disaster. How do we know she did? Doctors can be bought, just like anybody else, and Mr. Gail Wynand is an expert in such matters. If we consider all this, we might well see the outlines of something that looks like a most revolting 'design for living.' "

"The position taken by the Wynand press," wrote a quiet, conservative newspaper, "is inexplicable and disgraceful."

The circulation of the *Banner* dropped week by week, the speed accelerating in the descent, like an elevator out of control. Stickers and buttons inscribed "We Don't Read Wynand" grew on walls, subway posts, windshields and coat lapels. Wynand newsreels were booed off the theater screens. The *Banner* vanished from corner newsstands; the news vendors had to carry it, but they hid it under their counters and produced it grudgingly, only upon request. The ground had been prepared, the pillars eaten through long ago; the Cortlandt case provided the final impact.

Roark was almost forgotten in the storm of indignation against Gail Wynand. The angriest protests came from Wynand's own public: from the Women's Clubs, the ministers, the mothers, the small shopkeepers. Alvah Scarret had to be kept away from the room where hampers of letters to the editor were being filled each day; he started by reading the letters—and his friends on the staff undertook to prevent a repetition of the experience, fearing a stroke.

The staff of the *Banner* worked in silence. There were no furtive glances, no whispered cuss words, no gossip in washrooms any longer. A few men resigned. The rest worked on, slowly, heavily, in the manner of men with life belts buckled, waiting for the inevitable.

Gail Wynand noticed a kind of lingering tempo in every action around him. When he entered the Banner Building, his employees stopped at sight of him; when he nodded to them, their greeting came a second too late; when he walked on and turned, he found them staring after him. The "Yes, Mr. Wynand," that had always answered his orders without a moment's cut between the last syllable of his voice and the first letter of the answer, now came late, and the pause had a tangible shape, so that the answer sounded like a sentence not followed but preceded by a question mark.

"One Small Voice" kept silent about the Cortlandt case. Wynand had summoned Toohey to his office, the day after the explosion, and had said: "Listen, you. Not a word in your column. Understand? What you do or yell outside is none of my business—for the time being. But if you yell too much, I'll take care of you when this is over."

"Yes, Mr. Wynand."

"As far as your column is concerned, you're deaf, dumb and blind. You've never heard of any explosion. You've never heard of anyone named Roark. You don't know what the word Cortlandt means. So long as you're in this building."

"Yes, Mr. Wynand."

"And don't let me see too much of you around here."

"Yes, Mr. Wynand."

Wynand's lawyer, an old friend who had served him for years, tried to stop him.

"Gail, what's the matter? You're acting like a child. Like a green amateur. Pull yourself together, man."

"Shut up," said Wynand.

"Gail, you are . . . you were the greatest newspaperman on earth. Do I have to tell you the obvious? An unpopular cause is a dangerous business for anyone. For a popular newspaper—it's suicide."

"If you don't shut your mouth, I'll send you packing and get myself another shyster."

Wynand began to argue about the case—with the prominent men he met at business luncheons and dinners. He had never argued before on any subject; he had never pleaded. He had merely tossed final statements to respectful listeners. Now he found no listeners. He found an indifferent silence, half boredom, half resentment. The men who had gathered every word he cared to drop about the stock market, real estate, advertising, politics, had no interest in his opinion on art, greatness and abstract justice.

He heard a few answers:

"Yes, Gail, yes, sure. But on the other hand, I think it was damn selfish of the man. And that's the trouble with the world today—selfishness. Too much selfishness everywhere. That's what Lancelot Clokey said in his book—swell book, all about his childhood, you read it, saw your picture with Clokey. Clokey's been all over the world, he knows what he's talking about."

"Yes, Gail, but aren't you kind of old-fashioned about it? What's all that great man stuff? What's great about a glorified bricklayer? Who's great anyway? We're all just a lot of glands and chemicals and whatever we ate for breakfast. I think Lois Cook explained it very well in that beautiful little—what's its name?—yes, *The Gallant Gallstone*. Yes, sir. Your own *Banner* plugged like blazes for that little book."

"But look, Gail, he should've thought of other people before he thought of himself. I think if a man's got no love in his heart he can't be much good. I heard that in a play last night—that was a grand play—the new one by Ike—what the hell's his last name?—you ought to see it—your own Jules Fougler said it's a brave and tender stage poem."

"You make out a good case, Gail, and I wouldn't know what to say against it, I don't know where you're wrong, but it doesn't sound right to me, because Ellsworth Toohey—now don't misunderstand me, I don't agree with Toohey's political views at all, I know he's a radical, but on the other hand you've got to admit that he's a great idealist with a heart as big as a house—well, Ellsworth Toohey said . . ."

These were the millionaires, the bankers, the industrialists, the businessmen who could not understand why the world was going to hell, as they moaned in all their luncheon speeches.

One morning when Wynand stepped out of his car in front of the Banner Building, a woman rushed up to him as he crossed the sidewalk. She had been waiting by the entrance. She was fat and middle-aged. She wore a filthy cotton dress and a crushed hat. She had a pasty, sagging face, a shapeless mouth and black, round, brilliant eyes. She stood before Gail Wynand and she flung a bunch of rotted beet leaves at his face. There were no beets, just the leaves, soft and slimy, tied with a string. They hit his cheek and rolled down to the sidewalk.

Wynand stood still. He looked at the woman. He saw the white flesh, the mouth hanging open in triumph, the face of self-righteous evil. Passers-by had seized the woman and she was screaming unspeakable obscenities. Wynand raised his hand, shook his head, gesturing for them to let the creature go, and walked into the Banner Building, a smear of greenish-yellow across his cheek.

"Ellsworth, what are we going to do?" moaned Alvah Scarret. "What are we going to do?"

Ellsworth Toohey sat perched on the edge of his desk, and smiled as if he wished he could kiss Alvah Scarret.

"Why don't they drop the damn thing, Ellsworth? Why doesn't something break to take it off the front pages? Couldn't we scare up an international situation or something? In all my born days I've never seen people go so wild over so little. A dynamiting job! Christ, Ellsworth, it's a back-page story. We get them every month, practically with every strike, remember?—the furriers' strike, the dry cleaners' strike . . . oh what the hell! Why all this fury? Who cares? Why do they care?"

"There are occasions, Alvah, when the issues at stake are not the ostensible facts at all. And the public reaction seems out of all proportion, but isn't. You shouldn't be so glum about it. I'm surprised at you. You should be thanking your stars. You see, this is what I meant by waiting for the right moment. The right moment always comes. Damned if I expected it to be handed to me on a platter like that, though. Cheer up, Alvah. This is where we take over."

"Take over what?"

"The Wynand papers."

"You're crazy, Ellsworth. Like all of them. You're crazy. What do you mean? Gail holds fifty-one per cent of . . ."

"Alvah, I love you. You're wonderful, Alvah. I love you, but I wish to God you weren't such a God-damn fool, so I could talk to you! I wish I could talk to somebody."

Ellsworth Toohey tried to talk to Gus Webb, one evening, but it was disappointing. Gus Webb drawled:

"Trouble with you, Ellsworth, is you're too romantic. Too God-damn metaphysical. What's all the gloating about? There's no practical value to the thing. Nothing to get your teeth into, except for a week or two. I wish he'd blasted it when it was full of people—a few children blown to pieces—then you'd have something. Then I'd love it. The movement could use it. But this? Hell, they'll send the fool to the clink and that's that. You—a realist? You're an incurable specimen of the intelligentsia, Ellsworth, that's all you are. You think you're the man of the future? Don't kid yourself, sweetheart. I am."

Toohey sighed. "You're right, Gus," he said.

XIV

"IT'S KIND OF YOU, MR. TOOHEY," SAID MRS. KEATING HUMBLY. "I'M glad you came. I don't know what to do with Petey. He won't see anyone. He won't go to his office. I'm scared, Mr. Toohey. Forgive me, I mustn't whine. Maybe you can help, pull him out of it. He thinks so much of you, Mr. Toohey."

"Yes, I'm sure. Where is he?"

"Right here. In his room. This way, Mr. Toohey."

The visit was unexpected. Toohey had not been here for years. Mrs. Keating felt very grateful. She led the way down the hall and opened a door without knocking, afraid to announce the visitor, afraid of her son's refusal. She said brightly:

"Look, Petey, look what a guest I have for you!"

Keating lifted his head. He sat at a littered table, bent under a squat lamp that gave a poor light; he was doing a crossword puzzle torn out of a newspaper. There was a tall glass on the table, with a dried red rim that had been tomato juice; a box containing a jigsaw puzzle; a deck of cards; a Bible.

"Hello, Ellsworth," he said, smiling. He leaned forward to rise, but forgot the effort, halfway.

Mrs. Keating saw the smile and stepped out hastily, relieved, closing the door.

The smile went, not quite completed. It had been an instinct of memory. Then he remembered many things which he had tried not to understand.

"Hello, Ellsworth," he repeated helplessly.

Toohey stood before him, examining the room, the table, with curiosity.

"Touching, Peter," he said. "Very touching. I'm sure he'd appreciate it if he saw it."

"Who?"

"Not very talkative these days, are you, Peter? Not very sociable?"

"I wanted to see you, Ellsworth. I wanted to talk to you."

Toohey grasped a chair by the back, swung it through the air, in a broad circle like a flourish, planted it by the table and sat down.

"Well, that's what I came here for," he said. "To hear you talk."

Keating said nothing.

"Well?"

"You mustn't think I didn't want to see you, Ellsworth. It was only . . . what I told mother about not letting anyone in . . . it was on account of the newspaper people. They won't leave me alone."

"My, how times change, Peter. I remember when one couldn't keep you away from newspaper people."

"Ellsworth, I haven't any sense of humor left. Not any at all."

"That's lucky. Or you'd die laughing."

"I'm so tired, Ellsworth. . . . I'm glad you came."

The light glanced off Toohey's glasses and Keating could not see his eyes; only two circles filled with a metallic smear, like the dead head-lights of a car reflecting the approach of something from a distance.

"Think you can get away with it?" asked Toohey.

"With what?"

"The hermit act. The great penance. The loyal silence."

"Ellsworth, what's the matter with you?"

"So he's not guilty, is he? So you want us to please leave him alone, do you?"

Keating's shoulders moved, more an intention than the reality of sitting up straight, but still an intention, and his jaw moved enough to ask:

"What do you want?"

"The whole story."

"What for?"

"Want me to make it easier for you? Want a good excuse, Peter? I could, you know. I could give you thirty-three reasons, all noble, and you'd swallow any one of them. But I don't feel like making it easier for you. So I'll just tell you the truth: to send him to the penitentiary, your hero, your idol, your generous friend, your guardian angel!"

"I have nothing to tell you, Ellsworth."

"While you're being shocked out of the last of your wits you'd better hang on to enough to realize that you're no match for me. You'll talk if I want you to talk and I don't feel like wasting time. Who designed Cortlandt?"

"I did."

"Do you know that I'm an architectural expert?"

"I designed Cortlandt."

"Like the Cosmo-Slotnick Building?"

"What do you want from me?"

"I want you on the witness stand, Petey. I want you to tell the story in court. Your friend isn't as obvious as you are. I don't know what he's up to. That remaining at the scene was a bit too smart. He knew he'd be suspected and he's playing it subtle. God knows what he intends to say in court. I don't intend to let him get away with it. The motive is what they're all stuck on. I know the motive. Nobody will believe me if I try to explain it. But you'll state it under oath. You'll tell the truth. You'll tell them who designed Cortlandt and why."

"I designed it."

"If you want to say that on the stand, you'd better do something about your muscular control. What are you shaking for?"

"Leave me alone."

"Too late, Petey. Ever read *Faust?*"

"What do you want?"

"Howard Roark's neck."

"He's not my friend. He's never been. You know what I think of him."

"I know, you God-damn fool! I know you've worshiped him all your life. You've knelt and worshiped, while stabbing him in the back. You didn't even have the courage of your own malice. You couldn't go one way or the other. You hated me—oh, don't you suppose I knew it? —and you followed me. You loved him and you've destroyed him. Oh, you've destroyed him all right, Petey, and now there's no place to run, and you'll have to go through with it!"

"What's he to you? What difference does it make to you?"

"You should have asked that long ago. But you didn't. Which means that you knew it. You've always known it. That's what's making you shake. Why should I help you lie to yourself? I've done that for ten years. That's what you came to me for. That's what they all come to me for. But you can't get something for nothing. Ever. My socialistic theories to the contrary notwithstanding. You got what you wanted from me. It's my turn now."

"I won't talk about Howard. You can't make me talk about Howard."

"No? Why don't you throw me out of here? Why don't you take me by the throat and choke me? You're much stronger than I am. But you won't. You can't. Do you see the nature of power, Petey? Physical power? Muscle or guns or money? You and Gail Wynand should get together. You have a lot to tell him. Come on, Peter. Who designed Cortlandt?"

"Leave me alone."

"Who designed Cortlandt?"

"Let me go!"

"Who designed Cortlandt?"

"It's worse . . . what you're doing . . . it's much worse . . ."

"Than what?"

"Than what I did to Lucius Heyer."

"What did you do to Lucius Heyer?"

"I killed him."

"What are you talking about?"

"That's why it was better. Because I let him die."

"Stop raving."

"Why do you want to kill Howard?"

"I don't want to kill him. I want him in jail. You understand? In jail. In a cell. Behind bars. Locked, stopped, strapped—and alive. He'll get up when they tell him to. He'll eat what they give him. He'll move when he's told to move and stop when he's told. He'll walk to the jute mill, when he's told, and he'll work as he's told. They'll push him, if he doesn't move fast enough, and they'll slap his face when they feel like it, and they'll beat him with rubber hose if he doesn't obey. And he'll obey. He'll take orders. *He'll take orders!*"

"Ellsworth!" Keating screamed. "Ellsworth!"

"You make me sick. Can't you take the truth? No, you want your sugar-coating. That's why I prefer Gus Webb. There's one who has no illusions."

Mrs. Keating threw the door open. She had heard the scream.

"Get out of here!" Toohey snapped at her.

She backed out, and Toohey slammed the door.

Keating raised his head. "You have no right to talk to Mother that way. She had nothing to do with you."

"Who designed Cortlandt?"

Keating got up. He dragged his feet to a dresser, opened a drawer, took out a crumpled piece of paper and handed it to Toohey. It was his contract with Roark.

Toohey read it and chuckled once, a dry snap of sound. Then he looked at Keating.

"You're a complete success, Peter, as far as I'm concerned. But at times I have to want to turn away from the sight of my successes."

Keating stood by the dresser, his shoulders slumped, his eyes empty.

"I didn't expect you to have it in writing like that, with his signature. So that's what he's done for you—and this is what you do in return. . . . No, I take back the insults, Peter. You had to do it. Who are you to reverse the laws of history? Do you know what this paper is? The impossible perfect, the dream of the centuries, the aim of all of mankind's great schools of thought. You harnessed him. You made him work for you. You took his achievement, his reward, his money, his glory, his name. We only thought and wrote about it. You gave a practical demonstration. Every philosopher from Plato up should thank you. Here it is, the philosopher's stone—for turning gold into lead. I should be pleased, but I guess I'm human and I can't help it, I'm not pleased,

I'm just sick. The others, Plato and all the rest, they really thought it would turn lead into gold. I knew the truth from the first. I've been honest with myself, Peter, and that's the hardest form of honesty. The one you all run from at any price. And right now I don't blame you, it *is* the hardest one, Peter."

He sat down wearily and held the paper by the corners in both hands. He said:

"If you want to know how hard it is, I'll tell you: right now I want to burn this paper. Make what you wish of that. I don't claim too great a credit, because I know that tomorrow I'll send this to the district attorney. Roark will never know it—and it would make no difference to him if he knew—but in the truth of things, there was one moment when I wanted to burn this paper."

He folded the paper cautiously and slipped it into his pocket. Keating followed his gestures, moving his whole head, like a kitten watching a ball on a string.

"You make me sick," said Toohey. "God, how you make me sick, all you hypocritical sentimentalists! You go along with me, you spout what I teach you, you profit by it—but you haven't the grace to admit to yourself what you're doing. You turn green when you see the truth. I suppose that's in the nature of your natures and that's precisely my chief weapon—but God! I get tired of it. I must allow myself a moment free of you. That's what I have to put on an act for all my life—for mean little mediocrities like you. To protect your sensibilities, your posturings, your conscience and the peace of the mind you haven't got. That's the price I pay for what I want—but at least I know that I've got to pay it. And I have no illusions about the price or the purchase."

"What do you . . . want . . . Ellsworth?"

"Power, Petey."

There were steps in the apartment above, someone skipping gaily, a few sounds on the ceiling as of four or five tap beats. The light fixture jingled and Keating's head moved up in obedience. Then it came back to Toohey. Toohey was smiling, almost indifferently.

"You . . . always said . . ." Keating began thickly, and stopped.

"I've always said just that. Clearly, precisely and openly. It's not my fault if you couldn't hear. You could, of course. You didn't want to. Which was safer than deafness—for me. I said I intended to rule. Like all my spiritual predecessors. But I'm luckier than they were. I inherited the fruit of their efforts and I shall be the one who'll see the great dream made real. I see it all around me today. I recognize it. I don't like it. I didn't expect to like it. Enjoyment is not my destiny. I shall find such satisfaction as my capacity permits. I shall rule."

"Whom . . . ?"

"You. The world. It's only a matter of discovering the lever. If you learn how to rule one single man's soul, you can get the rest of mankind. It's the soul, Peter, the soul. Not whips or swords or fire or guns. That's why the Caesars, the Attilas, the Napoleons were fools and did not last. We will. The soul, Peter, is that which can't be ruled. It must be broken. Drive a wedge in, get your fingers on it—and the man is yours. You won't need a whip—he'll bring it to you and ask to be whipped. Set him in reverse—and his own mechanism will do your work for you. Use him against himself. Want to know how it's done? See if I ever lied to you. See if you haven't heard all this for years, but didn't want to hear, and the fault is yours, not mine. There are many ways. Here's one. Make man feel small. Make him feel guilty. Kill his aspiration and his integrity. That's difficult. The worst among you gropes for an ideal in his own twisted way. Kill integrity by internal corruption. Use it against itself. Direct it toward a goal destructive of all integrity. Preach selflessness. Tell man that he must live for others. Tell men that altruism is the ideal. Not a single one of them has ever achieved it and not a single one ever will. His every living instinct screams against it. But don't you see what you accomplish? Man realizes that he's incapable of what he's accepted as the noblest virtue—and it gives him a sense of guilt, of sin, of his own basic unworthiness. Since the supreme ideal is beyond his grasp, he gives up eventually all ideals, all aspiration, all sense of his personal value. He feels himself obliged to preach what he can't practice. But one can't be good halfway or honest approximately. To preserve one's integrity is a hard battle. Why preserve that which one knows to be corrupt already? His soul gives up its self-respect. You've got him. He'll obey. He'll be glad to obey—because he can't trust himself, he feels uncertain, he feels unclean. That's one way. Here's another. Kill man's sense of values. Kill his capacity to recognize greatness or to achieve it. Great men can't be ruled. We don't want any great men. Don't deny the conception of greatness. Destroy it from within. The great is the rare, the difficult, the exceptional. Set up standards of achievement open to all, to the least, to the most inept—and you stop the impetus to effort in all men, great or small. You stop all incentive to improvement, to excellence, to perfection. Laugh at Roark and hold Peter Keating as a great architect. You've destroyed architecture. Build up Lois Cook and you've destroyed literature. Hail Ike and you've destroyed the theater. Glorify Lancelot Clokey and you've destroyed the press. Don't set out to raze all shrines—you'll frighten men. Enshrine mediocrity—and the shrines are razed. Then there's another way. Kill by laughter. Laughter is an instrument of human joy. Learn to use it as a weapon of destruction. Turn it into a sneer. It's simple. Tell them to laugh at everything. Tell them that a sense of humor is an unlimited virtue. Don't let anything remain sacred in a man's soul—and his soul won't be sacred to him. Kill reverence and you've killed the hero in man. One doesn't reverence with a giggle. He'll obey and he'll set no limits to his obedience—anything goes—nothing is too serious. Here's another way. This is most important. Don't allow men to be happy. Happiness is self-contained and self-sufficient. Happy men have no time and no use for you. Happy men are free men. So kill their joy in living. Take away from them whatever is dear or important to them. Never let them have what they want. Make them feel that the mere fact of a personal desire is evil. Bring them to a state where saying 'I want' is no longer a natural right, but a shameful admission. Altruism is of great help in this. Unhappy men will come to you. They'll need you. They'll come for consolation, for support, for escape. Nature allows no vacuum. Empty man's soul—and the space is yours to fill. I don't see why you should look so shocked, Peter. This is the oldest one of all. Look back at history. Look at any great system of ethics, from the Orient up. Didn't they all preach the sacrifice of personal joy? Under all the complications of verbiage, haven't they all had a single leitmotif: sacrifice, renunciation, self-denial? Haven't you been able to catch their theme song—'Give up, give up, give up, give up'? Look at the moral atmosphere of today. Everything enjoyable, from cigarettes to sex to ambition to the profit motive, is considered depraved or sinful. Just prove that a thing makes men happy—and you've damned it. That's how far we've come. We've tied happiness to guilt. And we've got mankind by the throat. Throw your first-born into a sacrificial furnace—lie on a bed of nails—go into the desert to mortify the flesh—don't dance—don't go to the movies on Sunday—don't try to get rich—don't smoke—don't drink. It's all the same line. The great line. Fools think that taboos of this nature are just nonsense. Something left over, old-fashioned. But there's always a purpose in nonsense. Don't bother to examine a folly—ask yourself only what it accomplishes. Every system of ethics that preached sacrifice grew into a world power and ruled millions of men. Of course, you must dress it up. You must tell people that they'll achieve a superior kind of happiness by giving up everything that makes them happy. You don't have to be too clear about it. Use big vague words. 'Universal Harmony'—'Eternal Spirit'—'Divine Purpose' —'Nirvana'—'Paradise'—'Racial Supremacy'—'The Dictatorship of the Proletariat.' Internal corruption, Peter. That's the oldest one of all. The farce has been going on for centuries and men still fall for it. Yet the test should be so simple: just listen to any prophet and if you hear him speak of sacrifice—run. Run faster than from a plague. It stands to reason that where there's sacrifice, there's someone collecting sacrificial offerings. Where there's service, there's someone being served. The man who speaks to you of sacrifice, speaks of slaves and masters. And intends to be the master. But if ever you hear a man telling you that you must be happy, that it's your natural right, that your first duty is to yourself—that will be the man who's not after your soul. That will be the man who has nothing to gain from you. But let him come and you'll scream your empty heads off, howling that he's a selfish monster. So the racket is safe for many, many centuries. But here you might have noticed something. I said, 'It stands to reason.' Do you see? Men have a weapon against you. Reason. So you must be very sure to take it away from them. Cut the props from under it. But be careful. Don't deny outright. Never deny anything outright, you give your hand away. Don't say reason is evil—though some have gone that far and with astonishing success. Just say that reason is limited. That there's something above it. What? You don't have to be too clear about it either. The field's inexhaustible. 'Instinct'—'Feeling'—'Revelation'—'Divine Intuition'—'Dialectic Materialism.' If you get caught at some crucial point and somebody tells you that your doctrine doesn't make sense—you're ready for him. You tell him that there's something above sense. That here he must not try to think, he must *feel*. He must *believe*. Suspend reason and you play it deuces wild. Anything goes in any manner you wish whenever you need it. You've got him. Can you rule a thinking man? We don't want any thinking men."

Keating had sat down on the floor, by the side of the dresser; he had felt tired and he had simply folded his legs. He did not want to abandon the dresser; he felt safer, leaning against it; as if it still guarded the letter he had surrendered.

"Peter, you've heard all this. You've seen me practicing it for ten years. You see it being practiced all over the world. Why are you disgusted? You have no right to sit there and stare at me with the virtuous superiority of being shocked. You're in on it. You've taken your share and you've got to go along. You're afraid to see where it's leading. I'm not. I'll tell you. The world of the future. The world I want. A world of obedience and of unity. A world where the thought of each man will not be his own, but an attempt to guess the thought in the brain of his neighbor who'll have no thought of his own but an attempt to guess the thought of the next neighbor who'll have no thought—and so on, Peter, around the globe. Since all must agree with all. A world where no man will hold a desire for himself, but will direct all his efforts to satisfy the desires of his neighbor who'll have no desires except to satisfy the desires of the next neighbor who'll have no desires—around the globe, Peter. Since all must serve all. A world in which man will not work for so innocent an incentive as money, but for that headless monster—prestige. The approval of his fellows—their good opinion—the opinion of men who'll be allowed to hold no opinion. An octopus, all tentacles and no brain.

Judgment, Peter? Not judgment, but public polls. An average drawn upon zeroes—since no individuality will be permitted. A world with its motor cut off and a single heart, pumped by hand. My hand—and the hands of a few, a very few other men like me. Those who know what makes you tick—you great, wonderful average, you who have not risen in fury when we called you the average, the little, the common, you who've liked and accepted those names. You'll sit enthroned and enshrined, you, the little people, the absolute ruler to make all past rulers squirm with envy, the absolute, the unlimited, God and Prophet and King combined. Vox populi. The average, the common, the general. Do you know the proper antonym for Ego? Bromide, Peter. The rule of the bromide. But even the trite has to be originated by someone at some time. We'll do the originating. Vox dei. We'll enjoy unlimited submission—from men who've learned nothing except to submit. We'll call it 'to serve.' We'll give out medals for service. You'll fall over one another in a scramble to see who can submit better and more. There will be no other distinction to seek. No other form of personal achievement. Can you see Howard Roark in the picture? No? Then don't waste time on foolish questions. Everything that can't be ruled, must go. And if freaks persist in being born occasionally, they will not survive beyond their twelfth year. When their brain begins to function, it will feel the pressure and it will explode. The pressure gauged to a vacuum. Do you know the fate of deep-sea creatures brought out to sunlight? So much for future Roarks. The rest of you will smile and obey. Have you noticed that the imbecile always smiles? Man's first frown is the first touch of God on his forehead. The touch of thought. But we'll have neither God nor thought. Only voting by smiles. Automatic levers—all saying yes . . . Now if you were a little more intelligent—like your ex-wife, for instance—you'd ask: What of us, the rulers? What of me, Ellsworth Monkton Toohey? And I'd say, Yes, you're right. I'll achieve no more than you will. I'll have no purpose save to keep you contented. To lie, to flatter you, to praise you, to inflate your vanity. To make speeches about the people and the common good. Peter, my poor old friend, I'm the most selfless man you've ever known. I have less independence than you, whom I just forced to sell your soul. You've used people at least for the sake of what you could get from them for yourself. I want nothing for myself. I use people for the sake of what I can do to them. It's my only function and satisfaction. I have no private purpose. I want power. I want my world of the future. Let all live for all. Let all sacrifice and none profit. Let all suffer and none enjoy. Let progress stop. Let all stagnate. There's equality in stagnation. All subjugated to the will of all. Universal slavery—without even the dignity of a master. Slavery to slavery. A great circle—and a total equality. The world of the future."

"Ellsworth . . . you're . . ."

"Insane? Afraid to say it? There you sit and the word's written all over you, your last hope. Insane? Look around you. Pick up any newspaper and read the headlines. Isn't it coming? Isn't it here? Every single thing I told you? Isn't Europe swallowed already and we're stumbling on to follow? Everything I said is contained in a single word—collectivism. And isn't that the god of our century? To act together. To think—together. To feel—together. To unite, to agree, to obey. To obey, to serve, to sacrifice. Divide and conquer—first. But then—unite and rule. We've discovered that one at last. Remember the Roman Emperor who said he wished humanity had a single neck so he could cut it? People have laughed at him for centuries. But we'll have the last laugh. We've accomplished what he couldn't accomplish. We've taught men to unite. This makes one neck ready for one leash. We've found the magic word. Collectivism. Look at Europe, you fool. Can't you see past the guff and recognize the essence? One country is dedicated to the proposition that man has no rights, that the collective is all. The individual held as evil, the mass—as God. No motive and no virtue permitted—except that of service to the proletariat. That's one version. Here's another. A country dedicated to the proposition that man has no rights, that the State is all. The individual held as evil, the race—as God. No motive and no virtue permitted—except that of service to the race. Am I raving or is this the cold reality of two continents already? Watch the pincer movement. If you're sick of one version, we push you into the other. We get you coming and going. We've closed the doors. We've fixed the coin. Heads —collectivism, and tails—collectivism. Fight the doctrine which slaughters the individual with a doctrine which slaughters the individual. Give up your soul to a council—or give it up to a leader. But give it up, give it up, give it up. My technique, Peter. Offer poison as food and poison as antidote. Go fancy on the trimmings, but hang on to the main objective. Give the fools a choice, let them have their fun—but don't forget the only purpose you have to accomplish. Kill the individual. Kill man's soul. The rest will follow automatically. Observe the state of the world as of the present moment. Do you still think I'm crazy, Peter?"

Keating sat on the floor, his legs spread out. He lifted one hand and studied his finger tips, then put it to his mouth and bit off a hangnail. But the movement was deceptive; the man was reduced to a single sense, the sense of hearing, and Toohey knew that no answer could be expected.

Keating waited obediently; it seemed to make no difference; the sounds had stopped and it was now his function to wait until they started again.

Toohey put his hands on the arms of his chair, then lifted his palms, from the wrists, and clasped the wood again, a little slap of resigned finality. He pushed himself up to his feet.

"Thank you, Peter," he said gravely. "Honesty is a hard thing to eradicate. I have made speeches to large audiences all my life. This was the speech I'll never have a chance to make."

Keating lifted his head. His voice had the quality of a down payment on terror; it was not frightened, but it held the advance echoes of the next hour to come:

"Don't go, Ellsworth."

Toohey stood over him, and laughed softly.

"That's the answer, Peter. That's my proof. You know me for what I am, you know what I've done to you, you have no illusions of virtue left. But you can't leave me and you'll never be able to leave me. You've obeyed me in the name of ideals. You'll go on obeying me without ideals. Because that's all you're good for now. . . . Good night, Peter."

XV

"THIS IS A TEST CASE. WHAT WE THINK OF IT WILL DETERMINE what we are. In the person of Howard Roark, we must crush the forces of selfishness and antisocial individualism—the curse of our modern world—here shown to us in ultimate consequences. As mentioned at the beginning of this column, the district attorney now has in his possession a piece of evidence—we cannot disclose its nature at this moment—which proves conclusively that Roark is guilty. We, the people, shall now demand justice."

This appeared in "One Small Voice" on a morning late in May. Gail Wynand read it in his car, driving home from the airport. He had flown to Chicago in a last attempt to hold a national advertiser who had refused to renew a three-million dollar contract. Two days of skillful effort had failed; Wynand lost the advertiser. Stepping off the plane in Newark, he picked up the New York papers. His car was waiting to take him to his country house. Then he read "One Small Voice."

He wondered for a moment what paper he held. He looked at the name on the top of the page. But it was the *Banner,* and the column was there, in its proper place, column one, first page, second section.

He leaned forward and told the chauffeur to drive to his office. He sat with the page spread open on his lap, until the car stopped before the Banner Building.

He noticed it at once, when he entered the building. In the eyes of two reporters who emerged from an elevator in the lobby; in the pose of the elevator man who fought a desire to turn and stare back at him; in the sudden immobility of all the men in his anteroom, in the break of a typewriter's clicking on the desk of one secretary, in the lifted hand of another—he saw the waiting. Then he knew that all the implications of the unbelievable were understood by everyone on his paper.

He felt a first dim shock; because the waiting around him contained wonder, and something was wrong if there could be any wonder in anyone's mind about the outcome of an issue between him and Ellsworth Toohey.

But he had no time to take notice of his own reactions. He had no attention to spare for anything except a sense of tightness, a pressure against the bones of his face, his teeth, his cheeks, the bridge of his nose—and he knew he must press back against that, keep it down, hold it.

He greeted no one and walked into his office. Alvah Scarret sat

671

slumped in a chair before his desk. Scarret had a bandage of soiled white gauze on his throat, and his cheeks were flushed. Wynand stopped in the middle of the room. The people outside had felt relieved: Wynand's face looked calm. Alvah Scarret knew better.

"Gail, I wasn't here," he gulped in a cracked whisper that was not a voice at all. "I haven't been here for two days. Laryngitis, Gail. Ask my doctor. I wasn't here. I just got out of bed, look at me, I've got a hundred and three, fever, I mean, the doctor didn't want me to, but I . . . to get up, I mean, Gail, I wasn't here, I wasn't here!"

He could not be certain that Wynand heard. But Wynand let him finish, then assumed the appearance of listening, as if the sounds were reaching him, delayed. After a moment, Wynand asked:

"Who was on the copy desk?"

"It . . . it went through Allen and Falk."

"Fire Harding, Allen, Falk and Toohey. Buy off Harding's contract. But not Toohey's. Have them all out of the building in fifteen minutes."

Harding was the managing editor; Falk, a copyreader; Allen, the slot man, head of the copy desk; all had worked on the *Banner* for more than ten years. It was as if Scarret had heard a news flash announcing the impeachment of a President, the destruction of New York City by a meteor and the sinking of California into the Pacific Ocean.

"Gail!" he screamed. "We can't!"

"Get out of here."

Scarret got out.

Wynand pressed a switch on his desk and said in answer to the trembling voice of the woman outside:

"Don't admit anyone."

"Yes, Mr. Wynand."

He pressed a button and spoke to the circulation manager.

"Stop every copy on the street."

"Mr. Wynand, it's too late! Most of them are . . ."

"Stop them."

"Yes, Mr. Wynand."

He wanted to put his head down on the desk, lie still and rest, only the form of rest he needed did not exist, greater than sleep, greater than death, the rest of having never lived. The wish was like a secret taunt against himself, because he knew that the splitting pressure in his skull meant the opposite, an urge to action, so strong that he felt paralyzed. He fumbled for some sheets of clean paper, forgetting where he kept them. He had to write the editorial that would explain and counteract. He had to hurry. He felt no right to any minute that passed with the thing unwritten.

The pressure disappeared with the first word he put on paper. He thought—while his hand moved rapidly—what a power there was in words; later, for those who heard them, but first for the one who found them; a healing power, a solution, like the breaking of a barrier. He thought, perhaps the basic secret the scientists have never discovered, the first fount of life, is that which happens when a thought takes shape in words.

He heard the rumble, the vibration in the walls of his office, in the floor. The presses were running off his afternoon paper, a small tabloid, the *Clarion*. He smiled at the sound. His hand went faster, as if the sound were energy pumped into his fingers.

He had dropped his usual editorial "we." He wrote: ". . . And if my readers or my enemies wish to laugh at me over this incident, I shall accept it and consider it the payment of a debt incurred. I have deserved it."

He thought: It's the heart of this building, beating—what time is it?—do I really hear it or is it my own heart?—once, a doctor put the ends of his stethoscope into my ears and let me hear my own heartbeats —it sounded just like this—he said I was a healthy animal and good for many years—for many . . . years . . .

"I have foisted upon my readers a contemptible blackguard whose spiritual stature is my only excuse. I had not reached a degree of contempt for society such as would have permitted me to consider him dangerous. I am still holding on to a respect for my fellow men sufficient to let me say that Ellsworth Toohey cannot be a menace."

They say sound never dies, but travels on in space—what happens to a man's heartbeats?—so many of them in fifty-six years—could they be gathered again, in some sort of condenser, and put to use once more? If they were re-broadcast, would the result be the beating of those presses?

"But I have sponsored him under the masthead of my paper, and if public penance is a strange, humiliating act to perform in our modern age, such is the punishment I impose upon myself hereby."

Not fifty-six years of those soft little drops of sound a man never hears, each single and final, not like a comma, but like a period, a long string of periods on a page, gathered to feed those presses—not fifty-six, but thirty-one, the other twenty-five went to make me ready—I was twenty-five when I raised the new masthead over the door—Publishers don't change the name of a paper—This one does—The New York *Banner*—Gail Wynand's *Banner* . . .

"I ask the forgiveness of every man who has ever read this paper."

A healthy animal—and that which comes from me is healthy—I must bring that doctor here and have him listen to those presses—he'll grin in his good, smug, satisfied way, doctors like a specimen of perfect health occasionally, it's rare enough—I must give him a treat—the healthiest sound he ever heard—and he'll say the *Banner* is good for many years. . . .

The door of his office opened and Ellsworth Toohey came in.

Wynand let him cross the room and approach the desk, without a gesture of protest. Wynand thought that what he felt was curiosity—if curiosity could be blown into the dimensions of a thing from the abyss —like those drawings of beetles the size of a house advancing upon human figures in the pages of the *Banner's* Sunday supplement—curiosity, because Ellsworth Toohey was still in the building, because Toohey had gained admittance past the orders given, and because Toohey was laughing.

"I came to take my leave of absence, Mr. Wynand," said Toohey. His face was composed; it expressed no gloating; the face of an artist who knew that overdoing was defeat and achieved the supreme of offensiveness by remaining normal. "And to tell you that I'll be back. On this job, on this column, in this building. In the interval you will have seen the nature of the mistake you've made. Do forgive me, I know this is in utterly bad taste, but I've waited for it for thirteen years and I think I can permit myself five minutes as a reward. So you were a possessive man, Mr. Wynand, and you loved your sense of property? Did you ever stop to think what it rested upon? Did you stop to secure the foundations? No, because you were a practical man. Practical men deal in bank accounts, real estate, advertising contracts and gilt-edged securities. They leave to the impractical intellectuals, like me, the amusements of putting the gilt edges through a chemical analysis to learn a few things about the nature and the source of gold. They hang on to Kream-O Pudding, and leave us such trivia as the theater, the movies, the radio, the schools, the book reviews and the criticism of architecture. Just a sop to keep us quiet if we care to waste our time playing with the inconsequentials of life, while you're making money. Money is power. Is it, Mr. Wynand? So you were after power, Mr. Wynand? Power over men? You poor amateur! You never discovered the nature of your own ambition or you'd have known that you weren't fit for it. You couldn't use the methods required and you wouldn't want the results. You've never been enough of a scoundrel. I don't mind handing you that, because I don't know which is worse: to be a great scoundrel or a gigantic fool. That's why I'll be back. And when I am, I'll run this paper."

Wynand said quietly:

"When you are. Now get out of here."

The city room of the *Banner* walked out on strike.

The Union of Wynand Employees walked out in a body. A great many others, non-members, joined them. The typographical staff remained.

Wynand had never given a thought to the Union. He paid higher wages than any other publisher and no economic demands had ever been made upon him. If his employees wished to amuse themselves by listening to speeches, he saw no reason to worry about it. Dominique had tried to warn him once: "Gail, if people want to organize for wages, hours or practical demands, it's their proper right. But when there's no tangible purpose, you'd better watch closely." "Darling, how many times do I have to ask you? Keep off the *Banner*."

He had never taken the trouble to learn who belonged to the Union. He found now that the membership was small—and crucial; it included all his key men, not the big executives, but the rank below, expertly chosen, the active ones, the small, indispensable spark plugs: the best leg men, the general assignment men, the rewrite men, the assistant editors. He looked up their records: most of them had been hired in the last eight years; recommended by Mr. Toohey.

Non-members walked out for various reasons: some, because they hated Wynand; others, because they were afraid to remain and it seemed easier than to analyze the issue. One man, a timid little fellow, met Wynand in the hall and stopped to shriek: "We'll be back, sweetheart, and then it'll be a different tune!" Some left, avoiding the sight of Wynand. Others played safe. "Mr. Wynand, I hate to do it, I hate it like hell, I had nothing to do with that Union, but a strike's a strike and I can't permit myself to be a scab." "Honest, Mr. Wynand, I don't know who's right or wrong, I do think Ellsworth pulled a dirty trick and Harding had no business letting him get away with it, but how can one be sure who's right about anything nowadays? And one thing I won't do is I won't cross a picket line. No, sir. The way I feel is, pickets right or wrong."

The strikers presented two demands: the reinstatement of the four men who had been discharged; a reversal of the *Banner's* stand on the Cortlandt case.

Harding, the managing editor, wrote an article explaining his position; it was published in the *New Frontiers*. "I did ignore Mr. Wynand's orders in a matter of policy, perhaps an unprecedented action for a managing editor to take. I did so with full realization of the responsibility involved. Mr. Toohey, Allen, Falk and I wished to save the *Banner* for the sake of its employees, its stockholders and its readers. We wished to bring Mr. Wynand to reason by peaceful means. We hoped he would give in with good grace, once he had seen the *Banner* committed to the stand shared by most of the press of the country. We knew the arbitrary, unpredictable and unscrupulous character of our employer, but we took the chance, willing to sacrifice ourselves to our professional duty. While we recognize an owner's right to dictate the policy of his paper on political, sociological or economic issues, we believe that a situation has gone past the limits of decency when an employer expects self-respecting men to espouse the cause of a common criminal. We wish Mr. Wynand to realize that the day of dictatorial one-man rule is past. We must have some say in the running of the place where we make our living. It is a fight for the freedom of the press."

Mr. Harding was sixty years old, owned an estate on Long Island, and divided his spare time between skeet-shooting and breeding pheasants. His childless wife was a member of the Board of Directors of the Workshop for Social Study; Toohey, its star lecturer, had introduced her to the Workshop. She had written her husband's article.

The two men off the copy desk were not members of Toohey's Union. Allen's daughter was a beautiful young actress starred in all of Ike's plays. Falk's brother was secretary to Lancelot Clokey.

Gail Wynand sat at the desk in his office and looked down at a pile of paper. He had many things to do, but one picture kept coming back to him and he could not get rid of it and the sense of it clung to all his actions—the picture of a ragged boy standing before the desk of an editor: "Can you spell cat?"—"Can you spell anthropomorphology?" The identities cracked and became mixed, it seemed to him that the boy stood here, at his desk, waiting, and once he said aloud: "Go away!" He caught himself in anger, he thought: You're cracking, you fool, now's not the time. He did not speak aloud again, but the conversation went on silently while he read, checked and signed papers: "Go away! We have no jobs here." "I'll hang around. Use me when you want to. You don't have to pay me." "They're paying you, don't you understand, you little fool? They're paying you." Aloud, his voice normal, he said into a telephone: "Tell Manning that we'll have to fill in with mat stuff. . . . Send up the proofs as soon as you can. . . . Send up a sandwich. Any kind."

A few had remained with him: the old men and the copy boys. They came in, in the morning, often with cuts on their faces and blood on their collars; one stumbled in, his skull open, and had to be sent away in an ambulance. It was neither courage nor loyalty; it was inertia; they had lived too long with the thought that the world would end if they lost their jobs on the *Banner*. The old ones did not understand. The young ones did not care.

Copy boys were sent out on reporters' beats. Most of the stuff they sent in was of such quality that Wynand was forced past despair into howls of laughter: he had never read such highbrow English; he could see the pride of the ambitious youth who was a journalist at last. He did not laugh when the stories appeared in the *Banner* as written; there were not enough rewrite men.

He tried to hire new men. He offered extravagant salaries. The people he wanted refused to work for him. A few men answered his call, and he wished they hadn't, though he hired them. They were men who had not been employed by a reputable newspaper for ten years; the kind who would not have been allowed, a month ago, into the lobby of his building. Some of them had to be thrown out in two days; others remained. They were drunk most of the time. Some acted as if they were granting Wynand a favor. "Don't you get huffy, Gail, old boy," said one—and was tossed bodily down two flights of stairs. He broke an ankle and sat on the bottom landing, looking up at Wynand with an air of complete astonishment. Others were subtler; they merely stalked about and looked at Wynand slyly, almost winking, implying that they were fellow criminals tied together in a dirty deal.

He appealed to schools of journalism. No one responded. One student body sent him a resolution signed by all its members: ". . . Entering our careers with a high regard for the dignity of our profession, dedicating ourselves to uphold the honor of the press, we feel that none among us could preserve his self-respect and accept an offer such as yours."

The news editor had remained at his desk; the city editor had gone. Wynand filled in as city editor, managing editor, wire man, rewrite man, copy boy. He did not leave the building. He slept on a couch in his office—as he had done in the first years of the *Banner's* existence. Coatless, tieless, his shirt collar torn open, he ran up and down the stairs, his steps like the rattle of a machine gun. Two elevator boys had remained; the others had vanished, no one knew just when or why, whether prompted by sympathy for the strike, fear or plain discouragement.

Alvah Scarret could not understand Wynand's calm. The brilliant machine—and that, thought Scarret, was really the word which had always stood for Wynand in his mind—had never functioned better. His words were brief, his orders rapid, his decisions immediate. In the confusion of machines, lead, grease, ink, waste paper, unswept offices, untenanted desks, glass crashing in sudden showers when a brick was hurled from the street below, Wynand moved like a figure in double-exposure, superimposed on his background, out of place and scale. He doesn't belong here, thought Scarret, because he doesn't look modern—that's what it is—he doesn't look modern, no matter what kind of pants he's wearing—he looks like something out of a Gothic cathedral. The patrician head, held level, the fleshless face that had shrunk tighter together. The captain of a ship known by all, save the captain, to be sinking.

Alvah Scarret had remained. He had not grasped that the events were real; he shuffled about in a stupor; he felt a fresh jolt of bewilderment each morning when he drove up to the building and saw the pickets. He suffered no injury beyond a few tomatoes hurled at his windshield. He tried to help Wynand; he tried to do his work and that of five other men, but he could not complete a normal day's task. He was going quietly to pieces, his joints wrenched loose by a question mark. He wasted everybody's time, interrupting anything to ask: "But why? Why? How, just like that all of a sudden?"

He saw a nurse in white uniform walking down the hall—an emergency first-aid station had been established on the ground floor. He saw her carrying a wastebasket to the incinerator, with wadded clumps of gauze, bloodstained. He turned away; he felt sick. It was not the sight, but the greater terror of an implication grasped by his instinct: this civilized building—secure in the neatness of waxed floors, respectable with the strict grooming of modern business, a place where one dealt in such rational matters as written words and trade contracts, where one accepted ads for baby garments and chatted about golf—had become, in the span of a few days, a place where one carried bloody refuse through the halls. Why?—thought Alvah Scarret.

"I can't understand it," he droned in an accentless monotone to anyone around him, "I can't understand how Ellsworth got so much power. . . . And Ellsworth's a man of culture, an idealist, not a dirty radical off a soapbox, he's so friendly and witty, and what an erudition!—a man who jokes all the time is not a man of violence—Ellsworth didn't mean this, he didn't know what it would lead to, he loves people, I'd stake my shirt on Ellsworth Toohey."

Once, in Wynand's office, he ventured to say:

"Gail, why don't you negotiate? Why don't you meet with them at least?"

"Shut up."

"But, Gail, there might be a bit of truth on their side, too. They're newspapermen. You know what they say, the freedom of the press . . ."

Then he saw the fit of fury he had expected for days and had thought safely sidetracked—the blue irises vanishing in a white smear, the blind, luminous eyeballs in a face that was all cavities, the trembling hands. But in a moment, he saw what he had never witnessed before: he saw Wynand break the fit, without sound, without relief. He saw the sweat of the effort on the hollow temples, and the fists on the edge of the desk.

"Alvah . . . if I had not sat on the stairs of the *Gazette* for a week . . . where would be the press for them to be free on?"

There were policemen outside, and in the halls of the building. It helped, but not much. One night acid was thrown at the main entrance. It burned the big plate glass of the ground floor windows and left leprous spots on the walls. Sand in the bearings stopped one of the presses. An obscure delicatessen owner got his shop smashed for advertising in the *Banner*. A great many small advertisers withdrew. Wynand delivery trucks were wrecked. One driver was killed. The striking Union of Wynand Employees issued a protest against acts of violence; the Union had not instigated them; most of its members did not know who had. The *New Frontiers* said something about regrettable excesses, but ascribed them to "spontaneous outbursts of justifiable popular anger."

Homer Slottern, in the name of a group who called themselves the liberal businessmen, sent Wynand a notice canceling their advertising contracts. "You may sue us if you wish. We feel we have a legitimate cause for cancellation. We signed to advertise in a reputable newspaper, not in a sheet that has become a public disgrace, brings pickets to our doors, ruins our business and is not being read by anybody." The group included most of the *Banner's* wealthiest advertisers.

Gail Wynand stood at the window of his office and looked at his city.

"I have supported strikes at a time when it was dangerous to do so. I have fought Gail Wynand all my life. I had never expected to see the day or the issue when I would be forced to say—as I say now—that I stand on the side of Gail Wynand," wrote Austen Heller in the *Chronicle*.

Wynand sent him a note: "God damn you, I didn't ask you to defend me. G W"

The *New Frontiers* described Austen Heller as "a reactionary who has sold himself to Big Business." Intellectual society ladies said that Austen Heller was old-fashioned.

Gail Wynand stood at a desk in the city room and wrote editorials as usual. His derelict staff saw no change in him; no haste, no outbursts of anger. There was nobody to notice that some of his actions were new: he would go to the pressroom and stand looking at the white stream shot out of the roaring giants, and listen to the sound. He would pick up a lead slug off the composing room floor, and finger it absently on the palm of his hand, like a piece of jade, and lay it carefully on a table, as if he did not want it to be wasted. He fought other forms of such waste, not noticing it, the gestures instinctive: he retrieved pencils, he spent a half-hour, while telephones shrieked unanswered, repairing a typewriter that had broken down. It was not a matter of economy; he signed checks without looking at the figures; Scarret was afraid to think of the amounts each passing day cost him. It was a matter of things that were part of the building where he loved every doorknob, things that belonged to the *Banner* that belonged to him.

Late each afternoon he telephoned Dominique in the country. "Fine. Everything under control. Don't listen to panic-mongers. . . . No, to hell with it, you know I don't want to talk about the damn paper. Tell me what the garden looks like. . . . Did you go swimming today? . . . Tell me about the lake. . . . What dress are you wearing? . . . Listen to WLX tonight, at eight, they'll have your pet—Rachmaninoff's *Second Concerto*. . . . Of course I have time to keep informed about everything. . . . Oh, all right, I see one can't fool an ex-newspaper woman, I did go over the radio page. . . . Of course we have plenty of help, it's just that I can't quite trust some of the new boys and I had a moment to spare. . . . Above all, *don't come to town*. You promised me that. . . . Good night, dearest. . . ."

He hung up and sat looking at the telephone, smiling. The thought of the countryside was like the thought of a continent beyond an ocean that could not be crossed; it gave him a sense of being locked in a besieged fortress and he liked that—not the fact, but the feeling. His face looked like a throwback to some distant ancestor who had fought on the ramparts of a castle.

One evening he went out to the restaurant across the street; he had not eaten a complete meal for days. The streets were still light when he came back—the placid brown haze of summer, as if dulled sunrays remained stretched too comfortably on the warm air to undertake a movement of withdrawal, even though the sun had long since gone; it made the sky look fresh and the street dirty; there were patches of brown and tired orange in the corners of old buildings. He saw pickets pacing in front of the *Banner's* entrance. There were eight of them and they marched around and around in a long oval on the sidewalk. He recognized one boy—a police reporter; he had never seen any of the others. They carried signs: "Toohey, Harding, Allen, Falk . . ." "The Freedom of the Press . . ." "Gail Wynand Tramples Human Rights . . ."

His eyes kept following one woman. Her hips began at her ankles, bulging over the tight straps of her shoes; she had square shoulders and a long coat of cheap brown tweed over a huge square body. She had small white hands, the kind that would drop things all over the kitchen. She had an incision of a mouth, without lips, and she waddled as she moved, but she moved with surprising briskness. Her steps defied the whole world to hurt her, with a malicious slyness that seemed to say she would like nothing better, because what a joke it would be on the world if it tried to hurt her, just try it and see, just try it. Wynand knew she had never been employed on the *Banner;* she never could be; it did not appear likely that she could be taught to read; her steps seemed to add that she jolly well didn't have to. She carried a sign: "We demand . . ."

He thought of the nights when he had slept on the couch in the old Banner Building, in the first years, because the new presses had to be paid for and the *Banner* had to be on the streets before its competitors, and he coughed blood one night and refused to see a doctor, but it turned out to be nothing, just exhaustion.

He hurried into the building. The presses were rolling. He stood and listened for a while.

At night the building was quiet. It seemed bigger, as if sound took space and vacated it; there were panels of light at open doors, between long stretches of dim hallways. A lone typewriter clicked somewhere, evenly, like a dripping faucet. Wynand walked through the halls. He thought that men had been willing to work for him when he plugged known crooks for municipal elections, when he glamorized red-light districts, when he ruined reputations by scandalous libel, when he sobbed over the mothers of gangsters. Talented men, respected men had been eager to work for him. Now he was being honest for the first time in his career. He was leading his greatest crusade—with the help of finks, drifters, drunkards, and humble drudges too passive to quit. The guilt, he thought, was not perhaps with those who now refused to work for him.

The sun hit the square crystal inkstand on his desk. It made Wynand think of a cool drink on a lawn, white clothes, the feel of grass under bare elbows. He tried not to look at the gay glitter and went on writing. It was a morning in the second week of the strike. He had retreated to his office for an hour and given orders not to be disturbed; he had an article to finish; he knew he wanted the excuse, one hour of not seeing what went on in the building.

The door of his office opened without announcement, and Dominique came in. She had not been allowed to enter the Banner Building since their marriage.

He got up, a kind of quiet obedience in his movement, permitting himself no questions. She wore a coral linen suit, she stood as if the lake were behind her and the sunlight rose from the surface to the folds of her clothes. She said:

"Gail, I've come for my old job on the *Banner*."

He stood looking at her silently; then he smiled; it was a smile of convalescence.

He turned to the desk, picked up the sheets he had written, handed them to her and said:

"Take this to the back room. Pick up the wire flimsies and bring them to me. Then report to Manning at the city desk."

The impossible, the not to be achieved in word, glance or gesture, the complete union of two beings in complete understanding, was done by a small stack of paper passing from his hand to hers. Their fingers did not touch. She turned and walked out of the office.

Within two days, it was as if she had never left the staff of the *Banner*. Only now she did not write a column on houses, but kept busy wherever a competent hand was needed to fill a gap. "It's quite all right, Alvah," she said to Scarret, "it's a proper feminine job to be a seamstress. I'm here to slap on patches where necessary—and boy! is this cloth ripping fast! Just call me when one of your new journalists runs amuck more than usual."

Scarret could not understand her tone, her manner or her presence. "You're a lifesaver, Dominique," he mumbled sadly. "It's like the old days, seeing you here—and oh! how I wish it were the old days! Only I can't understand. Gail wouldn't allow a photo of you in the place, when it was a decent, respectable place—and now when it's practically as safe as a penitentiary during a convict riot, he lets you *work* here!"

"Can the commentaries, Alvah. We haven't the time."

She wrote a brilliant review of a movie she hadn't seen. She dashed off a report on a convention she hadn't attended. She batted out a string of recipes for the "Daily Dishes" column, when the lady in charge failed to show up one morning. "I didn't know you could cook," said Scarret. "I didn't either," said Dominique. She went out one night to cover a dock fire, when it was found that the only man on duty had passed out on the floor of the men's room. "Good job," Wynand told her when he read the story, "but try that again and you'll get fired. If you want to stay, you're not to step out of the building."

This was his only comment on her presence. He spoke to her when necessary, briefly and simply, as to any other employee. He gave orders. There were days when they did not have time to see each other. She slept on a couch in the library. Occasionally, in the evening, she would come to his office, for a short rest, when they could take it, and then they talked, about nothing in particular, about small events of the day's work, gaily, like any married couple gossiping about the normal routine of their common life.

They did not speak of Roark or Cortlandt. She had noticed Roark's picture on the wall of his office and asked: "When did you hang that up?" "Over a year ago." It had been their only reference to Roark. They did not discuss the growing public fury against the *Banner*. They did not speculate on the future. They felt relief in forgetting the question beyond the walls of the building; it could be forgotten because it stood no longer as a question between them; it was solved and answered; what remained was the peace of the simplified: they had a job to do—the job of keeping a newspaper going—and they were doing it together.

She would come in, unsummoned, in the middle of the night, with a cup of hot coffee, and he would snatch it gratefully, not pausing in his work. He would find fresh sandwiches left on his desk when he needed them badly. He had no time to wonder where she got things. Then he discovered that she had established an electric plate and a stock of supplies in a closet. She cooked breakfast for him, when he had to work all night, she came in carrying dishes on a piece of cardboard for a tray, with the silence of empty streets beyond the windows and the first light of morning on the rooftops.

Once he found her, broom in hand, sweeping an office; the maintenance department had fallen apart, charwomen appeared and disappeared, no one had time to notice.

"Is that what I'm paying you for?" he asked.

"Well, we can't work in a pigsty. I haven't asked you what you're paying me, but I want a raise."

"Drop this thing, for God's sake! It's ridiculous."

"What's ridiculous? It's clean now. It didn't take me long. Is it a good job?"

"It's a good job."

She leaned on the broom handle and laughed. "I believe you thought, like everybody else, that I'm just a kind of luxury object, a high-class type of kept woman, didn't you, Gail?"

"Is this the way you can keep going when you want to?"

"This is the way I've wanted to keep going all my life—if I could find a reason for it."

He learned that her endurance was greater than his. She never showed a sign of exhaustion. He supposed that she slept, but he could not discover when.

At any time, in any part of the building, not seeing him for hours, she was aware of him, she knew when he needed her most. Once, he fell asleep, slumped across his desk. He awakened and found her looking at him. She had turned off the lights, she sat on a chair by the window, in the moonlight, her face turned to him, calm, watching. Her face was the first thing he saw. Lifting his head painfully from his arm, in the first moment, before he could return fully to control and reality, he felt a sudden wrench of anger, helplessness and desperate protest, not remembering what had brought them here, to this, remembering only that they were both caught in some vast, slow process of torture and that he loved her.

She had seen it in his face, before he had completed the movement of straightening his body. She walked to him, she stood by his chair, she took his head and let it rest against her, she held him, and he did not resist, slumped in her arms, she kissed his hair, she whispered: "It will be all right, Gail, it will be all right."

At the end of three weeks Wynand walked out of the building one evening, not caring whether there would be anything left of it when he returned, and went to see Roark.

He had not telephoned Roark since the beginning of the siege. Roark telephoned him often; Wynand answered, quietly, just answering, originating no statement, refusing to prolong the conversation. He had warned Roark at the beginning: "Don't try to come here. I've given orders. You won't be admitted." He had to keep out of his mind the actual form which the issue of his battle could take; he had to forget the fact of Roark's physical existence; because the thought of Roark's person brought the thought of the county jail.

He walked the long distance to the Enright House; walking made the distance longer and safer; a ride in a cab would pull Roark too close to the Banner Building. He kept his glance slanted toward a point six feet ahead of him on the sidewalk; he did not want to look at the city.

"Good evening, Gail," Roark said calmly when he came in.

"I don't know what's a more conspicuous form of bad discipline," said Wynand, throwing his hat down on a table by the door, "to blurt things right out or to ignore them blatantly. I look like hell. Say it."

"You do look like hell. Sit down, rest and don't talk. Then I'll run you a hot bath—no, you don't look that dirty, but it will be good for you for a change. Then we'll talk."

Wynand shook his head and remained standing at the door.

"Howard, the *Banner* is not helping you. It's ruining you."

It had taken him eight weeks to prepare himself to say that.

"Of course," said Roark. "What of it?"

Wynand would not advance into the room.

"Gail, it doesn't matter, as far as I'm concerned. I'm not counting on public opinion, one way or the other."

"You want me to give in?"

"I want you to hold out if it takes everything you own."

He saw that Wynand understood, that it was the thing Wynand had tried not to face, and that Wynand wanted him to speak.

"I don't expect you to save me. I think I have a chance to win. The strike won't make it better or worse. Don't worry about me. And don't give in. If you stick to the end—you won't need me any longer."

He saw the look of anger, protest—and agreement. He added:

"You know what I'm saying. We'll be better friends than ever—and you'll come to visit me in jail, if necessary. Don't wince, and don't make me say too much. Not now. I'm glad of this strike. I knew that something like that had to happen, when I saw you for the first time. You knew it long before that."

"Two months ago, I promised you . . . the one promise I wanted to keep . . ."

"You're keeping it."

"Don't you really want to despise me? I wish you'd say it now. I came here to hear it."

"All right. Listen. You have been the one encounter in my life that can never be repeated. There was Henry Cameron who died for my own cause. And you're the publisher of filthy tabloids. But I couldn't say this to him, and I'm saying it to you. There's Steve Mallory who's never compromised with his soul. And you've done nothing but sell yours in every known way. But I couldn't say this to him and I'm saying it to you. Is that what you've always wanted to hear from me? *But don't give in."*

He turned away, and added: "That's all. We won't talk about your damn strike again. Sit down, I'll get you a drink. Rest, get yourself out of looking like hell."

Wynand returned to the *Banner* late at night. He took a cab. It did not matter. He did not notice the distance.

Dominique said: "You've seen Roark."

"Yes. How do you know?"

"Here's the Sunday makeup. It's fairly lousy, but it'll have to do. I sent Manning home for a few hours—he was going to collapse. Jackson quit, but we can do without him. Alvah's column was a mess—he can't even keep his grammar straight any more—I rewrote it, but don't tell him, tell him you did."

"Go to sleep. I'll take Manning's place. I'm good for hours."

They went on, and the days passed, and in the mailing room the piles of returns grew, running over into the corridor, white stacks of paper like marble slabs. Fewer copies of the *Banner* were run off with every edition, but the stacks kept growing. The days passed, days of heroic effort to put out a newspaper that came back unbought and unread.

XVI

I N THE GLASS-SMOOTH MAHOGANY OF THE LONG TABLE RESERVED FOR the board of directors there was a monogram in colored wood— G W—reproduced from his signature. It had always annoyed the directors. They had no time to notice it now. But an occasional glance fell upon it—and then it was a glance of pleasure.

The directors sat around the table. It was the first meeting in the board's history that had not been summoned by Wynand. But the meeting had convened and Wynand had come. The strike was in its second month.

Wynand stood by his chair at the head of the table. He looked like a drawing from a men's magazine, fastidiously groomed, a white handkerchief in the breast pocket of his dark suit. The directors caught themselves in peculiar thoughts: some thought of British tailors, others —of the House of Lords—of the Tower of London—of the executed English King—or was it a Chancellor?—who had died so well.

They did not want to look at the man before them. They leaned upon visions of the pickets outside—of the perfumed, manicured women who shrieked their support of Ellsworth Toohey in drawing-room discussions —of the broad, flat face of a girl who paced Fifth Avenue with a placard "We Don't Read Wynand"—for support and courage to say what they were saying.

Wynand thought of a crumbling wall on the edge of the Hudson. He heard steps approaching blocks away. Only this time there were no wires in his hand to hold his muscles ready.

"It's gone beyond all sense. Is this a business organization or a charitable society for the defense of personal friends?"

"Three hundred thousand dollars last week. . . . Never mind how I know it, Gail, no secret about it, your banker told me. All right, it's your money, but if you expect to get that back out of the sheet, let me tell you we're wise to your smart tricks. You're not going to saddle the corporation with that one, not a penny of it, you don't get away with it this time, it's too late, Gail, the day's past for your bright stunts."

Wynand looked at the fleshy lips of the man making sounds, and thought: You've run the *Banner*, from the beginning, you didn't know it, but I know, it was you, it was your paper, there's nothing to save now.

"Yes, Slottern and his bunch are willing to come back at once, all they ask is that we accept the Union's demands, and they'll pick up the balance of their contracts, on the old terms, even without waiting for you to rebuild circulation—which will be some job, friend, let me tell you—

686

and I think that's pretty white of them. I spoke to Homer yesterday and he gave me his word—care to hear me name the sums involved, Wynand, or do you know it without my help?"

"No, Senator Eldridge wouldn't see you. . . . Aw, skip it, Gail, we know you flew to Washington last week. What you don't know is that Senator Eldridge is going around saying he wouldn't touch this with a ten-foot pole. And Boss Craig suddenly got called out to Florida, did he?—to sit up with a sick aunt? None of them will pull you out of this one, Gail. This isn't a road-paving deal or a little watered-stock scandal. And you ain't what you used to be."

Wynand thought: I never used to be, I've never been here, why are you afraid to look at me? Don't you know that I'm the least among you? The half-naked women in the Sunday supplement, the babies in the rotogravure section, the editorials on park squirrels, they were your souls given expression, the straight stuff of your souls—but where was mine?

"I'll be damned if I can see any sense to it. Now, if they were demanding a raise in wages, *that* I could understand, I'd say fight the bastards for all we're worth. But what's this—a God-damn intellectual issue of some kind? Are we losing our shirts for principles or something?"

"Don't you understand? The *Banner's* a church publication now. Mr. Gail Wynand, the evangelist. We're over a barrel, but we've got ideals."

"Now if it were a real issue, a political issue—but some fool dynamiter who's blown up some dump! Everybody's laughing at us. Honest, Wynand, I've tried to read your editorials and if you want my honest opinion, it's the lousiest stuff ever put in print. You'd think you were writing for college professors!"

Wynand thought: I know you—you're the one who'd give money to a pregnant slut, but not to a starving genius—I've seen your face before—I picked you and I brought you in—when in doubt about your work, remember that man's face, you're writing for him—but, Mr. Wynand, one can't remember his face—one can, child, one can, it will come back to remind you—it will come back and demand payment—and I'll pay—I signed a blank check long ago and now it's presented for collection—but a blank check is always made out to the sum of everything you've got.

"The situation is medieval and a disgrace to democracy." The voice whined. It was Mitchell Layton speaking. "It's about time somebody had some say around here. One man running all those papers as he damn pleases—what is this, the nineteenth century?" Layton pouted; he looked somewhere in the direction of a banker across the table. "Has anybody here ever bothered to inquire about *my* ideas? I've got ideas. We've all got to pool ideas. What I mean is teamwork, one big orchestra. It's about time this paper had a modern, liberal, progressive policy! For instance, take the question of the share-croppers . . ."

"Shut up, Mitch," said Alvah Scarret. Scarret had drops of sweat running down his temples; he didn't know why; he wanted the board to win; there was just something in the room . . . it's too hot in here, he thought, I wish somebody'd open a window.

"I won't shut up!" shrieked Mitchell Layton. "I'm just as good as . . ."

"Please, Mr. Layton," said the banker.

"All right," said Layton, "all right. Don't forget who holds the biggest hunk of stock next to Superman here." He jerked his thumb at Wynand, not looking at him. "Just don't forget it. Just you guess who's going to run things around here."

"Gail," said Alvah Scarret, looking up at Wynand, his eyes strangely honest and tortured, "Gail, it's no use. But we can save the pieces. Look, if we just admit that we were wrong about Cortlandt and . . . and if we just take Harding back, he's a valuable man, and . . . maybe Toohey . . ."

"No one is to mention the name of Toohey in this discussion," said Wynand.

Mitchell Layton snapped his mouth open and dropped it shut again.

"That's it, Gail!" cried Alvah Scarret. "That's great! We can bargain and make them an offer. We'll reverse our policy on Cortlandt—that, we've got to, not for the damn Union, but we've got to rebuild circulation, Gail—so we'll offer them that and we'll take Harding, Allen and Falk, but not To . . . not Ellsworth. We give in and they give in. Saves everybody's face. Is that it, Gail?"

Wynand said nothing.

"I think that's it, Mr. Scarret," said the banker. "I think that's the solution. After all, Mr. Wynand must be allowed to maintain his prestige. We can sacrifice . . . a columnist and keep peace among ourselves."

"I don't see it!" yelled Mitchell Layton. "I don't see it at all! Why should we sacrifice Mr. . . . a great liberal, just because . . ."

"I stand with Mr. Scarret," said the man who had spoken of Senators, and the voices of the others seconded him, and the man who had criticized the editorials said suddenly, in the general noise: "I think Gail Wynand was a hell of a swell boss after all!" There was something about Mitchell Layton which he didn't want to see. Now he looked at Wynand, for protection. Wynand did not notice him.

"Gail?" asked Scarret. "Gail, what do you say?"

There was no answer.

"God damn it, Wynand, it's now or never! This can't go on!"

"Make up your mind or get out!"

"I'll buy you out!" shrieked Layton. "Want to sell? Want to sell and get the hell out of it?"

"For God's sake, Wynand, don't be a fool!"

"Gail, it's the *Banner* . . ." whispered Scarret. "It's our *Banner*. . . ."

"We'll stand by you, Gail, we'll all chip in, we'll pull the old paper back on its feet, we'll do as you say, you'll be the boss—but for God's sake, act like a boss now!"

"Quiet, gentlemen, quiet! Wynand, this is final: we switch policy on Cortlandt, we take Harding, Allen and Falk back, and we save the wreck. Yes or no?"

There was no answer.

"Wynand, you know it's that—or you have to close the *Banner*. You can't keep this up, even if you bought us all out. Give in or close the *Banner*. You had better give in."

Wynand heard that. He had heard it through all the speeches. He had heard it for days before the meeting. He knew it better than any man present. Close the *Banner*.

He saw a single picture: the new masthead rising over the door of the *Gazette*.

"You had better give in."

He made a step back. It was not a wall behind him. It was only the side of his chair.

He thought of the moment in his bedroom when he had almost pulled a trigger. He knew he was pulling it now.

"All right," he said.

It's only a bottle cap, thought Wynand looking down at a speck of glitter under his feet; a bottle cap ground into the pavement. The pavements of New York are full of things like that—bottle caps, safety pins, campaign buttons, sink chains; sometimes—lost jewels; it's all alike now, flattened, ground in; it makes the pavements sparkle at night. The fertilizer of a city. Someone drank the bottle empty and threw the cap away. How many cars have passed over it? Could one retrieve it now? Could one kneel and dig with bare hands and tear it out again? I had no right to hope for escape. I had no right to kneel and seek redemption. Millions of years ago, when the earth was being born, there were living things like me: flies caught in resin that became amber, animals caught in ooze that became rock. I am a man of the twentieth century and I became a bit of tin in the pavements, for the trucks of New York to roll over.

He walked slowly, the collar of his topcoat raised. The street stretched before him, empty, and the buildings ahead were like the backs of books lining a shelf, assembled without order, of all sizes. The corners he passed led to black channels; street lamps gave the city a protective cover, but it cracked in spots. He turned a corner when he saw a slant of light ahead; it was a goal for three or four blocks.

The light came from the window of a pawnshop. The shop was closed, but a glaring bulb hung there to discourage looters who might be reduced to this. He stopped and looked at it. He thought, the most indecent sight on earth, a pawnshop window. The things which had been sacred to men, and the things which had been precious, surrendered to the sight of all, to the pawing and the bargaining, trash to the indifferent eyes of strangers, the equality of a junk heap, typewriters and violins— the tools of dreams, old photographs and wedding rings—the tags of love, together with soiled trousers, coffee pots, ash trays, pornographic plaster figures; the refuse of despair, pledged, not sold, not cut off in clean finality, but hocked to a stillborn hope, never to be redeemed. "Hello, Gail Wynand," he said to the things in the window, and walked on.

He felt an iron grate under his feet and an odor struck him in the face, an odor of dust, sweat and dirty clothing, worse than the smell of stockyards, because it had a homey, normal quality, like decomposition made routine. The grating of a subway. He thought, this is the residue of many people put together, of human bodies pressed into a mass, with no space to move, with no air to breathe. This is the sum, even though down there, among the packed flesh, one can find the smell of starched white dresses, of clean hair, of healthy young skin. Such is the nature of sums and of quests for the lowest common denominator. What, then, is the residue of many human minds put together, unaired, unspaced, un-differentiated? The *Banner,* he thought, and walked on.

My city, he thought, the city I loved, the city I thought I ruled.

He had walked out of the board meeting, he had said: "Take over, Alvah, until I come back." He had not stopped to see Manning drunk with exhaustion at the city desk, nor the people in the city room, still functioning, waiting, knowing what was being decided in the board room; nor Dominique. Scarret would tell them. He had walked out of the building and gone to his penthouse and sat alone in the bedroom without windows. Nobody had come to disturb him.

When he left the penthouse, it was safe to go out: it was dark. He passed a newsstand and saw late editions of the afternoon papers announcing the settlement of the Wynand strike. The Union had accepted Scarret's compromise. He knew that Scarret would take care of all the rest. Scarret would replate the front page of tomorrow's *Banner.* Scarret would write the editorial that would appear on the front page. He thought, the presses are rolling right now. Tomorrow morning's *Banner* will be out on the streets in an hour.

He walked at random. He owned nothing, but he was owned by any part of the city. It was right that the city should now direct his way and that he should be moved by the pull of chance corners. Here I am, my masters, I am coming to salute you and acknowledge, wherever you want me, I shall go as I'm told. I'm the man who wanted power.

That woman sitting on the stoop of an old brownstone house, her fat white knees spread apart—the man pushing the white brocade of his stomach out of a cab in front of a great hotel—the little man sipping root beer at a drugstore counter—the woman leaning over a stained mattress on the sill of a tenement window—the taxi driver parked on a corner—the lady with orchids, drunk at the table of a sidewalk café— the toothless woman selling chewing gum—the man in shirt sleeves, leaning against the door of a poolroom—they are my masters. My owners, my rulers without a face.

Stand here, he thought, and count the lighted windows of a city. You cannot do it. But behind each yellow rectangle that climbs, one over another, to the sky—under each bulb—down to there, see that spark over the river which is not a star?—there are people whom you will never see and who are your masters. At the supper tables, in the drawing rooms, in their beds and in their cellars, in their studies and in their bathrooms. Speeding in the subways under your feet. Crawling up in elevators through vertical cracks around you. Jolting past you in every bus. Your masters, Gail Wynand. There is a net—longer than the cables that coil through the walls of this city, larger than the mesh of pipes that carry water, gas and refuse—there is another hidden net around you; it is strapped to you, and the wires lead to every hand in the city. They jerked the wires and you moved. You were a ruler of men. You held a leash. A leash is only a rope with a noose at both ends.

My masters, the anonymous, the unselected. They gave me a penthouse, an office, a yacht. To them, to any one of them who wished, for the sum of three cents, I sold Howard Roark.

He walked past an open marble court, a cave cut deep into a building, filled with light, spurting the sudden cold of air-conditioning. It was a movie theater and the marquee had letters made of rainbows: *Romeo and Juliet*. A placard stood by the glass column of the box office: "Bill Shakespeare's immortal classic! But there's nothing highbrow about it! Just a simple human love story. A boy from the Bronx meets a girl from Brooklyn. Just like the folks next door. Just like you and me."

He walked past the door of a saloon. There was a smell of stale beer. A woman sat slumped, breasts flattened against the table top. A juke box played Wagner's "Song to the Evening Star," adapted, in swing time.

He saw the trees of Central Park. He walked, his eyes lowered. He was passing by the Aquitania Hotel.

He came to a corner. He had escaped other corners like it, but this one caught him. It was a dim corner, a slice of sidewalk trapped between the wall of a closed garage and the pillars of an elevated station. He saw the rear end of a truck disappearing down the street. He had not seen the name on it, but he knew what truck it was. A newsstand crouched under the iron stairs of the elevated. He moved his eyes slowly. The fresh pile was there, spread out for him. Tomorrow's *Banner*.

He did not come closer. He stood, waiting. He thought, I still have a few minutes in which not to know.

He saw faceless people stopping at the stand, one after another. They came for different papers, but they bought the *Banner* also, when they noticed its front page. He stood pressed to the wall, waiting. He thought, it is right that I should be the last to learn what I have said.

Then he could delay no longer: no customers came, the stand stood deserted, papers spread in the yellow light of a bulb, waiting for him. He could see no vendor in the black hovel beyond the bulb. The street was empty. A long corridor filled by the skeleton of the elevated. Stone paving, blotched walls, the interlacing of iron pillars. There were lighted windows, but they looked as if no people moved inside the walls. A train thundered over his head, a long roll of clangor that went shuddering down the pillars into the earth. It looked like an aggregation of metal rushing without human driver through the night.

He waited for the sound to die, then he walked to the stand. "The *Banner*," he said. He did not see who sold him the paper, whether it was a man or a woman. He saw only a gnarled brown hand pushing the copy forward.

He started walking away, but stopped while crossing the street. There was a picture of Roark on the front page. It was a good picture. The calm face, the sharp cheekbones, the implacable mouth. He read the editorial, leaning against a pillar of the elevated.

"We have always endeavored to give our readers the truth without fear or prejudice . . .

". . . charitable consideration and the benefit of the doubt even to a man charged with an outrageous crime . . .

". . . but after conscientious investigation and in the light of new evidence placed before us, we find ourselves obliged honestly to admit that we might have been too lenient . . .

". . . A society awakened to a new sense of responsibility toward the underprivileged . . .

". . . We join the voice of public opinion . . .

". . . The past, the career, the personality of Howard Roark seem to support the widespread impression that he is a reprehensible character, a dangerous, unprincipled, antisocial type of man . . .

". . . If found guilty, as seems inevitable, Howard Roark must be made to bear the fullest penalty the law can impose on him."

It was signed "Gail Wynand."

When he looked up, he was in a brightly lighted street, on a trim sidewalk, looking at a wax figure exquisitely contorted on a satin chaise longue in a shop window; the figure wore a salmon-colored negligee, lucite sandals and a string of pearls suspended from one raised finger.

He did not know when he had dropped the paper. It was not in his hands any longer. He glanced back. It would be impossible to find a discarded paper lying on some street he did not know he had passed. He thought, what for? There are other papers like it. The city is full of them.

"You have been the one encounter in my life that can never be repeated . . ."

Howard, I wrote that editorial forty years ago. I wrote it one night when I was sixteen and stood on the roof of a tenement.

He walked on. Another street lay before him, a sudden cut of long emptiness and a chain of green traffic lights strung out to the horizon. Like a rosary without end. He thought, now walk from green bead to green bead. He thought, these are not the words; but the words kept ringing with his steps: *Mea culpa—mea culpa—mea maxima culpa.*

He went past a window of old shoes corroded by wear—past the door of a mission with a cross above it—past the peeling poster of a political candidate who ran two years ago—past a grocery store with barrels of rotting greens on the sidewalk. The streets were contracting, walls drawing closer together. He could smell the odor of the river, and there were wads of fog over the rare lights.

He was in Hell's Kitchen.

The façades of the buildings around him were like the walls of secret backyards suddenly exposed; decay without reticence, past the need of privacy or shame. He heard shrieks coming from a saloon on a corner; he could not tell whether it was joy or brawling.

He stood in the middle of a street. He looked slowly down the mouth of every dark crevice, up the streaked walls, to the windows, to the roofs.

I never got out of here.

I never got out. I surrendered to the grocery man—to the deck hands on the ferryboat—to the owner of the poolroom. You don't run things around here. You don't run things around here. You've never run things anywhere, Gail Wynand. You've only added yourself to the things they ran.

Then he looked up, across the city, to the shapes of the great skyscrapers. He saw a string of lights rising unsupported in black space, a glowing pinnacle anchored to nothing, a small, brilliant square hanging detached in the sky. He knew the famous buildings to which these belonged, he could reconstruct their forms in space. He thought, you're my judges and witnesses. You rise, unhindered, above the sagging roofs. You shoot your gracious tension to the stars, out of the slack, the tired, the accidental. The eyes one mile out on the ocean will see none of this and none of this will matter, but you will be the presence and the city. As down the centuries, a few men stand in lonely rectitude that we may look and say, there is a human race behind us. One can't escape from you; the streets change, but one looks up and there you stand, unchanged. You have seen me walking through the streets tonight. You have seen all my steps and all my years. It's you that I've betrayed. For I was born to be one of you.

He walked on. It was late. Circles of light lay undisturbed on the empty sidewalks under the lampposts. The horns of taxis shrieked once in a while like doorbells ringing through the corridors of a vacant interior. He saw discarded newspapers, as he passed: on the pavements, on park benches, in the wire trash-baskets on corners. Many of them were the *Banner*. Many copies of the *Banner* had been read in the city tonight. He thought, we're building circulation, Alvah.

He stopped. He saw a paper spread out in the gutter before him, front page up. It was the *Banner*. He saw Roark's picture. He saw the gray print of a rubber heel across Roark's face.

He bent, his body folding itself down slowly, with both knees, both arms, and picked up the paper. He folded the front page and put it in his pocket. He walked on.

An unknown rubber heel, somewhere in the city, on an unknown foot that I released to march.

I released them all. I made every one of those who destroyed me. There is a beast on earth, dammed safely by its own impotence. I broke the dam. They would have remained helpless. They can produce nothing. I gave them the weapon. I gave them my strength, my energy, my living power. I created a great voice and let them dictate the words. The woman who threw the beet leaves in my face had a right to do it. I made it possible for her.

Anything may be betrayed, anyone may be forgiven. But not those who lack the courage of their own greatness. Alvah Scarret can be forgiven. He had nothing to betray. Mitchell Layton can be forgiven. But not I. I was not born to be a second-hander.

XVII

IT WAS A SUMMER DAY, CLOUDLESS AND COOL, AS IF THE SUN WERE screened by an invisible film of water, and the energy of heat had been transformed into a sharper clarity, an added brilliance of outline for the buildings of the city. In the streets, scattered like scraps of gray foam, there were a great many copies of the *Banner*. The city read, chuckling, the statement of Wynand's renunciation.

"That's that," said Gus Webb, chairman of the "We Don't Read Wynand" Committee. "It's slick," said Ike. "I'd like one peek, just one peek, at the great Mr. Gail Wynand's face today," said Sally Brent. "It's about time," said Homer Slottern. "Isn't it splendid? Wynand's surrendered," said a tight-lipped woman; she knew little about Wynand and nothing about the issue, but she liked to hear of people surrendering. In a kitchen, after dinner, a fat woman scraped the remnants off the dishes onto a sheet of newspaper; she never read the front page, only the installments of a love serial in the second section; she wrapped onion peelings and lamb-chop bones in a copy of the *Banner*.

"It's stupendous," said Lancelot Clokey, "only I'm really sore at that Union, Ellsworth. How could they double-cross you like that?" "Don't be a sap, Lance," said Ellsworth Toohey. "What do you mean?" "I told them to accept the terms." "*You* did?" "Yep." "But Jesus! 'One Small Voice' . . ." "You can wait for 'One Small Voice' another month or so, can't you? I've filed suit with the labor board today, to be reinstated in my job on the *Banner*. There are more ways than one to skin a cat, Lance. The skinning isn't important once you've broken its spine."

That evening Roark pressed the bell button at the door of Wynand's penthouse. The butler opened the door and said: "Mr. Wynand cannot see you, Mr. Roark." From the sidewalk across the street Roark looked up and saw a square of light high over the roofs, in the window of Wynand's study.

In the morning Roark came to Wynand's office in the Banner Building. Wynand's secretary told him: "Mr. Wynand cannot see you, Mr. Roark." She added, her voice polite, disciplined: "Mr. Wynand has asked me to tell you that he does not wish ever to see you again."

Roark wrote him a long letter: ". . . Gail, I know. I hoped you could escape it, but since it had to happen, start again from where you are. I know what you're doing to yourself. You're not doing it for my sake, it's not up to me, but if this will help you I want to say that I'm repeating, now, everything I've ever said to you. Nothing has changed for me.

695

You're still what you were. I'm not saying that I forgive you, because there can be no such question between us. But if you can't forgive yourself, will you let me do it? Let me say that it doesn't matter, it's not the final verdict on you. Give me the right to let you forget it. Go on just on my faith until you've recovered. I know it's something no man can do for another, but if I am what I've been to you, you'll accept it. Call it a blood transfusion. You need it. Take it. It's harder than fighting that strike. Do it for my sake, if that will help you. But do it. Come back. There will be another chance. What you think you've lost can neither be lost nor found. Don't let it go."

The letter came back to Roark, unopened.

Alvah Scarret ran the *Banner*. Wynand sat in his office. He had removed Roark's picture from the wall. He attended to advertising contracts, expenses, accounts. Scarret took care of the editorial policy. Wynand did not read the contents of the *Banner*.

When Wynand appeared in any department of the building, the employees obeyed him as they had obeyed him before. He was still a machine and they knew that it was a machine more dangerous than ever: a car running downhill, without combustion or brakes.

He slept in his penthouse. He had not seen Dominique. Scarret had told him that she had gone back to the country. Once Wynand ordered his secretary to telephone Connecticut. He stood by her desk while she asked the butler whether Mrs. Wynand was there. The butler answered that she was. The secretary hung up and Wynand went back to his office.

He thought he would give himself a few days. Then he'd return to Dominique. Their marriage would be what she had wanted it to be at first—"Mrs. Wynand-Papers." He would accept it.

Wait, he thought in an agony of impatience, wait. You must learn to face her as you are now. Train yourself to be a beggar. There must be no pretense at things to which you have no right. No equality, no resistance, no pride in holding your strength against hers. Only acceptance now. Stand before her as a man who can give her nothing, who will live on what she chooses to grant him. It will be contempt, but it will come from her and it will be a bond. Show her that you recognize this. There is a kind of dignity in a renunciation of dignity openly admitted. Learn it. Wait. . . . He sat in the study of his penthouse, his head on the arm of his chair. There were no witnesses in the empty rooms around him. . . . Dominique, he thought, I will have no claim to make except that I need you so much. And that I love you. I told you once not to consider it. Now I'll use it as a tin cup. But I'll use it. I love you. . . .

Dominique lay stretched out on the shore of the lake. She looked at the house on the hill, at the tree branches above her. Flat on her back, hands crossed under her head, she studied the motion of leaves against the sky. It was an earnest occupation, giving her full contentment. She thought, it's a lovely kind of green, there's a difference between the color of plants and the color of objects, this has light in it, this is not just green, but also the living force of the tree made visible, I don't have to look down, I can see the branches, the trunk, the roots just by looking at that color. That fire around the edges is the sun, I don't have to see it, I can tell what the whole countryside looks like today. The spots of light weaving in circles—that's the lake, the special kind of light that comes refracted from water, the lake is beautiful today, and it's better not to see it, just to guess by these spots. I have never been able to enjoy it before, the sight of the earth, it's such a great background, but it has no meaning except as a background, and I thought of those who owned it and then it hurt me too much. I can love it now. They don't own it. They own nothing. They've never won. I have seen the life of Gail Wynand, and now I know. One cannot hate the earth in their name. The earth is beautiful. And it is a background, but not theirs.

She knew what she had to do. But she would give herself a few days. She thought, I've learned to bear anything except happiness. I must learn how to carry it. How not to break under it. It's the only discipline I'll need from now on.

Roark stood at the window of his house in Monadnock Valley. He had rented the house for the summer; he went there when he wanted loneliness and rest. It was a quiet evening. The window opened on a small ledge in a frame of trees, hanging against the sky. A strip of sunset light stretched above the dark treetops. He knew that there were houses below, but they could not be seen. He was as grateful as any other tenant for the way in which he had built this place. He heard the sound of a car approaching up the road at the other side. He listened, astonished. He expected no guests. The car stopped. He walked to open the door. He felt no astonishment when he saw Dominique.

She came in as if she had left this house half an hour ago. She wore no hat, no stockings, just sandals and a dress intended for back country roads, a narrow sheath of dark blue linen with short sleeves, like a smock for gardening. She did not look as if she had driven across three states, but as if she were returning from a walk down the hill. He knew that this was to be the solemnity of the moment—that it needed no solemnity; it was not to be stressed and set apart, it was not this particular evening, but the completed meaning of seven years behind them.

"Howard."

He stood as if he were looking at the sound of his name in the room. He had all he had wanted.

But there was one thought that remained as pain, even now. He said:

"Dominique, wait till he recovers."

"You know he won't recover."

"Have a little pity on him."

"Don't speak their language."

"He had no choice."

"He could have closed the paper."

"It was his life."

"This is mine."

He did not know that Wynand had once said all love is exception-making; and Wynand would not know that Roark had loved him enough to make his greatest exception, one moment when he had tried to compromise. Then he knew it was useless, like all sacrifices. What he said was his signature under her decision:

"I love you."

She looked about the room, to let the ordinary reality of walls and chairs help her keep the discipline she had been learning for this moment. The walls he had designed, the chairs he used, a package of his cigarettes on a table, the routine necessities of life that could acquire splendor when life became what it was now.

"Howard, I know what you intend to do at the trial. So it won't make any difference if they learn the truth about us."

"It won't make any difference."

"When you came that night and told me about Cortlandt, I didn't try to stop you. I knew you had to do it, it was your time to set the terms on which you could go on. This is my time. My Cortlandt explosion. You must let me do it my way. Don't question me. Don't protect me. No matter what I do."

"I know what you'll do."

"You know that I have to?"

"Yes."

She bent one arm from the elbow, fingers lifted, in a short, backward jolt, as if tossing the subject over her shoulder. It was settled and not to be discussed.

She turned away from him, she walked across the room, to let the casual ease of her steps make this her home, to state that his presence was to be the rule for all her coming days and she had no need to do what she wanted most at this moment: stand and look at him. She knew also what she was delaying, because she was not ready and would never be ready. She stretched her hand out for his package of cigarettes on the table.

His fingers closed over her wrist and he pulled her hand back. He pulled her around to face him, and then he held her and his mouth was on hers. She knew that every moment of seven years when she had wanted this and stopped the pain and thought she had won, was not past, had never been stopped, had lived on, stored, adding hunger to hunger, and now she had to feel it all, the touch of his body, the answer and the waiting together.

She didn't know whether her discipline had helped; not too well, she thought, because she saw that he had lifted her in his arms, carried her to a chair and sat down, holding her on his knees; he laughed without sound, as he would have laughed at a child, but the firmness of his hands holding her showed concern and a kind of steadying caution. Then it seemed simple, she had nothing to hide from him, she whispered: "Yes, Howard . . . that much . . ." and he said: "It was very hard for me—all these years." And the years were ended.

She slipped down, to sit on the floor, her elbows propped on his knees, she looked up at him and smiled, she knew that she could not have reached this white serenity except as the sum of all the colors, of all the violence she had known. "Howard . . . willingly, completely, and always . . . without reservations, without fear of anything they can do to you or me . . . in any way you wish . . . as your wife or your mistress, secretly or openly . . . here, or in a furnished room I'll take in some town near a jail where I'll see you through a wire net . . . it won't matter. . . . Howard, if you win the trial—even that won't matter too much. You've won long ago. . . . I'll remain what I am, and I'll remain with you—now and ever—in any way you want. . . ."

He held her hands in his, she saw his shoulders sagging down to her, she saw him helpless, surrendered to this moment, as she was—and she knew that even pain can be confessed, but to confess happiness is to stand naked, delivered to the witness, yet they could let each other see it without need of protection. It was growing dark, the room was indistinguishable, only the window remained and his shoulders against the sky in the window.

She awakened with the sun in her eyes. She lay on her back, looking at the ceiling as she had looked at the leaves. Not to move, to guess by hints, to see everything through the greater intensity of implication. The broken triangles of light on the angular modeling of the ceiling's plastic tiles meant that it was morning and that this was a bedroom at Monadnock, the geometry of fire and structure above her designed by him. The fire was white—that meant it was very early and the rays came through clean country air, with nothing anywhere in space between this bedroom and the sun. The weight of the blanket, heavy and intimate on her naked body, was everything that had been last night. And the skin she felt against her arm was Roark asleep beside her.

She slipped out of bed. She stood at the window, her arms raised, holding on to the frame at each side. She thought if she looked back she would see no shadow of her body on the floor, she felt as if the sunlight went straight through her, because her body had no weight.

But she had to hurry before he awakened. She found his pyjamas in a dresser drawer and put them on. She went to the living room, closing the door carefully behind her. She picked up the telephone and asked for the nearest sheriff's office.

"This is Mrs. Gail Wynand," she said. "I am speaking from the house of Mr. Howard Roark at Monadnock Valley. I wish to report that my star-sapphire ring was stolen here last night. . . . About five thousand dollars. . . . It was a present from Mr. Roark. . . . Can you get here within an hour? . . . Thank you."

She went to the kitchen, made coffee and stood watching the glow of the electric coil under the coffee pot, thinking that it was the most beautiful light on earth.

She set the table by the large window in the living room. He came out, wearing nothing but a dressing gown, and laughed at the sight of her in his pyjamas. She said: "Don't dress. Sit down. Let's have breakfast."

They were finishing when they heard the sound of the car stopping outside. She smiled and walked to open the door.

There were a sheriff, a deputy and two reporters from local papers.

"Good morning," said Dominique. "Come in."

"Mrs. . . . Wynand?" said the sheriff.

"That's right. Mrs. Gail Wynand. Come in. Sit down."

In the ludicrous folds of the pyjamas, with dark cloth bulging over a belt wound tightly, with sleeves hanging over her finger tips, she had all the poised elegance she displayed in her best hostess gown. She was the only one who seemed to find nothing unusual in the situation.

The sheriff held a notebook as if he did not know what to do with it. She helped him to find the right questions and answered them precisely, like a good newspaper woman.

"It was a star-sapphire ring set in platinum. I took it off and left it here, on this table, next to my purse, before going to bed. . . . It was about ten o'clock last night. . . . When I got up this morning, it was gone. . . . Yes, this window was open. . . . No, we didn't hear anything. . . . No, it was not insured, I have not had the time, Mr. Roark gave it to me recently. . . . No, there are no servants here and no other guests. . . . Yes, please look through the house. . . . Living room, bedroom, bathroom and kitchen. . . . Yes, of course, you may look too, gentlemen. The press, I believe? Do you wish to ask me any questions?"

There were no questions to ask. The story was complete. The reporters had never seen a story of this nature offered in this manner.

She tried not to look at Roark after her first glance at his face. But he kept his promise. He did not try to stop her or protect her. When questioned, he answered, enough to support her statements.

Then the men departed. They seemed glad to leave. Even the sheriff knew that he would not have to conduct a search for that ring.

Dominique said:

"I'm sorry. I know it was terrible for you. But it was the only way to get it into the papers."

"You should have told me which one of your star sapphires I gave you."

"I've never had any. I don't like star sapphires."

"That was a more thorough job of dynamiting than Cortlandt."

"Yes. Now Gail is blasted over to the side where he belongs. So he thinks you're an 'unprincipled, antisocial type of man'? Now let him see the *Banner* smearing me also. Why should he be spared that? Sorry, Howard, I don't have your sense of mercy. I've read that editorial. Don't comment on this. Don't say anything about self-sacrifice or I'll break and . . . and I'm not quite as strong as that sheriff is probably thinking. I didn't do it for you. I've made it worse for you—I've added scandal to everything else they'll throw at you. But, Howard, now we stand together—against all of them. You'll be a convict and I'll be an adulteress. Howard, do you remember that I was afraid to share you with lunch wagons and strangers' windows? Now I'm not afraid to have this past night smeared all over their newspapers. My darling, do you see why I'm happy and why I'm free?"

He said:

"I'll never remind you afterward that you're crying, Dominique."

The story, including the pyjamas, the dressing gown, the breakfast table and the single bed, was in all the afternoon papers of New York that day.

Alvah Scarret walked into Wynand's office and threw a newspaper down on his desk. Scarret had never discovered how much he loved Wynand, until now, and he was so hurt that he could express it only in furious abuse. He gulped:

"God damn you, you blasted fool! It serves you right! It serves you right and I'm glad, damn your witless soul! Now what are we going to do?"

Wynand read the story and sat looking at the paper. Scarret stood before the desk. Nothing happened. It was just an office, a man sat at a desk holding a newspaper. He saw Wynand's hands, one at each side of the sheet, and the hands were still. No, he thought, normally a man would not be able to hold his hands like that, lifted and unsupported, without a tremor.

Wynand raised his head. Scarret could discover nothing in his eyes, except a kind of mild astonishment, as if Wynand were wondering what Scarret was doing here. Then, in terror, Scarret whispered:

"Gail, what are we going to do?"

"We'll run it," said Wynand. "It's news."

"But . . . how?"

"In any way you wish."

Scarret's voice leaped ahead, because he knew it was now or never, he would not have the courage to attempt this again; and because he was caught here, he was afraid to back toward the door.

"Gail, you must divorce her." He found himself still standing there, and he went on, not looking at Wynand, screaming in order to get it said: "Gail, you've got no choice now! You've got to keep what's left of your reputation! You've got to divorce her and it's you who must file the suit!"

"All right."

"Will you? At once? Will you let Paul file the papers at once?"

"All right."

Scarret hurried out of the room. He rushed to his own office, slammed the door, seized the telephone and called Wynand's lawyer. He explained and went on repeating: "Drop everything and file it now, Paul, now, today, hurry, Paul, before he changes his mind!"

Wynand drove to his country house. Dominique was there, waiting for him.

She stood up when he entered her room. She stepped forward, so that there would be no furniture between them; she wished him to see her whole body. He stood across the empty space and looked at her as if he were observing them both at once, an impartial spectator who saw Dominique and a man facing her, but no Gail Wynand.

She waited, but he said nothing.

"Well, I've given you a story that will build circulation, Gail."

He had heard, but he looked as if nothing of the present were relevant. He looked like a bank teller balancing a stranger's account that had been overdrawn and had to be closed. He said:

"I would like only to know this, if you'll tell me: that was the first time since our marriage?"

"Yes."

"But it was not the first time?"

"No. He was the first man who had me."

"I think I should have understood. You married Peter Keating. Right after the Stoddard trial."

"Do you wish to know everything? I want to tell you. I met him when he was working in a granite quarry. Why not? You'll put him in a chain gang now or a jute mill. He was working in a quarry. He didn't ask my consent. He raped me. That's how it began. Want to use it? Want to run it in the *Banner?*"

"He loved you."

"Yes."

"Yet he built this house for us."

"Yes."

"I only wanted to know."

He turned to leave.

"God damn you!" she cried. "If you can take it like this, you had no right to become what you became!"

"That's why I'm taking it."

He walked out of the room. He closed the door softly.

Guy Francon telephoned Dominique that evening. Since his retirement he had lived alone on his country estate near the quarry town. She had refused to answer calls today, but she took the receiver when the maid told her that it was Mr. Francon. Instead of the fury she expected, she heard a gentle voice saying:

"Hello, Dominique."

"Hello, Father."

"You're going to leave Wynand now?"

"Yes."

"You shouldn't move to the city. It's not necessary. Don't overdo it. Come and stay here with me. Until . . . the Cortlandt trial."

The things he had not said and the quality of his voice, firm, simple and with a note that sounded close to happiness, made her answer, after a moment:

"All right, Father." It was a girl's voice, a daughter's voice, with a tired, trusting, wistful gaiety. "I'll get there about midnight. Have a glass of milk for me and some sandwiches."

"Try not to speed as you always do. The roads aren't too good."

When she arrived, Guy Francon met her at the door. They both smiled, and she knew that there would be no questions, no reproaches. He led her to the small morning room where he had set the food on a table by a window open to a dark lawn. There was a smell of grass, candles on the table and a bunch of jasmine in a silver bowl.

She sat, her fingers closed about a cold glass, and he sat across the table, munching a sandwich peacefully.

"Want to talk, Father?"

"No. I want you to drink your milk and go to bed."

"All right."

He picked up an olive and sat studying it thoughtfully, twisting it on a colored toothpick. Then he glanced up at her.

"Look, Dominique. I can't attempt to understand it all. But I know this much—that it's the right thing for you. This time, it's the right man."

"Yes, Father."

"That's why I'm glad."

She nodded.

"Tell Mr. Roark that he can come here any time he wants."

She smiled. "Tell whom, Father?"

"Tell . . . Howard."

Her arm lay on the table; her head dropped down on her arm. He looked at the gold hair in the candlelight. She said, because it was easier to control a voice: "Don't let me fall asleep here. I'm tired."

But he answered:

"He'll be acquitted, Dominique."

All the newspapers of New York were brought to Wynand's office each day, as he had ordered. He read every word of what was written and whispered in town. Everybody knew that the story had been a self-frame-up; the wife of a multi-millionaire would not report the loss of a five-thousand-dollar ring in the circumstances; but this did not prevent anyone from accepting the story as given and commenting accordingly. The most offensive comments were spread on the pages of the *Banner*.

Alvah Scarret had found a crusade to which he devoted himself with the truest fervor he had ever experienced. He felt that it was his atonement for any disloyalty he might have committed toward Wynand in the past. He saw a way to redeem Wynand's name. He set out to sell Wynand to the public as the victim of a great passion for a depraved woman; it was Dominique who had forced her husband to champion an immoral cause, against his better judgment; she had almost wrecked her husband's paper, his standing, his reputation, the achievement of his whole life—for the sake of her lover. Scarret begged readers to forgive Wynand—a tragic, self-sacrificing love was his justification. It was an inverse ratio in Scarret's calculations: every filthy adjective thrown at Dominique created sympathy for Wynand in the reader's mind; this fed Scarret's smear talent. It worked. The public responded, the *Banner's* old feminine readers in particular. It helped in the slow, painful work of the paper's reconstruction.

Letters began to arrive, generous in their condolences, unrestrained in the indecency of their comment on Dominique Francon. "Like the old days, Gail," said Scarret happily, "just like the old days!" He piled all the letters on Wynand's desk.

Wynand sat alone in his office with the letters. Scarret could not suspect that this was the worst of the suffering Gail Wynand was to know. He made himself read every letter. Dominique, whom he had tried to save from the *Banner* . . .

When they met in the building, Scarret looked at him expectantly, with an entreating, tentative half-smile, an eager pupil waiting for the teacher's recognition of a lesson well learned and well done. Wynand said nothing. Scarret ventured once:

"It was clever, wasn't it, Gail?"

"Yes."

"Have any idea on where we can milk it some more?"

"It's your job, Alvah."

"She's really the cause of everything, Gail. Long before all this. When you married her. I was afraid then. That's what started it. Remember when you didn't allow us to cover your wedding? That was a sign. She's ruined the *Banner*. But I'll be damned if I don't rebuild it now right on her own body. Just as it was. Our old *Banner*."

"Yes."

"Got any suggestions, Gail? What else would you like me to do?"

"Anything you wish, Alvah."

XVIII

A TREE BRANCH HUNG IN THE OPEN WINDOW. THE LEAVES MOVED against the sky, implying sun and summer and an inexhaustible earth to be used. Dominique thought of the world as background. Wynand thought of two hands bending a tree branch to explain the meaning of life. The leaves drooped, touching the spires of New York's skyline far across the river. The skyscrapers stood like shafts of sunlight, washed white by distance and summer. A crowd filled the county courtroom, witnessing the trial of Howard Roark.

Roark sat at the defense table. He listened calmly.

Dominique sat in the third row of spectators. Looking at her, people felt as if they had seen a smile. She did not smile. She looked at the leaves in the window.

Gail Wynand sat at the back of the courtroom. He had come in, alone, when the room was full. He had not noticed the stares and the flashbulbs exploding around him. He had stood in the aisle for a moment, surveying the place as if there were no reason why he should not survey it. He wore a gray summer suit and a panama hat with a drooping brim turned up at one side. His glance went over Dominique as over the rest of the courtroom. When he sat down, he looked at Roark. From the moment of Wynand's entrance Roark's eyes kept returning to him. Whenever Roark looked at him, Wynand turned away.

"The motive which the State proposes to prove," the prosecutor was making his opening address to the jury, "is beyond the realm of normal human emotions. To the majority of us it will appear monstrous and inconceivable."

Dominique sat with Mallory, Heller, Lansing, Enright, Mike—and Guy Francon, to the shocked disapproval of his friends. Across the aisle, celebrities formed a comet: from the small point of Ellsworth Toohey, well in front, a tail of popular names stretched through the crowd: Lois Cook, Gordon L. Prescott, Gus Webb, Lancelot Clokey, Ike, Jules Fougler, Sally Brent, Homer Slottern, Mitchell Layton.

"Even as the dynamite which swept a building away, his motive blasted all sense of humanity out of this man's soul. We are dealing, gentlemen of the jury, with the most vicious explosive on earth—the egotist!"

On the chairs, on the window sills, in the aisles, pressed against the walls, the human mass was blended like a monolith, except for the pale ovals of faces. The faces stood out, separate, lonely, no two alike.

706

Behind each, there were the years of a life lived or half over, effort, hope and an attempt, honest or dishonest, but an attempt. It had left on all a single mark in common: on lips smiling with malice, on lips loose with renunciation, on lips tight with uncertain dignity—on all—the mark of suffering.

". . . In this day and age, when the world is torn by gigantic problems, seeking an answer to questions that hold the survival of man in the balance—this man attached to such a vague intangible, such an inessential as his artistic opinions sufficient importance to let it become his sole passion and the motivation of a crime against society."

The people had come to witness a sensational case, to see celebrities, to get material for conversation, to be seen, to kill time. They would return to unwanted jobs, unloved families, unchosen friends, to drawing rooms, evening clothes, cocktail glasses and movies, to unadmitted pain, murdered hope, desire left unreached, left hanging silently over a path on which no step was taken, to days of effort not to think, not to say, to forget and give in and give up. But each of them had known some unforgotten moment—a morning when nothing had happened, a piece of music heard suddenly and never heard in the same way again, a stranger's face seen in a bus—a moment when each had known a different sense of living. And each remembered other moments, on a sleepless night, on an afternoon of steady rain, in a church, in an empty street at sunset, when each had wondered why there was so much suffering and ugliness in the world. They had not tried to find the answer and they had gone on living as if no answer were necessary. But each had known a moment when, in lonely, naked honesty, he had felt the need of an answer.

". . . a ruthless, arrogant egotist who wished to have his own way at any price . . ."

Twelve men sat in the jury box. They listened, their faces attentive and emotionless. People had whispered that it was a tough-looking jury. There were two executives of industrial concerns, two engineers, a mathematician, a truck driver, a bricklayer, an electrician, a gardener and three factory workers. The impaneling of the jury had taken some time. Roark had challenged many talesmen. He had picked these twelve. The prosecutor had agreed, telling himself that this was what happened when an amateur undertook to handle his own defense; a lawyer would have chosen the gentlest types, those most likely to respond to an appeal for mercy; Roark had chosen the hardest faces.

". . . Had it been some plutocrat's mansion, but a *housing project*, gentlemen of the jury, a housing project!"

The judge sat erect on the tall bench. He had gray hair and the stern face of an army officer.

". . . a man trained to serve society, a builder who became a destroyer . . ."

The voice went on, practiced and confident. The faces filling the room listened with the response they granted to a good weekday dinner: satisfying and to be forgotten within an hour. They agreed with every sentence; they had heard it before, they had always heard it, this was what the world lived by; it was self-evident—like a puddle before one's feet.

The prosecutor introduced his witnesses. The policeman who had arrested Roark took the stand to tell how he had found the defendant standing by the electric plunger. The night watchman related how he had been sent away from the scene; his testimony was brief; the prosecutor preferred not to stress the subject of Dominique. The contractor's superintendent testified about the dynamite missing from the stores on the site. Officials of Cortlandt, building inspectors, estimators took the stand to describe the building and the extent of the damage. This concluded the first day of the trial.

Peter Keating was the first witness called on the following day.

He sat on the stand, slumped forward. He looked at the prosecutor obediently. His eyes moved, once in a while. He looked at the crowd, at the jury, at Roark. It made no difference.

"Mr. Keating, will you state under oath whether you designed the project ascribed to you, known as Cortlandt Homes?"

"No. I didn't."

"Who designed it?"

"Howard Roark."

"At whose request?"

"At my request."

"Why did you call on him?"

"Because I was not capable of doing it myself."

There was no sound of honesty in the voice, because there was no sound of effort to pronounce a truth of such nature; no tone of truth or falsehood; only indifference.

The prosecutor handed him a sheet of paper. "Is this the agreement you signed?"

Keating held the paper in his hand. "Yes."

"Is that Howard Roark's signature?"

"Yes."

"Will you please read the terms of this agreement to the jury?"

Keating read it aloud. His voice came evenly, well drilled. Nobody in the courtroom realized that this testimony had been intended as a sensation. It was not a famous architect publicly confessing incompetence; it was a man reciting a memorized lesson. People felt that were he interrupted, he would not be able to pick up the next sentence, but would have to start all over again from the beginning.

He answered a great many questions. The prosecutor introduced in evidence Roark's original drawings of Cortlandt, which Keating had kept; the copies which Keating had made of them; and photographs of Cortlandt as it had been built.

"Why did you object so strenuously to the excellent structural changes suggested by Mr. Prescott and Mr. Webb?"

"I was afraid of Howard Roark."

"What did your knowledge of his character lead you to expect?"

"Anything."

"What do you mean?"

"I don't know. I was afraid. I used to be afraid."

The questions went on. The story was unusual, but the audience felt bored. It did not sound like the recital of a participant. The other witnesses had seemed to have a more personal connection with the case.

When Keating left the stand, the audience had the odd impression that no change had occurred in the act of a man's exit; as if no person had walked out.

"The prosecution rests," said the District Attorney.

The judge looked at Roark.

"Proceed," he said. His voice was gentle.

Roark got up. "Your Honor, I shall call no witnesses. This will be my testimony and my summation."

"Take the oath."

Roark took the oath. He stood by the steps of the witness stand. The audience looked at him. They felt he had no chance. They could drop the nameless resentment, the sense of insecurity which he aroused in most people. And so, for the first time, they could see him as he was: a man totally innocent of fear.

The fear of which they thought was not the normal kind, not a response to a tangible danger, but the chronic, unconfessed fear in which they all lived. They remembered the misery of the moments when, in loneliness, a man thinks of the bright words he could have said, but had not found, and hates those who robbed him of his courage. The misery of knowing how strong and able one is in one's own mind, the radiant picture never to be made real. Dreams? Self-delusion? Or a murdered reality, unborn, killed by that corroding emotion without name—fear—need—dependence—hatred?

Roark stood before them as each man stands in the innocence of his own mind. But Roark stood like that before a hostile crowd—and they knew suddenly that no hatred was possible to him. For the flash of an instant, they grasped the manner of his consciousness. Each asked himself: do I need anyone's approval?—does it matter?—am I tied? And for that instant, each man was free—free enough to feel benevolence for every other man in the room.

It was only a moment; the moment of silence when Roark was about to speak.

"Thousands of years ago, the first man discovered how to make fire. He was probably burned at the stake he had taught his brothers to light. He was considered an evildoer who had dealt with a demon mankind dreaded. But thereafter men had fire to keep them warm, to cook their food, to light their caves. He had left them a gift they had not conceived and he had lifted darkness off the earth. Centuries later, the first man invented the wheel. He was probably torn on the rack he had taught his brothers to build. He was considered a transgressor who ventured into forbidden territory. But thereafter, men could travel past any horizon. He had left them a gift they had not conceived and he had opened the roads of the world.

"That man, the unsubmissive and first, stands in the opening chapter of every legend mankind has recorded about its beginning. Prometheus was chained to a rock and torn by vultures—because he had stolen the fire of the gods. Adam was condemned to suffer—because he had eaten the fruit of the tree of knowledge. Whatever the legend, somewhere in the shadows of its memory mankind knew that its glory began with one and that that one paid for his courage.

"Throughout the centuries there were men who took first steps down new roads armed with nothing but their own vision. Their goals differed, but they all had this in common: that the step was first, the road new, the vision unborrowed, and the response they received—hatred. The great creators—the thinkers, the artists, the scientists, the inventors—stood alone against the men of their time. Every great new thought was opposed. Every great new invention was denounced. The first motor was considered foolish. The airplane was considered impossible. The power loom was considered vicious. Anesthesia was considered sinful. But the men of unborrowed vision went ahead. They fought, they suffered and they paid. But they won.

"No creator was prompted by a desire to serve his brothers, for his brothers rejected the gift he offered and that gift destroyed the slothful routine of their lives. His truth was his only motive. His own truth, and his own work to achieve it in his own way. A symphony, a book, an engine, a philosophy, an airplane or a building—that was his goal and his life. Not those who heard, read, operated, believed, flew or inhabited the thing he had created. The creation, not its users. The creation, not the benefits others derived from it. The creation which gave form to his truth. He held his truth above all things and against all men.

"His vision, his strength, his courage came from his own spirit. A man's spirit, however, is his self. That entity which is his consciousness. To think, to feel, to judge, to act are functions of the ego.

"The creators were not selfless. It is the whole secret of their power—that it was self-sufficient, self-motivated, self-generated. A first cause, a fount of energy, a life force, a Prime Mover. The creator served nothing and no one. He lived for himself.

"And only by living for himself was he able to achieve the things which are the glory of mankind. Such is the nature of achievement.

"Man cannot survive except through his mind. He comes on earth unarmed. His brain is his only weapon. Animals obtain food by force. Man has no claws, no fangs, no horns, no great strength of muscle. He must plant his food or hunt it. To plant, he needs a process of thought. To hunt, he needs weapons, and to make weapons—a process of thought. From this simplest necessity to the highest religious abstraction, from the wheel to the skyscraper, everything we are and everything we have comes from a single attribute of man—the function of his reasoning mind.

"But the mind is an attribute of the individual. There is no such thing as a collective brain. There is no such thing as a collective thought. An agreement reached by a group of men is only a compromise or an average drawn upon many individual thoughts. It is a secondary consequence. The primary act—the process of reason—must be performed by each man alone. We can divide a meal among many men. We cannot digest it in a collective stomach. No man can use his lungs to breathe for another man. No man can use his brain to think for another. All the functions of body and spirit are private. They cannot be shared or transferred.

"We inherit the products of the thought of other men. We inherit the wheel. We make a cart. The cart becomes an automobile. The automobile becomes an airplane. But all through the process what we receive from others is only the end product of their thinking. The moving force is the creative faculty which takes this product as material, uses it and originates the next step. This creative faculty cannot be given or received, shared or borrowed. It belongs to single, individual men. That which it creates is the property of the creator. Men learn from one another. But all learning is only the exchange of material. No man can give another the capacity to think. Yet that capacity is our only means of survival.

"Nothing is given to man on earth. Everything he needs has to be produced. And here man faces his basic alternative: he can survive in only one of two ways—by the independent work of his own mind or as a parasite fed by the minds of others. The creator originates. The parasite borrows. The creator faces nature alone. The parasite faces nature through an intermediary.

"The creator's concern is the conquest of nature. The parasite's concern is the conquest of men.

"The creator lives for his work. He needs no other men. His primary goal is within himself. The parasite lives second-hand. He needs others. Others become his prime motive.

"The basic need of the creator is independence. The reasoning mind cannot work under any form of compulsion. It cannot be curbed, sacrificed or subordinated to any consideration whatsoever. It demands total independence in function and in motive. To a creator, all relations with men are secondary.

"The basic need of the second-hander is to secure his ties with men in order to be fed. He places relations first. He declares that man exists in order to serve others. He preaches altruism.

"Altruism is the doctrine which demands that man live for others and place others above self.

"No man can live for another. He cannot share his spirit just as he cannot share his body. But the second-hander has used altruism as a weapon of exploitation and reversed the base of mankind's moral principles. Men have been taught every precept that destroys the creator. Men have been taught dependence as a virtue.

"The man who attempts to live for others is a dependent. He is a parasite in motive and makes parasites of those he serves. The relationship produces nothing but mutual corruption. It is impossible in concept. The nearest approach to it in reality—the man who lives to serve others—is the slave. If physical slavery is repulsive, how much more repulsive is the concept of servility of the spirit? The conquered slave has a vestige of honor. He has the merit of having resisted and of considering his condition evil. But the man who enslaves himself voluntarily in the name of love is the basest of creatures. He degrades the dignity of man and he degrades the conception of love. But this is the essence of altruism.

"Men have been taught that the highest virtue is not to achieve, but to give. Yet one cannot give that which has not been created. Creation comes before distribution—or there will be nothing to distribute. The need of the creator comes before the need of any possible beneficiary. Yet we are taught to admire the second-hander who dispenses gifts he has not produced above the man who made the gifts possible. We praise an act of charity. We shrug at an act of achievement.

"Men have been taught that their first concern is to relieve the suffering of others. But suffering is a disease. Should one come upon it, one tries to give relief and assistance. To make that the highest test of virtue is to make suffering the most important part of life. Then man must wish to see others suffer—in order that he may be virtuous. Such is the nature of altruism. The creator is not concerned with disease, but with life. Yet the work of the creators has eliminated one form of disease after another, in man's body and spirit, and brought more relief from suffering than any altruist could ever conceive.

"Men have been taught that it is a virtue to agree with others. But the creator is the man who disagrees. Men have been taught that it is a virtue to swim with the current. But the creator is the man who goes against the current. Men have been taught that it is a virtue to stand together. But the creator is the man who stands alone.

"Men have been taught that the ego is the synonym of evil, and selflessness the ideal of virtue. But the creator is the egotist in the absolute sense, and the selfless man is the one who does not think, feel, judge or act. These are functions of the self.

"Here the basic reversal is most deadly. The issue has been perverted and man has been left no alternative—and no freedom. As poles of good and evil, he was offered two conceptions: egotism and altruism. Egotism was held to mean the sacrifice of others to self. Altruism— the sacrifice of self to others. This tied man irrevocably to other men and left him nothing but a choice of pain: his own pain borne for the sake of others or pain inflicted upon others for the sake of self. When it was added that man must find joy in self-immolation, the trap was closed. Man was forced to accept masochism as his ideal—under the threat that sadism was his only alternative. This was the greatest fraud ever perpetrated on mankind.

"This was the device by which dependence and suffering were perpetuated as fundamentals of life.

"The choice is not self-sacrifice or domination. The choice is independence or dependence. The code of the creator or the code of the second-hander. This is the basic issue. It rests upon the alternative of life or death. The code of the creator is built on the needs of the reasoning mind which allows man to survive. The code of the second-hander is built on the needs of a mind incapable of survival. All that which proceeds from man's independent ego is good. All that which proceeds from man's dependence upon men is evil.

"The egotist in the absolute sense is not the man who sacrifices others. He is the man who stands above the need of using others in any manner. He does not function through them. He is not concerned with them in any primary matter. Not in his aim, not in his motive, not in his thinking, not in his desires, not in the source of his energy. He does not exist for any other man—and he asks no other man to exist for him. This is the only form of brotherhood and mutual respect possible between men.

"Degrees of ability vary, but the basic principle remains the same: the degree of a man's independence, initiative and personal love for his work determines his talent as a worker and his worth as a man. Independence is the only gauge of human virtue and value. What a man is and makes of himself; not what he has or hasn't done for others. There is no substitute for personal dignity. There is no standard of personal dignity except independence.

"In all proper relationships there is no sacrifice of anyone to anyone. An architect needs clients, but he does not subordinate his work to their wishes. They need him, but they do not order a house just to give him a commission. Men exchange their work by free, mutual consent to mutual advantage when their personal interests agree and they both desire the exchange. If they do not desire it, they are not forced to deal with each other. They seek further. This is the only possible form of relationship between equals. Anything else is a relation of slave to master, or victim to executioner.

"No work is ever done collectively, by a majority decision. Every creative job is achieved under the guidance of a single individual thought. An architect requires a great many men to erect his building. But he does not ask them to vote on his design. They work together by free agreement and each is free in his proper function. An architect uses steel, glass, concrete, produced by others. But the materials remain just so much steel, glass and concrete until he touches them. What he does with them is his individual product and his individual property. This is the only pattern for proper co-operation among men.

"The first right on earth is the right of the ego. Man's first duty is to himself. His moral law is never to place his prime goal within the persons of others. His moral obligation is to do what he wishes, provided his wish does not depend *primarily* upon other men. This includes the whole sphere of his creative faculty, his thinking, his work. But it does not include the sphere of the gangster, the altruist and the dictator.

"A man thinks and works alone. A man cannot rob, exploit or rule—alone. Robbery, exploitation and ruling presuppose victims. They imply dependence. They are the province of the second-hander.

"Rulers of men are not egotists. They create nothing. They exist entirely through the persons of others. Their goal is in their subjects, in the activity of enslaving. They are as dependent as the beggar, the social worker and the bandit. The form of dependence does not matter.

"But men were taught to regard second-handers—tyrants, emperors, dictators—as exponents of egotism. By this fraud they were made to destroy the ego, themselves and others. The purpose of the fraud was to destroy the creators. Or to harness them. Which is a synonym.

"From the beginning of history, the two antagonists have stood face to face: the creator and the second-hander. When the first creator invented the wheel, the first second-hander responded. He invented altruism.

"The creator—denied, opposed, persecuted, exploited—went on, moved forward and carried all humanity along on his energy. The second-hander contributed nothing to the process except the impediments. The contest has another name: the individual against the collective.

"The 'common good' of a collective—a race, a class, a state—was the claim and justification of every tyranny ever established over men. Every major horror of history was committed in the name of an altruistic motive. Has any act of selfishness ever equaled the carnage perpetrated by disciples of altruism? Does the fault lie in men's hypocrisy or in the nature of the principle? The most dreadful butchers were the most sincere. They believed in the perfect society reached through the guillotine and the firing squad. Nobody questioned their right to murder since they were murdering for an altruistic purpose. It was accepted that man must be sacrificed for other men. Actors change, but the course of the tragedy remains the same. A humanitarian who starts with declarations of love for mankind and ends with a sea of blood. It goes on and will go on so long as men believe that an action is good if it is unselfish. That permits the altruist to act and forces his victims to bear it. The leaders of collectivist movements ask nothing for themselves. But observe the results.

"The only good which men can do to one another and the only statement of their proper relationship is—Hands off!

"Now observe the results of a society built on the principle of individualism. This, our country. The noblest country in the history of men. The country of greatest achievement, greatest prosperity, greatest freedom. This country was not based on selfless service, sacrifice, renunciation or any precept of altruism. It was based on a man's right to the pursuit of happiness. His own happiness. Not anyone else's. A private, personal, selfish motive. Look at the results. Look into your own conscience.

"It is an ancient conflict. Men have come close to the truth, but it was destroyed each time and one civilization fell after another. Civilization is the progress toward a society of privacy. The savage's whole existence is public, ruled by the laws of his tribe. Civilization is the process of setting man free from men.

"Now, in our age, collectivism, the rule of the second-hander and second-rater, the ancient monster, has broken loose and is running amuck. It has brought men to a level of intellectual indecency never equaled on earth. It has reached a scale of horror without precedent. It has poisoned every mind. It has swallowed most of Europe. It is engulfing our country.

"I am an architect. I know what is to come by the principle on which it is built. We are approaching a world in which I cannot permit myself to live.

"Now you know why I dynamited Cortlandt.

"I designed Cortlandt. I gave it to you. I destroyed it.

"I destroyed it because I did not choose to let it exist. It was a double monster. In form and in implication. I had to blast both. The form was mutilated by two second-handers who assumed the right to improve upon that which they had not made and could not equal. They were permitted to do it by the general implication that the altruistic purpose of the building superseded all rights and that I had no claim to stand against it.

"I agreed to design Cortlandt for the purpose of seeing it erected as I designed it and for no other reason. That was the price I set for my work. I was not paid.

"I do not blame Peter Keating. He was helpless. He had a contract with his employers. It was ignored. He had a promise that the structure he offered would be built as designed. The promise was broken. The love of a man for the integrity of his work and his right to preserve it are now considered a vague intangible and an inessential. You have heard the prosecutor say that. Why was the building disfigured? For no reason. Such acts never have any reason, unless it's the vanity of some second-handers who feel they have a right to anyone's property, spiritual or material. Who permitted them to do it? No particular man among the dozens in authority. No one cared to permit it or to stop it. No one was responsible. No one can be held to account. Such is the nature of all collective action.

"I did not receive the payment I asked. But the owners of Cortlandt got what they needed from me. They wanted a scheme devised to build a structure as cheaply as possible. They found no one else who could do it to their satisfaction. I could and did. They took the benefit of my work and made me contribute it as a gift. But I am not an altruist. I do not contribute gifts of this nature.

"It is said that I have destroyed the home of the destitute. It is forgotten that but for me the destitute could not have had this particular home. Those who were concerned with the poor had to come to me, who have never been concerned, in order to help the poor. It is believed that the poverty of the future tenants gave them a right to my work. That their need constituted a claim on my life. That it was my duty to contribute anything demanded of me. This is the second-hander's credo now swallowing the world.

"I came here to say that I do not recognize anyone's right to one minute of my life. Nor to any part of my energy. Nor to any achievement of mine. No matter who makes the claim, how large their number or how great their need.

"I wished to come here and say that I am a man who does not exist for others.

"It had to be said. The world is perishing from an orgy of self-sacrificing.

"I wished to come here and say that the integrity of a man's creative work is of greater importance than any charitable endeavor. Those of you who do not understand this are the men who're destroying the world.

"I wished to come here and state my terms. I do not care to exist on any others.

"I recognize no obligations toward men except one: to respect their freedom and to take no part in a slave society. To my country, I wish to give the ten years which I will spend in jail if my country exists no longer. I will spend them in memory and in gratitude for what my country has been. It will be my act of loyalty, my refusal to live or work in what has taken its place.

"My act of loyalty to every creator who ever lived and was made to suffer by the force responsible for the Cortlandt I dynamited. To every tortured hour of loneliness, denial, frustration, abuse he was made to spend—and to the battles he won. To every creator whose name is known—and to every creator who lived, struggled and perished unrecognized before he could achieve. To every creator who was destroyed in body or in spirit. To Henry Cameron. To Steven Mallory. To a man who doesn't want to be named, but who is sitting in this courtroom and knows that I am speaking of him."

Roark stood, his legs apart, his arms straight at his sides, his head lifted—as he stood in an unfinished building. Later, when he was seated again at the defense table, many men in the room felt as if they still saw him standing; one moment's picture that would not be replaced.

The picture remained in their minds through the long legal discussions that followed. They heard the judge state to the prosecutor that the defendant had, in effect, changed his plea: he had admitted his act, but had not pleaded guilty of the crime; an issue of temporary legal insanity was raised; it was up to the jury to decide whether the defendant knew the nature and quality of his act, or, if he did, whether he knew that the act was wrong. The prosecutor raised no objection; there was an odd silence in the room; he felt certain that he had won his case already. He made his closing address. No one remembered what he said. The judge gave his instructions to the jury. The jury rose and left the courtroom.

People moved, preparing to depart, without haste, in expectation of many hours of waiting. Wynand, at the back of the room, and Dominique, in the front, sat without moving.

A bailiff stepped to Roark's side to escort him out. Roark stood by the defense table. His eyes went to Dominique, then to Wynand. He turned and followed the bailiff.

He had reached the door when there was a sharp crack of sound, and a space of blank silence before people realized that it was a knock at the closed door of the jury room. The jury had reached a verdict.

Those who had been on their feet remained standing, frozen, until the judge returned to the bench. The jury filed into the courtroom.

"The prisoner will rise and face the jury," said the clerk of the court.

Howard Roark stepped forward and stood facing the jury. At the back of the room, Gail Wynand got up and stood also.

"Mr. Foreman, have you reached a verdict?"

"We have."

"What is your verdict?"

"Not guilty."

The first movement of Roark's head was not to look at the city in the window, at the judge or at Dominique. He looked at Wynand.

Wynand turned sharply and walked out. He was the first man to leave the courtroom.

XIX

ROGER ENRIGHT BOUGHT THE SITE, THE PLANS AND THE RUINS OF Cortlandt from the government. He ordered every twisted remnant of foundations dug out to leave a clean hole in the earth. He hired Howard Roark to rebuild the project. Placing a single contractor in charge, observing the strict economy of the plans, Enright budgeted the undertaking to set low rentals with a comfortable margin of profit for himself. No questions were to be asked about the income, occupation, children or diet of the future tenants; the project was open to anyone who wished to move in and pay the rent, whether he could afford a more expensive apartment elsewhere or not.

Late in August Gail Wynand was granted his divorce. The suit was not contested and Dominique was not present at the brief hearing. Wynand stood like a man facing a court-martial and heard the cold obscenity of legal language describing the breakfast in a house of Monadnock Valley—Mrs. Gail Wynand—Howard Roark; branding his wife as officially dishonored, granting him lawful sympathy, the status of injured innocence, and a paper that was his passport to freedom for all the years before him, and for all the silent evenings of those years.

Ellsworth Toohey won his case before the labor board. Wynand was ordered to reinstate him in his job.

That afternoon Wynand's secretary telephoned Toohey and told him that Mr. Wynand expected him back at work tonight, before nine o'clock. Toohey smiled, dropping the receiver.

Toohey smiled, entering the Banner Building that evening. He stopped in the city room. He waved to people, shook hands, made witty remarks about some current movies, and bore an air of guileless astonishment, as if he had been absent just since yesterday and could not understand why people greeted him in the manner of a triumphal homecoming.

Then he ambled on to his office. He stopped short. He knew, while stopping, that he must enter, must not show the jolt, and that he had shown it: Wynand stood in the open door of his office.

"Good evening, Mr. Toohey," said Wynand softly. "Come in."

"Hello, Mr. Wynand," said Toohey, his voice pleasant, reassured by feeling his face muscles manage a smile and his legs walking on.

He entered and stopped uncertainly. It was his own office, unchanged, with his typewriter and a stack of fresh paper on the desk. But the door

719

remained open and Wynand stood there silently, leaning against the jamb.

"Sit down at your desk, Mr. Toohey. Go to work. We must comply with the law."

Toohey gave a gay little shrug of acquiescence, crossed the room and sat down. He put his hands on the desk surface, palms spread solidly, then dropped them to his lap. He reached for a pencil, examined its point and dropped it.

Wynand lifted one wrist slowly to the level of his chest and held it still, the apex of a triangle made by his forearm and the long, drooping fingers of his hand; he was looking down at his wrist watch. He said:

"It is ten minutes to nine. You are back on your job, Mr. Toohey."

"And I'm happy as a kid to be back. Honestly, Mr. Wynand, I suppose I shouldn't confess it, but I missed this place like all hell."

Wynand made no movement to go. He stood, slouched as usual, his shoulder blades propped against the doorjamb, arms crossed on his chest, hands holding his elbows. A lamp with a square shade of green glass burned on the desk, but there was still daylight outside, streaks of tired brown on a lemon sky; the room held a dismal sense of evening in the illumination that seemed both premature and too feeble. The light made a puddle on the desk, but it could not shut out the brown, half-dissolved shapes of the street, and it could not reach the door to disarm Wynand's presence.

The lamp shade rattled faintly and Toohey felt the rumble under his shoe soles: the presses were rolling. He realized that he had heard them for some time. It was a comforting sound, dependable and alive. The pulse beat of a newspaper—the newspaper that transmits to men the pulse beat of the world. A long, even flow of separate drops, like marbles rolling away in a straight line, like the sound of a man's heart.

Toohey moved a pencil over a sheet of paper, until he realized that the sheet lay in the lamplight and Wynand could see the pencil making a water lily, a teapot and a bearded profile. He dropped the pencil and made a self-mocking sound with his lips. He opened a drawer and looked attentively at a pile of carbons and paper clips. He did not know what he could possibly be expected to do: one did not start writing a column just like that. He had wondered why he should be asked to resume his duties at nine o'clock in the evening, but he had supposed that it was Wynand's manner of softening surrender by overdoing it, and he had felt he could afford not to argue the point.

The presses were rolling; a man's heartbeats gathered and re-broadcast. He heard no other sound and he thought it was absurd to keep this up if Wynand had gone, but most inadvisable to look in his direction if he hadn't.

After a while he looked up. Wynand was still there. The light picked out two white spots of his figure: the long fingers of one hand closed over an elbow, and the high forehead. It was the forehead that Toohey wanted to see; no, there were no slanting ridges over the eyebrows. The eyes made two solid white ovals, faintly discernible in the angular shadows of the face. The ovals were directed at Toohey. But there was nothing in the face; no indication of purpose.

After a while, Toohey said:

"Really, Mr. Wynand, there's no reason why you and I can't get together."

Wynand did not answer.

Toohey picked up a sheet of paper and inserted it in the typewriter. He sat looking at the keys, holding his chin between two fingers, in the pose he knew he assumed when preparing to attack a paragraph. The rims of the keys glittered under the lamps, rings of bright nickel suspended in the dim room.

The presses stopped.

Toohey jerked back, automatically, before he knew why he had jerked: he was a newspaperman and it was a sound that did not stop like that.

Wynand looked at his wrist watch. He said:

"It's nine o'clock. You're out of a job, Mr. Toohey. The *Banner* has ceased to exist."

The next incident of reality Toohey apprehended was his own hand dropping down on the typewriter keys: he heard the metal cough of the levers tangling and striking together, and the small jump of the carriage.

He did not speak, but he thought his face was naked because he heard Wynand answering him:

"Yes, you had worked here for thirteen years. . . . Yes, I bought them all out, Mitchell Layton included, two weeks ago. . . ." The voice was indifferent. "No, the boys in the city room didn't know it. Only the boys in the pressroom. . . ."

Toohey turned away. He picked up a paper clip, held it on his palm, then turned his hand over and let the clip fall, observing with mild astonishment the finality of the law that had not permitted it to remain on his downturned palm.

He got up. He stood looking at Wynand, a stretch of gray carpet between them.

Wynand's head moved, leaned slightly to one shoulder. Wynand's face looked as if no barrier were necessary now, it looked simple, it held no anger, the closed lips were drawn in the hint of a smile of pain that was almost humble.

Wynand said:

"This was the end of the *Banner*. . . . I think it's proper that I should meet it with you."

Many newspapers bid for the services of Ellsworth Monkton Toohey. He selected the *Courier,* a paper of well-bred prestige and gently uncertain policy.

In the evening of his first day on the new job Ellsworth Toohey sat on the edge of an associate editor's desk and they talked about Mr. Talbot, the owner of the *Courier,* whom Toohey had met but a few times.

"But Mr. Talbot as a man?" asked Ellsworth Toohey. "What's his particular god? What would he go to pieces without?"

In the radio room across the hall somebody was twisting a dial. "Time," blared a solemn voice, "marches on!"

Roark sat at the drafting table in his office, working. The city beyond the glass walls seemed lustrous, the air washed by the first cold of October.

The telephone rang. He held his pencil suspended in a jerk of impatience; the telephone was never to ring when he was drawing. He walked to his desk and picked up the receiver.

"Mr. Roark," said his secretary, the tense little note in her voice serving as apology for a broken order, "Mr. Gail Wynand wishes to know whether it would be convenient for you to come to his office at four o'clock tomorrow afternoon?"

She heard the faint buzz of silence in the receiver at her ear and counted many seconds.

"Is he on the wire?" asked Roark. She knew it was not the phone connection that made his voice sound like that.

"No, Mr. Roark. It's Mr. Wynand's secretary."

"Yes. Yes. Tell her yes."

He walked to the drafting table and looked down at the sketches; it was the first desertion he had ever been forced to commit: he knew he would not be able to work today. The weight of hope and relief together was too great.

When Roark approached the door of what had been the Banner Building, he saw that the sign, the *Banner's* masthead, was gone. Nothing replaced it. A discolored rectangle was left over the door. He knew the building now contained the offices of the *Clarion* and floors of empty rooms. The *Clarion,* a third-rate afternoon tabloid, was the only representative of the Wynand chain in New York.

He walked to an elevator. He was glad to be the only passenger: he felt a sudden, violent possessiveness for the small cage of steel; it was his, found again, given back to him. The intensity of the relief told him the intensity of the pain it had ended; the special pain, like no other in his life.

When he entered Wynand's office, he knew that he had to accept that pain and carry it forever, that there was to be no cure and no hope. Wynand sat behind his desk and rose when he entered, looking straight at him. Wynand's face was more than the face of a stranger: a stranger's face is an unapproached potentiality, to be opened if one makes the choice and effort; this was a face known, closed and never to be reached again. A face that held no pain of renunciation, but the stamp of the next step, when even pain is renounced. A face remote and quiet, with a dignity of its own, not a living attribute, but the dignity of a figure on a medieval tomb that speaks of past greatness and forbids a hand to reach out for the remains.

"Mr. Roark, this interview is necessary, but very difficult for me. Please act accordingly."

Roark knew that the last act of kindness he could offer was to claim no bond. He knew he would break what was left of the man before him if he pronounced one word: Gail.

Roark answered:

"Yes, Mr. Wynand."

Wynand picked up four typewritten sheets of paper and handed them across the desk:

"Please read this and sign it if it meets with your approval."

"What is it?"

"Your contract to design the Wynand Building."

Roark put the sheets down. He could not hold them. He could not look at them.

"Please listen carefully, Mr. Roark. This must be explained and understood. I wish to undertake the construction of the Wynand Building at once. I wish it to be the tallest structure of the city. Do not discuss with me the question of whether this is timely or economically advisable. I wish it built. It will be used—which is all that concerns you. It will house the *Clarion* and all the offices of the Wynand Enterprises now located in various parts of the city. The rest of the space will be rented. I have sufficient standing left to guarantee that. You need have no fear of erecting a useless structure. I shall send you a written statement on all details and requirements. The rest will be up to you. You will design the building as you wish. Your decisions will be final. They will not require my approval. You will have full charge and complete authority. This is stated in the contract. But I wish it understood that I shall not have to see you. There will be an agent to represent me in all technical and financial matters. You will deal with him. You will hold all further conferences with him. Let him know what contractors you prefer chosen for the job. If you find it necessary to communicate with me, you will do it through my agent. You are not to expect or attempt to see me. Should you do so, you will be refused admittance. I do not wish to speak to you. I do not wish ever to see you again. If you are prepared to comply with these conditions, please read the contract and sign it."

Roark reached for a pen and signed without looking at the paper.

"You have not read it," said Wynand.

Roark threw the paper across the desk.

"Please sign both copies."

Roark obeyed.

"Thank you," said Wynand, signed the sheets and handed one to Roark. "This is your copy."

Roark slipped the paper into his pocket.

"I have not mentioned the financial part of the undertaking. It is an open secret that the so-called Wynand empire is dead. It is sound and doing as well as ever throughout the country, with the exception of New York City. It will last my lifetime. But it will end with me. I intend to liquidate a great part of it. You will, therefore, have no reason to limit yourself by any consideration of costs in your design of the building. You are free to make it cost whatever you find necessary. The building will remain long after the newsreels and tabloids are gone."

"Yes, Mr. Wynand."

"I presume you will want to make the structure efficiently economical in maintenance costs. But you do not have to consider the return of the original investment. There's no one to whom it must return."

"Yes, Mr. Wynand."

"If you consider the behavior of the world at present and the disaster toward which it is moving you might find the undertaking preposterous. The age of the skyscraper is gone. This is the age of the housing project. Which is always a prelude to the age of the cave. But you are not afraid of a gesture against the whole world. This will be the last skyscraper ever built in New York. It is proper that it should be so. The last achievement of man on earth before mankind destroys itself."

"Mankind will never destroy itself, Mr. Wynand. Nor should it think of itself as destroyed. Not so long as it does things such as this."

"As what?"

"As the Wynand Building."

"That is up to you. Dead things—such as the *Banner*—are only the financial fertilizer that will make it possible. It is their proper function."

He picked up his copy of the contract, folded it and put it, with a precise gesture, into his inside coat pocket. He said, with no change in the tone of his voice:

"I told you once that this building was to be a monument to my life. There is nothing to commemorate now. The Wynand Building will have nothing—except what you give it."

He rose to his feet, indicating that the interview was ended. Roark got up and inclined his head in parting. He held his head down a moment longer than a formal bow required.

At the door he stopped and turned. Wynand stood behind his desk without moving. They looked at each other.

Wynand said:

"Build it as a monument to that spirit which is yours . . . and could have been mine."

XX

O N A SPRING DAY, EIGHTEEN MONTHS LATER, DOMINIQUE WALKED
to the construction site of the Wynand Building.

She looked at the skyscrapers of the city. They rose from unexpected
spots, out of the low roof lines. They had a kind of startling suddenness,
as if they had sprung up the second before she saw them and she had
caught the last thrust of the motion; as if, were she to turn away and
look again fast enough, she would catch them in the act of springing.

She turned a corner of Hell's Kitchen and came to the vast cleared
tract.

Machines were crawling over the torn earth, grading the future park.
From its center, the skeleton of the Wynand Building rose, completed,
to the sky. The top part of the frame still hung naked, an intercrossed
cage of steel. Glass and masonry had followed its rise, covering the rest
of the long streak slashed through space.

She thought: They say the heart of the earth is made of fire. It is held
imprisoned and silent. But at times it breaks through the clay, the iron,
the granite, and shoots out to freedom. Then it becomes a thing like
this.

She walked to the building. A wooden fence surrounded its lower
stories. The fence was bright with large signs advertising the names of
the firms who had supplied materials for the tallest structure in the
world. "Steel by National Steel, Inc." "Glass by Ludlow." "Electrical
Equipment by Wells-Clairmont." "Elevators by Kessler, Inc." "Nash &
Dunning, Contractors."

She stopped. She saw an object she had never noticed before. The
sight was like the touch of a hand on her forehead, the hand of those
figures in legend who had the power to heal. She had not known Henry
Cameron and she had not heard him say it, but what she felt now was as
if she were hearing it: "And I know that if you carry these words
through to the end, it will be a victory, Howard, not just for you, but for
something that should win, that moves the world—and never wins acknowledgment. It will vindicate so many who have fallen before you,
who have suffered as you will suffer."

She saw, on the fence surrounding New York's greatest building, a
small tin plate bearing the words:

"Howard Roark, Architect"

She walked to the superintendent's shed. She had come here often to

726

call for Roark, to watch the progress of construction. But there was a new man in the shed who did not know her. She asked for Roark.

"Mr. Roark is way up on top by the water tank. Who's calling, ma'am?"

"Mrs. Roark," she answered.

The man found the superintendent who let her ride the outside hoist, as she always did—a few planks with a rope for a railing, that rose up the side of the building.

She stood, her hand lifted and closed about a cable, her high heels posed firmly on the planks. The planks shuddered, a current of air pressed her skirt to her body, and she saw the ground dropping softly away from her.

She rose above the broad panes of shop windows. The channels of streets grew deeper, sinking. She rose above the marquees of movie theaters, black mats held by spirals of color. Office windows streamed past her, long belts of glass running down. The squat hulks of warehouses vanished, sinking with the treasures they guarded. Hotel towers slanted, like the spokes of an opening fan, and folded over. The fuming matchsticks were factory stacks and the moving gray squares were cars. The sun made lighthouses of peaked summits, they reeled, flashing long white rays over the city. The city spread out, marching in angular rows to the rivers. It stood held between two thin black arms of water. It leaped across and rolled away to a haze of plains and sky.

Flat roofs descended like pedals pressing the buildings down, out of the way of her flight. She went past the cubes of glass that held dining rooms, bedrooms and nurseries. She saw roof gardens float down like handkerchiefs spread on the wind. Skyscrapers raced her and were left behind. The planks under her feet shot past the antennae of radio stations.

The hoist swung like a pendulum above the city. It sped against the side of the building. It had passed the line where the masonry ended behind her. There was nothing behind her now but steel ligaments and space. She felt the height pressing against her eardrums. The sun filled her eyes. The air beat against her raised chin.

She saw him standing above her, on the top platform of the Wynand Building. He waved to her.

The line of the ocean cut the sky. The ocean mounted as the city descended. She passed the pinnacles of bank buildings. She passed the crowns of courthouses. She rose above the spires of churches.

Then there was only the ocean and the sky and the figure of Howard Roark.

The End